'Rich description, a beautiful setting, wonderful detail, passionate romance and that timeless, classic feel that provides sheer, indulgent escapism. Bliss!'

Amazon.co.uk review

'I thought Ms. Fielding had outdone herself with her second novel but she's done it again with this third one. The love story took my breath away ... I could hardly swallow until I reached the end.'

Amazon.com review

**Praise for *Masquerade* (winner of the Silver Medal for romance at the IBPA Benjamin Franklin Awards):**

'Secrets and surprises ... Set in Spain in the 1970s, you'll be enveloped in this atmospheric story of love and deception.'

*My Weekly*

'Hannah Fielding writes of love, sexual tension and longing with an amazing delicacy and lushness, almost luxury. Suffused with the legends and lore of the gypsies and the beliefs of Spain, there is so much in this novel. Horse fairs, sensual dreams, bull running, bull fighters, moonlight swims, the heat and flowers and colours and costumes of the country. A superb read.'

Amazon.co.uk review

'This was honestly one of the most aesthetically pleasing and sensual books I've read in a long time.'

Amazon.co.uk review

'*Masquerade* contains the kind of romance that makes your heart beat faster and your knees tremble. This was a mesmerising and drama-filled read that left me with a dreamy feeling.'

Amazon.co.uk review

'This engrossing, gorgeous romantic tale was one of my favorite reads in recent memory. This book had intrigue, mystery, revenge, passion and tantalizing love scenes that held captive the reader and didn't allow a moment's rest through all of the twists and turns ... wonderful from start to finish.'     Goodreads.com review

'When I started reading *Masquerade* I was soon completely pulled into the romantic and poetic way Hannah Fielding writes her stories. I honestly couldn't put *Masquerade* down. Her books are beautiful and just so romantic, you'll never want them to end!'

Goodreads.com review

**Praise for *Legacy* (final book in the Andalucían Nights trilogy):**

'*Legacy* is filled to the brim with family scandal, frustrated love and hidden secrets. Fast-paced and addictive, it will keep you hooked from start to finish.'     *The Lady*

'Beautifully written, and oozing romance and intrigue, *Legacy* is the much-anticipated new novel from award-winning author Hannah Fielding that brings to life the allure of a summer in Cádiz.'

*Take a Break*

'In the vein of *Gone With The Wind*, this particular book is just as epic and timeless. Written with lively detail, you are IN Spain. You are engulfed in the sights, sounds and smells of this beautiful country. Great characters ... and a plot with just enough twists to keep it moving along ... Start with book one and each one gets better and better. I applaud Ms Fielding's storytelling skills.     Amazon.com review

'Flawless writing and impeccable character building. *Legacy* takes the readers on a journey through the passions and desires that are aroused from romantic Spanish culture.'     Goodreads.com review

'Totally recommended … With its gorgeous settings in the Riviera and Italy, this novel is a treat for all the senses, a kind of modern Beauty and the Beast, with secrets, villains and dangers in the palace where the beast Umberto has retreated. Meanwhile, music makes a beautiful redemptive healing thread throughout the novel, thoroughly apt and marvellous.'

Lindsay's Romantics

'One of the most beautiful romantic storylines that I have read in quite some time … I felt like I was at the opera from the comfort of my sofa while reading this beautiful story.'

Bookread2day

'A beautiful, emotional tale which will leave a smile on your lips at the end.'
Book Vue

'Words almost escape me with how beautiful this story was … A truly wonderful, romantic story that will sweep you away …'

Debra's Book Café

# SONG OF THE NILE

HANNAH FIELDING

LONDON
WALL
PUBLISHING

First published in hardback and paperback in Poland in 2021 by London
Wall Publishing sp. z o.o. (LWP)

First published in eBook edition in Poland in 2021 by London Wall
Publishing sp. z o.o. (LWP)

HB ISBN 978-83-956892-6-0
PB ISBN 978-83-956892-5-3
EB PDF ISBN 978-83-667980-2-1
EB ePub ISBN 978-83-667980-3-8
EB MOBI ISBN 978-83-667980-4-5

10 9 8 7 6 5 4 3 2 1

Print and production managed by Printgroup, Poland

London Wall Publishing sp. z o.o.
Hrubieszowska 2, 01-209 Warsaw, Poland
www.londonwallpublishing.com
www.hannahfielding.net

*To my dear granddaughter, Philae, with my love
and hope that you grow up to be a kind and wise woman,
as was your great-grandmother Philae.*

*The dead cannot cry out for justice.*
*It is a duty of the living to do so for them.*

Lois McMaster Bujold

# PROLOGUE

*Luxor, Egypt, 1938*

A wave of anticipation ran through the crowded courtroom. A murmur rose among the assembly as the three judges, like ominous crows in their black coats and red sashes, filed back into the room. Mounting the platform, they took their places at the desk, looking down on the well of the court. Facing them, the lines of wooden benches that made up the gallery were filled with people, their glances flickering to the defendant's cage at the side of the courtroom, while members of the press, for whom this trial had already provided significant headlines, leaned forward in their chairs. The self-important lawyers who had sat laughing, chattering and making cynical remarks turned their full attention to the magistrates and the room fell into the deepest silence.

The man standing inside the iron cage looked drawn, his face unshaven, his clothes hanging loosely on him. At the appearance of the judges he straightened and his dark eyes sought out the face of the teenage girl seated in the front row of the public benches, next to a grey-haired woman who gripped her hand tightly. The girl's expression held so much anguish and fear as she stared back that the man in the dock looked pained; he gestured sadly with his shackled hands, as though trying to reach out and give her some comfort.

'This court has found Ayoub El Masri guilty of the theft and illegal possession of Egyptian antiquities and therefore has sentenced him to five years in jail with hard labour.' Another whispering current coursed through the well of the court, then deadly silence once more.

All eyes were on the man as he gripped the bars that held him prisoner. His face suddenly drained of colour and his breathing became short and laboured. Bringing his bound hands up to his chest, he staggered sideways, then crumpled to the floor of the cage. The young girl who had been watching the proceedings with such dread cried out and ran forward, desperately pushing her way past the officials to get to the cage, but her screams were drowned out by the chaos that ensued. Gasps and shouts went up; a handful of men swarmed around the iron door as it was unlocked and several officials rushed in to tend to the figure collapsed on the floor.

People were on their feet, jostling to see what was happening. Inside the cage, a young man was shouting to the officials to give him room, telling them he was a doctor. It seemed like an eternity to the girl as she fought her way to the front, where she clutched at the bars of the iron pen, her eyes wild with panic. The young man was kneeling, his strong hands clasped together on top of the older man's chest, pushing down with rhythmical compressions. The girl shouted the doctor's name, tears streaming down her face, but he kept going without lifting his head. Finally, he stopped and slumped back on his knees, and only then did he look up, straight into her eyes, his own grave gaze flooded with compassion. The next thing she knew, two maternal arms enfolded her, pulling her away, while sobs shuddered through her and the world slid into darkness.

# CHAPTER 1

*Luxor, March 1946*

Aida El Masri was jolted out of her deep reverie and back to the present as the cream-and-grey 1936 Bentley came to a slow halt in front of a pair of gates.

'We've arrived,' announced the portly man sitting by the young woman's side. 'I'm very happy that you've decided to come home, Aida. The *khadammeen* servants have been waiting impatiently for you, too. There's been a great atmosphere of joy and festivity at Karawan House since I announced your return.'

Aida smiled at Naguib Bishara. He'd been a very close friend of her father as well as his lawyer. Right to the end he had done his utmost for Ayoub El Masri and she would always be grateful for that. 'It's good to be back, Uncle Naguib.'

As the car's engine idled, waiting for the gatekeeper to appear, Naguib's charcoal eyes were warm as they settled on her. 'I'm not sure that many of them will recognise you now. You've grown into a lovely young woman, but there's hardly anything of you left.'

Aida laughed. 'No more of *Osta* Ghaly's excellent cooking, that's the reason. Rationing helped too. We didn't have all that butter and sugar you had here.'

Naguib hadn't changed much, apart from his hairline which was rapidly receding towards an ever-growing patch of sparse grey hair at the back. Above a long and mobile mouth, he had of late grown a Charlie Chaplin moustache too – Aida had known him without one and she didn't think it suited his smooth, rounded jawline. He had the sort of face you forget even while you're looking at it, and maybe that was why he had decided to grow it. He still appeared to enjoy his food, however, judging from his waistline. Her mouth twitched with suppressed amusement. 'Does *Osta* Ghaly still make his delicious *konafa*?'

Naguib chuckled loudly, patting a well-rounded stomach. 'Unfortunately, yes!' He raised his bushy black eyebrows conspiratorially. 'And his *basboussa* is still the best in Luxor, though you must never tell him or it will go to his head.'

Aida's smile became wistful as she gazed out of the open window at the tall palm trees edging the El Masri Estate, so integral to all the estates of Upper Egypt; she had always found the sound of their soft swishing at twilight so evocative and romantic. Breathing in the warm air, she sighed. It was the unmistakable scent of Egypt: the fusion of pungent earth and spices, of goats and chickens, and the distinctive tang of the cotton fields. She was finally home.

Eight long years had passed and the world had been ravaged by war since Aida had fled to England. She had never dreamed she'd be gone so long. Just for one year, she'd told herself, until the scandal had died down. She had been barely eighteen then, alone in the world except for a single relative, her English mother's brother. George Chandler, a former MP living in the home counties before the war, had no children of his own and welcomed the daughter of his late sister with open arms. And so it was Aida began her self-imposed exile at his house in Berkshire.

Tragic though Aida's circumstances were at that time, it seemed that fate, while callously closing one door for the young woman, had decided to open another. She always dreamed of becoming a nurse, ever since she had spent hours as a child hiding in the gardens of Karawan House when she was supposed to be in the kitchen helping her nanny, *Dada* Amina, with her prized date jam. There, she pored over history books about Florence Nightingale, 'The Lady with the Lamp' in the Crimean War, and Edith Cavell, the nursing heroine of the Great War. Finding herself in England, Aida had seen her opportunity to bring her dreams to fruition. With Uncle George's help, she enrolled as a trainee nurse at the Royal London Hospital. Any romantic notions Aida might have harboured about her destined profession had been instantly dispelled by the long hours of work, attending lectures and studying for exams, not to mention scrubbing bedpans and making beds, all to the exacting standards of the fearsome matrons and sisters.

Then war had broken out in Europe and, even if she had wanted to, Aida could no longer return to Egypt. For the next six years her life took yet another direction. As the bombs dropped on the East End of London, her hands-on training became accelerated by necessity. She nursed soldiers maimed at Dunkirk and bound the wounds of burned pilots from the Battle of Britain, as well as looking after injured civilians caught in the Blitz. By now, Uncle George had come out of retirement and moved to Chelsea to help the war effort by working in the newly formed Ministry of Supply in the Strand. On those few occasions when she had time off, Aida would often stay at her uncle's flat and George would take her to tea at The Ritz, a popular meeting place for politicians, aristocrats and minor royals. The glamour of those occasions was in sharp contrast to the ugly suffering she witnessed on a daily basis in her work.

If the death of her father had begun Aida's passage to adulthood with a cruel jolt, the crucible of war completed it in a baptism of fire. The chubby and confused teenager who had left Egypt grief-stricken spent the war years growing into a resilient and focused young woman. Yet while she was able to help mend the broken bodies of so many casualties of war, she carried her own pain inside like an angry wound that would not heal. Now, after what seemed a lifetime away from her country, she was back in Egypt … here to clear her father's name.

The creaking sound of metal broke into Aida's reverie as Kherallah the *ghaffir*, rifle slung across his back, opened the gates. Dressed in a loose snowy *galabeya*, crowned with an enormous white turban, he raised his arm in salute as the car glided past, his face lit up with a smile that revealed dazzling white teeth. Aida waved at him. Good, loyal Kherallah. He had been gatekeeper for as long as she could remember. As a lad he had worked under his father, who had also been Ayoub El Masri's gatekeeper and guardian of the estate before Kherallah took over.

Through the mango and guava trees, the bright glow of their fruit startling in that place of shadows and silence, loomed the pink house where she had been born: Karawan House, named after the nightingale. Aida loved the beautiful but sad legend about the bird, which *Dada* Amina used to tell her when she was a child. In Arab tales, the rose was believed to have originated from a sweat droplet fallen from the prophet Mohamed's brow. Legend has it that from the time the first rose was created from this droplet all roses were white, until a nightingale fell in love with one of the blooms and pressed its body so hard on the petals that the thorns of its stem pierced the nightingale's heart, turning the white rose to red with its blood, as well as creating the sad notes of the wounded bird's song. Aida's eyes travelled over the exterior of the building. Once so full of life and laughter, it seemed that Karawan House finally lived up to its name. After all these years, and with her father gone, it seemed shrouded in melancholy and drained of its former colour.

The finely carved old mansion that had been solidly built was now in bad repair. It displayed a neoclassical dark pink and cream crumbling stone façade with arches, pediments, columns and elegant, narrow windows masked by faded green wooden shutters. Its central structure was flanked by two lower wings, holding a ballroom and terrace on one side and a *jardin d'hiver*, the equivalent of an English conservatory, on the other, which was a suntrap even in winter. All the front rooms in the house looked out over the river and the desert, but the view from the back rooms was just as magnificent, taking in the grounds, with palm trees and green fields in the distance. It was not the most imposing house around, but it was grand enough, and despite losing her mother when she was only seven, Aida had enjoyed a happy childhood there with her father and *Dada* Amina. During term-time she had attended Cheltenham Ladies' College, a boarding school in England, but whenever she could, she returned to her beloved home in Egypt for the holidays.

The car came to a halt at the foot of broad white marble steps, which swept up to the veranda that ran along the façade of Karawan House, and Saleh the driver rushed round to open the door for Aida. Ragab the gardener, who had tended the gardens since Aida was a tiny child, walked up the drive with great dignity to shake her hand, his deep, gentle eyes proclaiming him a man close to nature. '*Hamdelellah Al Salama ya Sit*,' he whispered, bowing a fraction with reverence.

'*Allah yé sallémak, ya Ragab*,' Aida said, returning his welcoming greeting. She hadn't forgotten her Arabic, and it felt both strange and homely to be speaking the language again. The words came creakingly to the surface of her mind as if they had been deposited all these years somewhere in the pit of her stomach.

The mansion's carved oak front doors were open and the numerous smiling staff of Karawan House stood at the entrance to welcome back their *Sit* Aida. There was *Osta* Ghaly, the kind, plump old cook who would secretly give Aida delicious sweetmeats when she was a child, conjured up in his kitchen where she was not allowed; Bekhit, the head *suffragi*, attired in his spotless white robe, red sash and red *tarboosh* – a man of great age who had been in the family's service for fifty years; his eldest son, Guirguis, an alert young man with intelligent dark eyes that never seemed to miss anything, who would take over his father's position one day, although remaining under Bekhit's orders for now, while being trained for the job. There was Radwan the scullion, known as *filfil*, pepper, because he always interfered in other people's arguments like pepper thrown into food; and his cousin Hassan the cleaner, a quiet youth who smiled a lot but didn't say much. Both young men were the sons of *fellahin*, country folk, whose families had worked on the El Masri land for many generations. Then came Fatma, the washerwoman of the flashing gold teeth; Naima the maid, a young girl of seventeen who was only a child when Aida had left; and finally, *Dada* Amina, who had brought up her father Ayoub before caring for Aida.

Small and chubby, with curly black hair tied back under a triangular headscarf and wearing a flowery *galabeya* robe, *Dada* Amina had been a close confidante and second mother to the young Aida, the bond between them strengthening even further after Eleanor El Masri was diagnosed with cancer and died quickly afterwards. Though she was kind and possessed an exceedingly soft and sweet expression, *Dada* Amina was far from being a pushover and had kept the somewhat rebellious only child in check as she grew up. Once Aida had become a young woman, *Dada* Amina remained at Karawan House in the formidable role of housekeeper.

All these people had been in the service of Ayoub El Masri when he died, and Aida had insisted they should be kept on after his death even though she herself was making a hasty departure for England. Naguib, who had taken on the management of the El Masri Estate, had agreed, knowing that his friend Ayoub would have been proud of Aida's loyalty to their household *suffragis*, many of whom had become almost part of the family. Today, the return of *Sit* Aida was regarded with obvious excitement. They beamed as, smiling, Aida shook hands with them one by one, thanking each of them for having looked after the family home during her long absence. When she reached the end of the line, Aida's reunion with her old nanny was much more emotional. *Dada* Amina hugged the young woman to her heart and kissed her with tears glistening in her dark eyes.

'Aida, *habibti*, my darling, all grown up!' she exclaimed, holding Aida at arm's length to inspect her. 'Did you never eat during the war, *ya binti*, my child? You look so different, almost another person. But I would recognise you anywhere, *ya danaya*, my dear child … *Allah*, what have you done to your hair? You look like a film star! *Baeti zay el amar*, you have become as beautiful as the moon … Oh, it's good to see you again!' Fresh tears sprang from *Dada* Amina's eyes as she clung to the girl whom she had missed as much as she would a daughter of her own.

Aida wiped her own damp cheeks and spluttered out a laugh. 'And you haven't changed at all, *Dada* Amina. Tell me, what keeps you so young?'

Naguib interjected, 'Oh, bossing us all around and making sure we do what we're told, isn't that so?', giving *Dada* Amina a cheerful wink and laughing heartily at his own joke.

Time may not have changed *Dada* Amina, but not so Aida. The housekeeper was right: she felt like a different person. It now seemed an eternity since that far-off afternoon, eight years before, when she had seen her father, Ayoub El Masri, standing behind bars like a caged animal in the dark courtroom, and had witnessed his demise minutes after the verdict was pronounced. Branded a thief, the shock had been too great for the renowned archaeologist and, within minutes, he had died of heart failure. It was a tragic finale to his life, and a brutal end to the insouciant days of Aida's childhood. The memory of those first weeks of stark despair made her shiver.

Although she had no doubt about her father's innocence, Aida
had fled to England to get away from the hectoring of journalists
and the malevolent tongues of society, who were quick to seize
upon the scandal. The identity of the real culprit had been
revealed to Aida the day her father was arrested, and she had
carried the truth with her all through the war years. Now that
she was back in Luxor, she would do her utmost to find the proof
she needed to confront the coward who had let her father – his
neighbour and long-time friend – go to jail. The same man who
had ultimately caused Ayoub's death.

*       *       *

Once the moment of demonstrative homecoming had passed,
the staff dispersed, each going back to his job, except for *Dada*
Amina, who accompanied Aida and Naguib Bishara into the house.

The hall of Karawan House was large and light. Its floor was
made of cream calacatta marble, imported from Italy when
the house was built in the early nineteenth century, its veins
of gold giving it warmth and depth. The space was dominated
by a grand wooden staircase, each side of which stood a pair
of ionic columns in the same expensive warm stone. A magnificent
Baccarat chandelier hung from the lavish ivory-coloured ceiling,
whose decorative plasterwork panels were gilded and enriched
by beige and brown low-relief details of various birds of Egypt.

*Dada* Amina led them across the polished tiled floor into
the long, rectangular drawing room, made bright by four tall
windows, their edges softened by faded damask curtains opening
on to a terrace. From here the view was breathtaking: the slow-
moving Nile lying like a pearlescent sheet, so still it seemed as
though you could walk across the water to the farthest bank,
where the pink hills of the Valley of the Tombs rose up, changing
colour as the sun rode the sky. During the day, feluccas,

the romantic gull-winged sailing boats used since antiquity, skimmed over the surface of the river like big white moths.

This room, like all others in the house, was done up in the formal English style – Ayoub and Eleanor had totally refurbished the house when they moved to Luxor, replacing the heavily gilded French furniture with the more sober and elegant Sheraton interiors.

Aida smiled at the familiar surroundings. A nostalgic pang of sorrow gripped her heart. Her father always said that her mother's hand was to be seen everywhere in the elegance of the Karawan House interiors. *She needed beauty all around her*, as he had put it. The room was still as Aida remembered it. Painted a sunny yellow, its walls were adorned with oil paintings by David Roberts, Prisse d'Avesnes and Augustus Lamplough, which depicted the landscapes of Ancient Egypt, the River Nile, the desert, as well as scenes from Egyptian life. The golden oak floor was covered with fine antique carpets from Iran and Turkey and at each end of the beautifully proportioned room a fine Adam fireplace was surmounted by a gilded mirror. Both were lit in winter as the nights in this part of the world, contrary to the mild daytimes, were bitterly cold. Beautifully inlaid *demi lune* tables in satinwood stood on tapered legs between the windows, topped with antique Chinese ochre vases made into lamps, and in the middle of the room a large round table held a vase which *Dada* Amina always made sure to fill with sweet-smelling flowers from the garden, even when the house was empty. A set of deep-seat sofas and armchairs upholstered in pale celadon green damask faced each fireplace; Aida remembered nestling with her mother as a small child on one of those voluminous sofas while she read her stories, feeling the comforting rise and fall of Eleanor's breathing against her cheek. Growing up, all she had to rely on were memories such as these, and the reminiscences of her father and *Dada* Amina.

Aida's mother Eleanor and her family were passing through Egypt on their way back from India to England when she had met Ayoub El Masri at a drinks party at the British Embassy in Cairo. Ayoub was already a well-known and erudite archaeologist, renowned in his field, who had led many excavations and saved numerous Ancient Egyptian artefacts from destruction. Eleanor was young, beautiful and intelligent. It was love at first sight and the two had eloped and married very shortly afterwards. The ensuing scandal caused Ayoub, an only child who had lost his parents when he was still in his teens, to be disowned by the rest of his family and wide circle of friends, and Eleanor to be cut off from her own.

At first, they had been snubbed by the outraged Egyptian and British social circles – mixed marriages were not viewed with a benign eye in those days. Though he was originally from Cairo, Ayoub and his new wife moved to the quieter town of Luxor in Upper Egypt, where he could allocate more time to his excavation work while keeping an alert eye on the land he had inherited from his parents.

Society watched the golden couple furtively, and as Ayoub grew in status and his wife charmed her entourage, becoming an accomplished hostess, together they made valuable new friends in Luxor ... and enemies too, because as the old Arabic saying goes: *Envy is the companion of great success.* And when that happens, as *Dada* Amina was always fond of telling the young Aida, 'Who can pride himself on escaping the evil eye?' It had not gone unnoticed by an older Aida that the El Masri family seemed destined to be blighted by suspicion and controversy.

Aida followed Naguib towards the large sofas and chairs by the fireplace while *Dada* Amina left the room, closing the door quietly.

'Come, Aida, let's sit down. I know you must be tired, but we need to talk,' the lawyer said, as he took a seat in one of the high-backed armchairs.

'You look quite worried, Uncle Naguib. Is anything the matter?'

'You are right, I *am* worried. About *you*, Aida.' Naguib took out his black-stemmed pipe and filled the bowl with tobacco.

'About me? There's no reason to be worried about me.' Aida sank back into the sofa. 'I've survived the war, haven't I? Trust me, that wasn't a piece of cake, so I can look after myself.' She looked at him quizzically. 'Is it money? I haven't touched my inheritance, so unless something really untoward has happened I should be all right on that front.'

'No, no. My dear Aida, you are a very rich girl. Ayoub left you a great fortune, which is still intact since you did not give me or anyone else a power of attorney before leaving.' With a whoosh of a match, Naguib lit the brown bowl of his pipe. 'My concern is that you're a young woman on her own. It is a bad thing for a girl to be left fatherless, and no man to protect her,' he said. The vibrancy and laughter that characterised Naguib's personality had left his voice and he spoke sternly.

'Yes,' Aida replied faintly.

'You have no brothers, no family.'

'I know that I have no one here in Egypt, Uncle Naguib.'

'You have the Pharaonys. Your families were always very close … and in some ways they are your only family now. Of course you also have me – something you can always count on – but I'm not getting any younger and life is unpredictable, as you have seen.'

*The Pharaonys.* For a moment, the familiar face of a young man swam into Aida's mind – dark, disapproving eyes that turned her inside out. Eyes that had fixed on her the moment her father had died with compassion and regret. The image had haunted her painfully over the years, but now Aida's face closed, her jaw set stubbornly. 'The Pharaony family are of no interest to me.'

Naguib's small shrewd eyes fixed on her as he puffed on his pipe. 'Don't tell me that you still believe that Kamel Pharaony was behind that nasty business with your father.'

'Yes, I do believe it. Nothing has changed as far as I'm concerned.'

'But Kamel and Ayoub were best friends! What have you ever had to substantiate such an accusation, Aida?'

Aida took a breath. She had bottled up her resentment for so long that now she found it strangely difficult to speak. 'Even though I have no proof, my information at the time came from a reliable source ... The Nefertari statue belonged to Kamel Pharaony. He had brought it to our house earlier that afternoon.'

Naguib shook his head. 'You know that Kamel denied that, so why do you persist in thinking such a thing?'

Aida paused. 'Because my father was out, Kamel gave it to the maid, Souma Hassanein. He told her to put it in my father's study and that he'd come back in the evening to discuss the authenticity of the piece with him. Those were her words.'

Naguib's eyes widened. 'She told you this? Kamel would never have entrusted a valuable piece to a servant. He is one of the most cautious men I know.'

'Maybe, but Souma swore on her child's head that that was what happened.'

The only problem was that the maid had disappeared before Aida could call on her to repeat her claims. Still, would it have helped anyway? A *khadamma* would never have been taken seriously.

Judging by Naguib's expression, she had been right. 'You can't believe servants' gossip.'

'Gossip?' Aida kept her tone even, not wanting him to think she was still the hysterical, grief-stricken teenager. 'Someone like Souma wouldn't have been able to make up something like that. Those were exactly the kind of words Kamel Pharaony would have used. Besides, why would she lie to me?'

Naguib shrugged. 'Who knows? One can never be sure what ulterior motives these people have. Your father never liked Souma anyway. I know that a few days before the incident he caught her rummaging in some papers that were no business of hers, and he told her off. He only took pity on her because her husband had abandoned her and she needed a job to feed her son. He didn't trust her, but Ayoub wasn't a man to take the bread from a child's mouth, so he kept her on. As our Arabic proverb says, *Etak el shar le men ahssantou eleh*, beware of him to whom you have been charitable.'

Aida frowned, digesting this new information. 'Maybe, but I still don't see what she had to gain by telling me such a story.' Of course she had considered that Souma might have lied but she had gone over the maid's words in her mind so often that nothing else made sense, except that she was telling the truth. But why would Souma be interested in her father's papers? The old anger welled up inside Aida. She looked down, her fingers twisting the corner of a cushion. 'Poor Father died far too young. He didn't deserve what happened to him. Part of the reason I've come back is to clear his name.'

Naguib gave her an indulgent look. 'How do you think you'll be able to do that, *ya binti*, after so many years? I believe just as strongly as you do that Ayoub was innocent, but sadly, the real culprit is probably far away now.'

She raised her head. 'Is he? Well, as the other saying goes, *the corn passes from hand to hand, but comes at last to the mill.* Whether it's Kamel Pharaony or someone else, I will catch whoever was responsible for my father's death.'

'That won't be as easy as you think, Aida. Have you forgotten so much of where you come from? People here will not approve of a woman digging around and asking questions. Anyhow, where would you start?'

'With the only thread I have to follow. Souma, I'll find her somehow.'

Yet Naguib's words sank in heavily. Coming back to Luxor, Aida knew that she would have to navigate the conservative values of Egyptian society with some self-restraint. Egypt had remained in its own cocoon during the war and its society had failed to be touched by any form of sexual liberation, even in upper-class circles. It had been so different in wartime England. There, Aida had experienced the kind of social freedom in which her independent nature revelled. Suddenly she felt very isolated and alone in this place where she used to belong.

Naguib sighed. 'Well, all I can say is that Souma is long gone now, and the harm she did cannot be undone.'

Aida glanced at him. It was ingrained in her to respect her elders but she deliberately refused to see his meaning. 'I'm sure I don't know what you mean, Uncle,' she responded stubbornly.

'You know that your father and Kamel Pharaony had spoken about an alliance between your two families. Kamel had asked for your hand on behalf his son Phares just before the tragedy. It is well known that you were almost engaged.'

'Yes, that is so, but my father had never given his answer.'

'Things have changed now. You are not that young anymore and their son Phares still wants to marry you …'

Why was he telling her this? He had no right to speak sternly to her. She had barely stepped back on Egyptian soil and was already being pushed into a marriage of convenience.

With a slight lifting of her head she said gently, 'I have no intention of tying myself to someone I don't love.'

'In Egypt, *habibti*, the knowing and loving come after marriage.'

'Not always. What about my parents? They married for love, did they not?'

'Your parents were unusual, and look where it got them. Your father was disowned by his family for following his heart, not his head.'

'Maybe,' she agreed grudgingly. 'But in the last eight years I've learned that life is too precious and short just to throw it away.'

Naguib gave a frustrated wave of his pipe. 'But you would be doing the opposite of throwing away your life, you would be rebuilding it.'

'Please, Uncle, let me finish … Marriage would be an important part – the most important part – of my life, and I must get it right. Though we grew up together, Phares is much older than I am. Even in those days I barely knew him.'

Naguib's bushy brows shot up. 'Oh, come now, Aida! You and Phares were hardly strangers. He often dropped by to visit your father and talk about his work. Phares took an interest in Ayoub's findings, I seem to remember. Your father was very fond of the boy.' He gestured with his pipe as an afterthought. 'And you were often at Hathor or El Sharouk.'

To be pressed on her past feelings for Phares made Aida shift uncomfortably. 'What I mean is, I didn't know Phares as I would someone my own age. Besides, that was a long time ago, Uncle. You can't expect me to commit to a man who is almost a stranger to me now.' She gazed into his heavy-lidded eyes, which were watching her intently. 'My father would never have forced me to marry someone I do not love.'

'I am not forcing you, my dear. How could I? I have no power over you, I can only advise. You are a grown woman now. It is true that you look younger than twenty-six, but at your age most Egyptian women already have a string of children. I am speaking to you as if I were counselling my own daughter, merely trying to help you see things clearly. What you have been through hasn't been easy. Phares understands that.' Naguib leaned forward. 'He was there that day. He knows how dreadful it was for you. The poor boy tried to save your father.'

Aida blanched, trying to keep the emotion from her voice. He had gone too far. 'Are you saying that's a reason for me to marry him?'

'No, no, of course not, *habibti*.' Naguib's expression softened. 'Look, all I'm saying is that Phares is a good match. When you were younger, the two of you always seemed to have something to say to each other, which is a good sign, no?' He raised a thick eyebrow knowingly. 'I recall that you seemed to like him when you were a teenager. Is that not so?'

Embarrassed to be discussing such things with Uncle Naguib, Aida gave a brittle laugh. 'When I was younger I had a schoolgirl crush on Phares, no more. We were worlds apart in our thinking, and there was no question of love between us.' Hearing the words leave her mouth, that odd feeling of unease returned.

'There are other factors to consider,' Naguib pressed on, regarding her through a tendril of pipe smoke. 'Your father's *esba*, estate, is in a pitiful state, because without a power of attorney, no one could do anything about it. If you wanted to sell it today, I doubt you would get a reasonable price for it. Having Kamel oversee that side of things has been very useful, Aida. Plus, the Pharaonys' land borders yours, so it would be normal for your two families to unite.' The voice was deep, grating, and after eight years of absence, Aida found it foreign, instantly conjuring up the ruthless facet of a different world with customs her father himself had disobeyed by marrying a foreigner, and had paid the price.

Aida gave Naguib a mutinous look. 'That is no reason to give up my freedom. I'm still not sure what my plans are. I may want to go back to live in England.'

'You have always been headstrong, with a streak of recklessness that worried your father.'

'No, I've always known what I wanted. I didn't want to leave Egypt, and even when I was at school, I always preferred coming home to be close to my father. Now he is gone, things are different. There are greener pastures out there.'

The lawyer shook his head disapprovingly. 'Adventurousness is not a good trait in a woman. One day you'll get yourself into trouble, and God help you if people who care about you are not around to help.'

At this moment, *Dada* Amina came in bearing a tray of tea and a plate of *konafa* and *basboussa*, dainty little pastries made with nuts and syrup.

'*Osta* Ghaly made them especially because he knows how much *Sit* Aida is fond of them,' she chuckled. She glanced at Aida as she set down the plate on the table. 'And now that you are back, we must feed you properly again.'

Aida burst out laughing, a crystalline laugh that used to echo through the house before she had left. *Osta* Ghaly added coconut and orange flower water to his *basboussa* to give the cake his personal touch and she had always found it delicious. 'I will go to the kitchen later, like I used to when I was a child, and thank him personally.'

*Dada* Amina beamed. 'That will be very kind of you, *ya Sit, ya amira*. Thank you.'

After she had left the room, Naguib looked at Aida, sitting in front of him, and she read the disapproval still shadowing his features.

'You say you are thinking of going back to England? That is a bad idea, *habibti*. Your place is in Egypt. Don't forget that you are Egyptian.'

'Yes, but I am also English.'

The lawyer shook his head. 'You are someone here. Your father was a loved man, *Allah yerhamoh*, may God rest his soul.'

Aida sent him an arched look. 'You seem to forget how much he was criticised after the trial.'

'Society is fickle. That was a long time ago and memories fade. You carry the El Masri name, which is a respected one in Egypt. In England, as far as I know, you are no one.'

Her face flushed with irritation. 'That's not so. My uncle was a respectable MP who worked hard during the war to make sure people didn't starve, and I have made many friends there. I went to school in England, remember?' Aida knew that she was being deliberately stubborn, but in this country where men thought they had the right to rule women as they pleased, she felt slightly vulnerable and needed to mark out her position immediately.

Naguib remained undeterred. 'England is going through bad times. The war has ravaged Europe and people are emigrating to Australia, New Zealand and America, where there are economic opportunities. You already have assets here – ones that need looking after. The house and the land are in a sorry state. To bring Karawan House back to its former glory and for the land to deliver the crops it did before the war, you will need to spend a great deal of money, which you have, of course. As I've said, you are far from being a pauper, but it is much too heavy a burden for a woman alone to bear, and that is where you would benefit from marrying Phares Pharaony.'

'I'm quite able to stand on my own two feet and besides, how do you know that Phares still wants to marry me? He used to disapprove of me, thought I was too liberal and impulsive, although he probably considered that I was young enough to be tamed by a husband one day.'

'As you know, although I am not Kamel Pharaony's lawyer, he is a good friend of mine. When a few weeks back I told him you were coming home, he asked me to test the waters, find out if you would still consider marrying his son. It would be an alliance between two great families and would multiply both your riches. Not only that, but Phares is an eminent general surgeon now, fast becoming a legend in the medical world. He is well-respected.'

Phares, a surgeon … Aida was not surprised that he had become successful. He had always been driven by his love of medicine and his dreams of becoming a surgeon. She thought wryly of how protective he had always been towards others – an innate caring quality – though when they were younger, Aida had been infuriated by it whenever it had been directed towards her.

Naguib emptied his pipe into an ashtray. 'Anyhow, the Pharaonys have been very decent. They kept a vigilant eye on your land and they even hired a few *ghoufara* to look after it, especially at night. The trafficking in antiquities and hashish since the war has increased tremendously and the smugglers and *mattareed*, outlaws, tend to hide in the grounds of empty, unguarded estates. Sometimes they even try to appropriate the land, squatting on it, and the police have great difficulty in getting them out. I wouldn't dismiss an alliance with the Pharaonys so cavalierly, *habibti* … Think about it.'

'Uncle, it was in their interests to guard my land since it adjoins theirs. No one does anything for nothing in this day and age.'

'You are much too young to have such cynical thoughts, my dear child. The Pharaonys are good people, and they are well intentioned. I take it you will at least see Camelia while you are here?'

Camelia Pharaony was Phares's younger sister and she and Aida had been close friends since they were little girls. For that reason, even though Aida had wanted nothing to do with the Pharaony family after she'd left for England, she found it hard to bear a grudge against Camelia herself. Still, they hadn't corresponded during the war and Aida wondered if they would even get along anymore.

'Yes, of course,' she answered hesitantly. 'We have a lot to catch up on.'

'Perhaps she will make you see sense.'

Aida reached for a knife to cut a small piece of *konafa*. 'Please, Uncle Naguib, don't insist. The matter is closed. Let's enjoy *Osta* Ghaly's wonderful pastries and talk about something else.' She pushed a plate across the table in his direction.

Naguib hesitated, then smiled in resignation. 'As you wish, my dear.' He took a piece of *basboussa* and demolished it in a couple of bites. 'I'll let you relax for a few days before taking you around the property with Megally. You remember him, the estate manager? He would have come to meet you today, but I'm afraid his wife is very ill in hospital.'

'Yes, yes, of course I remember Megally. Poor man. Is he still working? He must be quite old by now.'

'Yes, and he's very good with the *fellahin*, the workers. They have great respect for him.'

'I do hope his wife will be all right. In the meantime, I'll reacquaint myself with the estate. Also, please could I take a look at the accounts? Perhaps next week?'

Naguib wiped the crumbs from his mouth and pushed himself slowly out of his chair. 'Yes, of course. The books are already in your father's office. And now I must go. Your aunt Nabila is cooking tonight and that's something worth getting home early for.' He chuckled to himself. 'I'll call by again soon.'

Aida accompanied Naguib to the front door, said her goodbyes and made her way back down to the kitchen to thank *Osta* Ghaly for his delicious pastries.

*   *   *

Up in her bedroom, Aida looked around her. It was a beautiful, gracious room, spacious and light, hung with English chintzes and furnished in English fashion. For Aida's sixteenth birthday, Ayoub had totally refurbished his daughter's bedroom. 'You're no longer a child and should have the bedroom of a young lady now. Your mother would have enjoyed doing it up for you and I hope I have done her proud,' he had told her when, after a week spent in Cairo with Camelia Pharaony, Aida had come back to Luxor for her birthday and discovered the surprise.

The nursery had been turned into the most luxurious room Aida could have dreamt of, painted in different shades of soft green, its silk curtains patterned with colourful fruit. She looked around her to find it unchanged. The wide single bed, covered in a silk peach bedspread and draped with a mosquito net, faced the two French windows that opened on to a narrow veranda, and in one corner of the room two comfortable armchairs sat either side of a small round table.

Next to one window stood a delicate painted escritoire and chair; in front of the other, an elegant mahogany dressing table and mirror with its old Roman *curule* seat covered in velvet. In between the two, an Italian ebonised mahogany table held a number of photographs of Aida at different stages of her life as well as photographs of Eleanor and Ayoub. A tall, painted parcel-gilt glass cabinet bookcase took up much of the left wall, and on the opposite side was a large mahogany wardrobe and cheval mirror.

Aida sighed as she looked at the pretty chintzes, the David Roberts' prints of Egyptian monuments that adorned the walls, the miniature dolls' tea set and bibelots of frail china in the glass cabinet, which her parents had brought back from England one Christmas, the gleaming silver ornaments representing various Egyptian artisans and sellers. Each item had a memory connected to it. She went to the table which held her history in photographs and picked up the last picture she'd had taken with her father only a few days before the tragedy. She seemed so young – a child – so different to the way she looked today. As *Dada* Amina had said: almost a different person.

The mirror returned the reflection of a young woman with burnt gold hair, styled in Rita Hayworth fashion. When she left Egypt, it had been in a short bob, to the nape of her neck, but in spite of its having been fashionable during the war, she had let it grow, and had treated herself to a proper hairstyle before leaving England. Brushed back simply from her face, with a flat crown and parted on the side, it now undulated in a rich and shining cascade past her shoulders.

Unusually large almond-shaped sapphire eyes fringed by thick, dark, almost-too-long lashes gave her face a mysterious and languorous expression. With just a suggestion of shadow underneath them tonight, they gazed back at her critically. She was rather pale. Her cheeks had lost their youthful glow – the lack of sun, the endless grey and drizzle of the English weather, hadn't suited her. She had also grown taller, much taller, and had lost the extra pounds that her father had indulgently called puppy fat. The roundness of her face had given her a look of plainness when she was a girl, but now the sharpness of her elegant cheekbones contrasted strikingly with her full lips. Yes, it really was a different woman that stood in front of the cheval glass. But Uncle Naguib was right: she still didn't look her age, a fact which irritated her because when people first met her they tended not to take her seriously.

Aida stepped on to the veranda. She felt singularly lonely as she looked out on to the velvety night, reminiscing. It was hard to think of a future back in Egypt without her father. Beyond the house where the clear sky came down to the sand, the afterglow of pink faded to yellow and mother-of-pearl, giving way to a blue sky of twinkling stars. It reminded Aida that she had changed continents and climate in less than twenty-four hours, and that in this part of the world darkness came quickly.

The days here were short, and twilight, the loneliest of hours, was unknown. The sun went down dramatically – bang – just like that, below the rim of the desert. For the last fifteen minutes, feluccas were drawing in beside the banks of the Nile, with a creaking of windlass and the whine of great sails, their chains rattling as they moored. A scene her eyes had settled upon many times before, but had never really registered the beauty and serenity of it. How unlike the world she had left behind was this remote universe of sand, water, palm trees and statues; how different from the images of war she had witnessed, how wonderfully peaceful and removed from reality! Now, as she closed her eyes and breathed in the warm night, she could hardly believe that she was back.

Aida loved this land where she had grown up. Everything was familiar; she fitted in here and would have never left if her father hadn't died in such tragic and shocking circumstances. She would have probably married Phares. She had carried a torch for him since her early teens, spellbound by his charisma, even though the six years that separated them meant that she hadn't had much to do with him. Just enough to know that she regarded him with as much frustration as admiration. It had been the same for as long as she could remember.

When she was much younger, Aida had found the teenage Phares a source of annoyance: the overbearing older brother who always knew better. His sister Camelia, who was a year older than Aida, would often invite her over to Hathor, the Pharaonys' family home, in the school holidays. Phares would sometimes make an appearance when he was still living at home, studying for his college exams. One afternoon, when Aida was nine or ten, he had caught her hurtling down a garden slope far too quickly on her bicycle. When he had called out to her to stop, she had lost control of the handlebars and ended up in a hedge with a badly grazed shin. Phares had quickly helped her into the kitchen, all the while admonishing Aida for her reckless behaviour.

'If you hadn't shouted at me, I would have been fine,' she had protested vehemently.

But Phares would have none of it. 'Girls aren't meant for wheels, they should stay on their feet,' he had told her with a stern look. And while silently outraged by his response, she appreciated how much care he took in cleaning the blood off her leg so that it didn't hurt too much.

Another time, Aida had found an injured bird in the gardens of Karawan House. She and Camelia had been working out what to do with it when Phares arrived to fetch his sister home for supper. Immediately taking charge, he had instructed Aida to find a well-ventilated box and a small towel. Returning with it, she was told by Phares that he would take the bird back to Hathor. Aida had objected immediately. 'But it's my bird, I found it!' she cried. 'I can look after it here.'

'It needs to be kept still. Warm and quiet,' Phares told her as he placed it in the box. 'Undisturbed by you noisy girls.' With that, he strode off with the bird in the box, his sister Camelia following at his heels, throwing Aida an apologetic look. The next day, when Aida rushed over to the Pharaonys' house to see the little bird, Phares told her that it had recovered and flown away. Aida remembered the equal feelings of relief and disappointment that had washed over her, and witnessing the apparent confusion on her face, Phares had smiled indulgently, his stern features softening as he did so.

As she grew into a teenager, Aida's feelings regarding Phares became more confusing to her, and she was acutely aware of the times he returned home from medical school in France. Increasingly, she noticed a restlessness in him and was told by Camelia that when he wasn't studying, he would disappear into the depths of the desert to spend time with the Bedouins in their camps. For the young Aida, discovering this unexpected wild side to Phares intrigued her even more, for reasons she couldn't fathom.

One time she had been picking flowers with Camelia in the gardens at Hathor when she saw Phares arrive with a group of friends. Among them was a local girl, Isis, who was walking far too close to him for Aida's liking. Dark and statuesque, the older girl was laughing at something Phares had said, and Aida's stomach experienced a sudden uncomfortable lurch, a feeling unlike anything she'd felt before. For the first time she felt every bit the chubby, awkward teenager, and when later that evening she had lamented her situation to *Dada* Amina, the nanny had shushed the youngster's frustrated tears, drying her face with a handkerchief.

'You will not be the duckling for long, *ya binti*. Every girl needs time to grow into her looks. One day you will become a swan, and men will be falling at your feet.'

Aida had given her a trembling smile and kissed *Dada* Amina fondly, feeling instantly better, but she continued to watch Phares, wondering why he made her feel so miserable and excited at the same time.

Whenever he dropped by Karawan House or they met at Hathor she began to feel physically strange, her pulse giving a little kick. It soon became clear to her that she had developed a crush on him. Mortified at the thought that he might find out, she took it upon herself to argue with him at every opportunity, whether it was about going to parties where there might be boys present or staying out after nine o'clock in the evening. All her foreign friends – Greek, Italian, Armenian or English – were allowed these privileges, yet she was not.

'Like it or not, Aida, you are Egyptian and for us, it's just not done,' Phares had told her impatiently.

Later, she complained to Camelia, 'Why is he always so concerned about my reputation? Doesn't he realise that I'm not a little girl anymore? I have just as much right to be independent as the English and Greek girls.'

Although he was never unkind, Phares in turn seemed to enjoy baiting Aida, which only made matters worse. Camelia, meanwhile, guessing her best friend's secret admiration for her brother, teased Aida about it and watched the sparring of the two with great amusement.

With a sigh, Aida opened her eyes, pulling herself away from those distant memories. To think that if things had been different, by now she would likely have been the wife of Phares Pharaony.

A scent of heliotrope and roses stole up from the garden below, mingling with the aromatic breath of eucalyptus trees and the piquant tang of orange blossom. It was very still; no sound at all save the occasional *ahem* of Kherallah as he went on his nightly rounds of the estate and the muffled cough of a hyena or a desert fox.

How wonderful it was to be back, and yet tonight the place was filled with ghosts. It was too quiet and a little desolate, and the young woman felt its silence almost as a reproach. Still, now she had come home. It didn't matter about Karawan House being shabby and neglected, about the weeding not having being done and the crops being poor. The warmth of *Dada* Amina's embrace and the household's welcoming reception of her removed all these things to the back of her mind. Karawan House had opened its arms to her and, deep down, Aida knew she would never want to go away again.

She paced slowly up and down the veranda, the anguish of the past becoming a searing torment. Naguib's words went round and round in her head: '*I wouldn't dismiss an alliance with the Pharaonys so cavalierly, habibti … think about it.*' Knowing how she felt about Phares, her father had welcomed the union at the time, even encouraged it, but that was before … How could she marry the son of the man who had betrayed her father?

A knock at the door drew her out of her reverie. '*Otkhol*, come in,' she called out, coming back into the room and closing the window to the increasingly chilly night air.

*Dada* Amina came in, bearing a tray with her dinner.

'What are you doing in the dark, *ya binti*?'

Aida flicked the light switch and the room was immediately bathed in a golden glow from the crystal Waterford chandelier. 'I was on the veranda. The nights are so beautiful here.'

'I brought your dinner up. I thought you'd be too tired to go downstairs after your long journey.'

'*Shukran*, I think I *am* tired, though I don't really feel it yet. I'm so excited to be back.' The flight had indeed been long – the BOAC Flying Boat had taken her via Marseille and Sicily before reaching Cairo, and then another plane to Luxor – but ever since Aida had gazed through the small aircraft window and spotted the pyramids of Gizeh in the distance, any trace of fatigue had vanished. 'Place the tray just there, thank you.' Aida smiled at her nanny and looked at the variety of dishes set in front of her on the little round table. 'Let me see, what do we have here?' She couldn't help but compare this lavishness to the meagre meals she had become accustomed to in England. 'Goodness, it looks wonderful! But why so much? This amount would feed an entire family in England.'

'They're some of the dishes you used to like.'

Yes, Aida could see that. There was *aish baladi*, the delicious native wholewheat bread that looked like a large flat stone, thick and airy on the inside with speckles of cracked wheat throughout; *shorbat adas*, yellow lentil soup; *keshk*, a tasty chicken dish made with yoghurt; *torly*, a tray of baked vegetables and tomato sauce; *ma shi warak enab*, vine leaves stuffed with a rice mixture of ground beef, onions and herbs; *salata baladi*, the equivalent of mixed salad, and a big plate of *basboussa*. The only consolation was that whatever food was left over would never be wasted – Aida knew it would automatically be shared among the servants to eat either in the kitchen or be taken home to their families.

'There are far too many dishes. One would have sufficed,' she sighed, looking at the food guiltily. 'In England, people live on the bare minimum. Everything is still rationed even though the war has ended.'

'That is why you have grown so thin. When you left Egypt, *konty zay el warda el mefataha*, you were like a flower in bloom.' *Dada* Amina put her hands on her own ample hips. 'You must eat and put on some weight.'

Aida laughed. 'Ah yes, I'd forgotten that in Egypt, beauty is measured with scales – curvy women are considered more beautiful.'

'You have grown into a beautiful lady, but you are a little pale.' The older woman settled herself into one of the armchairs in the corner of the room. '*Ostaz* Naguib told me that you are a nurse now. Ayoub *Bey* would be very proud of you.'

'Yes, I hope so.' Aida took the seat opposite. Being in her own room again brought back so many memories. She gave a quiet sigh. 'I miss him, *Dada*.'

Her old nanny nodded sadly. 'Me too, *ya binti*.' She gazed at Aida, her expression full of concern. 'I know how hard it was for you, *ya danaya*, that day Ayoub *Bey* was taken from us right before our eyes, may God rest his soul.' She crossed herself, tears welling up in her eyes. 'I held you in my arms like you were a baby again. It was terrible how you were afterwards, refusing to see anyone except me for days on end. I thought my little one would die of grief.'

Aida swallowed a lump in her throat and stared numbly at the floor. 'Yes, I think I did too. It hurts to remember.' She looked up and fixed a bright, brave smile on her face. 'But let's not speak of Father sadly. He would have been happy that I did my part for the war effort in England, at least.'

'*Allah!* He would have been worried sick about you every day.' *Dada* Amina drew a handkerchief from her pocket and wiped her eyes. 'I am just happy that it was God's will to spare you and return you to us.' Her watery gaze became suddenly intent. 'You were alone in England. I hope your English uncle looked after you properly. You must have had the eyes of many men on you.'

At this, Aida raised an eyebrow. 'Yes, Uncle George was very protective of me ... *Dada* Amina, what are you getting at exactly?'

'All I'm saying is that you weren't interested in any of the Egyptian men you met here, always wanting to go your own way. You were rebellious since the day you were born, just like your father.'

The old servant looked at Aida over her glasses. 'Phares *Bey* has never married, you know.'

Aida gave her nanny a sidelong glance. 'Really ... and why are you telling me this, *Dada* Amina?'

'There was once talk about a marriage between you and him. You may not have been engaged but since you were children there was an understanding, so to speak. Ayoub *Bey* was very keen on a union between your two families.'

'That was a long time ago. I've grown up since, and I'd no more marry a man I don't love than fly.'

*Dada* Amina shot her a look of astute surprise. 'Your heart has changed, then? You used to like Phares *Bey,* even though you used to be so rude to the poor boy.'

Aida frowned and reached for the flatbread, tearing off a piece. 'Most of the time he deserved it. Besides, what did I know about men and love at eighteen or life in general? Brought up like I was, protected in a cocoon.'

'You were brought up as a lady of your class should have been.'

'Well, I've changed. The world here is so cut off from reality. It's been frozen in the past. People live as our ancestors did thousands of years ago. Though I love this country, I'm not sure how I'll be able to adapt to it again. Perhaps it will have to accept my values, not the other way around.'

A shadow crossed *Dada* Amina's brow. 'Have you given your heart to a *khawaga*, a foreigner?'

Aida laughed. 'No, don't worry ... my heart has remained intact and is still mine to give, or not, *ala mazagui,* as I please.' She ate the bread, in truth wondering if she would ever find an Egyptian man who could make her truly happy.

Aida had never fallen in love. When she left Egypt, she had been an innocent teenager who had only mixed with families in her social circle who knew the rules of the game. If a young man was interested in a girl, there were no illicit meetings. He would '*dekhul min elbab*', 'enter from the front door, as the saying went in Arabic, and ask for her hand. The young couple would then use the period of engagement like a halfway marriage, in order to get to know each other. Although she had many suitors back then, Aida had turned them all down and Ayoub, a broad-minded man who himself had lived a great love story with his wife, was not one to enforce his will on his daughter on a matter as serious as marriage. When the subject had arisen, Aida had told her father how she felt about Phares, and Ayoub, who had always considered the young doctor dependable and serious with a brilliant future, was happy to entrust to him his dearly-beloved only daughter without a qualm. Still, nothing had been officially arranged; Ayoub had died under a cloud of disgrace, then Aida had left Egypt.

In the early days in England, lost and bereaved, Aida had had no impulse to do any of the bright things that other young girls took as a matter of course. Then, inevitably, what in the beginning had been no more than the restraints of her mourning became settled habit. Her training to be a nurse, then her work, absorbed her more and more. The misery she had witnessed in the hospitals compelled her to grow up overnight, not only leaving no place for love in her life, but also inculcating in her psyche a deep taste for her freedom.

Aida's thoughts were interrupted by *Dada* Amina's voice, saying, 'The Pharaonys have been good to us over the years. Since you're a trained nurse, why not ask Phares *Bey* to give you a job at his hospital?'

'His hospital?'

'*Da garrah add il donya*, he's a great surgeon now with his own hospital, El Amal. He had it built three years ago. You get much better care there than at the government hospital on the edge of town.'

'He must charge an arm and a leg if he's that important,' Aida muttered.

'*Abadan*, not at all. He has a department where he treats patients for free. He may be a proud man but he has always been kind and generous. Even as a boy, he used to give food to the beggars in the road.'

'Well, anyhow, I don't know why we're discussing Phares and his family. I want nothing to do with them.'

The old servant gave Aida a rueful look. 'Phares *Bey* has never married. You broke his heart when you refused his proposal, *ya haram*, poor thing.'

'For heaven's sake!' Aida jumped up from her chair and began pacing. 'We hardly knew each other.'

'*Allah! Habibti*, has the war addled your brain? How is that true?'

Aida knew she was on shaky ground with *Dada* Amina, who had witnessed all her emotional ups and downs when she was growing up. She tried a different tack. 'You forget that he'd been away for years when he was studying in France and only came back for the holidays.'

'Same as you.'

'Maybe. Anyhow, he disapproved of my thinking and my ways. He always said I was too liberal and impulsive. Phares was doing what every eldest son from a landed family does … wanting to add to his dynasty's riches. My land adjoined his land. I was the only heiress of the estate. My father had already put it in my name.' She flung her hand up in derision. 'By Egyptian standards it was a marriage made in heaven.'

'*La ya danaya*, no, my dear child, you're wrong. I used to see how Phares *Bey* looked at you when he came to visit. Even when you had those fiery arguments … I think that, deep down, he admired you.'

Aida stopped in her tracks, for a moment disconcerted by the idea that Phares Pharaony might have regarded her with anything approaching respect. She folded her arms. 'Well, all that is in the past and you can forget about our union … it will not happen.'

_Dada_ Amina sighed deeply. 'Does anybody know what fate has in store for us? *Al maktoub alal guibeen la bodda an tarah el ein*, what is written on the brow will inevitably be seen by the eye. What is written will be fulfilled,' she enunciated with confidence.

Aida laughed. 'Ah yes, your favourite saying. Well, fate or no fate, I'm telling you there will be no alliance between the El Masri and El Pharaony families. And now enough of that, I'm much more interested to know about you. How have you been all these years?'

'I can't complain. *Ostaz* Naguib took care of us, *Allah ye barikloh*, God bless him, and kept all our salaries going.'

'Well, I'm back now and there's nothing to worry about anymore. I will take care of everything,' Aida promised, though she was not feeling altogether as confident as she sounded.

As if sensing that the moment for trying to influence Aida had passed, *Dada* Amina gestured to the unopened luggage at the foot of the bed. 'You came with a very small suitcase. Where are all your belongings?'

'Life in Europe is still all about belt-tightening. No fancy clothes, I'm afraid. People have barely enough to eat.'

'*Ya haram*, poor thing. You must tell *Sit* Nabila to take you to her dressmaker *fil bandar*, downtown.'

'I'm better off going to Cairo for a week or so. I'll stay at Shepheard's Hotel. I'll go to Cicurel – they always had the latest fashion. Is Au Rêve des Dames, their haberdashery and ladieswear, still at 19 Kasr al-Nil Street?'

*Dada* Amina looked horrified. '*Maarafsh*, I don't know. One thing I do know is that you can't think of leaving us again when you've only just arrived,' she said sulkily.

Aida went to her old nanny and leaned over to put her arms around her. 'I'm not going anywhere yet, I have too much to do here first. And when I do, it'll just be for a few days.' She paused, choosing her words carefully. 'You said it yourself – I have nothing to wear and, besides, I need to pay my respects to the British Ambassador, Sir Miles Lampson. I have a letter from Uncle George to give him as they're old school friends.'

It had not escaped Aida that the ambassador would be a useful person to get to know. The Embassy was actively engaged in helping local Cairo law enforcement track down any smugglers of antiquities. The British prided themselves on their active involvement in trying to put a stop to the trafficking. If she was to play detective, then Sir Miles was a good place to start. Though Naguib was right, she was a woman alone and would need to tread carefully.

*Dada* Amina patted the side of Aida's arm as the young woman enveloped her in a hug. 'If you go to Cairo and stay at a hotel you'll be drawn into the social circle there and we won't see you again. When you return, you'll find it too quiet and will get fidgety, as when you were a young girl. Whenever Ayoub *Bey* took you to Cairo, you always found ways of staying longer.'

Aida frowned. She was not entirely convinced that people in Cairo would welcome her with open arms. Unlike Naguib, she was under no illusions that Egyptian society would have forgotten who she was. As soon as the news got out that Aida El Masri had returned home, her old acquaintances might turn their backs with the same scornful disapproval they had shown her when she fled Egypt. Still, if rebelliousness was in the El Masri blood, then so too was determination, and Aida would have to rely on this to carry her through.

'Maybe,' she answered pensively, releasing *Dada* Amina from her embrace. 'In any case, in those days I used to stay in Gizeh at Kasr El Ghoroub, the Pharaony House. I can't do that now.'

She looked wistful, remembering all those times with Camelia, to whom she hadn't spoken since she left Egypt. 'By the way, how is Camelia? Do you ever hear anything of her?'

'*Meskina Sit* Camelia, poor Mrs Camelia, her husband died in a car accident *alal tarik el sahrawy*, on the desert road between Cairo and Alexandria. They didn't have time to enjoy their married life.'

'Oh no!' Aida was horrified. In these last eight years Camelia had been married and widowed. Naguib had said nothing about it.

'Poor little one, she mourned the *Bey* like a turtle dove mourns his mate. *Dada* Fatma, who brought the *Sit* up and moved to Mounir *Bey*'s house when they were married, told me that day and night Camelia's eyes rained down tears ... she grew pale and wan as the young moon in the month of Ramadan.'

Aida loved the theatrical terms and imagery the *fellahin* sometimes used in their speech. Some of the phrases were so poetic that she had often thought to collect them in a scrapbook.

'Where is Camelia now?'

'She lives here at the Sunrise Farm Estate, *Esbat El Shorouk*, but I think that she often goes to Cairo. Especially when Phares *Bey* is at the Anglo-American Hospital in Zamalek.'

'Phares *Bey* works in Cairo too?'

'*Ommal*, of course, as I have told you, *da garrah add el dinya*.'

'I'll get in touch with Camelia. We were good friends. I can't blame her for what her father did,' she added, without thinking.

*Dada* Amina's eyes widened. '*Allah!* You still carry that idea around with you? Let it go, *habibti*. Kamel Pasha had nothing to do with your father's arrest. You are wrong, *ya binti*. I know that girl Souma filled your head with all this nonsense, but it was all lies, trust me.'

Aida lifted her head sharply. 'How can you know that? Why would she have lied?'

'*Eblees yaaraf raboh laken yatakhabeth*, the devil knows his Lord but still practises evil. Souma is a person who thrives on intrigue. You could never trust her.'

'Well, she was always pleasant around me. Anyway, if Souma wasn't telling the truth, I'm going to find out why.'

'Don't stir up a hornets' nest, *Sit* Aida. No good will come of it. Souma is long gone, and good riddance to her. You will only bring the evil eye closer by meddling.'

'I can look after myself, *Dada*, don't worry,' answered Aida, folding her arms. The conversation was going down a route she would rather avoid.

*Dada* Amina shook her head disapprovingly. '*Mafish fayda*, it's no use … you are so stubborn when you get an idea into your head.' She hauled herself out of her chair with a sigh. 'I will not waste my breath trying to convince you. I'd do much better to run you a hot bath so you can have an early night. Maybe when you're not so tired, you'll be able to think more rationally.'

Aida's irritation softened. 'I don't think so, but thank you, *ya Dada*, I would love a bath.'

It would be a change not to worry about hot water. In England, everyone had been careful with it as coal was rationed. For all the backward ways of Egypt, at least they still had their luxuries. Aida counted herself lucky that for the time being at least, she would enjoy everything her homeland had to offer.

Her mind returned to Camelia Pharaony. Tomorrow she would explore the estate and perhaps even try to see her friend if she was in Luxor.

*     *     *

Sheer exhaustion brought sleep to Aida that night. As dawn pointed, she was woken by the musical chant of the muezzin, half a mile away in the centre of Luxor, calling the Prophet's followers to prayer from the tall minaret of his mosque. She had always found that faraway sound rather romantic, floating like an echo over the countryside at sunrise or at dusk.

Aida sprang from her bed and pattered quickly across the room to the veranda to watch the sun come up. The moment was so short! Like dusk in this part of the world, there was scarcely a dawn – it was night, then day, as suddenly as a cannon's flash.

The whole of the sky was deeply flushed as the sun appeared low on the horizon, casting slender shadows on the gardens below and the date palms in the cultivated fields beyond. The Nile, the feluccas, the ancient city on the opposite bank were all tinged with colour. The air was like wine and held a thousand scents. Aida loved this hour when the countryside was waking: flocks of turtledoves were rustling round the trees, cocks were crowing, donkeys braying, water-wheels creaking.

She washed and dressed swiftly. Choosing a sleeveless white cotton broderie anglaise dress with a full skirt and a square décolleté, she girded her tiny waist with a wide blue belt. Slipping on a pair of white pumps, she crept noiselessly downstairs, out of the garden and into the fields that bordered the grounds. Today, she wanted to make a pilgrimage to the places she had always loved.

Her heart contracted as she set out on foot along the familiar road, which she had often taken on horseback at her father's side, at the end of which lay the trees dividing the El Masri land from the Pharaony Estate. As the sun was still gentle, she perched her sunglasses on top of her head to see the countryside in all its glorious colour.

The trees had been planted by an ancestor as an indelible marker between the two properties. In these villages so close to the Nile, when the river overflowed in early summer and flooded the fields, it often washed away any other boundary marks between the plots. In the past, landholders could have great difficulty in ascertaining the outer limits of the land they owned, resulting in family feuds that lasted for generations.

The sandy lane was fringed with date trees. Palm groves and cotton fields stretched afar on either side. The years seemed to roll back as Aida gazed around her, the pungent aroma of the sun-warmed earth and fecund smell of the Nile taking her back to her childhood. The *fellahin* were already hoeing and planting. The land was being prepared for the new cotton season. In one field a wooden plough was being pulled by two cows. Further away in another, groups of men were using picks to make even furrows in the ground, while others hoed the land between the rows of plants. A few women in long brightly coloured robes were coming and going on the path, carrying baskets on their heads and shoulders. One of them was returning from the river with a heavy pitcher on her head; Aida had always been fascinated by the gracefulness and amazing balance these peasant women had, their carriage that of a queen.

Groups of men by a stretch of canal near the road were hauling up water with a *shaduf,* an irrigation tool dating from the pharaohs, many of which could be seen up and down the Nile. It was composed of a long pole supported in seesaw fashion on an upright frame, from the end of which hung a wooden bucket to draw water from the river. Next to it the *saqia* waterwheel was turning, another irrigation mechanism devised by the Ptolemaic dynasty. Driven by buffalo, Aida had always been fascinated by it, watching for hours as it slowly lifted water and slopped it into irrigation ditches. She found it one of the most beautiful machines invented by man, combining aesthetic grace with bestial energy.

A *fellah* ambled past, dangling his legs and oscillating on the back of a small donkey. He smiled at the young woman. '*Sabbah El Kheyr, ya Sit,* good morning, my lady,' he said as he went by. Aida smiled in return and answered his greeting. She had no doubt that everybody at the *Esba*, and probably around Luxor, knew that the daughter of Ayoub El Masri was back.

She had been walking for an hour. By now, the sun was blazing down on her from a sky of cloudless blue. Aida loved the sun, although just now she was starting to feel it becoming almost too hot as she'd come out without a hat. The belt of high trees which separated the El Masri land from the Pharaonys' sugarcane plantation was now in view. She could either turn left down the path that bordered the trees and circle back homewards, or follow the wide side track in front of her, of which she had no recollection. She was not tired; on the contrary, this walk in the countryside, where the air was so pure in comparison to the polluted atmosphere of London, had energised her.

The new path proved delightfully cool after the sunny sandy lane. Soon it ran alongside another narrow canal banked by willow trees, their branches spilling into the water. On the other side of the path tall flame trees shed their mottled shade. The silence was deep; only her footfall could be heard, the hush broken now and again by the chirping of a bird.

On the opposite side of the canal Aida spotted a village where most of the *fellahin* who laboured on the El Masri land lived. A rabbit warren of low mud huts, they were all connected by the same crumbling walls. Their flat roofs were covered with cotton stalks, and they had no windows, only narrow doorways where a man had to stoop to enter. Black-gowned women sat on the ground, grinding corn or tending little odorous fires, their children in filthy rags staring at her, with matted hair and grime-encrusted faces. In one place a blindfolded ox patiently walked in an endless circle, turning the great flat wheel of a *saqia*; in front of a tiny whitewashed mosque an aged sheikh was expounding the chapters of the Koran to an attentive group of youths.

There were more paths opening on the right. Lost in thought, Aida turned down one of them, then down a second, until she found herself in an enclosed space where a group of buffalo were standing, one of them being milked by a *fellaha*. Aida realised that she was probably lost. The peasant woman flashed her a smile of welcome.

'*Sabah El kheyr ya Sit*, can I help you?'

'*Sabah El nour*, I think I'm lost. Where am I?'

'You're at *Esbat El Shorouk.*'

Aida frowned. 'The Sunrise Farm Estate? You mean this is Pharaony land?'

'*Aywa ya Sit*, yes, my lady.' The woman got up from her milking stool, dipped a tin cup into the pail of foaming milk and held it out to Aida. '*It faddally*, please have some.'

Aida did not like to drink milk which hadn't been boiled, but she took the cup so graciously offered. '*Shukran*, thank you.' She drank it, to the delight of the *fellaha*, who beamed at her, and thanked the woman again. Then she turned and headed back the way she had come.

She had been walking for almost half an hour when she realised that she must have taken another wrong turning. She found herself on a narrow track bordered by ancient fig trees planted closely together. Their interlacing branches formed a canopy above her head like a natural loggia, barring the entry of sunlight. Only glimpses of the hot blue sky could be seen through small gaps in the broken roof. Bees flew across her path, vanishing with a buzz into the juicy flesh of the ripe fruit that were bursting open from the heat.

Further along, as Aida emerged from the shadowed canopy, the track turned and opened out on to a great clear space with a house and a few carob and date palm trees. Low and built in stone, the house had whitewashed walls and blue wooden shutters, between which the leaded panes of glass of the windows shot forth flames of rose and green, orange and gold. A stream cooed on the side of the house and the long grass around it was dotted with clumps of colourful wild flowers.

. She remembered this old cottage of Kasr El Shorouk. How could she forget? How fantastic and beautiful and out of this world it was. Aida stood there on the edge of the sunlight with the dense trees behind her, watching spellbound as the door to the little cottage opened and a figure emerged. Without thinking, she quickly pulled her sunglasses down to cover her eyes.

A man strode forward. He was over six feet tall, with the supple, sinewy body of an athlete, and there was strength in the alert vigour of his movements. The breadth of his shoulders fitted with his height, and thick, unruly hair fell a little over a high forehead. He wore a cream cotton shirt with the sleeves rolled up to his elbows, and his long, muscular legs clad in a brown pair of riding breeches strode towards her.

'Where on earth have you come from?' he demanded. The voice was deep, almost curt. He had addressed her in perfect English. There must be something about her clothes or looks that branded her a foreigner. Aida recognised him immediately. He was as autocratic and arrogant as ever, she decided, and for a dizzy moment her heart stopped beating. However, it seemed that he hadn't recognised *her* – her face disguised by her sunglasses – and for the moment, it suited Aida to have the upper hand.

He was even more handsome and charismatic than she remembered, with a strong jaw and an almost golden tint to his tanned face as though he carried the reflection of his family's wealth and greatness in the very moulding of his features and the hue of his skin. She remembered the last time she had seen him, stern in a navy suit, finely pinstriped, wearing an expression that had unnerved her immeasurably. She took a deep breath and licked her lips, which had suddenly gone dry. A silent curse went through her mind. She hadn't seen him for eight years and it took no more than the sight of him for her to go weak at the knees.

Phares Pharaony. Phares, meaning knight, the man who had been the knight of her dreams until the day of the tragedy. He stopped in front of her and seemed not to notice how his proximity made her stiffen. His large almond-shaped eyes settled severely on her face, so startling in their density that they made Aida think of coals with a flame at the centre where passions might be quietly smouldering. They were fixing her now with a look that tested her nerves to the utmost limit.

She recalled how that same look from those eyes had made her feel like an irresponsible schoolgirl the day she dared to accuse his father of deceit and treachery. But eight years on, and they had a different effect, making her conscious of herself as a woman, and this strange new feeling was even more alarming.

'Who are you? And how did you get here?' The strong and dominant voice was achingly familiar.

'I'm afraid I'm trespassing,' she said, tilting her head up to him.

'You must have been aware of that for some time,' he observed with a significant glance behind her towards the path by which she had obviously come.

Aida was not going to tell him who she was, and that she had got lost. 'Maybe, but the countryside is so beautiful around here …'

'… That you decided to explore the place, even though you knew it was wrong,' he finished her sentence abruptly. His gaze travelled over her face as if trying to discern her expression behind the sunglasses then dropped to her lips, lingering there and making her heart beat frantically.

'Well, now I'll go back again.'

'Just like that.'

Aida's chin went up belligerently. 'Yes, just like that.'

'I've caught you trespassing and you will pay your forfeit, Miss ... What's your name?'

The rebellious teenager of eight years ago would have spluttered that it was none of his business, but Aida had grown more poised and confident since then. She kept looking at him, but didn't answer.

Phares regarded her coolly, a faintly mocking smile hovering about his full mouth. His eyes flickered over her hair. 'Okay, then ... Goldilocks.' Aida instantly recognised the same, sudden, unexpected flash of humour and tenderness in his smile that could transform his whole expression. Yes, she did feel like the girl who had gone for a walk in the forest and ended up at the three bears' house, somewhere she shouldn't have been.

Taking her cue from him, she entered into the game: 'Goldilocks came to no good.'

'That I can believe,' he replied, giving her a steady, appraising look ... There was something about the way he spoke, about the brightness and vitality of his gaze, the tanned bronze of his complexion, the crisp waves of his raven-black hair that made him seem twice as vividly alive as most of the men Aida had so far encountered in her life.

They didn't speak for a few moments. 'You must have been walking for quite a while to have come in from the back of the house and it's still early,' he observed pensively. 'Adjoining our land is the El Masri Estate. Presumably you crossed that property too. What were you doing out at the crack of dawn?' Phares glanced down at her disapprovingly. 'Has no one told you that it is dangerous for a *khawagaya*, I mean a foreign woman, to walk alone in these villages?'

She concealed her turmoil with an offhand smile. 'You surprise me. Since my arrival, I have only encountered courtesy here. I was kindly welcomed by one of your farm women.'

'Welcomed by one of my farm women?'

'Yes, she was milking, and very hospitably gave me a cup of milk.'

There was a sardonic tilt to his eyebrow. 'Really? And did you drink it?'

Aida nodded.

'You drank it, though I presume it hadn't been boiled?'

'I am not usually so ...'

'Reckless? Do you know that in this part of the world raw milk can cause tuberculosis?'

She folded her arms. This was just like the old Phares. 'How could I have refused such a spontaneous gesture?'

'You still haven't answered me. What were you doing out in the countryside at the crack of dawn? You must be a guest somewhere. We're too far from the centre of Luxor for you to be a tourist.'

'I was exploring this beautiful countryside.'

'You like our country?'

'Very much so.'

He smiled, showing a row of brilliant white teeth. 'It must seem quaint to you, as if suspended in another time.'

'That's what I like about it.'

'Come,' he said, his expression becoming imperious, 'I told you you'd have to pay a forfeit. You're going to have coffee with me.'

'I think I ought to go back.'

'You can go back immediately afterwards and I'll show you a much shorter way out of our *esba*, I mean our farm.' His voice was gentle, and when she didn't answer, his eyes became a velvety caress. 'Is my suggestion not clear enough?'

For a moment the coal flame dancing in Phares's black eyes had her hypnotised. Aida smiled, but remained silent.

'Come,' he said again, 'do as you're told.'

Aida started at the command, feeling a surge of indignation – she hated machismo in men, always had – but she smiled to herself. Phares hadn't changed; he'd always been bossy and slightly arrogant. 'I don't think so, thank you.'

Phares gave a soft laugh, watching her with amusement. 'I think you were going to accept my invitation, so what brought up the prickles, Goldilocks?'

She decided to ignore the taunt. He used to indulge in this sort of innocent banter when she was fifteen and in those days she was happy for the attention, now his patronising tone merely irritated her. 'You said there was a shorter way out of your property?'

'No coffee then?'

'No, thank you.'

'I'm coming with you.'

'If you give me directions, I'm quite capable of finding my way alone.'

'Possibly. But I'm not going to allow you to do so.'

Aida gave up. In silence they crossed the garden, striking through the Pharaony sugarcane plantation towards the Nile. Here, a path ran straight to the main road along the river, not far from the El Masri fields of cotton and the lane that Aida had taken that morning. It was less than half the distance of her morning walk.

'There you are,' said Phares. 'Now you're on the main road. And since you haven't told me where you're staying, I can't give you any more directions.' He studied her face intently. 'I assume you're a guest at one of the large farms beside the river. Whichever side you're on, in each direction you'll find a bridge which leads to the opposite bank.'

Aida smiled. 'Thank you very much.' She held out her hand. 'Goodbye.'

He took it in his own strong palm and as their skin touched it seemed to Aida that she was warmed from head to toe, making her almost gasp aloud. It was as if the firm hand holding hers infused its own vitality, an electric current galvanising her cold, bewildered self to life. Never in her life had a handshake caused that to happen. Right away she wanted to break the contact and, as if sensing this, Phares increased the pressure of his grip. Heart beating furiously, she stood looking up at him, into those magnificent dark, laughing eyes, and to her irritation, Aida felt her cheeks colour.

The sun meshed him in gold. He conveyed an air of inherent authority that seemed to be as much a part of him as his tall, sparse figure and raven black hair. 'I am Phares Pharaony ... Dr Phares Pharaony. Will you come and visit me again now that you know the way?' The initial hardness in his voice had disappeared and been replaced with a low-pitched warmth and vibrancy.

'Goodbye, Dr Pharaony.'

Phares was still holding on to her hand, locking it within his, as if telling her without words that she was now in the power of the Pharaony family and there was to be no escape from him. 'Say that you will come and see me again.'

His nearness overpowered her; he looked at her in a way that was overwhelming; not even when she was younger had she felt like this, and she wanted to distance herself from him to dispel the effect. Gently, she managed to disengage herself from his warm grip. 'Goodbye,' she said determinedly.

Phares flashed her an easy smile with those fine even white teeth showing again as his lips parted.

'Stubborn, aren't you? But I'm more stubborn still. I will find you and we will meet again before too long.'

'Will we?' she challenged him. '*I* don't think so.'

The air between them crackled with intensity and they stood there mesmerised for longer than Aida knew. In the silence, the young woman felt the atmosphere become charged with a force that seemed elemental ... as if a storm were coming.

Had Phares felt it too? For a second, a furtive questioning look flashed in his dark pupils, then he said abruptly, 'You must go, Goldilocks.' There was a low note of urgency in his voice.

'Yes, I must.' But Aida's feet were rooted, an odd glow of warmth rising in her face; she would not have moved unless Phares, with a nod and a smile, hadn't turned away at that moment and gone briskly off towards the path. Aida was freed then, and with a fleet step and a beating heart went speeding down the path alongside the Nile, still in a daze.

She was stunned by the feelings that had assailed her in Phares's presence – the same lightheadedness she felt years ago when he was in the same room, but with something more, a totally alien emotion that had stirred every nerve in her body. It must be the heat, she thought, or physical exhaustion, or perhaps the lack of food; she had gone out this morning without having any breakfast and now it was almost time for lunch.

The river was flowing timelessly between its banks, grey and tranquil amid green rushes, papyrus and other water plants. It had a romantic magic that was all its own – tranquillity plus mystery, ancient yet untouched by time – a magic that had surrounded her for the first eighteen years of her life. And now she was back and it was as if she had never gone away. Yet her future here was uncertain, complicated by the mission she had given herself. After all, eight years had passed …

If she was to believe Naguib Bishara's words to her yesterday, Aida supposed that once Phares knew who she was – and he would eventually – he would ask her to marry him; and she would of course dismiss him as she had previously.

But would she? The young man had always fascinated her, and still did.

Wouldn't she find it easier to investigate the truth if she didn't let on about her intentions and merely rolled with the waves? Wouldn't it be more astute to get closer to the Pharaony family instead of distancing herself from them? Still, that option, she decided, felt wrong. No, for so many reasons, Phares could never be hers nor she his.

Nevertheless, as she walked back to Karawan House *Dada* Amina's favourite quote rang like a presentiment in her ears: *Al maktoub alal guibeen la bodda an tarah el ein*, what is written will be fulfilled. Aida didn't know whether she wished this, or feared it.

# CHAPTER 2

Alone in his powerful MG TC two-seater, lost in thought, Dr Phares Pharaony was driving back from El Amal, his hospital in Luxor, to Kasr El Shorouk, his home on the outskirts of the city. The narrow, uneven road, which ran perilously close to the high bank of a deep canal, was teeming with the usual hordes of people and animals. He was accustomed to the familiar medley of large buffalos and their calves snorting; small donkeys trotting stiffly in the middle of the road, loaded with *berseem* – the native clover on which all animals were fed; mangy dogs barking; children shouting and running after the car; and the fowl, geese and ducks flying haphazardly about, clucking furiously. Sometimes this swarm of unruly, happy-go-lucky people and their flocks made him smile indulgently, but today, Dr Pharaony was grim-faced at the wheel. He blasted his horn irritably as the roadster constantly swerved from side to side while he tried to avoid collision with either man or beast by a hair's breadth, and the mass scattered wildly.

Strangely enough, the reason for Phares's black mood could be laid at Aida's door. The young doctor had spent most of his Sunday trying to find out discreetly the identity of the beautiful siren who had appeared so unexpectedly in his garden that morning, but his enquiries remained fruitless. No new group of visitors had arrived in Luxor, either by train or plane, during the last forty-eight hours. The only person who had come on the Misrair plane from Cairo the day before was *Sit* Aida, Ayoub El Masri's daughter, whom he remembered all too clearly had been a plump girl of no great beauty, albeit with intelligence and wit, and a fiery and reckless nature that he secretly admired.

Phares was blessed with striking good looks, as well as great charm, intelligence and a magnificent constitution, and had not lived to the age of thirty-four in monk-like austerity. Westernised, educated in France and well travelled, he'd had his share of passing affairs, like any other man of his age and background. Cairo being a cosmopolitan place, Phares hadn't needed to poach his pleasure among the more conservative Egyptian and Turkish families, but had found it in the company of light-hearted Western women who, like him, were looking for carefree passing flings.

Phares's experiences had given him insight and wisdom; he knew women very well, liked them tremendously and judged them shrewdly. He was a man of strong passions, firmly reined in – when he chose to do so – but he was far from a saint. Because of his wealth and good looks, any inclination he might have had towards excess could easily be indulged, but his innate strength of character had ensured that he'd become mature and ripened but not spoiled. Wise, kind and responsible, yet still quick to respond to the pleasures of life, he pulsed with life and energy.

However, despite his experience and sophistication, one thing so far had been lacking in him: Phares had never been in love. Not that this was of great relevance. In accordance with the custom of great landowning families, he was now of an age where society thought that he needed a wife. In fact, before the war there had been talk of him marrying Aida El Masri, the only daughter of Ayoub El Masri, his father's best friend and the owner of the neighbouring *esba*. Marriage to his childhood friend Aida would not have been without its challenges but it would have combined their estates, something his father Kamel had set his sights upon. In any case, that had been prevented by the sudden death of Ayoub El Masri, and Aida had left the country for England just before the war broke out, so matters had stood as before. And as the war continued, Phares had found neither the time, nor the reason, to marry, and his father Kamel remained hopeful that one day Aida would return and the knot would be tied, or the young woman would eventually sell to him. In either case the land would become part of the Pharaony estates.

Phares sighed. He knew that if Aida El Masri was back, his father would be raising his hopes once more that his eldest son would do his duty.

Hathor, the Pharaony residence in Luxor, named after the Ancient Egyptian goddess of love, rose against the sky above the eastern bank of the great river. An imposing wrought-iron gate announced the entrance to the *esba*; on one of its inlaid wooden panels was etched a mural of the nearby Temple of Hathor at Denderah, while on the other gate, a poem was carved in hieroglyphics, in which Hathor, goddess of the Nile, exalted her husband Horus, god of the sky.

Phares passed the gatekeeper's lodge and swept up the broad driveway of the noble house edged with elegant palm trees and crossed by gravel paths. Built of white sandstone in the old colonial style, it was square and pillared and substantial. A tall colonnaded porch dominated the entire frontage, and all along the upper storey, set further back, long, green-shuttered windows led from the first-floor bedrooms on to the balcony above. It was a gracious home and because it was so lovingly maintained and cared for, the years had been kind to it.

Coming to a stop in front of the fine marble steps leading up to the front door, Phares was surprised to see that the shutters of his father's apartment were wide open. His frown deepened. Kamel had left for Assiut earlier that week on business and was not expected to return for at least two weeks. He had planned to extend his journey to Cairo and then onwards to call on his elderly mother Fardus, who lived in the Pharaony family home in Alexandria and whom he visited every three months. It was not in the *pasha*'s habit to cut short these trips unless something of importance required a change of plan.

Phares was overcome by a wave of concern and he rushed up the steps; Kamel had a weak heart and the young doctor's immediate thought was that his father had been taken ill. As he reached the threshold, he was met by Daoud the head *suffragi*.

'*Masa' al-khayr ya*, Daoud, good afternoon. Why are the shutters of Kamel Pasha's apartment opened? Has my father returned?'

'*Masa' al-khayr ya Bey.* Yes, *Saat El Basha,* His Highness the *pasha* arrived about an hour ago. He told me to ask you to join him on the main terrace as soon as you came in. He is waiting for you.'

'Fine. I will join him immediately. Is he well?'

If Daoud was surprised by his master's question his impassive expression revealed nothing. 'Yes, he is well. He is having a glass of *karkadeeh*. Would you like one as well or would you prefer tea or coffee?'

'I will have the same as the *pasha, shukran.*'

While the outside of Hathor was stately – beautifully designed by an Italian architect to be a clear statement of wealth and status, with its balconies, porticoes and terraces well-hidden from the road by hedges of blooming tropical shrubs and great flowering vines – the interior of the house was no less impressive. Its hall was a large circular space with a considerable domed ceiling of night-blue Venetian stained glass, scattered here and there with tiny golden stars, and below this representation of the firmament, a floor of diamond-shaped white-and-grey granite and black tiles. On the right was the grand marble and wrought-iron stairway and gallery leading to the floors above; on the opposite side was the wood-panelled dining room, its dimensions ample for a banquet, elegantly furnished with highly

polished furniture upholstered with leather embossed with gold.
While the whole interior of the house was filled with exquisite
Persian carpets and was highly ornamented, often with gold leaf,
none of it was overdone. It was furnished in elegant European
style with corresponding furniture upholstered in delicate
brocades, all in the very best of taste.

Phares made his way down one of the many corridors to
the main terrace at the back of the house, where he found the *pasha*
waiting for him. Kamel Pharaony was seated in an armchair at one
of the small tables, sipping cold *karkadeeh*, an infusion of hibiscus
flowers renowned for lowering blood pressure – its effect somewhat
undermined no doubt by the large plate of pastries he was
comfortably working his way through.

Kamel beamed as Phares stepped on to the terrace. 'Ah, there
you are, Phares, my son.'

'I'm surprised to see you, Father. You were supposed to be
back on Sunday. When I saw your shutters were open, I was
worried. Is anything the matter?'

'No, no, no, nothing to worry about. Everything is great.'

Kamel Pharaony was a handsome portly man in his early
sixties, his skin tanned to a deep bronze and with thick white
hair and a big white curled-up moustache. An air of greatness
flowed around him. At first glance it might have been difficult
to credit that Phares and the *pasha* were father and son, but
the two proud faces, the brilliant dark eyes, high-bridged noses
and the charisma emanating from both men spoke of a strong
resemblance, and at a second glance their kinship was
unmistakable.

Kamel had never wanted to remarry after Gamila's death,
not only because he had loved his wife deeply, but also because
he did not want to bring a stepmother into his children's life.
A man of the world, farsighted and wise, he had realised that
he was young enough to remarry and have more children,

children whom in some sense might usurp part of the place Phares and Camelia occupied in his heart. Besides, he could not believe that any normal woman would not put her own children first. Added to this, there was the question of inheritance: what would happen to Phares and Camelia if something happened to him and he had had more sons? Phares hadn't needed his father to explain his reasoning to him; he understood and admired the sacrifice Kamel had made on his behalf, and was grateful to him.

'Sit down,' the older man commanded.

'I'll stand for a while if you don't mind,' Phares answered, leaning against one of the marble columns that lined the terrace. 'I've been too busy to go for my usual walk today.'

'Suit yourself.'

Phares eyed his father suspiciously. Kamel was acting out of character. He was usually calm and collected, but this evening he could sense a restless excitement in the old man. 'What's up, Father?'

'Well, you'll never guess …'

Phares's eyebrows went up enquiringly.

'Ayoub El Masri's daughter is back …'

Ah, so he was right. Now he had no difficulty in guessing at what was behind his father's strange behaviour. Phares shrugged nonchalantly. 'So? I don't see what's so surprising in that. She had to return one day. Her house is in a sorry state and if it hadn't been for us, her land would have fallen into the hands of squatters. It's high time she came back to Egypt to look after her affairs.'

'But, my son, can't you see? This is a wonderful opportunity.'

Phares's tall figure stiffened, his dark eyes growing wary. He readied himself for the onslaught, for he knew that the *pasha* was shrewd enough to have a hundred and one arguments to support his point.

The old man cast his son a keen glance, saying in a controlled voice, 'I know there have been other women you have considered, but I do not want to discuss that now. It was always accepted that you and Aida would be married … and if it hadn't been for that terrible tragedy, our two families would have united.'

Phares chose his words carefullly. 'And you think, after the accusation she made against you, she would welcome a proposal from me?'

The *pasha*'s face darkened. 'She was young and in shock. That was a long time ago. It is all forgotten.'

Phares raised an eyebrow. 'Yes, Father, it was a long time ago. Aida might be married by now or engaged. She must be in her mid-twenties and—'

'She is neither married nor engaged, I have checked,' Kamel cut in. 'You are my only son. Your sister will probably remarry one day, and move away from home.'

Phares crossed his arms. 'Camelia would never want to be far away from Hathor. She loves it here.'

'Anyhow, the *esba* and refinery are too big a load for a woman to carry,' Kamel continued. 'You are the one hope for our family business to survive and be handed down to the next generation. I know you are a medical man, but you have always loved the land. Happily, you have built your hospital nearby in Luxor, making your life here in Upper Egypt so you can commit yourself to both. All this will be under your control one day. If you and Aida El Masri were finally married, it would double the size of our estate and both families would benefit. She is alone in the world – we can support her. Anyhow, you are thirty-four and it's high time that you were married. I was already a father of two at your age. As we say in Egypt, *Baytun bila mra atin ka annahu maqbaratun*, a house without a woman is like a graveyard.'

Jaw tensing, Phares felt suddenly that he was a child of ten again but before he could offer a retort, Daoud appeared with a chilled glass of *karkadeeh* on a tray. Phares nodded his thanks and took a slow sip.

Once the servant had left, two pairs of eyes – so alike – met and measured each other. Phares knew that Kamel had the advantage of age: an expectation of subservience and obedience from his son was traditionally his right.

'Times have changed, Father. You can't force people into marriage nowadays,' he argued, trying to control the tone of his voice. Never one to be easily bullied, even when younger, now he was a man for whom, he knew, even his powerful father felt a healthy respect. The older man could, and did from time to time, lay certain commands upon him which he obeyed, but they had never concerned his private life. Phares knew that he wasn't prepared to tolerate interference in what he considered to be the most important decision he would ever make.

Kamel changed tactics. He smiled at his son, a mollifying smile whereupon the young doctor's eyes became warier still. Phares was very fond of his father, but he knew him well enough to be careful when he displayed this smooth blandness.

'You are right, my son,' the *pasha* conceded. 'Times have changed. There is no rush. I don't think the girl is going anywhere for the time being. I am told she had a hard time of it in the war. And now that she's come back to Luxor to take over her estate …' There was a hiatus in his speech, before he added pensively: '… she'll have her work cut out for her. This is the *Said*, Upper Egypt. It has never been easy for a woman in these parts to take on the management of an estate, let alone one as large as the Ayoub *esba*, which now of course is in a rather bad condition.'

Phares thought back to the rebellious teenager and wondered what kind of woman Aida had become. He had always found himself drawn to her unrestrained nature; she certainly knew her own mind and as such was a stimulating challenge, though he had never admitted that to anyone. 'From what I remember of Aida El Masri – if anyone can, she can,' he said. Perhaps her infuriating stubbornness would finally prove useful, he thought privately.

Kamel's look brightened. 'In that case, you and she would indeed make a strong partnership.'

Phares shot him a wry look. 'We would never agree on anything.'

Kamel frowned and took a sip from his glass of *kardadeeh*. 'You and I will discuss this matter again when I come back from my trip. I am leaving early tomorrow morning.'

'You needn't have come down to Luxor to tell me this,' Phares answered, endeavouring to keep the impatience from his voice. 'We could have talked over the telephone, or it might have waited. All this toing and froing is not good for your heart, Father. You know that.'

'Tut, tut, tut … you're a great worrier. I feel perfectly well. Never felt better, in fact. There is a flight from Luxor tomorrow morning to Cairo which I'll be taking and Camelia will come with me. She has a fitting with *Madame* Salha, who is making her dress for Princess Nazek's charity ball. Have you received an invitation?'

'Yes, I have. It arrived yesterday.'

'I presume that you will be going to it?'

'I'm not sure yet, but most probably. I am due a visit to the Anglo-American Hospital as I've an operation scheduled and the dates tie in nicely.'

'Very good, let me know as Camelia would like to attend the ball, and if you're not going to be there, I will ask your cousins Sélim or Amir to accompany her.'

'You can count on Sélim and his wife, I'm sure, if they're free, but I doubt very much that Amir will accept. You know how he feels about that sort of party. I'd be surprised if he's even received an invitation.'

The *pasha* shook his head. 'You are right. Well, *in shah Allah*, God willing, you'll be attending. If not, I will have to take your sister and forgo my game of bridge that evening.' Thereupon he stood up. 'I'll be in my study for an hour before dinner. I have some letters to write.'

'I'll see you at dinner then.'

\*    \*    \*

After his father left, Phares remained on the terrace, traces of the earlier frown still lingering on his brow. He moved towards the balustrade and let his gaze drift over the landscape, wanting to shake off his feeling of claustrophobia. The ornamental gardens were as large and spacious as if they were a whole estate in themselves, and of the three family houses that the Pharaonys owned in Egypt, this was the one he loved best, especially at this hour. The grounds were dotted with terraces and gazebos, marble balustrades and flights of steps, carved fountains and statues of nymphs, dryads, fauns and representations of those mythical figures and incidents from the songs of the bards. In many places, pergolas of vine, jasmine or mimosa shaded the lawns. Gardeners had been watering the beds and the air was laden with the heady scent of flowers. A whiff of woodsmoke stole towards him, mingling with the breath of the roses, and with it the gusts of fragrance from the flowering beans, the sweet and acrid scent that for so many spelt Egypt.

Beyond the gardens flowed the Nile, the waters of time, and further off slept the pyramids, silent witnesses of a great civilisation and the lonely immensity of the golden sands.

Now, in the distance, where the clear sky came down to the dunes, the crimson light of a desert sunset lay upon the horizon and the gold of evening was beginning to spread along the heavens. The palm trees rustled with the inevitable breeze that blew in stronger from the great river now that the day was done. The last green tint of twilight still lingered in the west, and standing out sharply against its strange clarity a train of camels rested for the night near the ancient caravan route through northern Africa.

Phares had always felt there was something almost ethereal about the desert evening. It was as if it helped those who knew to draw on its refreshing power to live through the breathless day. The thought came to him again as he watched a young gardener still drifting slowly hither and thither among the flower beds, armed with a huge watering can, from which came a gentle drizzling oddly at variance with its large proportions. The man's feet made no sound on the paths of beaten sand, and beneath his turban, his face looked calm, placid, like the face of a dreamy child. From somewhere in the orange grove close at hand came the impudent twitter of a flute, with now and then a strangely interpolated phrase of exquisite tenderness; and from farther away, nasal voices singing some weird chant resounded in the evening dusk. To someone unaccustomed to all things Eastern, these musical strains might have seemed bizarre to their ears, but because they were so familiar to Phares he found them sweet.

Even as a child, when he was not yet allowed to go far into the desert unaccompanied, Phares had dreamed of its exquisite silence. He had replayed in his mind the songs of the Bedouins that he had heard one night when out riding with his father. And once he was old enough to realise his dream, he discovered that the desert of his imagination had been but a pallid reflection of its true glory. As a teenager he would ride out into it alone and one night he stumbled upon a Bedouin tribe who had welcomed him in, taught him how to ride bareback and allowed him to help rear one of their foals, which he named *Zein el Sahara*, Prince of the Desert. From then on, Phares had been equally at home in the wilderness of burning sands as he was in the bustling metropolis of Cairo.

The Pharaonys owned twenty-two thousand acres in Upper Egypt in eighty-two villages in the Governorate of Qena. Most of the land was planted with sugarcane and cotton. Kamel had built a cotton ginning factory and talked about acquiring an oil refinery that he'd heard was for sale in Minieh. The marriage to Aida El Masri would connect two flourishing estates, adding many more acres to the Pharaony land holdings.

'All this will be under your control one day,' his father had said. It had always been understood that this would be the case, but hearing it was different – there was a finality to the words that made him feel trapped. There was a price to pay for such wealth and suddenly this reality was all too apparent. It was as if the matter was now cast in stone, and he would never be able to escape his fate.

Part of Phares longed to be free. Free of society's constraints, free of his filial duties, free of a job he loved but which took over most of his life – and above all, free of his large inheritance, which he viewed as a great weight and responsibility. He yearned to roam the world, his dream world, the world of the desert to which he felt so attuned.

Yet Phares was also part of a dynasty that had been built through hard work. He had obligations he could not ignore. Standing here looking out at the gardens, he thought of his grandfather, the man who had laid the first stone in the founding of the Pharaony wealth. Gamil Pharaony was Coptic, an ancient Christian community which prided itself on its aspirational values, and so Gamil, unlike some of the merchant class, had been educated as a boy before being apprenticed to a trader in Luxor who had taught him the business of freighting goods by felucca and barge between Cairo and Upper Egypt. In the 1860s and 1870s, Gamil Pharaony had seen the drive of Ismail Pasha, the Khedive of Egypt, to modernise the country and the young Gamil had understood the vast debts accumulated by the government to build the Suez Canal and other huge projects. With great pity Phares's grandfather had watched the *fellahin* who worked the land, who were squeezed with new taxes every year to service the government debt, and he had quietly blessed his father for pushing him into trade rather than working the land. He had therefore witnessed with some joy the year of dual control in 1880, when the English and French creditors established a commission sweeping away many of those taxes that had made land ownership such an unattractive business. By the early 1880s he had established his own trading business buying local crops for shipment to Cairo. Though not rich, he was liquid, and that was not all: he understood the potential of basin land. While it commonly yielded one crop because it flooded every year, he knew that if it could be kept drained with dykes and protective banks, it would be good for three.

Phares had been brought up to appreciate the courage of this quiet Coptic merchant who had gambled his trading profits to buy land being sold off by a government desperate to pay its debts. This was an opportunity. His grandfather had understood that the transition from the feudal control of the land by the aristocracy to a more modern system of freehold ownership by the population would be irreversible. His decision to invest was brave but right, and the family's fortune was established.

Still, his grandfather had not stopped there. He was not tempted to embrace all the modernism and foreign ideas that started to flow into his town in the suitcases of American missionaries and Thomas Cook's tourists. He brought up his son Kamel to know the value of money, and above all to love the rich Nile Valley soils that yielded their wealth to the family coffers. His last and strongest act to secure the family's position was to arrange his son's marriage to the daughter of another Coptic landowner, which resulted in a combined holding, insuring the Pharaonys' dominance in the region. This was the Egyptian way.

Although Phares enjoyed life to the full and was reluctant to change his chosen mode of existence, he understood all too well his own position. His Western education as a doctor, his hospital and research projects were all paid for by two generations who had committed to grindingly hard work. He understood even more clearly that his career path had run in a direction contrary to his father's instincts, yet Kamel had allowed him to follow it. Because of Kamel's generosity in encouraging him to forge a new direction, Phares now felt a deep sense of obligation to conform to his father's wishes. To secure more land with the marriage to Ayoub El Masri's daughter was the expression of a fundamental instinct that Kamel himself had learnt from Gamil Pharaony. How could Phares deny his father?

Aida El Masri. It had been years since he'd seen her. Evidently, she had decided there was still something for her in Egypt, though he'd privately thought she would stay in England for good. Phares had wondered about her surprisingly often over the last eight years, hoping her grief had subsided along with her anger at Ayoub's death. She had been almost hysterical, screaming out the most horrendous accusations about his father, and when he had tried to visit Aida – in part to soothe her fury, in part to defend Kamel – she had refused to see him. Would she really want to tie herself to the Pharaonys after damning them so emphatically before she left for England?

Phares sighed. He missed her father, Ayoub, too. He had greatly admired his father's friend and had hung about Karawan House as a boy, asking endless questions of the eminent archaeologist. Their conversations ranged widely over all kinds of subjects – Egypt's ancient past, politics, history, and particularly their shared fascination for the desert and the secrets it held. In fact, his genuine fondness for the El Masris had tempered any reluctance he might have felt in joining the two family estates through marriage one day to Ayoub's impetuous daughter. Then the terrible tragedy of Ayoub's death had seemed to break the bond between them, and while Phares continued to further his career and build El Amal hospital, all talk of marriage had largely ceased ... to the El Masri girl, that is. Gossip and speculation had simply moved on to a match with his old friend and anaesthetist colleague, Isis Geratly, but Phares's heart had never been truly engaged in that direction. Now that Aida El Masri was back in Luxor, his father was clearly intent on reviving the old family 'understanding' and had lost no time in appealing to Phares's sense of duty.

Still, although he had always known that he would marry eventually, and with time he would have committed to act upon the course he knew to be right, this morning had thrown him off balance. The sight of the prettiest and most delicious creature his eyes had ever seen had unsettled him deeply, and he was determined to find out who she was before she returned to her country. Of course he was realistic enough to know that nothing serious could come of a liaison with a foreigner, but more than ever, he was aware there was more to life than the blind obedience to convention.

Eyelids shut, Phares let his mind gently drift back to his earlier encounter with the beautiful stranger. He could still picture her so clearly. It was the young woman's hair that had struck him most: the thickest waves that glinted in the sunlight with almost the yellow of pure gold. It was drawn back from her wide, delicately curved forehead – in fact, her whole face was delicately curved, as was the shapely line of her eyebrows. He wondered at the colour of her eyes, hidden by her sunglasses, as she had stared back at him defiantly. Although she was fair, her complexion was not the pale pinkness of the many blonde Western and Scandinavian girls he met in Cairo, but the warm colour of honey with the perfect bloom and shiny quality of youth. An image of her sensuous mouth floated before his closed eyes and he felt a stir in his gut ... Those lips, gentle in their fullness, would be sublime to kiss. Her features were delicate, clear-cut and perfectly balanced; her body beautifully formed and proportioned. Goldilocks, he could tell, had the sophistication of a girl from a Swiss finishing school – she had clearly been brought up in luxury – and yet he thought, despite her spirited air of independence, there was about her the untouched look of an unawakened girl. She wore that combination of innocence and pride so easily and it chased around in his mind, intriguing and arousing him – a feeling which, now that he thought about it, was entirely new to him.

Whoever she was, she was exquisite, and the young doctor's heart, untouched until now, had instantly lost itself to this alluring stranger whom he feared he would never set eyes upon again.

Now, night lay over the desert. Not the thick, heavy night of Western climes, but the brilliant bejewelled night of Upper Egypt. From a background of blue velvet shone the great silver stars, almost barbaric in their radiance, and although the moon had not yet risen, there was little need for a lamp. No wonder starlight held such significance for the people of Egypt. Beneath its shine, Luxor lay in the distance, peaceful and quiet now that the toil of the day was over and the *fellahin* had departed for their huddled mud huts in the little villages close by.

All was still, save the whispering of hundreds of trees and the croaking of frogs on the shores of the Nile and its surrounding ponds. The great white Pharaony house lay apparently hushed in slumber.

Phares glanced at his watch: eight o'clock already. He'd better get ready for dinner; he shouldn't be keeping his father and sister waiting. As he set off along the veranda in the direction of his room, the animated smile of the beautiful stranger shimmered through his thoughts. He sighed. The return of Aida El Masri couldn't have come at a worse time.

*     *     *

The early-morning train from Luxor to Cairo drew out of the station, jerked, bumped, gathered speed and went racketing along the already hot, shining metal tracks. Though it was only seven o'clock in the morning, the fierce sun poured down on the roofs of the carriages; the air shimmered, silvery, in long waves of heat, and the golden dust of the desert came in through every chink, gritty and stifling.

Crowds of boys and men sat on the roof of the express, and the third-class carriages were packed with people piled in on top of each other with their animals and fowl. Aida sat alone in a large green leather seat in First Class, her window tightly shut, but whereas in other compartments the Venetian shutters were lowered against the sun, hers were pulled up. The false ceiling, with a wide space above it, cut down the sun's heat, preventing the interior of the carriage from being transformed into a rustic furnace.

Aida could have taken the local Misrair plane that travelled twice a week from Aswan to Cairo, via Luxor and Assiut, which would have reduced the time of the journey to an hour and a half, but she wasn't in a hurry, and wanted to refamiliarise herself with the colourful Egyptian countryside that she had missed so much during her long years of exile. Along one side of the rails ran a thin canal where women and children squatted in rows, laboriously washing the family clothes; on the other was a dirt road where men on donkey carts laden with newly cut sugarcane or *berseem* made their way to the fields.

As the train shuddered along the side of palm groves, sugarcane plantations and cotton fields, passing the circling blindfolded buffaloes turning their irrigation wheels while flocks of white cattle egrets trailed in the wake of ox and plough, Aida's gaze clouded over, her mind distracted.

Two weeks had already passed since her return to Egypt. By now she had recovered from the long hours of plane travel and was happy to be back in the sunshine, but she missed her job and the more hectic life she had led in England. For the first few days she had asked nothing more than simply to wander about the house and grounds, familiarising herself with old corners, gazing at an ancient tree or a hole inhabited by lizards ever since she could remember. Almost every square yard was peopled with the past, with friends who owned the local estates, and the memories of a plain young girl, still burdened with puppy fat and not quite out of the awkward age of her teenage years. Each encounter had its invisible button that opened its window on to the past. As she looked through it in her mind's eye, she saw little framed scenes which had taken place on that spot, ten, twelve years ago or more, dipped in the dye of pleasure, fear, joy, or deep sadness.

Aida had lost no time in paying a visit to Uncle Naguib and Aunt Nabila at their home in the countryside, Esbat El Fardouz – Paradise Farm, named after Uncle Naguib's mother. Another place of fond childhood recollections, it was a relaxed and lively house where people were always coming and going, turning up for tea unannounced and staying for dinner. Aunt Nabila had been overjoyed at seeing Aida again and the two women had spent long leisurely hours swapping stories of the past eight years. Nabila Bishara was active in many charities, including the Red Cross and Miss Lillian Trasher's orphanage in Assiut. She knew a great many people around Luxor, and was therefore a font of knowledge about its old families, particularly when it came to the list of Egyptian women who had landed British servicemen for husbands during the war. There were many times when Aida had spent an entire afternoon at Esbat El Fardouz without realising where the time had gone.

She had deliberately avoided going anywhere near Kasr El Ghoroub and the Pharaony land, in case she ran into Phares again. She had been deeply troubled by her reaction to the young doctor on their first meeting, and hadn't stopped thinking about him since. It was clear that her feelings towards Phares had merely been numbed for eight years and it had just taken this chance encounter to revive the old flame that had burned silent but constant all this time.

Yet, even at Karawan House, it was almost impossible to escape reminders of Phares. As she ambled through the gardens, Aida recalled the afternoon years ago – she had been perhaps fourteen or so – when Phares had found her curled up under the *shagar el jummayz*, sycamore tree, with a copy of Colette's *Chéri*. Devouring the tale of the affair of a courtesan and younger man and its world of sexuality and desire, Aida, thinking herself alone, had lost herself in the novel. She hadn't heard him approach and the heat had risen in her cheeks as he swiped the book from her hands, telling her it was hardly suitable reading material for someone her age. His critical but curious gaze had pinned her to the spot.

Acutely embarrassed and self-conscious, Aida sprang to her feet and snatched the book back. 'And who are you to tell me what is suitable? You're not my brother.'

'I'm as good as,' he replied, scowling at her rebuke.

Looking into the dark depths of his eyes, the feelings Aida had experienced were far from sisterly, as her racing pulse witnessed. 'You'll never be anything like a brother to me,' she blurted out, hardly realising what she had said.

If Phares understood her meaning he hadn't shown it, but Aida remembered the wounded look that struck his face before he strode off.

Eager not to dwell on such memories, Aida had thrown herself into the task of rebuilding the estate, a necessary job as well as a welcome distraction from her turbulent thoughts of Phares Pharaony. By the end of the week she had realised the scale of the work that needed to be done and suddenly the second week at 'home' had become busy and strenuous. The amount of land being cultivated needed to increase if the crop yield was to be revitalised, and that meant more *fellahin* and better agricultural equipment. All of this would take time to implement. Going over the books and around the estate with Megally, the old estate manager, was not an easy task, especially given that the whole business had to be carried out in Arabic. Although Aida still spoke it well, despite her long absence and it not being her first language, her reading and writing had suffered badly from neglect and were rusty to say the least. Uncle Naguib had come to her rescue a couple of times when she had tried to decipher the estate ledgers, but Aida was determined to prove to everyone, including herself, that she was up to the job and able to stand on her own two feet without help.

Still, she had to admit that she was out of her comfort zone. Managing a large estate was hardly what she was used to. Somehow, although she loved the remote peace of the countryside here, as well as its people, she missed the hustle and bustle of a big city. More than that, she missed nursing. Not only was she used to dealing with people from all walks of life, but the job of caring for the sick and disabled – alleviating pain, monitoring and advising patients – made her feel useful. She enjoyed giving back to society instead of just taking.

During her second week back, a letter had arrived from Princess Nazek, whom she had met on the plane home. They'd been sitting together among the dozen or so passengers, and the two women had immediately taken to each other, even though Princess Nazek was much older than Aida, and they had promised to stay in touch. Not only had she had liked the princess enormously, but the older woman had an air of spirited independence that Aida been drawn to. She might prove the kind of friend Aida sorely needed if she was to try and revive her old friendships in Cairo.

The letter was an invitation to the princess's annual charity ball in Zamalek on Gezireh Island in Cairo. Aida had immediately responded and accepted, without giving much thought to the fact that she didn't have an escort, and that it might be frowned upon among her social circle. A woman alone in Egyptian society was a vulnerable target of gossip and opinion, especially one like Aida with her English sense of entitlement to freedom. Still, it was too late to worry about that now, it would work out somehow.

'I'm going to Cairo on a shopping spree,' she had announced to *Dada* Amina one morning.

'You are not reasonable, *ya binti*. You will make yourself ill with all this coming and going,' *Dada* Amina exclaimed when Aida had asked her to prepare a suitcase.

'You told me yourself, I haven't any decent clothes to wear, *ya Dada*. Besides, I want to get in touch with all my friends. It's too quiet here.'

'Quiet is what you need, *Sit* Aida.'

'Perhaps I've just become too used to chaos and noise, and sleepless nights,' she said, smiling grimly. Aida still had nightmares about the Blitz ... the drone of planes above, the sirens and screams, the terrible wounds she had seen on patients in the hospitals. 'What I need is a bit of glamour in my life. I haven't been to a ball in eight years. I'm still young. I want to laugh and dance and have fun to make up for all that lost time ... I want to live again! Besides, the spring sales are on and I need a whole new wardrobe.'

*Dada* Amina shook her head disapprovingly. 'You need a good rest, that's what you really need.'

'I know, but this is also the beginning of the party season and if I want to be on any of the invitation lists, I must start showing myself in public,' she winked at her old nanny, 'and a ball given by an eminent princess is a marvellous opportunity.'

Uncle Naguib had also tried to persuade Aida to wait a few more weeks before going to Cairo. 'The wardrobe can wait, and there will be other balls,' he'd reasoned.

But Aida didn't want to miss this occasion; she remembered the balls she'd attended with her father, including one given at Abdeen Palace just a few months before Ayoub's death. That wonderful evening had left a lasting impression, remaining one of the happiest memories of her life.

'This one is rather special, Uncle. Princess Nazek and I really hit off. I wouldn't like to let her down.'

'You don't have an escort.'

'Does it matter?'

'Not that much nowadays, I suppose,' he said, grudgingly. 'I admit, the war has changed some of those old rules and the attitude is certainly more relaxed here, but there are still a few conservative Egyptian and Turkish families that insist on their daughters being escorted or chaperoned by a man.' He regarded her thoughtfully. 'Still, you are not a teenager anymore. You've lived abroad and you're a grown woman so perhaps it shouldn't matter that much.' So, Aida had left Karawan House with Naguib's blessing and a request that she call him from Shepheard's Hotel when she arrived.

As the train travelled steadily on, the river flowing gently beside it, smooth as glass, the land gradually presented the verdant richness of arable pasture. Presently, Aida's attention was drawn to it, finding that it had a life of its own, feasting her eyes on the placid beauty of the picture. Not an inch of the irrigated land was left uncultivated. They passed groves of date palms, young crops of barley, strips of purple flowering fava beans – the staple food of the *fellah* – and plots of vegetables and cotton. In every field there were *fellahin* hoeing, scything, harvesting and planting. A white donkey gambolled excitedly as it was let out of its stable into the noonday sun. A lad was plodding along the bank leading

a camel, and a couple of small boys in brown-and-white striped
pyjamas chatted as they made their way on the dirt road by
the side of the river, carrying loaves of *baladi* bread and some
sort of canister that Aida thought most probably contained lunch
for their fathers, who had been toiling away in the fields since
dawn. Seeing these colourful scenes of the *fellahin* at work, their
heavily laden animals, and the picturesque mud villages, Aida
felt that had it not been for the modern jarring element of the train
she might have imagined herself back in the time of the pharaohs.

Soon they were approaching Minieh and the train started to
slow down. The old town, with its little white houses and minarets
and its palm trees glowed in the sunlight.

The train pulled in at the station with a great shuddering of its
old carcass. No sooner had the engine stopped than copper-
skinned, half-naked, filthy-looking children, who didn't bother to
brush away the flies swarming all over their faces, ran up to
the carriages, smiling and waving their hands at the passengers.
Aida's heart went out to them. In this part of the world the death
rate in children was high because of disease spread by dirt. That
was one of the reasons why she had decided to become a nurse; it
was also why, in the past, she had so admired Phares's decision to
become a general surgeon. In addition, the young man once told
her of his dream of some day opening a hospital to cure the many
endemic ailments that existed among the poor, caused by
the ignorance and the squalor in which some of these people lived.

Rapidly, the train was boarded by a host of sellers carrying
fruit, hardboiled eggs, salted almonds, dried sunflower, pumpkin
and melon seeds, and biscuit rings covered in sesame seeds known
as *sammeet*, which were threaded hoopla-fashion on sticks
protruding from the rim of the seller's round basket. Aida
remembered how delicious they tasted and was tempted to buy
herself one to enjoy with her lunch, but refrained. When she was
a child *Dada* Amina bought them from a small bakery in one

of the poor quarters of Luxor but heated them in the oven before giving them to Aida to eat – to kill the bacteria.

Looking out of the window, Aida noticed a man hurrying along the platform towards the train. In his beautifully tailored beige suit, trim, soft-collared shirt, striped tie and highly polished shoes, he looked totally out of place among the unkempt medley of individuals milling around the station, and in striking contrast to the exotic, rural scene outside. Aida was intrigued. It was not often one saw such an elegantly turned-out person on the grubby platforms of Upper Egypt's stations, unless they were foreigners on guided Thomas Cook tours.

She didn't need to wonder for long as a few minutes later the gentleman walked along the corridor outside Aida's compartment, stopped and looked in through the open door. He smiled, pointing to the empty seat opposite her. 'Is that seat free, *mademoiselle?*' he asked in a cultured voice. Though he had addressed her in French, the rest of the phrase had been in English, and his command of the language was excellent, with just a trace of fascinating foreign accent.

'Yes, it is.'

'Do you mind if I share the compartment with you?'

'Not at all … please.'

The man bowed, set his small suitcase in the luggage rack above and settled in his seat, facing Aida.

'Thank you,' he murmured.

Aida looked up at him with a smile of acknowledgement. The eyes that met hers were so pale that they had a crystalline, luminous quality – in the mottled light of the small compartment she could not tell their colour. They were small and piercing, and set absolutely straight and quite close to each other. It was their expression that caught her attention and for the fraction of an instant made her feel as if she'd been turned to stone. That look held neither enchantment nor malevolence, it was simply steady.

Immutably, ruthlessly steady as if he could look through her to
the very depths of her soul, and although she had only mentally
given a shiver, he asked:

'Cold?' Without waiting for her answer he stood up and closed
the door of the compartment. 'I agree,' he said with a smile. 'There
is a slight draft. The doors in these trains never shut properly.'

'Thank you,' she murmured.

He seemed to be in his late thirties or early forties. Tall with
a wiry build and dark curly hair, he had a face that was thin and
sharply chiselled, dominated by a high, intolerant-looking hooked
nose, a nicely shaped goatee encircling beautifully shaped thin
lips, and black sideburns that thrust with a dagger-like precision
against his jaw. He looked vigorously powerful and in command.
No doubt this man was of Arab descent, not a Copt. His bearing
had the arrogance of a bird of prey rather than the haughtiness
of the proud pharaohs. The face of a red-tailed hawk, and with
those eyes!

As a bell rang somewhere and the train started again, she
glanced down at the platform to see a one-legged blind beggar
come limping towards the train, with a woman in tow carrying
a tiny baby. The pair were quickly intercepted by a policeman and
Aida felt her heart ache with compassion for these poor people. It
was a sight she had almost forgotten in her years away from home.

'You find Egypt dramatic?'

The question was asked in the deep, harsh, yet not unpleasant
voice of the man sitting in front of her.

Aida blinked at the question. This stranger had an uncanny
way of reading her mind.

She nodded sadly. 'Yes, I do ... so much poverty and squalor.'

He gave a hoarse laugh – a smoker's laugh. 'You should say
"so much paralysing ignorance and stagnation".'

Aida couldn't help but stare back at those glass-bright eyes.
'Should I?'

The stranger nodded. 'The dirtier a child, the better, says the average Egyptian parent, and that because they are great believers in what is known here as *El Ein*, the eye, the evil eye. They believe strangers have *El Ein*, and mothers, as well as the children themselves, are afraid if you look at them. You will find that many of them are given a charm to wear in the hope that the enviously admiring evil eye will be attracted by it and not the person wearing it. You can see those same charms on donkeys, camels and horses. Foreigners think they're just ornaments, of course, whereas to the superstitious Egyptian they have a deeper meaning.' Suddenly, the stranger stopped talking and smiled apologetically. 'But forgive me, here I am lecturing you and I haven't even introduced myself.' He lifted himself out of his seat, inclined his head and stretched out his hand, which was surprising cool as Aida shook it. 'Shams Sakr El Din, at your service.'

'Aida El Masri.'

'El Masri? You are Egyptian? I would have never have thought so. That golden hair, those sea-blue eyes and your beautiful peach complexion say otherwise.'

'My mother was English and my father, Ayoub El Masri, was Egyptian.'

His already tapered eyes narrowed further to slits and something passed in those small, piercing pupils ... Curiosity? Admiration? Surprise?

'You are the daughter of Ayoub El Masri, the great archaeologist?'

'Yes.'

'Where have you been hiding all this time? I am acquainted with most upper-class families of the *Said* and have never seen you around.'

'I've been away ... in England. I've just come back.'

'You grew up there?'

'No, in Egypt, but after my father passed away before the war I left for England.'

'So, you spent the war years there?'

'Yes.'

'It couldn't have been easy.'

'It wasn't.'

'And you've come back to stay?'

At this point Aida realised that she had been answering this man's questions automatically, as if the even tone of his deep voice was compelling her to reply. Shams Sakr El Din repeated his question.

'I have no plans for the time being.'

'Well, it will be my pleasure to show you around Cairo.'

'That's very kind of you.'

He took a card from the inside pocket of his suit and handed it to Aida. 'You can reach me at my home in Garden City or at my office downtown, next to the Turf Club.'

'Thank you.' Aida scrutinised the details on the card. Although there was something about him that made her feel uncomfortable, she was rather curious about this man. His name was printed in a raised elegant font: *Prince Shams Sakr El Din* and underneath, *Director*. So, the man was titled. She wasn't surprised; he was clearly very distinguished, with the confidence that comes automatically to the highborn. She glanced up at him. What was a prince doing on a public train? These people usually travelled by car, if not by plane.

Again, Shams Sakr El Din seemed to guess what Aida was thinking.

'I like travelling by train from time to time. That way, I get a more realistic view of the people of my country.'

Aida smiled at him. This man was like a figure from the *Arabian Nights* tales. Phares used to enjoy telling her and Camelia those stories when they were young. Thinking about Phares while talking to this man alone on a train gave her an uneasy thrill. 'Yes, I feel the same way. That's why I opted for this longer journey to Cairo instead of taking the plane.' Her attention returned to the visiting card. In the right-hand corner, over his office details, she read aloud: 'Chiffons à la Mode.'

The thin lips broadened into a wide smile. 'I own a chain of fashion boutiques in Cairo, Alexandria and Port Said. We sell haute couture clothes, mainly by Pierre Balmain, Worth and Schiaparelli. The items come to us directly from Paris and America. Our buyers have just returned from France, where they've secured some pieces by the new French designer Christian Dior for next year when he'll launch his latest collection.' He glanced out of the window at the passing landscape, then his steady gaze returned to Aida. 'I'll be giving my annual fashion show at Shepheard's Hotel in six weeks and I hope you'll be able to attend. Usually, it's at the Gezireh Sporting Club but this year it's a special occasion. Now the war is over, it's the first collection of the "New Look" so I think the ballroom at Shepheard's is far more glamorous.' He gave another glittering smile. 'If you give me your address in Cairo, I will send you an invitation.'

The annual Cairo fashion show was a major social event and Aida knew immediately that this show of Sakr El Din's would be one to which Cairo's beau monde would flock. Even more so if it was at Shepheard's.

'I don't have a flat in Cairo,' she said in answer to his request. 'Actually, I'll be staying at Shepheard's while I'm there.'

The prince looked outraged. 'A hotel? A young lady of your status?'

He was right. Even these days it would be slightly unusual for a young woman to stay alone in a hotel in the city, even one as prestigious as Shepheard's, but as she could no longer stay at the Pharaonys' house in Gizeh, Aida had little choice.

'I won't be staying long,' she explained with a smile. 'Less than a week.'

'No, no, no! That is not at all appropriate. Ayoub El Masri's daughter staying at a hotel? Your father, I am sure, would have never allowed that. My palace in Garden City is at your disposal, and—'

'That is very kind of you,' Aida interrupted quickly, 'but I'm sure my father would have found it even more inappropriate for me to stay at a gentleman's home, albeit one belonging to a prince.'

'*Touché*,' he replied with a half smile. 'I never met Ayoub *Bey*, but I heard a lot about him and I was a great admirer of his work.' Sakr El Din took a gold box from his inside jacket pocket. He opened it, offering it to Aida: 'Do you smoke?'

'No, thank you.'

'May I?'

'Yes, of course, please go ahead,' she said at once.

The prince chose a cigar, put his gold lighter's flame to it and then returned the lighter and box to his pocket. He drew on the cigar once or twice, and the aromatic smoke filled the air. For a short moment he sat silently, watching the young woman with narrowed brilliant eyes through the spiral of blue fog, reminding Aida more than ever of a desert predator.

'If you are at Shepheard's, will you allow me to call on you during your visit?'

'That's very kind of you, but as I said, I'm not staying long. Only a few days to pay my respects to the British Ambassador.'

'Ah yes, Sir Miles Lampson.'

Aida looked surprised. 'Do you know him? He used to be a friend of my uncle's when he was High Commissioner.'

'I know him well. I'm acquainted with most of the staff at the British Embassy, but I think Sir Miles has gone away. We sometimes shoot wild duck together in the Fayoum, and hunt fennec in the desert.'

'Fennec?'

The prince laughed, showing almost pointed canines. 'Desert fox. They're found all over Egypt, but mostly in the desert. They're the smallest fox in the world, with very large eyes and ears.' His own eyes gleamed. 'Quite a handsome animal really.'

As the train puffed along, Aida and the prince continued to talk. He spoke to her about his business, but mainly his kingdom in the desert, Wahat El Nakheel, Oasis of Palms, and his castle, Kasr El Nawafeer, Palace of Fountains, which aroused her curiousity even further.

'What romantic names!'

'The desert is a very romantic place.'

Aida laughed. 'Hardly! It's known to be harsh and cruel.'

His lips curled in an enigmatic smile. 'Only for those who don't know it, *habibti*, my dear … The desert has many names, one of them is Paradise. One day we will ride together and I will show you its splendour,' he said slowly, with a note of meaning in his voice that sent a shiver of apprehension through Aida.

He looked every inch the powerful desert lord, and although she couldn't deny that he was extremely handsome and charming, there was something about Shams Sakr El Din that made her uncomfortable. The way he spoke to her was far too familiar and those eyes of his made her feel like a butterfly pinned under glass. He was certainly a fascinating character, and doubtless many women would find him irresistible, but the Arab prince left Aida with an uneasy feeling.

It was late when the lights of Cairo came into view and the train slowed to a halt amid the glare and bustle of Ramses Station. The great terminal was alive with hotel touts, who fell upon the alighting throng and enmeshed them like greedy spiders.

'*Hamdellelah all'salama, bon arrivée*, we're finally here,' said the prince, standing up and lifting down Aida's suitcase from the luggage rack before reaching for his own. 'Do you have a car waiting for you?'

'I have arranged for a taxi from the hotel to pick me up, thank you.'

'Allow me to give you a lift. Shepheard's Hotel is on my way. Besides, it will mean I won't have to say goodbye just yet. The journey from Minieh to Cairo has never seemed so short.'

For a second Aida hesitated, and then graciously accepted the prince's invitation. A decrepit porter appeared and took their luggage, lifted it on to the shoulder of his blue cotton gown, and flapped away before them in the crowd of people leaving the train.

As she followed the prince and the *shayyal* down the high steps to the platform, the young woman caught her breath. Cairo! The bustle, confusion, the shouting of porters, the babble of Arabic … After the slow pace and the relative quiet of the countryside the noise was music to her eager ears. Even the night air here was different: heavy, humid and slightly dusty. She could feel the moisture clinging to her clothes, and it felt thick as she breathed in the damp air, coating the inside of her throat. As in those far-off days, excitement rose in her. Spring in the *bandar*, in the town! It all came back in a flood of memories as Cairo swept her up in an embrace.

A black and silver Bentley Mark VI saloon was parked in the square in front of the station amid a throng of cabs and swarthy cab drivers in their red *tarbooshes*. Under the streetlights and in the shadow of tall buildings, a multitude of turbaned and long-robed people bustled in all directions. The porter, having given the suitcases to the uniformed chauffeur, took his fee, blessed the prince several times, then turned and disappeared among the motley masses.

'*Allal* Shepheard's,' the prince told the driver as the latter held the door open for Aida.

'The road from here to the hotel is closed, Your Highness,' the man answered in Arabic. 'There's been some sort of student demonstration and there are barricades and police on Opera

Square and Abdin Palace. We'll have to make a long detour to reach Shepheard's.'

'That's fine.' He turned to Aida and grinned. 'It seems fate is being kind to me today and I will have the pleasure of your company even longer, *Mademoiselle* El Masri.'

Aida acknowledged this compliment with a quiet smile and stepped into the car. Sakr El Din took his place beside her, pushing up a little too close for her liking. His keen glinting eyes were now near enough for her to determine their colour clearly: a golden amber, so pale they appeared yellow. *A desert prince with pale yellow eyes,* she thought. *How strange.* In this part of the world eyes were usually coal black, like Phares's. Maybe it was a legacy from a foreign forebear.

The prince regarded the young woman with a sardonic tilt of his eyebrows, as if divining her thoughts about him. His irises made Aida think of the desert sands, but with an arctic flame at the centre; they had a startling brilliance wherein either cruelty or passion could be smouldering. Aida didn't know a great deal about men, but she suspected if crossed, this one could be a dangerous enemy.

Prince Shams Sakr El Din's eyes narrowed until their yellow tint was lost in the shadow of his lashes, and Aida was perturbed to realise that she'd been staring at him. 'My mother, may *Allah* rest her soul, was French … hence my pale-coloured eyes,' he explained, his gaze seeming even more penetrating. 'Isn't that what you were wondering about, *Mademoiselle* El Masri?'

'Yes, absolutely. You have an uncanny way of reading minds.'

'Only yours. Has no one ever told you that you have a very mobile face?'

Aida smiled with embarrassment. 'I'm afraid I'm not very good at hiding my thoughts.'

'A dangerous foible in this day and age … you wouldn't make a good spy.'

'I wouldn't want to be a spy.'

'I would have thought you had just the right kind of adventurous spirit.'

She shifted uncomfortably. 'An adventurous spirit, maybe. But disloyalty and deceit, I'm happy to say, have never been in my nature.'

'Ah, my dear, but life sometimes has a compelling way of forcing you to do things that you wouldn't think yourself capable of. *Il ne faut jamais dire fontaine, je ne boirais pas de ton eau*, never say fountain, I will not drink of your water.' He looked away. 'In other words, never say never.'

Aida stared for a moment at the strong dark profile of the prince, outlined now and again by the passing light of the tall streetlamps. What did he mean? She didn't like the turn the conversation was taking and rather than get into an unpleasant argument, she too looked away and focused her attention on the old streets of Cairo.

The long car ride led through a maze of streets lined with tall buildings and across squares aglow with street light. Even though it was past ten at night, the whole place was swarming with a motley crowd. In all the narrow alleys and lanes *ckah-wehs*, cafés, were open, where a few coloured bulbs suspended here and there lit up the scene only dimly. Near the shops the street became brighter. There, great lanterns set off the brilliant hues of fruit and vegetables, and the magnificent fabrics, carpets, jewellery and nick-nacks of all kinds spread out before the eyes of the customer. Imposing mosques with elegant tall minarets rising up in prayer to the sky stood side by side with old palaces and grand hotels.

Natives, foreigners, soldiers, animals, cars, and *hantours*, light two-wheeled calashes drawn by a single horse, with a folding hood and seats for two passengers and another for the driver on the splashboard, struggled for supremacy in the streets. Aida wondered at the art with which those native coachmen patiently and adroitly steered their great carriages in that sea of traffic.

There were beggars, sellers, men in rich robes and coloured turbans, and women carrying heavy burdens on their head or a child upon their shoulder, all milling together in this immense human wave where everywhere was movement, brilliancy of colour, noise and agitation. Against this spangling backdrop, the women entirely dressed in black were the most striking; they were still wearing the *boorcko*, or the *habarah*, a veil dating from biblical times, which appealed to Aida's romantic imagination because it gave women's eyes a mysterious look. It consisted of a piece of linen or black muslin almost the length of the body, attached to a band around the forehead by means of a vertical piece of bamboo placed over the nose and the two outer edges fastened to the sides of the band, leaving the eyes visible. Such traditional figures mingling in the crowd seemed to Aida very much in tune with the old Arabian houses that bordered the roads and the gardens. Leaning against each other in that free and easy Oriental style, these charming houses with their secretive latticed windows and their cool, shady carved wooden *mashrabiya* balconies that jutted out from the storeys above, and all the characteristic detail of their façades, not yet lopped and trimmed by progress, reminded her of the sketches in her favourite book, *One Thousand and One Nights*, Arabian Tales from which her father read to her when she was a child.

Entranced, the young woman's attention was totally captivated by the vibrancy of her surroundings. More than ever, she realised how much she had missed Egypt and her heart was filled with an exhilaration at the thought that she was back in the country she loved, among these people who, despite their poverty, were happy-go-lucky and had always occupied a special place in her heart.

'You seem as fascinated by the scenes outside as the curious *khawagat*, foreigners who visit our country.'

Jerked out of her contemplation, Aida turned abruptly and stared up at the prince, whose lips curved in amusement.

'Yes, I'm so excited to be back. This is where I belong,' she enthused, eyes shining and her breathing a little faster.

'Excitement suits you, *ya bint el engelizeya*, daughter of the Englishwoman. Your eyes shimmer like jewels and your cheeks are coloured with the pink hue of dawn.' Behind those heavy lashes, Sakr El Din's gaze slid down over her, his pupils shining like silver blades, flickering with thoughts Aida was knowing enough to guess at, as they raked her face, pausing first on her eyes, then her lips and finally settling hungrily on her naked throat.

*A barbarian with a veneer of culture*, she told herself. Still, in some singular way – to her as to most women, she presumed – the prince had the mysterious, compelling allure of the desert, and Aida knew she should guard against it.

The car stopped in front of a prestigious three-storey building whose relatively sober façade was set back from the pavement and fronted by a broad set of steps flanked by two dwarf palm trees planted in giant decorated stone pots. The steps led up to the famous Shepheard's Hotel terrace and beyond that, to its entrance lit by wrought-iron wall lamps. These were both sheltered under an intricate *mushrabeya* canopy set on narrow columns that, during the daytime, protected visitors from the sun, and were guarded by a pair of small stone sphinxes taken from the Temple of Serapis at Memphis. The terrace, tiled with Moorish blue, green and orange motifs, was enclosed by a finely chiselled wrought-iron balustrade and set with rattan chairs and tables. In an elevated position, two metres above street level, it commanded a shaded view of the picturesque ceaseless stream of comings and goings along *Sharaa* Ibrahim Pasha, Ibrahim Pasha Street, below.

Two imposing doormen in scarlet-and-white uniforms, complete with red fez, stood at the entrance, while a couple of porters in kaftans with the name Shepheard's embroidered across their chests rushed forward to take care of Aida's luggage.

Aida turned to thank the prince and take her leave, but he had already stepped out of the car and was holding the door open for her.

'Thank you for your kind hospitality, Prince.'

He took her hand in both of his. 'It has been a pleasure to spend time in your company. As for hospitality, I hope that you will find the time to honour me with a visit to one of my palaces during your stay, however short that might be.'

Aida inclined her head slightly and smiled. '*In shah Allah*,' she said, trying to slowly disengage from his hold.

The prince tightened his grip before releasing her. 'Yes, as you say, *In shah Allah*, God willing ... but, more often than not, *man* has to be willing to cooperate in order to make things happen.' He murmured the second half of the phrase in the caressing, suave tone with which Aida was swiftly becoming familiar, though it was not much to her taste.

'Thanks again and goodnight.'

'Goodnight, *Mademoiselle* El Masri. It has been a pleasure.' As she started to climb the stairs, Aida heard him say behind her, 'I will be in touch.'

Aida did not look back and instead felt a familiar thrill of anticipation as she crossed the wide veranda and went through those hospitable doors; she'd enjoyed many happy times in this old hotel. Shepheard's was an institution, holding its own unique place in the affections of all who knew and loved Egypt.

The interior was true to its reputation of opulence, and more. It was done up in the pharaonic style, with the thick lotus-topped alabaster pillars in the main hall a copy from the ones at the Temple of Karnak in Luxor. The lobby was furnished with rattan chairs, the walls adorned with paintings and sketches of Ancient Egypt and there were beautiful ornate hourglass urns containing dwarf palms set here and there on small, delicate marble tables. A pair of tall, ebony caryatid light-bearers, in the image of topless pharaonic women with golden headdresses, stood like mute sentinels on low columns each side of the elegant double staircase that wound itself gracefully to the upper floors.

Having registered at the reception desk in the lobby, Aida made her way to the high Moorish hall through one of the four great, striped blue-tiled arches, modelled on the Mamluk architecture of medieval Cairo. The great hall was dimly lit by a coloured domed glass hung in the ceiling. The suite she had reserved was on the second floor and, feeling stiff after having spent long hours sitting in a train, she decided to walk up the stairs.

Although not so ornate as the ground-floor reception rooms and the main hall, the suite had elegant proportions and was just as luxurious. It consisted of a vast octagonal bedroom with a fifteen-foot ceiling, from which a Murano glass chandelier was suspended. An arch led through to a sitting area, the two rooms flowing into each other without barrier. A sofa, armchairs and coffee table made one end of the room sumptuously comfortable, while the adjoining one was furnished tastefully with built-in cupboards, a dressing table and finally, a spacious, sumptuous pink granite bathroom. The walls were hung with jade, yellow and off-white striped damask wallpaper and green velvet curtains were drawn across the three windows, one of which looked beyond the hotel gardens to an open-air public cinema that was showing Lauren Bacall's latest film, *Confidential Agent*.

It was already late and although the kitchens at the hotel were still open for dinner in the dining room, it had been a long, strenuous day and Aida was pining for her bed. She had a bath and ordered room service: turtle consommé, medallions of turbot in a creamy white-wine *Normande* sauce – a sauce made of fish stock, flavoured with white wine and enriched with cream and egg yolk – with steamed potatoes and leaf spinach. She had always ordered this dish whenever her father had taken her for lunch at Shepheard's.

As she prepared for bed, Aida found herself thinking about her encounter with Prince Shams Sakr El Din. She had no doubt she would be seeing him again … not that she would be instigating a meeting in any way, but he was clearly a determined sort of man and Aida had been aware of the predatory undercurrents vibrating around him. Still, she had never met anyone like him – he was a strange character, compelling even – and it was exciting to be courted. It was up to her to protect herself and make sure she did not get into any difficult situations with him.

As she waited for sleep, her thoughts roamed back to Phares. During that second week at Karawan House, while struggling with the management of her estate, Uncle Naguib had pleaded with her again to be sensible. He had met with Kamel Pharaony, who had been delighted to learn that Aida had returned and expressed again his personal hope that the two families might be joined with the marriage of Phares and Aida, fervently asking Naguib to reason with her. Now, as Aida's lids closed, Phares's handsome strong-featured face stamped with self-will, blood pride and charm swam in front of her eyes, unmistakable marks of his distinguished pharaonic forebears. She had always likened him to the beautiful statues she had been surrounded with since childhood and under whose spell she had fallen – there was a pagan quality to his looks: a full and passionate mouth that revealed strong white teeth when he smiled, and saturnine brows above coal-black eyes that smoked and sometimes mocked. Yet he had shown her that if his eyes could flash with pride, they could soften quickly too, with sympathy and kindness. And she would never forget the look Phares had given her that day in the courtroom, while he was bent over the figure of her father.

Doubtless he still remembered the actions of the fiery eighteen-year-old who, on that late afternoon eight years ago, had stormed into Hathor to confront Kamel Pharaony after Ayoub El Masri had been dragged away by two policemen and Souma Hassanein had poured out her shocking revelation. She had been beside herself with fury and grief, demanding that Kamel Pharaony should admit he was the owner of the Nefertari statue, rather than her father who was now dead because of Kamel's own cowardice. All the while Phares had listened patiently and said little, as far as she could recall, though she had been in such a state that her memory of that afternoon was hazy and fraught with emotion. At the time, Aida was left with a sense that he had been haughty, proud and angry, a stiff figure in his pinstriped suit looking down at her, condemning her uncontrolled outburst. Yet, truthfully, she couldn't remember any actual rebuke from him, only tolerance in the few words he spoke as he tried to calm her down. In the days afterwards, her pain and anger had been so ferocious that she'd refused to see Phares when he'd paid a visit to Karawan House the day before she left for England.

Perhaps he hadn't been judging her back then ... Maybe he hadn't come to the house to shame her for her accusations ... but her rage had been too strong for her to see clearly, and now, eight years later, she was no longer sure how she felt about Kamel's son. However, the intervening years had calmed her rage but not her resolve. Aida wondered if Phares had known about Kamel's guilt. She presumed back then that he had, but now she wasn't so sure. Still, he was the son of a traitor – his father had betrayed his best friend. How could she ever be part of that family?

# CHAPTER 3

A ida, fathoms deep in sleep, felt herself being drawn up from those blissful depths like a diver at the end of a chain. She tried to resist, but there was a noise that couldn't be ignored and eventually she surfaced to a sunlit world and the shrill ring of the telephone next to her bed.

The young woman reached out a lazy arm from under the cosy covers and grabbed the receiver. 'Hello?'

'Good morning, Aida? Have I woken you?'

Aida's laugh was crystalline, happy. 'Good morning, Uncle Naguib. Yes, I must admit I was fast asleep. What time is it?' She looked up at the sun blazing through the open windows, shining full on her face so that she almost had to shade her eyes.

'It's eleven o'clock. The train journey must have tired you.'

Aida sat up against the large plump pillows, pulling the telephone set on to her lap. 'Yes, I was exhausted and slept like a log. I feel wonderful this morning though.'

'Well, I did try and tell you to take it easy, at least for a couple of months, but there's no reasoning with you when you've decided on something.' He gave a throaty chuckle. 'Still, I'm happy that you've recovered and seem to be in good spirits. What are your plans for the rest of the day?'

'I'm not sure now. It may be a little late to go to the British Embassy, but I'll ring them. Mind you, I don't know if I'll be able to see Sir Miles tomorrow. I've been told he's away.'

'Told? By whom? Don't say you've already made friends at the hotel.'

'No, not exactly. I met a gentleman on the train who's apparently a friend of Sir Miles.'

'Who? A foreigner? Tell me, I might know him.'

'Prince Shams Sakr El Din.'

There was a pause at the end of the phone. 'Ah yes, I've met him. Only a couple of times, but I've heard a lot about him … A suave fox, that one, and by all accounts a little too fond of the ladies. Not that they don't seem to like him too. Apparently, they swoon as soon as he enters a room. But I wouldn't get too close, *habibti* … he has a shady reputation.'

'Well, don't worry, Uncle Naguib. I'm not here for long enough to get into any trouble, and I'm quite capable of looking after myself.'

'Ah, my dear, but you're a pretty girl and, as I've said, the prince has an eye for the ladies.' Naguib's tone became more serious. 'I'm told he keeps a large harem at his palace in the desert – and it isn't just made up of Arab women.'

Aida burst out laughing. 'Trust me, Uncle Naguib, I'm not about to join the queue. I personally don't find him at all attractive,' she lied, 'though I can see the appeal he might have.'

'I'm just warning you, *habibti*. If you've caught his eye, that one won't rest until he has you where he wants you.'

'Well, I say good luck to him.'

'Just stay away, Aida … I knew I should have come with you … Trouble has a knack of finding you.'

Aida heard the uneasy note in Naguib's voice and she could just imagine his concerned face. 'Please stop worrying, Uncle. I promise to be good and not to associate with strange men. After all, I've lived through a war and managed to keep safe,' she declared, a little irritated by his overprotectiveness. Aida was not in the habit of being told what she should, or shouldn't, be doing.

She thought she had left all that behind when she'd gone to England. As far as she was concerned, she had returned to Egypt a grown woman, perfectly capable of taking care of herself.

'Yes, all right, all right,' he said, capitulating. 'But don't stay away too long, there's work to be done here. Now that you're back, everybody on the estate expects it to be up and running at last, and as you already know, it won't be an easy task.'

'I'll be back in a couple of days and will buckle down to work, I promise.'

'Good … well, there's plenty of money in your account so go ahead and indulge yourself. I've opened accounts for you at Cicurel, Shemla, Sidnawi and Chalon.'

'That's wonderful. Thank you, Uncle Naguib. And please, don't worry about me.'

Having put the receiver down, Aida sat up against her pillows and phoned room service for some breakfast, before asking the switchboard to put her through to the British Embassy. The prince had been correct when he told her Sir Miles had gone away. But now the secretary on the other end of the line put an end to any hope Aida might have had of having a meeting with him in the future. He had a new job, the woman told her: Special Commissioner for Southeast Asia.

'Is it an important matter, madam?' the woman asked. 'If so, perhaps I could book an appointment with Mr Alastair Carlisle, one of our consuls … Let's see … He has a spare slot in his diary next week if that works for you?'

'Please don't worry,' Aida said quickly. 'It was only a courtesy call to pass on a message from my uncle in England. Nothing important. If it's all right, I'll drop off the letter instead, if you wouldn't mind forwarding it to Sir Miles?'

As soon as the conversation was over, she made a note of the name she had been given – Alastair Carlisle. Perhaps the next time she was in Cairo she could find another excuse to meet the consul. At least she had this new contact at the Embassy for the future.

Aida sprang out of bed and padded across the plush Persian carpet to one of the open windows. She hadn't noticed the night before that it had an outside balcony. The sun was fully up; Cairo shone in all her glory, her domes and spires glittering, white walls gleaming under an azure sky. The sunlight fell warmly upon Aida's bare neck and arms as she stepped outside, and she lifted her face to it happily. On a flat roof not faraway a little Egyptian boy was standing. He tossed a handful of grain into the air and a flock of doves appeared from nowhere, circled above his head, dipped and rose and was gone again.

Aida heard a knock at the door and came in from the balcony. Pulling on her dressing gown, she went to let in the *suffragi* bearing her breakfast. She drank her tea with a slice of toast and marmalade, had a bath and dressed. Aida was beside herself with excitement. She was going on a spending spree – shopping for clothes, a whole new wardrobe! For the past eight years, Aida – who had always been pampered growing up in Egypt – had had to make do and mend. In England the clothing coupons never went far enough, and she would save them for emergencies. Everything she owned had been kept in a small cupboard, and she had learned never to throw anything away.

Throughout the war years she had adopted the Parisian motto that had come out in *Vogue* magazine in 1941: '*Il faut* "skimp" *pour être chic*'. The phrase referred to the tight, short-skirted silhouette that had replaced the flirty fullness of dresses worn in the thirties. The new sculpted look was driven by the wartime rationing economy, but not only that, it gave the illusion of brisk competence. As *Vogue* put it, it looked 'sharp, cold and even bold'. If you kept your figure trim, it was most elegant, and luckily, Aida's puppy fat soon dropped off her, helped by the inevitable austerity of wartime. In no time she had lost two stone, and the new style suited her beautifully.

This morning she was dressed in what she called 'her staple suit' with black platform shoes. The cut of the suit of grey jersey wool with padded shoulders had been influenced by the austere style of military uniforms. It had a red trim in soft velveteen to brighten it up and Aida wore it over a white crepe blouse with three buttons covered in the same red material, and a red velveteen pillbox hat to match. Although the style was conservative and uniform-like, the tailoring was magnificent.

As she crossed the lobby and walked out into the bright sunshine, Aida did not feel out of place among the more glamorous outfits worn by the other women milling about the foyer. The doorman hurried to ask her if he could call a taxi or *hantour* carriage, but, thanking him, she said she would prefer to walk. She knew her way about Cairo well, and besides, she needed some exercise.

Aida set out, enjoying how being on foot made her feel part of the city. She headed down *Sharaa* Ibrahim Pasha, one of Cairo's main streets that ran from Ramses Railway Station to the gates of Abdin Palace. The street was only a stone's throw from *sharaa* Fouad, where she would find Cicurel and Shemla, two of the most prestigious department stores in Egypt. This part of town had submitted to Khedive Ismail's urbanisation project in the mid-nineteenth century, one that had changed the face of Cairo. Entire streets of traditional Oriental houses had vanished – the Cairene elite aspiring to a more European style – and between the Nile and the old town a whole new quarter of magnificent lacy boulevards had been built. The new features had a belle époque veneer as Italian, French and Austro-Hungarian architects went about creating a 'Paris of the Nile', with a twist here and there of Moorish decor to maintain the Islamic atmosphere.

The pavements were thronged with an international crowd. Aida could tell their nationality by the way they were dressed. Englishwomen in morning cottons made by local tailors; French and Italian girls beautifully turned out in light summer dresses, some of them showing a daring amount of bare skin; young Egyptian women in swinging black silk skirts, short black *abbas* wrapped around their heads and shoulders, filmy yashmaks below their large painted dark eyes, and tiny high-heeled shoes on small feet covered in white stockings. The men also were attired in a variety of clothes that pointed to their social status. Some wore linen and thin tweeds, others were in frock coats and *tarbooshes*, and many sported long, white kaftans and skullcaps. Every now and then a majestic sheikh passed her in richly embroidered silks, a flowing cloak and snowy turban, each one with their *Sibha*, Islamic prayer beads.

Brightly striped awnings shaded the shopfronts. Aida was amazed at the wealth and variety of the merchandise displayed. It seemed you could buy virtually anything in Cairo, though the war was not long past – if you could afford the inflated prices, of course. She couldn't help but feel a little shocked by it all and found herself gazing at the hundreds of silk stockings displayed in all their lustrous, almost forgotten sheen. Such luxuries were nowhere to be seen in London, even on the black market, until the American GIs arrived on British shores in 1942, bringing sought-after nylons in their ration packs. Aida remembered using Elizabeth Arden leg paint to imitate seamed stockings and sometimes, when she was short of cash, gravy browning and cocoa, which were cheaper and just as effective. Aida couldn't help but feel incredulous when she saw the rich panoply of frocks, hats, scarves and filmy underwear; kid gloves and soft leather shoes; creams, powders and expensive bottles of French scent. At the small tables outside the cafés, men sat placidly playing *tawla*, drafts, and sipping coffee – another rare commodity in Britain – while cars belted along the road, klaxons sounding, and *hantours* clattered by, their drivers cracking long whips and cursing the suicidal pedestrians who seemed happy to take their lives in their own hands and cross the roads in a haphazard fashion.

The Cicurel department store loomed into view, four storeys high. Aida paused outside and lingered a while over the displays in the wide plate glass windows that ran the length of the ground floor of the vast building. Although Cicurel was the larger of the two department stores, Aida had always preferred to shop at Shemla next door, and so she decided to try her luck there first. Her main concern was to secure a suitable gown for Princess Nazek's ball.

Shemla, though smaller, was just as grand, designed in the more comfortable and elegant French *fin de siècle* style. Aida entered the vast art deco marble hall of the luxurious emporium and glanced up at the mezzanine level above, supported by columns topped with acanthus leaves. Glass display cases filled with expensive French bottles of scent and well-known make-up brands were the first stop for customers, as well as gloves, beautifully embroidered small evening bags and purses, sequined shawls and silk scarves. The ground floor held the cloth department, well known in Cairo for selling imported silks, which sat alongside the hosiery and lingerie section, and deeper into the store lay the furniture and shoe departments.

Aida made her way up to the next floor, which housed the spacious haute couture atelier that sold clothes in the latest Parisian trends. After the fashion starvation she had experienced during the war years, she was overwhelmed by the profusion, diversity and splendour of the elegantly displayed daytime clothes, evening gowns, hats, bags and accessories. She didn't know which way to turn.

A shop assistant came to her rescue with a broad, slightly patronising smile. Dressed elegantly in a black suit and white silk shirt, her whole persona smacked of French couture, although Aida guessed she was either Greek or Italian.

'May I help you?'

'Yes ... yes, please. Umm ... I'm looking for an evening gown.'

'For what kind of special occasion? Daytime? Evening? Wedding ... or a ball, perhaps?'

'Yes, a ball ...'

The assistant smiled. 'That shouldn't be a problem. I'm sure that I have exactly what you're looking for. My name is Cleo, by the way.'

She led the way to a large fitting room with a sofa and two armchairs, a coffee table and a set of tall mirrors, set at different angles to afford various views of a client's reflection.

Cleo disappeared behind a curtain and was back within minutes carrying a number of gowns. 'These have just arrived from Paris last week,' she declared as she hung the garments on a rail in a corner of the changing room. There were four evening gowns, each more glamorous than than the one before. Aida was spoilt for choice. 'No one has seen them yet ...' Cleo added as she plucked a fabulous gown by Schiaparelli from its velvet hanger.

Aida tried out every one of the dresses and though each was prettier than the last – and she would have taken them all, had she been extravagant – none was quite right.

'All these dresses are spectacular,' she said, handing the last one back to Cleo, 'but they don't quite fit the occasion.'

'I have shown you the simpler, elegant dresses. But we do have a fancier, more ornate collection.' Cleo hesitated. 'May I ask if you require this gown for Princess Nazek's Annual Ball?'

Aida laughed at her astuteness. 'Absolutely – yes, you're right.'

'I think I have just the thing for you then, *madame*. It was delivered this morning, straight from the airport, and hasn't yet been released from our atelier. I haven't seen it myself, but the girls upstairs were really excited. As you know, these are unique gowns and our buyer had real difficulty in securing it.

Apparently one of the Monaco princesses had set her heart on it and at the last minute changed her mind.'

Aida's eyes widened. Hearing the shop assistant, she couldn't get over what felt like almost unimaginable luxury. 'Wonderful, thank you! I've just come back from England. There's little in the way of fashion there so I need a new wardrobe.'

Cleo's expression softened a little. 'In that case, please feel free to browse the rails while I fetch it. If anything catches your eye, we are able to order it for you even if it's not in stock.' Twenty minutes later she came back with a dress still covered in tissue paper. 'I'm sorry to have kept you waiting, but it wasn't supposed to be released until next week. I've had a bit of a job trying to convince *Madame* Reinach, the head of the department, to do so, but in the end, she agreed.' She gave a small, satisfied smile.

'Thank you, Cleo. I'm sure I'll love it. So far I've loved everything you've shown me.'

As she unwrapped the gown, Cleo described it, saying, 'It is called *Romance à Minuit*, designed by Balenciaga. You'll see why when I show you the colour. Midnight blue. Not the shades and tones you mentioned earlier, but I think it will suit you beautifully. The dresses I showed you before … each a work of art, of course, aren't … *comment dirais-je*?' She hesitated, looking for the right word. 'I would say they are more frivolous. This piece is in a different league. A creation, if you like, and a substantial one at that.'

Aida's impatience to see the dress was growing by the minute as, one by one, the layers of tissue paper were peeled off. Finally, freed from its wrapping, the garment appeared in all its splendour. Dazzling and decadent were the only words to describe it. Cleo helped the young woman put it on.

Aida couldn't help a smothered gasp as she viewed herself in the mirrors that showed off every aspect of her habiliment. The gown's sweetheart-shaped bosom had a band made out of gold leather strips embroidered with multicoloured pearls, stones and sequins. A thin, intricate filigree spaghetti strap with a similar embellishment rose from the band and encircled Aida's slender neck in a sparkling halter style. The tight bodice of lustrous midnight-blue taffeta flared into a short full skirt that billowed over a longer, full-length one. On one side of the waistline was a repeat of the bodice motif, a lavish bejewelled cluster in the shape of a horseshoe that drew attention to the fitted waist, while the shimmering weave of the material reflected the blue of her eyes and darkened them.

'*Magnifique*! You will take the room by storm when you arrive at the ball, *madame*. The dress really enhances your beauty. What do you think of it?'

Aida could hardly believe how glamorous she looked. 'What can I say? … It *is* really fabulous.'

Cleo nodded knowingly. 'Balenciaga today is recognised as the master of couture even by Coco Chanel. I personally love his dramatic style but he *does* charge the highest prices.'

The price was indeed high: almost a third of the total bill once Aida had finished her shopping extravaganza. To the clothes she had chosen she added shoes, bags, coats, a cape, nylon stockings which she had so missed, and some gloves. To keep her going for the next couple of days she was spending in Cairo, she picked out two or three outfits, some accessories, nightwear and lingerie, which she asked the shop to deliver to Shepheard's. As for the remainder, they were to be sent to her home in Luxor.

As she turned to leave the counter, she almost collided with a young woman who was walking past with a large shopping bag.

'Camelia!' she exclaimed, recognising her old friend.

Camelia Pharaony seemed to hesitate for a brief moment before crying out in surprise, 'Aida? Aida El Masri, *mish maaoul*! Impossible … Is it you? … I can't believe it! When did you arrive?'

Aida looked back at her, equally dazed. 'Only ten days ago.'

Camelia enfolded her in a warm hug. 'How long are you here for? Are you alone? Have you been to Luxor? Where are you staying?'

Aida laughed. 'Slowly, one question at a time! I've already been home and I only arrived in Cairo last night … and, yes, I'm here alone.' She couldn't help beaming at Camelia; there was clearly no awkwardness between the two of them and she realised how delighted she was to see her old friend. 'I was going to contact you while I was here so it's wonderful we bumped into each other.' She let out another laugh, almost of relief.

Camelia's dark eyes danced with excitement. 'Let's catch up while having a spot of lunch … unless of course you have other plans.'

'No plans. I'm staying at Shepheard's. Let's have lunch there.'

'Wonderful! Do you have a car?'

'No, I walked. It's such a lovely day.'

'Mine is outside. I've just come to pick up a dress that needed altering. I'll tell them to deliver it to the house instead. I'll be right with you.'

The luxurious navy-blue chauffeur-driven Cadillac was waiting on the pavement. Talking endlessly all the way to the hotel, the two women fell back into an easy rapport, with so much to catch up on that both were gushing to fill in the gaps of the last eight years. Like Aida, Camelia had undergone a complete metamorphosis: the chrysalis had turned into a butterfly. From the tomboy she had been at sixteen, she had become a sophisticated young woman, now dressed in the latest of Paris suits, her lustrous jet-black hair gathered up in a cloud of curls on the crown of her head and styled in the most recent fashion. She was pure Egyptian, like her brother Phares, with thick-lashed gazelle eyes the colour of black velvet which burned with an intense flame, giving away her passionate nature. Still, there lingered in their depths a graveness, a sadness even, that Aida silently attributed to her friend's recent loss.

At Shepheard's, Aida went straight to the reception desk to inform the concierge that she was expecting a large delivery from the Shemla department store later that day.

'I will be in the dining room, but could you please have it taken upstairs and put in my dressing room.'

'Certainly, *madame*. And also, while you were out a large basket of flowers was delivered for you. We have placed it in your bedroom.'

Aida raised an enquiring eyebrow. 'Flowers? For me? Are you sure?'

The concierge eyed her slyly. 'Certainly, *madame*. The gentleman left a card with this note. He asked me to hand it to you personally.'

Aida took it and immediately recognised the same royal crest from the card Prince Shams Sakr El Din had given her on the train. Her expression flickered with unease. Without opening it, she put the note in her pocket – she would read it later.

'Thank you,' she murmured.

'Something wrong?' asked Camelia, appearing by her side.

'I'll tell you over lunch. Come, we'd better go in or we'll never find a table.'

The high-ceilinged Moorish dining room at Shepheard's, like the rest of the hotel, was magnificent and was packed for lunch. The maitre d'hôtel greeted Aida and Camelia at the door and showed them to one of the last empty tables. The elegant room was cool, dimly lit by different-sized *Mamluk* copper lanterns suspended from keyhole arches. The walls were adorned with *tadelakt* plaster, *zellige* tiles, motifs carved in the top of the marble columns and leaf and flower designs. *Suffragis*, each clad in a white kaftan with red cummerbund, red fez and slippers, glided effortlessly around the tables, appetising dishes of food balanced on their outstretched hands. At the far end of the crowded room, on one side, stood a beautiful six-panelled *mashrabiya* arabesque screen, while nearby, a three-tier stone fountain, its cooling blocks of ice ringed by beautiful banked-up plants and flowers, cooed monotonously in the background.

Once seated, the young women ordered the set lunch for that day. A plate of *mezzeh*, Egyptian hors d'oeuvres, followed by grilled entrecôte served with Béarnaise sauce, French-style peas and new potatoes.

'Shall we have some wine?' Camelia asked her friend. 'This is a special occasion after all.'

'Why not? I haven't had a decent glass of wine for years. It was so expensive in England.'

Aida, along with Camelia, had been brought up in the Coptic community, where alcohol was only to be enjoyed in moderation, though a trip to Shepheard's and a reunion with a long-lost friend, both agreed, was cause for celebration.

Camelia turned to the maitre d'hôtel. 'A bottle of Gianaclis red, please.' She fixed Aida with a quizzical smile. 'Now then, tell me all about this gentleman who has sent you flowers. Is he English?'

Aida shook her head and gave a little laugh. 'No, far from it! He's an Arab prince.'

'You mean Turkish prince.'

'No, no … nothing to do with the royal family,' Aida explained, then saw the odd look on her friend's face. 'I'm not joking … really, he's an Arab who says that his kingdom – I can't remember the name now – is an oasis in the desert.'

'Where did you meet him? What's his name?'

'We met on the train. His name is Prince Shams Sakr El Din.'

Camelia paled at the name. 'You're not serious?'

'I promise you, it's true.' Noticing her concerned expression, Aida's curiosity sharpened. 'Why? What's the problem?'

'The problem is that he's known to be one of the worst womanisers in Cairo. King Farouk is an angel in comparison, *habibti*.'

The conversation paused while a waiter appeared with the wine, pouring two glasses, while another followed in his wake with a tray of *mezzeh*. The women waited until they left before continuing.

'Apparently, women find the prince irresistible,' Aida said with an amused smile, dipping a small triangular piece of *baladi* bread into a plate of *bissara* bean dip.

Camelia's dark eyes widened. 'Well, this woman doesn't. Trust me.'

'You've met him?'

'Yes, actually ... though there's enmity between our two families dating back three generations.'

Aida looked startled. 'For what reason?'

Camelia helped herself to some *warag enab*, stuffed vine leaves, and a couple of falafels. 'My great grandfather Boutros and the prince's great grandmother Gawahir were in love and tried to elope. Her brother Seif stopped them at the edge of the desert. He knifed his sister and then a fight ensued between him and my great grandfather. They were both found dead the next day, their bodies ravaged by vultures and hyenas.'

Aida shivered and put down her fork. 'What a dreadful story.'

Camelia nodded. 'My grandfather hated the Bedouins, but I think all that has been forgotten now. The prince has been to the house a couple of times, which is why I've met him briefly. My father initiated the peace. It seems they have some business together, but I've not seen the prince lately. I personally don't like him, and Phares loathes the very idea of him, though I'm not sure they've ever spoken. I'm told the man is quite civilised, having studied in France, and certainly a great charmer. But I know several respectable socialites whose wings have been burnt by his fire. Apparently, he's always on the lookout for beautiful women to add to his harem ...' Camelia gave her friend a knowing look. 'So, not someone whose company you should keep.'

Aida laughed and gave an emphatic shake of her head. '*Aasham ibliss fil jannah*', Satan's aspiration to Paradise! Well, he won't find success with me. I admit, he's a handsome man and I can well believe that women swoon around him, but believe me, I'm not that naïve, my dear.'

'By the looks of it, he has already cast his line.'

'Maybe, but I'm not about to swallow the bait.'

Camelia regarded her warmly before saying, 'It's strange how we can still talk freely to each other ... It's as if you'd never left.'

Aida smiled gently. It was impossible to imagine what her life would have become if she had stayed in Egypt. 'Yes, but a war has taken place in that time and I don't think anyone has remained the same.'

'Nevertheless, *habibti*, you are here now, and we should drink to your return.' Camelia lifted her glass and clinked it against Aida's.

'To reunions,' Aida grinned and took a sip of the delicious Egyptian wine. How fond she still felt of Camelia!

'We didn't feel it much here, the war, I mean,' continued Camelia, after the waiter had brought their entrecôte steak. 'Especially in Luxor. In Cairo, it was full of British soldiers on leave but Gizeh, Garden City, Zamalek and all this part of town were never bombed. Of course, it was different for Phares who stayed most of the time in Cairo or in Alexandria, working in hospitals with the wounded brought in from the desert. He saw the uglier face of the war.'

Aida felt a tremor in her heart at the young man's name.

Camelia's eyes became wistful. 'We'd be sisters-in-law today if you hadn't rushed off as you did. I think it hurt Phares a lot, even though he didn't show it, of course.'

Something in the tone of her voice made Aida think Camelia had felt wounded too. 'Phares and I were never in love.' She cut into her steak but didn't eat it.

Camelia looked sceptical. 'You have a short memory, *habibti*. I seem to recall otherwise, at least where *you* were concerned ... Don't you remember when we went riding that summer at the crack of dawn, just to catch a glimpse of Phares studying on the terrace? And when we used to go to the Gezireh Sporting Club to watch him playing polo ... and that time you asked me to steal one of his photographs, which you then kept under your pillow?'

'Don't be ridiculous, Camelia, that was puppy love – infatuation,' Aida protested, though her cheeks went slightly pink. 'Like your being in love with Rizk, the gardener's son, remember?'

Camilia's face brightened and suddenly she giggled. '*Touché* ... but not quite. I still think your feelings for Phares ran much deeper than you remember, or want to admit to.' Her expression stilled as she added cautiously, 'You would have married him if ... if you hadn't left Egypt.'

Aida stiffened at Camelia's veiled reference to her father's death. It was the one subject they hadn't discussed yet. She took another sip of wine and cut into her steak. 'Anyhow, your brother was never in love with me. He was just following his father's instructions ... doing the right thing for the family business.'

'That's not so. Phares was very fond of you and admired the way you had turned out, considering your mother died when you were very young. He always said you were not spoilt like most girls in our social milieu, but intelligent and strong, and that you'd make a wonderful nurse because of your compassionate heart. Your impulsive nature was the only trait he had reservations about, and deep down I think he even respected that.'

Aida gazed at Camelia intently. 'It would never have worked. There was no passion between us.'

'Your arguments were certainly fiery.' Camelia glanced at her knowingly. 'My brother is a very passionate person.'

'Maybe with another woman, but he never showed that side of himself to me. We never even held hands.'

'You were not yet his fiancée ... nothing was official. He isn't like most men –Prince Shams Sakr El Din, for instance – who enjoy courting, kissing and more intimate things as casually as a glass of wine. Phares lives by a different code. Pride runs in his blood. Passion is something he would reserve for the woman he marries.' Camelia sounded fondly exasperated. 'You can't deny there was something there between you.'

Aida shook her head. 'I was in awe of him, probably because he was the only good-looking and charismatic man I'd met ... and remember, by the time I was eighteen, he was already twenty-five. Back then I must have seemed very gauche to him, with my half-formed ideas about life and my flippancy. He had lived on his own and travelled the world. For him I was probably just a child. I would have bored him ... it would never have worked.'

Camelia took a sip of her wine and said nothing for a few moments. 'He's never married, you know,' she said finally. 'Although it's not for want of women trying. Heaps of beautiful heiresses, whom Aunt Halima has been parading in front of him for the past few years, the old busybody!'

Aida let out an irritated sigh. 'Anyhow, all that's water under the bridge now.' She needed to get off the subject of Phares, knowing only too well the effect the young doctor still had on her. Those were private feelings, not to be intruded upon by anyone, even Camelia. 'Enough talk about me. What about you?'

'There's not a lot to say.' Camelia's large dark eyes became more serious. 'You must have heard that I married.'

'Yes, *Dada* Amina told me,' Aida said softly.

'So, she must have also told you that Mounir, my husband, was killed in a car accident on the desert road.'

Aida reached across the table to squeeze her hand briefly. 'Yes. I'm so sorry for your loss, Camelia. *Dada* didn't go into details, she just told me that you're now a widow.'

Camelia sighed. 'Thank you, *habibti*. Yes. And as you know, life for a widow in our narrow-minded society is even worse than a single girl's. Wagging tongues never stop. Without her husband, a woman alone is an opportunity for a jolly good gossip.'

Aida was no stranger to such unwanted scrutiny. She had a momentary vision of that last afternoon she had spent at the Gezireh Sporting Club before leaving for England. As she sat, feeling her isolation, she could hear the none-too-discreet laughter and sneers of people who, before her father's indictment and death, had called themselves her friends. 'It must be very hard for you,' she commiserated gently, feeling a wave of sympathy for Camelia.

Her friend nodded. 'My father is always reminding me of my status. Phares is overprotective, too. He seems to forget that I'm a grown woman. Mounir used to leave me for weeks on end alone in our flat in Maadi while he travelled to his cotton mills in Mahallah, Kafr El Dawar and Damanhour. He never worried for a moment that I would get into any trouble.' She glanced at Aida with a faint smile. 'You're lucky you've escaped all that.'

'Did you love your husband?'

'He was much older than me. We had a good relationship. He made me feel secure. We were good to each other and never fought. So yes, I loved him very much.' The young woman gave a weak smile.

'No children then?'

Camelia shook her head unhappily. 'No, and to me that is a great sadness. I would have liked to have a child. At least my life would have more purpose to it.'

'So, what do you do with yourself?'

'I'm on a few charity boards and I ...' Camelia stopped suddenly as though she had been about to say something but held back.

'And?' Aida prompted.

'Oh … I occupy myself with one thing or another … You know, coffee mornings and the usual *wagibs*, duties that arise almost every week … funerals, christenings, weddings. There's always something.'

'No man in your life?'

Camelia gave her friend an enigmatic smile. 'How? When a widow is treated as a social pariah. The women are afraid for their husbands so they keep clear, and men treat you as a loose woman because they assume without a man to keep an eye on you, you're open to any overture. As for the men, you know what it's like here. In our circle there are few ways to meet a decent man. We are just creatures of pleasure to most of them, unless you find one who loves you. What about you, *habibti*? Did you marry in England?'

Aida shook her head. 'No, I was too engrossed in my work. The war broke out before I had time to finish my training and so I was thrown in at the deep end, learning to be a nurse on the job, plus I was seconded to lots of different hospitals for a while. In a way it was both heart-wrenching and exhilarating. You lived in a surreal world where you couldn't anticipate what tomorrow would bring. The suffering we saw was horrendous, but you didn't have the time to think, feel, grieve … everything changed so quickly from one minute to the next.'

Camelia's eyebrows rose. 'Not even a fling? I understand people pretty much threw caution to the wind … kind of living for the day.'

Aida drew an inaudible sigh. 'Not even a fling. At first, I was homesick and then I was working round the clock with the doctors and other nurses. Overtime was a way of life and I never seemed to stand still. But you're right, I knew a few couples who married in panic during the war and were divorced by the end of it. Still, that wasn't for me. I had more pressing things to deal with, like people who'd been badly burned in a blast or a fire, soldiers who had lost a limb or part of it …' She shook her head, pushing away the memories. 'It was horrendous, really. War is so wicked.'

Camelia's large expressive eyes were full of affection. 'You always said you wanted to be another Florence Nightingale, Aida. And with your sort of drive and dedication, I'm not surprised …'

They had worked their way through the two first courses and now the maitre d'hôtel came over to ask if they would prefer the *Mont Blanc Chantilly*, a dessert of puréed, sweetened chestnuts topped with whipped cream, or a basket of fresh fruit. Both women opted for the classic French snow-capped treat and a pot of coffee.

Camelia eyed her friend over her cup. 'How long are you here for?'

'I'm here for Princess Nazek's ball,' Aida answered. 'We met on the plane from London. I'll be going back to Luxor after that.'

Camelia's face lit up. 'What a marvellous coincidence! My father and I have been invited too. And Phares, but I don't think he'll go. You must come and stay with us.'

Aida tensed. Catching her breath, she felt the colour sweep up her face, burning into the roots of her hair. The last person she wanted to see was Kamel Pharaony.

Camelia's perfect black brows drew together. 'What's wrong, Aida? You've gone all red.'

'Just a headache. I get them sometimes.'

Camelia looked concerned. 'I'll tell you what we'll do. You'll pay your bill for one night and then we'll go home to the house in Gizeh. You remember Kasr El Ghoroub, don't you? We spent such lovely times there.' She smiled encouragingly.

Aida remembered all right. She had loved staying at the Pharaonys' house, because more often than not Phares was there too, training at the hospitals in nearby Cairo during the day, and in the evening after supper he had frequently sat around with Camelia and Aida, listening to music and chatting until the early hours of the morning. Sometimes all three of them would go riding in the desert, and once or twice he had treated them to the cinema. On one very special occasion, Phares and his cousin Amir had taken the girls out to a nightclub on the pyramids' road, where Phares had danced with Aida under the stars. She remembered it so well. She had just turned sixteen, and that evening was the first and only time he had held her in his arms. For once Aida had been forced into bewildered silence in his presence as his strong hand rested lightly on her back and she felt the nearness of his hard chest, though no doubt Phares was completely unaware of her dizzying turmoil. For years after she had left Egypt, no matter how hard she tried to bury her mind's precious souvenirs from those carefree days, the memory of that particular warm summer night lingered like a wonderful dream. Every so often, when the atrocities she had faced day after day became too overwhelming, she would seek refuge in those cheerful memories, trying to recapture the faraway times when she had been carefree and happy.

Now, the thought of returning to Kasr El Ghoroub filled Aida with dark apprehension. For so long she had condemned Kamel Pharaony in her mind, convinced that he had betrayed her father. Even if she'd been wrong, Aida wasn't sure if she was ready to face him again. The last time she had seen him was that terrible afternoon of her father's arrest. Her brow furrowed under the strain of trying to push it from her mind.

'Can we leave it for the next time I come to Cairo?' she answered eventually. 'I … I really wouldn't like to impose on your father.'

Camelia looked at her curiously. 'On the contrary, Papa would be offended if you refused … Anyway, do you have an escort for the ball?'

'No, I must admit that I don't.' Aida knew this would provide another problem.

'It would be badly looked upon if you arrived without a chaperone.'

'I'm not a debutante anymore. During the war I often left the hospital late at night or in the early hours of the morning to go home.'

The beautiful brunette was having none of it. 'Yes, but you were in England and that was wartime.'

'Oh, Camelia, why must we argue? We've just found each other again. I can't bear your being annoyed with me,' Aida said, embarrassed by the persistent note in her own voice.

'Listen, it's just that both Papa and Phares will be furious with me if they find out that I knew you were in Cairo and let you stay alone at a hotel. That's even worse than not having an escort!'

'You don't need to tell them,' she said tentatively.

'Sooner or later they'll find out. Look, it's just a few days at our house, and it'll be like old times. Unless of course …' Camelia blinked, and something flickered across her face. She looked at her friend anxiously. 'Unless you still harbour those horrid thoughts about my father. Surely that was just your grief speaking?' she said tentatively. 'I never thought you meant it seriously …'

'Let it go, Camelia.' Aida's voice was quiet, although she could feel her agitation mounting.

'You do, don't you? You still think the statue belonged to Papa.'

'Forgive me, Camelia, but I don't know what to think anymore. I just know my father was framed somehow.'

'Your head is full of unfounded notions.'

'Maybe, but I need to find out the truth and clear my father's name.'

Camelia's eyes were wide. 'I can understand that. In your place I would have wanted to do the same, but you're going about it in the wrong way.'

Aida frowned. 'Perhaps, but I need to handle this in my *own* way. There's nothing more to be said or done about it.' A moment of awkward silence fell before Aida's expression softened. 'I value your friendship, Camelia. I hope you haven't taken umbrage at what I've said.'

Camelia met her friend's gaze, her expression earnest. 'I value your friendship too, Aida, and I will stand by you. Though I sincerely believe there has been a huge misunderstanding and that my father had nothing to do with what happened.'

'Thank you,' Aida murmured, and refrained from adding, *That remains to be seen.*

Camelia looked at her friend askance. 'I still think that you shouldn't be staying at the hotel alone and that we should all go together to Princess Nazek's ball. It'll be twice as fun preparing for a party together like we used to in the old days. I've missed you so much,' she ended wistfully.

Camelia was obviously lonely and was reaching out to her, and Aida was deeply touched by the young widow's avowal of friendship. Eight years was a long time, yet their closeness hadn't altered and they were as comfortable with each other as they had ever been. Camelia was one of the few real friends she had in Egypt. It would be nice to take up where they had left off. Aida didn't relish the idea of meeting Kamel Pharaony again, but sooner or later she would run into him; Cairo's social circle was as big as a pocket handkerchief, and she might as well get this first face-to-face over and done with. Besides, now that she was back in Egypt she was beginning to question everything she thought she knew.

Aida smiled fondly at her friend. 'You don't give up easily, do you?'

'Not when it's important,' replied Camelia resolutely. 'Our friendship is something I take seriously and I won't let you throw it away just because some poisonous person made accusations against my father. If you wish to clear your father's name, I also need to rid you of the suspicion that fills your mind. Which means your meeting *my* father again.'

Aida looked at her warmly. She had a point. 'I'm really touched by your friendship, Camelia.'

'Then you will come and stay with us,' she stated rather than asked.

Aida gave a brief capitulating laugh. 'How can I not after such an invitation?'

After they'd finished their coffee and the plate of petit fours that accompanied it, Aida asked the maitre d'hôtel to add the bill to her account and the two women left the dining room via the front desk, where Aida cancelled her reservation for the rest of her stay.

Together, they went up to her suite, where Prince Shams Sakr El Din's huge basket of flowers was displayed on the table in the middle of the room.

'You haven't read the note.' Camelia gestured at the opulent display. 'I noticed you put it in your pocket unopened.'

Aida stopped next to the table. 'Ah yes! I didn't like the way the concierge was looking at me, so I just shoved it away and then forgot about it.'

She took the note out of her pocket. The handwriting was left-slanting, small and angled. Aida had once been interested in graphology and she judged that the prince's letters denoted a highly intelligent but rather cold nature with strong powers of concentration, an analytical, manipulative mind and an aggressive, impatient personality. An interesting character, she thought, with a wicked provocative strain that spelled danger. Intriguing, but one to beware of.

*My dear Miss El Masri,* she read aloud, *Would you please do me the great honour of accompanying me tomorrow night to the opening ball of the season. It is given by a good friend of mine, Princess Nazek. It will take place at her palace overlooking the Nile on Gezireh Island. I was going to attend it on my own, but my pleasure will be so much greater if you agree to be my partner for the evening.*

> *Your faithful servant,*
> *Shams Sakr El Din*

Aida laughed. 'So, I *do* have an escort after all.'

'You're not going to accept? You've only met the man briefly ...' her friend protested, appalled.

'Why shouldn't I? This is a perfectly civil invitation.' *And a very convenient one at that,* Aida admitted silently to herself.

'I just told you about his reputation.'

'So what? He will be escorting me to a ball, nothing more,' Aida said cheerfully, gathering the few things she'd had time to unpack and returning them to her suitcase.

Camelia crossed to the window and looked out at the bustling Ibrahim Pasha Street below. 'Have you forgotten the wagging tongues of Cairo society? Your name will be linked with his, and every respectable young man will look upon you as ... as ... well, you know what I mean.'

Aida continued folding her clothes. 'Come on, Camelia, don't be so narrow-minded.'

Camelia glanced over from the window. 'I'm not narrow-minded, you know that *habibti*, but other people are. This ball is an opportunity to meet all the eligible young men in Cairo. That's why my father is so keen for me to attend. He's even cancelled his precious evening of bridge to escort me as Phares couldn't promise to be there. He never knows if he'll be called upon for an urgent operation ...'

Aida preferred not to think about whether or not Phares would attend, so her expression remained shuttered. 'I'm not interested in Egyptian eligible young men. They are so bigoted and set in their views.'

Camelia arched a brow. 'That's a sweeping statement, and a damned stupid one too.'

'Look, it's just that I've become used to much more independence than women have here. I could never live the parochial life most of these so-called prospective husbands have to offer.'

'My father will not allow you to be taken to the ball by this man,' Camelia declared flatly.

Aida looked up from the suitcase and her eyes hardened. 'With all due respect, I don't see that this matter is Uncle Kamel's business.'

Camelia walked over to her friend, her tone conciliatory. 'You know how it is, Aida. He will feel responsible for you, especially if you're staying under his roof.'

'Well then, I'll stay at Shepheard's as originally planned,' she retorted in a firm voice.

Camelia gave a small sigh. 'You're being unreasonable.'

'Maybe, but I won't have anybody dictate to me.'

'No one is trying to dictate to you. For what it's worth, you can do whatever you like and my invitation still stands. Papa will probably make some sort of remark, but he won't interfere, I'm sure.'

'I wouldn't like to put him in that sort of uncomfortable situation,' Aida said coolly. 'So, if you don't mind, I'll spend the next two nights at the hotel and I promise you that when I come to Cairo in the future, if you're also here I will stay with you.'

Aida proceeded to ring reception in order to undo her cancellation, but was informed that the room was already taken and there were no other rooms available for a week.

Frustrated, she turned back to Camelia. 'It looks as if the gods are conspiring against me,' she said with a wry look. 'I could of course stay at the Semiramis, or the Continental ...'

Camelia rolled her eyes. 'But you're not, because you aren't *that* insensitive. I'd really be hurt.'

Aida regarded her friend thoughtfully. She would have to meet Kamel Pharaony again at some point, she reasoned, so why not now? And when she did, she would hold her head high and look him in the eye.

Finally, a mixture of stubborn pride, curiosity and fondness for Camelia cemented her decision. 'And also because in my heart of hearts I really *would* like to stay at Kasr El Ghoroub, just like in the old days,' Aida admitted. 'I suppose now I'd better send a note to the prince and decline his invitation.' She sighed and looked at her friend sheepishly. 'Of course you're right, he would probably get the wrong idea and that would land me in trouble.' She realised that in their disagreement she had started playing devil's advocate, but then all too quickly had become caught up in the game.

'*Now* you listen to me,' Camelia said with mock exasperation.

'I knew all along it would be foolish to let the prince escort me, but you know how I am. I hate being told what to do, it just brings out the worst in me,' Aida admitted with a grin.

The two friends hugged each other fondly. Before leaving the room, Camelia rang home to tell the servants to prepare a room, and Aida called the hall porter to come and take down her luggage. She then asked Camelia if they could make a detour via the Embassy so that she could drop off her uncle's letter for Sir Miles.

Camelia's car and driver were waiting outside Shepheard's front entrance and as they left the hotel together, Aida wondered uneasily how it would be to return to the Pharaonys' house in Gizeh after all these years – and what she would see in the eyes of Kamel Pharaony when she saw him again.

# CHAPTER 4

K asr El Ghoroub was situated high up on the edge of the desert only six miles southwest of the bustling centre of Cairo. Settled in the shadow of the pharaohs, facing five and a half millennia of history, the house itself crested one of the few hills dotted around the landscape, where the land changed suddenly from sand to lush green vegetation.

The grand house, whose high walls ran parallel to one of the main canals, was approached by a long drive, flanked by majestic palm groves. It had been built in white marble by a French architect at the turn of the century and though European in design, its spirit was that of Ancient Egypt.

It was surrounded by extensive grounds, carefully planned and kept watered by pumped irrigation, and divided into a variety of sections, encompassing orchards of pomegranate, mango and citrus trees, and great *gemmayz*, the sycamore figs so popular with the Ancient Egyptians. Tall, elegant acacias with their huge twisted trunks loomed gracefully amid the red-berried indigenous *withania* shrubs, large ponds planted with delicate white and blue lotus lilies, and beds of chrysanthemums, chamomile, irises and poppies.

Elsewhere, more conventional flowers had been planted. At one side of the house a riot of gold and red climbing roses and white jasmine tumbled over a gazebo, and at night, the gentle fragrance of those cascades floated up into the cool air, making the atmosphere balmy and sweet smelling. The elegant fusion of the mansion, the grounds and the stunning setting contributed to an overwhelming sense of serene luxury.

The big gate of the walled entrance was bolted and barred, but a hoot from the approaching Bentley's motor horn brought two Arabs in grey robes and turbans on their heads speedily to the spot. As the car glided through the opening, Aida gazed out of the window from the back seat as she sat beside Camelia. Her eyes traced the outline of spiky birds of paradise lining the drive in thick, exotic shrubs, the sight of their orange and indigo flowers reminding her of the times she had spent in these beautiful gardens when she was younger. Memories rushed back and with them, pain. It was not surprising. This place held bittersweet associations.

Against the cloudless blue sky, the house on its eminence presented breathtaking views, especially at sunset. All the main rooms, pillared balconies and terraces overlooked the garden, the canal, the three great pyramids and the far-reaching desert beyond, with its illimitable leagues of sand humped into fantastic mounds and chains of low hills, the lonely monotony broken here and there by tiny oases of palm trees and tamarisk bushes.

The sumptuous drawing rooms, carpeted and filled with plants, the beautiful paintings and bas-reliefs framed in the walls, the heavily sculpted ceilings from which hung handsome chandeliers, the luxuriously decorated corridors that ran from one end of the house to the other, and the beautiful parquet floors inlaid with intricate designs of rosewood, all contributed to an impression of exquisite taste and elegant opulence that could intimidate a stranger – but not so Aida. For many years she had been almost part of the Pharaony family, regarding Kasr El Shorouk more or less as her second home. During the past eight years, she had tried to erase from her mind the wonderful childhood and adolescent memories attached to these people and places; she had done her best to ruthlessly smother any warmth that subsisted in her heart from those mellow, carefree days. Yet, as the Bentley stopped in front of the sweep of stairs that led to the main entrance of the house, and even before she had stepped out of the car, a surge of nostalgia brought a lump to Aida's throat, and she knew that nothing had been erased … nothing had been completely smothered or squashed – it all remained dormant but alive in the recesses of her mind, ready to arise at the first opportunity.

Kasr El Ghoroub was as imposing as she remembered, the carved stone framework of the entrance holding wooden double doors in belle époque style, each with ornate dark glass and wrought-iron panels. As she crossed the threshold, Aida welcomed the contrasting coolness of the interior on her skin.

'Isn't this wonderful, being here together again!' exclaimed Camelia, regarding her friend with brilliant eyes as they went through the palatial hall and up the broad marble staircase to the top floor, which was given over to guest bedrooms and a vast library. 'Exactly like the old days!'

'Yes, like the old days,' Aida murmured, an underlying sadness in her smile.

'With the difference that this time we won't be sharing a room. You'll have the privilege of using one of our guest bedrooms overlooking the canal and the pyramids.' Camelia paused on the landing next to Aida. 'Do you remember how we used to be in awe of those sumptuous bedrooms and dream that one day, once we were married, we'd be invited to some stately home and be allocated such a room? Personally, I find them rather overdone and a little gaudy now.'

The servants had already brought up the luggage via the back staircase and the door to the room Aida had been given was wide open, the place bathed in late afternoon sunlight. Its pale pink walls and friezes were delicately painted with representations of Ancient Egyptian mythology. One in particular had always fascinated Aida. It was an image of Hathor, the sky goddess of love, beauty and motherhood, bending over the horizon, a sycamore tree on either side swallowing and giving birth to the sun.

'Oh, my favourite room,' Aida breathed, gazing through the door. 'You remembered!'

Camelia strode past her into the room and turned back, looking pleased with herself. 'Of course – how could I forget? You used to insist on visiting this room every time you came to stay, just to look at this painting.' She eyed her friend with amusement. 'You never said why this bedroom was so special – it's neither the larger, nor the prettiest – but I always knew the reason.'

Faint colour suffused Aida's cheeks, but she said nothing. She too recalled why she favoured this room and this painting over the many others in the house. It had been a late afternoon, and the light shining through the tall French windows was very much like today. She had been standing outside the room with Camelia talking to Karima the maid, who was airing it for the guests who were due to turn up for the weekend, when Phares had come out of the library. He had commented on the painting and had likened Aida's profile to that of Hathor, adding that the Ancient Greeks identified the Egyptian goddess with Aphrodite and the Romans with Venus. After that, the three of them had gone riding in the desert to watch the sunset behind the pyramids and Phares had been particularly friendly towards Aida. From then on, Hathor's painting had remained dear to her heart.

'My father hasn't arrived yet, but he'll be here for supper,' Camelia said. 'I'll leave you now. It's been a long day and I'm sure you want to freshen up. We'll meet downstairs in an hour on the terrace outside the dining room.'

At the door, she paused, smiling warmly at her friend. 'I'm so happy you've come back, Aida.'

*       *       *

Aida bathed, washed and dried her hair, applied a hint of make-up on her cheeks and lips, going through the motions like an automaton. Since she had set foot on the Kasr El Ghoroub Estate, a whole raft of emotions had assailed her, leaving her confused and troubled. In one sense, being back in a place that held so many wonderful memories should have made her happy ... but now she was going to come face to face again with Kamel Pharaony. She was going to eat his food ... sleep under his roof ... be civil, polite, pretend ... For so long she had nurtured a hatred for this man, imagining how one day she would unmask him as the liar and traitor that he was. The man who had, to all intents and purposes, killed her father. In her eyes his cowardly refusal to admit that he was the one who had brought the antique Nefertari statue to be authenticated by Ayoub was as condemning as if he had planted a knife in his friend's heart.

Yet a kernel of doubt had lodged in her mind. If only she could talk to Souma Hassanein again. Knowing that her father hadn't trusted the maid was too important to ignore. Not that it was enough to erase her anger and distrust of Kamel Pharaony. It had resided in her for too long.

Damn it, she resented being in this awkward situation.

Still, she would remain detached. It was what had carried her through the past eight years, and it would do the same for her now. Besides, once the ice was broken, she could avoid Kamel and spend her time in Cairo with Camelia.

*Cairo ... Phares's hospital was in Cairo.*

The painting of Hathor caught her eye again and the memory of Phares's dark, curious gaze just days before shimmered in her mind. Would he suddenly appear at the house while she was staying? Nervous excitement fluttered in her stomach but she breathed it away, annoyed at her body's involuntary reaction to the merest thought of him.

Aida crossed to the wardrobe. She took a deep breath; for now, she needed to focus on the evening ahead. As the Pharaony family always dressed for dinner, whether in Cairo, Alexandria or Luxor, Aida chose a black velvet dress with green tulip taffeta sleeves and a square neckline. The formality of it was an added help to her this evening. She slipped into classic black suede narrow-heeled shoes and went down to the terrace.

Crossing to the balustrade, she paused to gather herself. A deep silence reigned over everything. Outside, in the soft dusk of the evening, the whitewashed house gleamed brightly against the lush green of the garden. The birds were settling to sleep in the tall trees, the flowers drooped their heads drowsily as they stood in their brilliant rows. Beyond the walls of the estate, where the clear sky met the sand, the crimson light of a desert sunset lay upon the horizon, reflecting in the canal and casting a mystical glow over the hoary remains of antiquity that heightened their melancholy grandeur.

'Aida? Aida, *ya binti*, welcome back – how wonderful to see you again!'

The young woman recognised the deep voice that sounded so much like Phares's. She turned to face Kamel, every muscle of her small figure braced for the encounter. For a moment she said nothing. She felt suddenly as though her whole body had been plunged into an icy bath and she needed a moment to recover her breath after the immersion.

Before Aida could speak, Kamel had advanced towards her, coming quite close, as if he meant to take her arm to draw her nearer to him. Aida, with an uncontrollable instinct, drew away. Suddenly the scene that had occurred all those years ago replayed in her mind for the hundredth time. With it came the sense of impotence, of dreadful, helpless despair, that had seized her on that afternoon at Karawan House when she had stood there watching as her father was taken away like a common thief. Ayoub El Masri – the kindest, most honourable and principled of men – framed by two policemen.

Noticing her recoil, Kamel frowned slightly. 'Why, what's the matter Aida, *ya binti*? Don't you recognise your uncle Kamel?' He gave a low, uneasy laugh as though taken aback by Aida's cool reception. 'It's true, my hair has grown white and there are a few wrinkles on my face that were not there before, but I hope I haven't aged to the point of being unrecognisable. You, on the other hand, have turned into a beautiful young lady.'

Aida flushed quickly, struggling to meet his eyes, despite her previous resolve. 'Good evening, Uncle Kamel. I … you startled me. I didn't hear you coming.'

Kamel smiled complacently, restored to good humour. 'Ah yes, you were far away in your thoughts. Still the dreamer, eh?'

Aida kept her expression bland, though inwardly her emotions were writhing. 'Without dreams, we reach nothing.'

She became aware of the clicking hum of cicadas which had begun their nightly chorus in the gardens beyond.

'Camelia told me that you are a qualified nurse now.'

'Yes.'

'It must have been hard during the war in England.'

'It was.'

'Were you located in London?'

'Yes.'

'So, you worked in the London hospitals? Quite horrendous for a young woman, I assume.'

'Yes, it was.' The turmoil Aida felt inside her somewhat paralysed her, and the monosyllablic answers were the best she could manage at the moment.

'Phares also worked in the hospitals during the war, mainly in Alexandria. He never spoke much about the horrors he saw there, but we, his family, knew how distressing he found it. We saw it in his eyes – they were always veiled with sadness.'

An awkward silence hung between them, filled only by the night sounds of the garden. Aida looked out at the oncoming twilight, unable to engage on such a personal topic with him. Just being here almost felt like a betrayal of her father.

*Oh, why had she agreed to come?*

In the eastern sky, where the daylight lingered, a young moon hung, a thin fairy sickle in heaven's pale-green fields, and one silver star peeped forth shyly to bear her company.

Kamel continued smoothly, as if he wasn't aware of her reticence. 'I am very happy that you ran into Camelia. You know she lost her husband shortly after they were married?' Sighing, he took a pack of cigarettes from his pocket and lit one. He leaned against the balustrade, joining her in contemplating the darkening sky.

'Yes, she did tell me. How did it happen?' Aida didn't want to engage him further with the question but couldn't help herself; Camelia hadn't gone into details about Mounir's death.

'It was at dusk. Mounir was coming back from Alexandria on the desert road. Some half-witted truck driver tried passing without seeing what was coming in the opposite direction. A hill concealed the oncoming traffic and the truck ran into Mounir's car, travelling towards it in the opposite direction. The collision was fatal. Mounir died on the spot.'

Instinctively, Aida turned to look at him. The dark eyes that met hers were oddly without guile, simply sad. She answered falteringly, 'Poor Camelia, what a terrible shock.'

Kamel gave a quiet smile, which reminded her of Phares's so that for a moment she forgot her grievance, and said, 'I am determined to help my daughter regain her joy in living. I have a feeling you can help me in so doing.'

She looked wary. 'Me?'

'I saw her briefly just now when I came in. The transformation is extraordinary. Sympathy is all very well, but she has been receiving too much of it and it was making a martyr of her. Believe me, Aida, *ya binti*, she has never been so lively. You are a breath of fresh air, I can see it already. Phares will be happy, too, that you've come back … er, to stay, I hope …' He glanced at her, adding in the same breath, 'You know, he has never married.'

Aida stiffened, but she hadn't time to answer as Camelia erupted on to the terrace, followed by a *suffragi* carrying three glasses of Egyptian wine. 'I thought it a good idea to open a bottle of our best Gianaclis to celebrate Aida's return.' Camelia clasped her friend's arm and gave her an affectionate peck on the cheek.

'Thank you, Camelia, that's very sweet of you.' Aida smiled awkwardly and accepted the glass of wine. It was a welcome distraction, and she needed something to ease her nerves.

Kamel shot Aida a smile, as if to say, 'I told you so', before looking warmly at his daughter. '*Kheir ma amalty ya binti*, you did well, my child.'

He ushered them towards a cluster of comfortable rattan armchairs, where glass lamps, which had been lit on a low table, emitted a soft glow in the fading light. Aida soaked in the familiarity of this corner of the terrace where she and Camelia had often run about as children; many Pharaony soirées had also begun here with music and the bubbling chatter of a cosmopolitan crowd that included Egyptian families, Greeks, Italians, Armenians, and French and British ex-pats.

To Aida's relief the evening continued more easily than she'd expected, if only because the conversation had not immediately slid into more personal matters, which spared them all from wandering into the troublesome territory of the past. The three of them sat under the stars, breathing in the air of a balmy night and sipping their wine as they discussed the upheavals occurring in the world after the war. In fact, Egypt itself was looking at a new era – uncertain though it was – with the proposal of the Labour government in England to finally withdraw British troops from the country, alongside the disintegration of the Wafd – the traditional national party – which had been in power for so long. The Pharaony family had always been interested in politics and supported the monarchy, so it was natural that when at least two members of the family were present in the same room the conversation inevitably centred around those subjects.

Egyptian politics was in turmoil, they all agreed, giving militant nationalism the chance to harness the general discontent of a rapidly growing working class. Only a few months earlier, Kamel told Aida, riots and demonstrations by students and workers in Cairo had resulted in British service clubs being torched.

Aida listened with growing fascination. Of course, she had seen the Pathé News reports and followed what was going on in Egypt in the newspapers, but to hear about these events first-hand was compelling.

'British people were attacked and killed. It was a terrible business,' Kamel declared with a frown.

Camelia interjected. 'And our king is too busy gallivanting around to pay attention to negotiations with the British, or to look at the social conditions of his own people.'

Kamel's mouth curved laconically as he glanced at Aida. 'Now my daughter has started on her soapbox, we'll never hear the end of it.'

Aida regarded Camelia with surprised curiosity. Her friend had certainly shown little interest in politics when they were teenagers. 'Isn't it true though that Farouk isn't loved like the boy king he was a decade ago?'

'No,' agreed Camelia, pointedly ignoring her father's gentle mockery. 'In fact, the people now loath him for his foolish excesses and empty gestures. Throwing gold coins at the poor during his royal visits won't make them love him. If we don't want the *fellahin* to revolt, then we must give them proper living conditions, not grinding poverty.'

Kamel raised his eyebrows. 'What, you would have us give up our land?' He pulled the bottle from the ice bucket and refilled their empty glasses.

'We don't have to sacrifice the land, Papa. Not if we can invest our wealth in education programmes and charitable work. Isn't the privilege of our class also to be guardians of the nation? Do we not have a duty to protect our own people?'

It seemed that Camelia had become a much deeper thinker now that she was older, Aida thought approvingly. 'There's also the question of diseases caused by contaminated drinking water,' she threw in. 'Diseases that are entirely preventable with decent sanitation.'

Camelia nodded as she picked up her glass. 'Yes, all part of the reforms the King has been promising and not delivering.'

Kamel lit a cigar. 'Farouk might not be as popular as he was when he was young, but as I've said to you before, he is Egypt's righteous king.'

Camelia sent her father an exasperated look. 'Righteous king? He's a puppet of the British!'

'Farouk knows he must play a long game, my child. He wants independence from the British as much as all of these radical nationalists who are demonstrating and rioting in the streets of Cairo and placing bombs in cinemas.'

'Papa, if he was a stronger leader and had a government who stood up to the British, those nationalists wouldn't need to resort to such things.'

'So, what are you saying? We should have a violent revolution, like the communists want?' Kamel shook his head emphatically. 'No, no. I want the British out of Egypt as much as the next man, but there are ways of making them leave without violence.' He regarded Camelia with a mixture of concern and disapproval. 'I'm all for women's education, *habibti*, but I'm not sure I like the idea of you reading Marx. And it has not escaped my notice that you've been seen at the Mena House Hotel having tea with Fatma Morsy and Naima Said. Feminists and communist intellectuals, both of them, by all accounts.'

Camelia gave a laugh which to Aida sounded a little forced. 'Fatma and Naima are old schoolfriends. You know that, Papa.'

Kamel drew on his cigarette, peering at her through the wafting smoke. 'I don't remember you seeing much of them until recently. I don't want them filling your head with ideas that will get you in trouble, that's all.'

Camelia sipped her wine quickly. 'Anyway, Papa, at a time like this how can you mix with the British and have them as your friends at the Turf Club, but then say you also want the British out?'

'It's not that simple, *habibti*. Wanting Egypt to govern her own affairs doesn't mean one can't have British friends.'

'And having tea with feminists and intellectuals, Papa, doesn't mean one wants to start a revolution.'

Kamel took one look at Camelia and burst out laughing, a deep, rumbling infectious sound. '*Touché, habibti*. Well, I'm glad at least that my little girl has grown into a woman who can think for herself!'

Aida saw the undisguised fondness for his daughter in Kamel's expression, and the way his dark eyes glittered so warmly reminded her once more of Phares. He turned to Aida, the laughter lines in his face etched strongly; she didn't want to like his smile but she couldn't help finding it genuine and kindly. 'Come, let's go and eat,' he said. 'All this talk has made me hungry.'

They graduated to the great dining room furnished just as Aida remembered it, in Louis XV highly ornamental but tasteful style. In the middle of the room an extending table, raised on cabriolet legs and normally seating eighteen people, was greatly reduced in size for the evening and was surrounded by jade leather upholstered chairs, which echoed the striped jade-green and silver-grey curtains of the French windows running along three sides of the room. Tall mirrors above two curved side buffets made the room look even larger and airier.

Aida glanced around the room. The only other ornament on the walls was still the full-length portrait of Kamel's grandfather, Samweel Pharaony, who, just before dying, had bought from Khedive Ismail the land on which Kasr El Ghoroub was built in 1880, when urbanisation of that part of Cairo began. As she took her seat on one of the dining chairs, the beautiful silverware and crystal glasses laid out before her, Aida was reminded how lucky she was to be part of the rich upper class in Egypt.

Dinner was served, beginning with cold *mezzeh*, and Aida's thoughts were interrupted by Kamel's voice again: 'So, Aida, I am glad we will all be attending Princess Nazek's ball together.'

Aida glanced up quickly to see Camelia flash her a knowing grin as if to say, *I told you so*. She ate a tiny piece of *baladi* bread dipped in *tahina* and replied nonchalantly, 'Yes, it was lucky that Camelia and I bumped into each other so soon.'

'I wasn't planning to go myself but Camelia needs a chaperone of course, and unfortunately, Phares can't commit to coming. He might be needed at the hospital. It's a shame if the two of you don't get the chance to catch up on such a marvellous occasion.' Kamel smiled broadly at Aida and raised his glass of red wine as if in a toast to their friendship.

*There it was.* It was inevitable that the conversation would eventually come round to Phares. Aida took in a silent breath. 'I hear that Princess Nazek has invited more than a thousand people,' she said, attempting to deviate. 'All the jet set, that's for sure – foreigners as well as locals. It seems as though most of Cairo will be there.'

'Let's hope so,' said Camelia. 'Then I can have fun telling you all the latest gossip about each of them.'

Kamel chuckled. 'In that case, Aida, my dear, you are in for a long evening.'

Despite herself, her mouth curved into a smile as Camelia caught her eye. She was finding it increasingly difficult to be the frosty adversary of Kamel Pharaony.

At that moment a different *suffragi* entered the dining room, carrying a refilled carafe of wine. His face was long-featured with a small moustache, and after a moment Aida recognised him as Mohamed, one of the young men who had helped in the kitchen when Aida was a teenager. Judging by his appearance serving at table in his white robe and red sash, he now had a more elevated position in the house.

Kamel smiled at him as the *suffragi* refilled his glass. 'Ah, Mohamed, how is your father doing?'

'*Rabbena yakoun fi ounoh*, may God help him, he is still sick, *ya Bey*,' he answered.

Kamel looked pensive. 'I've known Abdel Razek most of my life. He may be getting on now but he's still always full of health and good spirits. This is not good. Where is he now?'

Mohamed's eyes looked sorrowfully at his employer but his demeanour remained dignified. 'At home, *ya Bey*. He has taken to his bed.'

Kamel wiped his mouth and put down his napkin. 'We will move him. He must go to my son's hospital, I will see to it.'

Mohamed looked suddenly wide-eyed. 'Hospital …?'

Kamel patted the man's arm. 'Do not worry about the money. Your father has been part of this household since I was a boy. I will pay for his medicine and hospital bills.'

Aida saw relief flood the man's face. Mohamed nodded vigorously. 'Thank you, *ya Bey*. May God keep you and reward you for your generosity.'

'And may God look over Abdel Razek,' answered Kamel with a nod.

Mohamed clasped his hands together and bowed deeply to Kamel, a broad smile transforming his face as he left the room.

Aida exchanged looks with Camelia, whose eyes sparkled with unspoken meaning as her gaze moved from Aida to her father, who had become lost in thought as he continued to eat.

Aida cleared her throat apprehensively and after a moment said, 'No doubt you will be in his prayers.'

Kamel looked up from his food. He frowned slightly, his dark eyes filling with sorrow as they met her own. 'Your father would have done the same. It is our custom, have you forgotten?'

A shadow of emotion and regret moved clearly over his face. Was it guilt? Shame, perhaps? No. Aida was forced to admit that Kamel Pharaony had the look of a man who missed his old friend, and for whom the ebb and flow of genuine grief was still present. Aida lowered her confused gaze to the array of dishes in front of her, unable to find any words in response.

The rest of dinner went smoothly. The food was delicious, and Aida made a supreme effort to join in the conversation. Kamel did not try to engage her in conversation about her father, but seemed to sense that for the time being it was a subject to be delicately circumnavigated. Nor did he attempt to quiz Aida about her personal life or push her into discussing marriage to Phares. Though his son was mentioned on many occasions, it was only in the context of how hard the young surgeon was working, or in relation to the latest news regarding the rest of the Pharaony family. Indeed, Kamel was naturally charming and pleasant for the entire evening, and Aida listened carefully to his views on social reform, acknowledging that his dealings with the *fellahin* on his Luxor estate seemed fair and compassionate, like that of a benevolent patriarch. He was not the brute she had painted him; there was no hint of any dishonesty or greed. In fact, Aida found him more and more difficult to hate. Still, until she knew the truth of who had framed her father, she would never be able to totally relax in his company.

The evening was finally over and after she and Camelia said goodnight in the corridor outside their rooms, Aida breathed a sigh of relief. She was her own mistress again. The hardest moment, when she had come face to face with Kamel Pharaony, had passed ... and it had not been the ordeal she had imagined. In fact, nothing about coming home was as she had thought. All she knew was that the whole mystery and trauma of the past had to come to some sort of resolution, and she'd need to go with it as the truths surfaced, as they surely would. She had little choice in the matter anyway.

*     *     *

It was dusk when they left for the ball next day in Kamel Pharaony's Rolls-Royce. The car glided slowly alongside the canal, the surface of which was as placid as glass, reflecting the golden sunset. Against the glowing light of the west the pyramids stood huge and purple in the distance, their inverted images smiling up from the watery mirror of the canal.

The high-wheeled carts, so out of place in urban, cosmopolitan Cairo, belonged here naturally, clattering over the uneven road, a stone's throw from the canal; there, the billowing sails of feluccas crowded with sheep were moving towards the bridge, creaking open slowly with the help of the most antique of machinery to let the high masts pass through.

As the Rolls-Royce turned the corner on to the main road, the three giants came clearly into view. They looked ruddy and appallingly steep, towering majestically in the sky like gigantic ghosts, their shadows lying sharp across the sands. Long caravans of weary camels strode silently by in the twilight, while a host of shrouded figures, some accompanied by their beasts, hurried on the way to their mud houses where, for most of them, a dinner of *foul*, tomatoes and *gargueer*, wild rocket, awaited them.

The broad, straight Pyramids Road that led back into the centre of Cairo was a legendary highway with a tramway cutting through it. Built in the 1860s as a showpiece boulevard – part of the ambitious and idealistic Khedive Ismail's dream of making Cairo the 'Paris of the Nile' – the well-kept road thronged daily with private cars, camels, donkeys and charabancs. The sides of the beautiful avenue were planted with *lebbek* trees, or 'woman's tongue', named for the sound the seeds make rattling inside the pods like gossiping women. Rough-barked with twisted branches, their slender leaves flung a dapple of shadow upon the ground during the heat of the day. In the distance, green and fertile plains stretched out of sight.

As they journeyed to Gezireh Island, Aida was freshly struck by the beauty of Cairo. The romance of Egypt's own belle époque was so evident here.

Camelia nudged her friend. 'A penny for your thoughts. You seem so far away.'

Aida glanced back from the window and smiled. 'Perhaps it's because I've been gone a long time, but I was thinking about Ismail Pasha, and what an incredible feat it was to transform the whole of Egypt the way he did. … The Suez Canal, of course, but also the schools, irrigation, agriculture, railways, roads.'

'Yes, it's true,' Camelia agreed. 'Khedive Ismail transformed our country. We have him to thank for Egypt being dragged out of the Dark Ages almost overnight.'

Aida gazed out of the car at a passing tram crowded with passengers, some hanging off the sides while holding on to the window bars as it headed into the centre of town. 'I'd forgotten how very European Cairo feels.'

'I love that about it too. Well, it's hardly surprising, I suppose. The Khedive was a well-travelled man, educated in Paris, of course. He was the most dashing of Egypt's rulers and a true Francophile. This road, for example, was built in honour of the last of the Empresses of France. Thanks to him, we can travel from the pyramids directly to the centre in no time.'

Aida gave a small sigh. 'Yes, but look at the consequences. I wonder how many people remember that this road was also built in twenty-four hours, with no heed paid to the human and financial cost. The debts he ran up to pay for Egypt's modernisation were crippling. He may have been the most dashing of our khedives, but he was also the most reckless.'

'Reckless or not, it was a wonderful idea, and without Khedive Ismail's dreams we wouldn't have all the things you talk about. Or the beautiful palaces, the opera, theatre. We certainly wouldn't have our house at the pyramids today.'

'True, but there was a price to pay.'

Camelia smiled ruefully. 'There is always a price to pay for progress, *habibti*, don't you think?'

Soon they were crossing the Kasr El Nil bridge, one of the four that connected Gezireh Island to the rest of Cairo. This 'garden island', renowned for its beautiful public parks planted with exotic species from all over the world, had been another spectacular experiment by Khedive Ismail. It was home to the famous Gezireh Sporting Club, the Anglo-American Hospital, numerous mansions, lofty civic buildings and various royal palaces, including Saraya't El Gummyz, Princess Nazek's Palace of Sycamores, now only minutes away.

The two young women were sitting in the back, each looking every inch the high society debutante. Aida was in her fabulous Balenciaga midnight-blue dress which needed no adornment, except for the small sapphire, gold and diamond crescent earrings her father had given her on her sixteenth birthday and a Victorian

matching bracelet that had belonged to her mother, a copy
of which was in the Victoria and Albert Museum's collection in
London. Her hair was parted in the middle, the soft waves pulled
back and up from her forehead and held in place with combs.
A dark blue silk shawl embroidered with gold and silver thread
was wrapped around her shoulders and her Charles Jourdan
high-heeled slip-on satin navy shoes gave the finishing touch to
her elegant Parisian look.

Camelia's gown was of pale peach chiffon organdie, which set
off her amazing dark eyes and glossy black hair. The bodice and
long skirt were plain but relieved by a deep pleated frill around
the shoulders and another deeper one at the bottom of the skirt.
The frills were stiffened, the one on the bodice standing out like
wings, the other foaming about her feet as she moved. She wore
a striking parure of diamonds which, she told Aida, Mounir had
given to her on their wedding day.

The gilded wrought-iron gates of Saraya't El Gummyz were
open and the Pharaonys' Rolls-Royce joined the queue of cars
proceeding at a snail's pace up the long driveway overarched by
old sycamore trees. The approach to the *saraya* ended in
a platform flanked with two vast car parks, where a couple
of porters in dark-green and gold kaftans, and other men in black
suits and *tarbouches* helped guests out of their cars. Aida, Camelia
and Kamel finally reached the platform and were directed to
a magnificent pergola-walk covered with flowering creepers,
which led to a courtyard at the front of the *saraya*, where croton
shrubs were planted in an array of colours, with leaves that went
from deep green with yellow speckles to flame red and blue-black.
In the middle of the courtyard warbled a beautiful octagonal
*fisqiya*, a fountain decorated with arabesque tiles and mounted
with a blue dome ribbed with gold.

The palace itself was lavishly built, in a style reminiscent
of medieval Turkey. The bronze double doors of the entrance

were set in a high archway adorned with jewels and decorated on either side with Princess Nazek's family's coat of arms. The trio were ushered into the grandiose hall by two black Nubian colossi dressed in gold embroidered liveries. The central part of the marble paved hall was over fifteen metres high and lit from above by a most beautiful Bohemian pale-green opaline chandelier of enormous circumference, with tiers and tiers of lights going upwards in diminishing circles. The walls were decorated with calligraphic sheets of wise sayings or verses from the Koran, set in ornate blue-and-ochre panels with gilded frames, an adornment influenced by the ancient belief that whoever wrote the *bismillah* – 'in the name of God, the Beneficent, the Merciful' – in beautiful calligraphic script would enter Paradise without judgement.

A wide granite stairway inlaid with a dark-green carpet led up to the ballroom on the first floor. At the top of the steps a major-domo wearing the Turkish *stambouline*, a smart black frock coat, was announcing the guests. As she reached the top, Aida could see him bowing in a deep *téménah*, signalling that the couple in front were obviously of royal blood. Aida had always found that form of Turkish curtsey elegant when properly done. It consisted of bending downwards with the right arm making a sweeping gesture towards the ground and then up over the head, enacting in mime the ancient oriental idea of putting ashes on the head as a sign of humility.

'Kamel Pharaony Pasha, Mrs Camelia Abel Sayed and Miss Aida El Masri,' announced the master of ceremonies as the trio approached the ballroom, which for the occasion shone in all its glory. Both young women glanced at each other, their radiant faces slightly flushed, eyes glittering like jewels with excitement. It had been years since Aida had mixed with the grandees of Cairo society and she took in everything with wide-eyed fascination.

They entered a room of soaring, magnificent proportions dominated by eight large and twenty-four smaller Moorish archways. It was decorated in wild, gilded Turkish Baroque, the walls hung with magnificent tapestries with arabesque floral designs typical of the late Ottoman period, and great mirrors flashing a million dazzling reflections from the chandeliers. Gilt and damask created a gorgeous contrast in the sumptuous furnishings. Beneath a row of stained-glass lunettes stood backless little sofas, in front of which were low rectangular coffee tables inlaid with mother-of-pearl. On top of them were set small plates of *mezzeh*.

The ballroom boasted a beautiful floor of pale-green marble parquetry and was illuminated by immense glittering candelabra. At the far end of the room, raised on a platform, a small orchestra was playing beautiful Strauss waltzes for the enjoyment of upper-crust guests selected from the Turkish nobility, titled Egyptians, diplomats and notable members of the expatriate community. Ladies blossomed forth like exotic flowers in bright reds, pale corals, soft greens, and various shades of purple – so suited to the Egyptian colouring – and men strutted around in bespoke black or white dinner suits, complete with red fez for most of them.

Princess Nazek stood at the top of the stairs, elegantly regal in a beautiful pale-gold dress with floating skirts, her necklace and tiara sparkling in the light of the chandeliers. She was chatting to a host of people who greeted her in turn before relinquishing her company to other guests keen for her attention. When Aida's few minutes with her came, the princess beamed, asked how her stay in Cairo had been and insisted that she come to the palace for tea soon. No sooner had the trio paid their respects to Princess Nazek than they were surrounded by Kamel and Camelia's friends. While effusive greetings were swapped, Aida's gaze swept the vast room, wondering if there was a chance that Phares would put in an appearance this evening. There were so many people crowding into the space that it was impossible to tell if he was here or not. With a faint sigh, she told herself to forget about him and just enjoy her evening.

'Ah, Kamel Pasha! Where have you been? We haven't seen you at the roulette table for a long time. All well with you?' The smooth, sophisticated voice came from behind Aida, and she stiffened, recognising it immediately as that of Prince Shams Sakr El Din.

'My dear Prince, I've taken up bridge instead. A much less stressful pursuit,' Kamel answered in a tone just as debonair.

'Ah, but a much more boring one, you must admit.' Turning to Camelia, he lifted her hand to his lips, murmuring '*Madame*', before directing his attention to Aida, his pale eyes narrowing. His voice thickened slightly: '*Mademoiselle* El Masri. It's a small world, is it not?'

Kamel Pharaony's eyebrows lifted a fraction. 'You know each other?'

'We met on the train,' Aida provided, her face set with a gracious expression.

Prince Shams Sakr El Din smiled briefly. 'I had the pleasure of *Mademoiselle* El Masri's company on the train from Minieh to Cairo. I'm delighted we meet again, *mademoiselle*.'

Just then there was a hiatus in the music while the orchestra chose a new waltz and he inclined his head slightly towards Aida, lowering his voice: 'I hope you will do me the honour of this dance.' Then, without waiting for her response, he nodded towards Camelia and her father – '*Madame* ... Kamel Pasha' – and took her by the wrist, drawing her on to the dancefloor.

Despite the spaciousness of the ballroom the crush was terrific, and Aida found that dancing in her elaborate gown was more of a masterful performance than a pleasure. Holding her tightly against his strong body, the prince whirled her around the edge of the ballroom twice without speaking, then stopped at one of the sofas. His reptilian eyes glittered. 'Shall we have a drink and a few *amuse-bouches*?' he asked, without letting go of her waist.

'Why not?' Aida capitulated, still a little bewildered by his gall. Although she couldn't really say she liked him, she had to admit that she found the prince somehow fascinating. Oh, she had no doubt that he was a predator, and a dangerous one at that, but he was different and exciting. Her father had always reproached her for tempting fate in one way or another – as a child, she climbed the highest trees; at the seaside she swam so far out she once had difficulty coming back and a boat of fishermen had rescued her. During the war, though she had loathed the suffering she witnessed, Aida found it exhilarating to walk back at night to the nurses' home through the dark streets of London, even during the curfews. She never went down to the shelters when the warning sirens went off, though she knew she was flirting with danger.

They were still standing at the edge of the ballroom. Letting go of her, Shams Sakr El Din beckoned to a waiter, who was hovering nearby, then turned back to Aida: 'What will you drink? Champagne? Princess Nazek's cellars are famous. Even during the war, she managed to keep them well stocked.'

'I'd love a glass of champagne. Thank you.' Although the Muslim religion forbade the drinking of alcohol, it was obvious to Aida that the Westernised royalty members ignored this particular rule. As for her, attending a ball was a rare treat; tonight, she could enjoy such an indulgence without censure and it brought an added element of excitement to the evening.

Having ordered their drinks, the prince steered her to one of the small sofas at the side of the room. When they were seated, he took from his inside pocket a gold box decorated with tiny precious stones and offered her a cigarette.

Aida shook her head. 'No, thank you.'

'Ah yes, you don't smoke – I forgot.' He helped himself to one and lit it. 'Why did you refuse to let me escort you to the ball?' he asked after he had inhaled deeply.

Aida suspected a wave of gossip was already rippling through the ballroom, speculating about the return of the daughter of Ayoub El Masri and how she was keeping company with the infamous Bedouin prince, Shams Sakr El Din, but she didn't care. She lifted her chin.

'We hardly know each other.'

'You don't strike me as a conventional woman.'

'You've just proved that you *don't* know me.'

There was a hiatus in the conversation while the waiter brought over their drinks and set them on the small table in front of the two-seater sofa. The prince lifted his glass to her. 'To the future,' he murmured and took a sip of champagne. 'And now to return to our conversation. You say I'm wrong to think that you are a nonconformist – what is it the lovely Isadora Duncan once said? *Most human beings today waste some twenty-five to thirty years of their lives before they break through the actual conventional lies which surround them.*'

'And the writer Lucy Maud Montgomery would answer her: *'As a rule, I am very careful to be shallow and conventional where depth and originality are wasted.*'

The prince regarded her through a curl of smoke with a look of surprised gratification. 'Beautiful, intelligent, and witty with it. A rare rose to add to my garden.'

'Your garden?' Aida did not like the sound of this.

The reptilian eyes narrowed again, and his smile was enigmatic. 'Yes, my harem.'

'Ah yes, I'd forgotten,' she replied drily. 'You couldn't be a respectable prince without a harem.'

'Doesn't it pique your female curiosity?'

'Not one bit. I find the concept somewhat barbaric and retrograde. Surprising in men of your education.'

Prince Shams Sakr El Din laughed, though it was more of a snort. 'Education has nothing to do with it, *habibti*. I can't believe you are so naïve about the world that you cannot understand the concept of the harem … a man's garden where many flowers bloom for his pleasure ... with different colours, textures, fragrances.' His gaze dropped to Aida's lips, then lowered to her throat and bare shoulders, shamelessly devouring with his eyes every bit of her bare skin.

All at once bewildered, amused and insulted by his undisguised admiration, Aida shivered internally and took a few sips of her champagne. During the war she had met men and women of all kinds, in the hospital wards, bars and bombed prisons. She was used to men looking at her with affection, gratitude, admiration, or sometimes with anger and even lustfully, but none had fazed her. And now, for a split second, the light that had lit up in the prince's pale yellow eyes made her flesh creep. Still, the rebellious part of her could not resist the provocation and was enjoying this little banter with His Highness ...

She set down her glass and gave him a mocking smile. 'You people of the desert have some charming philosophies when it comes to women, haven't you?'

'If you mean that we venerate them? Yes.'

'Like sex objects.'

He waved his cigarette dismissively. 'Why put it in such ugly terms?'

'Because these women in your harem are there for your pleasure. You said it yourself.'

'But they regard it as a great honour.'

'For heaven's sake, spare me the hypocrisy!'

'When you visit my kingdom in Wahat El Nakheel, you can ask them yourself.'

'I don't think there's much chance of me going there.'

'Are you afraid of me, *Mademoiselle* El Masri?'

'Certainly not,' Aida retorted, suddenly on the defensive.

He gave a low, private sort of laugh. 'Then you will come to Kasr El Nawafeer. I am organising a picnic at the oasis in a few weeks for the Cairo expatriate community. Everybody will be there ...' He adopted a gracious, accommodating look. 'It will give you a chance to ease yourself back into Cairene society after being a fish out of water for so long. Besides, aren't you just that little bit curious? Yes, you are. Admit it.'

Aida hesitated, taken aback by his cajoling charm. 'Perhaps.' She reached for her glass and allowed herself the shade of a smile. He was right. Everything inside her burned with curiosity to see the inside of his palace and what it was like to travel by camel to Wahat El Nakheel. It would certainly be an adventure, and something inside her still craved excitement. The bubbles in the champagne felt cool and invigorating on her tongue as she took another sip. 'I'll admit that I'm fascinated by the desert. I've never ventured far into it to know much about it, but it does appeal.'

His piercing gaze was unwavering. 'So, you will come.'

'At the moment I don't have any plans, but I might be going back to England.'

'Europe is not a happy place at the moment, and you strike me as someone who likes to have fun ... You'll be much better off sticking around here, in Cairo, where you will be mightily entertained every day. Trust me.'

Before Aida had time to answer, they were joined by a party of young socialites magnificently dressed in the latest Paris fashion, and blazing with jewels. They gathered around the prince, all talking and laughing at once. Most of them were women who looked at him with stars in their eyes as they embraced him in greeting. Aida was presented to each in turn, and they all sat around gossiping and talking sport and politics, the prince holding court, directing the conversation with artful finesse. Aida could now see why he had such a notorious reputation. He was not only a womaniser, but a stirrer – he spent his time flirting, cunningly manipulating the ego of each woman present, and sowing discord and jealousy among them. She found it a distasteful game, but the conversation was anything but boring.

He was a well-connected intellectual, after all. A man about town, he knew much about the complicated politics of Egypt, and Aida, who had been away for so long, was interested in learning anything that concerned her country. Anyhow, the ballroom was so vast that soon she had lost sight of Camelia and Kamel, and as she hadn't yet recognised anyone else that she knew, she had little option but to stick with him.

The ballroom opened on to an immense walled garden, where an enormous marquee had been set up for dinner on one acre of land. Inside the marquee, a long, narrow buffet table, covered in velvet *sirmas* embroidered with gold thread, stretched almost out of sight. Standing behind it, *suffragis* wearing kaftans in the family colours of dark green and gold served guests who wandered in to sit at round tables. The tent was lit with Turkish blue mosaic drop lanterns, and beyond this pool of light the rest of the garden lay deep in shadow.

Each of the tables surrounded by delicate gilt chairs sat ten people, and were covered with silk tablecloths bought in Smyrna, hand-embroidered with gold and silver thread. They gleamed with monogrammed flatware in gold vermeil finish and fine crystal glasses rimmed with gold that bore the family's crest, also etched in gold. At the centre of each table stood luxurious Turkish Ottoman royal glass vases dating back to the fifteenth century, etched and encrusted with crystal diamonds and gilded with gold leaf and platinum, each containing a tasteful display of yellow roses.

Having only ever attended one royal ball before, Aida had forgotten how lavishly these banquets were presented. A whole gamut of Turkish and European entrees, main courses and delicious desserts cooked to perfection were beautifully presented on trays inlaid with diamonds, the most impressive being a great model of the Cairo Citadel in ice, its doors and windows filled with caviar and with solid gold spoons to scoop it out. There were *kabak mucver*, zucchini puffs served with yoghurt and dill sauce; *mahshi*, a variety of vegetables stuffed with rice, mince and herbs; *borek*, filo pastry parcels of feta cheese, spinach and onion; *kofta wa kabab*, a mixture of chargrilled skewered meatballs and morsels of mutton. There were boned fowl of all sorts, cooked with pomegranate, spices and fennel, or stuffed with raisins, pistachio nuts and crumbled bread seasoned with herbs. Sometimes they were served in a sauce made of walnuts called *sharkasieh*, which Aida especially favoured. Otherwise, the lamb legs arranged on beds of pilaf rice, cooked with liver slices, currants, peanuts, chestnuts, cinnamon and a variety of herbs seemed to be very popular. Numerous dishes of veal and beef roasts surrounded by tender young vegetables perfectly braised in *samna*, clarified butter, also had a long line of guests queuing for them, and finally, there were *yakhnees*, or stews, and a wonderful array of fish dressed with sauces and aspic.

The delicious food and wine did its usual good work: tongues were loosened, eyes brightened, geniality engendered; and under the blue lamps that made conversation lingering and easy, the opulent and flamboyant scene seemed to Aida like a staged opera version of the fairy tales in *One Thousand and One Nights*.

Though her eyes searched for Camelia and Kamel, Aida had not been able to see them among the sea of guests, and so, after helping herself to a plate of food, she had no other alternative but to follow the prince to a table where four people were already seated: a grizzled, serene-looking Swede, a white-haired, rotund, gesticulating Italian, a girl with hair like a flame, whose slender shoulders were wrapped in a black shawl, and a moon-faced man, with steady blue eyes and a rare, beautiful smile. They all seemed to know him, and he them … yes, the prince knew a great many people, Aida thought as he carried out the introductions once again. By the looks of it, he was not only popular with women, but also with men, who had been greeting him cheerily throughout the evening and earnestly seeking his opinion about their various business ventures. Soon, two other ladies and their husbands, who it later transpired were English government officials, joined the table.

The prince was immediately monopolised by the redhead on his right, who was looking up at him with eager, sparkling eyes. Somehow rather relieved, Aida turned to the moon-faced young man seated on her left, who looked to be between thirty and thirty-five, fair with a receding hairline and a face dominated by a high forehead. As fortune would have it he was none other but Alastair Carlisle, the consul at the British Embassy with whom she had planned to arrange a meeting.

She smiled at him, taking a forkful of timbale made from stuffed olives and crayfish. He had an open and approachable manner and for that reason alone she was glad to engage him in conversation. Perhaps later she could discreetly enquire about his work at the Embassy and find out more about the stolen antiquities market.

'How long have you been in Cairo?' she asked.

'I was posted here four years after the war broke out.' He looked at her curiously. 'Are you Egyptian? You speak beautiful English.'

'My mother was English and my father Egyptian. I've just come back from England, where I spent the whole of the war.'

'That must have been frightful.'

'Yes ... much hardship and suffering. I worked in the hospitals as a nurse.'

'You said your name is El Masri?'

'Yes, Aida El Masri.

'Are you the young lady who rang yesterday asking about Sir Miles?'

'Yes, he's a friend of my Uncle George in London, who gave me a letter for him. I wasn't sure how to get hold of him now that he's left Cairo, so in the end I dropped it off at the Embassy.'

'Ah yes, things are changing pretty rapidly here at the moment. Though for Sir Miles, his new post in Southeast Asia is a case of out of the frying pan and into the fire, poor chap. Inevitable, really. As soon as the new Labour government were voted in, the writing was on the wall for Sir Miles – or Lord Killearn, I should say now. I have his contact details in Singapore. I'll make sure your letter reaches him.'

'You're very kind. Thank you.'

He paused. 'Do you mind me asking, do you live in Cairo?'

'Not at all. At the moment I'm staying with friends near the pyramids, but I'm going back to Luxor in a couple of days – that's really where I call my home.'

The consul gave her a sharp glance. 'Have you known Prince Shams Sakr El Din a long time?'

'No, I met him on the train from Luxor and bumped into him tonight.' Perhaps it was the prince's reputation but she felt the consul disapproved. She added demurely, 'He's rather taken me under his wing.'

Alastair nodded pensively. Aida thought he was going to say something, but instead he smiled and moved on to different subjects.

The desserts display was just as spectacular. There was *om ali*, a delicious Egyptian dish served hot and rather like bread and butter pudding, but with almonds, hazelnuts, raisins, pistachios and a lot of cream; large trays of baklava pastries, beautiful-coloured crystal bowls of *kazandibi*, baked custard with *mastica* served with pomegranate ice cream and morello cherry sauce; *meyve tatlisi*, pears poached with saffron, figs and apricots, served chilled with cardamon ice cream, huge gold plates of *revani*, a moist semolina and orange cake soaked in orange syrup and served with honey yoghurt sherbet; and finally, a bombe of *dondurma*, an ice cream made with milk, sugar, *salep* orchid flour, and mastic. Princess Nazek's guests were spoilt for choice.

Aida helped herself to a big bowl of *om ali*. It had always been her favourite pudding when *Dada* Amina made it from an old El Masri family recipe, though she had yet to find one that tasted half as good as hers.

After dinner, the music in the ballroom started again for those who were not keen on local entertainment. To the delight of the Egyptian and Turkish guests, Kawkab Al Shark, Star of the East, were to take the stage – the Arabic singer Om Kalthoum, always known as *El Sit*, the Dame, and her male counterpart, Abdel Wahab – and this famous musical duo would be performing their greatest hits in the sumptuous reception room of the *saraya*.

The prince gave his attention once more to Aida midway through dinner, to the irritation of the enthralled redhead beside him, and their conversation had become easier now that he had cordially introduced her to the other guests at the table. He accepted a liqueur from a passing waiter and turned back to her.

'Are you fond of Egyptian music?'

'Not really. It's a little too repetitive for my liking and goes on for too long.'

He laughed. 'You surprise me. Om Kalthoum is the greatest female Arabic singer in the world. The variations in the intonations of her voice are quite extraordinary. Two years ago, King Farouk awarded her the *Nishan el Kamal*, one of the highest orders, a decoration normally reserved for members of the royal family. She usually refuses to sing at private parties, you know.'

'I'm sorry, I know she's a great star, but on the whole, I find Egyptian music monotonous. I must admit, we never listened to it at home, so my ear is not used to it, and that might be the reason I don't understand it. But please don't let me stop you from going to listen to the performance. I realise it's a very special event. Anyhow, I should be looking for Camelia and Uncle Kamel.'

This was true, she hadn't seen them all evening.

'No doubt they will be attending the performance.'

Aida laughed. 'Uncle Kamel maybe, but not Camelia. She shares my views. But please, don't let me keep you, go ahead. No doubt Camelia and I will find each other eventually, especially now that the ballroom will be relatively empty.'

He leaned towards her, a little too close for comfort. 'I feel I'm deserting you,' he murmured.

Aida felt suddenly uneasy again. 'Not at all … I'm quite capable of looking after myself.'

'Will you keep the last dance for me?'

The prince had been courteous and had more or less looked after her all evening and although Aida didn't like to commit, there was no reason why she shouldn't save it for him.

She forced a smile. 'Yes, of course I will.'

'Thank you. So, *à tout à l'heure* then.'

Aida wandered off towards the ballroom, where Alastair Carlisle immediately joined her.

'Not a fan of Arabic music, Miss El Masri?'

'No, not really.'

'Well, that's my luck. Care for a waltz, or would you prefer to be a spectator?'

'Actually, I'd like a glass of water.'

'So, let's go and ask for it from one of those smart *suffragis* standing in attendance all over the place – though I doubt very much they'll offer plain water. It'll most likely be flavoured with rose or orange blossom.'

'Actually, I quite like that.'

They found a *suffragi* who was going around with a tray of *sharbat ward*, a cordial made of rose petals and lemonade, and a plate of Turkish delight. They each helped themselves to a glass and found a little bench outside the ballroom on the terrace, from where a few guests were still ambling back inside through rows of arched Moorish porticos to catch the performance.

The air was beginning to cool, and here, at the back of the palace, the sculpted gardens were lit by lanterns among the shrubs and trees, creating little dancing shadows here and there.

'I didn't want to say anything over dinner, but I'm rather relieved that Prince Shams Sakr El Din is only a new acquaintance of yours,' Alastair remarked as they sat down.

Aida feigned surprise. 'Why is that?'

'A rather shady gentleman, our Bedouin Prince Charming.'

'In what way?'

'During the war, we suspected he was supplying arms to the Germans.'

Aida's brows shot up. 'Arms? Surely not! How would he get hold of them?'

'Oh, there are a million ways, my dear. One of them being bribery, of course. As you know, Egypt unfortunately is a very poor and corrupt place. Before the war, we knew that the prince was involved in another sort of trafficking, the nature of which I am not free to disclose, I'm afraid,' he added, seeing her quizzical look.

'Any proof?'

'We have never been able to pin anything on him … He's too crafty. A real desert fox, that one. I would avoid him if I were you.'

'Well, the war has ended, so trafficking arms to the Germans doesn't apply anymore,' Aida said defensively. She didn't like people meddling in her affairs, especially if they implied she was being hoodwinked and wasn't capable of looking after herself.

The consul paused. 'It seems that he's still up to something … He's a big fish. We're keeping an eye on him.'

'You mean trafficking?'

'Umm.'

'Hashish?'

'Among other things … There could be antiquities involved.'

Aida stilled. 'Antiquities?' Her mind immediately jumped to the stolen Nefertari statue that had been her father's undoing. 'What makes you say that?'

'We have our reasons.'

She hesitated, weighing up how much to say to Alastair at this point. 'I'm sure you must know about the case of my father, Ayoub El Masri, just before the war. He was wrongly accused of theft of an antiquity.'

Alastair's face became suddenly guarded and grave. 'Yes, I'm aware of your father's trial, though I wasn't working at the Embassy at the time.' He gave her a knowing look. 'I'm sorry for your loss. I know your father was a well-repected figure.'

Aida's gaze was scrutinising as she fixed him with her big blue eyes. 'No doubt the statue my father was accused of stealing was a trafficked piece, and the Embassy would have some theory about where it came from or who else might have been suspected at the time.'

He sighed. 'I can't tell you more, Miss El Masri, I'm sorry. Even if I had any information about your father's case, I'm not at liberty to discuss Embassy business and I've already said too much. My intention was merely to warn you off the prince. He has quite a reputation with the ladies and he seemed rather taken by you. You're a nice young woman, and with your uncle being a friend of Sir Miles …'

Aida could see she would get no further with her fishing. She smiled graciously, 'I appreciate your concern but you have nothing to worry about as far as I'm concerned.'

Strange though, she thought, her mind returning to the suave Bedouin prince. This was the third person warning her off Shams Sakr El Din, and yet he seemed to have an army of male and female followers. It didn't surprise her that he was at the centre of gossip – after all, he was a gentleman Bedouin, and Egyptian society was not without its prejudices, a truth she had experienced at their hands eight years before for rather different reasons. Was his reputation really deserved, or was it all born of hearsay and disapproval? She had never been a person with preconceived ideas, she reminded herself, so she would find out for herself.

Alastair and Aida sat a little longer on the terrace. The consul was interesting company and they talked about the war and their respective experience of it, and of this and that, but as time went on, it was getting chilly and so they decided to go back inside.

They were soon joined by the prince, whose gaze flicked straight to Aida.

'Ah, there you are! I've been looking for you. I see that in my absence you've been entertained by the lovely Alastair.' His smile was slightly mocking. 'Flowers and gardens and bees to honey, *habibti*. Come, let's dance,' he added, taking her elbow rather too possessively, she noted, which she didn't like at all. '*El Sit* has finished her performance and I can listen to Abdel Wahab any time,' he added, drawing Aida towards the dancefloor.

As she turned her head slightly, considering how she could best extricate herself from the prince's grip, with a sudden jolt she spotted two familiar men in the crowd, deep in conversation, both of whom shared the same proud, charismatic demeanour. One of them was Phares Pharaony.

Aida blinked, for a moment disorientated by his sudden appearance. Her heart skipped a beat. So, he had come after all. She had almost resigned herself to not seeing him tonight but there he was, his dark unruly hair tamed into thick waves combed back from his forehead. He was standing talking to his father next to one of the French windows that led into the garden. Noticing that they were both looking at her, she felt the colour rise to her cheeks. Phares in particular was staring at her, seemingly sharing the same surprise and confusion. His gaze seemed to grow in intensity, and she found it impossible to read from across the room.

'Anything the matter?' asked the prince as he began to whirl her around the room, his mouth close to Aida's ear.

'No, no,' she replied quickly, but more than anything now she wanted to twist out of the Bedouin's grasp.

As they swished past Phares, Aida saw his eyes flare at her. She drew in a ragged breath, scorched by the angry fire she read in their dark depths.

'Is anything wrong?' the prince asked again.

She kept her eyes fixed on his shoulder. 'I'm starting to get tired, I suppose. It's been a long evening.'

'The waltz after this is the last one. It's past two o'clock in the morning and the carriages will be arriving any minute now. You did promise me the last dance,' he reminded her smoothly.

Once again, they twirled round the room but when Aida looked again towards the French windows where she had spotted Phares, he wasn't there anymore. Camelia had taken his place next to her father and was watching her friend with a half smile.

The dance ended soon after that, much to Aida's relief.

'Will I see you again before you go back to Luxor?' the prince asked, clasping her hand captive in both of his.

'I'm afraid not. I'm not sure yet, but I might be leaving tomorrow evening if I find a place on the flight.'

'If you don't, do you promise to ring me?'

She tried to pull away gently, but he held her hand fast. 'I really ...'

He didn't let her finish and pressed two fingers to her lips, a very intimate gesture which was quite risqué in such narrow-minded society. 'Don't answer now, have a think ... I've given you my details ...'

Aida didn't answer. She wasn't really listening, and gave a distracted nod. Feeling smothered, she had only one thought in her mind: to get away from him.

She had no doubt that the Pharaonys would reprimand her for letting herself be monopolised by one man all evening, particularly one like Prince Shams Sakr El Din. Clearly, in their eyes, Aida was still promised to Phares. Not only that, but her open fraternising with the prince linked their names together, and with no official engagement between them, any respectable Egyptian family would deem it unacceptable – only foreigners behaved in this dissolute way. Furthermore, the prince was a notorious womaniser, and a Muslim at that, whereas Aida was Christian; even if she *was* romantically interested in the prince, it was a hopeless situation which precluded any idea of marriage between them. In her reckless mood Aida had quite enjoyed herself, and even if she did feel largely uncontrite about her self-indulgence, now she was slightly exhausted by the dancing and the wine she had drunk with dinner.

Finally, Sakr El Din disappeared into the crowd. She glanced around the ballroom, which was presently emptying as people lined up to take their leave of Princess Nazek. Kamel, Camelia and Phares were nowhere to be seen. Aida wasn't particularly worried about that – they had probably gone ahead and she would meet them at the car. The queue of departing guests had lengthened tremendously in the last few minutes; it would take her almost a quarter of an hour to reach her hostess if she joined it now. Hot and light-headed, she decided to take some air and headed for the same French windows where she had spotted Phares earlier.

It was one of those heavenly Egyptian nights, with a sky of velvet pricked by scintillating stars and a warm, caressing air. It felt good to be alone for a while. Aida stood leaning against the terrace parapet, taking deep breaths of the night air which was faintly scented by a flowering jasmine shrub whose delicate cream-coloured flowers hung down the wall.

It took a few minutes for her to realise another scent had joined it – the drifting aroma of a strong but not unpleasant tobacco. An expensive brand. She recognised the distinctive fragrance immediately, remembering it from years ago, when it had always given away the presence of the smoker, making her pulse quicken as it was now. In an almost Pavlovian response, a hot tingle ran down her spine.

Aida cast a look behind her to where the shadows were almost black, faintly discerning a tall shape and the orange glow of a cigarette as it was drawn upon, making the tip glow hotly. He approached her slowly with the lithe, elegant movement of a big cat.

'Phares,' she breathed.

He was so handsome tonight in his conventional evening suit fitted superbly to his wide-shouldered, lean and powerful frame. He stood towering over her, relaxed, half smiling, yet exuding animal virility, the narrowed lids of his large burning eyes raking over her face. Everything about him spoke of brute strength, which only served to make her feel more vulnerable – a familiar sensation that sent her reeling back to that awkward teenager, caught in his devastating gaze.

'So, Goldilocks, *you* are Aida El Masri?' His eyes held hers in a long, almost intimate encounter and it was like the first clash of foils in a fencing duel – light, instantly withdrawn, but a clash all the same. Echoes of past confrontations filled Aida's mind but this time it had a different edge that made her pulse kick madly. 'I told you we'd meet again. Somehow I remember that teenage Aida differently. Funny, eh?'

His tone was like the jab of a spur and Aida leapt recklessly to answer him. '*I* remember you exactly as you are, as you always were, Phares Pharaony,' she said.

He chuckled. '*Touché*! And how is that, might I ask?' he taunted, his barely disguised mockery infuriating her.

'Arrogant, haughty and narrow-minded.'

'Is that how you see me?'

'That is how you are.'

'How do you know? You've been away for eight years.'

'Leopards don't change their spots,' she answered tightly.

His gaze softened, and his voice fell to a low purr. He smiled wistfully. 'You've changed. I didn't recognise you the other day.'

'Obviously.' She didn't know whether to be irritated by this or oddly pleased that she was unrecognisable now from the sturdily built young girl who had secretly pined for him.

Her eyes fell to his mouth as it blew out a long trail of smoke. He was watching her now through the faint film of blue haze and in spite of her unspoken resolve to remain at a safe distance from this man, something inside her was melting under the mingled amusement and sensuality of that look. If only she wasn't still desperately attracted to him. How ironic that everyone was trying to protect her from Prince Shams Sakr El Din, while it was the man standing before her who represented a far greater danger.

Aida ignored his comment. 'Where are Uncle Kamel and Camelia? I lost sight of them.'

'I guess you were too busy lapping up His Highness's saccharine compliments.'

'Oh, for heaven's sake, Phares, spare me your sarcasm! Prejudice and bigotry ... I certainly haven't missed that in the last eight years.'

Phares laughed lazily. 'Well, I've missed the barbs on your tongue. In that respect you haven't changed either.' He exhaled smoke and his dark eyes dwelt pensively on Aida's face, holding her mesmerised – so intense and prolonged was his look, she felt involved in the deepest intimacy.

Why was it that whenever they had a conversation, without fail, she ended up being on the defensive? Even after all this time. It had always been that way with Phares; he had the knack of stirring her emotions and getting under her skin, and now that she was a grown woman, her physical reaction to him was even more potent.

Nothing had changed.

The quicker she rejoined the others, the faster she would end the perilous direction this *tête à tête* was taking. She had been here before, and more often than not her quick temper and 'barbed tongue', as Phares put it, had let her down. Tonight she didn't feel she was up to fencing with him. She remembered those heated discussions which invariably ended with her being in the wrong, as far as Phares was concerned, and decided to change the subject.

'I'm sorry I kept you waiting,' she said quietly. 'I assumed you'd all gone before me and would be waiting for me at the car. The queue was long so I came out for a breath of fresh air.'

'Father and Camelia were the first to leave as he's catching a plane for Alexandria early tomorrow morning and needs to get some sleep.' Something sparked in his dark eyes. 'So, I'm afraid you're lumbered with me as I offered to wait and take you home.'

Illogically, Aida's pulse quickened. 'Well, we'd better be going,' she said, an imperial lilt to her voice as she moved past him, heading for the ballroom.

'Whoever said mastery was primarily a masculine trait …' Phares mused in a low voice. The words stroked across her shoulder in a soft hypnotic drawl as his hand enclosed her elbow in a light grip, sending a shiver across her bare skin, but she pulled free, quickening her step to get away from him.

The crowd had thinned and they joined the queue silently, paid their respects to their hostess and walked slowly down to the car park. The air was warm and sweet with the overpowering scent of plants, the tangle of shrubbery starred with the cream blossom of jasmine. Something odd and compelling stretched between them so that Aida had the strongest premonition that she must not touch him.

In silence they walked to his cream roadster. Its top was down. He glanced at her briefly, his expression unreadable. 'Will the breeze spoil your hair?'

She stood awkwardly by the car door. 'Don't worry about my hair.'

'It's beautiful. This new long hairstyle suits you.' Phares's hand lifted, and afraid that he was going to touch a tendril, Aida drew back sharply. He saw the movement but made no comment as he opened the car door for her.

'I thought you weren't coming to the ball,' she said once they were driving out of Gezireh.

'As it turned out, the only operation scheduled for today was cancelled, and I finished my rounds early. I dressed at the hospital, which is on the island anyhow, and was able to make it on time.'

'I didn't see you all evening, nor Camelia or your father. I did look for them.'

Phares's jaw tightened, making the muscle flex. 'It would surprise me if you were aware of anyone except that Bedouin prince who was all over you.'

'What doesn't surprise *me*, however, is that you are as overbearing as ever.'

'Claws out again, tigress?' Phares's voice was idly amused, his eyes slightly mocking as he turned to look at Aida. He grinned, his gaze flitting over her, and she shook her head as if warding off the devilry that flared in his coal-black irises: that mysterious force which seemed to leap forth at her.

It was a blue night. The two-seater, open to the cool air, sped along the silent, empty road. The stars burned hazily ahead. A cool wind whipped at Aida's hair as she rested her elbow on the edge of the door, her chin on her fist. She inhaled deeply. This was what she had missed: the fresh and invigorating smell of the desert, and that special lightness in the atmosphere which the bombs in London, the fires and the city's perpetual traffic turned to the smell of fumes.

Still, the atmosphere inside the car was pregnant, filled with a heavy pulsating throb that had nothing to do with the sound of its racing engine. The miles of slumbering Cairo flew by. The jet-black stare of the driver seemed focused on nothing in particular, yet Aida was aware that he saw everything to right and left, strong hands on the wheel, relaxed yet alert like a steel spring. His coiled strength, only inches away from her, made her aware of him in a more disturbing way.

Had she thought that nothing had changed? She was wrong. The slow heat building between them was something new and unmistakable. Something she would have longed for as the foolish, besotted teenager all those years back but that now left her confused and wanting to deny its existence.

The cream roadster breasted a steep hill, and the canal and palm groves that bordered the wall of Kasr El Shorouk came into view, but instead of turning left where he should have, Phares drove on, past Mena House, the luxury hotel and competitor of Shepheard's, then up an even steeper hill, beyond which Aida knew nothing lay but the site of the pyramids and the limitless stretch of rolling dunes, home to small colonies of Bedouins and *matareed*, outlaws.

Unnerved by his silence and the prospect beckoning of being alone with him in the desert, she questioned sharply, 'Where are we going? This isn't the way to the house.'

'Why are you sounding so panic-stricken, Goldilocks? This isn't the first time we've driven into the desert together. I seem to remember you welcomed those little jaunts.' He flashed a grin at her. 'Is the thought of being alone with me so appalling, *habibti*?'

When she met this observation with contemptuous silence, he continued, slightly regretful, 'Now that you've returned, I'd planned – had looked forward – to spending some time alone with you. It's such a fabulous night, don't you think?'

She gazed out at the dark canopy of night above them, the spicy warmth of the air caressing her face. Yes, she silently admitted, she had forgotten how wonderful it was at night-time here.

'You used to accompany your father on his desert trips, as I recall,' he murmured.

'Only a couple of times. I don't feel I know it well,' she replied, surprised that her emotions didn't contort at his mentioning Ayoub.

'Nothing compares to desert nights,' he continued, 'when the stars hang low like big silver flowers in the sky, so close to earth. Almost as though a man might stretch up his hand and pluck one to offer his beloved, and the moon steals from behind some chain of dunes to add her gold magic to the scene. It's been ages since I've ventured into these solitary parts.'

Aida shifted in her seat, puzzled by the dreamy overtone that had developed in Phares's voice. It was almost as if ... but she couldn't make it out. This was so out of character ... 'You never struck me as a poet,' she couldn't help but remark.

He deserted his poetry to flash her a derisory look. '*Habibti*, your head was always full of preconceived notions. You're still rather good at jumping to conclusions, aren't you?'

They had reached the top of the hill where the imposing three pyramids appeared, like mysterious giants, mute witnesses to centuries of history, presiding over the graceful shadowy sand hillocks of the Arabian Desert and dark clusters of palm trees, towering up into the clear sky.

Phares pulled up at the side of the road. 'Just look at that! Isn't it fabulous? It never ceases to amaze me.'

Aida said nothing, but gazed in awe upon this handiwork of a bygone age. Its spell was indeed irresistible.

They got out of the car, and Phares walked a few steps away from her, loosening his tie, undoing the first two buttons of his shirt, which gleamed snow-white against his tawny-skinned throat. There was a remoteness about him now, more than simply the physical distance between them. He was splendid in his dinner suit, standing tall and lithe, his strong, proud profile almost like a son of Ancient Egypt masquerading in the clothes of a less ominous civilisation. Phares had always reminded Aida of the awesome figures carved upon those kingly tombs four thousand years ago. And tonight, as he stood looking out over the vast space of sand in the indigo atmosphere of the slumbering desert, he seemed more than ever in tune with the mystery and emptiness which lay for miles beyond. She felt that she could have been in the presence of King Mena himself, come to life. What thoughts were going through his head? Why had he brought her here? Was he trying to revive old memories. If so, to what end?

Despite their frequent differences of opinion, Aida had always known that Phares held some affection for her, but she had also been aware that he didn't love her or desire her as a man would a woman. She had been his younger sister's best friend and a good catch – one who would help grow the Pharaony family wealth. In those days she hadn't cared about that, her secret whole desire being to spend the rest of her life with him; and while eight years ago she had been prepared to compromise, today she was not. Even if there hadn't been the contentious issue of her father's death between them, her pride would never allow her to agree to a loveless marriage and where Phares was concerned, not only her pride, but her heart. No, it would be too hard to live with him, knowing his feelings for her were no more than those of an elder brother.

The dry night air nipped shrewdly, and lifting her eyes to the sky, Aida saw a slim virgin of a moon glide through the firmament, trailing a veil of light among the glowing Southern stars. The desert was a place of enchantment: silent, mysterious, illimitable. Aida felt the mystery of it more than ever ... how wonderful it would be to be out here alone with someone you loved and who returned the feeling. She sighed internally.

'Have you come back to stay?' Phares's tone was casual; he wasn't looking at her, but she gave a start.

'I haven't decided yet,' she answered brusquely, startled by his deep voice resonating in the silence. His question sent a flood of thoughts into her mind, of why she had returned to Egypt, of what she had set out to do ... of her father.

He turned and walked back to stand beside her. He seemed so tall when he came as close as this.

'Why the defences, Goldilocks?'

'Defences?' she repeated, as the meaning of the word drifted slowly into her consciousness. 'What do you imply by that?'

'You're so touchy ...' Phares smiled, hitching up a trouser leg and resting his foot on a heap of stones. 'You're so transparent. Even after eight years, you can't deceive me so easily ... but we have much to discuss, don't you think?'

She knew what he was alluding to ... So Uncle Naguib was right: the Pharaonys were still hoping that she would tie the knot with Phares and hand over her land to her husband like a good little Egyptian wife. Still, she wasn't going to make this easy for him.

'What do you mean?'

'It might be a little early to bring this subject up, but sooner or later we would have to talk about it ... clear the air. There's too much at stake here.'

Her heart was beating. Had Camelia told him that she was still brooding on the past? Was he going to propose to her there and then?

'Please stop talking in riddles and come to the point.'

He gave an impatient intake of breath. 'Never look back,' he chided her. 'All the yesterdays are gone as though snuffed out like candles. A little of their smoke might linger to fog the mind and cloud the heart, but it is always better to look forward.'

She crossed her arms and half turned away. 'You've not only become a poet, but a philosopher now ...'

'Don't mock, Aida. I'm being serious.' He sighed. 'I hope you can believe me when I tell you that I'm really sorry about what happened with your father.'

'Sorry!' Aida turned on him, all her pent-up rage unleashing blindly and the youthful prettiness wiped from her face as if by some profaning hand. 'Sorry! My God, what good is your sympathy to me? My father was an innocent man who was blamed for something he would never have done! Our families were close friends. My father was even thinking of tightening this bond by a further alliance – our marriage. And all I know is that our maid swore on her child's life that your father brought the Nefertari statue to our house!'

For a moment Phares said nothing, though a shadow passed over his jet-black pupils. Then he spoke slowly in a low voice: 'So you really still think that of my father, Aida?'

'What else should I think, Phares?' she returned sharply. Seeing Kamel Pharaony again had made her faintly uneasy about her long-held hatred for him, but now all that uncertainty was swept away by the old rawness of anger. 'It's the only evidence I have of my father's innocence, and nothing else makes sense.'

'So you judge my father, who you've known your entire life, without having all the facts and because of the word of your maid?' His tone was still quiet, but his gaze had hardened, his eyes fixed on Aida's face.

Not wanting to hear his denials and criticism, the young woman shook her head without answering.

Phares leaned closer to her, his voice low and steady. 'Listen to me, Aida. Your father was a great man. I respected him as much as if he were my own family. I miss him too. Do you think my father believes he was guilty of stealing that statue? Do you think *I* believe it? If your maid accused my father falsely, there was a reason.'

'And what *reason* would Souma have for that?'

He paused and scanned her face intensely. 'You want to know the truth?'

'Yes.' Aida lifted her chin haughtily, anger lending a defiant sparkle to her eyes. 'Or what you consider the truth.'

'So why don't you take my hand and we can look for it together? Marry me, Aida, and I promise you that I will do my best to seek out the person who caused our two families such grief.'

Suddenly she burst into laughter, which though a trifle theatrical was still genuine. How painfully ridiculous her situation now seemed. The son of the man she had blamed for her father's death was now offering to help her – *and* marry her.

Phares started slightly and looked sternly at her. 'I am asking you to become my wife … offering to help you … and your only response is to laugh? Where has this harshness come from, Aida?'

She didn't answer. There was such anguish in his face that she averted her gaze, and for a while both stood silently, looking into the peaceful night that was so at odds with the crackling atmosphere of their stormy exchange.

An owl hooted, the long-drawn, melancholy cry sounding indescribably forlorn in the stillness.

'Marry me, Aida … I'll make you happy. We'll have a wonderful life together.'

A little breeze wandered fitfully over the dunes, whispering faint promises of the joy of a life at Phares's side … with him standing there proud and powerful like an Egyptian god.

The temptation was overwhelming. The still night, the beauty of the starlit desert, the silence, and the ominous presence of those great mute giants had all stirred strange emotions in Aida's heart. It was as if the devastating resolve to avenge her father, the hatred she had nurtured for so long towards Kamel Pharaony, and by extension his son, was duelling with a warm compassion, so instinctive to her, which had once been nearly extinguished.

Aida felt her judgement misting over, her resolution fading. 'It's all very well for you … *you* have nothing to lose.'

'Neither have you.'

'*I* would have everything to lose. My land for one, which would be amalgamated with the Pharaony riches and over which I would lose all control. Besides, contrary to what you might think, I have changed. I am no more the naïve little girl in plaits that you once knew, who would be content with what you call *un mariage de convenance.*'

'You would be cared for and treated like a queen, instead of toiling alone, as you will have to if you decide to look after your affairs yourself.'

'I have estate managers, lawyers and accountants for that, thank you,' she threw at him.

Phares raked a hand through his hair. 'Look, Aida. You're not in England here, you come from Luxor. We're not even talking about Cairo or Alexandria. You're in the *Said*, in Upper Egypt, where women are—'

'Considered second-class citizens? Don't say it,' she cut in as she felt the burning heat rise to her cheeks.

He shook his head. 'No *fellah*, lawyer or manager would respect the orders of a woman alone. Like it or not, that's the way here. If we married, all of those problems would be solved.'

'Though I might have been happy to go ahead with the plans my father and yours had arranged eight years ago, it is quite different today. I've seen things that have changed me. The *world* has changed, Phares. I want much more out of life.'

He looked at her impatiently. 'Still the same rebellious, stubborn girl. You haven't changed that much. I would have thought that England, the war, would have subdued you, but it seems to have had the reverse effect.'

Aida's shock at his insulting arrogance gave in to an almost uncontrollable burst of wrath. 'What do you know about the war?' she said, her voice trembling with suppressed rage. 'There was no war here, no real restrictions, only hollow indulgence. Most people sat at grand hotel terraces indulging in careless enjoyment, drinking, gossiping and fornicating.'

Phares's jaw stiffened but he merely gave her a hard stare and shook his head, chastening her because now she remembered how involved he'd been at the hospitals for the wounded at Alexandria.

'Again, you jump to conclusions without knowing all the facts. I can see that you have been badly scarred by the war. But now, everything a woman could ever need or want is within your reach and you insist on pushing it away. I don't understand you.'

She took a step back. 'I don't expect you to understand me, or understand anything about what *this* woman needs or wants. Egyptian men ... *bah!*' Aida shrugged with contempt. 'You're all the same. Calculating, chauvinistic and emotionless.'

At this his eyes became so narrowed that it was impossible for her to read their expression. 'Emotionless, eh?' His voice, though still quiet, contained a strange vibrancy that caused a tingle to run up Aida's spine. He took a step towards her. 'That is a very dangerous thing to say to a man who has any self-respect at all.'

'Oh, is it?' she taunted. 'And why is that?'

He took another step. 'Because, you see, he will in all probability have the urge to disprove your statement.'

'And you see yourself playing such a role?' Aida forced a peal of incredulous laughter, seeing that she had finally succeeded in riling him. 'I always knew you were arrogant, but I didn't understand the extent of your conceit.'

Her heart leapt to meet the sudden dangerous flare that ignited in the depths of those fathomless eyes. How magnificent he looked ... seductive ... irresistible! Something stirred in her loins – a need she had never felt before.

'Must I prove to you how well *I* understand *you*?'

Phares had drawn very near her, his dark face almost against her own. Then, pressing his hard body deliberately close to hers, he bent her head back with surprising force and kissed her full on the lips. He kissed her long and vigorously, his mouth sensuous and demanding, rendering her completely insensible.

Dazed and confused, she thrust him from her. 'Why did you do that?' she demanded breathlessly.

He was still gazing mercilessly into her startled eyes. 'That's a foolish question, Aida,' he said. 'You ought to know the answer.'

'I don't!' Her heart was thudding in wild sledgehammer blows against her ribs.

'Don't look so violated, Goldilocks,' he murmured. 'Why not be honest, and acknowledge that your body betrays you? It says *you excite me*.'

The allegation scandalised her and his calm smile was infuriating. 'Are you daring to imply I invited this assault?' she stormed, wiping a shaking hand across her mouth. 'If it was to amuse yourself, you're more despicable than I thought.'

'You find me wanting in a great many ways,' he replied dryly. 'It's a pity, since I had high hopes for the future ... Come, let's go home before I do something we'll both regret.'

The stinging edge in Phares's voice made Aida flinch away from him. She moved blindly towards the car in silence, filled with new bewildering emotions. She was bitterly conscious of his broad frame just behind her, watching her retreat. If she were honest, she would admit that when his mouth left hers she could have cried out. It was like being bereft, cut off from an essential life force. Electrifying pulses still throbbed through her.

There was no wind tonight, yet at this moment there was a rustle, a sigh among the stones and the palm trees as a small eddy of sand drifted across the young woman's face. A breath from the desert, no more. Yet an imaginative soul might have thought that the old gods had stirred, had softly laughed – that they had known what Aida did not know …

The stars were still thick overhead; the thin crescent moon still smiling gallantly upon the three colossi, which rose majestically in the silvery beams. But Aida's heart was heavy, tears of humiliation hovering behind her eyes as they drove back to Kasr El Ghoroub.

# CHAPTER 5

Next day dawned brilliant. Kasr El Ghoroub sparkled in the sunshine, its climbing roses and jasmine hanging in heavy, drooping clusters, and in the surrounding gardens the pink petunias and purple orchids flagged somewhat in the glare of the new day. Out in the desert the sand shone like closely packed particles of gold. The air was hot and clear, with the peculiar soft freshness of the Egyptian early morning, and the distant pyramids were veiled in a purple mist, which lay like a faint bloom upon the austere stone outlines. The sky, blue and cloudless, the sand rolling away in endless yellow waves, the pink glow on the faraway dunes combined with an exquisite clearness of effect which enchanted Aida. For the past eight years, she had grown used to grey skies, faint colour contrasts, and an unvarying monotony of green and brown.

She and Camelia had just come on to the terrace to have breakfast.

'I really don't understand why you've suddenly decided to leave for Luxor today,' Camelia told her friend as she helped herself to a slice of *roumi* cheese and *baladi* bread, which had been made on the premises in an old-fashioned mud oven. 'You said you were here for a couple of days.'

'I promised Uncle Naguib that I'd be back immediately after the ball,' Aida answered in a matter-of-fact tone. 'There's a lot of work to be done and I have no excuse to let it pile up more.'

'I'm sure all this has to do with Phares bringing you home last night.'

Aida did not look up from buttering her toast. Involuntarily, her mind filled with the memory of being with Phares in the desert the night before ... of his powerful body against hers ... the wild thrill of his insatiable kiss ... the way he had revealed her vulnerability with such shocking ease ...

'You're reading too much into this,' she lied.

'No, I'm not. I haven't seen Phares this morning. He left very early for the hospital, but I heard you come in last night and I'm sure you didn't come straight from the ball. It was very late.' Camelia eyed her friend curiously. 'Where did you go?'

Aida felt herself blush. Under the pretext of wiping her mouth, she used her napkin to hide her telltale guilty expression.

'We went for a drive to the pyramids.'

'What were you doing out there?'

'Phares was fooling around, as usual,' Aida mumbled as she bit into the slice of toast without looking at her friend.

'Phares does not fool around. I have a good idea why he took you out there.' Camelia's voice bore an edge. 'Why do you insist on looking at it that way? A romantic setting, a handsome man in playful mood, and what do you do? You sneer.'

'I'm being honest. Besides, he ignored me all evening. How could he expect me to fall into his arms at the snap of his fingers?'

'He hadn't recognised you, and when I pointed you out, at first he didn't believe me.'

'As the saying goes: *out of sight, out of mind.*'

'Hardly. He couldn't keep his eyes off you and was in a shocking mood for the rest of the evening because that Bedouin was monopolising you.'

'What was stopping him from coming up to me if that was the case?'

'As I said, he hadn't recognised you earlier and so you hadn't been introduced.'

*We hadn't been officially introduced, but we had met,* Aida thought to herself, recalling their brief encounter on that sunny morning at Kasr El Shorouk not so long ago.

'You've changed, Aida. It took *me* a few seconds to place you when we bumped into each other at Shemla. Eight years is a long time. When you left, you were what the British call a "bonnie lass". Look at you … you've come back a stunningly beautiful young woman, elegant and sophisticated. Men at the ball were devouring you with their eyes. One by one, through the evening, they came up to my father, asking who you were. I'm sure your uncle will have them queuing to ask for your hand after yesterday.'

Rather than being flattered, Aida glared at her. She was about to say something, but Camelia raised her hand. 'Don't look at me like that. I know what you think of girls who see a prospective husband in every male on their horizon, but my point is that I also think my brother's feelings for you run much deeper than any of us imagined. Seeing you again has triggered something in him that he's ignored up until now.'

Aida helped herself to a cup of coffee and tried to ignore her friend's last comment. The idea that Phares might harbour deep feelings for her penetrated her poise, sending her thoughts in directions that were far too dangerous. 'You've changed too,' she smiled wryly. 'You used to be very down-to-earth. While I devoured Delly's romantic novels, you were much more interested in Agatha Christie's murder mysteries. Now it seems you're a real romantic.'

Camelia shrugged. 'It's just that I know my brother well, and his reaction to seeing you yesterday was out of character. It was also very revealing. Even my father noticed it. He was quite pleased when Phares offered to bring you home.'

Aida sighed and sipped her cup of strong coffee, lost for a moment in a chaos of conflicting thoughts. If ever the time came when she needed a confidante, Camelia would be that person, but Aida was not yet ready to talk. There were emotions which she had to understand, had to come to terms with. How she had imagined her return was very different from reality. Nothing was turning out as she had expected. Besides, she felt like a beetle under a microscope. She didn't like the way everyone had been plotting and planning, putting pressure on her since she had come back to Egypt. Maybe it was time to make her own position perfectly clear once and for all.

'I think you should all stop scheming, because nothing's going to happen between your brother and me. No marriage, no Pharaony-El Masri alliance, and I've no intention of giving up my land.'

Camelia paused, gazing at her friend speculatively. 'Want to talk about it? I can be very impartial, you know?'

Aida looked up sharply to frown at her friend. 'No, Camelia. And I do *not* want to talk about it anymore.'

'All right, no need to get upset.' Seeing the look on Aida's face, Camelia immediately backed down. 'Let's change the subject.'

The two women were silent for some moments.

'How was it with the prince?'

'He's a very charming and interesting man.'

'He stuck to you all evening.' Camelia's tone was carefully neutral.

'I know, and I realise how that must have seemed. Believe me, I did look for you, but I couldn't see you.'

'It was a real crush. One of us caught a glimpse of you from time to time, but you were either dancing or already seated for dinner. After dinner, Papa and Phares went to listen to Om Kalthoum.'

Aida glanced at Camelia over her coffee. 'What about you?'

'Oh, I just went for a stroll in the grounds.'

'Anyway, I also met one of the British consuls, Alastair Carlisle. I sat next to him at dinner. Do you know him?'

Aida felt her friend stiffen. 'I've met him a few times. He's an English spy.'

'What do you mean?'

Frowning, Camelia cut up another slice of *roumi* cheese into small pieces. 'They're all spies, these diplomats – you know, the socialite types who move from party to party, making so-called polite conversation, while all the time they're trying to extract sensitive information that might give insight to our country's affairs. Then they spend the next day on their typewriters reporting what they've heard.'

Aida raised an eyebrow. 'You never struck me as being anti-British.'

'I'm not, I'm just telling you the facts.'

'But don't you think it's a bit of a generalisation? Besides, a year ago the world was still at war, and allegiances among the Egyptian population, as I understand it, were quite ambiguous. It seems a lot of Egyptians were pro-Germany.'

'The local support for the Germans was not a reflection of their embracing antisemitism or European fascism,' Camelia said, her voice gaining fervour. 'They were simply voicing a protest against the British occupation. A lot of us hold them responsible for the absence of autonomy in our country. When Rommel landed in the Western Desert and engaged the Allies at El Alamein, we viewed that battle as the first step in Egypt's liberation from British control. That is all.'

'*We*? You're speaking as though you share those views.'

'I certainly do.' Camelia's large eyes flicked downwards. 'But I speak for myself. Papa and the rest of the family have a different view. As you know, he thinks Egypt is better off under the British, even if they are responsible for keeping our weak king in power for their own ends. He doesn't trust that Egypt is capable of self-rule.'

Aida put down her coffee cup, regarding her friend thoughtfully. 'You know, that's another way you've changed, Camelia. You were never interested in politics.'

Camelia stirred her coffee slowly. 'Mounir was extremely nationalistic. He was an interesting and passionate man who taught me a lot about the history of our wonderful country.'

'So really you *are* anti-British.'

Her friend looked up. 'It's not that simple. Throughout the war, Egypt made an important contribution to the Allied effort. Now the British are in debt to us for the first time. We were hoping to be rewarded for our support by a British declaration of complete independence when the war ended. Instead, we have been sorely disappointed by their refusal to change the status of our country, despite all the best efforts of Prime Minister Sidqi. All the talk of independence was nothing more than a sham, so is it any surprise that the British have forfeited what little goodwill they had left?' Camelia's large eyes had grown even more expressive. 'It's no wonder there have been massive strikes and demonstrations, people dying.'

'Is Phares of this opinion too?'

Camelia sighed and shook her head. 'Nothing has any importance for Phares apart from his patients, his operations, and his hospital – he is totally dedicated to his work.'

'That's a wonderful thing.'

'*Yaany*, maybe, but it's not a healthy way of living. That hospital, El Amal, is his life. Do you know, he makes a habit of turning up unexpectedly in various departments – the kitchens, laundry, path lab, X-ray room – quietly watching what's going on for a few minutes, then leaving without speaking to anyone?'

Aida nodded approvingly. 'That just shows he has a passion for efficiency. It's good that he keeps everyone on their toes.'

'Yes, yes, I agree, *habibti*. But he's not getting any younger and there's more to life than work.' She shrugged. 'He's thirty-four. At that age he should be married and know the joys of raising a family. All his friends are married. Their children adore him.'

Camelia flashed her friend a sideways look. 'He's very good with them, you know. He'd make an excellent father.'

Aida's heart turned over; she tried not to dwell on the thought of having children with Phares. 'You're saying that he has no other life than his work? No girlfriends?'

'Of course he has girlfriends ... foreigners, you know. But none whom he would actually think of marrying. They're just a pastime for him.'

'Why is that?'

'Because he believes that he must marry someone *min toboh*.'

Aida nodded. *Min toboh* – marrying someone cut from the same cloth. She knew the expression well; it was popular in most Egyptian circles, rich or poor, Christian or Muslim. Sticking to someone from the same race, religion and social background was paramount for an Egyptian. Aida's father had ignored this golden rule by marrying a foreigner and had suffered the consequences. But there was a whole other community in Egypt, one drawn from half the races of Europe. French, Italians, Maltese, Greeks and Armenians ... Unlike the real Egyptians of the Coptic and Muslim communities, these big families frequently intermarried until all trace of their original ancestry was hopelessly confused; a happy, wholesome, polyglot crew, speaking half a dozen languages fluently, and none correctly.

'There's no shortage of nice Coptic girls,' Aida pointed out. 'You've said yourself that your Aunty Halima has been introducing Phares to a string of suitable young ladies, yet none seem to please him.' She arched an eyebrow. 'Perhaps your brother is just a misogynist?'

Camelia burst out laughing. 'I would say quite the reverse. He genuinely likes the company of women – and they're all over him. You should see the nurses at the hospital.' She wiped her mouth with her napkin and waved it dismissively 'It's quite embarrassing really, all of them mooning over him whenever he walks into a room. I know he's had plenty of mistresses, although he keeps very quiet about it. He has some sort of *garçonnière*, a bachelor's apartment next to the hospital in Gezireh. And there's the cottage on the estate in Luxor. I think he takes his women friends there too. So, you see, Aida, my brother has no problem with women.'

A shadow passed over Aida's heart. For the second time that day she recalled the three bears' cottage at El Shorouk – so it was Phares's private little love nest. How very ironic. She managed a nonchalant smile. 'From what you say, there isn't much difference between your brother and Prince Shams Sakr El Din, whom you all criticise for just that reason.'

Camelia laughed. 'Ah, *habibti*, you're trying to score points now …'

'Maybe,' Aida conceded thoughtfully, and they left it at that. She poured herself some more coffee. 'When are you going back to Luxor?'

'I have a few jobs to finish here,' Camelia answered, sitting back in her chair, 'but I'll be back before the end of next week. I have to organise the big annual *Sham El Nessim* party we're giving, *in shah Allah*, God willing, at El Shorouk. You'll come, of course.'

Aida nodded, smiling. 'Yes, of course.'

She remembered those huge *Sham El Nessim* parties the Pharaonys held on the banks of the Nile at their estate. The celebration always fell on the Monday following Easter Sunday. Aida and her parents used to attend every year. Originating from the Ancient Egyptians' agricultural spring festival, known as the feast of *Shamo*, this celebration of the 'renewal of life' coincided with the vernal equinox, the date of which was not fixed, but determined by looking at the direction of the light at sunrise over the pyramids. The ancients marked it with a feast at the foot of the Great Pyramid, imagining this day represented the beginning of creation. When the festival and its fertility rites were later attached to Christianity and the celebration of Easter, its Coptic name, *Tshom Ni Sime*, was used – *tshom* meaning gardens and *ni sime*, meadows – before finally adopting its modern name, which literally means 'smelling the fresh breeze'. After the seventh-century Arab invasion, *Sham El Nessim* became a non-religious festival celebrated by all Egyptians regardless of faith.

Nowadays, with winter behind them, families in their summer clothes flocked to the countryside early in the morning to enjoy the fresh breeze and celebrate spring with a picnic consisting of coloured boiled eggs, spring onions and strong-smelling, salted *melouha*; seer, a freshwater fish considered a delicacy in Upper Egypt and in the north; and *feseekh*, a grey mullet found in the Mediterranean and the Red Sea and prepared in the same way. In Cairo, Egyptians crowded the open green spaces to enjoy the spring air, even if that meant sitting on grassy verges next to the road.

The few times when the Pharaonys spent the Easter holidays in Alexandria, Aida had stayed at the San Stefano Hotel with her parents, not far from the Pharaony house in Ramleh. It had its own private beach, and so the early morning picnic had taken place on the seashore. Aida gave a wistful sigh. Those happy-go-lucky times seemed so far away now.

After breakfast, Aida went up to her room and packed, then came back down again to say goodbye to her friend. Camelia walked with her to the grand front door, already open to the view of the tall acacias lining the long drive. A cheerful-looking man with a greying moustache dressed in a beige suit took Aida's case, carrying it down to the Bentley parked at the foot of the steps.

Camelia kissed Aida on both cheeks. '*Osta* Fathi will accompany you to the airport.' She paused. 'Can't I persuade you to change your mind?'

'No, trust me … much better if I leave today.'

'Did you and Phares have a quarrel?'

Aida levelled a stare at her friend.

'Drop it, Camelia, please.'

'Very well, *habibti.* I'll see you then for Easter?'

'I'm invited to Uncle Naguib and Aunty Nabila's for Easter, but yes, I'd be delighted to join you for *Sham El Nessim.*'

'Well, if I don't see you before then ...' Camelia smiled, 'take good care of yourself and stop brooding. Call me when you're back in Luxor.'

Aida thanked her friend and climbed into the back of the car, and as the Bentley made its way down the drive towards the gates of El Ghouroub, she breathed a little easier.

*       *       *

At the wheel of her new burgundy Ford convertible, Aida drove out of Luxor market. She had gone to the *souk* to order nuts, dried fruit and a variety of sweetmeats that would be distributed to the staff of Karawan House for Easter and *Sham El Nessim.* The heat had lessened; dusk was not far off. Although business was over for the day, most of the women still clutched stalks of bananas and sugarcane, standing among their hencoops with peering round-eyed children to stare at the newcomer. As she manoeuvred the car through the narrow streets, Aida's mind was preoccupied as usual.

In the days that followed her return to Luxor, she had found it difficult to put Phares out of her mind. There was a strange stirring in her heart that had never been there before. Her whole being reached out towards this new and intangible feeling, one that was quite beyond her narrow experience. It felt so real, yet somehow impossible to put into words.

She had attempted desperately to fill every hour of the day, trying not to think of what had happened with Phares at the pyramids, but to no avail. Although work on the estate was absorbing and she gained some satisfaction from taking control of her own affairs, Aida found that she missed nursing. But when she thought of her work in the London hospitals, her thoughts only naturally brought her back to Phares. How wonderful it would be if he could give her a job at his hospital. Surely they would value her experience? Still, after the other night there was undoubtedly a rift between the two of them. She should let some time pass before asking for favours.

Leaving the confines of Luxor, Aida drove with the bonnet down, feeling the breeze lifting the hair at her temples. A blue haze clung to the far-off dunes, giving way slowly to rising temperature. Ahead lay the colourful, cultivated fields of sugarcane, broad beans and cotton. She took the dirt road that led straight across the plain, roughly parallel with the river. Uneven and potholed in places, it meandered in a lazy fashion as if bent on whims of its own, and the car lurched and swayed in spite of her expert driving. There was a much better asphalted road, which would have led her straight to the estate, but it was further away; it would have added fifteen minutes to her journey and she was already late for Uncle Naguib, with whom she had an appointment to discuss some of the problems she'd had with Megally, the estate manager.

The sun was setting, casting a pink glow over the fields and date palms. In a few moments it would disappear and the countryside would suddenly be shrouded in darkness. The road thronged with natives and animals on their way home – the usual routine at dawn and dusk. The *fellahin*'s camels and patient donkeys jogged beside carts laden with local peasant women coming back from the fields. Aida was making slow progress, but she didn't really mind. Feasting her eyes on the scene, she realised how much she had missed all this. She was sure it could not have changed since the days of the pharaohs.

It wasn't quite dark yet. A pale, opalescent gleam lingered in the sky, falling on the clustered figures in the road. The colour of the women's clothes and the contrasting drabness of the men's merged into the strange half-light, softened to a muted kaleidoscope against the backdrop of slanting palms. No, this certainly wasn't London, with its chaotic streets ravaged by bombs, the buildings in ruin, ambulances tearing up and down, sirens blaring. Aida had forgotten how primitive the people were in this place she had chosen to live. It was as though they had been spirited right back to the beginning of the century.

Soon the road began to wind between tall hedges of sugarcane ready for cutting. This was Pharaony land. The unfenced acreage from here to the extensive cottonfields a few miles ahead belonged to Phares's family. The moon had risen, swinging into the empty blueness of the sky, and a light wind wafted the cane into a waving silver sea. The scenery was lovely, just as Aida had always remembered it …

She slowed down as she steered the car across the narrow wooden bridge over the Nile. The ground was soft here, almost like quicksand. As Aida rounded a corner, the car skidded in the mud and she lost control of the wheel. Unable to steer, she stamped hard on her brakes, sending the vehicle hurtling sideways, narrowly avoiding collision with a man on horseback who came out of the shadows.

In the dazzle of the headlights the horse and rider, who had lifted an arm to shield his eyes from the glare, looked massive – like one of the Four Horsemen of the Apocalypse. Aida could see the whites of the horse's eyes rolling, the only movement of man and beast, who stood as still and threatening as an enormous bronze statue.

A deep voice swore in Arabic, making Aida jump, and the rider moved away from the beam of her headlights.

'Well, well, well, Goldilocks! What are you doing taking a turn at that speed – and at night as well?' Phares stared down at her, the sleeves of his white shirt rolled up to reveal muscled forearms flexing against the reins. 'You startled my horse, you could have killed us all.'

Aida's heart skipped several beats and she swallowed hard. 'I'm sorry,' she murmured rather nervously, 'I lost control of the wheel at the turning. The ground is so muddy.'

'Do you even have a driving licence?' he asked curtly.

Outraged by his arrogance, she found her voice. Turning glittering, angry eyes on him, she retorted hotly, 'Yes, of course. What do you think?'

Phares leaned forward and stroked his horse's ears. 'Well, maybe you should take the test again.'

Aida gritted her teeth. She really didn't want to enter into another argument with him. Their last meeting had left her humiliated and confused and she wasn't about to encourage an encore.

'I thought you were still in Cairo,' she said testily.

He straightened in the saddle. 'Well, as you can see, I came back.'

Rider and horse moved out of the road and on to the verge. Phares signalled her to drive on, but as Aida turned on the ignition, as hard as she tried, the car wouldn't start.

It was her turn to swear under her breath.

'No wonder your engine's stalled, *habibti*. Has no one told you there's another road? You should have come that way. Not only is this one hopeless by car, but the bridge back there is rickety. You could have found yourself in the river.' Even in the dim light Aida could feel his gaze travelling over her, appraisingly. 'You've been in London too long. I think you've forgotten what our country roads are like ... Luckily, we're not far from the estate. We'd better fetch some help.'

Aida stepped out of the car, slamming the door. 'Don't worry, you don't need to accompany me. I'm perfectly capable of walking a couple of miles,' she said, locking her car.

'Don't be ridiculous. You're coming with me.' Phares jumped off his horse and, reaching into his pocket, took out a torch.

'Oh, you're lending me your horse?' Aida said, somewhat taken aback. Perhaps he was a gentleman after all.

His eyes glinted in the torchlight. 'No such luck, young lady. You can ride pillion. Come on, let me give you a leg up.'

She was acutely aware of him standing next to her. '*Sharing a horse? No way!*' she exclaimed, appalled by this suggestion but unable to control the excitement that coursed through her at the idea of sharing a saddle with him.

A smile strayed into his eyes. 'What are you afraid of?'

'People will gossip.'

'I never heard such nonsense! You forget that my grandfather and grandmother stamped on that myth a long time ago.'

Aida knew the story of Phares's grandparents, Sélim and Gamila. Though very much in love and officially engaged, they had to respect the custom which dictated that they should not see each other until they were married, except on special occasions when both families were gathered. They used to meet in secret, and finally, tired of the gossiping of their neighbours, they both decided to give the people of Luxor something to talk about. One day, with their parents' blessing, Sélim took Gamila on horseback through the town to the market. Subsequently, they went riding together most days and even though it was unheard of at that time, people soon became used to it.

'*We* are not engaged,' Aida replied roundly.

'Oh, but make no mistake, *habibti*, we will be. As sure as I see you now standing in front of me,' he murmured under his breath.

At that moment, seeing him standing there lit by the moon that had risen from behind a clump of ragged palms, Aida could have smacked the mock-serious expression clean from his face.

Phares made an impatient sound in his throat. Before Aida knew it, his hands were on her waist and he swung her up into the saddle. Soon he was astride the beast behind her, and they were away.

Phares's steely clasp crushed her to his broad chest. Locked between his powerful arms, she felt herself tremble as his burning lips brushed the side of her ear, his warm breath fanning her cheek. 'Don't worry, I won't let you go, Goldilocks,' he whispered, sending an unwelcome but nonetheless delicious quiver down her spine.

Night lay mysterious and silver upon the face of the desert. In the sky, the great bright stars hung in clusters. Like a huge plate of gold, the yellow moon was still low in the midnight-blue canopy, entangled, or so it seemed, in the branches of the tall trees. Its pale light turned the countryside into an enchanted fairyland lit by a magic lamp.

Through the shadows they sped. Soon, from the road bordered by palms and sycamore trees, they emerged into the open. Fields of sugarcane swayed on both sides and the wind tugged at Aida's hair. The air was soft and balmy. Phares's chest was hard against her back, the movement of the horse rhythmic beneath her thighs. She was acutely aware of him seated behind her, recognising in the way he held her that his need mirrored her own. A sensuous warmth spread through her body, making her light-headed, so much so that she wished he would kiss her as he had at the pyramids. She leaned into him, gently resting her head against his shoulder, wanting to connect further with his muscled body.

Had Phares sensed this? The tension between them was so electric that Aida could not see how he could ignore it. Presently, he slowed the horse and his arms tightened around her, pressing her to him; his strong fingers holding the reins slid over hers and Aida felt her skin burn where they touched. The longing welled up in her, a craving to be in his arms. Her heart was racing, her breathing coming fast with a short, staccato rhythm.

One hand pushed up her blouse and slid beneath it, for a moment resting palm down and motionless against the bare skin. The contact sent a sharp flame of desire shooting through her, warmth flooding her loins, and an almost imperceptible moan escaped her lips.

Then, although they were still half a mile away from the Pharaony house, Aida realised Phares was leading the horse off the road, taking them on to a narrow path bordered with centuries-old sycamores.

'Where are we going?' she ventured in a hoarse voice.

'To a game park.'

His somewhat ambiguous tone set a quiver of apprehension shivering along her spine.

'A game park?'

'Yes, a place where we can continue our games without running the risk of being disturbed, *chérie*.'

Aida's throat went dry. His words acted like a cold shower, sobering her at once.

'What do you mean?'

He didn't answer, but brought the horse to a halt and dismounted. There was something unnerving in the way he was looking up at her now, his eyes on her face, studying her with an intensity that made her tremble. From his face to his muscle-bunched shoulders, to the legs that were firmly planted on the rough ground, there was tension. Beneath his tan he was pale, and his eyes burned with a familiar, dangerous flame she was beginning to recognise.

She stared back at him silently, her heart thudding crazily against her ribcage.

'Don't bat those innocent eyes at me, Goldilocks. It won't get you anywhere. Desire is not a game. You refuse me and yet your body does not. I think you may find,' he added very softly, 'that you are not a girl anymore.'

Aida flinched. What had she got herself into? This was not what she wanted … or was it? She took in his black hair, windswept over his brow, his full lips and strong jaw, the muscle that ran down his neck flexing, and the raw hunger in his dark gaze. 'I know you wouldn't hurt me,' she said jerkily, though she raised her chin in defiance.

'So you decided to take advantage, eh? Like to provoke, excite and ignite a man's desires, do you?' A low, dangerous note came into his voice. 'Well, this man is going to show you that playing with matches has its own dangers.'

His possessive glance outraged her. Her eyes blazed jewel blue as hot blood rose to her cheeks. Though Aida felt bonelessly weak, she stared at him, wanting him so badly that every nerve tingled in shock. 'You wouldn't dare!'

Before she knew it, she was off the horse, prisoner of Phares's powerful embrace, his body pushing against hers as he folded himself around her. Aida's every nerve was sensually alive with her longing for him; his strength was so overpowering, she could not have pushed him away. Not that she tried.

Of their own volition, her arms lifted and she locked her hands behind Phares's neck, her lips parting instinctively, inviting his assault. And then she remained quite still as his head descended and for a moment they traded breaths, their lips almost touching. Then he crushed her possessively against him, moulding her soft body to the hard length of him before his ardent mouth found hers, forcing back her head until she was utterly consumed by his kiss. His tongue was tantalising in the warm secret places of her mouth; he tasted wonderful … a delicious mixture of fresh tobacco and mint.

Somewhere inside her was the knowledge that she should not be behaving in this way, that young Egyptian unmarried women, true virgins, did not conduct themselves with such wantonness. Purity and innocence were virtues men looked for in a woman when choosing a companion in this highly conservative country; and Phares, with all his foreign education, his travelling and his *soi-disant* enlightening experience was, in Aida's opinion, just as chauvinistic as the rest of them. On top of that, in his eyes Aida belonged to him, even though she had turned down his offer of marriage ...

And now his hands began to move over her, exploring her shoulders and her throat, sliding down to her waist, shaping themselves to the soft curve of her hips, and she moved instinctively against the thrust of his arousal, saying without words the way she also felt about him.

Phares's fingers tangled in her hair, the silky golden curls tumbling about her shoulders as they escaped their combs. 'You're the sexiest woman I've ever met,' he whispered between kisses. 'I could drink you in one go and still feel thirsty for you.' His mouth gentled, tasting, tenderly biting, and Aida responded avidly, her breasts, the nipples firm, urging his caresses as they pressed against his muscled chest.

He stroked them lightly over the flimsy fabric of her dress, sending the most acute sensations to the nerve centres of her upper body and causing her to shudder from head to toe. Tremors of unfamiliar need rippled through every inch of her flesh, numbing her brain. She was not thinking anymore. Her qualms forgotten, only two things were real: the silence of the night and these delicious sensations that were rippling through her like quicksilver. The roar and hum of Luxor was inaudible here. Civilisation seemed so remote from this sleeping deserted place to where she had been charmed away by her mesmerising pharaoh. From somewhere far off on the banks of the Nile came the sound of a young Arab's flute, and the whole land slumbered as though in an enchanted sleep.

Now Phares was lifting her skirt, tracing the long, smooth muscles at the front of her thighs, letting his thumbs curve upwards until he found the lacy edge of her panties. Her focus blurred, her lips parting as he slid his thumb beneath the lace. Only then did an alarm bell go off in Aida's head.

'No,' she cried out, sobering suddenly and pushing him back.

Phares lifted his head, his arms loosening their hold. 'This was rather more than I had in mind, *chérie*,' she heard him say a little hoarsely. His face was unreadable; the hard, passionate mouth parted in what might be a smile, or was it a sigh?

'That's all right,' she said softly. 'I should have stopped you sooner.'

His mouth twisted derisively. 'You should have but actually I was thinking of myself.'

Aida's breath caught in her throat as she jerked her head up to look at him. The coldness she now read in Phares's glittering ink-black eyes froze her to the core.

'You really are angry with me?' she said uncertainly.

He fixed her with a dark, impenetrable look. 'Not angry ... disappointed.'

Aida felt a warmth colour her cheeks. She bit down on her bottom lip, finding it hard to bear the disapproval written all over him. Why did he always make her feel like she had done something wrong? He had brought her here to 'teach her a lesson', and now he was *disappointed* that she had responded to his advances? She was used to his patronising objection to her comparatively liberal ideas and attitudes, upon which he had always frowned, but this was quite different: he was condemning her!

Embarrassment turned to fury at his hypocrisy.

'I can go back alone, the house isn't far now.'

'On foot?' He gave a mirthless laugh.

'Believe me, I'm perfectly capable.'

'I won't let you do that. No, Aida, I'm not letting you out of my sight until you are safely home.'

'But I *want* to go back by myself,' she insisted hardily.

His tone was clipped. 'Learn to give in gracefully, if nothing else. You're coming with me!'

Aida stood defiantly on the path, hands clenched into fists as she glared up at him. His face, set hard, was a shock to her. It could be a trick of the moonlight, but it seemed bone white and drawn; she could see the veins in his neck stand out as his jaw clenched. In the penumbra, he suddenly looked taller, rather menacing, and disturbingly male.

With a bound, Phares was back in the saddle. 'Step into the stirrups,' he growled, his eyes holding hers. She obeyed – the hypnotic effect of his gaze so compelling that she felt wholly dominated. His arms encircled her, but this time there was a lack of intimacy in his embrace and she knew that the overwhelming connection between them earlier was now broken.

The moon slid out of sight behind a far-off cloud, plunging the night sky into darkness as they rode back to Aida's home, extinguishing the glitter of the calm waters of the canal and the silvery patina on the palms.

*     *     *

Hours later, Phares was finally back at El Shorouk. He paced the room, trying to rub the tension from his neck.

On arrival at Karawan House he and Aida had found Naguib Bishara on tenterhooks as he waited for her. The older man's face had lit up with the most enormous smile when he saw the couple arrive together. Obviously misunderstanding the situation, he had clearly thought that the young doctor had been invited for dinner. He was on the point of leaving when Phares quickly clarified the situation, insisting that he wanted to supervise the retrieval of Aida's Ford convertible, adding that it was only proper as the young woman's delay was all his own fault. Then, reassured that Aida was safely at her house, Phares had gone back to the roadside with a mechanic who maintained the fleet of Pharaony cars. There, he made sure the vehicle was checked thoroughly before being delivered to Karawan House.

By the time he had dealt with the matter, it was past midnight. Busying himself with the car had taken his mind off the turmoil that had warred inside him earlier, but now he felt a storm of feelings rising up again.

Phares had gone through half a pack of Gitanes while waiting for the vehicle to be examined. Smoking usually did the trick, but still he was restless – restless and ashamed. He had gone too far with Aida; she was inexperienced and he should have known better. He wasn't himself at the moment: the way he was behaving with her was so out of character, but all the while he tried to argue in his own defence, he couldn't ignore his foibles. Phares was too honest for that.

He showered and changed into a pair of loose jeans. It was late … already almost two o'clock. Still too charged up, he knew that if he went to bed now, he wouldn't be able to sleep. Where had all this come from? Phares cast a swift glance out of his bedroom window. The Nile, the patriarch of rivers, lay silver and serene in the moonlight. Centuries had come and gone and there he was, the 'Father of All Life', flowing gently in the sweltering darkness, suffering no change that seemed of any account. He wondered at the placid beauty of the picture, and a sudden urge to be near the river possessed him; maybe his agitated soul would become transfused by its imperturbable tranquillity.

Wandering out into the garden he went to the waterfront and sat down on the grass, leaning his back against a large flame tree. The soundless shore was a graceful arc of sand, the moonlight lying across it making it appear as white as snow, while on the farthest bank, a grove of trees was lit by the stars burning hazily overhead. Nestled in between, the Nile meandered through the land like an undulating cobra in smooth, seductive curves: beautiful, cool and secretive. The heavy scent of orange blossom seemed to drench the entire landscape, its potent nightly scent making him slightly lightheaded. His temples beat like drums and his head was aching.

Aida … he couldn't get her out of his mind. A longing filled him, a yearning he had dreamed about but never before experienced, despite his many relationships. From the age of sixteen, women had paraded through Phares's life, and his bed. None had had this effect on him: even Nairy, whose enticing erotic games had for a while satisfied his needs. Aida was different. She was a puzzle to him – she always had been.

Aida El Masri. Ever since they were children he had been drawn to the spirited personality of his sister's best friend. There was a wildness to her that had always interested him, and while Phares often found himself exasperated by her unruly ways, a part of him secretly admired the girl for her audacity. When he thought about it, he remembered that she had been quite pretty too, despite the hint of puppy fat remaining as she reached her teens. He recalled striking eyes that glistened with life, like the blue waters of an oasis. Admittedly, her looks hadn't registered much with him on those summer holidays from medical school. More often than not he had been too busy admonishing Aida for her latest escapade, or baiting her for his own amusement.

It seemed the girl who had always managed to get under his skin was still plaguing him.

But now it was different.

Ever since the day he had laid eyes on Aida at the cottage, he had been brimming with a senseless desire to possess her. Then the sweet confusion of spotting her again at Princess Nazek's ball had been multiplied by the realisation of her identity. His limbs had frozen, along with his brain.

*His beautiful stranger was none other than Aida El Masri?*

That magnificent dress she had worn moulded seductively to her waist and when his eyes had wandered to the lush swell of her flesh above, it made his heart pound in his chest.

This was little Aida El Masri, standing there like a vision, like a woman; and ever since that evening, Phares had been thrown into a turmoil of confusion.

She made the blood burn in his veins, his loins aching with an overpowering need that had kept him awake night after night. He seemed to have no control when in her presence. There was something sensual in her voice, which in womanhood had deepened to a warm contralto, and the generous mouth that begged to be kissed. The seductive allure in the way she moved made him instantly want to run his hands all over the curves of her beautiful body; and then, most of all, there was such innocence in the fine bone structure of her face and the depth of those large, lustrous eyes, the deep colour of the Mediterranean sea. Eyes which, now he had looked into them again after so many years, were still so wonderfully blue and clear, and seemed to study his in an almost detached way. Aida El Masri had grown from an awkward, moody teenager into a fiery temptress who had turned Phares into someone he himself barely recognised.

Twice now he had made a fool of himself; twice he had lost his self-control. And to save his pride, he had managed to deflect attention away from his own unbridled lust. He had used Aida's inexperience with men, had taken advantage of her innocence … oh yes, he knew that she was pure, despite a body that called out to be loved, and savoured every kiss, every caress. The slightest touch fuelled her senses. They had only skimmed the surface of lovemaking and her reactions had not been those of a jaded woman. She was still fresh, a budding flower waiting to bloom, and of that he had no doubt.

The memory of his disappointment when she had pushed him away was as nothing to the guilt which gnawed now at his insides. He wanted Aida. He wanted her for his wife, but more than that, he wanted to get to know her again – this girl with such an independent spirit, who had been through so much and had grown into a woman who was as fascinating to him – and complicated – as she was beautiful.

The tragedy of Ayoub El Masri's death eight years back had scarred Aida, of that he was certain. It was a terrible business which Phares would never forget either. How could he? The devastated look on Aida's face when he had knelt beside Ayoub's lifeless body, unable to resuscitate him, was one that would be forever etched in his memory … and, too, her distraught appearance at El Shorouk the day after the trial. Phares had hoped that her initial animosity to his family had died a natural death with time … but no. It was clear tonight that Aida still carried a heavy burden of grief and anger, and he had badly misjudged her feelings.

He picked up a smooth stone and threw it absentmindedly into the river, watching its distant splash as it hit the surface of the water.

Thinking of how Aida had thrown his offer of marriage back in his face, he winced inwardly. He hadn't been enough for her, it seemed. Incensed, all his pent-up desire had boiled over. Phares knew that he'd been conceited and totally selfish. If only he had been reasonable in the way he had spoken to her they wouldn't have quarrelled, and there might still be some hope for them to have a future together.

As it was, he couldn't envisage them ever getting together now. He had lost her. Lost the wild, free spirit he admired despite himself. Her mocking words reverberated in his head. *I remember you exactly as you always were, Phares Pharaony. Arrogant, haughty and narrow-minded.*

He picked up another stone and hurled it with angry force into the water. He should have handled her more carefully but could she not see that he was trying to protect her?

He began to feel angry with Aida again ... angry, because she wouldn't let go of the foolish and unfounded accusations she'd made against his father. If he could only lay his hands on the person who had filled her head with such calumnious charges, but the El Masris' maid Souma Hassanein had disappeared immediately after Ayoub's arrest and all his efforts to find the woman had been fruitless – it was if the ground had swallowed her up. That in itself was the greatest proof that the maid's allegations had been pure fabrication. Still, one question never ceased hammering at him: why should a woman who'd been virtually a stranger to the Pharaony family invent such a story? What did she have to gain? Even if she had a bone to pick with Ayoub, or even Aida, why had she involved Kamel Pharaony? Had someone else put her up to it?

Sighing, Phares closed his eyes and struggled against the overwhelming anguish washing through him.

The only way to conquer Aida was to find out the truth about how the Nefertari statue had landed at Karawan House, and exonerate both their fathers: Ayoub from theft and Kamel from betraying his best friend. But for now, he needed to find the right time to speak to Aida, to apologise for his behaviour.

*       *       *

During the following days Aida avoided the Pharaony Estate, reluctant to put herself in the way of Phares's sarcastic comments again. There was hot rebellion in her heart and yet also a terrible, gnawing regret for this latest wedge between them. It was made worse by the knowledge that she had acted so wantonly. This, coupled with the horrible things she had said to him that night at the pyramids, left her uneasy with guilt, despite her anger. In fact, where Phares was concerned, nothing about Aida's feelings was clear to her. Deep down she knew that on the morning she had first seen him again, somewhere a door had closed on her antipathy towards him, but a new one was yet to open.

Aida was also aware of a certain restlessness at being home, a feeling that the life which eight years ago had completely satisfied her was somehow now lacking in purpose. She had lost her father, of course, and had gone through a war. So much had happened to her, and she had learnt from an early age that in life nothing ever remains static.

So, helped by *Dada* Amina, she busied herself with the preparations for Easter and *Sham El Nessim*. There were the eggs to boil and colour and the salted fish to prepare. Both customs were attached to rituals that dated from the days of the pharaohs. Aida had grown up with these traditions which Ayoub never broke, and this year she planned to revive them. As she had been invited to Uncle Naguib's for Easter, she offered to bring over the eggs and fish.

The colouring of eggs was mentioned in the pharaohs' *Book of the Dead*, and in Akhnaton's chants: '*God is one. He created life from the inanimate and he created chicks from eggs.*' A symbol of life to Ancient Egyptians, they had decorated the eggs in various patterns, writing their wishes on the shells. Then they would tuck them in baskets made of palm fronds and hang them on trees or the roofs of their houses in the hope that, by dawn, the gods would answer their wishes. As a child, Aida used to write her wish on a couple of eggs, much like children write letters to Father Christmas, and hide them in a large basket among all the others she and her father had assembled between them. If her wish had been for a toy of some sort, she'd always find it on her bed; and if it were some other sort of wish, Ayoub always tried to grant it to her, whether it was a picnic on a felucca on the Nile or a night-time visit to the Temple of Karnak when the moon was out.

Fish were highly valued in Ancient Egypt and, as such, were a crucial part of the Easter festivities. They were easily caught when the waters receded from the annual Nile flood, which enriched the earth and left them trapped in natural pools, and their abundance symbolised fertility and wellbeing. Salted seer fish, or *melouha*, was offered to the gods in Esna in Upper Egypt to ensure a good harvest, and indeed the city's ancient name was Lathpolis, the pharaonic name for the fish before it is salted. Most people bought the *melouha* ready-made, but both the Pharaony and Ayoub families had it prepared at home, the elaborate process having been passed down from father to son.

A week before *Sham El Nessim*, *Dada* Amina had herself been to the market to buy the fresh seer which had to be washed thoroughly, then dried for at least twenty-four hours until it turned white and the skin was crusty and hard. As a child, Aida used to watch her at work at the large kitchen table, filling the gills of the dried seer with coarse salt so they remained open, covering the rest of the fish in salt and placing it in clear polythene bags. When she was older, Aida would be allowed to help the housekeeper create neat parcels to ensure warmth and avoid air, doing this meticulously so the fish would not become contaminated. The *melouha* was ready once the seer turned silvery and shiny.

Easter parties the day before *Sham El Nessim* were always hosted by Uncle Naguib and Aunt Nabila at Esbat El Fardouz, Paradise Farm, and the festivities always had a delightfully informal air, characteristic of the place. A few miles from Luxor's centre, the estate was not on the banks of the Nile, but much further into the countryside. It nestled among the single-storey mud houses thatched with straw in which the hens roosted, and was surrounded by the sweet-smelling flowering bean fields, intersected by canals and full of dark Nile silt. On this occasion, cloth for a new kaftan and food were distributed to all the *fellahin* and their families.

Although in an elevated position, Esbat El Fardouz did not hold itself above the poorer dwellings in spirit, bound together as they were by the land, with the unbreakable bonds of the lush Egyptian countryside. There were no great walls surrounding the property, only tall palm trees soaring overhead, and although not as large as either Kasr El Shorouk or Karawan House, Esbat El Fardouz was nonetheless an estate of considerable size. Naguib and his wife Nabila were loved by the *fellahin* who worked on their land, and although it was a Christian celebration, the couple treated Easter as an *eed* – a feast for everyone – to be celebrated before next day's *Sham El Nessim*, which the Bisharas always spent at the Pharaonys.

Naguib and Nabila's guests consisted of a group of middle-class professionals: doctors, lawyers and accountants from Luxor and Aswan, whom Aida had never met. They came with their children and grandchildren and were a lively and friendly but unsophisticated group who talked a lot, laughed a lot and ate even more. Each brought with them their special dish to be shared at a large buffet set up in the garden, where the decorated eggs formed a colourful centrepiece. Guests sat themselves either in the shade on the terrace on comfortable chairs and sofas or at large, round tables on the grass, surrounded by trellises of sweet peas and herbaceous borders of delphiniums, peonies, lupins, phlox, snapdragons and asters in blues, burgundies, purples and gold. It was a civilised but noisy affair – everyone mingling happily, all speaking at once as Egyptians are prone to do, and tucking into the vast array of dishes.

Aunt Nabila was an excellent cook. She owned an upmarket bakery where she sold her cakes, speciality breads and pastries. She always joked that the reason Naguib married her was for her cooking. Her *fitir*, Aida's favourite, was known all over Luxor. A hot dish made of layers of stretched and folded pastry dough brushed all over with *samna baladi*, clarified butter, it was baked until crusty and served with molasses and *kishtat laban*, a thick cream made from buffalo milk. 'A recipe for a heart attack,' Aida had often heard

Phares describe it as he watched her and Camelia tuck into large sheets of *fitir* whenever it appeared on the breakfast table.

Nabila Bishara was a beautiful woman with smiling hazel eyes and chestnut hair, who always reminded Aida of a lioness. She had been like a surrogate mother to her ever since Eleanor El Masri died, and ever protective, she now immediately busied herself reintroducing Aida to the Bisharas' circle of friends.

'I bumped into Camelia Pharaony while having lunch yesterday at the Winter Palace Hotel,' Nabila said, as they wandered over to a group of guests. 'She told me she'd invited you to the Pharaonys' brunch party tomorrow.' She gave Aida a knowing look, her eyes shining. 'You are going, aren't you, *habibti*?'

'Well, I have accepted.'

Aunt Nabila smiled. 'Good. The Pharaonys give wonderful parties, and *Sham El Nessim* is one not to be missed.' She picked up two glasses of white wine from the buffet table and handed one to Aida. 'And you and Phares … you are getting to know each other again?'

*You could say that,* Aida thought wryly with a slight flush in her cheeks at the recollection of what had happened between them only a few nights before. She accepted the chilled wine her aunt offered and took a sip. 'We spoke at Princess Nazek's ball,' she answered non-committally.

'You two must have even more to talk about now. Phares is such a hard-working doctor and you being a nurse. Come to think of it, Naguib should talk to him about you going to work with him at his hospital.'

Aida's face brightened. 'Do you think he will? I must admit, I'd love to have something useful to do again.' If Uncle Naguib were to approach Phares it would be so much easier than if she were to do so. Particularly at the moment.

'Of course, *habibti*. You and Phares would work well together.' Nabila squeezed Aida's arm affectionately.

Suddenly the idea of working with Phares threw Aida slightly off balance. Seeing their conversation was heading in a direction she would rather avoid, she took another sip of wine and asked: 'Who do you think will be at the brunch tomorrow?'

'Oh, all of the big families in Luxor. Plus, the Williamses, the Lesters, the Carlisles and other British Embassy people from Cairo, I should think.'

'Alastair Carlisle? Yes, I met him at Princess Nazek's party. He'll be a friendly face.'

Aunt Nabila patted her hand. '*Habibti*, they'll all be friendly, I'm sure. Everyone is pleased you're back and wants to see you again. Come, there are more guests wanting to meet you. I'm sure they're all wondering who this beautiful young woman is, and don't realise it's our little Aida come home again.'

She laughed and kissed Nabila fondly on the cheek, dutifully accompanying her to a new group of cheerful guests, many of whom, she soon realised, had known her and Ayoub, and were keen to find out how Aida's life had been in England. All without exception took the opportunity to commiserate with her about her father's death, and although they did not dwell on what was such a painful subject for Aida, it was clear the Bisharas' circle was united in declaring the whole business of Ayoub's trial a fiasco. Aida was grateful to feel the warmth of this friendly, genuine crowd and they reminded her of all that she had missed about Egyptian family life.

It was during lunch, while Aida was settled at one of the round tables in the garden, that Phares Pharaony's name had arisen.

'Have you been to his new hospital, El Amal?' asked Samiha, one of the younger women, a neighbour of the Bisharas who had brought her three young children. She was addressing a plump woman with a hooked nose and shiny black eyes sitting opposite her.

Aida pricked up her ears.

'Yes, it's wonderful. He's done a really good job of it. All the equipment is state of the art. Isis Geratly showed me around. She's a lovely girl.'

'I agree, a brilliant doctor too, by all accounts. I've never heard of a female anaesthetist before.'

'Yes, yes, very impressive. Times are certainly changing.'

'Mind you, she must be almost thirty now, and not yet married. What a waste.'

The plump woman leaned forward to take a large piece of *mahallabeya*, an Egyptian custard donut covered in syrup. 'I'm told she's had many suitors, but she's turned them all down. Ghalia, the *khatba*, matchmaker, says that she's jinxed. Someone has made her an *aamal*, cast an evil spell on her.'

'Nonsense,' replied Samiha. 'She has her eye on Dr Phares, that's all. She's been in love with him for ever. Six months ago, there was talk of an engagement, but it seems to have gone quiet lately. Still, she's ambitious in every way, if you know what I mean, so I wonder what's going on there.'

Aida's spoon had paused in her *fitir*. Perhaps the women had forgotten that she was there, or that she had once been promised to Phares, in any case they continued merrily in their speculation.

'Yes, I heard,' said the other woman, munching on the *mahallabeya* enthusiastically. 'I think it's because of that Armenian girl. You know, Nairy Paplosian, the model. Apparently, a couple of years ago he wanted to marry her, but his father put a stop to it. I'm not surprised – imagine a Pharaony heir marrying a small-time Armenian jeweller's daughter …'

'A misalliance … unheard of in such a conservative family.'

'Nairy is Phares's *grand amour*, I'm sure of it. He still sees her when he goes to Cairo. I spotted them a few months ago in Gezireh, coming out of a building next to the Anglo-American Hospital. I think he keeps a *garçonnière* there.'

'Have you finished gossiping, you two? *Eib ya sitat, ya mohtarameen*, shame on you, honourable ladies,' said a rotund little man with a neat moustache, shaking his head as he got up from the table to go and inspect the buffet for a second time.

Samiha laughed. 'Don't be a hypocrite, Botros. You enjoy a good gossip just as we do.' Still, she quickly changed the subject to the more mundane topic of the soaring price of sugar.

One of the reasons why Aida had been happy to leave Egypt was because of this type of gossip, which Ayoub had also deplored. 'You can't sneeze in Luxor without everybody knowing about it,' he used to tell her. Aida knew these casual conversations concerning other people occurred in all societies, but the communities in Egypt were small. Before you knew it, one embroidered word had led to another, and a minor incident soon ended up blown way out of proportion.

Although her foolish heart had been thumping so hard against her ribs she'd thought it would break, Aida had tried to assume a blank look throughout the women's exchange. Anyway, they had been far too engrossed to notice her sitting at their table.

So, Phares's heart belonged Nairy Paplosian.

Dismayed at the ungovernable manner in which her feelings had reacted to this news, Aida now suppressed them even more determinedly. The knowledge was bitter, but it was ridiculous to have been surprised that Phares had attachments, she told herself. Women always wilted under his charm.

He had a presence, an aura that commanded attention wherever he went. Perhaps it was a product of his profession. Maybe he had cultivated that air of authority to inspire confidence in nervous patients looking for reassurance. Still, Aida had to admit, Phares had everything a woman desired: looks, wealth, position and a kind heart – even if a lot of the time he was arrogant and full of himself. It would be illogical for him to have still been free after eight years.

Although she had never met Nairy Paplosian, Aida had seen photographs of the beautiful model plastered all over Egyptian glossy magazines like *El Kawakib*, and she had seen the fashion diva's face on posters all over Cairo, advertising her forthcoming film.

As for Isis Geratly, the elegant anaesthetist, Aida knew her well. Closer to Phares's age, she had grown up as part of the same close circle of children whose parents owned estates around Luxor and the neighbouring villages. Aida had never liked her much. She had to confess that she had been jealous of Isis's looks and confident behaviour, at a time when Phares viewed Aida as little more than an unsophisticated, rebellious butterball. An intelligent girl, Isis had always played up to him, pressing their shared interest in medicine, although hers was by no means driven by the same passion to improve the health of the *fellahin*. In fact, Aida often suspected that Isis had followed Phares into medicine partly as a way of staying close to him. It was no surprise therefore that she had joined him at his hospital.

Still, thinking back now, she remembered her father saying that he wasn't the least duped by Isis's phony affectations. 'She's very much like her father,' he used to say, 'all puff and no consistency or weight.' Ayoub had made his own assessment of Isis's father, Adly Geratly, a noted historian. Geratly was a lecturer at Cairo University and a commentator on policy regarding heritage; in many ways he was considered ahead of his time, but according to Ayoub – who was a stickler for detail – he often based his arguments on inadequate research.

Now, try as she might to reason with herself, the day seemed suddenly meaningless to Aida. She had found the food delicious up until then, relishing each delicacy which marked this special occasion; now she might have been eating sawdust from the way it stuck in her throat. How was it possible that in such a short time Phares's handsome features had been carved on her heart, his magic touch stencilled upon every inch of her body, and the poetic words he'd uttered that night at the pyramids imprinted on her mind? He had stirred new emotions in her, set her senses on fire, and aroused the devil in parts of her she had no idea could spring to life. What a fool he'd made of her. He had even tried to persuade her to *marry* him ... and all the time he had two other women in tow. Hell would freeze over before she'd let that son of a b— touch her, Aida vowed fiercely.

It was a pity she had promised Camelia she would attend the *Sham El Nessim* party at Hathor the next day. Of course she could make her excuses and say she was ill. She could blame the heavy food for giving her indigestion, but somehow Aida couldn't escape the fact that she wanted to see Phares, needed to see him again, and she hated herself for her weakness.

Still, Aida was a young woman of pride and independence and as she stole some time to herself by wandering through the gardens down to the orchards of mango and guava trees, she remembered that Phares held not one, but two hiding places where he could indulge in his carnal pleasures ... Yet he had twice virtually abducted her, driven her to the pyramids and spoken to her of marriage, of caring for her, of treating her like a queen ...

The heavy disappointment in her heart gave way to a hot anger in her belly. How dare he treat her this way? Phares Pharaony, a born philanderer, had played on her inexperience with men. He had toyed with her senses and then made her feel as though she had been the one to blame for succumbing to him.

Had he meant her to feel that way, pushing her to the limit, testing her to see how far she would be led into his game? If he was truly interested in making her his wife, perhaps he wanted to find out whether Aida's years in England during the war had weakened her morals and turned her into a wholly unsuitable match. After all, he was an Egyptian man steeped in the traditional culture of his country and tribe. There was undoubtedly a darker side to him of which his sister was either unaware or ignored. The way he had treated Aida was cruel and heartless, and she pitied anybody who made the mistake of getting involved with Phares Pharaony. It was probably indicative of his chauvinistic attitude towards women that he wasn't yet married, but judging by the conversation she had overheard today it was not for want of opportunity. She'd been a gullible fool, playing right into his hands, and it was a good thing that *she* had not the slightest intention of marrying him.

Well, now he could carry on with both of his mistresses, damn him!

With this renewed resolution, Aida endeavoured to smother the last spark of fire that had burned in her heart for Phares all these years.

The meal dragged on until late afternoon. All the while, Aida pasted a smile on her face, taking part in the lively celebrations as best she could, not wanting to let the Bisharas down by brooding in a corner. When it was over, she took her leave, relieved to escape back to the sanctuary of Karawan House.

She wished heartily that she had found happiness in England and had stayed away from Egypt altogether. Still, no matter how much she tried to convince herself that Phares wasn't going to have any effect on her life, Aida had a disquieting premonition of change already looming on the horizon – and not change for the better, either.

# CHAPTER 6

*Sham El Nessim* dawned as one of those mornings when one felt that life could not be sweeter. Karawan House, with its pink walls smothered in scarlet oleander and plumbago, looked over its green lawns shaded by heavy branches of cream bougainvillea, drowsing dreamily in the early golden sun. From its elevated position next to the Nile, the gilded rolling dunes of Thebes were clearly visible across the miles of sparkling water. In the sycamores, the birds burst forth in vociferous chirping, heralding the birth of spring.

Aida had risen early. *Dada* Amina woke her up at the crack of dawn with a plate of spring onions that she encouraged Aida to inhale. This custom of breathing in onions was another ritual inherited from the Ancient Egyptians from a legend found on a papyrus, which told the story of a much-loved young prince who was struck down by an unknown disease and bedridden for years, during which time the people abstained from celebrating festivals in sympathy for the King Pharaoh and his son. The king summoned the archpriest of the Temple of Oun, who diagnosed the boy's sickness as having been caused by evil spirits. The priest ordered that a ripe spring onion be placed under the patient's head. He then sliced a second onion and put it on the boy's nose so that he would breathe in the vapours. The prince soon recovered and festivities were held in the palace to mark the occasion, which coincided with the beginning of spring.

Throughout Aida's childhood, Ayoub had made sure that ancient rites such as this were observed, and it was with a nostalgic sentiment that the young woman had decided to keep them alive, much to the delight of *Dada* Amina, who went a step further and, like many modern Egyptians, hung bunches of spring onions at the front door to Karawan House 'to keep the evil eye away' and prevent envy.

Although Aida had not slept well that night, on waking and going out to her terrace, the exciting freshness of a new day, all golden and smiling, had lifted her spirits. Having almost three hours before she was due at Hathor for the brunch party, she took her time preparing for the occasion, carefully going over the new clothes she had bought in Cairo.

Finally, she decided upon a bright-blue polka dot summer dress with puffed sleeves and a full skirt caught up in a belt that hugged her wasp-waisted figure. The pearl buttons fastened all the way down, a practical style popularised by the fashionable Hollywood starlet Phyllis Brooks, and gratefully embraced by wartime women habitually in a rush. Aida's feet were clad in a pair of Salvatore Ferragamo plaited raffia and cork wedge-sole peep-toes which, since the war, had been all the rage because of the restriction on raw materials. A small blue sapphire cross on a gold chain was the only jewellery she wore and with her honey-blonde hair cascading down her shoulders in sleek waves like a curtain of silk and just a hint of mascara and carmine lipstick, there was an untouched air about her that presented a picture of extreme youth with a provocative touch of elegance.

Aida drove to Hathor. As she approached it, the sun filtering through trees threw torch-like beams on the lush green garden, which lay like a cultured diamond in the barbaric setting of the desert's sand and rocks, with the Nile glittering at its feet.

When she arrived, the wide heavy doorway was open to the villa. The interior was filled with roses and lilies, and guests were welcomed at the door by *suffragis* in blue-and-white striped *shahi* material kaftans and showed into the garden, where tables had been set out under a huge loggia covered in vines. Aida glanced up at the familiar blue stained-glass domed ceiling as she was led through the house and felt that same ripple of memories as when she had visited the Pharaonys' house in Cairo. The very air here was flavoured with potent recollections of the past, and a grandeur that was unforgettable. She loved the sense of spacious elegance of the house, the cool beauty of silky Persian rugs on the polished hall floor, the walls against which family portraits glowed, the furniture and pedestals incredibly lovely in shape and design, the strange mingling of simplicity and wealth – and everywhere, flowers, their colour, their fragrance, invading shadowy corners.

In the garden the sun spilled down on the crimson, violet, primrose and blue petals of flowers, brilliant beacons to the bees circling around. The air was filled with the sound of cicadas mingling fluidly with that of muted voices rising and falling, punctuated occasionally by soft feminine laughter as guests drifted around. Waiters hovered among them with trays of lemonade, wine and cordial. There were about seventy guests in all, mainly made up of families from large estates and a few noted foreigners from the diplomatic corps, chatting and drinking in small groups. A very different affair to the lunch she had attended the day before at the Bisharas. As a girl, Aida had been accustomed to the luxurious status of Hathor, but today she was inclined to see it anew through fresh eyes. Yes, she noted, there was a definite aroma of richness in the air, expensive cigars, exclusive scents and *signé* clothes – the war had definitely passed Luxor by.

She stiffened when she caught sight of the unmistakable figure of Phares's aunt coming towards her, clutching a glass of *sharbat ward* cordial. The eldest sister of Kamel Pharaony, and a spinster, Aunt Halima lived at Hathor, where she had acted as housekeeper since Camelia's marriage to Mounir, five years before. Short and round, she had eyes of an extraordinary shade of brown, the only redeeming feature in a face that told a tale of regular displeasure. The occasional strand of her once black hair could still be seen though the lifeless grey nest of tight and somewhat frizzy curls that framed her round face.

Aida knew Aunt Halima had always disliked her; nevertheless, she gamely fixed a smile on her face.

'So, Aida El Masri is back, eh?' Halima said, coming to a halt in front of her and looking Aida up and down sourly. 'You had some flesh on you when you left but now you've turned scrawny. All that bad English food, I shouldn't wonder.'

As Halima herself had always reminded Aida of an angry fat pigeon, the young woman wasn't surprised at such a remark but refrained from rising to the bait, knowing it would only invite more rancorous comments. 'Aunty Halima, it's been a long time. How are you?'

'Well enough. Trying to look after what's left of my family. I heard you didn't find a husband in England so I suppose you're back here to make eyes at my nephew again.'

Aida's nostrils flared with suppressed irritation. 'I can assure you, Aunty, I have no intention of—'

'Well, Phares has plenty of other *respectable* Coptic girls to consider,' Halima interrupted, plucking a *mezzeh* from the tray of a passing waiter, 'so you'd better set your sights lower. Isis Geratly is here with her father. A girl from a fine family. Phares gave her a job working side by side with him at his hospital. She has been a great help to him while he's been building up his clinic.' Aunt Halima clearly felt the need to say no more. She gave Aida a final sullen stare as she munched her falafel and marched off in the opposite direction.

*Poisonous old witch.*

Aida took a deep breath to calm herself down. She looked about her and spotted Phares immediately. He was standing a few feet away, engrossed in deep conversation with Alastair Carlisle and two other portly Egyptian men. His arm was lightly imprisoned in the grasp of a woman with her back to Aida, who wore a fashionable cream linen dress with broad bands of blue, red, green and yellow around the waist and flared skirt. Her thick black hair was coiled on the crown of her head in a braided chignon and as her classic profile turned towards Phares with a smile and a murmured comment, Aida saw that it was Isis. She noticed the young doctor's mouth widen in easy response, his head slightly inclined, dark eyes resting on his companion's upturned face with thoughtful appraisal. There seemed to be a definite rapport between the two of them.

Even as a girl, Isis Geratly had always been attractive, poised and sophisticated; now, as a young woman, she was beautiful, elegant and charismatic. Aida felt a hard knot slowly forming inside her. Here was one of those 'respectable Coptic girls' who were falling over themselves to become Mrs Phares Pharaony, she thought darkly.

'Aida, how lovely you look!' She spun round to see Camelia, who had detached herself from a group of foreign ladies and was rushing to greet her. A beaming smile lit up her fine features as she welcomed her friend with the usual greeting reserved for feast occasions.

'*Kulle sana w'inty tayyeba, habibti*, may you be well every year, my dear!'

'*W'inty tayeba*, and you too,' Aida replied, her dark thoughts evaporating at the sight of her friend's delighted face.

'Was that Aunty Halima I just saw talking to you? I bet she was overjoyed to see you, no?' Camelia's mouth quivered with amusement.

'*Mmm*, I've never seen that woman overjoyed about anything.'

Camelia laughed out loud. 'Come, let me introduce you to people.'

The two women moved away, passing some guests who were having their glasses topped up. One of them, a bespectacled Egyptian man in a pale suit surveying the room as he sipped his drink, caught sight of Camelia and quickly detached himself from the group.

'Camelia, *Kulle sana w'inty tayyeba, habibti*, another wonderful *Sham El Nessim*. Let me say, your family always gives the best parties,' he exclaimed smoothly. His light brown eyes were brightly alert behind his round spectacles, though his smile, which revealed a slight gap between his front teeth, seemed slightly vacant. With an uncomfortable jolt of recognition, Aida saw that it was Adly Geratly.

The years had barely changed Isis's father and his even, quite handsome features were strikingly similar to his daughter's, as was his studied air. As a child, Aida had not met him often as the Geratlys tended to frequent the high-society parties more than the informal gatherings that the El Masris preferred, and now she hoped that she would not have to make awkward conversation with him for too long.

'*W'inty tayeba*. Thank you, Uncle Adly.' Camelia shot Aida a look before continuing, 'Of course this year is a particularly special one because our dear Aida is back with us. You remember Aida El Masri?'

Adly Geratly turned his inquisitive eyes on Aida and she registered his fleeting surprise as he shook her hand. 'Of course I remember Aida,' he said without hesitation, his voice pleasant and not particularly deep. 'All you girls grew up together. Welcome home, *habibti*. I didn't realise this party was in your honour.' He smiled, peering at her through his glasses.

'Thank you, Adly *Bey*,' answered Aida.

'You've been away from our country a long time.' He gave her an inscrutable look. 'Are you back to stay for good?'

Aware that she was being appraised, Aida's answer was non-committal. 'Well, I have a lot of work to sort out on the estate.'

She accepted a glass from the tray of lemonade a *suffragi* was passing around and smiled at him blandly as she took a sip.

'Of course Aida is staying,' said Camelia, nudging her friend affectionately as she helped herself to a glass too. 'She belongs here, with us.'

Another male voice entered the conversation. 'Well, that is rather good news.'

Aida turned around with a laugh, relieved when she saw that Alastair Carlisle had joined them. 'Mr Carlisle, how lovely to see you again.'

'Likewise, Miss El Masri. I must say, it would be a shame to lose such a charming member of our community again.'

'Indeed,' chimed Adly Geratly. 'I was just saying, Alastair, that Aida has been gone too long.' His gaze returned to her. 'You must feel like a foreigner after living in England for so long. I'm sure Isis would show you around all the old places when she has time.'

Aida was reminded why her father had disliked Adly so much. There was an air of condescension in the way he continually smiled as he spoke, and how he liked to be the focus of attention. Aware that he was attempting to deflate her, she answered lightly, 'Oh, I don't need to bother Isis, thank you. Phares has already offered to take us around Cairo, isn't that right, Camelia?' She flashed her friend a mischievous look.

Camelia hid her surprise admirably. 'Ah, yes, of course ... we are both looking forward to it, *habibti*.'

'That is excellent,' said Geratly, though his smile faded slightly. 'Phares is a dutiful brother.' He turned to the consul: 'Speaking of duty, Alastair, how are your investigations going into those recent tomb lootings in Qurna?'

'Now then, Geratly, you know I'm not at liberty to discuss our activities,' Alastair answered pleasantly.

'So, no leads then,' the other answered, lighting a cigarette.

Alastair would not be drawn. 'Suffice to say, these lootings would be curtailed if the Qurnawis weren't living in the tombs and mining for valuable artefacts.'

'Qurna is a problem that isn't going to go away,' interjected Camelia. 'The war has taken the tourists from Egypt, so it's no surprise that desperate *fellahin* have been looting.'

'The Egyptian authorities want to solve that problem by getting the Qurnawis out somehow,' said Alastair.

'But surely it's the same all over Egypt,' offered Aida. 'These antique dealers are getting their hands on stolen antiquities all the time. While foreign Egyptologists are here selling these artefacts for thousands of pounds to their foreign buyers, there will always be looters. They are simply supplying a market.'

'Yes, yes, that is true, young lady,' said Geratly, regarding her through a blue haze of smoke. 'But one must understand, these objects have always been taken and sold on.' He gave a huff of amusement. 'Even the Egyptian Museum is selling genuine artefacts in its gift shop. And after all, who owns the past? Can we claim ancient artefacts as our cultural property? We ourselves are almost an entirely different culture to our Ancient Egyptian ancestors, are we not? I have written a paper on just such a subject.'

Aida raised an eyebrow. 'There are many Egyptians who would fiercely disagree with you, Adly *Bey*. My father certainly would have been hotly opposed to that line of thought. He argued passionately for preserving our antiquities here in Egypt.'

'Ah yes, as I recall, your father often enjoyed baiting me on this subject.' He produced another thin smile and stared at her with a sad shake of his head. 'A tragic business, his death. Ayoub was a talented man. Such a waste.'

His affectation of sincerity made Aida's hackles rise but she kept her tone neutral. 'Many would say that our connection to our ancestors is bound up with our identity as a nation. They have a value to us that is unique.'

'And do you share this sense of identity, Aida?' Geratly looked at her unblinkingly. 'I mean, only your father was Egyptian.'

'You must forgive me, Uncle Adly,' interjected Camelia with forced brightness, throwing a look at her friend, 'but I must steal Aida away. We'll soon be opening the buffet for breakfast and there are so many people wanting to meet her again after so long.'

'Yes, I'm sure,' answered Geratly with a distracted smile, his gaze already roaming beyond them.

Brunch was delicious, the company lively and fun, but Aida's throat felt constricted. All through the morning she mingled with the guests talking, smiling, and performing her movements mechanically, almost like a robot. No matter how much effort she made not to follow Phares with her eyes, he was like a magnet to her senses. For Aida, the swirling kaleidoscope of colour, the brilliant and elegant men and women, the beautiful grounds with their specimen trees and vivid-hued flowers under a cloudless azure sky were drowned out of consciousness; everything was a void in which Phares's dark head and face stood out starkly, the centre of the small universe of laughing, warmly admiring friends and relations, and Isis taking his arm as they moved from group to group, casual and easy, as though she had done it a hundred times before. For a split second, Aida deeply resented him – it was as though he was deliberately shutting her out.

In order to fight her restless absorption with him, she assumed a bright exterior and attempted to chat cheerfully to women, and rather flirtatiously with men. With mingled irritation and self-pity, she fell to giving a reasonable performance of a young woman enjoying herself and her successive partners laughed appreciatively, gazing admiringly at her, doing their level best to stay with her until their wives and fiancées galloped in to break them up.

Isis did not leave Phares's side, and he seemed attentive to her in the most natural of ways: sitting, talking with gleaming amusement-filled eyes, one hand gesturing, the other holding a glass. During brunch he once looked up abruptly mid-sentence and trapped Aida's gaze, his black brows lifting. As she met his intent coal-black stare, her heart fluttered. He smiled and winked at her, and she managed to raise her glass of wine and smile coolly back at him.

After brunch it was time for the garden entertainment. The Pharaonys' guests gathered first to watch a juggler who also swallowed knives and ate fire and then a conjurer, the *háwee*. This one called himself the 'Gully Gully Man' – the reason for it becoming quickly clear when he began to perform his tricks. Instead of blowing through the *háwee's zummárah*, the large shell used by most sleight-of-hand performers, he would cry out, '*Gully, gully, gully, gully*'. To Aida's delight, as she took her seat next to Camelia, she recognised him as the same old Nubian magician who used to enliven her birthday parties when she was a child.

After executing a few amusing tricks – drawing a great quantity of coloured silk handkerchiefs from his mouth and blowing out fire, then placing his skull cap in a large covered box, saying his magic words, uncovering the box and producing a small army of chicks – the conjurer asked for someone in the audience to entrust him with a valuable ring. Camelia reached forward and offered him her diamond engagement ring.

Taking the ring, the magician put it in a small box. '*Gully, gully, gully, gully*,' came the magic words, and then, '*Efreet*, change it!' Opening the box, he showed the audience a cheap white metal ring, which was met with amused murmurs. Closing the box and opening it again, he produced a lump of metal which he declared to be the ring melted, and offered it to Camelia, who insisted with a laugh on having her ring back in its original state. The conjurer then asked her for one Egyptian pound to recast it and, closing the box again and uttering the *gully gully* incantation, he opened it and took out the original ring.

The next entertainment act was a dance show by a Brazilian couple, Sabina and Thiago Madriguera. Delighted, Aida clapped her hands with joy, recognising them as the pair who had lit up London during the war, and whose dance classes she had attended once or twice. In 1942 they had taken over a warehouse in the capital's Covent Garden and turned it into a dance centre where they taught sensuous, flamboyant dances like the samba, tango and rumba. Every Saturday night men and women congregated there to drink and take part in a dancing competition. One could hardly move in the press of bodies and those dance evenings were always full of uniforms of all nations, men and women home for a short leave and then gone.

Thiago and Sabina were both in their thirties, a good-looking, lively pair. Aida wasn't the only one who had adored their dance evenings. Many others had appreciated how they had helped wartime Londoners escape the mundane, the misery of rationing and the hard, physical work involved in most people's jobs. Their motto, 'Dance as if you are making love to your partner here on the floor', helped break the ice among strangers. Thanks to Sabina and Thiago, you could live your dreams for a few hours and come out of their dancehall lighthearted, transported to another world for a short while. Aida had been one of the lucky ones who had attracted Thiago's eye for regular special lessons, but she hadn't taken him up on his offer. Meeting individuals who were 'here today, gone tomorrow' was a poignant part of her day-to-day life on the wards, and she preferred to read a book, go to the cinema, or just sleep whenever she had any time to spare.

Having performed their act, Thiago announced he would like to choose someone from the audience to help him with his next – a tango. His eyes roamed the tables and he headed towards Aida, but before he could state his request, Phares had left his seat next to Isis and was whispering urgently to him and then to Isis, who rose to her feet. The dancer bowed to Phares's command and escorted Isis out of the circle of tables as everyone applauded.

Aida froze in her chair. What was Phares doing? How dare he! Had he thought her incapable of assisting in the act? Isis, of course, was as much at home in the limelight as sitting there at the table, and it had all happened so fast and Phares had handled the situation so smoothly that she was sure that few people guessed the dancer had been fobbed off with the one he hadn't chosen. Aida couldn't help but take it as a personal slight, though she hid it well, cogniscent of the fact that she was Phares's guest.

As a violinist and accordion player started up their tango music, Aida forced herself to stay in her seat while the elegant Isis, clearly delighted to be clasped in Thiago's confident embrace in front of the assembled guests, was instructed in the steps of the dance. Although Isis executed the moves imprecisely, she was eminently watchable; below her cinched waist, the flared skirt of her dress swished becomingly around her long legs as she moved, and her perfect glossy chignon accentuated her graceful neck and classic beauty. Aida's gaze flickered over to where Phares was sitting, pensive and unmoving, seemingly riveted by the dance. Her heart gave a painful squeeze and she looked away, her eyes determinedly watching the musicians.

After the dance act, in an effort to get away from it all for a few moments, Aida went to sit in the shade of a sycamore, trying to concentrate on the scenery of the Nile as though it were a colourful film unrolling before her. Behind her in the garden, tiny puffs of smoke floated up into the soft spring sunshine from the delicious aroma of spit-roast lamb, koftas and kebabs, gently cooking on the charcoal fires. The air was warm and from time to time the refreshing breeze whispered in the trees, making the leaves rustle with a light swishing sound. Most of the guests had left after the performance, including Isis, and only a handful remained for an early supper. Although Aida had been eager to return home after such a frustrating day, she had stayed on because Camelia had very sweetly asked her to. She felt sorry for her friend who, despite putting on a brave face in public, Aida sensed was still grieving for her husband.

A movement caught her eye through the trees. Holding a basket of coloured eggs, Phares, jeans encasing his narrow hips and sinewy thighs, was ambling towards her. The tan of his muscled forearms stood out against a short-sleeved shirt in the palest of blues that clung to his broad chest, imparting a leopard's grace to every lithe movement. He came to a stop under the tree and stood looking down at her, feet slightly apart, big and powerful and devastatingly sexual.

Exposed to a virility that was normally hidden beneath his more formal or riding outfits, a frisson crept up Aida's spine. The churning, treacherous feeling was back inside her. She wanted badly to run, yet another part of her wanted just as much to stay. Aida only wished she could sort out what she *did* feel right now.

Silently, Phares stretched out the basket towards her.

Aida swallowed to clear the peculiar tightness in her throat. 'Thank you,' she murmured as she helped herself to a royal-blue coloured egg.

Phares sat next to her on the grass and placed the basket between them. Saying nothing, his serious gaze flickered over her, a trace of questioning in the depths of his eyes.

He picked up a red egg and surrounded it with his fingers, leaving just a small part uncovered. 'Want to crack an egg?'

Without looking at him, Aida hit the top of the egg with her blue one, cracking it with the first tap.

'You're going to break my heart.'

'Really? Who says?'

'Isn't it a traditional belief that the person whose egg is cracked will have their heart broken?'

Only then did Aida lift her head to meet his smiling face. 'No, you've just made that one up to flirt with me.'

'Can't people flirt and yet remain friends?'

She shook her head. 'No. Men start by just flirting then they – they ...'

'Can't you say it?' Phares grinned. 'Well, there isn't any harm in any of that. It's all rather delicious, *chérie* ... for the woman as well as the man.' His eyes were full of devilry.

Aida ignored the remark. 'The way the story goes is that the one whose egg doesn't break will have good luck in the future. Maybe I'll be fortunate enough that you'll leave me alone.'

Aida felt Phares stiffen, but he didn't respond to her barbed comment.

'I thought of coming over to Karawan House the other day, but I reckoned you'd be busy with the preparations for Easter, so I decided it would be better if I spoke to you today.'

Aida's heart was pounding, but she managed a cold response. 'Speak to me? About what? Haven't you said enough?'

'More than enough.' He paused. 'I wanted to apologise for my behaviour.'

She glanced up at him, eyebrows raised. 'Gosh ... I'm impressed. The great surgeon Phares Pharaony apologising?'

Phares's eyes flashed but his voice remained neutral. 'Don't mock, Aida. This is already hard for me.'

'I can imagine. It must be the first time in history.'

'Why are you attacking me?'

'I'm not, I'm just being direct. You've always known that I'm not afraid to speak my mind.'

'True,' he whispered, fixing on her face.

Those dark eyes lashed into her soul, stripped away all protection against him. Their force sent a dread shooting through her being. Try as she might, Aida had to admit she was not yet immune to their caressing fire, even from a distance.

There was a long moment of silence filled with a strange tension as they watched a couple of feluccas glide by at walking pace, carrying families who had been celebrating *Sham El Nessim* on the river, or coming back from the one public garden in Luxor.

Phares moved closer and in that rich deep voice that never failed to stir her, said, 'You're very subdued today.'

She avoided his eyes, refusing to succumb to his easy charm.

He inclined his head. Amusement coloured his voice. 'You're sulking.'

'I may have many failings, but that is not one of my traits.'

'Are you still angry with me?'

Aida lowered her head again, saying nothing.

'I've apologised, haven't I?'

In her mind's eye she could just see Phares's provocatively raised brow.

Though her voice was cool, her eyes were stormy as they wandered up to his firm chin and well-defined lips. 'Arrogant you've always been, but I've never known Phares Pharaony to be rude to a guest before … and today you were deliberately rude to me.'

Dark pupils flashed. Outraged dignity animated his features. 'Rude? When was I rude to you? And since when have you been a guest? Have I not known you for most of your life?' he demanded, his face set. 'Do we not share a special relationship, far removed from that of a host with a casual guest?'

Aida was silent, thrown by his response. *Special relationship?*

His eyes bored into her. 'Why are you deliberately misconstruing my actions?'

Aida's abashed gaze lowered, her cheeks becoming rapidly scarlet. How could she explain her confused feelings? At this moment she resented him for so many things.

Phares drew in a tight breath and his tone hardened. 'Answer me.'

'Why did you do it?' she murmured, staring down at her hands in her lap.

'Do what?' You mean when I stopped that Brazilian lothario from making a spectacle of you in front of everybody? You think I haven't read about his exploits with women? ... Dance as if you're making love ...' He broke off with a sound of disgust.

'It isn't up to you to decide what I should or shouldn't do,' she retorted hotly. 'I'm quite capable of running my own life, even if I don't have a father.'

A muscle jerked suddenly at the corner of Phares's mouth and the expression in his eyes changed from scorching fire to soft velvet. 'All right, all right, Aida ... maybe I was wrong, *chérie*. I didn't think for a moment that you would take umbrage.' He held out his hand as he spoke and after a brief hesitation, Aida placed her slim one into it. His head bent, cool lips caressing her fingers.

Achingly, she wanted to run them through his thick locks of hair and drown in his dark gaze. She felt all at once as if his actions, words, emotions were as deep and unfathomable as the bottom of a well. It was this that both exhilarated and frightened her. Had it not been for the long-held antagonism she nourished for his father, she would have given in to him right then and there, if only for the sense of excitement he awakened in her.

Phares's fingers tightened on hers. 'Why must we quarrel each time we meet? You've changed, Aida, since you've come back from England.' He studied her intently. 'I would have said that you had grown up more, if you didn't still have the touchiness you had when you were young. You've hardened, but you've not learned restraint. You do not control your emotions, you still explode too easily.'

'If I've changed, then all I can say is that it's a pity you haven't! You're just as arrogant as you always were. Arrogant and narrow-minded.'

Aida moved her fingers, still in his grasp, and his hand tightened on them cruelly.

'Phares, you're hurting my hand!' she protested, but his grip only loosened slightly.

'It is nothing to what I would like to do to you,' he said. His eyes were black, probing her face, and she caught her breath beneath his smouldering gaze.

'You can't run my life,' she said quietly, slowly slipping her hand free. 'Whether you realise it or not, you have no right and I will never give you that right.'

'You mean you don't want me in your life?'

'Of course I do ... but not as a husband, a brother or a guardian, just as a friend.'

His brow creased. 'But I am your friend.'

'Well, then your concept of friendship and mine are far apart.'

'I am only trying to protect you, as I would Camelia.'

'Yes, I can see that, and that's the problem.' She gave a frustrated sigh. 'You want me to live in a sheltered world, not a real one. The real world is the one I joined eight years ago when I left Egypt. I can't blame you for wanting to keep up the illusion, but yes, I have changed.' She looked down, pulling at a tuft of grass. 'Maybe it was a mistake to come back. Perhaps returning to England is the only way for me to find fulfilment and a normal life.'

'You love this land.'

'You're right, I love Egypt, but I can't bear the narrow-mindedness of the people here ... the restrictions placed on women in a society where man is king. It's a high price to pay.'

'It doesn't need to be that way,' he murmured.

Aida stared up at his face, shocked by her own yearning to touch him. She remembered this sensation from her youth: the way her skin tingled with unforgettable excitement. There was an odd flicker in his eyes before his gaze turned to scan the river, pensively. They sat together, yet Aida knew they could not have been further apart. Even so, it was impossible not to be aware of the man next to her. His clear-cut profile, the faint emanation of an expensive masculine fragrance when he stirred beside her, her hunger for his arms around her, moved her profoundly.

Talking with Phares like this was somehow even more painful than fighting with him, especially as he had been attending to Isis's every need all day. Only now that the young woman had left did he bother with Aida, grudgingly sparing her his time. She wondered if he was going to marry Isis; there seemed to be a definite rapport between the two, and Aida had made her rejection of his proposal clear. Though Isis wasn't a person she could ever really like, she had to admit that the woman was poised, worldly and confident – all the things Aida realised she wasn't. With the added advantage of being a doctor, she was the kind of wife a man like Phares needed. At the thought of Isis sharing his life, the blood beat in her temples. Still, as confused and dispirited as she felt, she had to admit to feeling a painful sweetness in having Phares all to herself for a while, and she decided to make the most of it.

As if he had read her thoughts, his eyes kindled and he met her wary gaze. A shadow of a smile touched his lips. 'Shall we be friends this evening?' He reached out to cup her cheek in his hand.

Aida swallowed the lump in her throat. 'Yes … yes, please. I really don't like fighting with you, Phares.'

All at once he leapt up as though her answer had breathed a new vitality into him. '*Yalla*, come on! It's still early. Let's not waste this beautiful evening.' He stretched out his arm commandingly. She took in the broad shoulders, the easy movements of an athlete, as she allowed him to pull her up. 'Let's take a felucca,' he suggested.

'What, now?'

'Yes. It's a fine evening.

'But …'

Ignoring her hesitation, he continued, 'Have you brought a jacket?'

'No. Anyhow, there's no wind, the river looks very still ...'

He gave her one of his enigmatic smiles. 'Ah, it appears to be still,' he said, 'but beneath the surface there are secrets hiding and reeds whispering of things past and those to come.'

Aida could see Phares was in one of his mercurial moods. 'I didn't say I would come.'

'But, of course you will! I'll fetch us both something warm to wear.'

'No, but wait a minute, Camelia might ...?

'Camelia will not object.' Phares grinned. 'She likes her brother to be happy, and going for a sail in a felucca with you just now will make me happy.'

'All right then, I'll go and thank her and explain.'

'No. Wait here. No need to draw attention ... there are still a few busybodies around who will be delighted to read more into this than it is. We don't want to start tongues wagging,' he said, and moved off towards the house.

It was so like Phares to take for granted that she was happy with this arrangement. Aida smiled to herself and wistfully watched him walk away, aware of his long, lazy stride and the crisp curling of his thick, dark hair.

He was back in no time, carrying two sweaters and a small cool bag. Although the brightness at this hour was not as dazzling as earlier, he had put on sunglasses. Taking Aida's hand silently, he led her to a gate at the back of the garden and down a short track to where the Pharaonys' felucca awaited at a private landing stage to carry members of the family or their guests through an ancient world of relics and ruins.

The *reis*, the skipper of the felucca, in long white gown and green turban, was crouching in the shade of a clump of palm trees on the bank where the boat was moored, drinking tea with a couple of other boatmen. He scrambled to his feet as Aida and Phares appeared. '*Salam ya Bey*,' he uttered in a deep, guttural voice. Phares greeted him kindly, then told him he would be taking the boat out alone. He helped Aida aboard, and she watched from the seat that ran along the side of the felucca as Phares took his place at the end of the long, elegant boat and tucked the tiller under his arm.

He sat very straight, still and dark against the back of his seat, raven glints in his hair. Although Aida couldn't read his eyes, she could read both challenge and danger in that chiselled face, which she found thrilling.

He was the most self-contained and certain man she had ever met. He said whatever it pleased him to say, prepared at a whim to flaunt convention with such suavity that Aida wondered just how far he meant to go with her. Alone with him, away from prying eyes, in the romantic setting of a felucca on the Nile, her intuition grasped at the fact that it would be dangerous to dwell upon his undoubted charms. A man like that could create hell for a woman, she thought. But not her. She had too much common sense for that ... or did she?

A great inner sigh raked her. Phares had roused in her a craving for adventure, and in that moment she didn't care about anything other than to live for the moment and savour every last drop of pleasure this outing offered.

Phares had been right: the breeze on the beautiful river shining like glass in the splendid light was stronger than it had seemed from the bank. Filling their sails, it carried them along at a brisk rate, the smooth surface rippled in the wind like the curls of a sheep's back. The scent of beans in flower was carried to them by a light mist, and Aida inhaled deeply their sweet fragrance. The view slid by, of feluccas dozing with folded sails, lying on their sides like seabirds asleep; endless fields of corn, wheat, beans, cotton and sugarcane stretching afar; and the tiny, unreal villages, their mud walls and winding ways fringed by palms looking like bottlebrushes.

They passed dovecotes taller than the houses: massive earthen domes with niches for nesting, stuck full of posts at the top on which the pigeons could perch or use as supports for their nests. Donkeys grazed on the bank wherever it was clear of reeds, and a caravan of camels kicked up dust as they ambled along a narrow path on the edge of the desert where it bordered the Nile, lined with acacias rising above all other trees. Aida had never noticed before the variety of trees that graced the shores of the river, all of which were native to Egypt. There was the delicate tamarisk, with its bluish-green feathery blooms, the thick-trunked mulberry, with its light-green leaves and edible fruit, the wind-breaking casuarinas, with their long pine needles, the tall eucalyptus, with its camphor-producing pale leaves, and, of course, the sycamore, 'the tree of love' of the Ancient Egyptians. This tree they prized above all others, its dense foliage providing welcome shade, while the rosy, plump figs that grew on the trunk in clusters gave their life-prolonging benefits.

They had been silent since the beginning of their journey. Aida now lay on the edge of the felucca, making ridges and furrows with her fingers in the water, with half an eye on her companion, unable to bring herself to talk first.

'You're rather quiet, *chérie*.'

'It's so peaceful on the water. There's not a soul in view.'

'It's a beautiful land.'

She glanced up and smiled.

'Beautiful, but limiting.'

Phares was silent and although Aida couldn't be sure where his gaze fell, she sensed him watching her. 'You know, all those years during the war, I always wondered how the headstrong Aida El Masri was faring,' he said finally. 'You've never mentioned your life in London.'

'You never asked.'

He grinned. 'That's because you were too busy arguing to give me a chance.'

It was such a typical response from him that Aida laughed, despite herself.

'I always thought you'd make a good nurse,' he added. 'You have a compassionate heart.' His face was unreadable again behind his sunglasses. 'Camelia told me you began your training at the Royal London Hospital.'

'Yes, and the war completed it, I suppose. I learned so much in those years.'

'Were you there for the whole of the war?'

'No. After 1941, they often loaned us to hospitals outside London and we were bussed out to the home counties. There were months on end when I didn't know where I'd be stationed, or for how long.'

'That must have been difficult for you. So much unknown.'

She shrugged. 'No more than for anyone else. We were all in it together. In some ways, I was grateful to be so busy and not have time to think too much about the horrendous things we witnessed.'

Phares turned his head slightly. 'Yes, no one can see that sort of suffering and be untouched by it.'

Still reclined on the edge of the felucca, she looked up at him pensively. 'Your father ... he told me that you worked in the hospitals in Alexandria during the war. They must have been crying out for experienced doctors like you.'

'Yes, I began working at the Anglo-American Hospital at the start of the war and then spent a couple of years at the British General Hospital in Alexandria, and some time in Suez too. There were some French and Italian doctors, but it was run by the Royal Army Medical Corps so it was mainly British doctors and nurses stationed there. I knew when the war broke out that they would need as many trained medical staff as possible.'

Remembering how she had so scornfully dismissed his wartime experience, Aida winced inwardly with shame at her misjudgement. 'Look, I'm sorry about what I said before about you having no idea of what it was like – the war, I mean. I realise now how wrong I was. What *was* it like for you?' she asked quietly.

Behind his dark glasses Phares seemed to be scanning the edge of the river. 'As you said, we did what we needed to do. So many wounded came in from hospital ships from places like Tobruk or ambulance trains where they were too seriously injured to be treated at the dressing stations. El Alamein was the worst. Many of them ended up in Alexandria or Suez. Most of the time I was operating on men who had lost their eyesight from mortar bombs or assisting with amputations.' His head turned back towards her. 'I saw many of the British nurses come and go, sent to other places whenever they got the order. Often on the move and with no warning, just like you.'

He must have sensed that the atmosphere had become suddenly solemn and stopped abruptly. 'Come, we have plenty of time to talk about the war. It is too beautiful here to mull over such dark things. Now we must look to the future, don't you think?'

'Yes, whatever that might be,' Aida answered wistfully. 'The world has changed.'

'Not here. Look around you.' He paused, regarding her face. 'The desert, the Nile … its majesty is timeless. This is *your* world.'

Aida sighed. 'I don't know if I fit in here anymore.'

'Haven't you already had a chance to find out what life would offer you if you were to leave? Can England give as much? Think of all you have … all you *could* have if you just stopped thinking emotionally?'

'I'm at an age when my horizons have just begun to widen.'

'You're at an age when every sensible woman should be married, have a home, a husband and children.'

Aida stared out across the water. 'I would have to fall in love first, don't you think?'

Phares's smile was faint and mocking. 'What you would have to do is learn how to curb your belligerence and that overwhelming need you have for independence.'

She kept her eyes on the scenery. 'That is the failing of Egyptian men,' she answered impudently. 'They see a woman speaking her mind as belligerence and her desire for independence as a threat.'

Phares gave a low laugh. 'You are wrong, *habibti*. I am not threatened by you, just exasperated.'

'*You* exasperated by *me*?' Aida had to bite back a grin at the insufferable man.

'Yes, *habibti*. Men do not like the kind of wilfulness in women that ignores reality.'

'Honestly, Phares, faint wonder you're still a bachelor! Marriage is a joining of equals. Have you never been in love?' Aida couldn't stop herself from asking.

'It depends what you call love. Women have a different perspective of love from men.'

Aida glanced up at him, still trailing her fingers in the water. 'Really, and what, pray tell, would that be?'

'Women want to be desired and cherished. They look for acceptance and respect, security and fidelity. In fact, everything a man would be looking for in a relationship, but the difference is that women are much more insecure and emotional, and take everything personally. That makes them moody, possessive, jealous ...' He met her gaze directly. 'Rationality goes out the window with a woman as soon as she thinks she's in love.'

'And that doesn't apply to men?'

'No, most men are first and foremost pragmatic. They look at a relationship as a whole, and either it suits or it doesn't. Of course there's always the odd exception, as with women.' Phares flashed his devastating grin, doubly effective after so much arrogance.

'You really believe that, don't you?' Then, with an annoyed toss of her head, she added, 'I wish you'd take off those glasses.'

Phares obeyed. His jet-black eyes glittered over her face, startlingly candid. 'In answer to your question, yes, I believe it.'

His velvet gaze slid across the rest of Aida's body, light and knowing, in a way that completely robbed her of breath. Something odd and compelling stretched between them so that she had the strong premonition that if she touched him this evening, there would be no turning back. Just talking to him was loaded with a kind of unabated excitement. She was coming to realise he had a practised way with women. In fact, he was a past master at this game.

It was evident that he had brought her here for a reason. If Phares was in love with the notorious model Nairy Paplosian, and Isis Geratly was the obvious choice of wife for him, what did he want from *her*? Her body? Her land? Both? And where did that leave her?

'But enough of my views on relationships.' He went straight to the point: 'How many love affairs?' he asked crisply.

There was an ironic slant to her fine brows. 'To my endless chagrin, I can't actually lay claim to a real love affair.'

Phares shook his head slowly, his glance spiked with amusement. 'You ask me to believe that? Women, the attractive ones, are always in love or not in love with someone. I haven't met a single one able to resist the compulsive urge to complicate her private life. Are you telling me that you are different?' His eyes moved over her with disconcerting thoroughness. 'That with all the freedoms and promiscuity going on during the war, you took no part?'

Aida regarded him solemnly, her lips faintly parted with an unspoken protest that died on her lips. She shook her head. 'No, as I said, work took over completely. Overtime was a way of life and I never seemed to stand still.'

'So, you're no puritan?'

'No, I'm just not that type of woman. I accept that plenty of them want to express their freedom, just as men have always done – and yes, circumstances during the war made it acceptable – but I wanted my own kind of freedom, I suppose. It's simply not in my nature to need the attention of men all the time. I enjoyed my work. It fulfilled me, and I didn't want any distractions from it.' Aida felt herself flooding with colour as she gave way to her frustration at making him understand. 'I'm my own person, Phares!'

Her response earned an odd glance from him. His dark eyes flickered with amused satisfaction.

'Yes, you certainly are, *chérie.*'

Aida avoided his penetrating stare. She returned her gaze fixedly to the passing scenery: a triad of shaggy black buffaloes up to their shoulders in the river and dozing as they stood; a spreading sycamore fig, in the shade of which lay a man and camel asleep; a fallen palm uprooted by the last inundation, its fibrous roots still clinging to the bank, its branches in the water.

As the felucca approached the shores of Luxor, broken pillars of temples were outlined against the horizon. Aida didn't look up; she couldn't face the expression in Phares's eyes, nor risk him reading in her own how she felt about him. She continued to consider the landscape, ever rich in tropic beauty – the sweep of the majestic river, the eternal silence of the sand plains, and the desert hills that lay in the distance. Here, it was impossible to separate the Egypt of the past from the Egypt of today, she mused.

Dragging her eyes away, she turned towards him.

Phares was watching her. 'Shall we go for a walk into the desert?' he asked, his eyes shadowed with some knowledge she was finding increasingly irresistible. 'The countryside is so peaceful and beautiful at this time of the day. There's not a soul in sight – just the silent gaze of our ancestors. The sun will soon be going down and tonight is a full moon.' His dark-timbred voice had dropped to an intimate undertone.

Oh, he was clever! An urbanely clever, dangerous man who knew exactly which of her buttons to press. His words were conjuring images, arousing sensations that made Aida feel exhilarated, keyed up like a child about to start out on a forbidden adventure. She slanted a glance at his straight profile, the faint curve of self-mockery to his shapely mouth. All at once she wanted to touch him, so badly she dared not think about it. She was feeling a sense of affinity as if she'd known Phares in some other lifetime. What a fool! He was right, she was completely ruled by her emotions.

The pre-sunset breeze on the Nile was cool and moist, stroking her skin and making her hair lift and fan around her face. She turned towards Phares, pleasure melting in her blue eyes, filled with an intense love for this wild, mysterious land. She couldn't help the excitement tightening inside her like a closed fist and she heard herself whisper: 'True, this is the best time of all!'

Phares spun his head as if she had thrown something at him, pinning her gaze. For a stricken minute she felt herself transparent. Every thought, every desire, everything she had ever felt and tried to hide, there for him to register.

'Yes, the best,' he said softly, in such a way and in such a voice that, if she could, she would have run from him as if he were the devil himself.

They moored on a deserted shore under a willow tree, a mile and a half from the Temple of Karnak. The sun was still high in the sky, but subdued. The atmosphere was so clear, the desert breeze so pure it seemed impossible that this could be the same land which at noonday was like a furnace of molten brass, upon which the sun, from a glaring, cloudless sky, rained its pitiless flood of scorching heat and blinding light. '*There is something almost ethereal about the desert evening. It helps those who know its power of refreshment to live through the breathless day,*' Phares had remarked to Aida years ago when on one of their riding outings in the desert, and on this particular evening, the delicious freshness was almost divine.

Aida felt secure. He knew this part of the desert well. Ever since she could remember, he had been going for long hikes out here, on foot or horseback. He carried the two sweaters they'd brought with them. 'The weather's still mild,' he said, 'but by the time we make our way back, it'll be cold. Desert nights can be freezing. I'll leave the bottles of wine in the boat, we'll be happy to have them when we return. The alcohol will keep us warm.'

There were almost no ruins of value here as they were too far from the great temple for that – only a few mounds of stone, two sets of broken columns with a pediment lying across them that must have been part of a lesser temple, although there were still inscriptions that could be seen on the three pieces. In her imagination Aida repopulated the scene with figures of priests and worshippers from far-off days, restoring the fallen temples to their former glory, and could almost think she saw the processions winding round the walls of their temple, hearing the trumpets, harps, and sacred hymns in honour of the great pharaohs.

They had not spoken since leaving the boat and now she broke the silence: 'It was a great *Sham El Nessim* party. They were always lovely.'

'Yes, Camelia organised it almost single-handed this year. This sort of thing gives her something to take her mind off Mounir's passing. It's been very hard for her.'

'How very sad. It seems she loved her husband very much.'

'Yes. And it shows it isn't absolutely necessary to be in love to make a marriage work.'

Aida laughed. 'But you've just said that Camelia was in love.'

'No, I said she loved him, but I didn't say she was in love with Mounir when she married him. For her, he ticked all the right boxes. She made a rational decision, knowing the main ingredients were there to make the marriage successful. I think it was one of your English Restoration rakes, the Duke of Buckingham, who said that "all true love is founded on esteem". Mounir was a great man. He was many years older than my sister but he was well established, wise, respected in the community and kind. There was mutual understanding, respect and admiration between them. The rest came later.'

Aida stole a glance at him. 'So that's the way you see marriage.'

'Pretty much.'

'How very unromantic.' Before she could stop herself, she added, 'Is that the way Isis Geratly sees it too?' and wanted to bite off her tongue as soon as she had uttered those words.

'I don't know what Isis thinks. The subject has never occurred.'

*Well … she might as well go on.*

'Oh, come on, Phares.'

'What do you mean?' he replied easily.

'Rumour has it you are almost engaged to her.'

'And you believed it, I suppose.'

'The way she was hanging on to you today only confirmed the gossip. As for your behaviour … I won't even bother to comment.'

Phares gazed at her for a moment, his expression ironical. 'Do I detect an undercurrent of jealousy?'

She felt her cheeks warm. 'Don't flatter yourself. I just find it outrageous that you can offer to marry me when you've already tied yourself to Isis Geratly.'

'You're such a bundle of contradictions, *habibti*.'

'I don't know what you're talking about.'

Phares paused for a moment and his eyes seemed to change subtly from fire to velvet. They were cooler, clearer, and very frank. A half smile hovered around his mouth. 'Come on, Aida, credit me with a little sense. Eight years ago, you had a crush on me. True, we had an awkward relationship, but we were almost engaged.'

Aida came to a halt next to a tall column, her eyes flashing with indignation. 'Eight years ago, I was an overprotected child who didn't know much about life, or about anything much, least of all about men. Today, I'm a woman.'

Phares stopped too and his gaze slid over her. 'Yes, now you are a grown woman ... but even back then you were aware enough to look at me the way a woman instinctively looks at a man ... the way you still look at me when you think no one else is noticing. You haven't been kissed very often before, have you, *chérie*? Yet in my arms you come to life, you ...'

'Stop right there!' she exclaimed, almost unable to believe what he was saying, except it had a ring of truth about it. 'If you think that just because I haven't had much emotional experience you're going to bamboozle me into your bed, you're mistaken.'

Phares's eyes became serious. 'No, Aida. I have asked you to marry me. I am asking you again to be my wife.'

Though suddenly the very idea made her heart beat with a crazy quickness, her mind thrust a warning sign in front of her. 'Nice try. Tell me, Phares, how many women are you leading on a string? Dangling the great juicy carrot of becoming Mrs Phares Pharaony, wife of the great surgeon, owner of thousands of *feddans*, not to mention all the other riches you will inherit once you are head of the family?'

He tossed her a glittering look. 'I have never asked anyone to be my wife. Sure, I have always intended to marry some day. I am not the kind of man to lead a celibate life. Besides, someday I want children, the heirs to this estate that you mention so disparagingly, which employs a considerable number of people who count on it for their livelihoods.'

'Have you not asked Isis to marry you?'

'Never. Isis is a valued colleague whom I've known all my life. Our parents are friends and yes, to be honest, the idea did cross my mind at one time but as you can see, it never materialised.'

'Why, because of your love for Nairy Paplosian?' she blurted, and again bitterly regretted that she had let her mouth run away without thinking.

Phares drew a deep breath, his nostril tightening. The darkening of his narrowed eyes gave him both a sinister and sensual look. 'I see you've been busy, *chérie*,' he mocked. 'My private life is none of your business. Still, I will do you the courtesy of indulging your curiosity. Nairy was my mistress at one time. There was never any question of marriage. We had an arrangement, you might say. A contract between two adults who were attracted to each other and understood full well what they were getting into. Like any contract, this one came to an end. About six months ago.' He inclined his handsome head. 'Satisfied?'

Aida stared at him, a small frown unconsciously creasing her brow, until he reached out a finger and smoothed it away. His own expression was uncertain as he searched her face.

'Why don't you say something?' he asked.

What could she say? It was in the past and she should let it go. She turned away silently, loins melting with need of him. He was so beautiful, it hurt when he looked at her like that.

They had reached an elevated position in the desert which allowed a most enthralling panoramic view of the surroundings wrapped in a glory of hues in the light of the setting sun. Purple shadows were cast by the dunes and the far-off mountains. The sky had turned all red to the right, all pink to the left. The ochre and greys of sandstone, the dark granite and pale limestone cliffs blended exquisitely with the tawny yellow of the desert; the rich green of the banks and the blue of the river snaking away from them gave combinations and contrasts of colour in which Phares and Aida's eyes revelled.

They stood transfixed as, at the edge of the horizon, a ripple of flame and liquid gold marked the sun's course, lending colour to the growing twilight. In a few minutes the sky was melting from flaming red to purple, amethyst, golden yellow, soft pink, faded green, pale blue. And now the earth and the sky were suffused with a delicate pink tinge of the afterglow.

All the time Aida was conscious of the nearness of Phares's lithe, muscled body, of the tang of his skin with its faint fragrance of some expensive aftershave, of the fire smouldering in her own body. A wish flared briefly that he didn't have to be quite so ruggedly handsome, quite so outrageously masculine.

'This is the most fairy-like and magical effect of colour I have ever seen ...' she murmured at last.

'It is even more glorious at sunrise.' His eyes were fixed on the breathtaking painting in front of him. 'The peculiarity in Egypt,' he murmured, 'is that light and colour return after an interval of ashy grey, like the coming back to life of a corpse. Nowhere else would you witness such a miracle.' He paused, his gaze still on the horizon. 'Never leave this land, Aida. You are part of it, and it is part of you.'

She watched him, her heart thudding. Not for the first time she mused that he might well have been a descendant of some pharaonic prince. The distinct contours of his bold features, the dark eyes, the fineness of hands and wrists, the whole suppleness and easy muscular grace, showed breeding – the innate dignity of an ancient race. He belonged to the desert and yet his mantle of Western civilisation lent a touch of originality to the man on whom it rested.

A full golden moon was rising over the desert. Slowly, it swam into view, a great plate of gold as yet low down in the sky, entangled, or so it seemed, in the branches of the tall palm trees that dotted the land around them.

The air was soft and warm. From far away came the thin and reedy note of a native flute, piping one of the melancholy chants of the lovesick nomads of the desert; and the odd little tune, full of unhappy modulations, seemed somehow fitting to the wonderful black and gold of the night.

'Listen,' Phares said, suddenly attentive. 'There must be a caravan of *ghajar*, gypsies, not far from here. Come, let's follow the music.'

Aida shivered. 'Why? My father always said they're a thieving lot who like nothing better than to traffic antiquities.'

He shrugged. 'They have that reputation, but they're not the only thieves in the desert – especially around here. I'd be more inclined to fear the *matareed*, the outlaws that live up there.' He pointed to the chain of mountains edging the horizon.

Aida frowned. 'I don't like the idea of going there,' she said pensively.

'Don't tell me you listen to all that rubbish about them having sorcerers who can give you the evil eye? You surprise me. A free-spirited, independent young woman like yourself having such superstitions?'

'I never said that,' she retorted, annoyed by his presumption. 'What I do believe is if for some unknown reason they take against someone, they can be ... unpleasant.'

Phares's smile was ironic, teasing. 'Come now, *habibti*, fancy being afraid when you have me to protect you!'

He seemed set on his idea of finding the gypsies and Aida followed him half-heartedly. There were no stars in the sky and with the sudden nightfall, despite the brilliant moon, the desert seemed a gloomy, haunted place. Instead of the tranquil atmosphere she had felt at sunset, there was a sort of restlessness, an electricity in the breath of the night.

They soon spotted the caravan under a clump of palm trees. By the looks of it the evening meal was being prepared and around the fire were grouped men and women, camels, donkeys, and a few black goats. The grunting camels sprawled on the ground, their burdens beside them, and each time one of them moved there sounded the clank of a bell.

Around the biggest fire and lit by its fitful flame, a group of musicians had gathered. The light fell on their painted lutes, *darabukeh* drums and tambourines, making their swarthy faces and glittering teeth seem to jump out of the darkness. Some played *rebabahs*, a kind of small, round long-necked violin with a metal spike that rested on the ground, and the high, warbling sound pierced the air like a human voice. As a night scene, nothing could be more picturesque than this group of turbaned Arabs sitting in a circle, cross-legged. In the midst of them a blind man sat singing with an old hag, and by his side was a boy playing a reed pipe, his eyes wide set in his music-haunted face. The blind singer was young and powerfully built, but very thin. As he sat there, his wasted form wrapped in a coarse cloth of striped yellow and crimson, he looked the embodiment of the musicians represented in sketches on the walls of temples and tombs of Ancient Egypt. He swayed while the musicians thrummed; the rest of the men and women softly clapped their hands in time, waiting their turn to chime in with the chorus.

As Phares and Aida approached the camp, a woman who had been seated at a table enjoying a *shisha*, a turquoise hubble-bubble, came towards them. Aida guessed she was in her fifties, although she could have been younger as the *ghajar* often aged quickly owing to their lifestyle and the unfriendly desert sun.

The *ghajareya's* face was carefully painted, her eyes large, deep-set, savage, sensual – their bewitching expression rendered more striking by the kohl that blackened the edge of the eyelids, both above and below the eye. Her nose was slightly flat and adorned with a gold nose-ring with a blue charm to keep away the evil eye. Her lips were full, her hair a deep, glossy black, which hung on each side of her face in thick plaits. Her nails and toenails were stained the deep orange of henna, regarded by many Egyptians as a sacred embellishment. A blue thin vertical line straddled by two blue dots was tattooed on her chin. She wore a golden pair of very wide trousers, the *shintiyán*, made of cotton with a full, multicoloured striped shirt that stopped just above the knee. An embroidered kerchief, doubled over diagonally, encircled her waist loosely. Around her neck and on her arms were chains of gold and precious stone amulets that clanked like a country cart as she moved. *Doubtless all her riches*, Aida thought as she watched the woman stroll nonchalantly towards them.

'*Salam aleykom*, peace be on you,' she said as she reached the couple.

'*Wa aleykom el salam*, and on you,' Phares answered.

The woman's shrewd eyes moved from him to Aida. 'How can I help you?'

'We were just passing when we fell upon your camp.'

'*Marhaba*, welcome. My name is Ghalya. *It faddalou*, join us,' she said, before calling out, 'Hind, prepare a *shisha* for the *Bey* and a glass of *sharbat* for the *hanem*.'

Aida nudged Phares and whispered sharply, 'Let's go.'

To her irritation, Phares ignored her and smiled at Ghalya, turning on the charm. '*Shukran*, that's very kind of you. I have never seen you around here before. Do you often pass this way?'

'We come by once every four or five months, depending on the weather. We're originally from Ras Gharib on the Red Sea.'

'That's a long way away.'

'Yes, *ya Bey*, and the desert is *ghaddar*, treacherous, as you know,' she smiled back, enigmatically.

'How long will you be staying there?'

'It depends on the weather. The season of El Khamaseen sandstorms will be here in a week, so we will be going back soon. We need them to be behind us, *ya Bey*. Waiting for these gales of dust to pass would take too long. Our cousins from the Beni Gharib tribe will come tomorrow, then we will decide.'

Aida watched the exchange uneasily. Why did she have the strange impression she was *de trop*? She nudged Phares's elbow, but the gypsy woman turned towards her with a sly look. 'Why are you afraid, *ya bonaya*, my child? Why are you in such a hurry to leave us?' Her black, kohl-lined eyes glittered. 'Maybe I can help you in your uncertainty ... I tell the fortune, past, present and future.'

Aida knew that the *ghajareya* was trying to reel her in and would use any argument to manipulate her into parting with some money. Having grown up in Upper Egypt, she fell into the familiar way of speaking that *Dada* Amina had always used with the *ghawazy* and Bedouins, echoing her phrases: 'I am not afraid, and *shukran*, there is nothing to help. Past, present and future are in the *gheeb*, the unknown, and in the hands of *Allah*,' she retorted coolly.

They had reached the campfire. The air was thick with the acid tinge of hashish, familiar to Aida because she had often smelt it in Cairo bazaars, like the Khan Khalili. A younger woman appeared with the hubble-bubble for Phares and a glass of rose cordial for Aida. A much younger version of Ghalya, the girl couldn't have been more than eighteen, with unruly black hair pulled straight back on each side of her forehead in small braids, joined together behind her head. Around her neck, wrists, ears and ankles she wore her dowry, made up of a triple necklace of large, hollow gold beads, gold disk earrings decorated with gold granules, and two bands of gold with snake heads, twisted together and interlaced as a bracelet and anklet. Her enormous dark eyes, bordered with kohl, immediately settled on Phares.

Ghalya made the introduction. 'This is Hind, my daughter.' Then, turning to the young girl, she ordered, 'Dance for the *Bey*.'

'No need for that,' Phares protested, but the group of musicians began to play, while Hind, tying a scarf around her hips without delay, had already started her undulating dance.

Ghalya pulled Aida by the arm. 'Come, *ya bonaya*. Let's sit in the sand, here next to the fire. I'll tell you *el ghayeb will maktoom*, the unknown, and what is written.'

'I'm not interested to know the future.' Aida tried to draw away. 'My life is quite straightforward and I don't believe in destiny, thank you.'

'I can see a lot of turbulence in your heart and events as strong as an earthquake awaiting you.'

Irritated, Aida snapped, 'I really don't understand what you are talking about. As I've said, I'm the one in control of my life. Anyhow, *Allah* is there to show me the way if I get lost.'

The *ghajareya* laughed. '*El maktoob alal guibeen lazim te shofou'l ein*, what is written on the forehead must be read by the eyes. That which is destined to be will be fulfilled.' She lifted her face to the sky, pointing at it with one finger. 'You cannot escape what *Allah* has written for you in the heavens.'

Not quite knowing how it happened, Aida found herself sitting on a large red woven cloth spread out on the ground next to the fire with the gypsy woman seated opposite her, cross-legged.

A strange little shudder ran through her. She really had a bad feeling about this. Her eyes strayed towards Phares in the hope that he would rescue her from this ordeal, but like everyone else, his gaze was drawn to the swirling figure of Hind. Even Aida couldn't help but be riveted by the young *ghazeya*, as if held in a charm that she could not fight, like a moth to a flame.

The hypnotic allure of the *ghawazy* was famous. Egypt's most traditional dancers, their name meant 'conquerors' as they were said to invade the hearts of their audience. The dance of a *ghazeya* was earthy, exotic, abandoned, and the *ghawazy* were often paid to perform in courtyards, coffee houses and streets, and even at weddings and village celebrations. No man would dare marry a *ghazeya* but many a young man in the small villages of Upper Egypt had been initiated into the joys of sex by these bewitching dancers.

The gypsy's daughter was no less provocative a sight. The bright semi-transparent fuchsia body stocking below Hind's tight bodice revealed no actual flesh, but it clung to every curve, accentuated by the low shawl she had wrapped about her hips, which exposed bare thighs as she moved. She had undone the braids and part of her hair was fastened back over one small ear by a bunch of yellow jasmine. The rest cascaded on to her beautiful bare shoulders: rich, black and glossy. Her dark, luminous eyes flashed and her body, undulating like a snake with a lowering and raising of one hip only, moved in a kind of a rhythmic, gyrating hip walk, to the rattle of the small brass castanets in her hands.

A group of *A'l'mehs*, female singers, had appeared, also wearing dresses of vivid colours though much thicker in texture and not as clinging. They egged her on with clapping, singing, and *zaghareet* – those shrill, quavering cries of joy which in Egypt accompany happy events. A bottle of palm wine and some sort of goat's cheese and bread had been brought out to Phares. He was getting a king's welcome and Aida could see that he was enjoying himself immensely.

'If you are so enamoured with the *Bey*, why are you resisting him?'

Aida swung round and met the great dark eyes of the fortune teller watching her intently, a mischievous smile animating her wide mouth.

'I don't understand.'

The gypsy woman reached for a gazelle skin by the side of the fire and drew a large square in the sand with a stick. '*El*

*Bey raydaki fil halal*, the *Bey* wants you. Why do you rebuff him?'
She jiggled the bag before throwing its contents on to the square
in front of her. 'I don't need these to tell me how you feel about
him. Your eyes are enough, they devour him.'

'Nonsense!' Aida protested vehemently. 'He's like a brother
to me.'

'Brother, is it?' Ghalya let out a low, rusty chuckle. 'Already
I can see you are lying … not only to me, but to yourself. *Irmy
bayadik*, cross my palm with silver so I can tell you more.'

'I don't want to know more.'

'*Hal heya horreya am eindan yahwee ila dammar*, is it freedom
or a stubbornness that drops one into destruction?'

'What do you mean?'

'Throw your silver coins among my shells and I will tell you
the meaning in the sands.'

Reluctantly, Aida took out a couple of ten-piastre silver coins
and tossed them on to the square.

Ghalya studied the shells and gave Aida a cat-like stare; there
was a curious glint behind the dark lashes that she couldn't
quite interpret. 'I see anger … so much anger. You are like
the blind man who shuts his eyes and scorns.' As she spoke,
the *darabukeh* throbbed, and the monotonous *rebabahs*
furnished a soft but piercing bass. Smoke rose up and veiled
the blue flames of the fire. 'There is no darkness like ignorance.
*El zaher lena, wal khafy alal Allah*, what is manifest is for us,
and what is concealed, for God.'

The hidden meaning in the fortune teller's words was not lost
on Aida. Ghalya was surely referring to the betrayal of her father.
The young woman's gaze was drawn to the square in the sand
and, though she told herself that this was all trickery and
superstition, for some reason she feared what the *ghajareya* had
to say. Her instincts told her to flee, but her body was held
transfixed by an invisible power emanating from the square,

where the various shells and stones lay gleaming in the firelight as though they had a secret life of their own.

'*Man zara'a ar rih, hasada al asifa*, he who sows the wind harvests the storm.'

Aida glanced up, confused. 'The storm happened a long time ago. I am just searching for the real culprit.'

The fortune teller shook her head, her black eyes boring into Aida. 'No, that is not the storm I am seeing here. This one lies ahead of you. *Ma Kul maawoog arraqaba jamal*, not everything with a crooked neck is a camel, and there is none more blind than he who doesn't want to see. The Nabi Mohamed *alayhi as-sal m*, peace be upon him, said, "Beware of suspicion, for suspicion is the worst of false tales." And I am telling you, beware of impulsiveness or you might end up like a blind person swimming in the sea.'

Aida stiffened, her face hardening. 'I have no proof, but I will find it. I will do whatever it takes to find the truth.'

'It is true that he who takes revenge erases shame but you must choose your battles carefully and not jump to conclusions. *Al nar wala al aar*, rather be touched by fire than by dishonour.'

Aida frowned. 'You don't need to tell me that. I know it already and I don't see what it has to do with my quest.'

The fortune teller shook her head once more and mumbled, as if to herself, 'I tell her "It's a bull", she says "Milk it".' She was staring long and hard at Aida as though to convey her message without uttering words.

Ghalya kept silent for a long while, toying with the shells, picking them up and throwing them back on to the sand. The flames danced, throwing shadows on her lined face, which in the half-light took a sinister mien, her eyes looking darker and enormous, her brows jet black and thick, her nostrils open and wide.

Far away, a jackal gave its weird cry, tearing the night as it hunted its prey.

At length the *ghajareya* looked up. 'The doors of luck are almost closed for you. Winds do not always blow as the vessels wish ... evil is at work. I can almost hear *ibleess*, the devil, laughing as he dares the power of *Allah* to bring peace in your heart and around you. I will not hide from you that there is great danger ahead, but I can also see a glimmer of hope ... Then maybe, if you're lucky and if God wills, you will have a last chance for happiness. My final advice to you is to strike the deal in the field rather than dispute on the threshing floor. It's not too late yet. The heart is an astrologer that always divines the truth ... Remember, forewarned is forearmed.' Collecting her shells, she tidied them back into the gazelle skin and rose to her feet.

Aida remained seated for a short moment, trying to hold on to the cryptic words of the *ghajareya*, then got up and followed Ghalya to where Phares was sitting.

The dance, which had begun with some degree of decorum, soon deteriorated into a provocative, almost lascivious, show, with Hind shooting lustful glances at her male audience and making indecent gestures as the music took on a more rapid cadence. Sometimes she uttered a shrill cry, as though to spur the zeal of her musicians, while between her fingers her noisy castanets clacked unceasingly.

With an increased motion of her nimble frame, clicking her finger cymbals in time with every shake and shudder of her hips, she now came close to Phares, holding out her arms, shaking them from shoulder to wrist with an imperceptible quivering, moving them apart with soft, quick motions like those of the wings of a hovering eagle. Presently she was bending over him completely, then backwards, shoulders in a stiffened pose, her whole body slightly arched, flesh rippling into bronze ridges, the back of her head almost touching Phares's lap as she gyrated her belly.

Aida's gaze fixed on Phares, watching for his reaction. He seemed perfectly at ease with this display. She couldn't help her mind filling with images she tried instantly to push away. Could it be, as a teenager, Phares had experienced his rite of passage with such a girl?

Her eyes followed the young *ghazeya* with an aching heart until, in a sudden torment, she turned away, no longer able to stand the sight of the sleek, rose-coloured body circled around Phares. She had the galling knowledge that it was jealousy that was making it impossible for her to watch the dance to its conclusion. Yes, she *had* been jealous of Nairy Paplosian the day before, and of Isis Geratly this morning, and now this. It seared her like a red-hot poker. Had her puppy love for this man turned into something deeper? Allowing the painful truth to surface, unlocked from its prison deep inside her, she took a half-frightened breath and held a hand to her heart, which pounded with the desperation of something trapped. For Aida, in that moment, the moonlit desert was a place of horror, the yellow moon a leering goblin whose mocking eye seemed to lay bare the shameful secret of her own heart. She felt the ardent gaze of the fortune teller and turned to face her.

'Don't be afraid,' Ghalya murmured. 'Love hurts. The pain you are feeling now is meant to wake you up. Take heed before it's too late.' Detaching a beautiful talisman from around her neck, she handed it to Aida. 'This *aqiq*, carnelian, will protect you and keep you from *wellad el haram*, the sons of evil. Always have it around your neck, for not even *el jin el ahmar*, the red genie, will be able to help you if you get separated from it.'

Aida hesitated before thanking the woman and taking the amulet. She flushed and her eyes went from Ghalya to her daughter. In an accelerated collision of her brass castanets, Hind was swinging around Phares, ending in a deep curtsey which had her almost prostrated at his feet, and Aida couldn't help the slight shiver that ran through her once again.

Only then did Phares fling a look in her direction, slanting her a lazy smile as he stood up. Hind had disappeared into one of the tents and Phares came towards Ghalya. He reached for his wallet from the back pocket of his jeans and took out a couple of Egyptian notes, which he slipped into her hand.

'Thank you for your hospitality. Your daughter is a wonderful dancer and your palm wine was very good.'

'We aim to please, *ya Bey*.'

Turning to Aida, Phares took her hand. 'Come on, *chérie*, let's go.'

As they were about to leave, the fortune teller fixed Phares with her eloquent, enormous eyes, for a moment holding his mesmerised velvet dark gaze in her grip. '*Sahib al-haq lahu maquam wa lahu maqal*, the man who is in the right has both stature and the last word.'

A glorious smile spontaneously curved Phares's full mouth. 'Thank you for your vote of confidence. *Maa al salama*.'

'*Allah maak*, God be with you,' she replied, handing him a short chain with a small, golden charm. 'You are a man of the desert. You will understand the message.'

Phares grinned. '*Ummal*, of course. *Shukran*.'

'*Afwan*, you're welcome.'

When they were far enough away not to be in earshot of the camp, Aida asked, 'What did she mean?'

'About the charm?'

'Yes.'

He handed her the chain. 'You'll notice that the charm is a carved camel.'

She examined it. 'Yes, so what?'

'The story goes that because the camel has such patience and endurance he is the only infidel admitted into paradise.'

She gave the charm back. 'I don't like these people,' she said moodily. 'They tell you things that stick in your mind and influence your judgement.'

'Maybe ... but the way they live, with nothing else to distract them but the sand and the sky, often makes them wise.'

They went back by a different route. The moon had risen to its full splendour by now, illuminating ancient brick mounds of some forgotten city, with palm trees and fragments of arched foundations, and a wall and doorway here and there. An old vulture, asleep on the rim of a lotus capital under a twisted sycamore, woke up in great consternation as they went by; he winged his way along a dark colonnade of a ruined temple into the silvery moonlight, and finally settled on the peak of a glossy obelisk. The sky was flooded with light, against which the tall date palms stood out as though etched upon their background by some fairy hand. The scene was one of enchantment again: a symphony in silver and black that set Aida's sensitive blood racing with its suggestion of infinity and mystery. There were no stars visible in that brilliant radiance, only a great white moon hanging there, a serene and lovely goddess, in the exquisite heavens.

They walked back to the boat without speaking as though something of the silence, the immensity of the desert itself, had found its way into their hearts.

# CHAPTER 7

When they reached the boat, the temperature hadn't dropped, as Phares had predicted, and there was no whisper of a breeze. For Aida, the air felt uncannily warm, almost fiery against her cheek. She undid the first button of her dress and, dipping her handkerchief in the water, passed it over her throat and her upper chest to refresh herself.

'It's so hot,' she whispered, fanning herself with a small fan she always kept in her bag.

'I'm afraid we're going to have to wait for a while before we leave. There's no wind and I wouldn't like us to be stranded in the middle of the river.'

He pulled out the cool bag from under the bench and took out the two bottles of wine and a few *kahk*, round cakes made with semolina, stuffed with ground dates and nuts. He grinned. 'This will keep us out of trouble for a while. It might be a long night.'

The silence around them was profound, broken only by the echo of a distant laughing bark of a hyena or the wail of a jackal. Aida's senses, keyed up by Phares, her encounter with the gypsies and the fortune teller's words, were almost preternaturally acute. She felt unnaturally vital and awake, intensely aware of Phares's presence beside her in the boat. Even in the darkness she sensed his jet-black eyes brooding disturbingly. She saw the lines of his mouth, that charming mouth which so many women found attractive, and felt in every pulse a most unusual excitement which, though almost oppressive, was yet bewilderingly sweet.

Phares poured them both a glass of wine and offered her a cake before lighting a cigarette. He leaned back against the cushions, regarding her between his long, thick lashes. Aida's eyes met his and she saw a glittering curiosity in them, a desire to probe into her reserve.

'You look pensive and very beautiful.'

She gave a half smile. 'I was just thinking that those fortune tellers are quite a dangerous species.'

'Oh? Why is that?'

She shrugged. 'Well, they put things into one's head ... you know.'

A glimmer of rueful amusement leapt into his eyes.

'Because she guessed you are in love with me?'

Aida gave him a startled look. 'I'm not.'

'You might be without knowing it.' He leant towards her, his eyes slipping to her mouth, to her throat and to the front of her dress that revealed part of the curve of one breast.

'There's more to love than ... than liking the look of someone,' Aida replied sharply, reading the innuendo in his question. She had no doubt that Phares was well aware of her attraction to him.

'True,' he chuckled, 'but it starts the ball rolling.'

'Anyway, how do you know what she was saying? I should have thought you hardly noticed me.' Her pulse was beating madly because he *had* noticed. 'You seemed far too enthralled.'

'It's said of the Pharaony men that they can be absorbed in the sensual beauty of a woman and work out the details of a business deal at one and the same time. We do it like breathing, didn't you know that?' He raised a quizzical eyebrow and drew in a deep intake of smoke. 'You think there was something significant in the way I watched the *ghazeya* dance?'

'Wasn't there?' she challenged him. 'You looked totally captivated.'

'She was very beautiful, but it is not her that captivates me, *chérie*. She didn't move me one bit in the way you think ... in the way *you* have, ever since you've come back into my life.'

Aida was slightly embarrassed beneath his penetrating gaze, with an intense feeling that many things between herself and Phares would be better left unsaid. Her heart was beating with a primitive longing as his scrutiny burned into her like a hot poker, thrusting her into a new world of conflicting emotions. She didn't answer, but at the same time could not turn away from him.

Silence settled between them as it had done so often during their walk earlier. Although he did not speak as he considered her through the blue veil of smoke spiralling up from his cigarette, Aida understood the message in his narrowed eyes as clearly as though he had drawn her into his arms and was kissing her.

They sipped their wine for a while. The alcohol was having a beneficial effect on Aida, and she felt herself relaxing, a sense of wellbeing flooding her. Phares filled their glasses again, then lounged among the cushions, spreading his arms along the back of the seat.

'Such a night!' he whispered, his head thrown back as though in pagan worship of the stars, which were so brilliant above the river.

The moon tiptoed stealthily from behind a weeping willow tree like a flirtatious nymph and bathed the countryside with its mischievous light. Aida was taken by the charm of the moonlit Nile at this hour, its shining surface reflecting the willow and the softened shimmer of the countryside. Every distant sound seemed musical and the air was tangy with the earth and foliage, which had been sun-drenched all day. Nature was tranced and the world enveloped in a dream.

'Come sit next to me,' Phares said at length, eyes sparkling with devilry. Beneath his black brows they had the intensity of ebony, and their language was plain.

Aida's body was rigid with tension. She met his gaze with a show of bravery. 'No.'

'No?' he purred, his voice low and hoarse. He drained his wine in one go and put his glass aside. He leaned back against the cushions and she could see the outline of his virility against his tight jeans.

'No,' she murmured again, but could feel how her body betrayed her resolution as he suddenly moved close to her and placed his hand on her arm, eyes smouldering. She wanted to turn away, but like someone in a dream she couldn't break the spell that held her there. Her head felt light. *It's the wine*, she thought. She could feel the warm pulsating energy in him that wouldn't be reined in for much longer, not if she allowed him to sit this close.

The moon had shifted so its rays now cast soft shadows on Phares's face, which held a slumberous, sensuous expression. He reached out and ran his fingers over her lips, and she saw the moon agleam in his eyes and felt the instant response of her senses.

Some instinct gave her the strength to tear herself away from him. 'You're drunk,' she said, trying to control the quiver in her voice.

'And you are trembling, *chérie*. Why is that?'

'W-when a man's been drinking …' Aida took a breath, forcing out the words, 'any woman's fair game, isn't she?'

'Is that what it's all about? You think that at this moment I could lie with any woman? Do you think that I could be fooled by my own biology and that of the woman in front of me, like some ignorant teenage boy?'

'Oh, you're very experienced, I'm sure.' She had to say these things or leave her heart and body – all her senses that were crying out for him – entirely unprotected. Aida was simply a means to an end for him. Phares didn't love her. He just felt like having her … and once he'd had her, she'd be at his mercy, she and her land!

As if he knew what was going through her mind, Phares's smile was charm itself and he leaned forward on one elbow. 'There's no one like you, *chérie*. Elfin-blue eyes, fairy-like blonde hair and a mouth an angel might envy. You're as unique as this carnelian you're wearing, and I want you, Aida El Masri.'

At the sound of his voice – provocative, musical, caressing – heat shot through her, but the slumbering uneasiness stirred in her heart again and she thought of Nairy and Isis and the rumours that surrounded him.

Still, Phares's haunting male scent filled her head as he leaned so close. Aida trembled. Although the air had now cooled down, her body felt feverish. His glance whipped at her face with amused challenge.

'There are many superstitions connected with carnelian, as the *ghajareya* told you, one of them being a means of warding off the evil eye.' The moon glided out from behind a passing cloud and his face loomed back out of the darkness. 'But what she didn't tell you is the most remarkable claim ever recorded: that of the carnelian not only having the ability to protect one from impure thoughts but also the power to … how does the phrase go … erase the pain of "virgin purity by lust defiled".'

Aida edged a little away from him, hiding her nervousness behind a flippant reply. 'Fortunately, right at this moment I'm not likely to suffer either of those ailments, so I have no use for any such talisman.'

'How can you be so sure?' he countered, a quick lick of flame in his eyes. 'You're fully aware of my needs.'

'I'm *sure*!' She looked down, her heart thumping, resenting the ease with which he could set her pulses racing.

'And I'm fully aware of yours.'

For a moment she stared back at him, like a gauzy moth infatuated with a flame, and he turned away, his profile without expression, aloof, for all its splendid dark arrogance. Then abruptly, still looking ahead of him, he raked a hand through his hair and said roughly, 'I can't take any more of this. If we have to start from scratch, then we'll do it, but I'm not going to believe you felt nothing at all when I kissed you the other night. It was real for both of us, I'll swear to that.' He turned to look at her, saw the stunned blue eyes and stopped right there, his own expression altering.

For a moment neither of them moved, then he sat up and pulled her into his arms, his hand threading into her hair, finding her mouth with an urgency which jolted Aida out of her stupor. She was instinctively swept away ... this longing and need to touch and be touched ... this voice inside her that was screaming yes, yes, yes to the sweet, primitive hurting and giving until there was nothing ... nothing but Phares and being part of the wild, throbbing heart of him.

There were questions to be asked and to be answered, but for now they could wait. The spark he struck on touching her was bright and hot, flaring immediately into a flame of desire like nothing she had ever experienced before in her life. For Aida, all that mattered now was the feel of this man's muscular chest against her, of his lips on hers, of the warmth and pleasure spreading through her like sunlight pushing back the shadows.

Phares's hands dropped to her shoulders and trailed slowly down her arms, transmitting a new need to touch that shivered through Aida's skin. His eyes were locked on to hers, compelling her acceptance. She saw the conflict rage in them, felt the tension of his fiercely imposed control. The powerful strength of his desire stirred a turbulent storm inside her head, swimming with the intoxication of his caress.

Yes, she wanted him … all of him, and now. He knew. The knowledge blazed in his eyes. He said nothing, neither did she. There was no need for words anyway. And then, gently, he began to unbutton her dress. There could be no going back to whatever their relationship had been before.

In a flash, Phares had pulled the cushions off the seats and on to the floor and had pushed Aida back gently so she was lying in front of him. He didn't lie down next to her but slowly edged the fabric of her dress away, slipping it off her shoulders to expose her body. She watched him stare down at her, as though stunned. The primeval, almost savage, look in his eyes ignited every wanton flame in her veins.

'You are beautiful, Aida … made of pearl and moonbeams,' he whispered huskily, his gaze hot upon her. 'A mesmerising masterpiece of our creator.' Drawing a ragged breath, he brushed her skin lightly from top to bottom with a trembling hand before tracing his palm over the curve of her breasts. 'Under the stars, your skin is as mysterious as the covering of a waterlily bud.'

Aida sighed and a shudder rippled through her as her breasts tightened and she felt her nipples jutting high and taut. His burning gaze never leaving her face, he faintly circled one aureole with a finger and then the other, in a maddening, leisurely fashion.

A strangled cry escaped Aida's lips, her gaze watching his caressing hand, expressing in equal measure strength and grace and a certain violence held in check.

'Is this what you want?' he murmured as he dropped his head to take one hard crest in his mouth in a blind movement of longing. Her breath sucked in and she closed her eyes to savour the ecstasy of his gentle torture, arching her back needily against his mouth.

'You want more, *chérie*?' He moved to the other peak and now drew hungrily on it in a rhythm that echoed inside her body.

Licking and biting, tugging and rolling, he teased almost savagely, kneading the other breast with just as much relentless torment, the moan in her throat urging him on, craving the pain and the pleasure he was giving her.

Aida could feel the hardness of his desire throbbing against her. 'I want to please you too,' she whispered suddenly, as her fingers buried themselves in the crisp thickness of the dark curls of his hair.

Phares looked up. 'Shush, *chérie*, you are pleasing me more than you think. The night is long.' His voice was hoarse, his eyes glittering, almost feverish. Discarding his shirt in one swift movement, he lay beside her and covered her lips with his, his warm hands now roaming caressingly over each curve of her body. His lips moved probingly against hers, the tip of his tongue moving sensually around its groove, flicking in and out slowly, sending heat coursing through her veins. Aida's head swam with the intoxication of his kisses. Needing more of him, her hands moved to find the front of his trousers and, zipping them open, she slid her fingers into the heat of his virility and sensually fondled the silken skin of his masculinity. Phares caught his breath and moaned, before dipping into the velvet darkness of her mouth.

No more playful kisses: he let loose the rapacious craving he had so clearly struggled against. His mouth seemed to explode into hers with a hungry passion, wild for the taste of her, demanding a response that matched his need.

This was no mere melding of mouths. It was a fierce claim on all that she was, a driving, heart-pounding, unbridled search for what was, and what could be, between them, a giving and taking that sent streams of exultation bursting through her.

Aida's heart was racing so that she could scarcely catch her breath. Everything inside her was mounting to a crescendo and she responded to this new urgency as if hypnotised. Consumed by the flame of desire, she became the flame herself, instinctively using her lips, her hands, her whole body to express her passion and to increase Phares's arousal.

At length, he lifted his head, staring down into her face. 'Let me feel you.' His voice was low and husky as he let his palm slide down her flat stomach to her mound of Venus.

A frisson crawled up her spine, part dread, part her body's traitorous response to the anticipation of him touching her so intimately. 'No, no, not there,' she pleaded.

'Relax, *chérie*. I won't hurt you, I promise. On the contrary, I'll make you see the sun at midnight in a dark sky without stars.'

'No,' she whispered again, even though she could feel the scorching fire pulsing between her legs. Somehow, talking about it seemed to kindle her need.

'I can't resist anymore,' he breathed unevenly, his mouth brushing against her temple. 'I'm dying for you.'

'Don't say that … please.' It was wrong and yet here in the golden blaze of the moonlight it was inevitable. A night made for love, except … oh, she couldn't think anymore, she wanted so much for him to touch her … appease the fire that was torturing her.

'Have you never been touched there?'

'Never.' Aida's throat constricted, but she forced out the words. 'Once, a few years ago, I got carried away at a New Year's Eve party and the young man I was dating that night tried to touch me, but he disgusted me and I pushed him away and fled.'

'You never touched yourself, never tried to pleasure your lonely nights?'

She looked horrified. 'Never.'

He gave a shaky laugh as though bemused by what was happening. 'Oh, Aida, my beautiful pearl. Let me show you how your body can reward you when you let go. I will go very slowly and only if you want me to.'

Aida felt fear and shyness invade her as she looked at him so big and dark under the silvery moon, his black hair disordered on his brow and a slight quirk to his mouth.

Phares arranged her with a care as tender as it was teasing. She went to stroke him once again and gently he removed her hand from his throbbing need. 'I'm burning for you, *chérie*, and it's better if you don't touch me or you'll soon make me lose all control.'

'But I want to feel you ...'

'Shush, trust me. Lie back and relax. You will enjoy it, I promise.'

Phares pushed up her knees, to find the small lacy triangle that covered the most intimate core of her, and she stared into his soul-stealing eyes. Shame filled her, yet she could not silence the ache for his touch burning through her and the yearning to submit to it. Deft fingers caressed the damp fabric and she moaned as she spread her legs wider instinctively, unconsciously asking for more.

'You're so damp, I can feel how much you want me ... let me caress you, *chérie*.' His voice was hoarse and low, charged with pent-up desire. But Aida was beyond listening. His words were coming to her through a mist of sensations as he eased the lace panties down over her hips and stroked her legs apart, caressing the inside of her thighs, his warm palm making her shudder and give in to the ecstasy gradually creeping up her body.

She gasped at the contrasting contact of cool air on her burning flesh and followed it with a stunned cry of pleasure as Phares's cool fingers gently parted the outer tender lips, uncovering the small bud of her desire lying like a lustrous pearl at the centre of a pink oyster, waiting to be loved.

Aida heard him stifle a gasp. 'You are so wondrously beautiful,' he whispered.

At his words, she felt a renewed wave of heat and moisture invade her loins and she opened her legs wider to give Phares free access to stroke her swollen centre, arching her back, moving the lower part of her body up and down in a rhythmic cadence, inviting him to release the tension that was building up to an unbearable torture.

Phares didn't disappoint. His touch was sensuous, and Aida felt the shock of it right through to her bones as he teased, fondled and played erotically with the receptive swollen flesh, the desperate sounds she made seeming to inflame and increase his desire to please her. 'You are so beautiful, so ready to be worshipped. You can't know how sweet and soft and inviting you are! I want you with every atom of my body,' he murmured, caressing her intimate folds before lowering his head and taking her in his mouth.

Aida cried out at the contact of his lips. He kissed her for a long time, with a depth and sensuality, a power and a promise, taking her into the warmth of his mouth, drinking her, his tongue probing and licking, and from time to time adding to those caresses the fiery touch of his fingers, leaving her reeling: every inch of her alight, every thought a meaningless jumble.

Aida burned from the inside out, certain she was going to ignite. There was no longer need for her to tell herself not to think as the slow flames of desire flooded her with mindless heat. The magic was voracious, like a forest fire consuming everything in its path. More, more, more … her mouth was dry, she was licking her lips, she wanted it never to stop.

When she could go no further, she closed her eyes tight, letting the pleasure cascade through her, a long, sobbing breath escaping her throat as he made her peak again and again until she was shuddering and crying out so loud that she startled the dozing birds in the willow tree, while everything broke within her flesh in a wild spasm. Phares collapsed beside her, panting, trembling, his body jerking convulsively as he called out her name, Aida's pleasure having unexpectedly become his.

They remained motionless for a while, satiated and spent, then Phares slid his arm around Aida's waist and drew her to him, laying her sleepy head on his shoulder and stroking her cheek with a very gentle finger before cradling her in his arms. The air was cold now, though there was still no wind. He had left their sweaters on the cushions beside them and they pulled them across their bodies, not wanting to let go of each other. 'We will have to spend the night on the boat, *chérie*. Cuddle up to me and I will keep you warm,' he whispered, enfolding her further in his embrace.

Aida loved feeling Phares at her side, the heat of his body seeping warmth into her own. She sighed with contentment as she huddled against his length, laying her head snugly in the hollow of his shoulder – it fitted just right. They were together in the misty cold air of the desert night, cloaked by stillness. The flapping winged *bennu* – the grey long-beaked heron that the Ancient Egyptians revered as a deity linked with the sun, creation and rebirth – silently came to visit them, along with the bright-eyed, timid fox. The slow, soft fall of the heavy night-dew enveloped them, while the petrified desert lying behind them hid its secrets from the rest of the world.

*       *       *

Following her night of passion with Phares, Aida was assailed with disturbing doubts. Although she realised that she had never felt so good as when she had been in his arms, Aida was more than ever uncertain about his feelings towards her. Sunshine threw a totally different perspective on their moonlight interlude, and it left her perplexed about how she wanted this chapter in her life to move forward.

Still huddled together as the night slipped away, in silence they watched the long fingers of pale, golden light stripe the land as the sun tinted the distant heights of the dunes to a pale rose. The Nile gleamed with delicate mother-of-pearl reflections as gradually sky and river became blue and the north wind began to blow.

'We'll go back now,' Phares said, 'and we'll announce our engagement immediately.'

Aida's heart slammed against her ribs and she sat up suddenly. 'Engagement?'

Still reclining on the cushions, his dark brows drew together. 'Why do you sound so surprised, *chérie*? Didn't you enjoy our night together?'

She stared down at him, unnerved by his brooding intensity and mystified by his words. 'Surely one can't base a marriage on one night of pleasure?'

'Don't look so anxious.' His laughter was softly taunting. 'We have a head start on most couples who decide to get married.' He reached out and ran a finger up her forearm, heat in his gaze. 'A man and woman who can spark each other the way we did last night can set off more explosive reactions in each other. Aren't you curious to know how much more I can teach you? Yesterday was just the tip of the iceberg ...'

His touch made her skin shiver but nothing he said made her feel as though she could trust her heart to him. She moved off the cushions and sat on the bench, gazing at the river, flat as a mirror in the calm of the transparent air. 'Phares, we want different things from life. Isn't it better we just remain friends?'

'Friends?' Phares sat up, his eyes darkening. 'What we did last night had nothing to do with friendship, Aida. You wanted me in the same way a woman wants a man. I want to marry you because we cannot go on like this – we don't *need* to go on like this. I am a normal man with normal needs. I want you as a wife, not as a friend, not as a sister. I want to come home to you every evening, to reach for you in the night ... touch you, smell you, taste you without feeling guilty. I reined myself in this time, but I cannot vouch what will happen if I have you in my arms again.'

Aida felt herself blush to the roots. There was no denying it. The images that filled her mind at those words excited her, but it was exactly that excitement that drove her to resist what Phares was asking for. It would never be enough and she would be destroyed.

She turned her head towards him. 'There will *not* be a next time, I will make sure of that,' she said with emphatic finality, trying to belie the yearning that she feared was so blatantly written on her face. 'I admit what we had just now was certainly more than enjoyable … it was enthralling. But I could never envisage marrying someone just for the promise of physical pleasure. The day I marry, it will be for love … and love had no place in what happened between us last night.'

Though Aida saw the shock in Phares's eyes at the forcefulness of what she'd said, the corner of his mouth half lifted in a smile. 'You forget, *chérie*, that as my wife you'll have a few more diamonds to deck that beautiful fair skin of yours. You'll want for nothing.'

Her eyes widened. 'You think I care about all that?'

'Perhaps not,' he said, his look softening. 'But life would be a hell of a lot easier for you. No more worries about Karawan House's extensive renovations, and we could live there if you wanted. We can sort out the accounts, and with some Pharaony capital, your land will yield twice as much produce. In a material sense—'

'I had never realised you were so materialistic, Phares,' Aida cut in. 'There is more to life than jewellery, riches and satisfying one's lust. Besides, I don't want Pharaony money.'

Phares let out an irritated sigh. 'Don't be naïve, Aida. You're a woman alone in Egypt. If you decide to return to England, as you suggested yesterday, what would happen to Karawan House and your estate? You're a very rich girl and your property is deteriorating by the day. What will you do, sell it?'

'I don't know, I haven't thought about it,' she replied testily. 'You can't expect me to make snap decisions about the future as soon as I arrive. I don't want to sell Karawan House or the estate, I never shall, but I haven't had time to live in it long enough to think about what I'll do. I know that your father has made an offer to Uncle Naguib to buy it, but you can tell him from me that I'm not interested in his proposition.'

Phares's tone became persuasive. 'This is not about the land. Of course your land would be an added bonus, but that's not why I'm asking you to be my wife. Maybe originally that is how it was, but since you've come back …'

'Since I've come back, nothing's changed. If anything, the situation has become more complicated,' she shot back, though she had no desire to try to articulate her feelings any further.

His gaze was unwavering. 'It is not complicated, Aida. You want me and I want you. We were promised to each other years ago and now we can unite our families. It makes sense for us to marry.'

Aida wrestled with the twisted skein of emotions inside her, and she wondered why this confrontation was making her pulse race in a strange and terrible way. She wanted to lash out at him, hurt him, provoke him into telling her that he wanted her because he loved her, and that she was all he needed.

'What a romantic proposal,' she answered sarcastically. 'What makes you think I want to unite with your family anyway?' And before she could stop herself, the old anger and suspicion resurfaced. 'Do you forget that *your* father is to blame for *my* father's death? Yesterday hasn't changed any of that.'

Phares's eyes were like volcanic glass, warning her that she had pushed him too far. In a single stride he was next to her, hands fastened upon her shoulders, warm and hard, relentlessly pulling her upright from where she sat on the bench. Giving her an angry shake, he bent his mouth close to her face. 'Don't be a child! Without your blind accusations and your stubbornness we'd be married today with a pack of children. I'd have a purpose in life beyond work and you wouldn't be roaming aimlessly like a lost soul, prey to a lonely life and wasted youth, fighting a battle that cannot be won for the simple reason that the culprit must be far away by now and you haven't a chance in hell of clearing your father's name on your own.'

He stared down at her, at her hair half flung across her eyes, the buttons of her dress still half undone. His face was lean, hard, and the look on it made her breath catch. Her pulse beat heavily in the silence that hung between them.

'Let me go,' she whispered, turning her head away.

'Look at me,' he ordered.

She gazed up at him. For a brief moment the atmosphere between them was alive with vibrations, swift missiles of thought and feeling that flew from his eyes into hers, exploding in little shafts throughout her body. There was something in his eyes that seemed to touch her deep down, where her jumbled feelings were most vulnerable and yet desperate to remain undetected.

He was not hurting her but he was making it impossible for her to struggle, holding her so tightly that she could hear his heart thumping in his chest. She felt the burning imprint of his hard-muscled body begin to stir hers to an even greater response than the night before. He lowered his head, his ardent gaze boring into her belligerent blue eyes, searching for answers even she herself didn't know.

'Aida, Aida,' he murmured at last, close to her mouth. 'If you had allowed me all those years back, I would have been the doting father whose loss you feel so keenly, the sympathetic brother you never had, a protective husband content to lie like a dog at your feet, a gentle, considerate lover sensitive to your every need. I would have shielded you against anyone who tried to hurt you. But instead you chose to leave, and now you come back more beautiful and desirable than ever, awakening the beast contained within every man … I want you, Aida, with every fibre in my body, every cell in my brain. I think I've always wanted you. And it may have escaped your notice, but I always get what I want … and despite your stubborn resistance I know you want me too.'

Aida strove to control the heady mixture of feelings that welled up in her. She looked up, not yet conquered, full into his eyes.

'Maybe you've never met your match before,' she breathed, her eyes flashing a blue flame. 'Perhaps I'm not of the same breed as the women you're used to.'

Phares laughed softly as her words tailed away and he pressed himself against her, making her knees almost give way. She felt the potency of his desire pushing against her, sending hot spears of need quivering deeply along every vibrant nerve, confirming what she had tried so desperately to deny.

She felt his fingers relax their hold round her shoulders a little, but he didn't let her go at once. Instead, he murmured in her ear, 'The proof of the pudding is in the eating, *chérie*,' before taking her lips in a most sensuous kiss, his tongue wandering into the intimate recesses of her mouth, a never-ending kiss that seared right through her bones.

Despite herself, Aida felt her hips mould themselves to his and gave herself up to the pure magic of Phares's caresses as his hands roamed her body. Her fingers encircled his neck, seeking the warmth of his thick, raven-black hair as she returned his kisses; then leaving her lips, his mouth sought out the angle of her jaw, the hollow beneath her ears, the smoothness of her neck down to her shoulders.

It was only when his exploring fingers started to slide her dress off her shoulders, exposing one of her breasts, that she struggled against him in spite of her wild longing, and managed to break free momentarily from the spell he was weaving.

'No,' she breathed, almost in a swoon. 'This is madness!' She staggered back, pulling the top of her dress back on, running distraught fingers through her dishevelled hair. 'Please, Phares,' she whispered, staring at him wide-eyed and vulnerable. 'Please don't, it's not fair.'

'Aida,' he coaxed, 'don't pull away from me.' He stepped forward as if to take her in his arms again, but she backed away, her hands held up to ward him off. His breathing was irregular as he murmured, 'Opportunities are precious, life is fleeting. Yesterday we were young, tomorrow we shall be old. Remember that, Aida. One day you and I will marry.'

'It is not possible,' Aida replied, trembling.

'All things are possible, if one wishes them to be. Ah, Aida, you are like most women! You fear what you most desire.'

His obsidian gaze was lit with intensity. 'Give me a chance. Give *us* a chance. Fine, I admit I've been going too quickly. In my panic to lose you, I've rushed things. I let you leave eight years ago, because I didn't realise what we could have together. We're meant for each other. No man and woman were ever better suited to one another than we are.'

He took a step nearer and studied her face. 'And, Aida, believe me, I will do everything in my power to help you clear your father's name, one way or another, even if it takes a miracle.

'Say you'll marry me – if you want to wait, so be it, I'll wait as patiently as I can, but let's get engaged.'

He spoke with such passion, Aida didn't know what to think. *Was this a declaration of love?* she wondered, her heart beating faster. 'What are you saying?'

'*Rihlat al-alf mil tabda bikhatwa*, a journey of a thousand miles starts with one step. Let's take it one day at a time and learn to know each other.' He came closer, bending forward, and Aida felt his lips touch her forehead with extreme tenderness. 'I'm going to Cairo for a couple of weeks. I won't press you for an answer today, just think about what I've said and we'll talk again on my return.'

There was a new expression in his face, one she had never seen before.

Aida sighed. He was saying a lot, but not the three short words she longed to hear – which would have swayed her: *I love you.* Still, she could feel herself weakening in the face of such passion.

'Fine, we'll talk about it on your return.'

His eyes filled with devilment. 'Then shall we seal this contract with a kiss?'

'No, we shall not,' she said emphatically, although she still craved the delicious impression of Phares's mouth on her lips.

'Your wish is my command, *chérie.*'

Phares took his place again at the end of the long, elegant boat with the tiller resting underneath his arm, while Aida sat on one of the seats at the side of the felucca. He manoeuvred the sailboat into the middle of the river and they set off through the fresh morning air.

On the banks of the Nile the sands sparkled with a peculiar glitter like some mysterious treasure, making Aida feel as though she was still caught in a dream. She gazed uneasily at Phares, whose face was turned to the sun. Perhaps it was inevitable that she had not been able to resist the dark fascination of this pharaoh, this man who despite not having a drop of Arab blood running in his blue veins had somehow soaked up the instincts of those desert dwellers who raced their horses on the dunes, with falcons on their wrists and an almost barbaric glint in their eyes.

Phares was like the soul of Egypt itself that coursed through her veins … she could run from him for a while but he would always draw her back to him.

\*　　\*　　\*

When they arrived at Karawan House, *Dada* Amina greeted them with a huge smile. Aida breathed a silent sigh of relief. As she had hoped, the old servant had taken for granted that she had spent the night at Hathor with her friend Camelia, like she used to in the old days. Not for a second had it crossed this simple, kind woman's mind that Aida had been up to anything untoward.

After Phares left, having politely refused *Dada* Amina's offer of coffee, explaining that he was needed at his hospital, the housekeeper took a close look at Aida's face.

'You look tired, *habibti*. I bet you were up half the night gossiping with Camelia,' she said. 'Just like old times, I expect.'

Aida gave a weak smile, feeling slightly flustered. 'Yes, it was. I think I need a bit of time in my room, maybe catch up on some sleep.' *Dada* Amina wasn't quite ready to let her off the hook. 'It was a good party, yes? You seemed to be getting on well with Phares *Bey*.'

She turned away, evasive. 'Yes, it was kind of him to give me a lift home.' She gave a small yawn as though to mark the end of the conversation and, making her excuses, headed for the staircase.

Aida could feel *Dada* Amina's disappointed eyes on her back but she couldn't talk – not now. There was so much going on in her head … so many crazy thoughts to sort out … and she needed to do so without her old nurse's advice – or Phares's overbearing presence, for that matter. His proximity stopped her from thinking rationally. Mind you, she was too tired to ponder it all in any rational way, and realised it would be wiser to sleep for a few hours. She was on too much of a high to assess all that happened and what it meant to her. Her whole body was aching, her cheeks burning as her mind relived the night of passion they had shared.

Restlessly she went to her bathroom to shower. Hot water needled her skin, running in rivulets down the breasts he had stroked so tenderly. Tremors curled like a snake across her stomach and down her thighs, reminding her of his fingers' warm touch, and she trembled, missing him … needing him … wanting him.

Phares hadn't deflowered her, but he had taken away her innocence; he had kept his word; he had shown her 'the sun at midnight in a dark sky without stars' and she knew that she would never be the same again, never be able to look at her nakedness without thinking of his kisses and the ecstasy of his touch.

Still, she needed to remember one thing: she was not the only woman in his life.

The things he had said to her, about dying for her, burning for her: they had all been said to other women in order to make weak fools of them, Aida was sure of that. The way he kissed, the way he touched, proved Phares was a practised seducer. He had used her to assuage the fire that Hind the gypsy dancer had lit in him, she told herself stormily. That, with the wine and the hashish he had no doubt inhaled from the hubble-bubble, the desert air, the romantic moonlight, her own need to touch and be touched … as well as an overwhelming desire for him … all of these things had contributed to what had finally happened.

Then there were those rumours about Isis Geratly and Nairy Paplosian. Although when Aida faced him with the gossip about Isis, Phares had brushed it away as mere fabrication, she knew that there is no smoke without fire. But Isis was not the one Aida feared the most: her real rival was surely Nairy, Phares's beautiful Armenian mistress, the woman he really loved, but who would never be accepted into his prim circle. Aida remembered her father telling her that many Egyptian men entered into a marriage of convenience and kept a mistress on the side. The wife was often only too pleased to rid herself of what she considered a degrading act, the only use of which was to have children. Sexual pleasure was regarded as the province of men. Ayoub and Eleanor had of course been modern in their thinking, and Aida could never accept any sort of marriage of convenience. For her, fidelity was one of the most important bases for marriage and she expected her husband to be as faithful and devoted to her as she would be to him. Could Phares be that kind of husband?

Stepping out of the shower, Aida was drawn to the mirror and she stood staring at herself, at the passionate flare to her nostrils, the kiss-bruised look of her lips, the darkly glowing pleading in her eyes beneath the tumbling hair that Phares had run his hands through so hungrily. He was right: she was a woman who needed a husband and children. Alone for too long, she now recognised a long-buried yearning for a family of her own. Maybe she had been a fool to resist his proposal. She could still feel his skin against her own, his hands on her body, the long, hard length of him pressing against her, the power of his burning passion she had not been able to resist in the dense black shadows and silvery shafts of moonlight that had enveloped their night of romance.

It had been a sensual captivation which had nothing to do with the heart, she told herself. Not once had Phares uttered the word love, it had all been about longing and desire and pleasure. She had responded to the carnality with a wild abandon that brought the shamed blood rushing to her cheeks.

Something so savagely sensual bore no relation to love.

Phares had aroused her to an animal sensuality. It would be beneath her to give in to such lowly instincts; she would not allow him to make of her an odalisque, with no freedom or will of her own, a simple extension of the great Phares Pharaony – a mere heap of curves and limbs to be caressed.

Had she really promised to think about marrying him?

Aida closed the shutters and climbed into bed. Restlessly, she twisted and turned between the sheets in the wide double bed, flagellating herself with all the might-have-beens, her thoughts lingering longest on the bond she felt with this man, the like of which she had never felt with anyone else. And when they were not bickering defensively with each other, she recognised the warm companionship and mutual understanding that had been there all those years ago.

The temptation to become Phares's wife, to be totally his, possessed by him, to sleep and wake up in his arms every morning of her life was overwhelming. She had never given it much thought, but now she knew. She could never marry someone that didn't excite her in the way he did, and she doubted very much that person existed.

Still, there remained the eternal thorn in Aida's side … Kamel Pharaony, the man who had surely played some part in her father's death. How could she marry his son? How could she live in the same house as the one person she blamed not only for bringing about Ayoub's demise, but sullying the reputation of an honourable man who all his life had been known for his integrity? So, Phares had promised to help her clear her father's name? How could he when the culprit was his own flesh and blood?

Yet if she held fast to her rejection of him for that reason, which meant so much to her, she must sacrifice all the joy and peace and fulfilment she had felt in Phares's arms last night and again this morning. Either way, it was a ruinous choice that would leave her incomplete.

Demons continued to gnaw at Aida like rats in a corn vat until, finally exhausted, she closed her eyes with half a sigh and sank into oblivion.

*     *     *

The Jeep turned swiftly out of the gateway of El Amal hospital with a small, derisive touch of the horn, Phares's way of saying goodnight to the *ghaffir* guarding the gates. It had been a busy day. One of the factories in Luxor had caught fire and fifteen men and women had been brought to the hospital suffering shock and burns. All the staff had been working flat out for the past five hours, dealing with the emergency in addition to their routine work. Phares had performed two scheduled operations – and one including the division of the obturator nerve to enable a spastic child to walk – before rolling up his sleeves and helping on the wards. Only once he was satisfied all that needed to be done was completed, and that his presence wasn't required anymore, did he call it a day.

He took a handkerchief from his pocket and wiped the sweat from his face. It was a hot and humid night. He glanced at the Rolex on his wrist: almost midnight. He would have liked to go home to shower, but he still had some work to take care of. Nothing to do with the hospital, this was private. He sighed wearily.

Night and silence had descended over the land. To his right, the moon made a shimmering pathway across the Nile; to the left, the fields gave up their fragranced sweetness. As he drove swiftly, heading for his cottage a mile away from Luxor, the lights of a few private villas glimpsed through the sycamore trees went out one by one. Luxor was going to sleep. The water and the land were bathed in soft silver moonlight, the peaks of the distant desert hills no longer stood out against the dark night sky.

For the first time since he set foot in the hospital that morning, Phares allowed himself to think of Aida and the night of passion they had shared. All day he had fought against that memory, and now wondered why he wanted so badly to marry her. With his natural aversion to emotional dependency, was he the right kind of man for her? Could he give her the sort of unconditional love she wanted? He had made some impulsive declarations on the felucca that now surprised him. Dammit, she put fire in his blood, making him feel things over which he had no control.

The potent pleasure he had felt at her enjoyment had been a rude awakening. He had never felt that way about any woman before. Up until now, for Phares sex had just been an exchange of caresses between two consenting people, the only purpose of which was mutual pleasure. And although what had occurred between Aida and him had been little more than heavy petting, the intensity of his release had been so much greater than anything he had experienced before. The power of his craving for her disturbed him now. Wasn't he better off just accepting the Aida of the present, enjoying a relationship with her and letting this marriage project remain in the past?

*Give it up*, he told himself as he pressed his foot on the accelerator. *Do the sensible thing and marry Isis. Let go of this new complication in your life.*

Excitement vied with apprehension, but to be controlled by his emotions rather than his intellect was a new experience for Phares, one he did not like. Particularly where Aida was concerned. She'd always exercised some strange, maddening power over him, even when they were younger and he had just seen her as an impudent, headstrong young girl.

He played back the various conversations they'd had since Aida's return. Most were disastrous – she acted as though she hated him. Still, in his arms she'd lost control and despite her obvious innocence become the most generous lover he'd ever had, giving herself completely, without a shadow of inhibition. This was no mere girlish infatuation ... but what exactly did Aida feel for him?

She was an interesting study. He could never reconcile her personality – passionate, ardent, fierce towards her enemies – with her delicate features and rose-petal skin. Aida's blue eyes were surely never meant to hold those mysterious flashes of fire and light; that sensitive mouth was never intended to give utterance to the wild, reckless, sometimes harsh words in which so many of her thoughts were clothed.

Indeed, Phares saw more keenly than ever the fiery soul that dwelt within that appealingly feminine exterior. Physically, Aida was astonishingly strong; he found her mentally alive, alert, vivid, almost startlingly so. Violent in her likes and dislikes, she gave the impression that she could be a splendid friend and an equally wholehearted adversary. Her will was indomitable, except when she was in his arms; her temper hot, and her heart …

It was there that the mystery lay.

Such a mystery only added to the complication of his feelings for Aida. He couldn't claim it was love, yet it went far beyond ordinary desire. He wanted nothing less than her complete surrender.

His problem was how to get her to want him enough to be his wife. Had she actually said she was happy about his proposal? No, she hadn't. Many words had streamed out of her, but she hadn't really said anything at all when he got right down to it. Was she truly refusing him because of what had happened eight years ago, or because she just didn't trust him? Both, probably …

His frown deepened. And then there was his promise to her. For eight years the truth about who had framed Ayoub El Masri had remained unknown. It had always troubled him that Aida had suspected his own father and had left Egypt without seeing Phares. He'd never had the chance to convince her that she was wrong about Kamel. Now things would change.

He parked the Jeep in a lane close by and walked to the cottage. The shadows were deep over the garden, although it was a clear moonlit night and he could see for miles. The atmosphere was heavy without the slightest breath or sound; the trees themselves slumbered in the starry silence. Even the croaking of the frogs had stilled; it was as though the whole world slept.

He made his way quickly there through the dark shadows, and without turning on the light, went to a locked cupboard in the back room he sometimes used as a bedroom. He pulled a set of keys out of his pocket and unlocked the cupboard. A shaft of moonlight fell on to a large safe that took up the whole length and breadth of the cupboard. Phares dialled the combination and with a click, the door swung back to reveal the most beautiful head of Ramses II. The details of the piece were exquisitely rendered. It was as if life had been breathed into it by the sculptor's hand.

Phares stroked the object pensively, then, pulling a towel from a nearby shelf, he wrapped the pharaoh's head in it, locked the safe and cupboard and quickly returned to the car. Without wasting any time, he exchanged his day clothes for a dark kaftan, throwing a scarf over his shoulders. He headed back towards Luxor and then on to the new road that had been built during the war across the desert from Luxor to the Red Sea.

This was not the first time he had taken this road at night to reach his destination. He had used various methods in the past, all equally charming and necessary for his purpose: floating swiftly in a felucca under a strong breeze down the Nile, as he had done the day before with Aida; riding slowly upon his horse Antar; driving up the old highway in a more or less comfortable horse trap. This time Phares had intended to ride his horse, but he had been delayed at the hospital and would miss this month's meeting if he didn't use the Jeep.

As he drove, he felt his heart thumping hard against his ribcage. However dangerous, he loved these nights of adventure riding through the dunes. Every time he made this journey, whether by car or on horseback, he felt at one with the desert as he passed these ancient temples, imagining their secret world of pomp and pageantry, but which were now just echoes of his ancient history. The moon's silver sheen glittered over the white dust that lay so thick upon the road. Now and then, bats dipped down through the air and darted off again, shrieking, but otherwise the great stillness of night was everywhere, not to be broken until he reached the rickety bridge that led to the opposite bank of the Nile.

Phares stopped the Jeep and tied the scarf around his head in a makeshift turban before crossing the bridge and taking the road beside the river. It wasn't long before he came to Kurna, a typical village of mud huts, a few low, whitewashed houses, a miniature minaret set on a tiny white cupola'd mosque, and the inevitable grove of palm trees planted for their pleasant shade. A few shadowy robed figures passed in the night, sometimes with dancing lanterns in their hands. Unlike Luxor, Kurna was not asleep tonight; the yellow gleam of lights shone through unglazed windows. The Jeep glided as silently as possible on the soft dusty sand covering the road, yet those keen-eared peasants, more akin to the Bedouins of the desert than to the *fellahin* who worked in the fields, seemed to know as if by some sixth sense that a stranger was moving through their village at night, and they came in ones and twos to their doors to look at him, or peered quizzically out of windows. Although they appeared eerie in the unreal world created by a full moon, it didn't bother Phares, he was used to it. Had he been on his horse, they would still never have spoken to him, merely watching with curious eyes. Once or twice his horse had set a couple of dogs barking half-heartedly, which had brought someone to the door, and at those times he muttered a greeting which seemed to put them at ease, but he never stopped.

Leaving Kurna, the road branched off towards the west and he soon found himself in a dry sunburnt gorge where no vegetation could grow, where the soil was either rocky stone or arid sand and the only living things were snakes and scorpions. This was the famous Valley of the Tombs of the Kings, where the royal dead of the long-vanished Thebes had been laid to rest.

As the Jeep moved slowly through the narrow canyon, on each side the ragged cliffs, pink in daytime but silver under the moon, loomed high overhead like sentinels as if to guard the way into this once sacred place. All along the gorge stretched the tall silhouette of the ridge. Its isolation and lack of living green growth showed how suitable the place was for the melancholy purpose to which it had been appropriated – the hiding of the mummies of the kings of Egypt. The scene was unutterably desolate – wild, bleak and forbidding a valley as that of the shadow of death, which it really was – and yet for Phares there was a certain grandeur about its dreariness that made him dream, and his heart filled with pride at being a descendant of such a great civilisation.

The narrowing track between two jutting cliffs was bumpy, littered with fallen boulders, loose quartz and flints. Gaunt hills culminated in a single, square-shaped peak whose sloping sides were debris-covered. Here was the Place of Truth, dominated by this thrusting mountain called Al Qurn, the Horn, which bore down on the sixty-three royal tombs hidden under the pale scree of these valley walls, their square black entrances cut into the rock, giving no hint of the riches within. Phares shivered, feeling the weight of a dynasty of souls, of the mortals who believed themselves to be gods, whose tombs had been plundered with little respect for the sanctity of the place.

He scanned the deserted canyon as he drove along the track, and let out a breath when his eyes picked out what he was looking for.

Three men. One was mounted on an elegant white stallion; the other two had racing dromedaries, trained for speed and endurance by the Bedouins and worth their weight in gold to a smuggler. Able to cover seventy miles in a single night, castrated camels like these were taught never to utter a cry: highly useful for a rider needing to go undetected.

He stopped the Jeep at the bottom of a high cliff and got out, whilst the first man dismounted and strode hastily over the sand towards him, his blue garment over which he wore a vast *burnous* flapping against his brown legs, his rascally proud face and shining eyes alert like those of a hawk. Very tall and slim, his broad square shoulders gave an impression of forcefulness and endurance, his powerful frame rather like that of the camels, Phares thought. Carrying a long-barrelled rifle and a curved dagger wedged into his belt, his head was swathed in a scarf, his flowing robes criss-crossed with bandoliers of bullets.

All around, the sands lay silver and serene, broken into patches of black where the boulders cast their shadows. In the cloudless sky the big white moon hung motionless, as though arrested by the strange scene beneath.

'*Salam aleykom*,' the Bedouin greeted Phares when he reached the Jeep.

'*Wa aleykom el salam*,' Phares replied.

'The Bedouin are strong like the desert, soft like the sand, moving like the wind and forever free.'

Phares met the large striking eyes of the Bedouin, which were perfect luminous orbs of a green colour, the whites so pronounced as to give almost supernatural depth to the jet-black pupils. 'They are the emperors of the desert and no one can touch them,' he replied.

The two men looked at each other in silence for a few long moments.

'*El Sahara ghadara*, the desert is treacherous, especially at night. Have you lost your way?' the Bedouin asked at length.

'Yes, I am trying to get to the town of Luxor on the other side of the Nile and I seem to be going round in circles.'

'Turn round the way you came and drive along the shore of the great river until you find a bridge which will lead you to El Oxor.'

'Thank you. I have no money to reward you for your kindness, but maybe this will do,' Phares told the man, reaching under his seat.

He took out the precious head wrapped in a towel and held it out. Before taking the bundle, the man signalled to his companions to bring his horse and join him. It was only once the men on their camels had surrounded the Jeep that the Bedouin took the bundle from Phares and proceeded to unwrap it. Uncovering the head, which shone in the silvery light, the shadow of a smile passed over his angular face.

'That will do,' he said, and handed Phares a small jute bag. 'Be on your way and *Allah* be with you.'

'And with you. *Salam.*'

Before Phares had had time to blink, the Bedouin had mounted his horse and the three men disappeared in a cloud of dust, soon swallowed up by the shadows, the ravines and the cliffs.

Phares didn't leave immediately. He sat for a while in the open Jeep, savouring the velvety windless night. Shadows were sharp among the honeycombed sides of the gorge. Storks flitted uneasily around their rooftop nests, white and ghostly against a blue night sky brilliant with stars – a canopy of sapphires and silver, broken by occasional long-tailed comets, shooting restlessly from one spot to another in the patterned heavens. Phares had seen mirages by day, but the night, too, had its mysteries – cold and aloof, yet deeply romantic. He sighed deeply, wishing Aida was with him to share the magic of it all.

It was a long time before he started up the engine and began the long journey back, his mind brooding on his promise to Aida.

# CHAPTER 8

Although the days that followed *Sham El Nessim* were busy ones for Aida, they went by on legs of lead.

The work on the estate was complicated, especially as it was carried out in Arabic, which was not Aida's forte. Every other day she would need to look over the books and she was not used to the endless discussions about crops and livestock. The daily dealings with the *fellahin* were also difficult, because although they loved and respected her, these older men, some of whom had worked for her father, viewed with scepticism her ability to run such a large domain. To begin with, she was a woman, and they knew she had no real experience of the land.

As time passed, Aida began to grasp the logic in the advice given her by Uncle Naguib and *Dada* Amina. Marriage to Phares would be the ideal solution to these material problems.

It was not only the estate work that made the days seem arduous. Phares was away in Cairo for a couple of weeks and Aida could not keep her thoughts from straying to their wild night on the felucca. His touch had left upon her the forceful imprint of his personality, and if during the day she was able to push his memory away through sheer determination, at night it was different: he haunted her dreams over which she had no power. Although she thought she knew him quite well so his personality on the whole didn't frighten her, she also knew that there were women in his life and there always would be. She had

tried to imagine what it would be like married to Phares, living
in the family home with Kamel Pharaony and Kamel's elder sister
Halima, who had never liked her. It would be a strange life, not
at all the life she had planned for herself, but in time she would
get used to it, she supposed, and when they had children ... they
would, of course, have children. She had to remember, too, that
Phares was a loner. There was a side of his life in which she had
no part: the part of him that needed to escape the routine of life
and hankered for the wide-open spaces of the desert, for
the silence, the peace. Aida could never be part of that, even if
she married him, if only because she would be the woman who
would be his wife, cherished and protected, on a pedestal where
she must remain, like all married women in their circle.

At this point her thoughts would always flow back to Isis and
to Nairy ... Phares was a man with a great appetite and she would
never be able to rest assured that he wouldn't always be having
some sort of affair going on the side. How could she ever consider
linking her life to someone she couldn't trust?

So, it was on one of these musing afternoons that the invitation
to the fashion show of the year arrived. This haute-couture
extravaganza was to take place in one week's time in the ballroom
of Shepheard's Hotel. Aida had scarcely finished reading
the details on the card when she received a phone call from
Camelia inviting her to stay at Kasr El Shorouk for the event,
eager for her friend to spend some time with her in Cairo. They
agreed to leave the next day by plane, giving them a whole week
to explore the Musky bazaar and enjoy socialising at the Gezireh
Sporting Club, of which they were both members. The first polo
match of the season was to take place on the day after their arrival
and when Camelia told her that Phares would be participating,
a nervous thrill went down Aida's spine.

Although she had not been back to the club since her return
from England and she was slightly apprehensive at meeting

the circle of friends she had mixed with before the tragedy, Aida was elated at the idea of seeing Phares again. Not only that, but she would be staying under the same roof as him. The very thought made her whole body tingle with excitement.

*    *    *

The Gezireh Sporting Club, a British military club since the late nineteenth century, was an exclusive meeting place in Cairo where the Egyptian elite rubbed shoulders with British officials and cosmopolitan socialites. That afternoon the polo ground presented an animated scene.

The players had not yet appeared, but the ponies were on the field in the charge of their white-gowned *saises*, grooms. Nervous and eager, the animals' coats were gleaming, their small hoofs dancing with impatience. The pavilion and the rows of chairs were filling with spectators: men in cool linen, women in bright summer frocks and shady hats. In the brilliant sunshine, under a deep-blue sky, all colours were intensified: the vivid grass, the striped awning, the tall trees beyond. The very hot air had that dry and stimulating quality peculiar to Egypt, a heat that sharpened the senses, exciting and seldom exhausting.

Everyone seemed to know everyone else; as more and more people arrived cheerful greetings and laughter could be heard. Men already seated sprang up, women found their closest friends and sat down side by side, girls waved to each other and to young men. There was an air of ease and intimacy in the assembly, something very pleasant to those who belonged to the charmed circle, less pleasant for any who did not, as Aida had found out to her cost after the scandal of her father's trial. The volte-face happened overnight – suddenly she had been ostracised and isolated. She remembered clearly one instance when she had visited the club and was watching a tennis match: she had a chair in the centre of a row, but she might have been on a desert island, or indeed totally invisible. No one seemed aware of her; women talked across her as if she did not exist. Nevertheless, her presence had not gone unnoticed and she soon realised that everyone was whispering about her.

Today, although guarded, she was determined to keep her head held high. The premises at the club hadn't undergone any changes: as far as she could see, the eighteen-hole golf course, the immaculate tennis courts, the beautifully tended lawns and gardens were the same, and the red-brick tiled clubhouse with flower beds on either side of its straight driveway lay under the scorching sun just as she remembered it. Still, most of the people she'd known all those years back were not around anymore. The crowd today was largely British: army officers, agency officials, and administrators working for the Egyptian government as well as the royal family. And of course there were the rich Egyptians and foreign residents of Cairo with their wives and families.

Aida leaned back in her cane chair with a vague, thrilling sense of anticipation. She and Camelia had arrived at Kasr El Shorouk very late the night before and had not seen Phares. That morning, he had left for the hospital before the young women had woken up.

Aida had decided to wear one of the new outfits she had bought from the Shemla department store, a dashing bright-red frock with buttons scampering down the side to fasten in the new popular side-closing. Its gathered yoke-line culminated in a self-fabric belt with crossover buttoning. The tailored collar gave the dress a neat formality, while the handy little pocket on the bodice, mirrored again but tilted at the hipline on the skirt, added a charming, casual touch.

The players were now coming on to the field. She immediately spotted Phares's tall figure as he appeared with a *sais* leading his pony. Phares swung himself into the saddle, turning to wave towards the pavilion where Aida, Camelia and so many of his friends were gathered in the first and second rows. Catching sight of Aida, his smile lingered on her face, making her flush. He stood out among the others. Dark, handsome, deep-set black eyes, straight nose, strong mouth and chin: a rider par excellence, Aida thought, at one with his mount, his big frame showing the grace of perfectly trained muscles.

But he was not the only polo player Aida recognised. In his team she identified Alastair Carlisle from the British Embassy and in the other, she noticed, with an uncomfortable pang, Prince Shams Sakr El Din. The prince was quick to spot her in the group of spectators and, like Phares, acknowledged her presence with a tilt of his head, lifting his hand in a salute as he came on to the field, his penetrating eyes piercing right through her. A strange, apprehensive premonition shuddered through her as she met his gaze despite herself. Like a small bird fascinated by a snake, she was enthralled and helpless, hating and loathing its oppressor while succumbing to his charm.

'Look who's there,' Camelia whispered. 'I've never seen him on the polo ground before.'

The umpire threw in the bamboo ball between the two teams lined up in front of him in their helmets and knee guards, and the chukka started. The teams were well matched and the players first-class. The ponies' small feet thundered on the hard ground, that lovely thunder like no other sound on earth, up and down, wheeling, up and down again. Phares had the ball; leaning perilously from his saddle he followed through with his polo stick and scored a goal while the audience clapped and cheered.

'Bravo!' Camelia cried out.

'*Moheeb*, magnificent, bravo!' echoed the strong voice of a woman immediately behind them. Aida recognised it at once, and a little shiver of jealousy ran through her as she saw Phares's head lift a moment on hearing Isis Geratly cheer, his eyes searching the audience before a smile flashed across his face in their direction. A moment later, taking advantage of the three-minute interval between chukkas, Isis leant forward. 'Hello Camelia, what a surprise to see you in Cairo.' She nodded politely towards Aida. 'May I join you?' she asked, pointing to the empty chair next to Camelia.

'Yes, of course,' Camelia replied, smiling, though Aida could feel her lack of enthusiasm.

Isis looked stunning in a bottle-green day dress with a bias pleated bodice, green jadeite jewellery on her ears, at her wrists and on her fingers. Her head seemed almost regal with its shining coil of black hair pinned up high; her face beneath a picture of perfection with its finely arched brows, small mouth and narrow forehead.

'How long are you staying in Cairo?' she asked Camelia.

'For a week or so. We're here for the Shepheard's fashion show.'

Turning to Aida, the young woman continued her interrogation. 'Where are you staying? At Shepheard's?'

'No,' Camelia answered for her, almost defiantly. 'Aida is staying with us, at Kasr El Shorouk.'

Isis's round brown eyes stared unblinkingly at Aida, a stilted smile frozen on her beautiful face. 'How lovely for you! Aren't you lucky to have such generous friends?'

Refusing to be embarrassed by the stinging allusion she couldn't have missed, Aida replied simply, 'I know.'

Camelia was about to add something when the whistle announcing the next chukka silenced her. Aida's eyes were now on Phares. Flushed like a rose, lips parted with excitement, she watched the man who had occupied her thoughts day and night since their trip on the felucca. From time to time her attention strayed almost indifferently towards the other players; she studiously avoided looking at Prince Shams Sakr El Din, recognising the fascination the desert monarch held for her and wanting to sever any chance of a friendship burgeoning between them.

During the next break between chukkas, Camelia and Aida talked among themselves, purposely ignoring Isis. The latter swiftly disappeared, reappearing after the interval to sit with a group of her friends.

And now, during the final chukka, the ball was Phares's for the fourth time that day. Again, came the clapping, the hurrahs as he made the last goal of the game, securing victory for his team. Heart beating fast, Aida watched as he came towards them, a broad smile lighting his flushed face. He looked superb in his polo outfit, a towel slung around his neck.

'Aida, Camelia, how lovely to see you here! I didn't realise you knew that I was playing today.' As they stood to greet him, he gave each a peck on the cheek, his lips lingering a little longer on Aida's. His fleeting proximity and the powerful heat radiating from his muscular frame brought a swift recollection of the last time his body had been this close to her, and her pulse seemed to thunder as loudly as the ponies' hooves on the polo field.

Camelia's voice piped up: 'Papa told us this morning at breakfast. We felt it would be a great way of spending an afternoon. Aida hasn't been to a polo match since she left Cairo and we wanted to support you.'

His velvet jet-black eyes dwelled intensely on Aida's face, making her legs turn to water. 'Well, you definitely achieved your goal! Your presence made all the difference. You might even say that our team owes its triumph to you.'

Camelia laughed and nudged her brother affectionately. 'Don't be so modest. The team always wins when you're playing.'

Out of the corner of her eye, Aida could see Shams Sakr El Din walking into the pavilion with an assured step; to her horror, after uttering a quick, pleasant word of greeting for his friends, he wandered over to their little group. In her confusion, without thinking, Aida made the introductions.

The prince smiled graciously. 'Phares Pharaony, at last we are introduced officially after years of our paths almost crossing … By *Allah*! This is a trick of fate – a most delightful one.' And turning to Camelia, taking her hand and lifting it to his lips, he whispered, 'And your beautiful sister. *Enchantée, madame.*'

Shams Sakr El Din then held out his hand to Phares, which the young doctor accepted, his level gaze holding the Bedouin's. Electricity crackled in the air.

'A truce,' the prince proclaimed, and laughed.

'You think?' Phares replied coolly, his eyes narrowing to slits.

'Is it not so?' the other demanded. 'We meet here, in this beautiful garden, in the presence of these charming ladies. You and I, for the first time playing polo together, albeit on opposite teams. Is this not a sign?'

With a swift, almost imperceptible gesture he drew from somewhere – a pocket or his belt – a little toy dagger set with semi-precious stones such as Aida had seen sold in the Musky bazaar as souvenirs and which were usually used for slitting envelopes or the pages of an uncut book. With a twist of his long slim hands, he broke it at the hilt and flung it to the floor of the pavilion, between himself and Phares.

'Thus,' he said, seeming to consider that by his action he had finished something which no one present was aware had ever begun, and that all was made clear and satisfactory.

Phares seemed to have perceived the cloaked meaning of the gesture because Aida saw his face darken in a way she recognised when he was holding his anger back. Still, he said nothing, but looked directly at the prince in an unwavering stare.

'*Allah!*' the prince exclaimed, hands thrust out, palms upward – a gesture recognising his by-play had fallen flat. 'Do you not remember …? I can't believe you don't know …' There was a note of harsh reproach in his voice. 'Have you forgotten that your ancestor and mine met in a single combat to cleanse the honour of a daughter of the House of Sakr El Din? And how, when both fatally wounded, they cursed each other and all their descendants?'

Phares looked blank. 'I don't.'

'But, *habibi*, my dear fellow, the enmity between your house and mine is historic! I drank it in with my mother's milk as surely you did with yours. Though the shame was washed out, the memory remains.' His compelling yellow eyes betrayed a twinkle as they held Phares's cool gaze, his urgent voice holding an undertone of amusement which belied the force of his words. 'Can we ever be friends?'

Phares was saved from replying by Alastair Carlisle, who had just joined the group. The conversation quickly moved on to the match, and as other players from both teams and their friends came over, settling at the small tables in the garden just outside the pavilion as afternoon tea was ordered, all talk now revolved around the polo tournament.

Excitement was in the air, fostered by the spring weather – a time for engagements and weddings. This time of year, the days were dazzling, the sun hot, and the evenings like velvet. The intense heat of summer had not yet visited Cairo. There was a fresh tang to the mornings and a cool desert wind still sprung up about midnight, which made sleeping a comfortable thing. This was the time for gymkhanas, amateur singing galas, garden parties, dancing under the stars, and of course, picnics in the desert.

The prince was quick to choose a seat between Aida and Camelia, while Isis, who had by now joined the group, grabbed a place next to Phares.

*It's all so predictable*, Aida thought with a sinking heart as she watched her lay a possessive hand on Phares's arm and whisper something in his ear.

Her attention was broken by the prince's deep voice, his tone almost reproachful. 'I haven't seen you around since Princess Nazek's ball,' he told her, his pale eyes scrutinising her face.

'I've been in Luxor, trying to put my estate in some order.'

He nodded sympathetically. 'Yes, I can imagine that it is a great burden for a woman on her own.'

'Oh, I'm not alone,' Aida was quick to contradict him. 'My uncle Naguib is a great help and most of the people involved are experienced employees who worked for my father.'

'Well, you know you can always count on me for assistance. I myself own quite a large amount of land in Minieh, which I often visit. It's not that far from Luxor, and it would be easy for me to call on you if you needed help.'

Aida smiled awkwardly. 'You are very kind. I will certainly bear that in mind.'

A high-pitched female voice entered the conversation: a young Englishwoman sitting next to Alastair Carlisle. 'Are you giving your annual party at your oasis? I hope I'm not being too cheeky in saying I'd love to see your desert palace. My friends who went last year really enjoyed themselves.'

The prince flashed her a smile. 'Yes, of course. I'm a little late this year, having been busy organising the fashion show. The invitations are going out as we speak. I'll make sure you are on the list. This year I propose to organise the event differently. My guests will not drive to the edge of the desert and leave their cars there, as in previous years. Despite my men standing guard, there was some vandalism last time. I wouldn't want it to happen again so I will have a bus collect my guests and camels will carry you into the desert to Kasr El Nawafeer. Naturally you are all invited for the weekend.'

The proposition was met with cries of enthusiasm.

The prince's gaze switched back to Aida. 'I hope you will do me the great honour of accepting this invitation,' he said, bowing towards her. 'I will accept no excuses.' His voice flicked like a whip and his heavy seal ring caught a last bright ray of the setting sun as he laid a hand proprietorially over Aida's, making her shiver.

'But, of course,' she said, a forced smile quivering on her mouth. 'It sounds terribly exotic.'

'Camelia, Aida, I'm afraid it is time to leave.' Phares had stood up abruptly, his black eyes holding a meaningful gleam as they met hers. 'Father has invited some friends over for dinner and it'll take us a good while to get to Kasr El Shorouk. We'd better get a move on.' Turning to the group who were protesting loudly, he gave them his most charming smile, his teeth brilliant against the copper tone of his skin. 'There'll be many more occasions to get together, my friends, but you must excuse us today.'

Aida breathed an internal sigh of relief that she was able to escape the prince's possessive hold, and they left the pavilion in silence as they made their way to the car.

'What was all that about dinner? Papa left this morning,' Camelia asked her brother as soon as they were out of earshot.

'I know,' Phares muttered, frowning as he strode ahead, 'but it was the only way I could get you both away from that suave fox. How dare he paw Aida *einy einak*, in broad daylight! I had to do something.'

*Osta* Fathi was waiting for them with the Cadillac outside the clubhouse. Here, Phares took his leave: 'I have my own car. I'll shower and change and join you at Kasr El Shorouk.' Turning to Aida, he added, 'We could have an early dinner. Perhaps you would care for a horse ride after that in the desert?'

Aida's heart quickened at Phares's suggestion. Although she knew being alone with him again was dangerous in case she was to lose her self-control, she turned to Camelia for her approval. Knowing her friend didn't particularly enjoy riding, Aida didn't feel she should leave her on her own without checking first with her.

'Go ahead, please. There's something on the wireless I want to listen to tonight. They're reading passages from *Kifah Tibah*, Thebes at War. Naguib Mahfouz is my favourite writer, I don't want to miss it.' And with that, she climbed into the car.

Aida cheeks burned as she lifted her eyes to Phares, hoping he couldn't read too much into them. 'I haven't ridden in the desert for years. I'd love to go for a ride after dinner. Thank you.'

His eyes met hers with a glint of awareness. 'Our last escapade was rather successful, wasn't it?' he murmured. And as he held her blue gaze prisoner of his own, so dark and intense, Aida was aware that everything around her was quiet but for the cicadas who were ever present yet always unseen, like the motives of the human heart.

\*        \*        \*

After dinner, Phares was already waiting for Aida in the hall when she came down the grand staircase wearing fawn-coloured slacks and a man's shirt tied at the waist. As she took in his tall, lean frame, she couldn't help but feel that familiar stirring deep in her belly. Standing next to one of the long windows, one arm resting on the architrave, staring out into the night, he had a dignified and noble appearance, looking more than ever like the proud Copt he was, who held firmly to the traditions of his race and caste. His long legs were encased in black riding breeches, and he wore a white shirt open at the neck with the sleeves rolled up and knee-length boots of gleaming black leather; a powerful figure in his riding gear, full of vigour, the thong of a whip wrapped around his brown knuckles.

'Ready?' he asked as he turned towards Aida with a broad smile.

'Yes. I haven't yet had time to buy my riding gear, but I think this will do.'

His gaze moved over her appreciatively. 'Yes. You look good in trousers and the way you're wearing that shirt is very ...' he hesitated, then added, 'flattering. You need a riding hat though. You can borrow one of Camelia's from the tack room in the stables. She hasn't ridden much since Mounir died.'

'I feel bad leaving her alone this evening,' Aida murmured as they headed for the large wooden front door.

'I wouldn't worry. Camelia likes her own company and listening to the radio.' He gave her a warm look. 'She's really brightened up since your return. For the first few months after the accident she was almost a recluse.'

'It's terrible to lose a loved one, especially so suddenly,' Aida said, knowing the significance of her words but not caring.

Phares's lips twisted. 'Yes,' he muttered, his jaw tightening.

For a brief moment the atmosphere crackled with electricity, threatening to raise the usual wall of antagonism between them, but it evaporated as soon as they stepped out into the garden and a rush of cool, sweet air greeted them. Phares reached out for Aida's hand and regretting her earlier point-scoring, she didn't pull away.

Darkness had fallen. In the navy-blue sky the stars shone with an intense and lustrous brilliancy, blinking and winking in the early night. They went through a wrought-iron gate that led into the big gravelled yard of the stables, a long line of whitewashed brick buildings behind the house surrounded by high walls. Aida sniffed the air and found the smell of horses and hay a healthy dispeller of melancholic thoughts. Youths were busy about the place and though they eyed her furtively with curiosity, they did not speak to her, keeping their gaze to the floor. It was not protocol in Egypt for the yard hands to look at or converse with the guests, no matter how informal their dress or manner.

Phares approached a boy who was cleaning saddles and asked him about the foal whose mother had apparently been put down the week before. The boy set aside his cleaning rag and rubbed his palms down the sides of his narrow trousers, then led them across the yard and down a passageway. There in a scrubbed stall was the foal, firmly planted on its long legs, a black beauty with a cocky little tail and the promise of a proud mane along its silky neck. Aida knew little about horses but she could tell that the foal was exceptionally fine. She went forward to fondle the perked ears, and at once, the foal backed away from her and began to kick the wall with its back legs.

'Be careful,' Phares warned, pulling her back. 'He's young, but he's already spirited like his father, Zein el Sahara, Prince of the Desert, my best horse.'

'Was he in one of the stalls upstairs? I didn't notice him.'

'No, he's much too nervy to be among other horses. He has his own box outside, behind this stable block.'

'Are you riding him this evening?'

Phares shook his head. 'I only ride him when I'm on my own. For our evening stroll, I have chosen a beautiful fawn-coloured mare, Bint El Nil, Daughter of the Nile, for you, and for me, my other favourite mount, Bourkan, Volcano. Another spirited black horse, but older and wiser than Zein el Sahara. I named him Bourkan because when I give him free rein it sounds like an erupting volcano when his hooves start galloping.'

Aida's eyes followed Phares as he moved slowly but deliberately to stand in front of the foal, who immediately began to nuzzle his hand. 'Your love of horses and the desert is so strange,' she said finally. 'You were made to be a Bedouin.'

'Maybe that was who I was in a previous life,' he said, his eyes looking far away, as if he saw the immense desert before him.

She stilled. 'With a harem of women ... is that what you pine after?'

Phares sighed. 'Contrary to what you think of me, I'm not as one-track minded as you are. I might have known a lot of women, but that is not my sole objective in life. But sometimes, like you, I feel the overpowering constraints of our society and I long to break free of its chains. Still, most of the time I am well aware of how lucky I am to live the wonderful life I have, especially when I look around me and see all the misery in the world.'

Aida watched him thoughtfully, wondering what constraints Phares felt. Was he thinking of Nairy Paplosian and the customs controlling Egyptian society that looked unkindly on the mingling of blood and the mixing of social strata, condemning a person if they married outside their circle and their cast? A lump suddenly formed in her throat at the disturbing thought: it had happened to Ayoub when he had married her mother, an Englishwoman.

The stable hand returned with some cubes of sugar. Aida laid one on the palm of her hand and spoke seductively to the foal. He at once pricked up his ears with curiosity and took one or two sidling steps towards the sweet bribe she held out to him. The young animal quivered as he caught the scent of it, and the next moment his velvety muzzle was tucked in her palm and he was gobbling up the sugar. When it was all gone, he pushed his head against her, roughly but not spitefully, and allowed her to fondle his ears.

'He's beautiful.'

'He should be, he has a fine pedigree. Both his parents have won awards.'

Phares and Aida went back to the stable block, where their two mounts were waiting for them.

'She's lovely,' Aida exclaimed as she ran her hand down the glossy neck of Bint El Nil's pale satiny fawn coat.

'She should be. She's the descendant of Baz.'

'Baz?'

'Yes, it's a Berber name from the desert-born legend, *The Birth of a Stud.*'

Aida glanced at him, her eyes twinkling. 'I remember those days when you used to read me and Camelia tales from the *Arabian Nights*, but you never told me that one before.'

A flare of warm recognition lit his eyes and leaning up against the stable wall, he adopted the mien of raconteur, familiar to Aida from those far-off days.

'In a tale whispered through the ages,' he began, 'it is rumoured the mare was born from the breath of the Creator. No animal on earth could improve upon her nature or form. It's said that she was in foal and gave birth to a colt, and in time they were mated. For generations her descendants replicated her perfect beauty, intelligence, and agile strength. She was named Baz, and is the Eve of the Arabian horse breed. For thousands of years, the original shepherd's descendants bred the pure stock of Baz. Her family grew and branched out, as did her caretaker's, until the desert lands were renowned for both the nomadic Bedouin tribes and their unique hot-blooded horses.'

Aida smiled at him, for a moment transported to those carefree days of her youth. Then she asked, 'How did you come across her?'

'I have many friends among the Bedouins,' he said, checking the girth of Aida's mare was properly tightened, something Bint El Nil clearly did not like, for he had to speak to her in a low, gentle voice to get her to stand still so that he could help Aida up into the soft brown saddle.

She then watched as he mounted Bourkan, who did his best to get rid of his rider. Using his wits and horsemanship, Phares stuck on. Aida could see immediately that the the stallion was not only swift but free-spirited, occasionally giving way to youthful exuberance, dancing sideways as they went. But trained to the nth degree, he finally became amenable to Phares's touch on the rein, settling down to business, aware that a master was in the saddle. Phares recognised to a fraction the difference between high spirits and vice, and knew exactly how far he might indulge his Arab mount, and when he needed to bring Bourkan to heel without jerking the horse's sensitive velvet mouth unnecessarily. It was wonderful to watch the two wills, that of the man and his beast, fighting for supremacy.

A belated third-quarter moon lent an uncertain light, its pale bulk reflected in the tranquil bosom of the canal that lay along the way from Kasr El Shorouk to the Pyramids Road. As they rode, talking easily together, the broad expanse of the fields' waving green faded away into the illimitable distance. The scattered mud villages, huddling under clumps of palms, were mere ghostly sketches, like mirages in the night, and the pyramids stood high above on a surprisingly lofty bluff which marked the eastern edge of the eternal sands.

Soon, they reached the Great Pyramid. Here, on the edge of the desert, the night was lighter and the Nile Valley presented an almost unreal, haunting view.

'Shall we go down to the Sphinx?'

'Yes, it's never so impressive than by moonlight,' Aida replied keenly.

'I've seen him at various times of the day and at each hour I find he has a different expression but I think it's by moonlight that I like him the best.'

'You automatically say *he*. Is the Sphinx a man? Wasn't the Greek Sphinx of Thebes a woman?'

'Man or woman, it's the most extraordinary piece of sculpture ever wrought by human hands, even if its sex is lost in that pitiless, stony glare. I slept at its feet one night. My Bedouin friends disapproved because they say the place is haunted by the ghosts of the Arab cemetery just over the rise from the Sphinx.'

'Was it a good experience?'

Phares beamed. 'It was wonderful. The desert was an extraordinary pink colour in the moonlight.'

Aida smiled at his enthusiam. 'Did you see any ghosts?'

'There were a few Arabs crossing the cemetery in the distance. They did actually look like black ghosts. Anyone walking in the desert at night seems to be stealing across it. Strangely enough, a grey owl flew out from somewhere, I couldn't tell where, and sat on the Sphinx. It stayed there a long time before flying away. The moon gave it a curious ghostly sheen. A beautiful sight ...'

'The spirit of one of the Arabs lying in the cemetery perhaps.'

'Maybe. It did cross my mind.' Phares gave a low chuckle. He seemed completely at ease on horseback here in the desert. 'One feels very privileged to lie under a wondrous sky, gazing at the majestic calm of the Sphinx's face.' He turned to look at her, the glint in his eye visible in the dim light: 'We must do it together some time.'

At a walking pace they passed the Pyramid of Cheops, bore around its massive eastern face and down into a valley. The three great pyramids towered nearby, their silhouettes soft yet glowing in the magic of the moonlight. There was no one else about and the effect was so potent, all conversation between them was hushed in awe at the grandeur of those monsters of the past and the illimitable spaces of the billowy desert. It felt to Aida like passing over a recent soft snowfall, and she was lulled by the gentle, swaying motion of their mounts and numbed by the chill of the night.

Cantering now, they descended to the deserted hollow wherein lay the Sphinx. The huge sculpture, carved out of the solid rock of the plateau, was half buried in the sands. The moon softened the gaze of its sightless eyes and threw the sharp shadow of its mighty back on the face of the desert. In this soul-stirring atmosphere it wore the mystic look for which it was renowned, one which spoke of eternal secrecy. At a standstill on their horses, Aida and Phares did not speak but stared up at the mighty sandstone figure so disdainful of man, marvelling at the leviathan's length. It was almost terrifying in this vast solitude. Silent, menacing, a crouching half man, half lion lying at the edge of the desert, it gazed through human eyes towards the dawn.

'It makes you feel like an ant,' Aida whispered to Phares.

He nodded in agreement, then dismounted, tying Bourkan to a post before helping Aida down. In doing so, Phares kept his arm around her waist a fraction longer than necessary, their gazes tangling in the half-light. She stared back at him in a half-daze before he released her to tie the mare next to his horse. A new awareness crept into the air between them as they started to walk silently through the valley.

He turned suddenly to face her. 'Have you thought about our conversation the other day?'

'Yes.' She stole a glance at him from under her lashes, dreading the next question.

He had turned away from her and appeared to be totally absorbed in the view in front of him, his profile set in unreadable lines. 'Have you come to any conclusion?'

She almost held her breath. 'Not really, Phares.'

He said nothing, but Aida sensed he was brooding on his own thoughts. She wanted him to know she cared, wanted him to understand her dilemma, and searched her mind to explain more clearly what she felt.

'The situation between us is not simple, Phares ...'

Aida trailed off as he suddenly strode towards her. His hands closed around her shoulders as he pulled her against him, turning her face up to him so that she was forced to meet his penetrating gaze. 'Would it be simpler for you if I was Shams Sakr El Din asking you to marry me?' he said in a dangerously low voice. 'I saw the way he was looking at you at the clubhouse.'

Aida's eyes widened in surprise. 'The prince? No, he has nothing to do with...'

He hooked an arm around her waist and drew her sharply against his hard, strong body. Continuing as if he hadn't heard her, he growled, 'Because it's not him you want, Aida, it's me.'

The smell of his warm skin, of soap and fresh tobacco and maleness made her head spin. He was shockingly handsome in the moonlight as it fell upon his jet-black hair and proud features, haughty, arrogant and utterly mesmerising. Feeling his arousal hard against her, heat rushed down her body, pooling between her thighs. She wanted to give in to her desire for him right there and then but that would not make her situation any easier.

She inhaled raggedly. 'No, Phares. You've got it wrong. The last thing I want is to marry Prince Shams Sakr El Din. Besides, how could I? He's Muslim, you know that.' Aida was shocked by the unthinkable suggestion. 'It's just that I need more time,' she whispered. 'Give me more time … This is a lifelong commitment you're asking me to make.'

Staring back at him, Aida was aware of the hot and urgent desire flashing out at her, barely controlled. She knew how sorely she had tried his patience, how frustrated he must be in still finding her elusive. A flush of guilt pulsed into her cheeks and she looked down, struggling to justify her determination to follow her own instincts instead of considering his feelings.

Phares studied her face as though weighing up her answer and finally relaxed his hold on her. 'Whatever you want, Aida,' he conceded gruffly. 'You're like a hobby lantern, you know that?'

Aida understood perfectly what Phares meant. Those atmospheric ghost lights were like mirages seen by travellers at night, especially over swamps, resembling a flickering lamp. It was said to recede if approached, drawing anyone who came near it away from the safe paths. She could not afford to keep him waiting too long without running the risk of forfeiting everything if he turned away from her to Isis.

Her gaze flew back to his. 'I know I'm sounding so selfish.'

'It's your prerogative, you owe me nothing.'

Saying nothing more, he brushed the back of his hand to her cheek tenderly, his expression scorching but sad. There was something in his look that made her almost ready to agree to whatever he wanted even if she was not convinced that it was wise. She smiled gently. 'I promise to give you my answer before going back to Luxor.'

'And I will wait patiently.' His eyes glowed with anticipation. 'Let's go back now. I'm leaving early tomorrow morning for Luxor. I'll be back in a couple of days for the fashion show.'

They walked back to the Sphinx, where the horses were tied together. Phares helped her back on to Bint El Nil, then swung himself into the saddle, looking more than ever a dashing figure, as if he and his mount were one.

As they cantered back across the hard sand they spoke little, not because Aida had run out of conversation, but because she had the feeling that Phares was pensive and tired, wanting only to be left to his own thoughts.

As they reached the top of the hill, Aida suddenly found her saddle slipping, its girth strap having come loose. With it, she felt herself sliding sideways. The startled mare broke into a frantic gallop; Aida was falling and could not free her right foot from its stirrup. An instant of panic … the terrified thought of being dragged … the thunder of hooves behind her. The next moment she was caught, her foot miraculously freed, then somehow on Phares's horse, held fast and safe before him.

Aida turned to look up at him: 'Thank you.' Already breathless, the look in Phares's eyes, the clasp of his arm, rendered her more so. Looking ahead, she tried to laugh. 'How did you do it? …' Her voice died away.

His voice was low and gravelly near her ear. 'I did nothing. It is no extraordinary feat, trust me. No more than any Bedouin youth could have accomplished.'

'What about Bint El Nil?'

'She'll be fine. Our horses are trained to find their way back to our stables. She's young and won't go far. We'll probably find her back at Kasr El Shorouk on our return.'

Phares held her against his strong chest, his arm like a band about her, his muscular thighs bracketing her own.

'You seem to know the desert well, too. But how?' she managed to ask, although it was hard to keep her voice level while her whole body was being assailed by tiny jolts of excitement.

'The desert is what you make of it, *chérie*. You dream it, you have hopes about it, embellish it, and one day you discover it and you don't know what to think or say. It intimidates us into silence. You watch the sunset, you marvel at the subtlety of colours, and then you return to your inner self, to your thoughts. But the desert only makes sense if you take the time to stay in it. If not, it gives nothing. It remains a postcard, the image of a lacklustre memory.'

'Have you ever lived in the desert like the Bedouins?'

'No, but I'd like to.'

'But how could you ever? You're a civilised man, a well-educated surgeon.'

'You have no idea how seductive the desert can be on the senses, especially at night when all is silent and the stars flood the sky. It is like a woman,' he murmured, 'alluring and challenging, with depths in which a man might get lost forever. I have known it in all moods, yet each time I ride, its sweeping spaces offer something new.'

'You *do* love the desert, don't you?'

'Of course. The wild is a necessity for man's spirit and as vital to our lives as bread and water. Believe it or not, the way the Bedouins live is healthy: a regime of dates and water and sleeping under the stars. You will find that most of them have a serene expression, and they're rarely overweight. Some live to a hundred. They are much more attuned to nature than those in what we call the civilised world. I can assure you that on horseback you'll see, feel and enjoy more in one mile than you would in a hundred sitting in a car.'

'But the desert seems so wild. Unyielding ... cruel.'

'The soft and tender things are never as exciting as the more primitive ones. The hard-shelled passion fruit is more delicious than the peach once its shell is broken open. The dragonfly that eats the moth is magnificent in colour. The cactus, which we call the cruel flower, holds water for the man lost in the desert.' The arm around her tightened. 'I would have thought you of all people would understand this with your adventurous nature.'

He was right. How well he knew her. In turn, she wanted to discover more about this man to whom she was becoming increasingly drawn by the minute. His breath was warm against her neck as he leaned a fraction forward. 'There is a place to which I ride sometimes when the moon is full or when the dawn rises. It's all veined with blue and gold, the lapis lazuli blue of your eyes and the gold of your hair. I call it the Moonstone Oasis, because of the dreamy atmosphere that inhabits it, and never on this earth was there a place lovelier, or lonelier. Would you like to ride there with me one day, *chérie*?' His voice became a husky caress. 'I can imagine making love to you on its silvery sands.'

Phares had set her senses tingling unbearably. She looked back at her rescuer. Though his dark eyes blazed, raking over her feverishly, he remained silent as he turned Bourkan towards the shadows of the high, barren cliffs and mountains outlined on the horizon.

Phares now urged his horse into a canter. While the Arabian horse's gait was fluid, moving smoothly under Phares's command, Aida still had to adjust herself to its faster motion, aligning her back snugly against Phares's hard chest as he instinctively held her tight against him. Together, their bodies moved rhythmically as one. She felt his thigh muscles flex around her and the pleasurable hot ache that spread rapidly through her body was almost painful. Yet added to this familiar physical yearning was something more profound and serious within her, something of which she had so far been only vaguely conscious. Now, Aida responded with a drumming of pulses that made her dizzy – this was different to the stirring excitement of desire.

For a crazy instant, giving herself to the fresh breeze and the swift motion while he had spurred Bourkan on, something had tugged at Aida's heartstrings. Something directly opposed to the dark memories which she so stubbornly encouraged. She wished Phares was running away with her, forcing her to make up her mind, forcing her to admit to her true feelings for him.

At that moment Aida felt a sudden yearning to be free – free of old bitterness and resentments, from the taint of hatred which had gripped her and to which she had deliberately clung. She had prided herself on her refusal to forget, had believed herself incapable of doing so, her pain biting deep into her soul, and she'd been convinced it had left a permanent, unhealable scar.

Still, held like this in Phares's strong arms against his beating heart, upon a racing Arab galloping off into the desert, love, like a velvet fist, reached out and struck through her skin to her very heart and gripped her. All of a sudden, she realised what love and passion could be, coming alive as she had never done before. With a thrilling realisation she thought – *Oh yes, there is nothing in life I want more than to be Phares's wife.* Yet for now she would keep her secret warm in her heart until she could choose the right moment to tell him of her decision.

Soon they were back at Kasr El Shorouk. With slow steps they rode through the moonlit garden; overhead the starry sky and all around the tranquil night with its sleeping flowers and the incessant breathing of nature in the undergrowth and trees. As they made their way to the stables in silence, a golden beam flashed swiftly across the sky, and Aida pointed upwards to it with her whip.

'See there, quickly! Phares, a falling star! Wish something now before it vanishes!'

'The saying goes that it is a glistening flame thrown by one of the angels,' Phares answered, steering Bourkan towards the stables, 'that pursues an evil *djin* who crept into heaven to listen to the secrets of the future.'

'I prefer to think that it's the sign of the passing of a soul, and if we quickly make a wish, it will carry it to the throne of God,' Aida said with a crystalline little laugh, while a curious exhilaration ran through her because she knew her wish – or rather her prayer – was safe with God. Things would come right – she was sure of it now.

Later that night she stayed up for a long time, unable to sleep, reflecting on the sudden decision that seemed to have landed upon her out of the blue and thinking longingly about the life she would have with Phares.

They would travel, but her real home would be upon a cultivated strip between the Nile and the Western Desert, an exotic estate growing wonderful crops, guarded by brave *ghoufara*. She loved Egypt, and had assumed before her father's death that she would remain for the rest of her life here. In those days she had never wondered about her English roots, never really given thought to her dual nationality, even while at boarding school. She had been comfortable in both places. It was only after the scandal and the hardships of war in England that she had been aware of her Englishness. Back in Egypt now, she felt torn between her two bloods.

Aida sat on the balcony outside her room in a warm and sheltered corner, looking out across the rooftops and trees to the line of glinting gold which was the desert. She thought of Phares and how he had told her that he occasionally went out there, far into that vast emptiness, alone. She too loved the desert: she had tramped enough of it with her father, looking for buried tombs and undiscovered temples. Still, she had to admit that she loved it as a stranger, a visitor, an excavator. To her it was exotic, something wonderful to see, a place where she had camped with her father a few times, but which still held a lot of mystery. But to Phares, those sandy wastes were a part of his existence. That great family could have been descended from the pharaohs themselves: the desert was in their blood.

*     *     *

For the next two days Aida was walking on clouds. Her mind was made up; she was no longer torn by doubts. Something had happened to her in the desert with Phares two nights ago that couldn't be wholly accounted for by the romantic, whimsical moment on Bourkan when she wished they would escape together into the desert and she had glimpsed a new horizon. There was an unprecedented calm deep inside her as though at last she had found the centre around which all else must revolve.

Even so, she jealously kept her secret, not breathing a word even to Camelia although they spent all their time together, having breakfast on the terrace, lazing at the pool at the Gezireh Sporting Club, lunching at Mena House, or simply sitting in the garden in the evening, listening to the cicadas, chatting while drinking cold *karkadeeh*.

On one of those leisurely days they decided on a shopping afternoon in downtown Cairo, where, between Cherif and Fouad Streets, a wide variety of shops lined the pavements, selling antiques and art, expensive jewellery – the latter mostly owned by Armenians who were known to be the best artisans – and fashion items. These luxury boutiques brought in the latest fashions from France, but also offered silk and cotton fabrics in an array of rainbow colours.

She and Camelia made sure to visit the large department stores like Cicurel, Sidnawi, Challons and Gategno, all of which showcased the finest wares manufactured by the Italian, Greek and Jewish communities. Coming back through the dark winding alleys of the Musky bazaar, where every arch glowed with lanterns on crowded stalls and the aroma of coffeehouses suffused the air, they came upon a large open *siwan*, a tent-like room where a *zar* was taking place. Aida had often heard about this kind of religious ceremony which used drumming and dancing to bring on a trance to cure an illness thought to be caused by a demon, but she had never seen one in real life, only at the cinema.

She grabbed her friend's arm. 'Oh, Camelia, let's stop and watch! It's just starting.'

Camelia looked sceptical. 'I don't think it's a good idea. You look foreign and we'll stand out like sore thumbs.'

'Look, there are foreigners standing around. Please, Camelia, don't be a wet blanket. I've always been curious about this ceremony. *Dada* Amina is a great believer in it and I'm fascinated to know what she sees in these things.'

Camelia gave her a wry look. 'All right, but not for long. It's getting late. Really, Aida, you surprise me. It's such a primitive, ignorant custom, unworthy of an intelligent woman like you.'

Aida shook her head. 'Look, I know it's a healing cult and the poor people who come to these ceremonies suffering some kind of mental trauma need proper psychiatriatic help. I'm just curious to know what it's all about, that's all.'

Lanterns flared yellow along the walls of the *siwan*. Men turned their turbaned heads to eye the two young women from the tops of their bare heads down to their bare legs. In the centre of the room stood an altar made from a round brass tray placed on a tall bench. It was covered with a white cloth and laden with piles of nuts and dried fruits. A woman in a *milaya-laf*, that flowing black cloak which Egyptian women have worn for centuries, spooned a whitish powder from a small clay pot on to a saucer of smouldering charcoal. After she placed the saucer on the brass tray, smoke rose from it and a thick sweet scent of incense rose into the air.

The place was filling with people. Near Aida and Camelia, a plump woman dressed entirely in white was beating a *tar*, a sort of tambourine, while another was banging a *tabla*, a skin drum, with the flat of her hand. As they did so, a row of similarly dressed women had risen to form a line in front of the drummer.

A tall man in a white kaftan and a skullcap pleated and puffed like a miniature baker's hat was walking towards the row of white-clad women through the quieting crowd of onlookers, growing larger by the minute, who turned and bobbed respectfully. A moment later, the man paused in front of a figure Aida hadn't noticed before, who was seated behind the white-clad women, facing the wall. It was the cocoon-like figure of a woman, wrapped tightly in a white kaftan, her hands and feet covered in henna, eyes lined with thick kohl. Women were applying to her skin what Aida concluded must be the special *zar* fragrances *Dada* Amina had told her about, said to purify the soul as they are inhaled, and used as offerings to the *zar* spirits, especially frankincense. And a few minutes later, as the ceremony began, an aromatic thurible was passed among the audience so that they too might purify themselves.

Now the room was starting to divide itself in two: the sheikh and the musicians occupying one side of the *siwan*, the rest of the participants on the other. Aida looked on, fascinated. 'She must be the patient, and he's the sheikh who will lead the *zar*,' she whispered to the frowning Camelia, who, unlike Aida, was obviously hating every minute of this strange ceremony.

The sheikh turned his back on his patient and, clapping his hands, set a faster beat for the drum. Incense was filling the place now. People started to clap and Aida followed suit, while Camelia kept her hands folded tightly against her.

Slowly, the sheikh began to pivot slowly on the heel of his brown slipper, marking out a small circle; one of the clapping women in white followed his lead. He was turning rather slowly, his face blank yet serene, arms outstretched like wings. Aida could see this man had a real rapport with his audience. He was gradually drawing all the women in white into his ever-widening circle, leaving the immobile wrapped-up figure visible to everyone, hunched defenceless and alone while her friends and relatives circled to the drumbeat to help her in her sorrow.

*If I'd had a nervous breakdown, would I want a crowd of people hovering while I went through the cure?* Aida wondered.

Boom! Boom! Boom! Still more drums joined the measured beat, and the clapping rang out in a long, sharp sound. Fresh incense had been added to the saucer. White skirts and veils of the twirling women caught the air, clouds of cloth below those of the incense which rose, adding a pungent thickness to the air.

The patient now appeared standing, eyes half closed, abandoning herself completely. Her movements were increasing in intensity with the drumming, taking her in circles around the altar, as though freeing her body from the inside out. The rhythm of the beating drums focused every eye on what was happening and Aida felt herself being slowly drawn into the ambience.

Camelia nudged her. 'Let's go, Aida. You're getting too involved.'

'I'm fine really, don't fuss.'

Suddenly the sheikh tripped, but he regained his balance, revolving with his head at his knees, before bringing himself up in a twisted, violent writhing of his whole body. His pleated cap fluttered to the floor like a dead moth.

And now, as the audience stared, they saw that the serene flat face had been transformed. The sheikh was in a trance, his eyes wild and staring through strings of long black hair. He raised his hands higher, supplicating, drawing the spirit into dialogue, sweat running down his face, the drums accelerating to keep pace with his quickening, rhythmic whirling.

'Ahhhh! Ahhhh!' The women marked their turns with short, sharp cries. The incense and insistent drumbeat as well as the rhythmic perpetual turning were beginning to tell.

Aida shook her head, fighting off a sense of giddiness. The scene had actually seemed for a moment to move backwards and forwards before her eyes. Beside her, Camelia fidgeted uneasily.

The sheikh was now closing in on the crouched figure of the woman, closer in his turns until in an apparently chance movement he touched her. He whirled away, then whirled back and dragged her swiftly across the floor, sliding her deftly into the centre of the circle.

The patient sat, a faceless pathetic bundle, the only fixed point in the moving whirling group in the *siwan*.

'Ahhhh! Ahhhh!' The women closed in, forming a protective circle of white around the sick person, who began to bob back and forth slowly and rhythmically. Above the drums and clapping, Aida could hear a new sound, a tearing, convulsive sobbing. Boom! Boom! Boom! The drums were deafening.

'Ahhhh! Ahhhh!'

Pivoting, the sheikh whirled swiftly upon the patient like a fury and tore open the cocoon of her white dress. The circle of women in white fell back and the drums ceased suddenly. The woman screamed, exposed in her wrinkled cotton kaftan, her eyes glazed, face swollen with weeping, hair dishevelled and wild. '*Allah!*' she wailed. '*Allah! Ya Allah!*'

Trying to stand, she fell in a crumpled heap to the floor. The women in white carried her gently to a corner, cradled and comforted her, smoothing her hair while she wept bitterly and loudly, calling upon *Allah* for mercy and compassion.

'Have you seen enough? Can we go now?' Camelia asked, restlessly.

Aida was still scanning the tent, peering from the sheikh to the women in white and wondering if that was the end of the ritual. 'Shouldn't there have been a sacrifice? I'm sure *Dada* Amina told me that usually they sacrificed some sort of bird or animal.'

'I'm going,' Camelia said emphatically. 'I would let you stay for all the gory details, but it's dark and I don't want you wandering these dark alleys on your own so let's call it a day, shall we?'

Aida laughed. 'All right, all right, don't get stroppy. It was interesting, fascinating even. It's one of our Egyptian customs.'

'Not one we should be proud of.'

At that moment Aida caught sight of a man talking to the sheikh. Dressed in a worn baggy shirt and faded old trousers, he was a clear head taller than most Egyptian men and had the features of a black-eyed hawk, his piercing eyes fringed with dark lashes, his nose narrow with a vague hump and hook. His thick, tightly curled hair was sun-bleached to a pale brown that contrasted strangely with his deeply tanned skin, and a black straggly beard clung to his chin like winter-ravaged ivy tendrils.

The man looked oddly familiar. For a moment Aida couldn't place him, then her focus sharpened as it dawned on her where she had seen him before: Karawan House, years before. It was Souma Hassanein's brother, Atef.

In a split second Aida weighed up what to do. She turned to Camelia, trying to school her features into a neutral expression. 'Look, I'm going to stay for a minute. Do you mind terribly?'

Her friend shook her head in resignation. 'I'll wait for you outside. Don't be long, all right?'

As Camelia left, Aida moved slowly through the crowd to the edge of the tent near the entrance and waited. She watched as Atef murmured something to the sheikh, put his hands together in thanks and started back through the crowd, coming closer to the spot where she was standing.

Instinctively, she reached out a hand and grabbed the sleeve of his shirt. 'Atef Hassanein, is that you?'

The man's head jerked sideways, scowling, then seeing that Aida was a well-dressed European, his expression became somewhat puzzled.

'*Hadreteck meen*, who are you?'

She held herself confidently. 'I am Aida El Masri. You are Souma's brother, Atef, aren't you? She used to work for our family in Luxor.'

He could not conceal his surprise. '*Sit* Aida? Ayoub *Bey* El Masri's daughter? *Ahlan*, welcome.'

She needed to be direct and to the point and scrutinised the man closely. 'You remember my father so you'll remember too that Souma left our house suddenly after his arrest. Where did she go?'

Atef's gaze held a coiled wariness. 'Souma left Luxor while she could. May *Allah* protect you, *Sit* Aida, but I cannot speak to you anymore. Your father, *Allah yerhamoh*, may God have mercy on him, was a good man. His death was a terrible tragedy, but you must stay away from all this.' His speech was low and rapid, his hawkish eyes flitting to the left and right as he spoke.

Surveying the man's restless posture and his agitated expression, Aida could tell that he was afraid. 'What do you mean, Atef? You know my father didn't steal that Nefertari statue, don't you?'

'You don't want to get mixed up in all this. Let sleeping dogs lie, *Sit* Aida. *Wallahi*, I swear to you, as *Allah* is my witness, these are dangerous people … they have eyes and ears everywhere. If they find out I've talked to you, we'll both be killed.'

She stared into his dark face. 'If *who* finds out? Who are you talking about?'

Atef's gaze was caught by something behind her. He took a step away. 'I'm sorry, *Sit* Aida, forgive me.' Before she could ask him anything else he hastened towards a group of people leaving the tent and disappeared into the night.

She stood there for a moment before leaving, knowing it was pointless trying to follow him. She cast a glance around the tent, wondering who or what had made Atef bolt so suddenly, but in the smoky haze all she could see was the same group of people milling around. The plump woman had taken up her *tar* once more and was singing in a guttural voice.

Aida joined Camelia outside without a word of what had happened. She had to keep this to herself until she could think clearly about what to do. Children skipped around them as they went past the dark blind fronts of the Musky houses into a lit-up row of fruit stalls, still open although it was late. The insistent sweet smell of ripe guavas reached them, triumphing over all the other smells of the alley, and they paused to buy some of the pungent fruit before hurrying to where they had left *Osta* Fathi, the driver with the car.

*     *     *

On that last night before Phares's return, as she was undressing to get into bed, Aida heard a car drive up to the house. She ran to the window hoping it was Phares, but in the moonlight, it was clear enough for her to make out that it was not his car but a taxi. Soon, Camelia came running down the stairs as two men got out, carrying a third. Aida watched as she joined them, leading the three men into the house. A few minutes later, the two bearers hurried back to the taxi, which drove off silently. Shortly afterwards Aida heard a faint rap at her door.

'Come in,' she said, turning from the window.

The door opened and Camelia, white-faced and in tears, stood on the threshold.

Aida rushed to her friend. 'What's happened? Who was …'

Camelia brought a finger to her lips and whispered, 'Shush …' as she slowly closed the door behind her. 'Please come, I need your help,' she murmured, tears rolling down her beautiful face. 'Quickly! Sami has been hurt. I told him not to go … I knew it would be more dangerous than ever.'

Aida's brows knitted together. 'What's happened?' she repeated. 'Who's Sami?'

'It's a long story and I don't have time to give you details. Suffice to say a friend of mine has been hurt by a bullet and I can't call a doctor or take him to hospital.'

'You mean he's been shot?' Aida tried to keep calm.

'I thought they should bring him here. You're a qualified nurse, you've dealt with the wounded … I didn't know what else to do!' Camelia's eyes were wild with panic. 'Please come quickly, Aida, he's lost so much blood already.'

But Aida was already moving, snatching up her dressing gown and slipping it on over her underwear. 'What medical supplies do you have and where are they?' she demanded as she ran to the door, impelled by instinct.

'Phares sometimes performs minor operations on *fellahin* who've been hurt in the fields. Everything you need will be downstairs.'

Aida followed her breathless friend, both of them running through corridors and down the stairs to the basement where Sami lay on a small bed moaning, almost unconscious. He was young and well built, with a lean face that looked waxen despite his tanned skin, his brows drawn together in a grimace of pain. Aida immediately knelt down beside him and took his pulse: it was weak but steady. She unbuttoned his shirt to reveal a blood-soaked cloth tied tightly around a shoulder wound. She breathed a sigh of relief. Having dealt with many such cases in the war, she knew from experience that this was little more than a flesh wound. Sami was bleeding freely, but their main issue now was to remove the bullet and clean the area with antiseptic before infection set in.

Meanwhile, her friend was working herself into a frenzy of grief, sobbing almost uncontrollably. Aida, needing to keep a cool head, was brisk: 'Camelia, fetch me painkillers, antiseptic lotion, cotton wool, sterile dressings and a clean bandage. And stop that noise!'

Calmed by Aida's measured tone of authority, Camelia immediately went to a large medicine cabinet against the wall, unlocked it and hunted among the well-ordered medical supplies to find the items. Aida breathed another sigh of relief when she saw what a well-provisioned household it was, inwardly blessing Phares for it. A moment later and she was giving Sami a shot of morphine in his arm. Then with swift, deft fingers, she swabbed gently at the congealed blood around the wound, before probing it carefully to remove the bullet with a tweezer-like probe. By now, Camelia had stopped crying and looked on helplessly while Aida stitched and dressed the wound, until it was ready for the bandage.

'I've done all I can, now you must leave him to rest.'

Camelia went to her friend and put her arms around her, fresh tears rolling silently down her face. 'I will never forget what you've done tonight, Aida. Thank you.'

'Here ...' Aida felt in her dressing-gown pocket for a handkerchief and offered it to Camelia, looking at her with concern. 'He'll need an antibiotic. Check there are some in the cabinet. You don't want that wound to become infected.'

Camelia took the handkerchief, her huge eyes red and watery. 'Yes, of course. There are some, I'll get them now.'

'Good.' Aida was relieved, yet knew that Sami still needed careful supervision. 'You know, he should still be seen by a doctor, don't you?'

Camelia nodded, then retrieved the medicine from the medicine cabinet. 'You've been wonderful, Aida. I can't thank you enough. I don't think that a doctor could have done any better than what you've managed. But don't worry, his friends are coming back in a few hours. They're planning to take him to another friend's house, whose father is a doctor. Tonight, it just couldn't be done, it was too dangerous ... but you've saved him. God bless you.'

'I've given him a sedative so he'll sleep for the next six hours at least. Tell your friends they must move him carefully.' Her expression softened. 'You need to get some rest. I can see it's been a great shock.'

Camelia shook her head. 'I won't be able to sleep. I know you must be exhausted after the strain, *habibti*, but can I come up to your room for a while?'

Aida gave a sad little laugh. 'Strain? That was nothing.' Her eyes clouded as she remembered the suffering she had witnessed in the war hospitals. 'I've seen much worse that this.' She put an arm round Camelia's shoulder. 'Anyhow, I'm wide awake too. Why don't we have a cup of *teelio*? It's been so long since I've had some. It'll calm us down.'

Camelia's face brightened slightly. 'What a wonderful idea. Go to your room and I'll bring it to you. You didn't even have time to undress properly. I'm sorry, Aida.'

She smiled reassuringly. 'You were right to fetch me. Every minute counted. Your friend has lost a lot of blood.'

Aida went up to her room. Although she wasn't sure, she had an inkling of what all this was about. During her conversations with Camelia since her return, she had sensed her friend's nationalist sympathies and she had the suspicion that, even if she wasn't directly involved, she was somehow mixed up with the Nationalist Party, which had pitted themselves against a government too willing to accede to the British. Only the previous day, they had heard on the radio about another demonstration and more rioting that had broken out. Camelia had taken on the impassioned countenance Aida was starting to become familiar with. Her large eyes were fired with intensity as she described how it had been since the February student-led general strike.

'It will go down in history as one of Egypt's most infamous tragedies,' she said, her voice trembling with emotion. 'The police opened the Abbas flyover on the orders of the Prime Minister. They let the protesters on to the bridge and dozens fell over the side and drowned in the Nile. It was awful. They then rounded up the survivors and arrested them. There was such an outcry that Prime Minister Nokrashy had to resign. As you know, Ismail Sidqi took over … though I'm not sure he's much better.'

She had gone on to explain to Aida how the tragedy had triggered the student-led general strike, followed by clashes between Egyptian students and British occupation troops.

'The students went on to torch a British military camp.'

'Is that really a good idea? Surely we don't want more violence?' Aida had said quietly.

'Maybe if they don't, no one will sit up and take notice. Forty-seven students have died for the cause. If only Sidqi wasn't so old and ill. He hasn't the strength to lead the negotiations with the British.'

Sensing where Camelia's sympathies seemed to lie, Aida hoped that her friend hadn't become out of her depth. Frustration with the political order had created a boiling pot of activism, whether by supporters of the nationalist Wafd Party, the Muslim Brotherhood or the communists. It was clearly a dangerous time. After their last conversation, a feeling of disquiet had rippled

314 SONG OF THE NILE

through Aida, and now she realised she had been right. Her friend was clearly involved in some way. Now Camelia came back with the two cups of lime flower infusion. She had changed into her pyjamas and looked calmer, though her eyes were still rimmed with red.

The two young women sat on Aida's bed, like old times except for the worry on Camelia's face.

'I suppose I owe you an explanation,' she said at last, eyeing Aida sheepishly.

'I think I can guess … Which group are you working for?'

'Better you don't know,' Camelia answered quietly. 'But I'm not really part of the organisation, I just help from time to time.'

Aida threw her a sceptical glance. 'You must be helping a lot for them to risk bringing their wounded to you in the middle of the night …'

Camelia said nothing, but her large expressive eyes were full of confusion and uncertainty as they fixed on her friend.

Aida sighed. 'Does Phares know about this?'

Camelia gasped. 'No! And don't you dare tell him. Please, Aida, you can't!'

'Do you realise what sort of risk you're taking? Think how this could reflect on your family … on Phares's career.'

'Yes, but … but … this feeling of patriotism goes beyond that. Mounir would have encouraged me, I'm sure.'

Aida eyed her friend quizzically. 'Mounir? Are you sure? How do you feel about Sami? He's a very handsome man.'

'What do you mean?' Camelia replied feebly.

'Are you sure it's not your feelings for Sami rather than a powerful sense of patriotism that's motivating you?'

Aida saw her friend's cheeks burn red. 'How could I have any feeling of that sort for Sami when I still grieve for Mounir?'

'Love takes various forms. Your love for your husband still lies deep in your bones, but that doesn't prevent you having feelings for another man. Mounir will never come back, and the way you were crying tonight ...'

'Oh, Aida, you don't miss anything, do you? You're voicing something I have been denying to myself for some time. And Sami cares for me, too ... though he has never said so. I can read it in his eyes when he looks at me ... But there is no future for us, we could never marry. His father is a carpenter – can you imagine our family's reaction? Anyhow, Sami's too involved in politics ... He once told me that he was married to Egypt – the fairest bride he could ever wish for. Anyway, he is too proud to face a rejection, of course. Or elope, for that matter.' Camelia gazed at her friend wryly. 'But how come you are so perceptive about my feelings and so blind about yours?'

Aida laughed softly and shook her head, draining her cup. 'Don't change the subject. Anyhow, it's already past one o'clock and if you need to be awake for your friends, you'd better get some sleep.' She stood up, tying the cord of her dressing gown. 'And now I'd like to check on Sami once more before going to bed, and again in the morning before he goes.'

Camelia jumped up from the bed and put their cups on the tray. 'Let's do it, but I don't want him to see you in the morning. It puts you at risk.' Her beautiful face darkened. 'If he gets caught and is tortured, he could speak. I want you kept out of this.'

'But ...'

Camelia grasped her arm and fixed her with a haunted look. 'Please, Aida. Don't make me regret that I came to you. Trust me, I know what I'm talking about.'

\*     \*     \*

Aida was awakened next morning by the sound of Phares's murmuring voice below her window. She had forgotten to close her shutters the night before and the sunlight was pouring in bright against the walls of her bedroom and sprawling like a golden cloak across her bed.

Heart pounding, she leapt out of bed and ran to the window to make sure it was him. As she looked down, Phares, who was talking to the gardener, lifted his face up and waved at her.

'Good morning, *chérie*. How about I take you to the Khan Khalili this morning? Camelia has asked me to take her pearl necklace to be restrung. We'll have lunch at the El Malik restaurant just around the corner from there.'

'That sounds a wonderful idea,' Aida called back, unable to conceal her smile. 'I haven't been there for years. But aren't you going to the hospital today?'

'Today is my Sunday off. I took an early plane.'

'Give me half an hour to get ready and I'll be down.'

He nodded and waved. 'I'll be on the terrace having breakfast with Camelia.'

*I'm in love with Phares*, Aida said softly as she hurried to the bathroom. And he? He desired her, he had told her as much, but that was a far cry from being in love with her. No, she must not be so mad as to hope that Phares felt as she did.

Aida quickly chose a primrose crepe day dress, with dolman sleeves and a full skirt, printed with small sprays of wild flowers. She had bought it from Harrods in London on the eve of her departure and hadn't had a chance to wear it. She loved the way the loose sleeves were cut in one piece with the body of the garment, and how good it looked with the narrow red, varnished belt with a horseshoe buckle that cinched her waist. She slipped on a red peep-toe sling-back sandal with a French heel that made her legs look even longer, and after checking herself for the last time in the tall mirror, she grabbed a red bag and ran downstairs to join Camelia and her brother.

'You look radiant.' On seeing Aida, Camelia, who was alone on the terrace, greeted her friend warmly and poured her a cup of coffee. 'One would never guess that you were up half the night saving a life,' she added, lowering her voice.

'It's such a beautiful day.' Aida glanced around nervously before answering. 'Did your friend get off safely?'

'Yes, he was well enough to walk to the car with help. He didn't ask who had saved his life and I didn't tell him.'

Aida sat down, poured milk into her coffee, and after a few moments said warily, 'Do you realise the risk you're running?'

Camelia shrugged. 'Yes, but there was nowhere else they could take him. They rang me to ask if Phares was at home to see to Sami. I said he wasn't, but that I knew someone who I trusted to help.' She gave Aida a rueful smile, 'Thank goodness you were there when I needed you, *habibti*. I will be forever grateful.'

Aida sighed. 'Well, at least Sami is out of danger.' She paused a moment before asking, '*Would* Phares have helped?'

'Yes, because a life was a risk. You know Phares. He's not only a professional, but he's kind. But then,' she went on, 'he would have lectured me and made me promise not to become involved in politics. He'd have stopped me seeing my friends and would have watched me like a hawk.'

'Don't you think you *deserve* a lecture?'

Camelia regarded Aida over her coffee cup. 'Maybe, but one has to do what one has to do. I have a duty towards my country.'

'What about your duty towards yourself and your family? *I'm* supposed to be the adventurous and impulsive one,' Aida said wryly. 'You've always been level-headed and reasonable.'

'I'm not being impulsive.' Camelia raised her hand emphatically. 'On the contrary, I've given this much thought. I have a deep belief in the aims of this Nationalist Party. Listen, we need to liberate our country from imperialism and our impotent government. The system needs to be adjusted. This might take time and it will certainly claim lives, but it needs to be done for the good of Egypt and Egyptians. I can't expect you to understand, *habibti*, you've been away from Egypt for too long.'

Although her friend spoke quietly, the passionate intonation in her voice was unmistakable. Aida knew it was useless to argue with her.

'Don't judge me too harshly, Aida, I ...' Camelia trailed off as Phares stepped on to the terrace.

'What mustn't Aida judge you too harshly about?' he asked with a mischievous smile, but didn't wait for an answer. 'You girls never stop nattering. Don't you ever run out of subjects?' His dark eyes settled on Aida appreciatively. 'Good morning. You look beautiful, *chérie*. Yellow suits you.' He came to sit down, trailing his hand discreetly across her back as he did so, which immediately created a familiar little tremor in her stomach. Then bending his head, he gave her a peck on the cheek. He was wearing a dark-blue shirt belted into his jeans, and his thatch of black hair was wet and tousled; he had obviously just come out of the shower.

'You look quite fetching yourself this morning,' she said, excitement welling up inside her.

His devilish smile glinted at her, whiter than ever. 'Why only "quite fetching"?

'Stop teasing her, Phares,' his sister reproached.

'I've always teased her. She doesn't mind, do you, *chérie*?' He winked at Aida.

She rolled her eyes. 'I'm used to it by now.'

He gazed at her as if unable to tear his eyes away from her. Then remembering himself, he glanced at his watch: 'If we want to get to the Musky, have lunch and return in time to get ready for the fashion show, we'd best leave now. Are you ready, Aida?'

Aida turned to Camelia, taking in that she was still wearing her dressing gown. 'You're not coming with us?'

'No, thank you,' she replied, a slight smile on her face. 'It's very hot and if I spend the whole day at the Musky, I'll be wilting by tonight. I'll leave you two brave people on your own, but promise not to scratch each other's eyes out.'

Phares gave that infectious grin Aida had always found so appealing. 'We're doing rather well these days, aren't we, *habibti*?'

Aida felt the pink hue warming her cheeks and she shrugged. 'Come on, Phares, don't be irritating.'

His lips pulled down in mock offence. 'I'm very hurt.'

'No, you're not. You're an incorrigible tease, that's what you are,' Aida replied laughingly as she stood up. She turned to Camelia: 'You're sure you don't want to join us, even just for lunch?'

'No, really. Go ahead.'

A wave of excitement washed over Aida.

*A whole morning alone with Phares …*

'Come on, then,' he said, putting his arm around her shoulders. Instinctively her pulse quickened as together they stepped down into the garden and made their way to the front drive, where his car was waiting.

# CHAPTER 9

Cairo was humming like a great beehive beneath the clear blue sky. Aida and Phares crossed the thoroughly Europeanised west part of the city with its broad streets shaded by *lebbek* trees, and rows of great hotels, smart boutiques, churches, clubs and residences of the rich, where bougainvillea clambered in purple magnificence over porticoes. Dodging around the modern bulk of the opera house and the Turf Club, they skirted the Ezbekiyeh Gardens and, crossing the square where the various tram lines of the city met, they entered the real Cairo, the African Cairo, a totally new world which led to the bazaars and the Musky, or the Khan Khalili as it was known to Egyptians.

No more broad streets, no more fine buildings. It was one vast huddle of old structures, some of them rather fine examples of the architecture that prevailed in Cairo when the merchants were kings. Into the mass of close-packed houses was threaded a network of numberless deep, dark alleys and narrow lanes overhung with the pretty, wiry balconies of harems, almost meeting above the jostling crowds. They appeared secretive and mysterious; Aida wondered what lay behind them, her imagination conjuring up all sorts of romantic images.

The red *tarbooshes* and coloured turbans of the natives in a variety of costumes formed a bobbing sea on either side of the road lined with a brilliant assortment of sweetmeat shops, fabric stores and fruit sellers. Through the car's open window,

Aida watched the bright multitude thronging the streets in a motley picture of such effective colour schemes that never failed to enchant her eye. Her ears, too, were enthralled by the street cries and passing music, and the wailing prayers from the top of the tall minarets.

The old Turk who was setting up his cake stall in the recess of a sculpted doorway; the donkey-boy with his colourful caparisoned animal, waiting for customers; the beggar asleep on the steps of the mosque; the veiled woman filling her water jar at the public fountain – they all looked as if they had been put there expressly to be painted.

Phares parked the car in a side street not too far away from the main drag of the bazaar and he and Aida wended their way along the tortuous pavements lined with shops offering semi-precious stone necklaces arrayed in glittering splendour against a black background, stalls with engraved brasswork, and others that offered pearl inlayed items and *mashrabiya* carved woodwork.

At this time of day, the well-trodden route leading to the Musky was teaming with life. The sun was blazing, the sky an unbroken arc of blue, and there was a quality of magic in the atmosphere. Crowds were drifting to and fro, on and off the pavements, chattering and laughing in that happy-go-lucky way that Aida loved so much about the Egyptian people.

A man carrying on his head a tray of sugar plums and sweetmeat made of parched peas and sugar was singing rhythmically, '*Mulabesseyeh! Homasseyeh!*' Another cried, 'Figs, the food of sultans!' while yet another with a great bottle was attracting attention by clapping together his brass cups as he sang, 'Oh, here is the refresher of the body, O men!'

Many of the terms these sellers used to proclaim their wares were so vaguely poetic that it was almost impossible to guess what they were selling. '*Assal wa sukar, ya assal!* Honey and sugar! Oh, honey!' repeated an old man, when, in fact, he was carrying nothing but carrots. '*Raéhat el gannah*, scents of paradise!' called a young girl offering bunches of flowers. 'Oh, how sweet is this little son of the river! Better than almonds!' cried out a lupin seller. Aida loved the subtle psychology and charm with which these men and women laid out the qualities of their merchandise.

Phares's voice sounded next to her. 'Did you know that the origin of many of these handicrafts is clearly described in the pictures and hieroglyphics of the Ancient Egyptians?' he asked Aida, clearly seeing her absorbed delight in the passing scene.

'No, I've never given it any thought.'

'Some of the articles shown on these murals are still so dear to us that we cannot be persuaded to set them aside. Take baskets, for example. When the digging of the Suez Canal began, many wheelbarrows were brought from France for the work but not a single Egyptian labourer would use them for their proper purpose. All the thousands of tons of earth were transported in their familiar baskets of soft palm leaf, carried on their head or shoulders, exactly as you see them pictured on the walls of the ancient tombs and monuments.'

'Yes, look,' Aida said, pointing at a peasant on the opposite pavement trying to cross the road. He was carrying a pair of geese by the wings in that peculiar Egyptian fashion that she'd witnessed every day in the villages around Luxor. 'He might have stepped straight out of a painting in one of the old tombs. I see what you mean. The picture he makes is exact in every detail.'

Phares laughed. 'This is portrayed a hundred times a day if you watch the scenes, whether in the city or the countryside. See that old sheikh hobbling in front of us? He's supporting himself with a stick peculiar to the dervishes, which is always cut from an almond tree, with a particular crutch … There's often exactly such a stick in the hands of the deities represented by the Ancient Egyptians.'

'Oh, Phares, look!' Aida murmured. 'Shades of Scheherazade!' They stopped a while to watch an old man who was manipulating with his toe a string on a bow of wood, miraculously producing *mashrabiya*, the carved wood screening that provided window coverings for the harem quarters in the time of Scheherazade, but was now used as screens and doors.

Opposite, on the sunny side of the street, the tentmakers sat, catching the clearest light in which to stitch on to their cotton those complex abstract designs in orange, red and blue that always covered the walls at funerals, weddings, and in festival tents alike.

One of Aida's favourite streets was Souq El Dahab, the gold market. There were hundreds of pairs of earrings on show, crescents of heavy-worked gold and droplets of seed pearls. There were bracelets and gold beads, charms to hang about the necks of newborn babies, golden miniatures of the Koran that opened like lockets, crosses, and Coptic and pharaonic 'key-of-life' symbols swinging from delicate chains.

Phares stopped in front of a discreet shop with a front window displaying pieces of jewellery clearly in a different league to the gaudy offerings in the road. There was a gold pharaonic-shaped eye pendant with a blue bead in the centre which attracted Aida's attention.

'Let's have a look inside,' he said, and she wondered if Phares was so attuned to her thoughts that he read them.

There was a seat with velvet pads from which to admire the jewels on the counter at close range.

'Ah, Pharaony *Bey*,' exclaimed the shopkeeper, pushing up striped shirtsleeves held in place by arm bands. 'It's been a long time since we've seen you.'

'Work ... you know how it is, *Monsieur* Cohen.'

'Ah yes!' nodded the jeweller. 'How can I help you?' he added with a huge smile, coming quickly to the point.

'You have a pretty pendant with a pharaonic eye displayed in your window.'

'Ah yes, very beautiful, *ya Bey*. You have always had an eye for the best,' continued *Monsieur* Cohen as he moved to the window. 'Would you like to have a closer look at it?'

'Yes, please.'

'The stone, which you undoubtedly know is an AAAA turquoise, is of course of the highest quality. I bought it myself when I was in Tehran last month from a most reputable jeweller so I can guarantee its authenticity and value … A rare item of beauty.' *Monsieur* Cohen took out the coveted pendant and placed it on a black velvet tray.

Phares picked it up and scrutinised it, then passed it to Aida. 'What d'you think?'

The pendant was quite heavy, and the blue of the turquoise was deep, indicating optimum quality. 'It's beautiful,' she said, handing it back.

'It's very rare,' repeated the jeweller.

'Turn around,' Phares told Aida. 'Let me see how it looks on you.'

Her gaze flew to his. 'On me?'

'If you don't mind.'

She turned around and he fastened the chain around her neck. The sensuous movement of his thumb against the silkiness of her flesh caused a peculiar weakness that made her legs feel as though they were turning to jelly. Acutely conscious of the strength and heat of his fingers, she trembled internally under the deliberate provocation of his touch. She looked at herself in the table mirror on the counter and caught her breath. The gold and blue glowed magnificently against the rich texture of her honey-coloured skin.

'You must admit that it is a spectacular piece, and on *mademoiselle*, it is even more striking,' *Monsieur* Cohen encouraged.

'I agree. It was made for you, *chérie*.' Phares had not taken his eyes off her.

Aida hesitated, unsure what to think. 'You mean this is for me?'

'Who else?'

His powerful black eyes drew her into their caress.

'But, Phares …'

He hesitated, and then said flatly, 'Call it a brotherly gift.'

*A brotherly gift!* He didn't honestly expect her to be able to treat him as a brother, did he?

Just being near him like this recalled all too well the occasions he had seemed unable to keep his hands off her. Surely he was teasing her, giving her a taste of her own medicine? It was not so long ago that she had asked him to be a friend, a brother to her … How could she dismiss thoughts of his ardour, the feel of his skin against hers, the urgent hardening of his body and the passion which had swept her far beyond the limits of physical restrain? How could she forget the things he had taught her about herself? No, the link that bound them could not be put down to brotherly or sisterly affection …

Aida lifted her arms to detach the chain from around her neck.

Phares's eyebrows rose. 'I thought you liked it.'

'I love it, Phares.'

'Then keep it on. It will protect you from the evil eye.' Turning to *Monsieur* Cohen, he asked, 'Your best price?'

The jeweller fussed around them, stroking his head with its few remaining hairs brilliantined carefully to its bald surface. He spent a long time pretending to calculate the exact price he would accept for the pendant by gazing through the jeweller's glass held to one dark, faded eye. Finally, he smiled.

'Only for you, *ya Bey*, I will let the pendant and chain go for fifty pounds.'

'Thirty,' parried Phares.

'You drive a hard bargain, sir.' The man smiled. 'Forty-five.'

'I don't want it,' piped in Aida as she started to detach the chain from her neck.

The little man's face fell and he smiled again. 'For the *mademoiselle* here, I will let you have them for forty pounds.'

'It's a deal,' Phares replied, taking out his wallet.

*Monsieur* Cohen accompanied his happy clients to the door. 'Don't stay away so long this time, *ya Bey*,' he said as he shook their hands. 'I have some beautiful Kashmiri blue-velvet sapphires arriving in ten days.'

'I'll be in touch very soon, *Monsieur* Cohen.'

'Thank you, Phares,' Aida whispered as they left the shop. 'But you really shouldn't have.'

His gaze locked with hers. 'If you'd only let me, I'd cover you in jewels and silks.' He paused a moment and his eyes travelled over her face, moving downwards to dwell on the open neck of her dress, a little lower than her collarbone where the pendant rested, glowing in the sunshine. 'Many women would give their eye teeth for your skin. A man would never cease wanting to touch it.'

Under his intense look, Aida felt a pink hue rising to her cheeks.

They soon reached the tangle of labyrinthine bypaths wherein one could be lost for hours: the Musky. Aida loved the exotic scents, veiled light and smothered footfalls. The colour and strangeness of this Oriental bazaar had always fascinated her. In the past, she had spent many an hour rambling among its stalls, buying silks and bottles of scent and bits of beaten brass and silver. After the dazzling, sun-flooded streets, the Musky was dim, filled with flickering lights and shadows. After the noisy bustle outside it was quiet, mysterious, the only sounds the slip and patter of heelless shoes, the guttural low voices of the stallholders. Incense and perfumes, the smell of leather and coffee and spices and less delectable smells made the air heavy and exotic.

Phares and Aida threaded their way through the maze in the flickering shadows of the dim, mysterious aisles. They went past tiny shops offering exquisite items of inlaid work and mosaic.

The bazaar was a delightful beehive: some were blowing glass, others were weaving linen; even the lame and the blind seemed to be working. A bench was set in front of almost every shop where sat a venerable and turbaned patriarch, pulling industriously at his *narghileh.*

To her delight, Phares let Aida do the bargaining, causing much sonorous laughter among the stallholders. He found the process tiresome and she was a master at that game. The shopkeeper as a rule demanded more than he expected to receive and it was up to Aida to declare the price exorbitant, offering half the sum, which was of course rejected, but resulted in him lowering his price and both buyer and seller were satisfied. She loved this dance of negotiation that had been the way of things for thousands of years.

Aida bought a rug, a beautiful silver-encrusted black Bedouin kaftan and one of those baskets woven with palm leaves that Phares had talked to her about. Next, they stopped at a shop where youths were renovating *tarbooshes* using a machine that looked like a brass stove adorned with huge, brazen dinnerbells. Using an inner mould, Aida watched them press the red fezzes into smart and effective shapes. Phares finished paying for a new fez and they took their leave of the shopkeeper.

As they left the shop, he took her arm, directing her down a shadowed alleyway. Plainly he knew where he was going. He guided her through yet another labyrinth of narrow streets, some built with original bricks from which the earlier town had been constructed.

'Where are you taking me?' Aida asked, intrigued, as they reached a large green gate opening on to a dark and aromatic alley where cloaked figures shuffled silently past them and the exotic fragrances of Arabia filled the air.

Phares chuckled. 'Not to the slave market, if that's what you think, Aida. Oh yes, don't look so surprised. They still have them in some remote oases, where white women are sold into the ruler's harem.' A wide grin split his face. 'But don't worry, there's nothing of that sort around here. The police are vigilant.'

She shuddered, glad of his tall presence at her side.

They walked through the spice domain and its incense-laden atmosphere to the scent bazaar – the most delectable in Cairo, Phares told her.

'Sandal! Sandal!' called the merchants. 'Very rare, modom! Very cheap!' They spoke in broken English, obviously taking Aida for a tourist, asking her if she needed powdered baby crocodile skin to rub on warts or a bag of herbs to assure safe delivery of a child. But Phares answered them in Arabic and immediately they gave a charming, sheepish laugh and backed off.

Eventually, Phares turned into an open doorway. Suleiman Abdel Hadi, maker and vendor of perfumes, sat at a desk just inside the entrance to his shop. Incense was burning in a tiny crucible at his left hand, sending up thin blue aromatic smoke, which impregnated the air around him. A bony individual, he had a single eye and toothless jaws that broke into a smile as he recognised Phares.

'*Salam aleykom.*' He stood and stretched out a welcoming hand.

Phares nodded. '*Wa aleykom el salam.*'

'How can I help today?'

When her eyes had accustomed themselves to the darkness in the shop Aida saw that there were pyramids of spices and herbs, petals, crooked twigs and roots displayed in orderly fashion in open jute sacks. The shelves were stacked with bottles and boxes and the air was redolent with cedarwood, ambergris, sandalwood and other less familiar scents she couldn't quite recognise.

Phares whispered something to the old man, whose dried-walnut face again split into a broad, toothless smile.

'Come,' he said, signalling to Aida. 'Your beauty is that of the rose before it opens fully ... a bud which has not yet blossomed. But once open, the flower becomes warm and sensuous, and so it must be with your perfume.'

Aida lifted her blushing face to Phares with enquiring eyes.

'Suleiman is going to concoct a scent for you.' He smiled, his eyes becoming caressing black velvet. 'It will be your special fragrance, which will be redolent of you, only you,' he murmured.

She looked at him doubtfully. 'That's very kind, Phares, but shouldn't I smell it first? I'm not sure his idea of a nice fragrance and mine will correspond.'

'Trust me, *chérie*,' he said, an edge of amusement in his voice. 'Suleiman has mixed the most fabulous scents for famous actresses, princesses, and beautiful socialites. Did he not describe you correctly?' He leant forward, bending his head close. 'Are you not still an unopened flower?' he murmured huskily, close enough that she could feel his breath warm on her neck. She flushed, embarrassed, under the intensity of his stare as if she were standing naked before him, and only just stopped herself giving a flippant retort to hide her discomfort. She prayed that she wouldn't say or do something to rekindle that spark of discord, which thankfully seemed to have evaporated today, but which usually smouldered between them. They sat on rickety wooden chairs and drank cups of spiced black coffee, which a boy was sent out to fetch, in that age-old tradition born of the shopkeeper's desire to keep the customer in the shop a little longer, giving him time to look over all the merchandise.

While they were waiting, Suleiman rummaged among his wares, reaching with exquisite airs and graces towards an array of gummy bottles, measuring and pouring, sniffing occasionally, adding a pinch of this and a squeeze of that. Aida caught the elusive scent of lavender, of rose, and then a more subtle, spicy bouquet. The old man pounded something in a wooden bowl with a small pestle and the warm fragrance of carnations drenched the air. Finally, he went back to his place and asked

Aida to take a seat opposite him. 'Give me your wrist. Let me smear it with the perfume of Arabia.'

She held out her wrist hesitantly, and the old man smeared it with the oil he had concocted, asking her to wait a few seconds and then sniff it, which she did. The delicious fragrance filled her nostrils with full-blown roses, sweet almonds, airy musks, but also golden amber and sultry sandalwood, ending with the heady scent of carnation. Fresh, but also delicately warm. She sniffed again, then looked up at Phares before turning to the old man. 'Mmm ... I love it. Thank you.'

'I can smell it from here,' Phares told her, 'although he has only smeared a tiny amount on your wrist. It portrays fresh innocence well, but also undercurrents of rebellion and passion.' The black velvet caress in his eyes deepened into ardent black coals.

Aida flushed, embarrassed under their intensity as if she were standing naked before him. Clearing her throat, she turned to Suleiman: 'Does the scent last? It seems quite potent.'

The old man threw up his hands. 'Wash as energetically as Lady Macbeth and you shall not remove that aroma from the back of your wrist for days. Suleiman Abdel Hadi is a great *parfumier!*'

'What is it called?'

Old Suleiman's eyes travelled from Aida to Phares, and he smiled. '*Nasmet El Aroussa*, Fragrance of a Bride.'

Aida blushed a deeper red, feeling rather embarrassed at what he was obviously implying, but the fragrance really suited her. 'I'll buy it,' she told the man. 'It's lovely, thank you.'

'*I'll* buy it,' Phares cut in, taking out his wallet, his tone indicating that he would not stand for any argument.

Remembering her earlier prayer to avoid the confrontation that so often seemed to spark between them, she kept silent.

'Thank you,' she murmured.

They left the shop and went back the way they had come.

'I need to have Camelia's pearl necklace restrung,' said Phares as they threaded their way through the scent bazaar. 'It might take some time and I'll have to sit there while it is being done to make sure the pearls are not swapped. Would you like to come with me, or would you prefer to browse and we'll meet back here in twenty minutes?'

'I'd like to browse if you don't mind.'

They agreed to meet at El Malik, a restaurant serving the best in Egyptian specialities, which, although tucked in a side street close to the main gateway to the Musky, was very easy to find. Phares took his leave and Aida made her way to the candle shop. She wanted to buy some fragrant religious candles to put in front of the Virgin's statue in the garden where her father was burried. For Aida, as for most Copts, the fragrant wax and the labour of the bee, which dies when its work is accomplished, had a mystic significance. Drawn from the nectar of flowers, the wax was deemed the most worthy material for offerings.

As Aida entered the shop her eyes fell on the huge, pillar-like candles. She smiled. Custom dictated that a Coptic bridegroom must send a bouquet and wax candle to his bride the night before she left her father's home. The candle must be as tall as the bride, big enough to burn throughout the night in her bedroom. Would Phares send her a candle on the night before they were married? she wondered, a wistful smile on her lips.

Leaving the candle shop, she glanced at her watch. She had just enough time to get to the restaurant. It was two o'clock, the hour at which shops closed for the afternoon. Everywhere, doors were being closed against the heat and the lane was deserted.

She had almost reached El Malik when she caught the sound of footsteps coming towards her, a quick decided ringing on the cobbles, and a tall form emerged from the shadows, revealing itself as Prince Shams Sakr El Din. He was dressed in white, from his silk shirt and linen suit to impeccable leather moccasins, and looked as though he'd stepped right out of a fashion magazine.

Aida paled. He was the last person she wanted to meet today. She knew the antipathy Phares felt towards the prince. Not only that, she herself had her reservations – there was still something about him that made her feel uncomfortable.

'What a delightful surprise! The beautiful Aida El Masri in person,' he exclaimed, flashing a bright smile as he took her hand and brought it to his lips. 'I knew this would be my lucky day when I woke up this morning and you see, I was right.'

*Was it a delightful surprise?* Not for Aida. Quite the reverse, actually. She trembled inside, hoping desperately that Phares wouldn't arrive now. Their day had been wonderful so far and she knew him well enough to realise that an encounter with Shams Sakr El Din would be a mood changer.

The prince's eyes rested intently upon her face. 'What's wrong? Are you not glad to see me? Are we not friends anymore?'

'Of course we're friends,' she protested, swallowing the dryness in her throat, 'but …'

His pale gaze glittered. 'But you are waiting for someone … your friend, Phares Pharaony, I think. I saw you both earlier, coming out of the *aattar*, the perfumery.' He sighed heavily. 'I don't know why that man hates me. Maybe it's because I employ his young lady friend. It is common knowledge he's lost his head over her. I am told that despite their social differences they are completely …' he lifted two fingers and crossed them '… inseparable.'

He looked penetratingly into her face, as Aida felt the flush rise from her throat. Still she said nothing and simply lifted her eyebrows nonchalantly but he wouldn't let it drop.

'You know, that young Armenian model, Nairy Paplosian. She's my top *mannequin*. Very beautiful, of course.'

Aida felt a cold hand grip her heart, but from somewhere she dredged up enough poise to shrug, managing to feign ignorance. 'I wouldn't know.'

His eyes narrowed. 'No doubt you will see her at the fashion show tonight. You *are* coming, aren't you?'

'I wouldn't miss it for anything,' she replied, adding, 'I'm sorry, but I have to rush. I'll be late for Phares.'

'No problem. *Bon appétit.* And remember, don't be late tonight. It's very much on a first come, first served basis. Though it is by invitation, many guests have asked to bring friends, and who am I to turn potential customers away? I've made sure to reserve a table for you and the Pharaonys but come early – half the entertainment in these shows is to see and be seen. I'm sure you'll be more beautiful than any woman in the audience. Or on the catwalk, for that matter.'

His knowing stare made her flush and she found it hard to meet his eyes. 'Thank you. You're always very gallant.'

He inclined his head. 'I only tell the truth.'

He took Aida's hand and held it to his lips just as Phares turned the corner at the end of the alley. She saw him accelerate his step and as he reached them in a few swift strides, the glow in his black eyes reminded her of coals flung from a furnace. Aida felt the blood leave her face. He made no attempt to shake hands with Sakr El Din and the prince's lips curled faintly.

'Phares *Bey*! How opportune we should meet again,' he said suavely with a smile that did not reach his yellow eyes, which had narrowed to slits. 'You left rather promptly after the tournament the other day and I didn't have a chance to speak to you about tonight. With all the well-known Parisian names in couture taking part in the show, the response has been overwhelming. I was just telling Aida that I have reserved a table for your party next to the catwalk, which will afford you the best view.'

'That's very thoughtful, Prince. Thank you,' Phares's jaw tightened, and for an instant, Aida thought he was about to say something more, but then good sense seemed to assert itself. He forced a smile to his hard mouth, although the veins that stood out on his neck bore witness to his extreme state of tension.

The Bedouin's gaze flickered over Phares speculatively, and then he gave his attention to Aida. 'I hope you will be joining the party coming to my palace, Kasr El Nawafeer, the day after tomorrow. There'll be a camel race and an interesting couple of shows.'

Aida smiled nervously. 'Unfortunately, I'm going back to Luxor that day. I've already reserved my seat on the plane.'

'I'm sure you'll be able to change it. It will give me so much pleasure to show you around my oasis. There will be ...'

'I think you've heard Aida's response, Prince,' Phares cut in drily and Aida saw his fists clench slowly at his sides. 'I don't think it's appropriate for you to insist.'

'Well, it's my loss,' Sakr El Din answered, his lips stretched into a thin, horizontal line. 'I'm sorry I've been unable to convince you, *mademoiselle*.'

Phares took hold of Aida's arm. 'Come on, *chérie*. We'll never get a place at the restaurant if we don't hurry. It's already two-thirty ... Prince ...' He bowed to the Bedouin, then marched Aida off at a brisk pace.

El Malik was a truly authentic Egyptian eating place. Although it was utterly unlike the restaurants of the West, its popularity with both Egyptians and foreigners meant it was packed at all times of day and night. The cooking was done next to the entrance – an excellent tradition, Aida's father had always said, because not only are the odours wafted into the street, but the customer can see the food before it is cooked. In this way one was able to judge not only the quality of the raw ingredients but also the skill of the cook and the state of his utensils.

The place was teeming with people of all nationalities. A hubbub of laughter and different languages filled the room, which was furnished in a traditional Egyptian way. Guests sat on the floor on plush, brightly coloured cushions around a circular brass tray raised upon a wooden stool inlaid with mother-of-pearl and tortoiseshell. Disk-shaped cakes of bread cut in half were placed round the tray, served with sliced limes. An ebony spoon was set for each person and large bread loaves served as plates.

Phares had almost dragged Aida to the restaurant, tight-lipped, with a face like thunder. Only once they were seated next to each other on the large embroidered plumped-up cushions did he finally speak.

'One day I will knock that smug smile off His Highness's royal face.'

Aida glanced at him. 'Why do you resent him so much? He's not particularly likable, I admit, but he's always friendly and polite.'

'You know nothing, Aida,' Phares snapped. 'He has the personality of a fox and tiger combined. You'd do well to stay away from him.'

Although she sensed an undercurrent of threat in his advice to her, which usually would have made her prickle, Aida decided to keep the peace and ignore it. She smiled sweetly. 'He is too suave for my taste. Oily, if you know what I mean.'

'We're not going to spend the whole lunch analysing Shams Sakr El Din's personality,' Phares said gruffly. 'Let's order.' He signalled to one of the waiters, who came rushing over. 'What would you like to eat?'

'I'll have the kofta and kebab. I seem to remember they're renowned for them here.'

Phares's face suddenly relaxed. He let out a low chuckle, having regained his good humour. 'You haven't forgotten a thing, *chérie*. Don't ever tell me that you'll leave Egypt one day to live abroad.'

'I was very happy here,' she said, refraining from adding, *until my father died*. Instead, she kept her attention on the meal and smiled. 'What will you have, Phares?'

He leaned back in his chair. 'I'll order some *mezzeh* for us to start off with and I'll have *hamam bil ferik* to follow. Apparently, the pigeon and the green wheat sauce is delicious. They make it differently to our cook, *Osta* Anwar. His is always a little too heavy ... too much onion, I think.'

It was the Egyptian way to enjoy talking in depth about the food while at table and so Phares took time placing his order. He asked the waiter to provide cutlery because, although some Egyptians were accustomed to eating with their fingers and a spoon, it was not the tradition in more Westernised families like theirs.

After the waiter had gone, Phares's eyes sparkled playfully. 'Are you sure you won't have the pigeon too?'

Aida met his gaze, her pulse giving a little kick. In Egypt, pigeons were a special dish, regarded quite openly by the working classes as an aphrodisiac. A wife who wanted to please her husband would cook pigeons for him. A mistress would always cook *Gose Hamam*, a pair of pigeons, for her married lover when he visited her. Aida arched an eyebrow.

'I'm fine with the kofta, thank you.'

Phares felt in his pocket for his Gitanes, and Aida's glance was upon his hands as he took out a cigarette and tapped it on the pack. Lean, mobile hands which had caressed her with such maddening skill ... The emotion she felt at the recollection made her heart beat faster.

He lit a cigarette, carrying it to his lips and releasing the smoke on a somewhat troubled sigh. 'You haven't yet given me an answer. Have you not yet come to a decision, Aida?'

She stared back at him. Why was she hesitating? Why was she delaying? She knew she wanted to marry Phares and had promised to give her answer before going back to Luxor ... there was less than forty-eight hours left. Still, she sat there tongue-tied, unable to tell him that she loved him, that she wanted to share his bed, his life ... to be a part of his breath, his soul. He was like no other person she had ever known. Every nerve in her body was keyed up in his presence, yet she kept her feelings to herself as though tied by a powerful spell that forced her to remain mute.

Her mind wandered to the fashion show that coming evening, and she knew what it was that held her back. Marriage had to be based on trust, and there was still a kernel of doubt in her mind about Nairy Paplosian.

*It's common knowledge he's lost his head over her ...* While the prince's words about his 'beautiful mannequin' had frazzled her nerves, Aida knew he had been trying to bait her. She had refused to let such malicious gossip poison the new and wonderful feelings that had flooded her over these past days. In fact, she was rather surprised at how well she'd coped. She had tried very hard to be her usual self, and succeeded well enough, she hoped, to fool Phares. But inside, she couldn't help the creeping doubt that assailed her at quiet moments, when thoughts of Nairy came bubbling up, unbidden.

Tomorrow, she would ask Phares one more time about the Armenian model before giving him her answer, and then she would draw a line under this episode in his life and move on. For now she would say nothing; she would not let anything cloud this beautiful day.

Aida gave him a look as blue as the sky outside. 'Please, Phares, bear with me a little longer. I promise to give you an answer tomorrow night.'

His moody dark eyes slid up and down her face, lingering on her wide and generous lips, and then his gaze settled directly upon hers. 'Don't toy with me, Aida. I have never asked a woman to care for me with her heart.'

If only she could be sure of his.

'You prefer a woman to care for you with her body?' she fenced, trying to keep her voice even.

'That is all I have known or needed ... until you came along.'

He snapped out of his glum mood. The waiter had brought small dishes of delicious *mezzeh* to the table, and Phares's face brightened as if by magic. 'Right now, this man wants his lunch. Breakfast seems such a long time ago.'

Serenity had re-established itself between them and they ate heartily, chatting and laughing as though there had never been a cloud in their sky. Still, it wouldn't be long before the hand of fate dealt Aida a card with a sinister face on it, dark clouds looming behind it.

\*     \*     \*

Every New Year's Eve the ballroom of the glamorous Shepheard's Hotel would be converted into the Garden of Eden, a Chinese pagoda or any other scene that took the fancy of the management. Tonight, the sumptuous colonnaded ballroom was decorated with a coloured palette of blue and gold, reflecting the desert's natural beauty. Displays of waving palm trees and waxwork figures of camels and sultry Bedouins adorned various parts of the magnificent high-ceilinged room in which the blue lighting was designed to mirror a desert night sky illuminated by the moon and stars. Beneath it, the catwalk dividing the room in two was covered in a shimmering, almost translucent sheet of marble to represent the Nile. As if on its riverbanks, at tables and chairs on either side the prince's dazzling guests were seated, who had come to view the exciting 1946 avant-garde styles the Parisian couturiers had brought to Cairo for the *haut monde*'s delectation.

Although the showing of the collection was set for seven o'clock in the evening, by six-thirty, the ballroom was filled with men and women in the most elegant clothes. The place was tightly packed, round tables and chairs almost wedged against each other. On one side at the end of the room the Cairo Philharmonic Orchestra musicians were seated, tuning their instruments for the show. A buzz of chatter rose and fell in the heavily scented air, and the glittering candelabras reflected the sparkle of jewellery. Aida, Phares and Camelia had arrived well before the show in the Pharaonys' luxurious navy-blue Cadillac and had met up with a large group of friends that made up their party. It was agreed that they would all go on to the Mena House to have a light al fresco dinner and dance in the popular garden café with its unique vantage of the pyramids and distance from the noisier hub of Cairo.

Aida and Camelia were seated at the small table Prince Shams Sakr El Din had reserved for them next to the catwalk, while Phares stood chatting to Alastair Carlisle and a group of men at the next table. Camelia was surveying the room, talking animatedly, every now and then commenting on notable Cairenes, pointing out to Aida people she might remember, and speculating about the show.

'You know, the newspapers are full of all the avant-garde fashion houses at the moment,' she said, sipping her rose cordial, 'and Chiffons à la Mode seems to be high on the list of boutiques with these latest trends. I do love Christian Dior's new French look.' She grinned wryly. 'I must admit, the prince may be not be my choice of company normally but this is definitely the hottest ticket in Cairo.'

Aida nodded, glancing around the room. 'Yes, the place looks wonderful. Tonight will be quite a treat after the drudgery of the war years. I missed wearing lovely clothes. I spent most of my time either in nurse's uniform or practical slacks.'

Aida and Camelia were certainly dressed elegantly tonight, both looking as though they had stepped out of the pages of a fashion magazine. Camelia was radiant in a cloud of violet organza: a full-length evening gown with square drape shoulders and a beaded neck and waist panel. Her hair was sculpted into fashionable voluminous rolls at the top of her head and fastened in a chignon at the nape of her neck, a matching violet flower nestling to the side above her ear.

As this was an event not to be missed, and Aida had taken particular care with her outfit. Cleo had shown her the Grecian-style dress at Shemla and she had been attracted by its simple lines. The plunging V-neckline bodice with thick straps embellished with sparkling *ton sur ton* rhinestone jewels showed off enough cleavage to look sexy without being daring. Ruched to the waist and cinched with a glittering belt, its full-length skirt fell to the ground in shimmering layers of champagne silk chiffon. The gown gave her an ethereal silhouette, and as she walked, every delicate bone in her body made itself known, every beautiful line visible.

Over the years Ayoub had given first his wife, then his daughter the most fabulous pieces of antique jewellery purchased during his travels. Consequently, Aida had a huge collection of magnificent pieces: earrings, necklaces, bracelets, bangles and even headrests. Tonight, she had complemented her dress with a pair of Greek Serpentine gold arm bands from the fourth century BC and an interesting Hellenistic pair of twenty-four-carat gold Erotes and Isis crown earrings, embellished with garnet and glass. She'd left her neck and décolleté bare, judging that the dress itself had ample adornments as it was, and she didn't want to look like a Christmas tree. She had simply daubed behind her ears and on her wrists a little of the delicious, heady fragrance that Phares had bought for her.

She wore her hair differently tonight, using a thin braided piece the colour of her hair, twisted with strings of pearls to give it a Grecian look. Parted in the centre, her hair was combed smooth, pulled back and secured with small gold combs; the braid across her head was held in place with Bobbie pins. A pair of gold high Chilli sandal clogs completed her outfit, together with a gold beaded evening bag that had belonged to her mother and a gold lamé shawl. Before leaving the room to join the others Aida had glanced once more at herself in the mirror. The glamour of the event was not the only reason she wanted to look her best. Tonight, she would be in the same room as Nairy Paplosian, and the idea of seeing the Armenian model headline the show unnerved her.

Just a few hours before, as she had prepared herself for the event, Aida's head had been filled with Phares and the wonderful day they had spent together at the Musky. It had been perfect but for the short interlude when Shams Sakr El Din had made his appearance. Aida was curious about Phares's strong aversion to the prince. Could it be that he was jealous of him because Nairy was one of his models or was there another reason?

Nairy ... Aida had often seen her photograph in glossy magazines, but she had never met her in the flesh. In a few minutes that would change.

She glanced across at Phares, still deep in conversation with Alastair Carlisle. The dark formality of his dinner jacket and black tie made him seem even more charismatic and handsome if that were possible, coupled with his usual dashing masculinity. She pressed her hand to her stomach, trying to calm her nerves.

Phares caught her eye and a secret smile curved his lips. Glancing at his watch, he murmured something to Alastair and came to join them at the table.

He looked warmly at Camelia. 'You look magnificent. That amethyst colour suits your complexion. You look like those pictures of our mother. I'll be the envy of every man this evening, accompanied by two such ravishing ladies.'

His gaze travelled to Aida and stayed there. When she had first appeared in the drawing room dressed in her evening finery, his breath had visibly caught and his eyes held the feverish incandescence of desire that she was beginning to know. Now that same look returned and a tremor ran through her entire body.

'And you, Aida ...' he murmured, leaning close to her temple so that no one else could hear. 'You look like a summer dream wrapped in sunlight, *chérie*. Mmm ... and your fragrance evokes the gardens of heaven. I will never be able to smell a rose or carnation without conjuring your image.' Aida could feel the warmth of him heating her neck and inhaled his own masculine fragrance, a spicy balm of starched linen and clean male skin that made her almost lightheaded.

At seven o'clock exactly the overhead lights dimmed, the gold satin curtains draping the dais drew back to form an arch, in readiness for the start of the show. Silence descended on the crowd waiting in the darkened room. Aida watched as a single spotlight focused on the stage and moved to one side of the catwalk to reveal the orchestra. The music of sweeping violins filled the place as a coloured spotlight swirled and fixed over the entrance to the stage. Gasps were heard among the audience as the microphone announced the name of the modelled dress, *Clair de Lune*, and Nairy Paplosian made her entry.

Tall, slim, delicate and fabulous, the redheaded model with her pale skin and the most extraordinary grey cat's eyes stood for a brief moment at the entrance, soaking up the limelight. She wore a magnificent ball gown of foggy grey silk tulle. The flared skirt and train were arrayed with an overlay of scallop-moulded petals embroidered with feather-shaped opalescent sequins, rhinestones and imitation pearls. The shell forms of its skirt and the heart-shaped bodice, nipped in at the waist, were embellished with nacreous sequins, iridescent seed beads, aurora-borealis crystals and pearls. Her lustrous red hair was swept up in a Grecian chignon torsade, showing off a long pale neck, which she inclined gracefully, acknowledging the audience's applause before treading the path that lay in front of her.

Aida sat very still, an unpleasant feeling in her stomach. Nairy's wasp-waisted silhouette, she had to admit, looked like a glittering ethereal nymph appearing out of the Nile and her gaze went straight to Phares to see his reaction. She could only see his profile through the halo of smoke that encircled it, and he seemed to be sporting the inscrutable mask she had seen him wear from time to time. What were his thoughts at this moment? Was he wishing he could marry the gorgeous redhead instead of having to make a prescribed match – one not necessarily based on love?

'What a gorgeous creature!' Aida heard a man behind her say.

'I don't see why so much fuss is made about her,' answered his female companion. 'She's too thin and pale … a ghost.'

'She's fabulous! Honestly, haven't you got eyes? That Pharaoh man, what's his name, is very lucky. I certainly wouldn't push her out of my bed.'

'Shush, you idiot! He's sitting right in front of us.'

Camelia turned around and gave them a dirty look while a smattering of applause greeted Nairy, who was almost lost in the buzz of conversation and conjecture as she made her way slowly and gracefully along the room, almost in slow motion, stopping in front of every table, turning twice to show off her garment before resuming her gentle strutting journey down the catwalk. She was stunning.

The loudspeaker announced 'Dina, in *Nocturne*,' and this time a brunette appeared in a strapless, backless three-tier navy-blue evening dress in alternating velvet and chiffon layers with an embellished net upper bodice. But Aida was not paying attention: Nairy was about to reach their table and the orchestra was playing Perry Como's new hit, 'Prisoner of Love'.

The upturned almond grey eyes settled on Phares impudently. She smiled, turned and sighed, lifting her arm slightly as her hand went to her neck and slid down to her shoulder and arm caressingly before she continued down the catwalk.

'Dolores wearing *Inspiration*,' continued the presenter as a blonde young woman walked in, wearing a green jersey backless evening dress, with gathered crossover sash, which flounced at the front.

The parade continued as one after another the models walked in, displaying dresses that showed off Paris's corseted, full-bosomed and hourglass New Look. After the deprivations of the war, it was clear that French designers wanted to restore fantasy and luxury to women's wardrobes.

'Chantal wearing *Rêve d'un Soir*,' the presenter continued … 'Alia, with *Belle de Nuit*.' … 'Christiane wearing *Ma Première Soirée*, a dream of innocence in a silk voile pink evening gown with full skirt, gathered shoulder and bust panels, and edged with a blue velvet ribbon.' All the dresses of the collection had one thing in common: a fragile effect that merged Second Empire romanticism with the classical iconography of ideal and eternal beauty.

And now Nairy appeared again with *Chant d'Amour*, a romantic off-the-shoulder full-length black evening dress with ruched lace neckline and hem panels embellished with a beautiful red rose at her cleavage. Her voluminous Titian hair was adorned with another red rose which she wore behind her right ear, nestling among the sophisticated long glossy waves, the signature of so many Hollywood vamps. She was glowing, using those almost silver eyes and dark lashes with more deftness than ever.

This time when she stopped in front of their table, her cat's gaze settled on Aida, who met her stare with audacity. Beside her, she felt Phares stiffen in his chair, then Nairy's attention turned to him. Bending down, she whispered something in his ear, which Aida could not hear. Phares nodded almost imperceptibly and Nairy was on her way again.

Camelia frowned and leaned against her brother. 'What was all that about?'

Phares shook his head. 'Nothing … don't worry about it.'

Aida's heart gave a painful lurch, then thudded sickeningly against her ribs as Shams Sakr El Din's insinuations came flooding back to her.

The Collection was now nearing its end and when Chantal and Dolores came out in wild-silk bridesmaids' dresses, there was an audible murmur of anticipation. The slow strains of Mendelssohn's *Wedding March* seeped through the room and there was another wave of *ohs*! and *ahs*! as Nairy stood framed in the archway once more.

Her dress was a dream of innocence: a subtle blending of tulle and ultra-thin lace that appeared to reveal everything, yet revealed nothing. Apart from her face and hands, she was completely swathed in clouds of material, her hair adorned with a wax flower crown and long net veil. It was a masterpiece of cut and extravagance that could only have been worn to advantage by a girl with as fine a figure as Nairy Paplosian. Her hair was loose, falling in red flames to her shoulders, where it then curled softly upwards, and her face was devoid of make-up, save mascara and a pale gleaming silver lipstick ... the perfect angel.

It was a new facet of the Armenian girl's beauty that she was showing to the world. Gone was the femme fatale of the past two hours and in her place was a shy, gentle girl, whose defencelessness invited protection.

In time with the music she walked down the aisle without stopping. Aida was aware that every man in the room was now looking at Nairy boldly, demandingly, lustfully. She had no doubt the model's exposed vulnerability made each of them, including Phares, want to possess and protect this virginal beauty.

Aida's eyes dwelt on the dark head and handsome profile of the man sitting beside her and again her heart gave a painful little pinch. It was impossible to tell what thoughts were quickening in that shrewd, determined brain. The models paraded once more on the catwalk in their dresses before the show came to a thundering end and the room erupted with applause, roses thrown on to the catwalk, the audience shouting bravos from every corner of the room. The models left the stage and after a few moments of silence and a rolling of drums, Prince Shams Sakr El Din took their place, accompanied by Nairy Paplosian, his star model, in a silver lamé gown with plunging neckline.

After more cheers and showers of flowers, the prince gave a short speech in which he thanked his guests for coming and ended with a pledge: 'Glamour and sophistication, the ultimate dream, will be this year's motto of Chiffons à la Mode.' As his eyes tracked the room, they fell on Aida and he singled her out for an enigmatic smile.

She glanced at Phares, who was once again talking closely with Alastair Carlisle; she was relieved that he was neither looking at Nairy, nor had he noticed the prince's smile in her direction. Instead he seemed calm and aloof.

She sighed heavily. In spite of her close surveillance she had no idea whether he was in love with Nairy, or if the affair really was a thing of the past. So how, she asked herself despairingly, could she let herself love him? What was she getting herself into by agreeing to marry him?

*    *    *

The Mena House Hotel was almost as impressive as the monuments in whose shadow it nestled. Built on the edge of the desert in a beautiful garden and dominated by the Great Pyramid, it had originally been Khedive Ismail's hunting lodge until it was bought by Ethel and Hugh Locke-King, who had turned it into a luxurious hotel. Arabesque in design, it covered a huge space, combining the comforts of modern life with the joy of sand and sky. Luxurious and expensive, yet it had a homely air, its wide doors welcoming guests and making them feel at ease, as if they belonged.

The long, low building with its white façade, flat roofs, elaborate balconies and terraces paved with old tiles and mosaic floors, and its dark *mashrabiya*, was reminiscent of the world illustrated in the tales of *One Thousand and One Nights*. It boasted large and comfortable salons with carved wooden doors and brasswork, and a delicious Moorish dining room lit by a galaxy of antique lamps.

Over the years, annexes and terraces had been added to the main building of which the popular garden café was one. In 1937 it had been expanded to include an al fresco dancefloor and it was on that terrace that Phares and his friends were congregating this evening.

A velvety, windless night had descended over the countryside. There existed a strange contrast between the crowded, noisy terrace with its bevy of guests in glamorous glittering eveningwear, drinking, eating, chatting and flirting, and the peaceful stillness of the ancient land of Egypt surrounding them. Beyond the hotel's garden walls lay the desert, secret and mysterious, and tiny villages with patches of dense shadow and flickering lights, and here and there the blaze of a small open café. A radiant luminescence lay on the pyramids and desert. The tall group of palms lifted its branches calmly into the glory of the moonlight.

The ladies deposited their wraps and, piloted by Phares, made their way to one of the small tables that had been reserved for them in the garden café, dimly lit by candles and small lanterns hidden in the trees. The tables were crowded close together, colourfully decorated with smilax and roses. The place was thronged with beautifully dressed women, and men in conventional black and white or dress uniform, with rows of medals adding vivid touches of colour. Aida saw the scene as a glittering kaleidoscope of elegance, aristocracy, money and power.

Dishes of nuts and olives, tiny crisp biscuits spread with caviar, anchovies, *antipasti*, cream cheese stuffed with pimentos, already dotted their table. As usual, Phares had organised everything in advance, down to the smallest detail.

A Tzigane orchestra was playing on a dais, the first gypsy band to appear in Egypt since the war. The management had kept it as a surprise, springing it on their patrons tonight.

Nairy Paplosian was already there. A beautiful low-cut plain and close-fitting satin evening dress clung to her tall, slim figure, accentuating every curve like a loving caress. There were two gardenias low on one side of her head where the smooth red hair was gathered back into a great knot at her neck. Her almond eyes with their heavy lids stood out against the creamy pallor of her skin. She was surrounded by a court of heterogeneous men and women drawn from half the races of Europe.

Aida sat between Camelia and Alastair Carlisle with Phares opposite her, trying not to feel as though a knife was raking her stomach. The candlelight shone on her golden hair and cast deep shadows about her dark blue eyes. She was pensive.

Nairy's earlier open advances to Phares were troubling her – not that she could pin on Phares any untoward reaction, not even an answering look. Indeed, it was just that detached imperviousness of his that bothered her. Aida had watched him closely and he hadn't batted an eyelid at the coquettish movements Nairy had made, instead being as aloof to her as the Sphinx had appeared to her and Phares during their desert promenade the other night. For someone who was by all accounts deeply smitten by the sexy model, his attitude was too … unconvincing.

'She looks like a black snake,' Camelia whispered as she followed her friend's gaze.

Aida smiled at Phares's irrepressible sister. 'You don't miss anything, do you?'

'Not when it has to do with the people I care for.'

The food was excellent but Aida could barely swallow it, so anxious was she made by the presence of the young woman seated two tables away. Phares also seemed uneasy. Or perhaps uneasy was not the right word. Electric was more like it … focused, as though all his formidable resources, physical and intelligent, were concentrated on some problem ... and Aida was sure that the name of the problem was Nairy! Still, she ate her iced consommé, her *homard cardinal*, drank champagne and chatted inconsequentially all through dinner, laughing mechanically, barely conscious of anyone but Phares and Nairy.

She was thankful for Alastair Carlisle who never stopped talking and brought her all the society gossip from Cairo. His light-hearted chatter and entertaining anecdotes about the various places in the world he was posted before the war made her laugh, easing the tense atmosphere in the nicest way.

The band struck up with the first notes of Lucienne Boyer's wartime hit '*Que Reste-t-Il de Nos Amours*', and before Aida could bat an eyelid, Nairy was at Phares's side, laying a beautifully manicured white hand with long red nails on his arm with open acquisitive eagerness. She fluttered dark lashes, gazing at him with bold grey eyes as though she wanted to carry him off there and then. There was nothing of the innocent angel about her now. 'Aren't you going to ask me to dance?' she whispered, her openly sexual smile revealing in all its untamed greed the desires that prowled beneath a thin veneer of civilised reserve.

Aida's hands gripped each other tightly in her lap. It was impossible to tell what Phares thought of this open parade of emotions as he was so intensely shielded by the golden mask of his features. His eyes were lazily undisturbed: reserved as ever, he didn't seem to object to the way Nairy clung to his arm, and Aida found herself wondering painfully if the tune meant something to them.

'Come on, let's dance,' the model insisted, fixing her hungry eyes on him. Phares sighed, then glanced at Aida as though he thought she might say something, but all she did was look away. She wasn't going to diminish herself – her pride wouldn't permit it – and she carried on sipping indifferently at her wine.

Shrugging, Phares allowed Nairy to draw him out on to the dancefloor. Somehow, Aida made herself smile and pretend it didn't matter. She turned her face away from the dais; she didn't want to see that woman in Phares's arms, to see her deliberately provocative words and actions. In all honesty, he could hardly have refused without being rude, but Aida was not willing to think of it that way. Instead, she finished what was left of her drink and asked Alastair if he would refill her glass.

'She's certainly not trying to hide how she feels, is she?' he remarked, cocking an eyebrow. 'It's a wonder she doesn't just throw him down on the floor and have her way with him here and now.'

Aida ignored that remark and changed the subject, but, unwillingly, her eyes stayed on Nairy, watching her laugh, her beautiful head thrown back as she pressed her long, curvaceous body against Phares. Again, Aida had to fight back that tide of corroding jealousy that she had been trying to suppress since her meeting with Prince Shams Sakr El Din at the Musky: '*Despite their social differences they are completely inseparable.*' Yes, right now, she could certainly see that was true.

Camelia shot a sideways glance at her friend. 'She's drunk, and poor Phares doesn't know what to do.'

'Gossip has it—' Alastair started.

But Camelia cut in: 'Gossip is gossip, and none of it's worth believing.'

Alastair bit his lip and fell silent, realising his faux pas. Then, as if he'd had a sudden brainwave, he turned to Aida again: 'Would you care for a dance?'

She managed a smile and got to her feet, joined by a couple of others with the same idea. As she moved like an automaton around the dancefloor, she looked back at the tables. Nairy had returned to hers, but Phares was nowhere to be seen.

And then as the first notes of the old 1930s hit, '*Parlez Moi d'Amour*', were heard, Phares was at Aida's side. Smiling at Alastair, he asked politely, 'May I?' before almost pulling her out of the other's embrace. 'It's a rather special song.'

Alastair relinquished Aida gracefully and made his way back to their table. When she glanced up at Phares's face again, its expression of severity made her frown in puzzlement. His mouth was tight, eyes hard as jet. He seemed caught in the grip of some strong emotion, yet his voice betrayed nothing of this when at length he spoke.

'Relax, Aida. You're stiff as a poker.'

'How unflattering!' she retorted. 'I've never been told I'm stiff.'

He laughed, and in that instant all severity was dispelled.

'Perhaps I was a little strong in my description. You're tense. Is something wrong?'

She shook her head, feeling the pink rise to her cheeks, unable to explain the torture Nairy's presence had put her through all evening.

'No, nothing.'

And now they were dancing to the strains of the loveliest waltz ever written – Schumann's *Souvenir de Vienne* – and the gypsies played it like a rhapsody. It was amazing how these talented musicians could switch from one type of music to another, skipping from tune to tune without a single piece of sheet music to follow.

'You're more relaxed now.' He glanced down at her flushed face, and his eyes creased into a smile. Aida caught her breath, still bewildered to find that the touch of his hands was the most wonderful experience she had ever known. His arm about her was comforting ... protective.

'Are you tired? We'll go home after this dance, it's been a long day.'

She smiled up at him. 'Yes, I think that'll be wise.'

They went back to the table and waited for Camelia before bidding farewell to the few remaining late-nighters in their party.

*Osta* Fathi and the Cadillac were waiting for them outside and they drove home in silence.

Once at Kasr El Shorouk, Camelia immediately said goodnight, taking her leave of them and going up to her room. Aida was about to follow her up the stairs when Phares caught her arm. His eyes settled on her face and she noticed a brooding expression in them.

'Will you join me for a nightcap on the terrace? It's such a beautiful evening and I'm rather restless.'

She hesitated a moment. Her mind was already in turmoil and she needed some space to think things over. She was well aware that she had promised to give her answer to Phares the next day, but something compelled her to stay.

'Just for a few minutes,' she found herself saying.

She followed him into the dining room, where he took two cognac glasses and a bottle of Rémy Martin. Together, they stepped on to the terrace. It was a hot night. They stood by the balustrade, not quite together, looking over the still and sleeping garden and gazing up at the sky. Aida caught her breath in amazement.

'Oh, Phares,' she whispered, the full splendour of the firmament bursting upon her with a glory that was overwhelming.

Phares poured them each an inch of cognac. They stood a while sipping their drinks, silently aware of the spell of Egypt upon them both. The heavens were an arch of purest, darkest blue, bejewelled with burning, glittering points of light. So big and bright were the gleaming clusters hanging, trembling, in the vast space above that it seemed as though a man might reach up and pluck a great gold star from among its close-set sisters of the night. In England, Aida had heard the term starlight without realising in the least what it could mean: back there, the stars at their brightest conveyed little idea of any real power of illumination but out here on the edge of the desert it was easy to comprehend the meaning of the word, for the stars did indeed pour down a stream of radiance that, even without the waning crescent moon, managed to flood the countryside with a soft and brilliant light which turned the world to a garden of enchantment.

All the while Aida could feel the presence of Phares a few feet away, as though he was keeping his distance, and yet the air between them hummed with heightened awareness, making the downy hairs on her arms lift. She tried to display a cool exterior but couldn't help darting a glance at him.

He had turned his back to the scenery and for a long moment he looked at Aida, letting her see without evasion the open hunger in his eyes as they slid down the length of her silk chiffon dress and back up to her face. The silence between them seemed to roar, drowning out the cicadas singing in the grass.

Then, in a single stride he was next to her. 'I can't let you go, Aida. Give me your answer. Now.' His lips found hers and crushed them mercilessly, his tongue invading her mouth. He was like some supreme pharaonic god whose word was a law unto itself, whose command could not be disobeyed. Aida felt the power of him, the mastery and the arrogance. The heat and hunger of his kiss rendered her lost, confused, no longer wanting to resist. She couldn't help herself as her body began to respond to his touch, the need for him coursing through her veins, and she gave herself up to the dark, stinging rapture of the moment.

Phares dragged his mouth from hers and buried his face in her neck. 'Your scent is driving me crazy,' he said huskily, inhaling deeply. 'You go to my head like a drug … I want you with my body, my mind, with every last bit of me … I want you so badly, *chérie* …'

Somewhere in Aida's mind a rational voice was demanding proof that he loved her, telling her that she should not be allowing him to touch her until the moment he did. Yet the other voice inside her rang out more clearly.

It all came down to feelings, instincts, emotions – those vague, insubstantial things that weren't even easy to identify, let alone prove: thistledown floating on the summer air, moonshine, flickering shadows. She didn't understand them, but she knew what they told her.

*I love him*, she thought.

Finally disengaging from her, Phares met her troubled gaze. 'Has no one told you that you have eyes so big and blue that a man might dive into them and be drowned?'

Aida stared back at him mutely, stunned by the heat between them. Then he touched his fingers to his lips and put them gently, fleetingly, on her mouth, before letting them slide down over her chin to the long line of her throat, and further down to the valley between her breasts that were already aching for his touch, and down still further over the soft chiffon fabric of her dress outlining her hips to the warm, moist joining of her thighs.

Aida gasped, her head falling back under the shock of his touch, as she realised the extent of her own need for him – and the power he had over her. Her voice cracked as she breathed his name, imploringly, her dazed eyes fixed on the firm line of his mouth. She wanted his lips on hers, longed for them, thirsted for them, but she mustn't. She needed a clear head to think things over, and so with an almost insurmountable effort, she pushed his hand away.

Phares's breath caught in his throat. 'Why are you torturing me, Aida?' His eyes were bloodshot and she could see he was fully aroused.

'Forgive me, Phares. Tomorrow … I promise I'll sort all this out tomorrow,' she whispered, her eyes welling with emotion, her body still trembling from the excruciating battle with her senses she was putting herself through.

Phares raked a hand through his hair and tossed back the remainder of his drink in one gulp. 'Fine, I will wait until tomorrow lunchtime, because I want things to be right between us.'

She tried to bring her breathing back under control. 'I'm spending the morning with Camelia at Chiffons à la Mode.'

He turned and leaned his elbows on the balustrade, staring into the night. 'I'm leaving early in the morning. I have two operations and I'm at the hospital until two o'clock.'

'I'm having lunch with Camelia at Shepheard's. I'll see you in the evening.'

'But I want to have lunch with you at the Gezireh Sporting Club. Tomorrow you will give me your answer, *chérie*. Don't worry about Camelia, I will talk to her. She'll understand.'

'I don't think it's fair on her, but if you prefer it that way then I'll meet you at the club at two-fifteen.'

Only then did he turn to look at her. 'Good. I want you to have no regrets because there is nothing safe about the way I want you.' His smouldering gaze seemed to burn a hole right through her. 'The delicacy of your skin … your body stops my breath and makes me almost afraid to touch you … and yet, at the same time, I want to penetrate you so deeply that your flesh will hold the memory of me within it forever.'

No man had ever spoken to her like this before, arousing her so intensely, both emotionally and physically, simply by the sound of his voice, the message in his words.

Still, it was all about sex, only sex, not love. And although Aida could actually feel the sharp, excited pulse of her own arousal deep within her core where she ached physically from Phares's explicit description of his desire, she moved away from him.

'I must go in,' she said calmly, as if he hadn't spoken those passionate words. 'Goodnight, Phares. I'll see you tomorrow.'

With that, she hurried from the terrace before she had time to weaken beyond return.

# Chapter 10

Aida awoke as dawn was pointing. She slid out of bed and made her way to the window just in time to see Phares's car disappearing down the drive. Her heart started to beat at an accelerated pace and a soft warmth flowed through her whole body. It didn't seem to matter how stupid it was, the same thing happened whenever he was in the vicinity. Of late, her body had been affected this way even at the thought of him.

The half-aroused sun was trampling down the lingering shadows, spreading its ruby-tinted tresses over the blooms in the dew-washed garden. A pinkish light appeared in the sky, running in long lines as though marked with a crayon by an unseen hand. Less than a kilometre away, a muezzin would be mounting the tall minaret of his mosque to stand on a circular platform and call the Prophet's followers from their sleep, for it was *El Fagr*, the hour of first prayer.

At this early hour in the solitude of her room, as the events of the previous evening returned to her, a sense of foreboding seemed to settle into Aida's heart. Her mind was filled with Phares and yet she was afraid of trusting her own judgement. For like this dawn she was watching, a new sun was rising slowly, almost warily, over the horizon of her life; and although she strove to turn her eyes away, reluctant to give in to her love when she was uncertain of his, she could not blind herself altogether to this new and cheering warmth.

It was her own feelings that made her afraid … afraid of wanting him … of loving him, of allowing him even deeper into her heart when she knew that all he wanted was her body. And surely, he would tire even of that one day and go looking for greener pastures. *But it was too late*, an inner voice whispered to her, *he was already there.* From the way Nairy Paplosian had looked at Phares, Aida knew the model was in love with him, and this only increased Aida's sense of vulnerability; she was already feeling exposed and in danger. It was why she had held off accepting Phares's proposal for so long.

The answer stared her in the face. Her whole being wanted to marry Phares, but she would first have to ask him for honesty about his relationship with Nairy.

Aida heard Camelia leave her room and at last came down to earth. She glanced at the clock on her bedside table: almost seven-thirty already? She knew that her friend liked to go for an early walk in the grounds every morning before the sun became too hot. After breakfast, she and Camelia had planned to go together to Chiffons à la Mode, to take a closer view of the dresses that had been shown at the fashion show and maybe buy a dress or two. She wondered if Phares had told Camelia about their lunch meeting and that today, they would finally discuss their marriage.

Picking up the bottle of *Nasmet El Aroussa*, Fragrance of a Bride from the dressing table, she smeared a little of the delicious heady scent on her wrists and behind her ears and opened the drawer to retrieve the turquoise pendant Phares had bought her. As her eyes lingered dreamily on the necklace her gaze was caught by a flash of colour. There, in the bottom of the drawer, was the talisman that Ghalya the gypsy woman had given her, its flaming orange gemstone winking brightly. She picked it up and held it to the hazy morning light spilling through the window; the heart of the gem seemed to burn a fiery pulsing red.

Unbidden, the dark, kohl-rimmed eyes of the old fortune teller drifted back into her mind, along with a vague memory of the *ghazeya*'s words. What had she said? Something about the amulet protecting Aida from the dangers ahead. What 'dangers' had she meant?

'*Always have it around your neck,*' that's what Ghalya had said. '*The day you are separated from it, not even* el Jin El-Ahmar *can help you.*'

Aida frowned and shook her head, returning the amulet to the drawer where it seemed to stare back at her insolently. What superstitious nonsense! Was happiness not just around the corner for her and Phares? It was within her reach and she would grasp it.

Shutting the drawer quickly, Aida hurried downstairs to join Camelia on the terrace.

*    *    *

An hour later, Aida and Camelia were in town at Chiffons à la Mode. The place was packed with men and women fighting their way through to the grand room where the models were parading, once more showing off their fabulous gowns. The two friends decided to have an iced chocolate at the fashionable Groppi tea shop that lay between The Savoy and the Grand Continental Hotel before Camelia's appointment at the hairdresser's, and then meet in the afternoon after lunch. Phares had obviously told Camelia about his lunch date with Aida: it was obvious from the smug smile that played around his sister's lips which seemed to say, '*I'm in on the secret, and even though I'm not going to try and influence you, I know what your answer to Phares will be.*'

As the *suffragi* brought the bill, Aida asked, 'What will *you* be doing while I'm having lunch with your brother?'

Camelia shot her a sheepish look. 'I'm visiting Sami at a friend's house. He's convalescing there at the moment.' She eyed her friend warmly. 'I'll never be able to thank you enough for what you did, *habibti*. You saved his life.'

Aida hesitated. 'Is what you're doing wise?'

'It might not be wise, but one has to do what one has to do, so let's not talk about it.'

'Fine, Camelia, but I do worry about you. The police are everywhere and you know there's no mercy when they catch these rioters.'

Her friend sighed. 'Please, *habibti*, let's not go into it again. Do you mind a lot if I leave you now? If I hurry, I'm sure Spiro the hairdresser will see me now. His other clients are bound to be busy at Chiffons à la Mode. It'll mean that I can set off to see Sami a little earlier.'

Aida sat back, resigned. There was no reasoning with Camelia, she could see that. 'No, I don't mind, *habibti*. I'll go to the bookshop and buy some books to take back with me to Luxor. I can then hop in a taxi to go to Gezireh or I might even surprise Phares at the hospital.'

Camelia beamed. 'Yes, do that, he'll be thrilled.'

The two friends separated in front of Groppi's and Aida went off to browse the shelves in Dar El Kotob, one of the largest bookshops in Cairo. She was surprised to find that all the bestsellers she had read about were available, including *Arch of Triumph*, the new book by the exiled German writer Erich Maria Remarque, whose previous bestseller, *All Quiet on the Western Front*, had been such a success. Her interest was immediately piqued: the bittersweet love story set in France on the eve of the war had as its hero a German surgeon who found himself driven to help out two less skilful French physicians.

Delighted with her shopping, Aida glanced at her watch. There was nearly an hour to kill. Time enough to surprise Phares at the hospital. Not only was she curious to see where he worked, but as she hadn't yet investigated nursing opportunities in Cairo, it made sense to take a look around the place. Perhaps it was somewhere she herself might like to work one day.

She hailed a taxi and directed the driver to the Anglo-American Hospital in Gezireh. The town was crowded at this hour. Policemen in white uniforms and black berets stood atop stepladder towers in the grassy roundabout, channelling long lines of cars, carts and bicycles into the streets radiating from the central *medans* like the spokes of a wheel.

The taxi crossed the great Kasr El Nil steel bridge, its approach guarded by huge, imposing bronze lions, to Gezireh Island, where a long avenue of *lebbek* trees led to the Anglo-American Hospital. It drew to a halt at a pair of tall, black wrought-iron gates manned by a Sudanese *bawab*, and Aida got out, her pulse quickening uneasily. Suddenly she wasn't sure that turning up uninvited at Phares's workplace was such a good idea. He was undoubtedly very busy and wouldn't want to be distracted. Still, she told herself, she'd have a look around without bothering him, then make her own way to the Gezireh Sporting Club, which was only a ten-minute walk away.

The hospital was a typical anglicised villa in the same style as the majority of buildings on the island. Painted white, with tall, green-shuttered windows and a few verandas, it was set in a beautiful English garden with great flame trees, red and white oleander bushes and brightly coloured herbaceous borders. Aida had been born at the 'Anglo', as it was commonly known, a small hospital originally set up and funded by British and American companies in Cairo, essentially as a benevolent organisation. During the war, the Anglo had become a British-run military hospital and in 1944 had made world headlines when Lord Moyne, resident British Minister of State, was assassinated and was rushed there, eventually dying from his bullet wounds.

Aida, making her way towards the great arched entrance, suddenly stood quite still, like a rabbit fascinated by a ferret's glare.

In his white doctor's coat, Phares's tall silhouette appeared at the top of the stairs, Nairy Paplosian by his side. The model was smiling provocatively at him, her hand on his sleeve smoothing away an invisible piece of thread. As they came down the steps, Aida had just enough time to throw herself behind an oleander bush before they went right past her.

A chauffeur-driven green Ford Super Deluxe pulled up in front of the gateway, not far from where Aida was hiding, and the *bawab* scrambled to his feet to open the gates. Nairy stood on tiptoes, her slim and elegant body leaning passionately against Phares's, and kissed him.

Straight as a poker, he placed a hand on her arm. 'I'll be waiting for you this evening, six o'clock,' Aida heard him say as he pushed her gently into the car.

Nairy promptly leaned out of the window and called with a coaxing smile, 'Don't be late, *ya hobi*, my love.'

*Phares and Nairy were still lovers.*

Aida felt as if she had been doused in a bucket of freezing-cold water. Every particle of colour drained from her face, and then her cheeks begun to burn. Hands clenched, she stood paralysed by what she had just seen, her neck rigid with the effort of self-control. Jealousy, primitive and barbaric, possessed her, sending the blood to her head, rendering her unpredictable and frightened of the rage that was welling up in her.

Phares waited until the car had passed through the gates then slowly retraced his steps, looking pensive as he passed inches away from Aida. She nearly sprang out of her hiding place to confront him with what she had just witnessed but her pride wouldn't allow her to humiliate herself further.

Now she couldn't wait to get away. She didn't want to see any more, hear any more. Her mind reeled. Only an hour later and it might have been her in Phares's arms, celebrating the dawn of a new life together. The pain slashed at her, and she turned, fumbling her way blindly back through the gates of the hospital. At least she'd been spared that, if nothing else.

For a moment she stood on the pavement as if lost, not knowing what to do next, then she hailed a taxi and asked him to go to Kasr El Ghoroub. She would pack her bags and stay the night at a hotel. Tomorrow, she would fly back to Luxor as planned, and maybe after that she would return to England.

How naïve she'd been. Her uncle George always teased her for wanting men to be like the heroes in the books she read. '*Too many romantic novels, my dear … Men and women are not that way in real life.*' She guessed he was right.

At Kasr El Ghoroub she asked the taxi to wait for her while she packed her bags. Luckily, there was no one at the house to question her, so having gathered all her belongings pell-mell into a suitcase, she then phoned Shepheard's Hotel to reserve a room for the night. Nothing was available. She then tried other, equally luxurious hotels only to find that they, too, were full, due to the number of guests who had come into town for the fashion show the previous day. Finally, she managed to book a room at the Windsor and before leaving the house, wrote a brief and apologetic note to Camelia, telling her that she had decided to go back to Luxor a day earlier. She would explain everything, she promised, when her friend was next in Upper Egypt.

An hour later, Aida's taxi stopped in front of the entrance to the hotel whose stone façade and uniformity of windows was a faithful example of Colonial Era Neo-Mamluk architecture. Built at the turn of the century, the building was originally the baths of the Egyptian royal family, and then the Windsor served for many years as a colonial British officers' club before being bought by a Swiss hotelier, who made it an annexe of the Shepheard's Hotel, naming it the Hotel Windsor – Maison Suisse. The exterior had always reminded Aida of the interior courtyard façades of the sixteenth-century Wikalet El Ghoury, a caravanserai not far from the Musky.

The lobby was dark, double-height and narrow, with a tall reception desk where two smiling young men were registering new arrivals and dealing with guests. On the back wall was a hive of wooden pigeonholes for room keys, passports and guests' letters and to the right stood a Bakelite telephone switchboard, studded with rows of jacks and sockets.

After one of the genial young men had entered Aida's name into a large leatherbound guestbook, she was shown to the wooden carriage lift which took her up to her room on the third floor. The landing and corridor that led to bedrooms were hung with travel posters depicting horses galloping through the snow at St Moritz, Alpine walkers in Zermatt and colourful Swiss meadows carpeted with wild flowers, reminding Aida of the summer holidays she had sometimes spent with her father in Switzerland. The whole ambiance of the place spoke of faded grandeur, and although its understated charm would in usual circumstances have appealed to her, in the mood she was in, she didn't want to spend more than one night there.

After leaving the hospital, Aida had performed everything like an automaton, dazed as though in a dream. Now alone in her rather dark hotel room, the reality of what she had seen struck her once again with all the force of a thunderbolt. All she understood was that she wanted to burst into tears, to scream and howl her misery to the four winds.

She should have known: it had been staring her in the face and she hadn't wanted to see it. She had enjoyed being courted by Phares, her wanton body demanding her to be blind to the truth because she was so in love with him. He was a man like any other and in her mind's eye she tortured herself with images of him ... saw him dancing with Nairy as he had done last night ... Nairy the redheaded beauty with flaming hair, gluing her lissom model's body to his and looking so fair in contrast with his darkness; leading him into desire even as he led her through the rhythms of the dance. Pain twisted in Aida's stomach; she felt her antagonism towards them both like a bitter taste at the back of her mouth.

She remembered how Phares had kissed her and said those words to her only last night ... But then she reminded herself with a shock of revulsion that they had been words of lust, not love. She needed to get out, go for a walk, get some fresh air.

Aida changed into a pair of grey slacks and went out into Alfi Bey Street. The pavement outside the hotel was overrun by the crowded tables of the Parisiana Café, which occupied the ground floor. She was just about to cross the road when she heard someone calling her. She turned around. A large group of expats was seated at a couple of tables outside the hotel, and Alastair Carlisle was walking towards her.

'Aida, my dear, I saw you coming into the hotel earlier with a suitcase. I thought you were staying at the Pharaonys.'

'Hello, Alastair.' His sudden appearance had interrupted Aida's dark thoughts and now she struggled to school her features into nonchalance. 'I was, but they were called away to Luxor. As my plane ticket is for tomorrow morning and Shepheard's is full, I decided to spend the night here.'

His eyes gave a friendly twinkle. 'Ah, come and join us then. We're all very jolly this evening, looking forward to our excursion to Wahat El Nakheel, Prince Shams' oasis. It's all rather fascinating.' He leaned in conspiratorially and lowered his voice. 'To be honest, I'm using it as an excuse to see what kind of set-up he has. Very useful, if you know what I mean.'

'You're going to his oasis?' repeated Aida, only dimly registering the information.

'Yes. Each year, the prince invites a different group. This year, I'm one of the happy chosen, which suits me very well indeed.

'The only man, in fact, among a bevy of ladies.' He grinned. 'Nigel, Eve's husband, was supposed to come too, but the Embassy's sending him off to England tomorrow.' He regarded her quizzically. 'I take it you're not going?'

'No, I need to get back to Luxor,' she said quietly.

'Will you join us for a drink? They make delicious cocktails at the Parisiana. You know most of the gang.'

Aida looked into Alastair's good-natured face and her mood shifted slightly. Perhaps a drink and the friendly company of others was what she needed right now. 'I was going for a walk, but on second thoughts I think I would love one of the Parisiana's cocktails. I've often heard about them, but have never had one. It's the first time I've been here.'

'An experience not to be missed, trust me. My recommendation would be a pink gin. Did you know,' he said as they made their way to his table, 'that the drink was originally created by the Royal Navy? They used Angostura bitters as a medicinal treatment for their sailors, and the gin was added to make it more palatable. Their concoction is very good here,' he winked. 'Plenty of gin and not too heavy-handed on the Angostura.'

*    *    *

The Embassy contingent was an animated lot who, for the most part, had met Aida briefly before at the Gezireh Sporting Club. Alastair introduced her to the ones she didn't know, some of whom worked at the British Embassy. The Parisiana was the hub of writers, actors and an amalgam of industrious and prosperous elements drawn from the various native-cum-European communities of Cairo, and the atmosphere outside the café was buzzing with life. Soon, having ordered one of the excellent pink gins, Aida was very much at ease, chatting merrily, taking part in the lively conversation, speaking of mutual acquaintances and finding plenty to talk about: it quickly became evident that they had all been, at some time, in the same set.

At Aida's table were seated Simone Villiencourt, a young socialite whom she had often seen at the Club, looking very French in her pale pink organdie, her narrow face animated by big brown eyes that were so dark that it was difficult to tell whether they were brown or black; Eva Delamere, an Italian, golden-skinned beauty with a tumble of black curls and a ready smile who was gracious to everyone; her husband Nigel, the youngest English Consul, a rather stiff young man who didn't speak much; Sonia, a white Russian working at the British Embassy as secretary to one of the consuls, who was seated next to Alan Wendt, a handsome American army man who couldn't take his eyes off Aida; and James and Mrs Saunders, who were discoursing at length on the upcoming bazaar for the English church. Conversation moved freely and briskly back and forth among them all, and it would have been hard to find a more delightful and happy gathering.

Just as Aida was starting on her second gin, a silver Rolls-Royce stopped in front of the hotel, out of which stepped a tall man in a heavy white silk gown covered by a black *burnous*, on his head a white turban bound by camel-hair cords. He was followed by Prince Shams Sakr El Din in his usual immaculate white suit. Their deep conversation was broken suddenly when the prince noticed the group of foreigners at the table.

He stopped short, a broad grin lighting his face, then said something to the other man before the pair swiftly made their way over. Aida noted that the other man was as strikingly handsome as the prince and bore a strong resemblance to Shams, though the older man's hawk-like face was leaner and deeply lined.

Their arrival at the café had not gone unnoticed. Aida felt a stir in the group as most of the woman at her table, and even those seated at others, turned predatory eyes to look at the prince, who was his usual dashing self.

'Who is he?' asked Simone Villiencourt.

'Prince Shams Sakr El Din, scion of an old and distinguished Bedouin family. Immensely rich, charming and a wonderful host … a rattling fine fellow,' Sonia told her.

The prince held out his hands, smiling with delight. 'Ah, my friends, how lovely to see you. May I present my uncle, Sheikh Mahmoud Salah Sakr El Din.'

Introductions were made all around. Sheikh Mahmoud spoke excellent English with just a trace of an accent and the occasional unusual phrasing, both a little stilted and entirely charming. He appeared pleased to meet his nephew's friends and his loud voice boomed like a great bell, punctuated by full-throated and infectious laughter.

'Will you join us?' Alastair asked.

'My uncle and I are on our way to visit a sick friend who lives down the road, but it would give us great pleasure to join you for a little while,' replied the prince.

At Alastair's signal, an attentive *suffragi* brought two extra chairs, one of which he placed at Aida's side of the table. The prince immediately took it and squeezed it between Alastair and Aida, his grey eyes half merry, half rueful at having inveigled his way in. '*Etnein asseer lemoon*, two lemonades,' he told the *suffragi* awaiting his order.

Turning to Aida, he took her hand in both of his.

'So, we meet again, my dear,' he said, scrutinising her face with a keen, intelligent look.

She smiled demurely. 'Cairo is a small place.'

'Indeed it is, though the Parisiana is the last place I would have thought to see you.'

'Aida's friends have had to go back to Luxor urgently,' supplied Mrs Saunders.

Sakr El Din's eyes lit up with quick interest. 'Ah, some respite from your watchdog.'

'My plane ticket is for tomorrow,' Aida explained, refusing to be baited by the prince's provocative remark.

'Ah yes, I remember. That's why you said you couldn't make it to my oasis.'

'Correct.'

His pale hawk eyes darkened almost to hazel, boring into her blue ones. 'Are you sure you have to leave? Is there no way I can tempt you?' His thin lips stretched into a quizzical smile.

'Of course she'll join us,' piped up Mrs Saunders. 'I'm sure we can all squeeze on to the bus that Your Highness has so generously organised for us.'

'Come on, Aida, you can change your ticket for the Monday or Tuesday of next week, *ce n'est pas la mer à boire,*' threw in Simone. 'It's not that complicated, *non*?'

'When would you have such a great opportunity again to visit an oasis in the desert?' enthused Mrs Saunders once more. 'Besides, Wahat El Nakheel is famous for its beauty. In life, one must grab these lucky chances with both hands.'

Sakr El Din's gaze settled on Simone. 'I hope that you will be free to join your friends on this excursion tomorrow, *mademoiselle.*'

'That's so kind of you, Your Highness. I wouldn't miss it for anything. I've heard that it's Eden on earth. *Ah, le désert, quel rêve!*' she gushed, hugging herself coquettishly.

The prince inclined his head. 'Those are very kind words, thank you.'

Aida was tempted. After all, nothing was forcing her to go back to Luxor the next day. She hadn't yet told *Dada* Amina of her return, and Phares was too busy with his redhead mistress to care, she thought bitterly, although another part of her did wonder what would be his reaction when he discovered that the bird had flown the nest. He wasn't to know that she had seen him with Nairy at the hospital; already she must have offended his masculine pride by not turning up for lunch, perhaps concluding the reason for her absence was that she had decided not to marry him after all. Her heart squeezed painfully at the thought.

The only one who might become worried by her sudden departure would be Camelia, and Aida decided she would ring her tonight and explain.

She glanced up at the prince. All through the argument he had kept quiet, letting the others fight his corner. His eyes watched Aida's face steadily between the straight, narrow lids, and though they looked full at her, she could make nothing of that look.

Aida suddenly wondered what would be so bad in accepting his invitation. Apart perhaps from the two pink gins she had drunk on an empty stomach, which may have clouded her judgement, she couldn't say what had prompted her change of heart. Was it the fear of appearing unfriendly and ungrateful in front of her peers? Or could it be that she was surprised and slightly disappointed that the prince had remained silent and had not pressurised her himself? Aida had never considered herself a flirt, but was she slightly miffed that he might have lost interest in her? Had it made her want to rekindle his admiration?

She had to confess that her reaction was most likely an immediate consequence of the scene she had witnessed at the hospital, prompting in her a secret pleasure in doing something she knew perfectly well would anger Phares.

Whatever the answers, Aida turned to him with a demure smile and heard herself say: 'On second thoughts, Prince, I'd be delighted to accept your very kind invitation.'

'You are doing me the greatest possible honour,' he smiled, with a charming gravity that had a hint of mysteriousness.

'It's all my pleasure, really.'

'I will always wonder at the moods of women, changeable as those of the sea and the sands of the desert.'

Aida registered the glint of humour in his eyes. Was his amusement at her expense? Had he guessed the reason for her sudden change of heart? Did he think that somehow the callous hint he had made about Nairy and Phares's relationship had manipulated her into agreeing to join the excursion?

Glancing at Alastair, she noticed his expression was guarded. He was the only one who had not rushed to encourage her to join the excursion. He sat back watching the proceedings, lighting a cigarette. Did he disapprove of her going? Or perhaps he was being protective of her, as he had been at Princess Nazek's ball.

She shrugged mentally. To hell with all these men. It was hurting her head to think this much. From now on she would just concentrate on seizing every opportunity to have a good time, as per Mrs Saunders' wise advice.

The prince beckoned to the *suffragi* and paid his bill plus those of the two tables, under a shower of protests. 'As arranged, the bus will be waiting for you in front of the British Embassy in Garden City at seven-thirty sharp,' he announced.

Turning to Aida, he informed her in a quieter voice, 'I will have my driver pick you up ten minutes before. You'll join the bus at the Embassy as you will be going in convoy. Unfortunately, I will not have the pleasure of driving you myself as I must return to the oasis tonight to make sure the preparations are carried out properly.'

Aida's eyes widened, uneasy that he'd singled her out for preferential treatment. 'But …'

'Please, allow me this pleasure.' His voice was warm and vibrant, low-pitched, without harshness. 'My driver will bring you back at the end of the weekend as I will be staying on at Kasr El Nawafeer for some time.' That gracious bearing, that silken tongue, that perfect courtesy masked a determination that Aida, although recognising it, couldn't be bothered to combat tonight.

She nodded, contriving a pale smile. 'I'll be ready. Thank you.'

'Wear something comfortable and bring a hat,' he suggested, his gaze still lingering on her face although he was on the point of leaving. 'The desert is very hot, and I have planned some outside entertainment.'

As soon as the two men were out of earshot, the gossiping about the prince began again. Aida was tired now; it had been a long day. She was bruised, and all she wanted was to be alone in the sanctuary of her room. She'd need an early night if she was to be up early in the morning. She parted company with the jolly little crowd, who by now were quite sozzled, and made her way back inside the hotel.

It was already eight o'clock and she wanted to put in a call to Kasr El Ghoroub, but the hotel telephones were out of order. They would be repaired in the next two hours, she was told by the concierge. She asked if room service could bring up a large bottle of cold Evian water, a ham omelette and some fruit, and went up to her room, where she turned on the wireless. The news wasn't good. There had been further demonstrations; more people arrested. She wondered if they were friends of Camelia's.

Aida sat on the edge of her bed, staring blankly at the open window, listening to the noise of the street below. Phares was probably with Nairy, she thought gloomily. After her father's death she'd presumed nothing would have the power to shock her again, but seeing the pair together had upset Aida more than she'd imagined possible. All day she had been numb, the pain dormant deep inside her, but now a bitter jealousy gripped her as she imagined them together in his cosy love nest next to the hospital. She hated herself for being so weak, for wallowing in unrequited love like a foolish teenager.

Room service brought up her order, but Aida had no appetite and could hardly swallow anything. Once again, she tried to ring Camelia, but there was no answer. Sighing heavily, she climbed into bed, deciding that it was probably best to try ringing again tomorrow from the oasis. Surely there would be every facility at the palace, and she was certain her host wouldn't mind.

\*     \*     \*

It was with a sense of fatality that Aida dressed herself that morning to join the group that were going to spend the day at Wahat El Nakheel.

Despite her grievance against Phares, she knew she was acting impulsively just to spite him. Admittedly, deep down she herself didn't much like the prince, though something about him spoke to a darker side of her that she dared not scrutinise ... but it would be an adventure, she told herself, trying to rouse all the enthusiasm she could muster.

On the positive side, it would be the first time Aida had visited an oasis, and the party she was joining were a fun lot. Ever since she had returned to Egypt she had felt the pressure to be a good Egyptian girl, and she was growing heartily sick of it. She didn't want to be branded a wet blanket; she'd never thought herself a bore – quite the reverse, she'd always been the life and soul of a party.

Aida chose a practical pair of roomy navy trousers and a matching cotton shirt with long sleeves, which she thought suitable for the expedition. If she was going to be riding a camel, she should be comfortable. Clipping her hair back from her ears in two smooth waves, she donned a wide straw hat with white ribbons to protect her from the sun.

The prince's driver arrived punctually in a smart burgundy newly inaugurated model of the new Willys Overland Station

Wagon, and by seven-thirty, they had joined the bus waiting outside the British Embassy. By now, Aida was taking a guilty pleasure in the luxurious treatment that Sakr El Din was bestowing on her. To know she would be travelling in such comfort in convoy with the bus made her a little self-conscious. She remained in the station wagon instead of getting out to chat with her travelling companions, giving a friendly wave towards the group as they climbed on to the bus, all the while hoping they didn't think she was lording it over them.

The road led straight to the west between illimitable green fields, cut by flashing channels of water, where the *fellahin* were working, their long gowns tucked up about their waists. Here and there, built upon high stilts or in the branches of a lonely tree, she spotted a rickety platform upon which an armed man was standing, keeping watch over the crops in a vigil that would last through the night.

They drove out along a canal bank, the station wagon taking the lead, then struck into the desert on a dirt road. As the car bumped across the rubble, swaying perilously in the soft sand, Aida's eyes were riveted to the barren scenery rolling by. The miles were coming towards her, sliding beneath her, stretching out behind her. She was conscious of space and distance as never before and had plenty of time to reflect on the wisdom or otherwise of the step she was taking. Whatever risks or regrets that might arise, it was too late now.

It was another hour before they reached a flat plateau where camels awaited them, reclining and ruminating in the shadow of a clump of palms. The sun was already high, even though it was not yet nine o'clock.

'This is where we stop,' the driver told Aida. 'His Highness's men will take you from here. The rest of the journey will be by camel as the terrain is awkward for a car. The oasis is not too far.'

Even though she had grown up in Egypt, Aida had only ever ridden a camel once before, as a young teenager, and had not liked the experience at all. Still, that was years ago and doubtless it was time to give it another go, she told herself gamely. Suddenly forgetting for a moment her woes, she welcomed the novelty of it all and felt the excitement rise in her at the idea of this new adventure.

She got out of the car and donned her sunglasses as the driver approached three tall figures in large white turbans whom Aida assumed were the prince's dragomen. Bright-eyed, with hawk-like features, they wore long, spotless white coats and brown sandals, and she wondered how they were able to keep their robes so clean out in the desert. As her driver took his leave, one of the men approached her with a long, leisurely stride and bowed. 'Miss El Masri, it is our honour to escort you to Wahat El Nakheel, His Highness Prince Shams Sakr El Din's oasis. It is a short journey and we have plenty of water.' He smiled broadly, revealing a gap between his teeth, and gestured to the bus as it pulled up alongside them. 'And now you can join your companions.'

Tumult and joyous noise burst from the bus as its doors opened and the group disembarked. They made their way towards the desert transporters, laughing and joking, and quickly surrounded Aida, who was introduced to Marica, a redheaded Greek whose flaming mane brought out the freckles on her face, and her green-eyed friend Norma, an Armenian, both of whom Aida knew by sight from the Gezireh Sporting Club. Once she had endured the inevitable questions and teasing about her chauffeured car, she soon entered into the spirit of the day's expedition, a new wild, reckless mood taking her over. Even Alastair Carlisle, who had seemed circumspect about her coming, now smiled broadly, saying, 'Stick close to me, Aida. This is certainly going to be an experience and a half.'

The noise of the small crowd awakened the camels and for a few minutes much rumbling and grunting went on. With its hanging lower lip and large yellow teeth, drooping eyes and long lashes, and its ridiculous wisp of a tail, this large desert animal could never be described as a handsome creature, despite the decorative blue beads threaded in its trappings to ward off the evil eye. Aida wrinkled her nose; she didn't much like its smell either.

Alastair, who seemed to be an expert at camel riding, moved to help Aida on to her camel, which was still crouching on the ground.

'The worst part of every camel ride is the beginning and the ending,' he told her with mock seriousness. 'The sitting-down and getting-up bit is a complicated process at best. Try to seat yourself firmly in one go. These wretched animals have a habit of rising suddenly, before you're seated properly, and flinging you about.'

*Great!* Aida thought as she scrambled as nimbly as she could on to her camel's extreme summit. The beast rose with a forward lurch.

'Lean back!' commanded Alastair.

Aida did as she was told.

'Look out!' the consul called out as the camel strained his front legs, lurching backwards and almost unseating her.

'Lean to the front to counter the movement.'

Aida complied. The camel finally stood straight and she was aloft – *at the top of the world*, she thought, looking around her. At this height, if the animal were to become refractory, what could she do? She was sitting far too high to be able to steady herself with her calves, as she would on horseback. Aida soon realised that the bridle was of no use, having little influence on the beast, however hard she pulled on it.

'You look a bit doubtful, Aida,' Alastair called to her. 'Do you feel all right?'

'I'm fine, don't worry,' she replied gamely. 'I'll soon get the hang of it.'

He showed her how to cross her legs in front of the saddletree like the Bedouins and communicate her wishes to the camel by drumming with her heels on its withers, or with the single rope attached to the halter around its nose. Yes, that was better, Aida thought with satisfaction, she felt more secure now.

There was much squealing and exclamation from the little gang before they got underway. They walked in a solemn and a silent string, in awe of the great magnificence of the scenery, each camel led by two boys shrouded in white. The air was so clear and delicious, the sun's heat tempered by a wandering breeze, and the sand shone and sparkled.

Aida had pictured this ride across the desert as one long, monotonous procession over the scorched brown sand. Yet she discovered that here was not merely a land of endless shifting dunes, but those sandhills were no more alike than mountain pastures or green fields, and in the enfolding silence she was filled with amazement at the alluring scenes unfurling before her eyes in the hot Egyptian sun. There were so many strange and wonderful sights to be seen along their route – ruined temples, colossal sphinx-like figures in groves of tufted palms at the edge of tiny mud villages, each boasting their own white-walled mosque and colourful bazaar.

They swung on, some of them in continual danger of being thrown off, as one or two camels took no pains to make things pleasant for their riders, but Aida quickly got the hang of it. Soon, they left all signs of cultivation behind them and were crossing an expanse of golden sand, interspersed with patches of rubble, with no evidence of human habitation, no animals or even growing things, save the occasional low bush of camel thorn amid the huge dunes of sand that had been moulded by the winds into the semblance of sea waves.

The desert atmosphere, Aida found, was deceptive. Here, she saw the first mirage of the day. It was like looking at a fairy-tale city through the bottom of a glass; there were strangely shaped houses and castles, seemingly solid, yet none of them turned out to have any substance. Reality clashed with illusion as these mirages shimmered about them, strange and beautiful like dreams but so tantalisingly material. And it wasn't all cities and palaces: here and there, the vivid green of a watered plain leapt into sight, the river seeming almost within reach of the outstretched hand, only to vanish as if by enchantment as they seemed to get closer, leaving a burning yellow tint over everything.

They went steeply up a chain of mountains and then down a hillside towards the plain in which the oasis Wahat El Nakheel lay. Now there was a clear path zigzagging on a sharp incline. Aida gave a gasp. On one side a yawning abyss; on the other, bush-covered slopes.

Phares had been right. The desert, at first sight so alien and tedious, did develop its own magnetism after a while. This morning, Aida had discovered that the texture, colour and contours of its backdrop changed continually. Yes, she understood his fascination now. At the thought of him a knot formed in her throat ... Even if she had wanted to forgive him and give him a second chance, by agreeing to spend a weekend at the Palace of Fountains, she had burned her boats where the young doctor was concerned.

Suddenly Aida was distracted by the rapturous exclamations of the group. Coming out of her reverie she saw it: a fortress surrounded on all sides by a towering wall – a wall so high, only an agile Bedouin might scale it. At each corner was a white gate guarded by dark-skinned men, whose keen eyes ensured that no one got in or out without permission.

Their camel train made for the main entrance, and as it approached, guards pulled the high gates back, allowing the camels to amble in.

The oasis was nothing like the few single palms half buried in the sand that one imagines on hearing the word. Wahat El Nakheel fully deserved all Shams Sakr El Din had said of it. It lay in the midst of the burning waste like a green jewel – such a welcoming surprise after the expanse of golden sands they had trekked through for over an hour. At the top of a steep hill loomed Kasr El Nawafeer, the prince's Palace of Fountains.

'It's so green,' Aida exclaimed.

'That's because the oasis is fed with water via many springs,' provided Alastair, who'd kept close to her throughout the journey.

The houses were white and almost windowless. Their upper storeys were like closely barred cages: the world of the harem, the word in itself meaning prohibited. These quarters, where women with a slave mentality lived locked away from the civilised world, were sacred and inviolable: the master's dearest treasure which must be guarded from profane glances and frivolous influences. The courtyard doors of the houses were decked out with beautiful ironwork. As the camel train passed by, it happened that one of these doors was open and Aida caught a glimpse of a garden and its palm trees.

Everywhere, on ground not taken up with a road or a primitive house, a thick carpet of grass grew, dotted with brightly hued flowers.

They passed by the bazaar. The narrow alleyways were roofed in, heavily barricaded. The great square, where the market stood, was very much like a circus; the hub of a deeply interesting throng of people and animals – a moving pattern of every vivid colour imaginable in that intense heat and clouds of rosy dust. Aida marvelled at the picturesque crowd whose costumes were a kaleidoscope of colours, including those yet to be invented, it seemed.

There, under a medley of garish awnings, squatting on their haunches, were the storytellers, whose raucous, guttural voices rose and fell monotonously. Moving about among them were all the other entertainers: the jugglers, sword-swallowers, fortune tellers, magicians and fire-eaters. Pandemonium reigned.

The noise was tremendous. Every conceivable sound in the world seemed rolled into one harsh, deafening clamour – a babel of cries, laughter, music and singing. Strings of strong-smelling, ragged-looking camels with hairless necks were being driven away from the market. Lean little donkeys, a halo of flies around their heads, struggled slowly forward, bearing bundles of wood or carpets. Veiled women carrying pitchers on their heads passed back and forth. There were groups of turbaned Bedouins smoking *keef*, drinking tea and playing dominoes. Others were doing nothing so perfectly that they appeared to the uninitiated to be doing something.

At various vantage points closed sedan chairs had paused, inside of which veiled faces watched the scene, some with beautiful eyes. The tall, bearded black men who carried these litters guarded their female contents closely, trying as best they could to keep a clear space between them and the milling crowds.

Simone wanted to stop to watch the snake charmer seated cross-legged and playing his pipe, his mournful gaze fixed on the snakes writhing to his music, but the dragomen pressed on. It seemed the guests were already late for His Highness.

By now, the travellers were wilting. It may have felt like a short journey for the Bedouin dragomen but not so for this group. The last ten minutes spent climbing the hill had literally been the last straw. Even Aida, who as a girl had been accustomed to long horse rides in the desert fringes around Luxor, was beginning to feel weary and hungry, although gourds of water had been provided to slake their thirst on the journey. And so it was with great sighs of relief and smiles that the party finally approached a second gate leading to the palace.

Kasr El Nawafeer was at the top of a hill, surrounded by a high wall topped with iron spikes. Guarded day and night, the fortified enclosure gave no promise of the paradise within. After the aridity of the desert, the verdant beauty of the scene that opened up in front of them was dazzling: nature in her humble brilliance.

It was as if the place had been blessed with a gift from the sky: rain. A liquid magic that had washed the sand off a vibrant world that had always been there. Grass the shade of every dreamer's meadow; trees of a thousand green hues that whispered softly in the wind; flowerbeds in a riot of colour, their yellow roses like buds of pure gold. Here and there were ponds, with singing fountains that joined with the happy chorus of birds in the trees.

The palace itself, its many pointed towers giving it the look of an eccentric crown, was a strange mixture of architectural periods and styles: Arab, Moorish, Saracen, even Byzantine – each had its place in the scheme. In the fierce, lawless days of old it had changed hands frequently, as kinsman succeeded kinsman, with the result that many minds had gone into the fashioning and refashioning of the whole. Still, despite its mishmash and florid make-up, one couldn't deny its dignified magnificence.

On three sides of the building was a garden full of splendid trees and shrubs, with beds whose glowing blooms of geraniums, antirrhinums and roses, among others, betokened endless care and a truly marvellous system of irrigation. The front of the palace gave on to a big courtyard, in the centre of which lay a beautiful folly surrounded by twelve small fountains set in a circle which played eternally, their silver drops falling with a musical splash into a great marble basin where small and shining fish swam languidly. Over every available inch of wall space bougainvillea hung like a purple mist, and snowy jasmine filled the air with an indescribably sweet and cloying fragrance.

News of their arrival had already reached their host, who stood waiting in the doorway of the palace to receive them. Here in his desert home, Prince Shams Sakr El Din had discarded the European clothes in which Aida was accustomed to seeing him and he presented a truly regal figure as he greeted the group of foreigners.

Over an elaborate robe of thick and creamy silk he wore a splendid kaftan of green satin, heavy with golden embroidery. On his head was a magnificent turban, on the front of which blazed an enormous emerald, and on his slim hands glowed other precious stones set with all the cunning of the goldsmith's craft. A short, gold dagger was suspended from his shoulder by a silk cord tucked into his belt.

Seen thus, in all the richness of his princely Bedouin attire, Prince Shams Sakr El Din was a very striking figure, and even Aida admitted to herself that the flowing garments and wonderful jewels gave him an air of almost barbaric splendour.

Nothing could have exceeded the courtesy and stately sincerity of welcome the prince extended to his guests. As they entered the vast domed hall, Aida was reminded of some of the larger mosques she had visited long ago with her father. The walls had nooks and alcoves, each one featuring a spotlit antique treasure displayed in the most tasteful way. She had no time for a close survey, but from what she could tell, these statues and urns seemed to have their origins in Ancient Rome, Greece and Pharaonic Egypt. A wealth of museum-quality masterpieces displayed in this place of dim grandeur, with its marvellous mosaic floors, elegant pillars and frescoed walls. The whole was intoxicating in its lavishness and mystery.

'Welcome to Wahat El Nakheel and Kasr El Nawafeer,' the prince announced with evident pleasure. 'I hope you haven't been too tired by your journey. It's a particularly hot day today.'

'We've spent a most enjoyable time in the desert,' Mrs Saunders declared staunchly.

'Your dragomen were so thoughtful. They managed to spare us any undue fatigue,' Aida added politely.

Met with the graciousness of the prince's behaviour and surroundings it wasn't difficult to conceal her misgivings regarding her host. Her impulsiveness had brought her here, and it was only right to exercise good manners, even though she didn't entirely trust him.

'Splendid.' His piercing eyes glittered as he inclined his head fleetingly towards her. 'I'm sure you would like to refresh yourselves before lunch.'

They came to an archway hung with priceless tapestries. The prince held aside a curtain for them to pass through and they found themselves in a long corridor, at the far end of which was a flight of marble steps adorned with bronze statues holding electric torches. An elderly Bedouin woman in a black garment with a heavy silver hoop hanging in one of her misshapen ears stood at the top of the staircase.

The prince addressed the travellers: 'If you will permit it, Eysha will show you to your apartments and we will regroup here in half an hour.' He gave them an elegant bow, then disappeared back down the corridor while they climbed the stairs to greet the housekeeper.

The landing at the top of the stairs was huge, its walls adorned with large mirrors interspersed with statues and palm trees in tubs, its floors covered with the finest Persian carpets. Eysha led the way, depositing the guests one by one at their various apartments. Aida was taken to hers last of all as her quarters were rather far from the rest, on the top floor of a tower.

She walked through a heavy wooden door to find herself in a round room, the walls of which were dotted with small windows with a view of the palace gardens, the oasis and the far-off desert dunes. She had expected the furnishings of her apartment to be in Bedouin style: to sleep on a divan, to have simple bathroom facilities – certainly an absence of the luxurious baths she was used to – and to pile her clothes on a sofa or heap of cushions.

But the rooms that had been prepared were purely European and in impeccable taste.

The furniture was French, ornate, reminiscent in its lavish splendour of some big hotel in Paris. Indeed, Aida found herself transported to France as she beheld the magnificent satin curtains, velvet chairs, gilt mirror on the green walls, and heavily embroidered cushions and quilts.

*How startling,* she thought. *Paris in the desert!*

She showered quickly and changed into a lavender pair of pirate trousers in light cotton, with a matching top that had puffed, pleated sleeves. She had caught the sun: her eyes looked shiny, her cheeks and lips had a rosy glow. With her cloud of thick honey-blonde hair and her brilliant blue irises, she resembled a being from another world, far from this strange, glowing, languorous world of sun and sand.

Shams Sakr El Din led his guests into the semi-shade of a patio, where large ceiling fans were working heavily, disturbing the hot atmosphere and giving an illusion of coolness. Here were giant palm trees whose leaves protruded above the roofless patio to stab the blue sky, together with orange trees in tubs and masses of purple bougainvillea overhanging the white walls, giving here and there splashes of bright colour. The mosaic-tiled floor of the square patio was also shaded by the verandas of the first-storey rooms, shutting out some of the glare. There were faint but teasing smells everywhere – sandalwood, charcoal fumes, jasmine flowers and attar of roses. Here, too, was a fountain that splashed and tinkled melodiously in its basin, the sound of dripping water music to the ears of a hot traveller, mouth parched by the sun and fine sand of a journey across the desert.

The group sat on mattresses and cushions around a shared tray that reminded Aida of her lunch in the Musky with Phares. She couldn't believe it had only been a couple of days ago. Feeling the sting of tears welling up in her eyes, she made a determined effort to smother the pain that gripped her heart.

'I love the desert,' Simone exclaimed. 'There's an alluring quality to it that I'd heard about, but which I completely understand now.'

The prince lifted an amused eyebrow. 'Do you, *mademoiselle*?' He turned his head towards Aida. 'How do *you* see it, Miss El Masri?'

His question startled her from her private thoughts. 'I find it awesome, but frightening,' she replied after a moment's hesitation. 'It demands endurance and courage to approach its infinite spaces. It is beautiful and magnificent, yes, but also treacherous and cruel, and I don't trust it.' Unwittingly, her eyes locked with his as she spoke, and once more she had the feeling that she should not have come here.

Shams Sakr El Din held her gaze for a moment, as if reading her innermost thoughts. 'You are right to be wary of it, of course, because it is still an unknown entity to you. The desert can be brutal.' He took a leather case from a pocket in his robe, selecting from it, and lighting, a dark-leaved cheroot which emitted a pungent smoke. 'But, so can it be wondered at. It demands that man's brain provides the needs for his body and, yes, without knowing what it has to offer, it can seem menacing. One must have the sagacity of the serpent for the desert's fierce moods, and the gentleness of the dove for its tender moments.' He blew out a controlled trail of smoke, regarding Aida unblinkingly. 'And that, my dear, applies not only to its sands, but to the men who live upon it.'

Was there a double entendre in his words, or was she being over-sensitive? Aida chose to ignore it, thinking instead of Phares's love story with the desert ... *Oh, Phares.* How she wished he were here with her now.

'You seem to have a wonderful collection of antiquities,' Mrs Saunders interjected enthusiastically, smiling at the prince.

He turned to her, nodding. 'Yes, it is the most magnificent collection, I must admit. It has been handed from father to son over many generations. Each new scion has done his best to add to it a few more curious and beautiful items.' His glittering gaze slid back to Aida. 'It comes from a craving for all that is beautiful, rare and valuable ...' His pale eyes were blazing, his whole being vibrant with emotion.

Aida shuddered internally. She had no doubt that this last phrase had nothing to do with his collection of antiques. After a pause, he resumed his speech, his voice low and hoarse. 'To obtain for myself some of the treasures of the world, I would commit any crime, endure any hardship, perform any sacrifice.'

They drank *karkadeeh*, lemonade and *mayat ward*, pure well water flavoured with the petals of a certain rose only grown in the oasis, while servants brought big plates of large succulent dates, olives, purple figs and small-shelled nuts to the table.

Although Aida made sure her eyes strayed as little as possible in the prince's direction, he had seated himself next to her, and she was aware of his scrutiny, intense and smouldering, weighing on her all the while. She shivered with unease.

'By *Allah*, you have such blue eyes, Aida ... such a silky bow of a mouth ...' His whispered sigh wafted his breath over her face as he passed her a plate of stuffed dates. 'A man would accept damnation just to lose himself for a moment in the deep sea pools of your irises and brush his lips against the soft fullness of your lips.'

Flushing with embarrassment, she drew away from his display of open admiration, pressing herself into the far edge of her seat, anxious to escape his gaze. It was gleaming with an emotion that she recognised only too well, and as much as it thrilled her in Phares's eyes, it repulsed her in this man. She felt as trapped as a butterfly under a glass jar.

He laughed softly to himself. 'Nothing excites me more than a reluctant filly,' he muttered under his breath.

Following the prince's example, everyone helped themselves with their fingers to a first course of timbales of stuffed olives and crayfish. It was the accepted manner of eating for a man of the East, and he was obviously keen to make them go through the real experience of a meal in true Bedouin style.

'I have lived more in the desert than elsewhere,' Shams Sakr El Din told them, as they tossed the timbales awkwardly into their mouths. 'I share most of the ways of the tribesmen.'

'It amazes me that you don't spill rice and nuts all over you,' Aida replied edgily, taking a sip of her glass of hibiscus water.

'It is a knack to eat this way,' he said, leaning closer. 'Shall I show you?'

'No, thank you.' She shook her head, avoiding his glance. 'I'll soon get the hang of it.'

Then came a whole roast lamb, which was placed before the prince, who tore off juicy slivers and passed them to his guests. When the best bits were eaten, a servant removed the carcass and another plate took its place. Aida was used to the extravagance of entertainment in this part of the world, and even though she knew nothing was wasted – the remains fed a multitude of servants and their families – she looked upon it as a squandering of money. After having felt the deprivations of England, she found herself deploring it.

A mound of rice, binding a concoction of all kinds of fish and fried eggs, olives, fruit, vegetables and nuts, with a small pastry lid on top was brought to the table next. Every family had their own recipe for *magluba*, and the prince explained that his was an enhanced version of the original Sakr El Din recipe, created in honour of his guests. Steaming hot, it was decorated like a birthday cake with dates, mushrooms and hard-boiled eggs. After that came fat pigeons and roasted chickens, stuffed with olives and mushrooms, and then more lamb in the form of *mansaf*, the traditional Bedouin dish served at weddings and feasts. The lamb had been stewed over an open fire, then served in a dried yoghurt sauce, called *jameed*, on a bed of flatbread and rice, and sprinkled with pine nuts and almonds. Aida knew she couldn't decline any of it as it would have been regarded as a great insult.

After so many courses of protein dishes, the guests finally moved on to something sweeter. Biscuits dipped in molasses and a cake made of pressed, preserved fruits was brought next, followed by the last, but not least, of the dishes: the famous nut and raisin pastries *difr el hanem*, ladies' fingers, which Aida liked but could only nibble at because she had eaten too much already.

The meal finally done, vassals came round with scented water, pouring it over the guests' hands into big faience earthenware basins, before bringing in the coffee.

'That was a delicious lunch, Your Highness. *Suffra daiman*, may your table always be plenty,' Alastair declared, and the others clamoured their agreement.

The prince flashed a gracious smile. 'It is my pleasure, dear friends.'

'I couldn't eat like this every day,' laughed Simone. 'I'd be twice the size within a month.'

'Arab men like their woman to be curvy, isn't that so?' asked Sonia, her twinkling eyes devouring the Bedouin prince.

'Yes,' Simone chipped in. 'I read somewhere that Moors used to feed their harem favourites with stuffed dates and cream horns in order to make them so languid that all they wanted to do was laze about on silk cushions.'

Glints of sardonic amusement danced in Shams Sakr El Din's eyes. 'That may be the case for most men of my country, but passive submission in a woman holds no appeal for me.' His pale gaze fixed on Aida and she shuddered internally at the predatory smile that crossed his lips as he added, 'Ah, the joys of taming a shrew! Your great playwright Shakespeare understood that concept well enough …'

The other women seemed to revel in the prince's bold, risqué manner and a few mock-scandalised expressions passed between them. Alastair, meanwhile, kept a veiled eye on Aida. She couldn't be sure, but he seemed to be maintaining a guarded watch over her.

A silence hung over the table and then the prince stood up, everybody else following suit. 'You might like to have a stroll in the garden or a lie-down. Our show starts at six after the greatest heat of the day is over. Knowing you English love your riding, I've chosen a display of horsemanship to entertain you. Nomad horsemen will perform in competition with the equestrian guards of my palace.' He smiled smugly. 'I think you'll find that the feats performed by horses and riders alike take the gymkhana to new heights.'

As they were leaving the table, he leaned a little closer to Aida, his nostrils flaring slightly. 'You wear an intriguing perfume, fragrant yet sensual. Is it carnation?'

'Yes,' Aida felt anger boiling under her skin at his excessive attentions. 'Phares had it specially made for me. I wear it to please him.' She spoke pointedly, hoping that if he thought she belonged to another man, he would stop his slimy courting.

A fleeting flame flared for a second in Sakr El Din's eyes. 'You do many things to please the doctor, eh? So, how is it that you are here today on this escapade, which I'm sure would only displease him highly?'

The others had moved off towards the edge of the patio and were looking at the view.

Aida lifted her chin as confidently as she could. 'Phares and I are almost engaged, but that doesn't mean he owns me. And as I've never visited an oasis before it seemed a good idea to take advantage of your generous hospitality, as Mrs Saunders so astutely said. The opportunity might never present itself again.'

'Well, *habibti*, as I have told you before, you have done me a great honour in accepting my invitation. As for your young doctor, don't you think he will wonder how we passed the time in such close proximity?' His voice was a smooth murmur. 'Surely he saw us dance at Princess Nazek's ball, and I know I'm not exactly someone he holds dear. A jealous man ... Even though he clearly does not abide by the saying, what's good for the goose is good for the gander.'

Aida fixed him levelly with her most impudent look, though her throat felt painfully dry. 'Phares is not like that. Besides, we trust each other.'

'Don't be fooled, *habibti*. Whenever a man and a woman are alone there is a feeling in the air ... of a silent dicing with danger. Only between a man and a woman can there exist this awareness of a thousand subtle differences, each capable of arousing a thousand subtle sensations. The belief has always been that men are polygamous and women monogamous, but I have often realised the idiocy of this assumption.'

In the tense silence that followed his words a thousand crazy thoughts rushed through Aida's mind as her eyes skimmed the face and frame of the Bedouin. A dark ripple of awareness overtook her as she met his stare. Anxious to read his open desire in it, she looked around wildly to find that her friends had drifted away.

'Where are the others?' she asked, trying to hide her alarm.

'Oh, I wouldn't worry. They've probably wandered off into the garden or perhaps they've gone to their rooms for an afternoon siesta.' Again, his voice dipped huskily. 'Most of them don't have your vitality. It was a tiring journey after all.'

Aida prayed silently and swiftly for the return of her friends.

'How pale you are, my dear ... but lovely ... akin to pearls and milk and the finest silk.' He was looking at her lazily as though he sensed, and was enjoying, the fury building up inside her.

'Aida, there you are!'

Alastair Carlisle had suddenly appeared behind them, and she sighed audibly with relief. 'Yes, here I am.' She gave a tight little laugh. 'I was wondering where you'd all got to.'

'I'm sorry, we wandered off to look around the garden.' Turning to the prince, he remarked, 'You have the most beautiful collection of statues, Your Highness. Those four Italian fountain goddesses are quite magnificent ... and the other Greek and Roman sculptures ... all women, I note.' At this, he briefly met Aida's eye and once again she had the strange feeling that he was guarding her interests, her safety.

The prince laughed low in his throat. 'Yes, I like to surround myself with beautiful women. In stone and in the flesh.'

Again, a sharp glance from Alastair, then Aida quickly took her opportunity to get away. 'I think I might go and have a lie-down. I'll see you both at the camel race.' By now she was desperate to escape the cloying gaze of her host and the electric atmosphere she felt crackling around her.

'I will ring for Eysha to take you to your room.'

'No need, thank you.'

'The palace is a maze of dark corridors, I wouldn't want you to get lost.'

'I think I can find my way.'

'Suit yourself, *habibti.*'

Aida found her way back to her rooms without difficulty. Her head ached and her eyes burned. This really had been a mistake, she should never have come. When would she learn to curb her impulsive nature? She had often been told that one day it would lead her into trouble and she strongly suspected the day had come.

A cold sweat ran down her spine as she tried to recall the words of the fortune teller. Was this the 'great danger ahead' that Ghalya had predicted? Aida had never fancied herself superstitious – save in the matter of the new moon perhaps – and her mind had never been attracted to the subjects of clairvoyance, spiritualism and kindred doctrines. Still, she was forced to admit that since her arrival at Kasr El Nawafeer, and seeing Prince Shams Sakr El Din in his surroundings, she had an uncomfortable presentiment of evil. Something, it seemed, somewhere in the palace, threatened her; and yet through all her shrinking, she felt a potent lure as if the place and the man repelled and fascinated her equally.

Aida bathed her face and eyes in cold water and lay for ten minutes on her bed, but she was restless. She got up and looked out of the window at the splendour of the view. Far to the north, the great hills, bare on their tops, showed brown and gold against the vivid blue of the sky, more like masses of cloud than land. Nearer, on the lower slopes, their surface of yellowed grass was dotted with small herds of sheep or goats. Here and there among the herds, she could see odd splashes of white as the goatherds or shepherd girls moved among their flocks or rested on the slopes. A herd of gazelles leapt joyfully across the rocky track, littered with clumps of *talha, Acacia tortilis,* and disappeared behind some sand dunes. Further away, galloping across the landscape, was a silhouetted train of racing camels, directed by vassals in white gowns. Aida guessed they must belong to the prince and were being exercised.

Her eyes narrowed against the bright light. Was it another town she could see outlined there in the distance, dancing like a gold painting on the horizon? Surely not ... it was a mirage. She had seen enough of them during the morning's journey to recognise one. No wonder these people believed in djinns and spirits. Even in broad daylight, with the bright sunbeams on the undulating sand dunes making them look like a heaving ocean of gold, there was that strange sense of unreality. Nothing was real. So how could people behave normally? Herself included.

# CHAPTER 11

Although the late afternoon sun still shone royally overhead when the prince's guests congregated in the garden for the display of horsemanship, the fierce heat of its rays was tempered by a most delicious breeze which, blowing over countless leagues of sand, brought with it a fresh and life-giving breath of coolness that was welcome after the hot, still day.

Out in the desert the horizon's mirage shimmered like a band of liquid above the sparkling sand, but in the garden of Kasr El Nawafeer the green trees and sweet water were realities, and the fountains tinkled merrily as they flung their silver drops high into the air.

The tourney ground was a vast arena built in a semicircle with tiered seating above a performance area, like the Ancient Roman and Greek amphitheatres used for gladiator fights and other events and competitions. All around the arena, the spectators were ringed, men and boys in a motley crowd, wearing garments of every shade – gold, green, blue – brown faces working, brown hands gesticulating, bare feet shuffling in the sand.

In the place of honour, Prince Shams Sakr El Din's guests struck a note of alien coolness. Aida in particular stood out. The dark colouring of the other women in the party contrasted noticeably with her honey-gold hair and brilliant fairness, marking her out as the daughter of a land far removed from this fierce country of sand and sun and wild desert men.

Behind them, the green garden of the palace glowed like an emerald in the sunlight, its hundreds of palms like sentinels guarding this precious oasis in the heart of burning desert sand and rocks. All around, the air was loaded with the heavily sweet fragrance of the yellow jasmine that grew everywhere. The whole scene was an enchanting medley of colour and life. Blue sky overhead, the azure merging into green and then to flame in the west; the multi-hued garments of the crowd, vivid against the orange sand; the shining coats of the horses – bay, chestnut, glossy black and purest white; the bright native saddles – some brilliant vermillion, others decorated in gaudy hues; and everywhere, the sunlight, flashing on land and spear. Wherever Aida's eye turned there was life and radiance, and somehow, she forgot her woes. The blood coursed swiftly in her veins and her eyes sparkled as she drank in the extraordinary spectacle.

The prince did not sit next to Aida during the tournament. Shams Sakr El Din appeared to have forgotten her existence and she was grateful for the respite. He concentrated on Simone, whose simpering airs seemed to enchant him, and Sonia, who was also competing for his attention. Placed between Alastair and Mrs Saunders, Aida had a great time listening to the humorous running commentary taking place on both sides of her. Eva, Marica and Norma sat behind her, and judging by their constant chatter and raucous laughter, all three women were delighted by the proceedings.

The gymkhanas which Aida had attended at the Gezireh Sporting Club in Cairo, and Semouha in Alexandria, were mere child's play compared with the magnificent riding, galloping, tent-pegging and other feats in which the desert riders indulged.

Down over the sand thundered a wild cavalcade, robes flying, hawk-eyes flashing, weird and wonderful cries ringing through the air. So swift were their movements that it was difficult to follow them with the eye. They performed wonderful acrobatic feats, mounting their horses at full gallop, standing in their saddles, tossing from one to another their long spears, leaping, hurdling, exchanging horses in mid-gallop, and indulging in a hundred different tests of skill that showed off their splendid horsemanship.

To make matters more interesting, the event had been run on competitive lines, one party of equestrians attempting to outdo the other in the neatness and daring of their feats. The nomad riders, those desert tribes from which the *ghawazy* had originated, did indeed look even wilder than the Bedouins, but an easy camaraderie existed between the two groups. It was evident that in spite of the loud cries and vehement clamour, which at first alarmed Aida, the utmost good humour prevailed, although each party was intent on carrying off the honours of the day.

Although the nomad riders were in many ways the superior, Prince Sakr El Din's men rode handsomer animals than those of their rivals. As a result, the teams were evenly matched, giving a spice of piquancy to the entirely friendly contest.

Now, a shrill clamour was arising among the crowd of onlookers. The Bedouins, who at first had kept a respectful distance from the visitors, had gradually crept nearer to the semicircle of seats in front of the tourney, where the prince's guests were gathered. The prince explained to his party of foreign guests that this was a request for a contest of skills between the chief of Nomads and Sakr El Din himself. He stood up, eyes dancing, white teeth flashing in his bronze face, and took up the challenge with gusto.

Never would Aida forget the sight before her eyes at that moment. In front of her was the vast space of sand: gold and tawny now in the light of the setting sun. In one corner, the nomad riders sat in a group, magnificent desert men with aquiline features and flashing eyes, their large, sweeping gestures native to those who have their habitation in the empty spaces of the earth.

In the opposite corner, Shams Sakr El Din's men were grouped; and they too were splendid specimens of humanity, with quicker, more restless movements, as befitted those who dwelt in something more akin to civilisation than their nomad brothers.

For twenty minutes, the spectators were treated to an exhibition of such perfect horsemanship as was rarely seen, even in England, a country renowned for its skilful equestrians. As though the animals themselves entered into the spirit of the game, they too did their best, and honours were equally divided between the contestants.

At last, as if by a preconceived plan, the riders came sweeping back at terrific speed, each party making a wide detour in a semicircle, towards the impromptu stand where Aida and the other guests sat. Then, just as it seemed that the two leading horses must crash into one another, there was a sudden halt, a check, and two short, simultaneous cries. The animals were pulled up immediately in front of the visitors, each rider sitting like an image of bronze in his saddle for a second before leaping to the ground in a sign that the show was over.

After the game, prizes were given out and the radiant prince shepherded his flock back to the palace so they could prepare themselves before dinner. Cool rooms and fragrant baths awaited them after their festival of sun and sand, he promised them.

Towards the west, the sky was like an oriental tapestry woven in carmine and dusky gold, intermingled with the palest green. The rolling dunes that surrounded the oasis were tinged delicately with pink, and the distant hills veiled in a purple mist, which added to their stature and gave an imposing effect to their somewhat meagre proportions. The whole oasis was preparing for the rest that comes with evening. A muezzin wailed from his minaret platform, and then the tawny sky turned violet. Long strings of native labourers, in shapeless garments of blue or pink cotton, were making their way, some to the mosque, others to their little homes dotted around the oasis. A few yellowish dogs of dubious ancestry slunk at their heels, or turned aside to investigate some heap of delicious garbage with uncritical attention.

Having returned to her room, Aida found that there was a young Bedouin woman awaiting her in the bathroom. Although she knew that the custom of a servant drawing a bath existed in rich homes and palaces, she had been brought up by a Western mother, who had stopped helping her with her bath when she was five. *Dada* Amina had never understood this and had at first taken umbrage, jumping to the conclusion that in being denied her bathroom duties, they presumably didn't trust her.

Aida did not send the girl away, knowing full well that she would be reprimanded in a way that didn't bear thinking about. In these outlandish places it was not unheard of for recalcitrance to be met by whipping. Although Sakr El Din himself was an educated, seemingly civilised man, Aida had a sneaking suspicion that down here at Wahat El Nakheel, he operated very differently.

Having had her bath, she returned to the bedroom, where the young servant, whose name was Abla, waited to help her dress. Aida had brought with her an evening gown in heavy silk, not too revealing, which had horizontal gold and black stripes on the skirt and a plain black bodice with matching detailing on the cuffs of the three-quarter sleeves.

Abla deftly gathered her hair on the crown of her head and put on her pharaonic gold necklace, bought by Ayoub at auction the year before he died. Once she had donned a pair of matching gold earrings, giving the last touch to her elegant outfit, Aida looked positively regal. Before leaving the room, she slipped a couple of Egyptian silver coins into the girl's hand. She refused to take them at first, but at Aida's insistence, she accepted the tip gratefully, showering her benefactress with a deluge of blessings.

Night had fallen. It was warm, and dinner was to be served outside under the stars. The dining table was placed in the middle of a walled-in courtyard open to the sky, set round with dozens of tubs of orange trees and wonderful dwarf rose bushes, the fruit and blossoms imbuing the air with a wild and heavenly sweetness. The saffron glow of the lamps, around which moths clustered, brought out the luxurious soft sheen of the mellow carpets, cushions, hangings and copper ornaments. Overhead, the sky blazed with brilliant stars, and their light mingled with that of the lamps, which illuminated the table with its bowls of roses.

The prince had changed his afternoon clothes for magnificent silken robes of a wonderful creamy yellow, in which he looked a regal, very attractive figure. Something of the afternoon's glow seemed to linger about him still; his white teeth shone, and his eyes, which for the first time seemed darker tonight, glittered beneath the elaborate turban crowning his head. He talked easily with his guests and poured them glasses of ruby-coloured *karkadeeh*, made from the petals of the hibiscus grown in the palace's own garden. A small group of Bedouin musicians played in the background, and a singer was pouring his heart out in a sad Arabic lament that told of his lost sweetheart: '*She is like a gazelle emitting the fragrance of amber. She is like the sweet-smelling flower growing by the pond ...*'

At dinner, once again the prince did not seat himself next to Aida, but took a seat beside Simone, who seemed totally entranced with her host. The music drifted across the courtyard, and Aida glanced towards him, noting the alert, almost violent expression of his face, even in repose ... the curl of his lip, the intent, eager look in his bold eyes. She had never seen a countenance like it – fierce, hawk-like, cruel. Like the desert itself. He was a part of all this, as indigenous as the falcons, or the golden sand cats that lurked among the sandstone rocks. And yet, as she looked at him,

Aida was bound to admit that the width of the brow meant, surely, that there was a keen intellect there; and once, during the singer's perfectly rendered solo, an expression of pleasure crossed his face, as though the beautiful soft wailing of the music appealed to some touch of artistic spirituality within him. She glanced over at Simone, who was drunk with elation at the prince's conferring on her his mesmerising attentions. Aida disliked Shams Sakr El Din, but she had to admit that he was an interesting and charismatic figure, a fascinating man for whose love some women would scrap over like desert vixens.

The meal was unduly prolonged and the subject revolved around the gymkhana they'd watched. The group never seemed to tire of questioning the prince as to the meaning of this or that manoeuvre within the tournament. And Sakr El Din was only too ready to answer them all, turning courteously from one to another as he explained various points to them with an obliging smile.

'The camels will be leaving for Cairo early in the morning,' he told his guests as they left the table to return to their rooms for the night. 'Breakfast will be brought up to your room at six o'clock. You should be on your way by seven-thirty. It was my honour to have your company for the weekend and I hope you have enjoyed your time at Kasr El Nawafeer.' He bade them goodnight, and Aida heaved a sigh of relief that the day had gone by without incident.

*    *    *

That night, Aida was violently ill. Until dawn, she had been going backwards and forwards to the bathroom at regular intervals as strong bouts of nausea assailed her. Was this a touch of gastric flu or had she been poisoned? She wondered how the rest of the party were feeling. Did the prince have a hand in this?

After his cloying attentions, she no longer trusted his motives in bringing her here.

She must have dozed off because she thought she was swimming in the sea in Alexandria. The water was deliciously cold, and *Dada* Amina stood on the shore under the swaying pine trees calling to Aida, and she was anxious because she couldn't make out her words.

When she opened her eyes, she found Abla standing beside her bed, holding the breakfast tray and calling her. Almost at once, she closed them again, raising a hand to shield them from the glare of the lamp that the servant had turned on when entering the room. Weak and dizzy, it was as if a vice was squeezing her head, and from time to time, an acute pain shot across her closed eyelids. She tried to lift herself up, but fell back immediately on her pillows with a whimper. She hadn't known the human body could sink so rapidly into a revolting mass of nausea and pain.

Abla hurried off and came back with the prince and Mrs Saunders.

'She's not in a fit state to travel, especially by camel.' Sakr El Din's voice penetrated the febrile haze in Aida's mind.

'She needs a doctor,' affirmed Mrs Saunders.

'We have some of the best-trained physicians at the palace. I'll call for one immediately, but I think it's only a touch of sun. I'm sure Miss El Masri will be perfectly well enough to travel in the morning.'

Mrs Saunders sounded doubtful. 'But …'

'Please don't worry yourself. I'll take her back to Cairo in my private plane or deliver her to Luxor myself, if needs be.'

'I am loath to leave her here on her own.'

'My dear Mrs Saunders, she is not on her own here. Do not fret, I will look after her as if she were my own flesh and blood.'

The tone of the other's voice relaxed a little. 'In that case, Your Highness …'

Before Aida could rouse herself properly to protest, they had left the room and Abla was back with an ice pack, which she placed on the young woman's burning forehead.

Curled up on her side, hugging a cushion for comfort, Aida was so worn out that she drifted off to sleep, and although too drowsy to raise her head or speak, she was aware of people coming and going around her like figures on a screen.

When she awoke the next morning, she found herself in a different room, under a carved-wood ceiling, surrounded by walls of mosaic tiles and lace-like plasterwork. She was lying on an enormous carved bed, its brilliant blue silk coverlet reaching to the floor and canopied with spotless white net mosquito drapes, tied back with beautiful sashes. In one corner of the room was a large, modern-looking dressing table on which numerous toilet accessories were laid out, looking strangely out of place in the big Moorish room.

Puzzled at first, Aida ran dazed eyes around, an odd feeling sweeping over her as she realised that the large room, unlike the one in which she had gone to sleep, was utterly Eastern. Magnificent velvet hangings adorned the walls, embroidered with fabulous birds and beasts; a fine mesh of carved, silvery wood screened the long lattice-work windows, at the top of which featured a row of coloured-glass flowers and peacocks. Tinted lamps shed their light over the ivory and pearl inlays of the *mashrabiya* furniture standing on the splendid Turkish and Persian carpets that lay on the marble-tiled floor. She could smell a sensuous scent emanating from incense twigs burning in a copper brazier, sending up spirals of fragranced smoke.

*What day was it? How long had she been asleep?*

Aida shivered and hugged herself while a dark suspicion began to infiltrate her mind. Leaping to her feet, she ran to the heavy wooden door and wrenched at the handle, pulling it open. The doorway's beautifully carved arch framed a pair of eunuchs in long robes, their dark inscrutable eyes and black faces expressing no emotion. Reality suddenly sunk in: she was in Sakr El Din's harem.

Fury rushed through her. 'Where's the prince? I need to see him immediately!'

Silently, one of the men reached forward and with slow deliberation, his eyes fixed inscrutably on Aida, closed the door in her face.

Aghast, she gazed at the door, cold sweat running down her spine. She banged and kicked at it, but no one came to help her. With a sickening lurch she realised that she could scream the palace down and still there would be no one to hear her.

Aida looked round her. Noticing a heavily curtained recess, she sprang towards it and tore the drapes aside. She found herself facing a half-open door which led, she discovered, to another room laid out as an Eastern dining room, very much like the one in which she'd had lunch the day before, but much smaller and more intimate. The room was ornamented with several beautifully carved tables inlaid with mother-of-pearl, on which were placed pottery bowls full of roses. At the far end of the room was another door, but this was locked too.

She went back to the smaller room and gazed up eagerly at the *mashrabiya* windows which projected out from the room, overhanging the ground below. They were too high for her to be able to see out, so she hastily pulled up a chair against the wall and stood on it, peering through the slits below the carved wood latticework panels. Disappointment awaited her there too. No escape possible that way: the window looked out over a paved courtyard and was at least twenty feet above the ground. The drop, if she were to attempt it, would break her neck. Aida had to acknowledge finally, with a sense of foreboding, that there was no way she could escape unaided from these rooms.

The others had gone back to Cairo without her and would assume she was being looked after by Sakr El Din. She shuddered. What was in store for her? Now that the full impact of her situation hit her, most bitterly did she regret her folly in accepting the prince's invitation.

Aida was pacing restlessly up and down when suddenly the heavy door opened, making her almost jump out of her skin. She swung round, her eyes filled with alarm, fearing that it would be Sakr El Din. Instead, an old woman stood in the archway, dressed all in black, a heavy silver ring hanging from one of her thick, fleshy ears. She was not unattractive, though her coffee-coloured face was covered with innumerable wrinkles, out of which her black eyes gleamed brightly. Behind her came two young girls in robes, of whom one was Abla, carrying some beautiful clothes.

Aida's blue eyes flashed with apprehension. 'Who are you? What do you want? Where is Prince Shams Sakr El Din?'

The older woman looked at her blankly. 'I am Khadija, the prince's aunt.'

'Where is he?' Aida demanded haughtily.

'His Highness is awaiting you for the evening meal. He has chosen these garments for you and would be grateful if you wore them tonight instead of your Western clothes.'

Panicked, Aida ignored her response, instead saying, 'Why am I imprisoned in this room? I need to go back to Cairo, my family will be worried.'

The woman looked surprised. 'You are not a prisoner here, you are His Highness's guest.'

'He promised to fly me back to the city once I was better, and now I am fine.'

'The *khamseen* is on its way. It is neither possible for you to leave by land nor by air.'

Aida knew that the *khamseen* desert wind could be ferocious but she wondered if the prince's aunt was merely colluding with her nephew to keep her here. She looked at Khadija blankly then asked, 'What do you mean?'

'Just what I have said. Now, please, would you let Abla and Zuleika attend to your toilet?' the old woman asked, taking Aida by the arm and pulling her towards the bathroom.

But Aida thrust her aside. 'Let me go, let me go!'

The prince's aunt signalled to the two young girls, busy spreading the sumptuous garments out on the divan, and immediately they stopped what they were doing and rushed to catch hold of Aida.

She disentangled herself, panting angrily. Trying to remain calm, she told Khadija, 'Please tell them to go away. I can manage perfectly well on my own.'

Silently, the girls disappeared into the bathroom and went about filling the bath. Khadija's black eyes peered curiously at the young woman. 'It is the custom—'

'I don't care what your customs are,' Aida cut in, raising her voice once more. 'They aren't mine, and I won't have an audience while I take a bath.'

'His Highness's desires are paramount. These young girls are trained to follow his wishes in every regard.'

In the midst of the affray, the door to the dining area was pushed open and the prince himself entered the room.

'Let her go,' he ordered, 'and leave us.'

Khadija's expression grew conciliatory as she looked up at him. 'Release the *roumia*, foreigner, from your house, dear nephew. She is more trouble than she's worth. You don't need this wild animal among your peaceful kingdom. She is not even beautiful …'

The prince looked calmly at her, though his voice held an edge. 'Go now, Khadija, and thank you. I will take care of Miss El Masri.'

'I have only your welfare at heart, my nephew.' The old woman looked sideways at Aida. 'This blue-eyed *roumia* will bring only bad luck on you and your kingdom.'

'It is for me to say if she stays and when she leaves,' the prince replied drily. 'Since when do I take advice from a woman? Leave now! Have I not said that I will deal with this?'

'As you wish, dear nephew.' Khadija turned dark eyes laden with contempt on Aida, before pulling open the heavy door and breezing out, followed by Abla and Zuleika.

When the three women had left, an uncomfortable silence filled the room.

'Prince Shams Sakr El Din,' Aida said, mustering a dignified calm as she faced him, 'I feel perfectly all right now. If you will kindly arrange for a camel to be brought, I will take my leave.'

His yellow eyes were hooded as he replied quietly, 'What? Now? At night and with raging *khamseen* winds racing at one hundred kilometres an hour? I would be failing mightily in my host's duties if I let you leave. You are under my protection here.'

The fact that Aida felt about as protected as a hare in a snare was neither here nor there.

'Will the wind storm have passed by the morning?' she asked.

'The *khamseen* comes and goes, as I'm sure you are aware. Rarely more than once a week and lasting only a few hours at a time. Let's hope the storm will be over by morning, then I can fly you back to Luxor.'

In spite of her uneasiness, Aida had to admit that his words made sense, but then it didn't explain why he had moved her from the Western side of the palace. Why had he placed guards at her door? Everything indicated that she was Sakr El Din's prisoner.

'And now, *habibti*, will you do me the honour of having dinner with me?'

She eyed him warily. 'One more question.'

'Go ahead.'

'Why have I been brought to this part of the palace?'

He gave a saturnine smile. 'It is the most luxurious part of Kasr El Nawafeer.'

'Your harem, no doubt … Did you think I'd be flattered to be here?'

'I brought you to my harem because that is where I knew you would be properly cared for. My women are not allowed to circulate freely in the palace. I only wanted you to be comfortable and well looked after.'

He seemed so sincere that Aida began to doubt her fears, telling herself that it was absurd, ridiculous to be so fanciful.

'Very well, I will have dinner with you, but tomorrow we leave for Luxor,' she told him.

He inclined his head. '*In shah Allah*, God willing. And now, if you will step into the bathroom next door, you will find various requisites for a bath. I will go myself to bathe in my quarters as I have a fondness of a hot soak and a scrub, being not entirely the barbarian you seem to think I am. It would please me if you wore the garments I have provided for you, which are much more suited for this part of the palace than your Western clothes.'

His eyes swept over her from head to toe. It was a look that seemed to strip Aida's nightshirt from her body, a look that took in her soft skin and hidden curves, and all the self-control he seemed to be deploying couldn't hide the flame in his eyes.

She tried to keep her voice steady. 'Very well then, I will comply with your wishes. The gown is magnificent. I don't think I've ever worn anything as luxurious. Thank you.'

With a subtle smile that could have meant anything, the prince pressed long, lean brown fingers to his eyes, his lips and his heart. '*Salam aleykom*, my dear Miss El Masri, I will return in an hour and we will dine next door.'

A strange unsettled feeling came over Aida as he left the room. Despite his reassuring words, there lurked within her a most persistent feeling of dread at the thought of the desert prince. She went into the bathroom. A beautiful sunken lotus-shaped tub lined with blue mosaic tiles was set in the centre, filled to the brim with scented steaming water, which charged the air with its herbal balm. On a low cane table stood jars, soaps and a loofah; next to it on a stool was piled a stack of soft, fluffy towels.

As she dropped her nightgown to the floor and stepped into the hot water, Aida felt a tightening of nerves in her midriff, a quickening of her heartbeat as she realised her foreboding was not her imagination playing tricks. What gripped her now was a sense of that peculiar doom only a woman can feel when she knows herself at the mercy of a man to whom women are merely objects of pleasure or service. Once again, she damned herself for accepting this invitation, and again she thought of Phares's reaction when he should learn about her escapade. True, his own behaviour towards her was not snow white, but he was an Egyptian man after all, and still 'free'. She had not yet agreed to be his wife, and he had never even promised her his love. But now ... now she could not expect him to honour even his promise of marriage. She had been impulsive and childish, and she wondered how high the price of her folly would be.

She slipped into the fragrant water but it did little to soothe her anxiety. Again, Phares's face swam into view and she closed her eyes tightly against an anguish of regret. How could she ever face him now?

Aida had always known that her country's values were unforgiving, yet still she had behaved as though she was back in England, going where she wanted, doing whatever she pleased. Even if she somehow escaped from here, the fact remained: she was a woman alone in a Bedouin prince's palace. Everyone, Phares included, would assume the worst and her reputation would be in tatters.

*Why had she been so damned headstrong and naïve?*

More out of frustration than anything else, Aida picked up the loofah and gave herself a merciless scrubbing with the translucent bar of palm oil soap. Then, with a heavy heart, she climbed out of the bath and dried herself before going back into the bedroom, where the sumptuous array of Arabian clothes were laid out for her.

A knock at the door made her turn. Abla came in and bowed respectfully. 'His Highness, Prince Shams Sakr El Din, has sent me to help you with your garments and hair. You must look your best when you dine with him.'

A kind of numb acceptance took hold of Aida; besides, she wasn't sure what punishment would await the girl if she was to send her away. She smiled weakly.

'I will leave myself in your expert hands.'

Pleasure swept over the young girl's face. 'It is a great honour for me to attend to my lady. His Highness is obviously very taken with your beauty. Your presence has caused a great commotion in the harem.'

Aida frowned at the assumption that she was the prince's new mistress. It was insufferable. 'You can tell the women they have nothing to fear from me. I'll be leaving in the morning and there's no chance that I'll be coming back here again,' she snapped.

Abla said nothing, her dark lustrous eyes fixing on Aida's face with a blank expression as she began to help her with the fabulous clothes that had been chosen for her. Biting down on her lip, which trembled treacherously, Aida submitted to the girl's expert hands.

The trousers were of the finest midnight-blue pure silk, delicately interwoven with a gold thread and fastened to her legs at the bottom by beaded bands. They were so light, Aida barely felt their presence. Above them, she wore a short silk tunic of pearl and gold, and the front of the sleeves was open and linked by strands of pearls that reminded her of shackles ... *Jewelled shackles*, she thought. *How appropriate.*

Her honey-blonde hair was left unbound but threaded with fine strands of pearls and diamonds that gave her a glittering look.

Although she accepted the golden slippers, she flatly refused to dust her eyes with kohl; Abla told her it would produce a sensuous look, which Aida certainly didn't wish to convey. She also rejected the expensive jewels the servant girl produced, refusing even to look at them when Abla opened the lid of the black velvet box.

Aida stood in front of the mirror hardly recognising the image of the woman standing in front of her. She was certainly beautiful, mysterious and seductive, but the stranger who gazed back at her looked like a slave girl, brought in by caravan. She turned away in disgust, hating every aspect of herself and feeling a frantic urge to tear the garment piece by piece from her body.

As Abla's hand reached out to offer her an array of slim glass vials of fragrance, each one engraved with beautiful gold Arabian script, Aida pushed her away. 'Enough of this masquerade,' she whispered as tears welled up in her eyes.

'It is important that you smell most fragrant for His Highness.'

The thought of the scent Phares had given her came into Aida's mind. Carnations, a scent designed just for her. The little bottle lay in her bag. The prince had commented on it, had liked it. She gave a shudder, sure in the knowledge that she would certainly not wear carnation tonight. She held her wrist out to Abla sullenly. 'Choose whichever one you like.'

Then she was ready. Abla looked her over with a critical eye. 'You are very beautiful, my lady. His Highness will be pleased with you.' There was a note of meaning in her voice that sent a shiver through Aida. 'I will take you to the dining room now.'

'Wait,' Aida said. Going to her bag, she took out a wad of banknotes. 'Thank you, Abla,' she said, pressing them into the girl's hand.

Abla's eyes widened in surprise. 'You are too kind, my lady, but this is far too generous.'

'Please,' Aida insisted. The young Bedouin girl might be her one and only ally in the palace.

The girl took the money. Aida met her eyes, and for a moment wondered if she only imagined a fleeting look of sympathy in them.

'Thank you, my lady. May *Allah* bless and keep from you the children of evil.'

\*    \*    \*

Prince Shams Sakr El Din was waiting for her in the next room. The blue glass lamps on brass chains made a soft blue twilight, beneath which stood the crescent-shaped divan, the stools of red leather, the low carved tables silvered with arabesque details.

As Aida entered the lounging area, he rose and contemplated her in silence before coming towards her and lifting her hand to his lips. He led her to the table, seating her on the plush cushions with their bejewelled silk throws, and took his place beside her.

Behind those heavy-lashed eyes, he was an uncaring, ruthless brute, Aida thought, yet in his kaftan of sombre royal blue that matched hers, with his beautifully wrapped turban and bejewelled with the most awesome precious stones, there was no doubt he looked proud and distinguished.

*A barbarian cloaked in a deceptive coat of civilisation*, Aida told herself.

'By *Allah*, you are the most beautiful and delectable woman my eyes have ever laid upon!'

She stared back at him disdainfully. 'I feel like one of the concubines in your harem.'

'And is that so displeasing to you?'

'You have no right to treat me as one of those women. I am English.'

'You are partly Egyptian. That's why you have that fire in your blood that stirs mine with such power. Fire and frost, an interesting combination, don't you think?'

'What I think is that you are an unscrupulous barbarian. A despot who regards women as creatures of luxury, toys without minds or hearts of their own.'

'A woman has to be handled as one handles a spirited filly. I told you as much the other day. Shakespeare had the right idea. A real woman likes to feel that she is mastered.'

It was impossible to misunderstand his meaning now.

'Are you not impressed that the barbarian has an intellectual side to him?' he said, and she felt his pale, tawny eyes flicker over her skin.

Aida tilted her chin haughtily, regarding him with disdain. 'Quite frankly, it makes you even more of a monster.'

He cocked an eyebrow. 'Haughty too, eh?'

'Haughty? *Me?* You have some nerve! You, master of a kingdom which you rule with an iron fist, rushing girls into marriage with men they hardly know, who are twice their age, keeping a bevy of women prisoners, toys for your own *keif*, your twisted pleasure? And you have the audacity to call *me* haughty?'

Aida was defiant enough in this moment not to care if the prince completely lost his temper with her.

He swept a curt look over her face. 'You have the emotional intellect of a schoolgirl. You are less instructed in the ways of life than the youngest concubine in my harem. You need tuition in the ways of being a woman.'

'And you are going to be my teacher, is that it?' Aida tried to speak the words with a cool indifference, but the suggestion in his remark stoked her already smouldering fear of his intentions. 'You'd like to beat me down into a heap at your feet. I wouldn't even put it past you to use a whip,' she asserted more bravely than she felt.

Sakr El Din's eyelids drooped in a smile; a gleam lay behind the intense look he gave her. 'The aspects of a country formulate the character of a person. By living in the desert, your needs will undergo a change,' he said softly. 'You will understand that pleasure can be reaped from brutality, that pain when administered by an expert can lift you to unimagined ecstatic heights.'

'Damn you and your arrogance!' Aida's hand clenched around a finger bowl, and she was preparing to hurl the contents in his face when he reached forward and pulled away her hand.

'I wouldn't try it,' he murmured with blazing eyes. 'I might be tempted to give you a taste of that whip before you are properly prepared for its enjoyment.' He gestured to the meal set out so appetisingly on the low table. 'Come, the food will get cold.'

Aida battled with a sudden dizziness, and cold sweat trickled down her spine at his words. Now she had no doubt she was his prisoner; she must control her temper and keep her head in order to think calmly of a way of escaping.

Not only did the mounds of food look inviting, they smelled heavenly. Aida had not eaten since the night before and, despite her fear and fury, she felt her mouth watering.

The prince poured a pale golden wine into her crystal glass. 'Taste it, *habibti*. It is a wine distilled from the Zahdi dates, which are grown on oasis.'

She did so, out of curiosity, and found it potent but admittedly delicious.

'I thought the Muslim religion prohibited the drinking of alcohol.'

'So it does, but we export our wine to many countries, and of course there are plenty of foreigners in Egypt to sell it to.'

Aida ate the food in a kind of hungry spell. She knew she needed all her strength if she was going to try to escape. Her eyes fell on a saucer on which was the depiction of a gazelle in flight from a leopard … such an appropriate symbol.

As if reading her thoughts, something with which he had often surprised her, the prince's eyes narrowed until their pale golden irises seemed to be spears piercing her face. 'Do you imagine Cairo would be so easy for you to find?' he spoke mockingly. 'Even the bravest men in my oasis get lost in the desert and die. How do you think a mere young woman would fare? And what would you do if the storm overtook you, eh?'

She looked up at him, pushing her plate away. 'At least I wouldn't be your prisoner.'

'You might fall into hands less clean than mine.'

'Anything is better than being here.'

He quirked a black eyebrow at her defiant stance. 'You have a poor way of returning my hospitality.'

Her blue eyes flashed angrily. 'You're the last man to be sitting in judgement on me! If I'm ungrateful, it's because you've *kept* me here. And now, please, I would like to return to my room.'

Sakr El Din rested his turbaned head against the cushioning of the divan. He took a long, almost black cigar from a humidor and lit the end. 'Do relax against the cushions next to me, *habibti*, and stop your childish pantomime.'

Aida thrust aside his hand as he tried to pull her towards him. 'No,' she exclaimed, her eyes huge with indignation. 'Don't touch me, please. If you're going to keep me against my will, at least allow me a little dignity.'

'And what about mine, eh? You haven't stopped insulting me since the beginning of the meal.' He leaned towards her again. 'You have excited me … whet my appetite for games that nothing else can assuage.'

In a flash, he pushed the table away and pulled Aida on to the cushion beside him against his hard body. His face in the lamplight was savage, his eyes ablaze with temper and desire. 'You deserve the taste of the whip, my little filly, rather than my caresses. Be kissed instead of bruised, it will be far more pleasant.'

Aida fought him like a she-cat, but there was no getting away.

'You're just a barbarian, a savage in a golden robes. You disgust me,' she hissed, gritting her teeth as she continued to struggle in his arms, causing every nerve in her body to cry out in protest.

'Words I can silence with a kiss,' he murmured, bending over her and putting his threat into action. He took her lips with a fierceness that brooked no refusal. The strength in his arms could have cracked her body as he forced her to yield to his kiss. The warmth of his hard and unyielding body burned through the silk of her habit, and his fingers bit into her flesh. She shuddered with pain and fright, and like a wild thing continued to struggle, even going so far as to kick at him.

Suddenly, as though she weighed nothing, the prince lifted her up in his muscled arms and made his way to the bedroom. Although she cried out and fought with all her strength, she was but a toy in his grip. An incredible fury shook her. Like a young vixen, she sank her teeth into the side of his neck, and saw the drops of blood run on the bronzed skin.

*Oh God, what had she done!* At once she was torn between the delight of having hurt him and the fear of his retaliation. Yet he barely flinched. The door of her bedroom was thrust open and he carried her to the great bed, dropping her on to the lace and silk coverlet without ceremony before opening a drawer in a small table beside the divan and taking out a chain, cuffs and padlock.

'What are you doing?' she gasped as she struggled to get off the bed.

But he pushed her back silently, holding her down with the strong fingers of one hand, pressing into her breast, gripping her like the talons of a hawk. His eyes seemed to smoulder with points of fire in that dark, cruel face and she watched numbly as he cuffed her hands and feet and tied her with the chain, which he padlocked to the bed.

He stood there studying her, looking every inch a man without mercy in whom a rage of passion was building up.

'Are you planning to cane me?' Aida looked up at him, chin held high even though her spirit was flagging.

'Alas, I will have to postpone that delight until the morning. I have an important meeting to attend to tonight, but the anticipation of administrating all sorts of pain and pleasure to your fair flesh will increase my enjoyment all the more.'

'You won't get away with this. They will come looking for me … The Embassy, Phares, Uncle Naguib, everybody … I'm not alone in the world, I have friends,' she gasped.

Although she shrank inwardly with fear, Aida retained a cold look of dignity; it was the only way she had now to oppose him. She had learned that he liked to fight her; it awakened the animal in him and whet his sadistic nature.

His eyes raked over her face. 'Good luck to them, *habibti*. By the time they come, not even the blue devil, *effrit el azrak* will be able to find you.'

And with these words, he turned and left the room.

Aida lay silently on the bed and as awareness of what was in store for her sank deeper into her mind, the quietness became torment. With a sudden sob, she buried her face in the silk pillow. How fiercely she wished she could kill him. If there had been a knife to hand, she would have plunged it into him the moment she had a chance. She shivered and gritted her teeth, vowing never to resort to self-pity. She'd got herself into this mess and surely there was a way out. She imagined a hundred ways of escaping, but none seemed plausible. Finally, fatigue and desperation overcame her and she sank into a deep sleep.

Dawn was not far off when Aida fancied she heard someone moving around her bed and opened her eyes. In the shadows, she recognised Alba and Khadija. Alarmed, not knowing what was going to happen, she lifted herself up on one elbow.

'Quick, *roumia*, get dressed with these clothes,' Khadija urged, dropping some Bedouin robes next to Aida.

'Khadija? You're helping me …?'

'Yes, quick, before my nephew returns.' The old woman spoke under her breath as she swiftly unlocked the padlock holding Aida prisoner. 'You are creating too much trouble in our happy harem and His Highness will not listen to reason. Your screams last night were a disgrace, and will only encourage others to revolt.'

'Where are you taking me?'

'A horse is awaiting you at the door to the palace. Ali, Abla's brother, will take you to the edge of the oasis. From there, you are on your own.'

'Do you have a map of the desert?' she asked helplessly.

Khadija laughed scornfully as she undid the final cuff from Aida's foot. 'We have no maps here. Ali will give you a compass and a gourd of water. It's a good thing I have a kind heart and haven't poisoned you, or buried you alive in one of those ancient tombs of which my nephew is so fond.'

Aida rubbed her wrists, glancing around warily.

'Where is the prince?'

'That is no concern of yours. You'd better hurry before he comes back and all hell breaks loose. We will all be whipped, if not killed.'

'What will happen when he finds out I've escaped?'

'Heads will roll, I'm sure.'

Aida looked aghast. 'Yours?' Much as she had no liking for the woman, she wished her no harm.

Khadija shook her head. 'He would never suspect me.'

'Abla, then?'

'No, I will be her alibi.'

'Then whose?'

'I have no doubt he will find someone to blame.' She helped Aida put on a turban, draping the cloth about her shoulders; Aida had noticed commoners in the oasis wearing ones in this same style, quite different to the elegant headpiece worn by the prince. 'Hurry, we will go from the back door. Your disguise will protect you. Cover your face and do not speak to anyone.'

Keeping her head and eyes down, Aida followed Khadija and Alba through the dark corridors of the palace. They met no one as they passed along galleries with queer alcoves and recesses holding figurines, urns and other treasures; only the eunuchs, those mute sentinels, who were stationed at various doors, guarding the hapless female prisoners who lay behind the imposing and beautifully sculpted wooden portals. Soon they reached a long passage, at the end of which was a window. Here, Alba bade Aida goodbye and disappeared into one of the shadowy doorways.

'I'm afraid you will have to jump, *roumia*,' Khadija told her as they reached the window. 'It is not very high to the next floor and then down again to the back door of the palace, where Ali is waiting for you. I must go now. *Allah* be with you,' she added almost begrudgingly as she turned to go, 'although for the last two days you have sowed the devil's chaos at Kasr El Nawafeer.'

Aida watched Khadija's retreating figure and for a moment had to force herself to move. There was no time to be lost now; whatever happened, she must go forward. She looked out of the window. Five feet below, a balcony projected from a lower window. Once on the balcony, it would be easy to drop to the ground, and though there was the risk that someone might see her, as the sun was almost coming up, it must be faced boldly and at once. Any delay at this stage would be fatal.

Opening the lattice window, which swung widely outward, Aida crept through the opening and, balancing herself on the sill, looked down. Young dawn flooded the world and showed her plainly where to drop. Without stopping to think, she slid down from the window, hanging with her hand on the sill for a minute, before dropping as lightly as possible on to the stone floor of the balcony below.

Picking herself up, she crouched a moment in the half shadow of dawn, to make sure no one had overheard the movement, but the silence remained unbroken. By now physically exhausted, she dragged herself to the edge of the balcony and clambered over, catching as she did so the frill of her shawl and tearing the thin fabric with a small, rending sound that filled her with terror.

It was easy to slide down the supports of the veranda, and with one last breathless effort, she stood outside the palace, a prisoner no longer, but as free and unfettered as the sun beams which lit up the desert.

As she paused a moment, trying to collect her scattered wits and still the thumping of her heart, she heard an unmistakable sound from the belt of palm trees behind her. With a wild prayer for help on her lips and terror in her soul, she turned to see who had tracked her down. She heaved a sigh of relief as she saw a young man coming towards her with two horses.

Ali did not speak, but signalled her to get on to her mount. She swiftly climbed into the saddle of the beautiful bay horse, and once as she had done so he threw a heavy bundle of sticks on to her shoulders. Aida accepted her burden without complaint, knowing it would help her look more like one of the Bedouins, and dutifully followed Ali's mare as soon as he beckoned with his hand for her to follow.

They passed some men on the road, and Ali shouted to them in Arabic. The harsh, unpleasant tone of the dialect brought new fear to her heart. *Was he trying to start a quarrel?* But the men merely laughed, clearly mocking him, and went on their way. Aida would have liked to question the young Arab, but he wasn't the talkative type, seeking only to hurry them onwards, almost certainly fearing as the sun came up that there would be more people about and they might be stopped. Luckily, they passed through the remainder of the oasis unchallenged, and finally arrived at the large gates that Aida had come through almost forty-eight hours before ... so much had happened in such a short time.

Ali saluted the guards, who were half asleep and yawning, and suddenly Aida understood why Alba's brother had been moving so swiftly. If these men were the night shift ready to go home to their beds before the new patrol arrived, they would be much less inclined to cause problems. It had all been very well planned, obviously by Khadija.

Then the gates were open at last, and Aida found herself in the open expanse of the desert. Here, Ali gave her the compass and a gourd of water and with the simple words, 'Reeh will take you where you need to go', took his leave. To avoid arousing suspicion, he did not return to the oasis but galloped off in the opposite direction to that which Aida was to take.

She headed east, straight into the blazing red of the sun. The dawn wind was already whipping up the sand into little eddies as it blew across the impassable desert. As it rose, the sun struck long shadows across the dunes, for a moment turning the garish panorama to a thing of fairy lightness and purity of colour. Through tired eyes, Aida watched the slowly brightening hills of sand and could have wept for joy at the attendant warmth and cheer of the sunrise. She threw the bundle of sticks to the ground and rubbed her shoulders. She knew more or less where she was going and if her mount held up, it would take her just over an hour to get to the road where the group had picked up their camels.

Immediately Aida raised her whip and flicked the horse's flank; it leapt forward, then bolted like a red streak of lightning across the livid sands. Luckily, Aida was an excellent rider, and sensing at once the speed of which he was capable if he was given free rein, she crouched low in the saddle. The horse was aptly named. *Reeh* meant wind – and it wasn't hard to see why. In a moment he had taken the initiative, and was off like the thoroughbred he was, racing the desert wind with Aida holding tight to the reins, gripping the saddle with her knees. At first she was a little scared, then suddenly felt exhilarated once she realised that she was speeding away from Wahat El Nakheel and the prince.

The landscape fled by in a dazzle of gold. This heady sense of escape filled her being, to the exclusion of her fear of being lost in the desert. She had her leather gourd strapped to the saddle, and these desert-bred horses were curiously intelligent. There was every hope that Reeh would sense that they were on a familiar path to Cairo and which direction to take. Her confidence billowed like that of the large, windswept shawl she had tied around her shoulders like a cloak. What could go wrong now?

\*     \*     \*

Aida had been going for what seemed like ages, when Reeh suddenly stumbled on one of the sandstone rocks half buried in the sand. He crashed headlong almost before she realised what had happened, and with a scream she kicked free of the stirrups, before her legs and feet could get crushed beneath the weight of the agonised animal. She felt herself flying out of the saddle as Reeh rolled away from her, whinnying loudly with pain.

After landing in the soft sand, she lay shaken and breathless before her mount's distress brought her staggering to her feet, still dizzied by her fall. Lurching to Reeh's side, she flung a hand over her mouth when she saw how he was rolling his eyes and baring his large teeth in agony. She could tell at once that he had snapped a foreleg and pity for him mingled with the fear of being lost in the desert without a mount. She sank to her knees just out of reach of the horse's helpless, kicking legs. Though the sun was beating down, she felt shivery, torn between compassion for Reeh and an instinctive terror of the unknown.

She stifled a sob; there would be no escape from the prince after all. The desert was like his devilish incubus, she thought bitterly, helping him to trap her by planting that cruel stone, half hidden in the path of her galloping horse. And there across the surface of glaring yellow sand lay the trail of hoof marks leading to her.

The desert all around her felt like a trap, but somehow she had to muster the courage to set out on foot even though she knew that it was sheer lunacy. Anything was better than being recaptured by that beast of a man. Death, even? Aida resolutely drove that thought away and looked about her.

She couldn't bring herself to abandon Reeh, but as he ceased to thrash about, Aida unhooked the gourd, filled the cap with water and carefully tipped it into the horse's mouth. The animal gazed at her so pathetically when she did this that tears welled up in her eyes and she stroked his sweating neck, the pain-stretched muscles like cords beneath her hand. He had been so vital, so swift and proud, and now he lay in the hot sun with a broken leg and there was nothing she could do about it. She wished that she had a pistol to put him out of his misery. As a child, Aida had witnessed Karawan's estate manager Megally shoot a badly wounded horse so that the creature would not suffer. Outraged at first, it had taken her a while to understand the mercy of such an act.

She must move if she was to have any hope of making it to the road before nightfall and escaping the prince's fury. As she turned away, unable to bear the sight of the distressed animal, she knew that she had no choice but to leave him behind if she was to have a hope of saving her own life.

Aida slung the gourd across her chest and struck out alone across the sands, walking for hours under the fierce, insistent sun. The landscape was brassy and arid, a confusion of jagged peaks and twisted ravines. It might have all been cast in some heavy metal, so hard and massive was its surface, spread out under a sky hazy with heat. With gathering strength, the sun beat down on her and the crags of yellow and orange limestone whose uneven-edged cliffs quivered above her against the blazing sky.

On and on she stumbled, her slippers soon turning to rags which chafed the skin of her feet. Her blouse was soaked in perspiration, her hair clung damply to her skin. Muzzy-headed, she was keenly aware of her tongue swelling with thirst; the water in the gourd had run out long ago. She thought longingly of a glass of fresh water, then halted suddenly in her tracks and stared in the direction from which she had come.

She was lost! Totally lost! She had broken the first law of the desert, had wandered away from the relative sheltering protection of the oasis, and no one knew where she had gone. Pushing down her panic, she forced herself to keep moving, hoping that she would come across anything to help her find her bearings.

The afternoon came and went, and with the twilight, the desert grew cold. Soon the night surrounded her, swiftly, intensely dark. The moon would not rise till late and no stars were visible against the black pall of the sky. Aida could see nothing but a vast, dark plain stretching away into impenetrable gloom, offering no features by which she could steer a course to a village or other place of refuge.

She was shivering in the chill breeze that blew from the distant flats. She felt hollow, in need of food, having eaten nothing since the night before. Walking was becoming increasingly harder; she had never before realised how tiring the loose sand of the desert is to the feet. And still not a sound broke the stillness of the vast, empty sands.

As the night progressed, Aida grew ever more faint and weary; she could hardly drag one foot in front of the other and the bruises from her fall had made her feel stiff and sore. Finally, panting and dishevelled, she had to sit down on a stony mound, arms clasped around her knees as she realised with mounting horror her impotence.

Enormous vultures soared high over her head, emitting hoarse cries. No other sounds were to be heard save her breathing and the pounding of her heart. Unless help came – and without a miracle, no help would come – she was doomed. Every dread she had ever known, every frightful story she had ever read, every alarming picture she had ever seen, rose up to confront her in this hour of mortal dread. Without food or water, she must prepare to die in the desert. Even her fearless spirit quailed before the thought of that lonely death, a corpse for the hyenas and falcons to pick at. Cut off from all human intercourse, surrounded only by sand and sky, tears welled up in her eyes. She felt indescribably forlorn, in the dark, empty desert, with only the dark, empty sky overhead, and now she was to die alone in this harsh environment.

And then suddenly, all her nervous instincts alert, she raised her head and stared with hopeful eyes across sands misty with the coming of night.

A caravan … a train of camels and men. Was it a mirage?

She stood up and waved her hands wildly. With a croaking cry from her parched throat, she stumbled blindly in the direction of the caravan only to trip over the stone on which she had been sitting. Falling headlong, the sharp edge of it cut through the skin of her shin. The pain of the fall stunned her and then as her head crashed into the hard desert floor, she collapsed senseless on to the hot sand.

# CHAPTER 12

I t was a glorious sunset, the air clear and still, when Phares and two British officers set out on their horses to the desert oasis of Wahat El Nakheel. As the glittering golden sun marched towards the horizon, magnificent hues were flung upon the sky as from some unseen brush. Here was a kingly purple, there a transparent green until the whole firmament burned with splendid multicoloured fire; and when at length the sun sank, royal to the last over the rim of the world, a broad band of vivid red stained the sky from end to end.

As he rode Antar at a deadly speed, the hooves of his animal kicking up the sand, Phares's mind raced just as fast. The last forty-eight hours had been eventful, to say the least, culminating in a meeting with Alastair Carlisle that had led to this nocturnal expedition. First, the telecommunication he had received at the hospital that made his heart sink: it had come from the Maadi Police Station, informing him that Camelia had been among a group of writers and journalists who'd been arrested at the home of the head of a group of nationalists working against the King and the British. Well aware of what that meant – high treason and imprisonment – Phares had immediately dropped everything. He'd rung his father in Luxor, as well as *Ostaz* Nazmi, the Pharaony family's lawyer, and had driven off to Maadi to his sister's rescue.

He had spent the whole afternoon trying to negotiate Camelia's release, without success. Attempting to get hold of Alastair at the Embassy, he was informed that the young consul was away for the weekend and wouldn't be back in his office until the Monday. He had also tried to ring Aida, to apologise for missing their lunch appointment, but one of the servants at Kasr El Ghoroub told him that she hadn't been at the house since the morning.

Neither he nor *Ostaz* Nazmi had managed to get Camelia released and after several hours of fruitless enquiry and agitation, Phares had returned to the Anglo-American Hospital with a heavy heart. He prepared himself for a surgery that was both tricky and would take hours to perform: the removal of a tuberculosis gland from Nairy's mother's jaw. The biopsy proved his initial diagnosis of tuberculosis in the gland to be correct. It was considered a difficult and tricky procedure and this was one operation he could not reschedule. After a lengthy time in theatre, he had tried to ring Aida at Kasr El Shorouk, but had received no answer.

It was almost midnight when Phares had driven home hoping to find Aida awake. At the house another shock awaited him when Gomaa, the *suffragi*, presented him with the letter Aida had left for Camelia. Perusing it quickly, he then screwed it up in his fist, breathing a silent oath. He should have known that Aida's impulsiveness would get the better of her when she hadn't found him waiting for her at the Gezireh Sporting Club. Tired and furious with his sister, Aida and the world in general, he had saddled up Antar and spent the next few hours riding recklessly in the desert until, almost dropping with fatigue, he tied his horse to a palm tree and sank to the ground, where he lay for hours in a heavy, desperate slumber.

The *pasha* turned up in the morning and the rest of their weekend had been spent trying to pull strings to free Camelia from prison and avoid trial. Again, all their efforts had failed, and by the evening he and his father had to accept that their only resort lay in the British Embassy's intervention.

First thing on Monday morning, Phares had presented himself at the Embassy, asking to see the consul urgently. Alastair Carlisle had listened intently, then reassured Phares that he would take the necessary steps to free Camelia, on condition that she promised to cease her involvement in politics and cut all contact with her troublemaker friends. Apparently, she had been under surveillance for some time though the matter had only recently come to Alastair's attention. The consul warned that if Camelia were to appear on the authority's radar again, there was a limit to how much influence he could have a second time.

As Phares stood up, about to take his leave, Alastair glanced at him quizzically, staying him with a raised hand. 'I assume you did not get my message this morning?'

'Message? No, I left in a hurry.'

'It was about Miss El Masri.'

Phares frowned, lowering himself back into his chair. 'Go on.'

Alastair paused, retrieving a packet of cigarettes from his pocket. 'You are probably not aware that Miss El Masri made a last-minute decision to join the party going to Prince Shams Sakr El Din's oasis for the weekend.'

Phares stilled. 'No, I was not.'

The consul tapped a cigarette on the table before lighting it. 'As you know, we have been keeping a keen eye on His Highness for quite some time so I had my own reasons for being there, to get a look inside the fox's lair, so to speak. Miss El Masri decided to come at the last minute and though it wasn't my place to interfere, I did try to keep an eye on her. Where I now feel remiss is that we left her at the palace after she had come down with food poisoning or perhaps the effects of sunstroke. With matters coming to a head here, I had no choice but to leave for Cairo with the others. The prince assured us he would fly her back today.'

'You left her there?' Phares's face darkened. In the past, there had been incidents of vulnerable young foreign women going missing and sinister rumours connected them to the prince.

Alastair drew his eyebrows together. 'I'd been given to understand that she was quite ill and could not be moved. There was nothing I could have done really.'

'Yes, I suppose so.' Phares's eyes narrowed as he leaned forward in his chair, trying to control the dark fury building up in him at the thought of the Bedouin prince.

'Anyway, you might want to check that she really is brought back to Cairo today, the weather reports aren't looking too promising.'

Phares's jaw hardened. 'I will investigate.'

'And keep me posted?'

'Of course, as always.'

Alastair glanced at him meaningfully and out of habit lowered his voice. 'And about that other business ... my sources in Libya tell me that there will be another convoy of antiquities coming through the Western Desert soon, though no one is clear on timings. I need you to be ready. One of our men, Charles Montgomery, will go with you. He's also been primed. This could be El Kébir's biggest one yet.'

Phares met his gaze, understanding exactly the consul's meaning. For months now, he had kept this part of his life secret from everyone he knew. The man nicknamed El Kébir, the chief, had eluded capture for years. No one knew his identity and yet he was responsible for the most notorious antiquity smuggling operation in Egypt. It was like chasing smoke, but now that Phares had become an unofficial part of the consul's efforts to pinpoint the infamous head of the smuggling ring, with every dangerous mission he undertook, they were getting closer to El Kébir.

'You think this time, he'll have involved himself directly?'

Alastair nodded. 'That's what I'm hoping. He has always operated in the shadows but with this job he's likely to entrust it to someone high up. If we can get to that man, we may be able to get to El Kébir himself.'

Phares rubbed his chin pensively. 'We've both discussed this before, but El Kébir must have been connected to Ayoub El Masri's arrest all those years ago, yes?'

Alastair shrugged. 'I agree. But we've never had proof, as you know.'

'The El Masri's maid, Souma Hassanein. We need to find her. Aida is convinced she knows something.'

'The maid who apparently told Miss El Masri that it was your father who owned the Nefertari statue?'

Phares nodded. 'She conveniently disappeared as soon as Ayoub was arrested but no one knew where she went. At the time I thought it was Aida's grief making her cling on to the *khadamma*'s story. None of it made sense and then Aida went away and the trail went cold. Perhaps I should have tried to pursue it further, even though I didn't have your resources at my disposal at the time.' He raised grave eyes to the consul. 'If Souma Hassanein was paid to plant the statue at Karawan House, then we should try and pick up that lead now. The woman must still have family in or around Luxor. I've begun to ask discreetly among my Bedouin contacts. Can you put out the word among your people too?'

He nodded. 'Of course. It won't be easy after all this time, but we can give it a shot.'

Phares stood up. 'Much appreciated, Alastair. Now I must go and see if there's been any news of Aida at Karawan House.'

'Please let me know as soon as you hear anything about Miss El Masri,' said the consul, rising from his chair. 'She is a remarkable young woman and I feel a certain amount of responsibility for her. As for your sister, I will make sure she sleeps tonight at your home.'

Phares gripped his hand in a firm handshake. 'Thank you, I will not forget your kindness.'

Alastair patted Phares on the back. 'Come on, old chap, what are friends for? Besides, you've been risking your life helping us with our investigations. This is the least we can do.'

After leaving the Embassy, Phares had been besieged by thoughts as though chased by a pack of wild dogs but he forced himself to focus. On arrival at the Anglo-American Hospital, he had immediately called his father and their lawyer *Ostaz* Nazmi to tell them of Camelia's imminent release and arrange for them to pick her up. He had then rung Karawan House in Luxor to enquire about Aida. With a gnawing heaviness in his gut, he learnt that the young woman was not at her home and *Dada* Amina hadn't heard from her at all. Next, he had his secretary call all the Cairo hotels and when at lunchtime, he was told that there was no Aida El Masri staying at any one of them, he rang Alastair and immediately arranged for two officers to accompany him that night to Wahat El Nakheel. Phares's mind was swimming with grim possibilities and even though he could not be sure that Aida was in danger, his seething blood wanted him to break every bone in Sakr El Din's body.

By now, the Western Desert's orange moonlight had turned the expanse of sand that lay in front of Phares into a sea of tawny light as he pushed his mount Antar on towards Wahat El Nakheel. Occasionally, a gust of hot wind hit his face. With mounting anxiety in his heart, his black eyes had lost something of their habitual brilliance as images of Aida in danger danced before him like hideous mirages.

Anger also gripped him when he thought of her frivolous behaviour. How dare she disobey him and join the party. She knew how he felt about the prince but she hadn't cared about his feelings; she hadn't given a second thought to how it might look and how her own reputation would suffer. Most of all, she had potentially placed herself in jeopardy. There was much he admired, loved and respected in Aida, but also a great deal he deplored, not least her belligerent and impulsive nature. Was it madness to want to link his life to hers for ever, could a marriage between them be happy? They were so different.

Nevertheless, these considerations were outweighed by a desperate desire to see her safe, to hold her close. Beneath all his frustration with her was a longing so deep he was shaken by it.

Phares Pharaony was in love for the first time in his life.

He knew that now. In love, as only a man experienced in the ways of women and well-versed in affairs of the heart can be: utterly and irrevocably and with a strength of passion and depth of tenderness impossible for the most ardent of younger men. He wanted to share his life with someone, to have someone with whom to laugh and cry and rejoice, and most of all to have children ... many children. He wanted that person to be Aida.

Still, Aida rarely did anything she did not want to do. Maybe she had decided not to marry him after all and that was why she had accepted the prince's invitation: to prove her independence.

Was she angry at him? Or had her feelings for him finally cooled? In his arms, Aida had proved that she felt something for him beyond infatuation.

But could she *love* him?

He could see that Aida had changed since she'd left Egypt and the years of war had marked her, yet she still retained that purity and the passionate character he had always admired in her. A fire burned within her that communicated itself to him whenever she was close. She had become as necessary to him as breathing.

Phares's jaw tightened. Whatever it took, he would have Aida, heart and soul.

In the same way his desire for her had ignited her passionate nature, his love must now call forth the same love in her. He would sweep away her misgivings about his father and once they married, she would come to love him.

This latest escapade would force her hand. Surely now Aida would have to marry him? Too many people knew that she'd spent time at the prince's palace alone and Cairo's society was unforgiving, especially the circle in which they mixed. The foreign crowd didn't appreciate how far her reputation would be ruined – even Alastair, who had left her at the palace alone with barely a second thought. If Aida had to leave Cairo again, cast out by her social circle, this time he'd lose her for good. He couldn't let that happen. But for the time being, all Phares wanted was for Aida to be safe. He would never forgive himself for missing their rendezvous if anything had happened to her. An image of Sakr El Din flashed before him, making him grip the reins of his horse even more tightly.

The sky was now ablaze with stars and despite his anxiety, Phares's blood throbbed to the music of the unceasing desert refrain which rang in his ears as he hurried towards Kasr El Nawafeer. A refreshing breeze was blowing over the dunes, bringing a whisper of strange things in its breath – the rustle of palm trees swaying in the quiet night, the sudden cry of a desert animal as it slipped on its restless way beneath the silvered firmament, the stirring of the sands over long-buried mysteries. From time to time, if he felt that the two officers were slackening their pace, he'd cry out to them, 'Let's not delay, gentlemen, I implore you. Let's move on … time is precious!'

And suddenly they were in view of the oasis, lying in the distance under the purple vault of the desert night.

The three men were stopped at the gates of Wahat El Nakheel, but the guards moved aside when they saw the official papers they were carrying. The town was austere and calm, nothing stirred anywhere. The pallid houses appeared sharp and clear against the bright night: the wooden camel saddles hanging up by their doors, the flat roofs and thick mud walls broken by shafts of black shadow. Somehow, the scene bore the indefinable impression of terror.

They were stopped again at the palace gates. At the sight of the men, the guards who were smoking and laughing over some joke broke off at once. They passed the officers' papers from hand to hand, and after their close inspection, Phares and the two officers were allowed in.

A manservant ushered them into an immense, richly carpeted hall almost devoid of furniture, which they passed through into a large open courtyard with gardens and fountains. Before them rose one of the palace's wings, its many windows alight. A strip of red carpet with a red and white canopy above led to an open door.

Phares had no time to think as he and his companions were ushered through the door and handed over to yet more liveried servants, who led the men into a vast, Eastern-furnished room lit by eight chandeliers hanging from a painted ceiling and logs crackling in the huge tiled fireplace at one end. The room had a bright and welcoming warmth, though Phares felt none of it.

They did not have to wait long. Soon, Prince Shams Sakr El Din entered the room in all his sumptuous Bedouin attire. He stood a moment before them, the perfect host, smiling and saying all those pleasant, conventional things. Then he sat them down, ordered coffee and asked his servant to refresh his guests' horses. Only then, when his eyes turned back to his guests, did Phares see them narrow slightly, like the eyes of a watching cat, before regaining their normal dimensions.

The prince sat back in his seat and asked pleasantly: 'And to what do I owe this delightful visit, gentlemen?' He seemed amused, yet there was a hint of challenge in his manner, a touch of the master which Phares did not care for.

Slowly clenching one fist at his side, Phares could think of nothing else but the urge to wipe the smile off Sakr El Din's face and tear the place apart to find Aida. He only just managed to control himself, knowing that if he allowed his pent-up anger free rein, he and the officers were hopelessly outnumbered and it would not help Aida if his head were severed from his body.

Phares levelled an unflinching gaze at the prince. 'We are here to enquire about the whereabouts of Miss Aida El Masri, one of your weekend guests who stayed behind because she was taken ill.'

The prince nodded earnestly. 'Ah yes, Miss El Masri. She was indeed taken ill during the night and couldn't make it back to Cairo with the others in the morning. She slept all day and in the early evening, we had a very pleasant light dinner together, but she was still tired, she said. So, you can imagine my surprise when in the morning I was told that she had ordered one of the servants to saddle one of my best horses and had gone.' He raised his eyebrows. 'Has she not returned to Cairo?'

'No, the lady is missing,' provided one of the officers.

Phares's jaw tightened. 'You let her leave unaccompanied?'

'If I may remind you, I did not *let* her do any such thing. It was quite reckless, I must admit, for this young lady to take herself off in this way. I told her that I would fly her back in the morning, weather permitting,' the prince insisted.

Smothering the roiling anger eating up his insides, Phares replied, 'May we speak with the servant who provided the horse for her, and anyone else who might have seen her leave?'

'Yes, of course. Though I don't think that many would have been around. That night, we were holding the wedding celebrations of one of my cousins and most of my household would have been there.'

The prince rang and a servant appeared almost immediately. 'Tell Abdul Fattah to come and speak to the *bahawat*, gentleman.' Then, turning to his guests, he went on, 'The desert is a dangerous place at the best of times, and a *khamseen* has been threatening this part of the oasis for a couple of days now, though it hasn't struck us yet, but of course there could have been some turbulence. How well does Miss El Masri know the desert?'

Phares hesitated. This was something he was afraid of. It had been years since Aida had ridden out among the dunes, and certainly not this far. 'Not as well as any of us, but she is an excellent rider.'

The prince's pale eyes glittered oddly. 'This is very worrying news. I must send my men in search of her. They know the desert and its perils well, and if she is lying somewhere hurt, I am sure they will find her.'

Phares couldn't read the enigmatic expression on Sakr El Din's face and although he didn't trust him, instinct told him that Aida wasn't still at the palace. Making an escape on horseback sounded exactly like something she would do. Yet one thing he did know: he did not want the prince to be involved in any rescue mission.

'Thank you, that will not be necessary. This incident has caused you enough trouble and we wouldn't like to inconvenience you any further.'

'It is no trouble, really.'

At that moment, Abdul Fattah was shown into the room. A lithe-looking man of about forty, he had a chiselled face, a slightly curved nose, fleshy lips and small raven-black shifty eyes, which Phares immediately mistrusted. Yes, Abdul admitted, the lady in question had given him a five Egyptian pounds and had asked him to provide her with a good horse and a gourd of water.

Phares didn't believe him. Though he could certainly imagine Aida needing to escape the palace, and someone having helped her, if the man's story were true, and he had been the one to do so, then Phares had no doubt that the prince would have whipped his servant to death, at the very least for giving away one of his best horses.

Phares held the prince's pale gaze one final time as he rose from his seat. 'Until we meet again, Prince Shams Sakr El Din.'

As the three men took their leave, he watched as the prince's face hardened, his amber gaze icing over.

*     *     *

Dawn wasn't far off when the group on horseback started out. Phares had gathered a handful of trusted Bedouins who lived near the pyramids to help him in his search for Aida. The night was calm and the voices of the Bedouin riders, chanting as they rode, made no echo but moved over the desert like a wave of sound – eerie, magical, beautiful. In the darkness loomed the indistinct figures of the horses; now and then one could only hear the padding of soft hooves, or the creak of a saddle. Like riders from another world, they made their noiseless way among the hills.

A chill, light wind came over the Western Desert, sweeping in across the sleeping city only a few miles away, heralding the dawn. Stars went out as it passed, the skies paled and the street lights were extinguished. Behind them Cairo lay pallid, strangely tawdry, like an old hag showing her bones in the pale cold dawn. A finger of gold touched the tip of a minaret; into the silence came a deep bell-like note: *Allahu Akbar, Allahu Akbar, La illah illallah.*

Although he hadn't slept, Phares was unnaturally vital and awake as he settled into a swinging trot over the hard, firm sand. With the spectacular swiftness of the East the sun came up, its fiery rays touching the sandhills and the outlined mountains. Now the way ahead was easier to follow.

He squinted into the distance. If Aida had become lost, she could have ridden in any direction. It made sense for the men to divide into two parties and zigzag back to the oasis, trying to cover a wider area. So, Phares gave the signal to three of his men and they parted ways, the Bedouins galloping off in the opposite direction.

The horses were fresh and owing to the early start, good progress was made before the fierce noonday heat made a halt imperative. Luckily, a little shade was procured under a thick grove of palm trees and here, the remainder of the small party rested for as long as they dared before Phares urged them on. Aida might be out there somewhere and time was slipping through their fingers.

At four o'clock the sun's heat grew a little less powerful and travelling became easier. For hours they rode, scanning the shimmering horizon, but there was nothing but the vast yellow dunes and the empty azure sky. With moonrise a light breeze sprang up and Phares and his men rode on and on, close together, thankful for the refreshing coolness after the long, hot day, and watching the sparkling stars creep out in bright armies in the velvet sky, illuminating the surrounding desert with their brilliance. They had covered a considerable portion of the journey when the riders reached a small quarry and instinctively spread out. Picking his way among the stones and boulders, Phares suddenly slowed and then stopped, his heart giving a small jolt.

'My God!' With a shout he lifted his arm to the others, signalling them to halt. In the brilliant moonlight he could just make out a heap lying on the ground, which was neither a stack of stones, nor a boulder, nor a mound of sand.

Leaping off Antar, heart hammering, he swiftly made his way down through the rocks and sand. Reaching the bundle in seconds he threw himself beside the small white figure lying huddled and motionless.

The once-lively sapphire eyes were closed, the soft cheeks white as chalk, her lips parted; and all of a sudden earth and sky turned dark for Phares. He held her in his arms and could detect no sign of life. As he stooped over her, he saw that the thin cotton of her shirt was torn and hanging about her in soiled fragments. 'Aida,' he murmured, his hand going to her cheek. There was no response.

Love and grief tore through him but somehow the doctor in him took over. His fingers went to her neck. For a moment it seemed as though her heart throbbed too faintly for him to feel its pulse and no breath stirred from the bluish lips. Then he felt a pulse, weak and quivering, but it was there.

One of the Bedouin men strode swiftly over the sand towards them, his white garment flapping against his brown legs, his rascally face full of concern. He had brought over a gourd of water and Phares took it from him silently and held it to Aida's lips.

For an anguished moment her still form didn't move and Phares hesitated, wondering whether or not to apply some stimulant to help bring her back to consciousness. Then, as he sprinkled a few drops of water on to her pallid brow, the big eyes opened feebly and Aida gazed up into his face.

'Phares …' Her voice was very faint.

His heart slammed into his chest and all he could do was whisper her name.

Her brow furrowed weakly. 'What is it? Oh … I remember. I fell, didn't I?'

'Shush, *chérie*, you're safe now.'

He had brought several large silk handkerchiefs smeared with ointment with him, which he now took from his pocket valise and bound them around the wound Aida had sustained in her fall.

When he lifted his head, he saw that her eyes were closed again. He whispered her name and felt an enormous sense of relief when she stirred slightly and opened them.

'Phares …' She gave a faint smile and whispered something inaudibly, then closed her eyes with a sigh, too weary to keep them open any longer.

'I'm here, *chérie*.' Lifting the small figure tenderly into his arms, he gave her to the Bedouin to hold while he slid back in the saddle. Once he was securely seated, he took her from the man and pulled her up against his chest so her fair head lay against his shoulder. Enfolding her tightly in his embrace, he rode back to Cairo with his men.

*    *    *

Aida seemed to drift underwater, aware of voices that came to her from a distance, and then receded. There were conversations floating around her that she couldn't understand. One of them belonged to Phares. He'd come for her, and she wanted to reach out for him, but now she couldn't see where he was, just the blackness. Too tired to open her eyes, she gave into the blackness and sank back beneath the waves. And then she felt herself floating upwards to the surface of the water, the sun's rays striking warmly on her face.

She opened her eyes slowly. Wherever she was, it was dusk. Clumsily, she tried to sit up and as she did so, the sudden pang which went through her stiffened frame brought her to a full realisation of her surroundings. Still somewhat dazed, she looked round the hospital room with its cool pale walls, noticing that a nurse was sitting in a chair a few feet away, dozing.

Aida lay back and closed her eyes again. How long had she been here? Mind and body shuddered alike as images of what had happened began to form again in her head. She was so cold inside, as if her stomach were filled with ice. She swallowed hard, her throat sore and swollen with tension as she fought against remembering the details of her nightmare. Her entire body ached – so physically tired that she felt almost battered. Feverish and weak, it was as if she was suffering from a disease.

Sleep must have taken her again for when she opened her eyes once more, the clock on the wall opposite showed it was early. She must have slept through the night. She noticed that the nurse who had been dozing had left the room, and feeling a little stronger, Aida pushed herself up against her pillows and winced, everything now rushing back to her consciousness like water flowing through the floodgates of a dam.

*What had she done?*

Aida knew perfectly well that in Egypt, girls belonging to respectable families did not behave in the way she had. It was all very well being half English and having lived in England during the war, but she was half Egyptian too and now she was back in Egypt, where she intended to make her life. She sighed. When in Rome and all that. Even her father, who was regarded as broad-minded in comparison to his Egyptian peers, would not have condoned her behaviour. What had happened to her was no surprise, and Aida was too fair-minded and lucid not to admit it. It was not as if she hadn't been warned. She was lucky that she had escaped with only a few bruises and a harsh lesson that she would never forget as long as she lived.

Still, her mind was foggy and confused. What was Phares doing at that hour in the desert with a group of Bedouins? Surely he had come looking for her. He must have rung Karawan House and found that she wasn't there, but how had he guessed so quickly that she had gone to the prince's oasis?

She was so ashamed of her impulsive behaviour. How could she ever face Phares again? He would never marry her now. Her defence was jealousy – he had lied to her by saying that his relationship with Nairy Paplosian had ended months ago – but her pride would forbid her from ever telling him that she knew that he was still carrying on with the model. Still they were not officially engaged and Aida hadn't even given him an answer, so maybe she had no right to be either jealous or angry. As usual, she had gone off the deep end without considering the consequences of her actions, and she would now have to pay the price.

She remained there with her eyes closed, thankful at least that she was safe after her ordeal, but then her peace was invaded by the sound of squeaking hinges as the door was thrust open.

Her eyes snapped open as Naguib Bishara entered the room. The usual smiling, debonair expression on the lawyer's face had given way to a tightening of the lips and a grave mien that Aida had only experienced during the far-off days that had preceded and followed her father Ayoub's trial. She propped herself further up in bed, almost sitting, ready to face the music.

'Good morning, Aida.'

'Good morning, Uncle Naguib.'

'How are you feeling this morning? You still look very pale, but better than yesterday when they brought you in.'

'I feel a little weak and tired, but I'm fine, thank you. So, I've been here for a whole day?'

'Yes, *habibti.* Your aunt Nabila came to visit while you were sleeping. She's been worried sick.' Naguib sighed as he sat down in the chair next to Aida's bed. He gazed at her, his dark eyes concerned though reproachful. 'Aida, my child, how could you behave in this way? Didn't you realise the fearful risks you ran in going to Kasr El Nawafeer alone and what the consequences might be from such a foolish action, not to mention the utter madness of setting off into the desert on your own? Do you know how lucky you are to be alive? Will you never learn wisdom?'

Colour rose to Aida's cheeks and she stiffened, resentful of this criticism. 'I didn't go alone, Uncle, we were in a group. Had I not been taken ill, none of this would have happened and I would have returned with the others. As for my running off, I was *escaping* from Prince Shams, don't you see? The man's a madman, he wanted to keep me there as his prisoner.'

Naguib's eyes widened. 'We were told he was going to take you back himself on his private plane the next day.'

'That's what he told Shirley Saunders, but he handcuffed me and locked me up in the harem.' Aida couldn't keep the tremor from her voice. 'If it hadn't been for his aunt and a couple of servants who helped me escape, I doubt you would have seen me again.' She shivered and tears clouded her eyes.

Naguib's face darkened. For a moment he did not speak, then he reached for Aida's hand, which lay limply on the bed, and gave it a brief squeeze. 'I see. Do not worry, I will make enquiries. The man thinks he is above the law but I will find a way to deal with Prince Shams Sakr El Din.' He sat back and rested his elbows on the arms of his chair, interlacing his fingers. 'But in the meantime, my dear, our whole Cairene social circle has been talking about your disappearance. I'm afraid you have given cause for endless gossip and scandal. The prince is a renowned womaniser. People are already saying you feigned sickness to stay behind with him. It didn't help that your travelling companions told everyone that he was flirting with you during your stay.'

'But it isn't true!' she exclaimed, her voice now heated by hurt and anger.

Naguib lifted a calming hand. 'Yes, you and I know that.'

'What about Phares?'

'Phares loves you.'

'No, he doesn't.'

Naguib fixed her with a serious look. 'The man cares for you a great deal. He must do, because he stayed by your side for hours without sleeping, until he was called away urgently. He also told me when he brought you back that I mustn't worry about your reputation. He is still keen on marrying you and as soon as possible, too.'

Aida blinked in surprise. Phares wanted to marry her, *as soon as possible*. Why did he not want to distance himself from her now that that she had brought shame upon herself in the eyes of their social circle? Part of her rejoiced but the doubts would not be silenced. Phares wanted her, but his heart lay with someone else.

Aida glanced sharply back at Naguib. 'Yes, of course, he is still keen to marry my *feddans*, acres of land,' she replied bitterly.

'You must be aware of his affair with Nairy Paplosian, the well-known model.'

Naguib sighed and shook his head. 'If a man has a mistress, it doesn't necessarily mean that he loves her. Most young men have mistresses until the day they marry. Men's needs, *habibti*, are different to those of a woman. The affair usually ends when the man settles down.'

She turned her head away. 'Yes, yes, I know about all that.'

'I'm sure that Miss Paplosian is only a … let's call it a pleasurable entertainment for Phares. He is a man like any other, and the woman is a siren. You are not so innocent as to be unaware of the fact that a man may be deeply in love with one woman yet by no means impervious to the wiles of another. Especially when the woman he truly loves seems unattainable. And as I understand it, *habibti*, Phares has asked you to marry him a number of times and you have been evasive, to say the least. So, you see, there is nothing for you to worry about … Phares is seriously taken with you.'

Aida gave a hollow laugh. 'Well then, you haven't been listening to the gossip. She is the love of his life, Uncle. The only reason Phares is unable to marry this woman is because of their social differences. We're such a bigoted society, it would harm his career. I'm well aware that if he married me it would be the perfect match and he would be able to have his cake and eat it.'

'Not now, *habibti*,' Naguib said, a little more sternly. 'You are certainly not the perfect match for him anymore. I can name many young women who would provide Phares with as much land as you would. You are not the only rich woman around – Take Isis Geratly. She has had her eye on Phares for years and makes no bones about it, and she's an heiress to a lot of land.'

'Yes, but *my* land adjoins his, and Kamel Pharaony can't wait to have us married so he can get his hands on it.'

'That may be so, but Phares is his own man, Aida, and if he didn't love you, especially after your last escapade, he wouldn't

marry you. Think about it, *habibti*, but don't delay. Patience has
its limits. After another rebuff from you, I wouldn't blame Phares
if he gave up and turned to someone who would be grateful for
his proposal. There is no reason why a young man so in demand
should continue with a love that is unrequited.'

Aida sighed. 'I'll think about it, Uncle, but I won't deceive
myself with dreams filled with nothing but sweet air.' She paused
for a few seconds and then asked, 'When can I leave the hospital
and return to Luxor?'

'Doctor Amir would like you to spend another night under
observation. You could have died out there in the desert and he
wants to make sure you are totally recovered before you travel.
So, tomorrow, we will go back to Luxor together.' Naguib rose
from his chair. Moving over to the window, he stared out, hands
clasped behind his back. 'I should tell you that Kamel Pharaony
has been asking after you as well. He wanted to come and see you
but he needed to remain in Luxor for Camelia.'

Aida looked up in surprise. 'Camelia? Is she all right?'

He turned and gave her a knowing look. 'Not exactly. That is
why Phares was called away urgently. He's taken Camelia back
to Luxor. Like you, she's been reckless … Anyway, they have both
flown to Upper Egypt this morning, where she will hopefully
stay out of trouble.'

Aida was alarmed. 'What do you mean?'

Naguib levelled a hard stare at her. 'Did you know that your
friend is part of a nationalist organisation working to get rid
of the King and the British?'

'No, I didn't,' she lied.

'Well, she was arrested at the home of the head of Masr Lel
Masreyeen on Friday and was thrown into prison, where she
remained for the weekend until Phares was able to persuade
the Embassy to help him have her freed. The news of her release
came after you were brought here.'

'Oh, poor Camelia!'

Naguib flung his hands up. 'No, not poor Camelia ... reckless, unwise Camelia.' Exasperation filled his voice. 'Honestly, you're just as foolish as each other.'

Aida was concerned. 'Did they torture her, or harm her?'

'Not that I've heard.' He shook his head ruefully. 'Ah, Phares ... he's had a rough few days dealing with you two girls.'

'I'm sorry, Uncle Naguib. I behaved on impulse ... as usual.'

'Well, *habibti*, I hope you've learned your lesson.'

'I have, I can assure you.' Genuine regret tinged her voice. 'It was a very frightening experience.'

Naguib's expression softened. 'Your father always said you would have to learn the hard way. Poor Ayoub, how he used to worry about you.'

Aida gave a sad smile. 'If he hadn't died, I suppose I'd be married to Phares today.'

'Indeed, but that is all in the past. This is a situation that can rectified, and that now lies in your hands. And now, *habibti*, I must leave you as I have some work to attend to. I'll come back this evening and make sure you have everything you need. You must get your strength back now so that we can get you home to Karawan House.'

Once Naguib had gone, Aida rested her head against the pillows and closed her eyes, emotions warring with her reason. Uncle Naguib was right: when you added up all the disadvantages marriage to her must represent for Phares, the match must seem to him slightly dubious. Aida was the daughter of a man whom society had censured, a woman alone with no useful connections. Ayoub El Masri's daughter was impetuous, headstrong ... and a liability.

Marriage to Ayoub's daughter, though it would do Phares no real harm, would not exactly enhance his prestige – and he was an ambitious man. Only the land could compensate for these shortcomings – and her love perhaps. Aida knew now more than ever that she could not will herself to stop loving Phares. The fact was she couldn't imagine life without him. Perhaps she could dare hope to give flight to that flutter of optimism in her heart … If Phares was determined to have her, she'd be damned if she was foolish enough to let him go. Her mind was made up: she would set aside her pride and do whatever it took to make him love her.

Aida drew a deep breath. As for Nairy Paplosian, she would fight the woman with her very own weapons.

*Seduction is an art discovered by Eve and practised ever since by women determined to get their men.*

Aida had read that somewhere years ago. At the time it had faintly shocked her, but she felt differently now. Women had limited ammunition to aid them in the war of the sexes, so those they had must be used wisely and well.

She already knew how much Phares desired her – again and again he had made it plain, and she wanted him too, beyond all reason. If, as Uncle Naguib seemed to think, Phares's attraction to his model mistress was merely sexual then Aida would do her best to seduce him, please him and love him until he forgot Nairy Paplosian entirely.

\*   \*   \*

A flood of hazy morning sunlight poured into the long, walled garden, which lent an enchanted secrecy. It was planted from end to end with orange trees, their shining leaves glistening in the sun and here and there a round ripe fruit showed among the small waxen flowers. Creepers tipped by clusters of purple wisteria outlined the furthest wall, while a shabby pergola on a path leading to the river was covered in a luxuriant vine with thick, dark, lance-shaped leaves and balls of scarlet berries. The air was hot and sweet, heady with the scent of acacias, orange blossoms and roses, which clambered up the other walls among clematis and passion flowers. Two colourful hoopoes, one in the sweet-lemon tree, the other hidden somewhere in the mimosa hedge, called to each other in their enchanted notes like birds in a dream.

Aida was in the garden when Phares came looking for her. Wearing a loose blue button-down dress to keep cool against the coming heat of the day, she leant against the trunk of an acacia tree on the bank sloping down to the Nile.

She had been back nearly a week, but hadn't heard from him. She had tried to speak to Camelia over the telephone, but her friend was apparently shutting herself away, still in shock, refusing to take any calls.

Her heart raced as she saw Phares's tall, lean figure appear at the top of the terrace staircase that led to the garden. Beige chinos were belted to his flat, athletic waist, and a fine cotton shirt covering his broad chest and wide shoulders was open at the neck, bright white against his tawny skin. The curved fullness of his mouth, deceptively soft-looking, coupled with the lock of black hair that hung over his forehead, gave him a rugged, thrilling look that went straight to her heart. Deliberately, arrogantly, with even a touch of insolence, he ambled towards her.

'Aida, *chérie*, I thought I'd find you here. You look … much better.' He seemed to be wrestling with pent-up energy. For a moment his eyes swept over her in a possessive gaze, a mix of relief with something darker. 'You're far braver than I thought … and far more foolish. A bravado that could have cost you your life.' He gazed at her fiercely with eyes like obsidian. 'Damn it, Aida! What were you thinking?'

For a few seconds, she just looked at him with a catch of her breath. The pallor of her cheeks was replaced by two flames that flickered over her cheekbones and shot sparks into her eyes.

'I'm not proud of my escapade, Phares. I'm sorry—' she began, but he cut in, not giving her the opportunity to finish.

'That you should run off on a whim just because I wasn't at our lunch appointment shows how irresponsible and immature you are. My God, I could have been held up in an operation or had an accident! Didn't that even cross your mind? No, you ran off to that womaniser's palace, knowing it would infuriate me and putting yourself in very real danger.'

His words filled the air around them with tangible hurt and anger. Phares's eyes flashed bitter reproach as they dwelt on Aida's face, which had gone so white that her mouth looked bruised. He took a breath as if gathering his self-control. 'The word "honour" has meaning for all the Pharaony family, as you know, and I'm surprised it didn't hold more importance for you.'

'Honour?' In an instant, Aida's contrition turned to fury. Despite all she had promised herself, she was on the verge of retorting that it was he who'd had little regard for honour when he repeatedly asserted to her that his relationship with Nairy Paplosian was a thing of the past when she had not only seen him with the model, but had heard him arrange a meeting with her for that evening. Just in time she bit her tongue, silencing those irrevocable words that might have ended their relationship. This was not the right time to confront him, but she needed to know if he still wanted to marry her.

Straightening her back she took a step towards him and spoke with angry pain in her voice. 'I sincerely regret my behaviour. I was totally wrong, and would understand if you decided to withdraw your proposal.'

Phares didn't answer immediately. There was a quality of stillness about him that made her think of a panther – tensed to spring on its prey. The silence between them held the warning of a pounce.

'My proposal stands.' He angled a direct stare at Aida. 'And as you will be coming to this marriage with a large dowry – your land – you will hand it over to the Pharaony Estate as soon as we are married so that I can oversee its management properly.'

Her eyes widened. 'You can't be serious!'

'I have never been more serious.'

Of course Aida knew Phares was only claiming a right deeply ingrained in Egyptian culture. The sharing of land would symbolise their union, but for her, it would also mean the final surrender of her independence. Yet it wasn't only the issue of her land that pained her.

*Where in his declaration was there mention of love?*

If only Phares would say those words to her she would never care that he would always be the master. Aida had met a will stronger than her own and would do her best to obey … she was ready to be a loyal, faithful and supportive wife. If she could be sure he truly loved her, she could do all of that for him.

'I will never give up my land,' she murmured, almost desperately. 'You can have money in lieu, but never my land.'

'Those were the terms my father discussed with yours when he asked for your hand.'

'I'm sure my father would never have agreed to giving away all our land.'

'Correct. Not all your land, but part of it while he was alive and he could look after it. You know as well as I do that you are out of your depth running your estate so I've made it my sole condition.'

'*Condition*?' She scowled at him. 'You speak of marriage as though it's a cold transaction.'

He clenched his jaw. 'Why must you twist everything I say, Aida? You know there is more than that between us.'

'Yes, lust, that's all,' she shot back, the truth of it feeling like a chill down her spine.

'You think so?' His brows drew down like a visor, shadowing his eyes. 'In that case, lust, if nothing else, will force you to marry me.'

'Don't you think you're flattering yourself?'

'Am I, *chérie*?' He laughed and it rang out arrogantly in the quiet garden.

His eyes met hers, their quizzical depths as baffling as ever, and his hand brushed away a strand of hair that the breeze had driven across her face.

Aida sucked in her breath, instinctively putting a hand to her cheek and feeling its warmth. Being Phares's wife ... a tremor raced through her. No, she knew only too well that he wasn't flattering himself. His gaze, his brief touch, even his arrogant laugh reawakened in her that wild, strange ecstasy that could not be called love, but a hunger, a driving need that she shared with him entirely.

'Why are you always running away from me, Aida? What are you so afraid of?'

'I'm not afraid,' she lied, as a shiver snaked up her spine.

'And yet you ran straight to Sakr El Din's palace when I didn't turn up at the club.' His gaze fixed hard on her, mingled with taunting fury, pride and desire. 'Were you enjoying the prince's attentions so much, you wanted to see what it was like to become one of his harem?'

'You *know* that's not true,' she half gasped. She tried to move away but he inched closer, backing her up against the trunk of the acacia. 'I swear to God if that son of a *ibn el sharmouta* had touched you ...'

Her breasts were rising and falling in tandem with her rapid breaths. 'No! No, Phares, he didn't, I swear. I escaped before he could do anything.'

Phares seemed only slightly mollified. He braced his arms against the trunk of the acacia, trapping her between his body and the tree. His voice was dangerously soft. 'Because you are *mine*, Aida. You were always destined to be mine, and deep down, you know it. You will be my wife, and no man will touch you but me.'

Aida was trembling but she met his mesmerising gaze, saw the flare of his nostrils and the passion etched on his full, strong mouth. All her life she had been fearless, and there was a quality of elusiveness about her that charmed some and disconcerted others. Right now, however, she was at the mercy of her love and her need for this man … utterly defenceless.

Phares's eyes narrowed as he looked at her, his lips only inches away. 'There will be compensations, *chérie*. You know how flames kindle between us. The blue in your eyes is already darkening at the thought of your initiation to more carnal delights. Dare to tell me I'm wrong.' He caught Aida's slim body and pulled her against him.

Oh, that hardness, how she had missed it!

His eyes were brilliantly alive as they held her gaze … held it until she threw her arms around him, her hands pressed against the nape of his neck. She drew him in until their breaths mingled, tantalising, electric. Finally their lips met with a sensuousness that turned to hunger, and whatever her hesitation of a few minutes before, it was now abandoned as she sank into his powerful frame, melting into his strength. She was lost on the wave of his urgency as he pressed himself hard against her, enjoying his turbulent kisses and the feel of his hands on her body. All tenderness was gone as he claimed her mouth like a ravenous animal, thrusting his tongue into her mouth again and again, driving Aida to incoherence … to a wanton wildness of feeling. He broke away from her lips and kissed a scorching trail down her neck, every sensual word he murmured, every note in his voice making her senses beat like a forest fire. And then, he seemed to come down to earth and he pulled away from her, dropping his arms to his sides. His eyes twinkled with devilment and he laughed quietly, almost in surprise, although she saw through her own haze of thwarted desire the hot tide of blood mount under the skin of his throat and face, evidence of him battling to regain his self-control.

He stepped back. 'This is just a teaser, *chérie*, in case you'd forgotten … No more until our honeymoon. I haven't planned for an engagement period. You have one week. Prepare yourself for our wedding next Sunday.'

\*     \*     \*

While Phares was scrubbing up, his assistants knew better than to make conversation as they waited to help him don his surgical gown and cap. He was always quiet while getting ready to operate. It was his way of gathering his focus – to think about the procedure step by step. Sometimes, if it was a particularly difficult intervention he would pray before beginning work.

Today, his face was more intense than usual as the first patient was brought to the theatre, but for once his mind was not wholly on the imminent minor surgical operation.

Alastair Carlisle had finally received intelligence on El Kébir's latest smuggling operation in the Western Desert. The authorities only had wind of it in the last forty-eight hours so Phares had to act quickly. Tonight, he would be heading out of Cairo.

According to the Embassy's sources, an important convoy of stolen antiquities had already begun its journey south from Ras Gharib on the shores of the Gulf of Suez. From Ras Gharib, it would head for the Kharga Oasis, eventually bound for Dakhla, another oasis in the Western Desert. At Dakhla, it was to meet another convoy travelling down from Siwa in the north, which would take delivery of the goods to finally pass them on to Libyan traders, then across the Mediterranean to Greece and the rest of Europe.

This mission consisted of ambushing the convoy, and the seizure was to be made by a Kharga patrol of ten Sudanese guards appointed by the Embassy and two guides – one who knew the roads and local conditions, the other to control and read the tracks. The men would be under the command of Phares and Captain Charles Montgomery.

The Embassy had been informed that as one of the vehicles was to contain a priceless piece, the convoy would be overseen by one of the main leaders of the criminal organisation. If Phares and the others could capture this man, the police had no doubt they would be able to extract from him the names of the other leaders of the smuggling ring. Above all, El Kébir.

Tonight, he would be going by Jeep from Cairo to Assiut, then travelling over two hundred kilometres south into the desert with the Sudanese guards to Kharga, where they would abandon their Jeeps and use dromedaries to reach the outskirts of the Dakhla Oasis, the drop-off point for the smugglers. Travelling quietly by camel would allow them to go unnoticed since some of the local people might be El Kébir's spies, and they didn't want the conspicuous noise of vehicles alerting the convoy to their presence.

Phares had camped more than once in the seven oases of the Western Desert. He knew the Kharga, Dakhla and Farafra oases well, and even if the mission itself was causing him some apprehension, at least he was feeling confident enough about navigating the desert. Still, this mission was coming at a most inconvenient moment. What with the arrest and imprisonment of Camelia at the same time as Aida's reckless episode in the desert, his focus had been splintered in too many directions. Then there was the wedding too, which, now that he finally had it in his sights he was almost feverish to accomplish as quickly as possible before Aida changed her mind and decided to return to England.

His thoughts were interrupted by one of the nurses as she tied his surgical gown at the back. 'You look tired, Doctor,' she remarked. 'You've been working too hard. You look as though you could do with a vacation.'

Phares shook his head and smiled enigmatically. 'Time enough for that later.' Then, looking around him, he remarked, 'Where is Dr Isis? Has she not been informed that we have three operations today?'

'She called in sick. She was very apologetic, but she has laryngitis and a fever.'

'Is Dr Safwat here?'

'Yes. He's just come in and is about to scrub up.'

'Good.'

Phares sighed quietly. He was sure Isis wasn't sick. No doubt she'd heard about his engagement to Aida; by now the whole of Luxor was bound to be talking about it: servants' gossip travelled fast. She was probably sulking. She'd been acting even more possessively since Aida had returned to Luxor. Still, he couldn't help it if Isis was jealous: he had always been honest with her. She would have no problem finding herself a good husband: once she set her mind to it, Isis would pursue that as single-mindedly as everything else. Still, he hoped her resentment wouldn't lead to her resignation. On the other hand, even though she was a good anaesthetist, he could find another. If she did resign, then Dr Safwat was capable of holding the fort for the time being. Phares could help Isis find a good position at another hospital – he owed her that.

He flexed his fingers, staring at them thoughtfully. Sometimes it was terrifying, the faith patients had in him. At least today the interventions were fairly straightforward. He needed to conserve his energy for the next forty-eight hours.

*     *     *

It was growing late as Phares took the road out of Cairo. The sun was already setting, a ball of glittering gold swimming, so it seemed, in a lake of flame; the swift darkness of night would soon descend. He had packed his Jeep with a change of clothes for night, a filled water-skin, and a small amount of bread and cheese for the long journey ahead. Once in the desert, after leaving his Jeep, he would stow everything in the saddle bags of his *dhalul*, dromedary.

The temples on the banks of the Nile were already taking on the purple bloom of night, while the far-off desert hills began to look like a great black wall cutting across the horizon, casting deep indigo shadows and strange, eerie depths of blackness here and there. The Nile too was changing quickly to a sombre ribbon of ebony beneath the sentinel palms. At this hour there was no one on the agricultural road bordering the river, so Phares was able to speed ahead.

As he drove to Assiut, his mind turned over what was at stake if all went to plan. They would be one step closer to El Kébir, and hopefully also to clearing Ayoub El Masri's name. Strange to think so much had happened so quickly. Phares recalled the conversation he'd had with Alastair Carlisle at the beginning of this venture a few months back.

During the war, he had treated many British soldiers at the Anglo-American Hospital and had saved Alastair's brother's leg from being amputated. A solid friendship had sprung up between the two men, and in January of that year, when Mrs Carlisle had visited her son in Egypt, Alastair and his mother had been invited to stay at the Pharaony Estate in Luxor, where they were lavishly entertained by the Coptic family. It was there that the consul, a keen rider, had accompanied Phares one afternoon on a horse ride around the pyramids of Gizeh.

The sun had been dipping below the horizon, the shadow cast by the Great Pyramid stretching sharp and distinct across the stony platform of the desert, as they passed a group of pedlars offering their goods and picked their way down the long sand-slope to regain the road. It was then that some six or eight Arabs in fluttering white garments came out of nowhere and ran on ahead of them to bid the riders goodbye.

'You come again!' they said. 'Good Arab show you everything next time. You see nothing this time. You want buy *antikahs*?'

'Ah, *antikahs*, antiquities, the big word!' Alastair scoffed. 'It's everywhere, and even worse in Luxor, I suppose.'

'You mean the trafficking of antiquities?'

'Precisely. They're all at it ... Arabs, Copts. Perfectly polite, plausible, but mendacious, every one of them.'

'There are a lot of forgeries, of course, if that's what you mean.'

Alastair nodded. 'More forgeries than genuine antiquities are being sold, I think, because whatever the demand, the dealers are prepared to meet it.' He'd gone on to outline some of the work the Embassy had been doing in an attempt to curb the activities of a particularly large smuggling ring, one which seemed to have many branches across Egypt and beyond to Libya and Sudan. The scale of the operation had only increased during the war, alongside the trafficking of arms to the Germans, but so far none of the British agents had been successful in finding any significant leads.

As they rode slowly on, the consul gestured at the Great Pyramid behind them. 'We're not so concerned about the small-time forgers and sellers like those men.' He fixed Phares with a knowing look. 'It's the real antiquities that interest us.'

It was the first time his friend had opened up to this degree about his work, and Phares immediately sensed the subtle hint: 'Tell me, Alastair, how can I help?'

The consul gave a smile of satisfaction, as though that was the answer he'd hoped for. 'We know that you're a man of the desert, familiar with the sands almost as with the nomads who travel across them. We also know that you have many friends among the Bedouins and that they trust you. We are almost sure that many of the genuine antiquities are taken to Prince Shams Sakr El Din's oasis. Whether he holds on to them or sells them on himself, we don't know. We also have no idea of the identity of the big wig supplier, the man responsible for the illegal excavations and who actually provides these antiquities.'

'I had assumed that the looters were opportunists, and most of what is being sold on the black market is forgeries.'

'Believe me, the excavation of real artefacts happens alongside the work of forgeries. More and more diggers are colonising the western bank. They live rent-free among the tombs, driving donkeys or working in the fields during the day and spending their nights searching for treasure. We are aware that hundreds of families live in this grim way, spoiling the sites of the Ancient Egyptians for their livelihoods.'

'So, what is it you want me to do?'

'We need you to infiltrate the organisation so we can catch the person in charge of it. We are almost sure he resides in Luxor or its neighbouring districts. He goes by the name of El Kébir, or at least that is what our sources know him as, and he seems to inspire terror in anyone who has dealings with him. Very few of the opportunistic tomb looters would risk their lives going into competition with this man, and most are in his employ one way or another, through his deputies.'

Phares's brow furrowed. 'That's all well and good, Alastair, but I'm no connoisseur of antiquities. I wouldn't know how to tell the real from the fake.'

'That's no problem, we will provide you with the fakes. We've actually managed to penetrate a forger's workshop. They will copy anything, and I defy anyone, unless they're a real specialist, to tell the real from these forged ones.'

Phares stared ahead, deep in thought. 'How will this work?'

'We want you to put around the rumour that you are a buyer of antiquities. Forgers, diggers and dealers play into one another's hands and drive a roaring trade, so it will not be difficult to spread the word. Observe and you will see that every foreigner is plagued by sellers from the moment he lands in Luxor till the time he leaves. The boy who drives the donkey, the guide who leads people among the tombs, the half-naked *fellah* who flings down his hoe as you pass and runs beside you for a mile across the plain … all of them have an *antikah* to dispose of. And in the majority of these transactions the money will make its way to El Kébir. They will hear about your interest in genuine antiquities, believe me.'

From that day, Phares had been a recruit for the British Embassy. Now that Alastair made him aware of what was going on, it was as if he noticed illegal transactions being made everywhere. One time, a turbaned official had come to pay the hospital a visit and seeing in his office a few framed papyruses representing images of the Ancient Egyptian world, had warned against forgeries, hinting at genuine treasure to which he alone possessed the key to acquiring. Another time, at a *gahwa baladi*, old Egyptian café where he stopped after visiting a patient, an *effendi*, gentlemanly native, sitting next to him had, just by chance, possessed a wonderful scarab in his pocket for sale.

Phares drove for a few hours more to Assiut, where he booked into a hotel for the night. He was due to meet the patrol at dawn. They would ride by Jeep to Kharga Oasis and from there, would continue their journey by camel to Dakhla.

He didn't sleep well, aware that he'd had little time to prepare for this mission. It had been thrust upon him so suddenly, and he was aware of his own lack of experience. There would be guns involved and although he had once shot his ageing, rheumatic horse to put him out of his misery, an exchange of fire with other men would be an altogether different matter. Not only was he in the business of preserving lives, he was also concerned that his relative lack of experience might be fatal as he had no doubt the smugglers were properly equipped.

It was still very early when Phares finally decided to get up. The moon had long since paled to a wan ghost with the approach of day and a chill, almost cold breeze blew freshly from the desert. He bathed, shaved and dressed before ringing for the hotelier to bring up a cup of coffee, a few slices of *shamsy* bread and some *gibna adima*, a type of feta cheese. He ate standing at his bedroom window, waiting for the sunrise, preparing himself mentally and physically for the long, strenuous journey.

As he drove in his Jeep to the meeting place, somehow the sight of the broad river, brightening slowly beneath the rosy sky, brought him a small measure of tranquillity. For so many centuries the Nile had flowed between the palm-fringed banks, once the highway of a great civilisation and now the waterway for the agricultural commerce of his country. To Phares, the river was the symbol of eternity; as he watched the water move endlessly but without haste, he sensed death was not the end for man.

The call of the muezzin sounded from the minarets and rooftops of the city, while the boats began to move up and down the broad waterway. Big ones laden with grain floated downstream or tacked from side to side against the stiff breeze of early morning. The more cumbersome rafts began to move about slowly, clumsily, here and there.

Just as the last lingering call died away from some distant minaret, Phares glanced across at the river and saw a felucca carrying a group of men skim past, hugging the bank. The occupants looked to be white-robed Sudanese and he guessed immediately who they were. They must be on their way to picking up their Jeep and the two guides. A shiver of apprehension mixed with excitement ran up the young doctor's spine: the adventure was beginning.

Phares met with the remainder of the patrol outside Assiut, on the edge of the desert. The tallest of the white-robed men, the scarf of his turban covering the lower part of his face, introduced himself as Captain Charles Montgomery. Phares could see he was roughly the same age as himself, with lightly tanned skin over high cheekbones and a long aquiline nose, the whiter crow's feet around his alert blue eyes suggesting a temperament normally quick to laughter. There was something in his face that Phares found trustworthy and part of him relaxed slightly. The guides, also dressed in white *galaleeb*, had joined the Sudanese and he bowed to the assembled group with a greeting, '*Salam aleykom.*'

Montgomery shook Phares's hand firmly. 'Good to meet you, Doctor Pharaony. We appreciate your help.'

'It's been quite an education so far,' Phares murmured. 'Though, to be frank, I'm keener on using a scalpel than I am a gun.'

Montgomery laughed robustly, a reaction that had a further calming effect on him. 'Hopefully, it won't come to that, old chap. We're not expecting you to fight like an army pro.'

'Good to know. And if anyone gets wounded, you can be sure I'll be able to stitch them up satisfactorily.'

Another boisterous laugh from Montgomery. Grinning, he slapped Phares on the shoulder. 'Right, we'd better get moving. Let me introduce you to the rest of the party, then we can go over the details of the mission.'

Ten minutes later, as they climbed into the back of the Jeep behind the two guides, Montgomery handed Phares a rifle: 'I know I said you can leave the firepower to us, but you'd better have one of these just in case.'

Phares merely nodded, and they started on the long journey to Kharga.

*    *    *

The sun, high in the sky, was beating down on the eight figures on camels as they wound their way through the huge rocky spurs punctuating the desert sands on the last stretch of their journey.

Having swapped their Jeeps for camels, which had been waiting for them at Kharga, Phares and his men were finally nearing Dakhla. This was a place that had been used by smugglers for centuries. The Dakhla Oasis had been an important transit point for the desert caravans for over three thousand years. It had always been considered the southern and western Gate of Egypt, connecting it to southern Africa through Darb El Arbeen, the Forty-Day Way, a long caravan route for the transportation and trade of ivory, spices, gold, wheat and slaves, which took forty days to traverse through the desert.

Phares watched the passing sand dunes, his earlier weariness now replaced by adrenaline, knowing every track of man and beast on the few existing caravan roads interested the guards. He had learnt by mixing with the Bedouins that all tracks in open wastes where there was neither grazing nor water were significant. It was an axiom in the desert that the camel is slow and the Bedouin disdainful of time, therefore the least indication of speed in the tracks raised suspicion. Furthermore, it made sense that smugglers would only choose the caravan road because they'd know that in using it, their movements would soon be obliterated by the tracks of subsequent caravans.

A whistle went up as one of the guides suddenly brought his camel to a halt, pointing to some discoloured lines in the sand fifty yards away. He slid off the beast and went over to inspect them more closely, then beckoned the others over.

'Old tracks of a convoy,' the guide said. Phares and Montgomery were down on one knee, peering at the sand. 'Camels that have been watered here very quickly.' The guide pointed to faint pits in the sand. 'A lot of Bedouins too.'

The tracks themselves were almost completely covered by a dusting of sand, but Phares could see here and there straight lines of different hues only just visible. He and Montgomery, with the guide, followed the lines to the lee of the hill.

'You can tell by the tracks that it came this way a few weeks ago,' the guide told them, 'probably on their way to Qena. A very large convoy, over twenty men and twice as many camels.'

'And now they'll be on their way back.' Montgomery cursed quietly. 'That's more than we bargained for.'

'Well, at least we'll have the element of surprise,' said Phares dryly. 'And look,' he pointed to an old tower standing near a ridge of rocks not far away, 'we've got cover. What more could we ask for?'

The old tower, built no doubt by some chieftain of olden days as a stronghold from which to espy his enemies riding over the desert, was surrounded by a low wall made of mud hardened by the harsh desert sun into a rocklike substance. The men walked through the enclosure to the tower. Phares pointed, drawing Montgomery's attention to the crumbling masonry. By exercising a little care, it would surely be possible to climb up the outside walls to the remains of a flat platform near the top, from which could be obtained a good view of the desert beyond the sandhills and rocky outcrops.

The guards split up and chose the best spots to crouch in, vantage points behind the low enclosure wall or among the rocks, either of which would offer not only cover from enemy fire but a view of the track. Phares climbed cautiously up the ruined tower, armed with a pair of powerful field glasses through which he gazed eagerly southwards, in the wild hope of spotting the illicit caravan on its way into the heart of the desert.

Now it was a case of waiting.

Less than an hour later, Phares spotted a dark line of figures on the horizon, moving towards them. Scrambling down the tower to alert the others, he ran to join Montgomery, who had his back against a low ridge of rock, his gaze fixed on the track and the approaching camel train.

'It's them, got to be,' Montgomery murmured.

As the convoy grew closer, Phares counted twenty-six men riding on camels, the lower half of their faces covered by their turbans. Almost all had rifles slung across their backs. Interspersed among the riders, the rest of the dromedaries were laden with packs.

At Montgomery's signal, shots rang out as the guards fired continuous rounds at the convoy, sending the riders leaping from their camels on to the sand and running for cover behind rocks. Some were shielded by their animals as they ran with them, while others fired shots in retaliation.

Under the cover of fire from the Sudanese guards, Phares and Montgomery led two others with them, zigzagging across the boulder-strewn sand in the direction of the rocks behind which the smugglers had retreated.

Phares threw himself down as a bullet streaked past his ear. Montgomery grabbed his shoulder and pulled him behind a small sandhill. Raising their rifles to their shoulders, together they joined the other guards, firing at anything that moved in and around the outcrop of rock. Phares found it all too easy once he got started; it didn't feel that different from a game shoot, as long as he didn't think about their quarry being human.

Eventually all was quiet. Two camels lay dead in the sand, but the smugglers had completely vanished into the desert as though they had never been there.

Phares and Montgomery returned to the abandoned convoy of camels – thirty animals stood laden with antiquities, rifles and ammunition. Only now did Phares sling his rifle across his back. 'We didn't get a single one of them,' he told Montgomery, wiping the sweat from his brow.

Montgomery squinted into the distance, patting Phares on the back. 'Oh, they'll be back, don't you worry. We'll just have to be ready for them.'

'We'll be heavily outnumbered,' answered Phares, 'though at least we have most of their rifles.'

'In the meantime, we'd better get this lot moving. The longer we hang about, the quicker they'll be able to regroup. Once they put the word out, who knows how many others in their operation will come to boost their numbers.'

Phares noticed a furrow of worry had crept between Montgomery's brows. It was the first time he'd seen anything disturb the officer's otherwise habitually cheery countenance. Needing no further prompting, he set to work with the guards efficiently to gather the scattered camels to form a movable train.

Once they were ready to leave, Montgomery came to stand beside him. 'Hard to get things done in this heat,' he observed, wiping his brow. 'These white robes are a godsend. Can't see how you could survive in the desert wearing anything else.'

Phares leaned over and scrutinised the map while the officer outlined the route they'd have to take. 'The most dangerous bit is this gorge,' he said, pointing it out to Montgomery. Being familiar with the seven oases of the Western Desert, he knew this was the quickest route back. 'You realise this will take us a couple of hours to reach?'

Montgomery glanced at him, his frown deepening. 'We'll just need to be on our guard. The rock face either side of that gorge gives us nowhere to hide if they were to ambush us there.'

It was clear there was no other way of proceeding. Montgomery clearly knew the risk, but staying put was not an option.

Phares nodded grimly. 'Right, let's go. We need to get out of there before dark. Let's get on with it.'

\*     \*     \*

The first part of their journey had been uneventful. The camels were biddable and there had been little sign of life along the sun-baked desert track. Phares scanned the landscape of wind-worn rock formations and felt its barren beauty. Fluttering above, he watched vultures circling, marring the glass-blue sky like swirls of ash, their cawing the only sound in this immeasurable expanse.

*Awaiting their next meal,* he thought grimly to himself. *Most probably some animal carcass lying not too far away.*

He consoled himself that at least they had plenty of water. Along the way, he and Montgomery had spoken little and now they lapsed into uneasy and watchful silence as their caravan moved towards the limestone gorge. Its walls grew taller as they progressed into it, until at some point it seemed to Phares that the heights were bearing down on them. The sharp rock scintillated in the sun, accentuating the dizzying effect as he looked from left to right, his gaze attempting to follow the line at the top of the great escarpment on both sides, as well as the cracks and crevices in the limestone walls.

They heard the men before they saw anything. A rock dislodged, the scuff of a heel against the scree, a flash of white clothing, but it was enough. Realising they were sitting ducks, in an instant reflex Phares gestured to their Sudanese companions, waving them down. A warning swiftly followed by Montgomery's peremptory command:

'Get down! Find cover!'

Other than small knee-high ridges of rock and the odd boulder, there was little cover to be had. Phares instantly dismounted from his camel and ran for it, following Montgomery to a buttress-like rock protruding from the side of the gorge. Barely six-foot wide and only shoulder height, it would be enough for the moment, Phares thought as he crouched behind it, cocking his rifle. Even so, it was clear that they were trapped in the neck of a bottle, unable to go forward or retreat. At least Montgomery had checked that each man had a belt well stocked with ammunition.

As soon as the thought flitted into his mind it was met by a loud volley of gunfire coming from both sides of the gorge. Their assailants had the advantage of looking down on them from a height, but Phares and Montgomery were tucked into the cliff face, making them difficult targets to access. Their attackers would need to descend the rockface to come closer and then it would be up to their own small group to pick them off, one by one. At least, that was the hope. There was little point in firing wildly if they couldn't see their opponents: it would only use up bullets they could ill afford to waste.

Phares was surprised to find that he was icy calm. It wasn't the first time he had been under pressure – his training in emergency rooms had prepared him well for that, though his own life had never actually been at risk. His ears and eyes were sharpened by the extreme danger they faced now. Adrenaline gave him a feeling almost of invincibility.

'I can see one of them,' hissed Montgomery in a low whisper. 'Cover me, will you? I'll head for that next rock, I'll have visibility from there.'

Phares gave a curt nod and his companion took off, zigzagging as he ran, bent almost double, while Phares fired again and again, covering the officer.

Moments later, Montgomery's new position having been secured, Phares had the grim satisfaction of seeing their assailant tumbling down the rocky scree, killed with a bullet to the head. *Montgomery must be a crack shot*, he thought to himself, relieved that the British had at least thought to send one of their best marksmen on this mission.

Just at that moment, out of the corner of his eye he saw a swift movement. One of the smugglers had moved soundlessly into a position whereby he had a view of Montgomery's back. Without time to think, Phares ran out into the open, firing as he went. He saw his friend's startled face flick round, just as his assailant took a shot at him, but Phares got there first, his bullet catching the man in the shoulder, forcing him to shoot wide so that he missed Montgomery, his own bullet ricocheting off the rock. Another shot from Phares, and the man keeled over backwards.

This time it was Montgomery's turn to cover him as three or more assailants turned their fire on Phares. Shots whistled past his head as he hurtled full tilt back to the jutting limestone rock that he was fast beginning to think of as his friend and saviour.

Ears ringing, Phares didn't at first notice that the noise of gunfire had amplified. When he did realise it, he had only one thought: *More smugglers have come to join them. We're done for …*

He mentally prepared himself to go down fighting – keep it up for as long as he could – but then as he reached for his ammunition belt, he realised with a sickening sense of dread that he was out of cartridges. His mind frantically sought a next move, and then he saw Montgomery leave his position. Running in a crouch, the officer ran back in the direction of Phares, who was astonished to see a grin plastered over the man's face.

'We've got them on the run, old chap! One of our patrols – must have heard the gunshots and come to investigate.'

Indeed, Phares could hear the rifle fire receding audibly as the smugglers started to scatter. His spirits surged as reality hit him. All being well, he'd live to see the end of this; he'd live to take Aida in his arms. Relief washed over him and with it, a deep exhaustion. So far, adrenaline had kept him alert, but without it now, he felt in an imminent state of near-collapse.

'You go and check out what's happening. It's imperative we don't let them get away this time,' he told Montgomery. 'I'll join you, but first I need to pick up more ammunition. I'm completely out.'

'Righto. Though watch yourself, there may be one or two smugglers still lurking around.'

Phares headed into the open, making his way cautiously towards the camel train, which amazingly was still intact, the dromedaries waiting patiently for the return of their masters. The Sudanese guards had lived up to their indomitable reputation and were now in hot pursuit of the smugglers, determined not to let them get away a second time. For now, Phares was alone.

The sun was fading as dusk drew closer, staining the blue sky with a purple haze and lengthening the shadows of the dromedaries on the sand. As he approached the camels, there was a curious unsettled wave of movement in the line, accompanied by thick nasal calls, which Phares put down to his disturbing them. He made a few clicks with his tongue, mimicking the sound the Bedouins made to calm them, and proceeded to unstrap one of the packs he knew contained a stock of rifle cartridges.

He turned his back and in that moment sensed a motion behind him, a disturbance in the air; he jerked sideways and spun round just in time to see the glitter of a blade as it flashed past his shoulder. A Bedouin's body, lithe and whippet-quick, pushed into the thrust, grunting, the heft of his torso colliding with the camel's side. A sound filled Phares's ears, a screech emitted from the throat of the dromedary as the blade sliced into its haunch, missing Phares by inches, and then the Bedouin turned.

The scarf that had been wound around the man's face had slipped, and Phares saw two pale yellow eyes narrowed in hatred … a gaze he recognised at once: Prince Shams Sakr El Din.

The prince recovered himself quickly and stood back on the balls of his feet, ready to dart forward again, knife in hand.

'Prepare yourself, Pharaony. *Allah* won't be so kind a second time.'

Phares's eyes never once left the blade as he replied, 'Ah, Prince, so you finally show yourself. You surprise me. I thought you paid others to do your bidding when it comes to taking such risks. From what I've heard, you prefer lying on a sofa, having the women of your harem rub oil into you than getting your hands dirty.'

Both men were tall and strong, but his opponent had the upper hand, not to mention the only weapon. Phares sensed he had only one option now: to try and rile him with words must be his best hope and one look at the prince's seething face meant he knew he was on the right track.

'When something as valuable as this is at stake I make it my business to guard it personally,' snarled the prince. 'Shame you didn't do that with the El Masri girl you were making such a play for. Such rare beauty and a fiery spirit too. She put up a good fight, I must say.' He began circling Phares, raising the knife in front of him. 'She would have been my finest treasure. Shame.'

Phares clenched his jaw but kept his expression impassive, his eyes darting to the surrounding rocks for any possible weapon and back to the knife in Sakr El Din's hand. He tsked. 'You should have known Aida would never have lowered herself with the likes of you,' he chided, all the time slowly mirroring his opponent's movements.

The prince let out a harsh laugh but his eyes narrowed. '*The likes of me*? Well, after her little sojourn with me, I suppose the great Pharaony name won't be sullied by a match with *Mademoiselle* El Masri. The girl's reputation was shaky to start with … now, I imagine, it's in tatters. No Egyptian of any rank will want her. She might as well go back to England. They can have her with our blessing, eh?'

Phares felt his rage rising. 'Only a *gaban*, coward would behave as you did. As for reputations … after your countrymen hear of this, you won't find anyone in Egypt prepared to call you friend. Not even your master, El Kébir. He had you in his pocket but will do nothing to protect you now. Come now, Prince, you have nothing to lose. Tell me his name.'

The prince's face tightened in a snarl. 'Enough, Pharaony! At least I will have one less enemy after I've slit your throat. My ancestors will be satisfied I have ended the curse and restored the family honour at last. They'll rest easy in their tomb while you rot in hell!'

At this, he lunged at Phares, who darted back from the deadly blade. The knife caught the side of his robe, grazing the skin underneath, but it was a shallow flesh wound, barely a scratch. The prince recovered himself quickly and turned to make another slash at him, but Phares caught the other man's knife arm with his fist, a sharp blow that dislodged the dagger from his grip. The prince didn't try to retrieve it but threw himself on Phares, grappling him to the ground.

The sky above the gorge was now a burning orange and Sakr El Din's face lit by the fiery rays of the dying sun. Any semblance of suave, civilised sophistication had vanished, replaced by a mask of hatred and almost maniacal savagery.

On his back and winded, Phares felt the hard grip of fingers around his throat. His shoulders held down forcibly by the prince's knees, he found himself pinned to the hot desert sand while his attacker's fingers did their best to squeeze the life out of him. Phares refused to be beaten; he wasn't about to let Sakr El Din's slitted yellow eyes be his last sight on earth. His vision blurred a flame colour, spotted with black, as his right hand scrabbled frantically on the granular, hot surface of the sand.

'I'll tell Aida you said goodbye,' growled his opponent, a note of triumph in his voice.

The tips of Phares's scrabbling fingers met something hard … cylindrical. The handle of the dagger. Another desperate stretch and they closed around it.

The prince leaned down further and whispered, 'I'll enjoy visiting your woman one last time.'

Mustering all his strength, Phares seized his chance and gave a sudden and forceful jerk of his right shoulder. For a brief second the prince was unseated, his knees losing their hold, though his fingers still gripped Phares's throat. But now Phares had his right arm freed, and in that instant, with a roar of fury, he took a swing.

Above him, as the blade met flesh, the prince's face froze, eyes popping, and he gave a soft, surprised grunt as the blade penetrated the sinew of his neck. His fingers loosened their hold on Phares's throat, and for a moment the Bedouin prince sat atop him in this frozen state of startlement, before Phares gave a violent shove to topple him.

Kneeling above the dying Bedouin, Phares gripped him by the robes covering his chest. The words when they came were a hoarse, strangled whisper: 'Who is El Kébir? Tell me! Give us a name and we'll let you preserve some of that so-called family honour.'

The prince, his yellow eyes rolling back in his head, was unable to oblige, giving only a whistling sigh as he breathed his last.

*    *    *

When Phares finally arrived back at Hathor, it was two in the morning. Over-exhausted, he was now too keyed up to sleep, so sank down in a rattan sofa on the terrace, smoking and listening to the sounds of the night. The mission had been a triumph – of sorts. They had succeeded in capturing a handful of smugglers but he very much doubted any of them would have a clue as to the whereabouts or name of the kingpin they called El Kébir. With a man like that keeping to the shadows their only hope had been to get Prince Shams Sakr El Din to speak.

Phares ground his butt into an ashtray in frustration and immediately lit another cigarette. The homecoming of the two patrols bearing their prisoners had been greeted with approbation by the Embassy and noisy alacrity by the Egyptian police and government officials. Reflexively, his hand went to the cut on his side. Phares had never taken a life, only tried to save them, yet he found it hard to feel too much remorse about what he had done. He wondered how the news of the prince's death would be greeted at Wahat El Nakheel when eventually they found out. Would there be shrill, quavering cries of joy, *zaghareet*, behind the screened windows of their *mashrabiyas*? Would sheep be slaughtered for a festival? He imagined they might be happy to know the smugglers had been caught, but would they mourn the loss of their master? Phares, for one, did not.

In the meantime, Montgomery had told him that the powers that be would have to keep the prince's death under wraps for as long as they possibly could. It might be weeks until the news filtered out, and Phares was cautioned to keep it close to his chest or it might compromise the investigation. Still, all that could wait for the debrief with the Embassy.

He let out a deep sigh; he should take himself off to bed, but his mind was too active. With the capture of the smugglers, he'd hoped to get to the bottom of who had framed Ayoub El Masri with the stolen Nefertari statue. For Aida's sake he wanted the answer – it would be the best wedding gift of all, because it would lift the dark cloud that seemed to hover over their happiness. She needed – *they* needed – the truth brought to light. But time was marching on, and he was still no nearer to finding it. Perhaps Alastair would find some leads. If they could track down Souma Hassanein, they would surely be a step closer.

Meanwhile, the preparations for their marriage ceremony were underway. Camelia had promised to wait until the day before the wedding to go over to Karawan House and surprise Aida with details of their plans. For the first time that day, Phares smiled, thinking of Aida looking radiant and surrounded by all those clucking, boisterous women at her henna ritual, a ceremony that had almost disappeared among the Coptic Europeanised families, but was still kept among the *fellahin*. He stubbed out his cigarette and walked inside. There was plenty to be happy about, he told himself. Aida had promised to be his – and he wanted above all things to marry her – and his mission was over, at least for the time being.

He was pleased with the results the team had achieved in Kharga, but then again, he couldn't fool himself that the smugglers' network was destroyed. It would take more than that. Egyptian police knew how to make people talk, yet the Bedouins were tough men, slippery and clever like desert foxes, and it would be a mistake to underestimate them. This illicit commerce had been going on for a long time, Alastair had said, and it wouldn't be easy to drag the facts out of such hardened criminals. Antiquities were by no means the only merchandise these men traded in. Drugs, armaments during the war … they were up to every dirty trade one could think of – an utterly ruthless and undiscriminating lot.

Still, for now Phares resolved to put these concerns aside. He badly needed to sleep and the only sensible thing would be to wait until he was mentally refreshed before once again turning them over in his mind. Besides, in a few days he would finally be making Aida his wife, and that was all that mattered.

# CHAPTER 13

The wedding preparations had to be accomplished in only a week – an unusually brief time in Egypt – but the frantic pace seemed only to add to the number of festive elements involved. Uncle Naguib and Aunty Nabila organised work parties to make several hundred *bonbonnières*, which, given more time, would have been ordered from Groppi's tea shop. In addition, small, solid silver dishes had been bought from Zaghloul, a famous silver shop at the Musky, as gifts for the wedding guests. Each was to be filled with sugared almonds set around a chocolate truffle, the dainty parcel wrapped in white tulle tied with a satin ribbon set with a pink rosebud.

*Dada* Amina was beside herself with excitement and kept filling the house with incense to keep away the evil eye. She fussed and cooed and was full of wise advice: 'You will be living in your husband's home with his sister, his father and his aunt, who is an *aggraba*, a scorpion,' she declared resolutely. 'Don't let anybody come between you and him, *ya binty*, and don't listen to gossip. People are always envious of one's good luck.' And then again: 'Be content in your husband's company. Listen to him and obey him. Contentment brings peace of mind, and listening to your husband and obeying him pleases *Allah*.' And also: 'Never disclose a single one of his secrets and never disobey any of his orders, because if you disclose his secrets how can you ever feel safe from his betraying you? And if you disobey him, his heart will be filled with hatred towards you.'

Although Aida laughed whenever her old nanny began her lectures, she was grateful for her care and counselling. She was deeply fond of her, despite the woman's overprotectiveness and often simplistic remarks but even though *Dada* Amina was an uneducated woman, Aida had to admit that she was a sagacious old bird who had often persuaded her in the past to do the right thing.

Apart from the dress and the bridesmaids, Aida herself had nothing to organise. In Egypt, unlike England, it was the custom for all the planning and arrangements to be taken on by the groom's family. She had decided to wear her mother's wedding dress, a real masterpiece of ivory chiffon banded with gold lamé and pearls, designed in 1920 by the House of Worth. When she took it out of the tissue paper in its box to try it on, she found to her delight that it still looked new, and not only that: it fitted her to perfection. Her heart was suddenly filled with a nostalgic melancholy as she thought of her parents who wouldn't be there to attend her special day.

The wedding was to take place at Luxor's main cathedral in Sharia Maabad al-Karnak, Temple of Karnak Street, and *Abouna* Youssef, an old family friend who had christened both Aida and Phares, was to perform the ceremony. Aida would have liked Camelia to be her maid of honour, but she had yet to get hold of her friend, and so in the meantime, she had spoken to Aunt Nabila and decided to have five of the Bisharas' grandchildren, whom Aida had sent to Cléo at Shemlah in Cairo to get outfitted.

Still, notwithstanding her old nanny's bustling attentions, she was somewhat surprised at *Dada* Amina's relative calm. If Phares was away, as Aida presumed, and Camelia was confined to her room, who was dealing with the main preparations? A hushed atmosphere prevailed in the household and although the staff obviously knew about the wedding, they never spoke of it in front of her; indeed, whenever Aida entered the kitchen all conversation ceased abruptly and they continued about their work with sheepish expressions on their faces. Aida had also noticed that *Osta* Ghaly disappeared for long hours during the day, and she had a suspicion that he was making frequent visits to Hathor, although that, at least, was no real surprise. It was considered a kind of *cuisinier*'s etiquette for all good cooks to help one another with the preparation of their buffets at a wedding or a similar occasion, all the food being home-cooked by chefs employed by rich families in the neighbourhood.

The week passed in a flash, during which Aida walked around in a tremulous, glittering dream. Although he never came in person to Karawan House and there were no notes from him, Phares sent daily boxes of presents and bouquets of flowers for his bride-to-be in the week preceding the wedding. There were evening dresses, delicate and elaborate dresses of crepe de chine for morning wear, trailing silk and lace gowns for the afternoon. He sent slippers, and shoes with four-inch heels, and gossamer stockings and fine silk underwear trimmed with lace and bunches of rosebuds. His taste was impeccable. Aida had tried to ring him to thank him, but he was apparently away, and Camelia was still keeping to her room, she'd been told.

So, it was with some surprise that on the eve of the wedding, Aida received *Dada* Amina's announcement that Camelia was in the drawing room to see her.

Her friend, although looking a little drawn, greeted her effusively: '*Mabruk*, congratulations, Aida! You can't imagine how happy I am that you and Phares have finally decided to admit your feelings for each other and tie the knot.'

Aida instinctively rushed to her friend and drew her into a hug. 'My goodness, Camelia, *habibti*, how are you after your terrible ordeal?' She stepped away, holding Camelia's shoulders in both hands and scrutinising her with concern. 'I was told that you were in a depressive mood and wouldn't leave your room.'

Camelia waved her hand dismissively and laughed. 'Ah my dear, but that was the only way I could get on with the preparations for your wedding.' Then she laughed, her beautiful almond-shaped dark eyes twinkling mischievously. 'Phares and I wanted it to be a surprise.'

Aida joined in with her friend's merry spirit. 'Oh, how lovely! Thank you. I did feel that something was going on. *Dada* Amina was too quiet and *Osta* Ghaly kept disappearing after lunch every day, which he's never done before.'

Camelia linked her arm with Aida's and they moved to one of the sofas. 'I've been organising a henna night for tonight. I thought it might amuse you.'

'Goodness, I thought that sort of ceremony had gone out of fashion with the likes of us a long time ago.'

'Well, Phares and I thought you'd enjoy it. *Dada* Amina has prepared her own henna recipe and her cousin will paint the henna drawings on your hands and feet, if you like. If not, you can just have your fingernails and toenails coloured, like the pharaohs, a sort of royal Ancient Egyptian manicure.'

Aida beamed at her friend. 'Oh, thank you, Camelia, you're a real sister to me.' Her expression became more serious as they sat down. 'But tell me, what happened with you?'

A shadow passed over the beautiful face of her friend, who hesitated before answering. 'There was a *kapsa*, a raid, on Youssef's house. A large group of us were there to visit Sami, and also for a reunion.' She frowned. 'There's a mole in the midst of our party, but God only knows who they are.'

'My poor darling! Did they hurt you?'

Camelia's dark gaze turned to her, looking suddenly haunted. 'No, not me … not the women. But they dragged Sami out of bed, and I haven't had any news about him since then.' At that, her face puckered, her eyes filling with tears.

Aida took her hand. 'Can't Phares help? He seems to have some clout. He's the one who got you out, isn't he?'

Camelia shook her head sadly. 'Yes, my brother was instrumental in securing my release, and for that I owe him my deepest gratitude. I've promised him that I won't involve myself with the party any longer, much as it pains me. I tried asking him to find out about Sami too, but he won't hear anything of it. He's very angry with me, not least because apparently I was the reason he missed your lunch appointment at the Gezireh Sporting Club and for you going off in a huff to Shams Sakr El Din's party.' She shot her friend a tentative, reproachful look. 'By the way, I know I'm hardly one to speak, but that was a very unwise thing to do.'

'I know, and it's something I regret bitterly.' Aida chose not to tell Camelia about Nairy Paplosian and what she had seen at the hospital. She was trying desperately to forget that whole episode and start afresh. 'I acted foolishly and I've learnt my lesson.' She squeezed her friend's hand. 'I'm sorry it's caused you problems too.'

Camelia brushed away the dampness on her cheek. 'Well, let's not talk about all that. Both of us should put our troubles behind us now. Happy days are ahead for you and we must concentrate on those.'

Aida smiled warmly. 'I presume we're having the henna party here tonight.' Then, glancing at her watch, she exclaimed, 'It's already past ten. If I have to organise a dinner, it doesn't leave me much time. How many women are coming?'

'We'll only be about ten or twelve ladies, and your five bridesmaids of course. But you mustn't worry about dinner. Our cooks have been busy and everything will be delivered tonight.' Camelia looked sheepish. 'I've had to invite Isis Geratly. Phares insisted out of obligation. Our families have been friends for a long time and she is his best anaesthetist. I think Isis is very disappointed that Phares is not marrying her and frankly, he's afraid she might make trouble at the hospital. Although he never promised her anything, there was a lot of gossip about them … you know how it is here.'

Aida sighed. 'Yes, I know.'

How many women had been hoping that Phares would choose them to be his life's companion? After all her procrastination and foolish behaviour, she was lucky that he still wanted her to be his wife.

'It's going to be quite a big wedding,' Camelia continued. 'We've been invited to so many over the years, and you know the saying, *salaf wa dain*, a debt to be paid. We'll be about five hundred people in all.'

It suddenly hit home to Aida what a huge occasion it was going to be and her stomach fluttered nervously. 'It's amazing how you've been able to organise all this in less than a week.'

'Well, *Abouna* Youssef has seen both you and Phares grow up, and he knows you well enough to be certain there are no surprises there. He's a good man, and he adores Phares.'

'How did you manage to invite everyone? Five hundred people is a large number.'

*Kyrie* Vassilis at the Musky had the printing of the invitation cards done in twenty-four hours and *Osta* Fathi distributed them in Cairo. As for the guests who live in Luxor, I made the telephone calls myself and everybody has accepted.'

'I'm really touched, *habibti*. I don't know what to say.'

Camelia laughed. 'Then don't say anything, my dear, and enjoy! Phares is going to be busy too, setting up a tent, *siwan*, for the servants. It's a *baraka* … everyone will bless your union.'

'You've thought of everything.'

'It's been exciting and fun. Besides, it has stopped me from brooding about Sami and the party.'

'By the way, where is Phares?'

Camelia shrugged. 'I'm not sure at the moment but one minute he's in Luxor, the next he's off to Cairo. It seems he can't stay still. I think waiting for the wedding, and to see you, is driving him mad. He believes that absence truly does make the heart grow fonder.'

Aida laughed softly, remembering their meeting in the garden only a few days before. 'Yes, he intimated something of the kind the last time I saw him.'

Camelia stood up. 'Well, I'd better leave you now. Do you need anything from me?'

'No, nothing, thanks. You've done plenty.'

Aida accompanied her friend to her car and after waving her goodbye, went in search of the gardener in order to discuss which flowers he would pick for her to arrange in vases at the house. It was all very exciting, and she couldn't wait to see Phares the next day. He had been constantly in Aida's mind all week. In the early morning, when the air had a heavenly coolness and earth and sky were veiled in trembling white mist, he was there; and in the burning afternoons when the birds slept and the air shimmered under the sun he was there, as well as in the hushed and breathless evening when the leaves made fantastic shadows on the paths and the flowers stood white and motionless in the moonlight and the air was so sweet, every breath was a separate and distinct delight.

But it was mostly at night in her dreams that he came to her, a fascinating, naked Adonis, longing and hungry for her, his eyes sparkling wickedly. It was shameful how hot, how wet, she was for him each time, imagining him leaning on his arms above her, holding his weight tantalisingly away from her body, making her arch upwards and wriggle her hips towards his with her need to feel his strength, his hardness, his heat. Invariably she'd wake up gasping, still panting desperately in the midst of the sensual explosion that rocked her, tangled in a heap of bed linen, hugging her pillow.

Very soon now he would claim her, possess her. If only it might be as a man in love, and not only a lover experiencing simply that carnal desire.

Aida's breast lifted on a sigh. Phares would enslave her, but never love her. Their intimacy would be ecstatic, but he would take her only for pleasure … and just for a second, her heart ached.

\*     \*     \*

Aida spent a long time preparing for her henna night. As she bathed, she thought about the meaning of the ritual. It meant much more than any custom involved in a European hen night. She reminded herself that this was a marriage rite in which the bride symbolically left her identity as daughter in her father's house behind, entering into a new life stage as a wife whose life revolves around her husband's family. Furthermore, the red henna had an association with blood, her transformation from girlhood to womanhood, where her body became an object belonging to her husband. Aida did not much like the connotations behind the ritual, but she loved the theatrical quality of the ceremony and was looking forward to it. She didn't want to think more deeply about 'belonging' to Phares – it would only cause a confusing division in her mind, between herself as a modern Westernised woman and the one born into these ancient traditions.

Wearing old clothes, *Dada* Amina sat quietly most of the morning in the covered courtyard behind the kitchen preparing the greenish paste from her own recipe, mixing the henna powder with herbs and oil of clove, while chips of sandalwood burning in a tiny earthenware bowl scented the place. Aida had noticed the inconspicuous little bush from which the henna was produced, rather like privet, in a corner of *Dada* Amina's favourite courtyard. Without the paste applied to the tips of her fingers and the soles of her feet, no *fellaha* or Bedouin woman, no matter how poor, would feel properly dressed for her wedding day.

At six o'clock the *belláneh*, an expert in the art of sugaring, arrived at Karawan House. This method of waxing the larger as well as more sensitive parts of the body – the legs and arms, armpits and private parts – with a mixture of sugar, water and lemon was traditional in Egypt, especially before a wedding. Expertly exfoliated in this way, the skin becomes supremely smooth, soft and silken. Afterwards, perfumed oils were rubbed into the skin; no two fragrances ever alike as each woman made her own from pounded leaves and flowers, the recipes of which were a closely guarded secret. Aida had her own favourite scent, Elsa Schiaparelli's Le Roy Soleil. The Baccarat crystal fragrance bottle placed in a shell-shaped golden casket had been designed by Salvador Dalí to celebrate the end of the war. It was one of the presents Phares had sent her during their week of separation, along with an exquisite Bedouin dress woven with gold silken threads and fine seed pearls, which she would also wear tonight.

It was custom that the woman would have her toenails painted and adorn her feet with anklets, but wear no shoes – symbolic of her not leaving the house, but remaining in the harem. Aida had a couple of authentic ancient Egyptian gold anklets adorned with lapis, moonstone and turquoise, which she donned for the first time. She loved the chiming sound the jingling charms and singing bells made as she trod the ground lightly on tiptoes.

*Dada* Amina insisted on *kahalling* Aida's eyes, which she did by blackening the edge of the young woman's eyelids, both above and below the eyes, with kohl, a black powder the nanny produced by burning the shells of almonds. She applied it with a small, tapering blunt-ended probe from a beautifully engraved ivory kohl vessel that had belonged to Aida's grandmother.

By nine o'clock, Aida was ready to receive her guests. Despite her fairness and foreign looks, she could have stepped out of a famous Orientalist's painting, one by Édouard Richter or Carl Haag perhaps, dazzling in the light of all the Venetian chandeliers, sparkling like iridescent jewels. Beautiful blooms from the garden vivified the rooms with splashes of colour here and there, and a mixture of incense and the fragrance of flowers suffused them.

From the drawing room, Aida heard the women arrive and walk in procession around the outside of the house three times, chanting and carrying the bowl of henna paste, which they had set with five large candles in accordance with the old saying 'khamsa wa khumaysah', 'five fingers poked in the evil eye'.

On entering in their traditional kaftans, they were shown into the drawing room by Bekhit, the head servant. Aida breathed a sigh of relief, noticing immediately that Isis Geratly wasn't among the guests that made up the procession – she didn't want anything spoiling her enjoyment of the evening. It was with some relief too that she noticed that Aunt Halima did not have on her normally sour and miserable expression and instead was even pleasant to her, leading Aida to wonder whether Aunt Nabila had warned her to behave; still, she dearly hoped that Halima had had a change of heart and was now happy about this union.

Nabila started off the ritual by praying, while Aida sat as the young, unmarried virgin women walked in circles around her, holding candles. Once the prayers were over, everybody took a seat and Aunt Halima, who was taking Phares's mother's place for the ceremony, took some henna from a cup and tried to put it in Aida's palm. Following tradition, Aida then went through the motions of refusing to open her hand, which was symbolic of her asking for a commitment from the groom's family. The other then put a gold coin in her palm, communicating her acceptance of the responsibility to provide financial security for the new family. All this Aida conformed with willingly, accepting the coin and then the henna, and firmly putting aside in her head any of the modern implications of what these rituals symbolised.

Following this, the henna cup was passed from one guest to another, each of whom added a golden coin to the sticky paste and helped themselves to a lump of henna to colour their own palms. That being done, the guests sang folk songs and danced, and drank the delicate rose-petal *sharbat ward* cordial, while servants brought round plates of dried fruits, nuts and small plates of *mezzeh*.

While the guests indulged in the merriments, Nabawiya, *Dada* Amina's cousin, painted Aida's hands and feet with henna. Not wanting them to be overdone, Aida asked her to paint a sun on one hand and a moon on the other, and a couple of delicate geometric designs on her feet. While this was being done, she was fussed over by a bevy of young women, who busily provided her with small tidbits to eat and served her glasses of *sharbat* and lemonade. After Nabawiya had finished painting, Aida's hands and feet were wrapped in linen, which would be removed the next morning to reveal the beauty of the designs.

Camelia sang love songs, her voice lovely and melodious, accompanied by their neighbour Mariam on the piano. The others clapped and acted as a choir, while *Dada* Amina's neice, Magda, having tied her scarf tightly around her hips, performed a genteel version of the well-known Arabic belly dancing. Holding out a stick in front of her in both hands, she jerked her stomach up and down, her body rotating as she did so.

This joyous assembly continued their noisy merrymaking until the early hours when on Nabila's signal, they took their leave reluctantly. Kisses, hugs, *mabruks*, congratulations, filled the room until, finally, Aida was able to retire to her bedroom, exhausted but radiant, her heart full of dreams and love for Phares.

Tomorrow, she would finally be his.

*    *    *

The day of the wedding had arrived – bright and glowing, a perfect example of that still, exquisite weather that characterised this time of year. The Luxor skies were clear over the glistening Nile as the intense heat of the afternoon sun waned; beyond the El Masri property, the green fields appeared richly verdant and even the nearby slumbering villages with their dilapidated mud houses looked romantic, bathed in sunshine.

Radiant, despite the revelry of the night before, Aida descended the marble steps of Karawan House, her feet and hands adorned with her cousin's beautiful henna designs. She was surrounded by attendants: Uncle Naguib, who was to take the place of her father, her five bridesmaids, plus all the servants who wanted to wave her off. Just as she was about to get into the garlanded Bentley, a young *effendi* whom Aida had never seen before handed her a small yellow envelope. Perplexed, with a slightly strained look, she opened it. The scrawled message consisted of two lines.

'*Beware of the half-truths – you may have gotten hold of the wrong half. Ask Phares Pharaony where he spent these last two nights. It is no shame to be deceived, but it is if you are willing to stay with the deception.*'

The note was unsigned. Aida felt herself pale and swallowed hard, forcing back the tears welling up. Raising her eyes, she was about to ask the young messenger who it was who had sent him, only to find that he had disappeared.

'Anything wrong, *habibti*?' enquired Uncle Naguib. 'You've gone all pale. What was in that message?'

Although stunned by the contents of the note, Aida managed a weak smile and shook her head, refusing to let anything mar this day. 'Nothing, nothing, just a congratulatory note,' she murmured, disappearing quickly into the Bentley, which drove off immediately, leaving behind the *zaghareet*, the joyful trilling ululations from all the women.

A discreet phone call from Uncle Naguib to the *Omda*, Mayor of Luxor, had assured the closing off of certain streets leading to the cathedral. This was in keeping with the tradition that demanded the car carrying the bride should always turn to the right, thereby ensuring that she would always do the right thing after she was married.

The vehicle, escorted by a honking entourage of cars driven by Phares's friends, weaved its way through the streets of Luxor. Inside, Aida felt a hot stinging in her cheeks as she absorbed the meaning of the words delivered by the cryptic message. The build-up of emotion was almost more than she could bear, and for a wild moment she wanted to grab the wheel and wrench the car into the kerb, caring nothing for the consequences. But instead she calmed her racing heart and picked up her bouquet, burying her face in the cool, ferny orchids and roses and inhaling their scent. A faint image of Phares's concerned face as he scooped her up in his arms in the desert made her rationality return. The note had surely been written by someone who didn't truly have her best interests at heart, otherwise why hadn't they signed their name?

Still, the memory of Nairy Paplosian with Phares came rushing back to her in a series of vivid images: leaning over him at the fashion show; dancing with him later at Mina House, her body rubbing against his; and their kissing each other outside the hospital. Swift pain pierced through her, mingled with a melancholic sadness that made her want to scream and cry. The harrowing feelings remained locked up inside her, but it was as though all the dreamy excitement of the past week had been cruelly swiped away like a sudden thunderstorm on a beautiful summer's day.

Aida had just a moment's hesitation as she descended from the car. The priest *Abouna* Youssef appeared just then, coming forward to receive her from Uncle Naguib and deliver her to her future husband, as tradition dictated, in a symbolic gesture that mirrored God's bringing of Eve to Adam. As he took her slightly trembling hand and led her the few short steps to Phares, Aida knew her life was about to change for ever.

Her bridegroom was waiting for her, resplendent in his well-cut dark suit, a Hermès navy-coloured tie knotted with perfect precision under the tailored stiff collar of his crisp white shirt, a delicate white rose in his buttonhole. Aida's chest suddenly felt tight. Standing bronzed, tall and lithe, Phares looked nothing like the doctor he was. With his shock of black hair, slightly longer than usual, he had the appearance of one whom an artist would wish to immortalise in paint or marble. Was he nervous? Aida doubted it. Any fear and trepidation were hers and hers alone. But Camelia was there at the door, arranging Aida's trailing veil and smiling her congratulations and encouragement as though she knew what was going through her friend's head. Each carrying a candle, the five bridesmaids in their pink finery followed, symbols of the five wise virgins who had enough oil for their lamps as they processed at the wedding in Cana, Galilee.

Even if inside she did not feel as radiant as she should, at least Aida knew she looked the part. Her wedding dress was classic in style, superb in its detail, from the deep oval neckline down to the softly flowing skirt. The dress combined an acanthus leaf pattern with a four-and-a-half-yard scalloped antique lace train and veil, which she wore elegantly draped over her head. It was held in place by a Cartier orange-blossom tiara of small diamonds and pearls, given by Ayoub to Eleanor on their wedding day. The very perfection of the dress made Aida all the sadder for it was the kind of gown which any bride should be happy and eager to be married in.

A single strand of stunning pearls encircled her neck, a pair of baroque pearls adorned her ears, and the cascading bridal bouquet of stephanotis, white lace hydrangea, flannel flowers and white bougainvillea gave the final touch to the picture of innocence and purity that Aida portrayed as she stood for a few minutes before entering the cathedral while Camelia and the bridesmaids tidied up her fabulous train.

Her eyes finally met Phares's and he smiled down at her, his face gleaming with pride. 'You look stunning,' he said softly, his eyes crinkling slightly at the edges, caressing her features with a mixture of passion and tenderness.

She felt the breath tighten in her throat and looked away. She was acutely aware of his tall frame as he walked beside her, of his hand on her arm, but she didn't dare look back at him, keeping her eyes peeled to the entrance in front of her in case they gave away the turmoil within.

'Nervous, *chérie*?'

'Just a little,' she whispered, grateful that he had put her silence down to nervousness rather than guessing the true cause of her hesitation and confusion.

The priest and the chanting *shammamsa*, deacons, led the way into the cathedral. Stepping across the threshold, she began her slow walk up the aisle towards the altar on Phares's arm, followed by her elegant cortège of bridesmaids. As she did so, Aida felt certain that no other Pharaony bride could have entered into marriage with the same amount of dread and bitterness in her heart. The accompanying vocal music interspersed with cymbals and the triangle had always reminded her of the chorus of a pagan procession in the temples of Ancient Egypt as the pharaohs proceeded to worship their sun god. Today was no different, and its eerie, majestic sound gave her the unreal impression that this was all taking place in a dream.

The oak pews decorated with bouquets of white roses and tuberoses were crammed to capacity with locals who had known her since childhood, who were familiar with the scandal that had touched her father, who had for the most part condemned him, and whom she felt resented this marriage more than ever because they regarded Aida, being half British, as a foreigner. Not only this, but with that cloud still hanging over her because of the old scandal, they deemed her unsuitable to be the wife of one of the prize catches in the Coptic community. They looked at her with surreptitious curiosity, she knew; she could feel their eyes boring into her back as she moved along, wondering, surmising, their heads turning to gaze at her as she passed, and then quickly, almost guiltily, looking away, in case she read the disapproval in their eyes. As for her own eyes, she kept them fixed steadily on the great clusters of blooms massed at either side of the altar, her face set in a tight mask that betrayed not even a flicker of emotion.

The dying sun shone through the arched windows of the grand old cathedral with its coral pillars and Byzantine panelling. As Aida approached the altar steps, a last ray of sunshine began moving across the very stained-glass panel she had donated to the church before leaving for England eight years ago. It was one of many coloured panels gifted over the years by members of the rich Coptic families of Luxor to replace damaged ones. The orange light played upon Phares's head so that his dark hair took on the appearance of a fiery crown. Then, as she stood quaking by his side waiting for the ceremony to begin, the light progressed steadily across the inscribed glass, picking out each jewel-bright word etched on the pane so they felt seared upon her forehead: *Honi soit qui mal y pense* – Evil be to him who evil thinks.

She stared at it, transfixed. Was she not doing to Phares what these people had done to her father – judging him on the basis of questionable proof without giving him a chance to defend himself? Was she not letting her pride and jealousy gain the upper hand over her reasoning? 'The wanderer's tale awaits his arrival,' was a proverb that her wise Dada Amina often used to quote to her as a girl whenever Aida criticised a person behind their back without knowing the whole story.

Time moved in a series of impressions while the priest and chanting deacons blessed and celebrated the holy matrimony of the bride and groom in a royal manner. Everything had a mystique about it, from the azure haze of acacia wood incense and flickering candlelight to the opulent golden icons and statues of Jesus and Mary looking down on them.

As was customary, the ceremony of this two-thousand-year-old sacramental rite was conducted in Coptic and Ancient Greek. *Abouna* Youssef placed the priestly vestment over Phares – a reminder that the young doctor was now the priest in his own house, responsible for the spiritual wellbeing of his new family. Then he laid hands on Aida and Phares's heads, praying all envy, temptation and evil be cast away from them, thus making them one. Following this, he anointed them with holy olive oil and rings were exchanged, their right hands joined to secure their union. Finally, placing on each of them a crown fashioned from fine golden leather, which symbolised that they were now king and queen of their own small kingdom, *Abouna* Youssef gently pushed their heads together, indicating their mutual submission to each other.

Aida felt Phares's dark gaze upon her as they listened to the priest speak of submission of the wife to her husband, already presupposing the absolute love of the husband for his wife. Another wave of doubt shivered through her heart. These were profound words filled with meaning for couples whose hearts clamoured to be joined in holy wedlock and Aida wondered if those lovely ancient words had a significance for Phares or whether he was thinking they could never apply in their case, since his heart already belonged to someone else.

She suffered the rest of the ceremony in a state of limbo, detached as a newly departed spirit hovering above the heads of mourners at her bedside. Even Phares's kiss made scant impression upon lips frozen into the semblance of a smile. Had she been sure of his love, she would have felt differently. Still, now that they were officially man and wife, Aida threaded her arm through the crook of his and as the bridal procession moved slowly back down the aisle towards the cathedral entrance, to the sound of another hymn from the congregation, she returned those stares, full of prejudice, with defiance. It was not until they left the church and were being driven back to Hathor that she was shocked back to reality by Phares's breezy acceptance of a situation she was suddenly finding intolerable.

'Tired?' he asked, as the silence stretched between them.

The smile Aida gave him in reply was slightly strained.

'Why don't you lay your head on the back of the seat and close your eyes? I'm afraid we still have a long night in front of us before we are able to relax.' His eyes twinkled as they swept over her face tenderly. 'I can't wait to be alone with you, *chérie.*'

'Where are we spending the night? At Hathor?'

Phares lifted a brow. 'What on earth would make you think that I would want to spend our first night together at the house, eh?'

She blinked with surprise. He was right, it would have been out of character for him – Phares was all about adventure, new places, surprises.

'Everything has happened so quickly, I didn't think you would have had the time to organise anything.'

He grinned and bent his head towards her. 'Only a phone call to the Winter Palace Hotel. I've reserved their Emperor's suite, *chérie,* for our first night together. As for our honeymoon, that's a surprise. Just think, days and nights of surprises ...'

Phares stretched out his hand and covered hers, then lifting it to his lips he turned it over and placed his mouth in the centre of her palm so that she felt the warm pressure of his kiss on her skin. At the hot brush of his tongue, a thousand emotions assailed her and a deep, coiling sensation erupted in the pit of her stomach.

'You're trembling,' he murmured hoarsely, his eyes holding hers in some sort of spell. He glanced towards the chauffeur who was driving them back to Hathor. He leaned in closer, his voice dropping an octave as it caressed her ear like dark velvet. 'I wish we were alone. I've missed you ... I've dreamt of you every night. You do things to me I thought I was far too experienced to feel.'

The knowledge that Phares wanted her physically was like a heady wine, too tempting for Aida to resist. He made her feel so feminine. The longing welled in her: the desire to be in his arms, to make love with him. And like someone listening to a hypnotist, she murmured huskily, 'I want you too ...' and she truly did, but how could that be when she was so hurt and angry?

They finally arrived at Hathor, where guns were fired into the sky in celebration as the car glided through the open gates and they were met with exultant rhythms from drums and tambourines combined with trumpets. Aida couldn't help but be swept up in the excitement and jubilant noise as the beat of traditional wedding songs became punctuated by joyful, trilling ululations from the women: the famous *zaghareet Al Farah*, announcing the couple was back and that the wedding reception was about to begin. Aida and Phares were deposited at the front door to take part in the *Zaffa*, the traditional wedding procession. Golden light streamed from the house as doors and windows were flung wide, and a cheery hum of voices and the tinkle of glasses filled the air.

The *Zaffa* assembled at the front door and proceeded down the red carpet towards the *siwan*, a large tent with embroidered panels that had been erected in the front garden for the reception. First came the musicians – two parallel rows of young men dressed in traditional Egyptian kaftans playing the Middle-Eastern *bendir* drums, *mizmars*, bagpipes and horns – dancing, twirling and singing to the cacophonic and distinctive rhythm of the music. They were followed by Camelia and the young bridesmaids with their long candles adorned with ribbons and flowers, and then by the *Shamadan*, a belly dancer in a brightly coloured costume, balancing a candelabra on top of her head, swaying her hips and rotating to the music in front of Aida and Phares.

As the colourful, musical procession moved down the red carpet and approached the entrance of the tent where guests and family were waiting for the bride and groom, Aida felt as though she was part of some lavish film, swept up in the joyous spectacle, but almost detached, as though all of it was happening to someone else. She took a deep breath and must have gripped Phares's arm a little more tightly as he turned his head, his gaze lingering on her, smiling tenderly as they entered the *siwan*. Inside the tent was lavishly decorated with tuberoses and acacias, and lined with tables groaning beneath silver platters of roast turkey, frilled hams, pigeons in aspic, *foie gras*, caviar, Russian salad and other elaborate dishes, cakes from Groppi's trimmed with Egypt's national colours, together with fantastically shaped pastries and ices, while waiters were already circulating among the guests with glasses of champagne, lemonade and rose *sharbat*.

Aida could see the place was packed to suffocation with a heaving crowd. How beautifully dressed the women were, she thought, most of them in full-length gowns of brocade and silk, bejewelled with priceless accessories. Among the glamorous outfits, she recognised some of the dresses that had been modelled at Shams Sakr El Din's fashion show, a memory she quashed, preferring not to think of the prince tonight. The couple took their places in the reception line at the entrance of the tent to greet each guest, and the shaking of hands took so long, Aida wondered if people were going round and round again, there seemed so many. With half of them, she was aware of their fixed smiles and the scrutiny of their gaze upon her and could only imagine the hushed conversations that ensued as they left the line to gossip about her over the champagne and *mezzeh*. In those cases, she simply lifted her chin higher and smiled even more brightly.

Aida gave an inward sigh of relief on shaking the final guest's hand, and leaving her talking to Phares, she made her way across the lawn, heading for the cloakroom inside the house. She had only gone a few steps when Aunt Halima accosted her, regarding her coldly with shrewd, small black eyes. Whatever goodwill she might have found for Aida the evening before, it had now clearly vanished.

'Do try and look as if you are a bride, not a mourner.' She spoke drily, her mouth curling contemptuously. 'You don't know how lucky you are. I really can't understand what my nephew sees in you, a washed-out *khawagaya*, foreign woman, with a heart of ice.' And then, without waiting for Aida's answer, she turned on her heels and walked away.

Aida felt the colour storm into her cheeks. She hurried into the house, biting her bottom lip to stop the tears that were welling up and clenching her fists until her fingernails dug into her flesh. She wanted to cry until there were no tears left, but held her head high as she made her way to the cloakroom. Finally, she was alone. She sat down on one of the stools and glanced at herself in the mirror. True, her expression was more like that of a mourner than a bride.

*Buck up! Where is your self-confidence, your pride? Why are you giving satisfaction to these envious women who are so eager to sow discord between you and Phares? They'll only start rumours about you.*

She splashed cold water over her face and freshened her make-up. There, she looked presentable now. With one last glance in the mirror and a deep sigh, she left the room to join her new husband, who by now, she thought, must be wondering where she was.

The reception was in full swing when Aida joined Phares. He was surrounded by his friends, most of whom she had never met, who were congratulating him on the beauty of the young woman he had chosen to be his lifelong companion. He seemed to be taking advantage of this opportunity to show her off and was full of enthusiasm as he introduced her to his friends. Aida couldn't help but notice that he was glowing with happiness, proud as a peacock as he took her from group to group. To see him like this, she could have sworn that Phares was deeply in love with her and it made her wonder if she'd been mistaken all this time. Or was he simply an accomplished actor? She gazed at him with an inward sigh, wishing more than anything that it might be true.

There were no speeches – it was not the custom at Egyptian weddings. At length the buffet was open, during which the happy couple circulated from table to table. They would have an intimate dinner later on, behind closed doors, the prospect of which sent tiny flutters whirling inside Aida's stomach.

Once the buffet was cleared of all foods, the beautiful wedding cake decorated with doves, a horseshoe and bells was wheeled in amid the sound of bravos, *Allah ye barek*, *mabrouks* and the clamour of the *zaghareet*.

'Cut the cake!' everyone chorused.

With an ambiguous smile, Phares placed his hand over Aida's on the hilt of Gamil Pharaony's sword – the very one that had run through Prince Shams' ancestor – and plunged it into the white icing of Groppi's enormous five-tiered wedding cake. At this, there were congratulatory cheers, the clink of champagne glasses and laughter from the throng of guests.

As Aida looked up, her eyes caught those of Isis Geratly, who was standing among the crowd of well-wishers. There was so much venom in them that it was obvious that felicitations were far from the young anaesthetist's mind. No doubt she would gladly have hurled the cake to the floor and trampled to pieces every silver ornament that topped it. And it was at that moment that Aida knew without a doubt it had been Isis who had sent the vitriolic note she'd received moments before the ceremony. What had she hoped to achieve? Did she know something Aida didn't, or was she simply trying to drive a wedge between her and Phares?

At last came the moment for Aida to go upstairs and change for the honeymoon journey. Camelia showed her to one of the guest rooms, where a beautiful purple silk-shantung dress and a parure of purple diamonds had been laid out for her.

'Phares looks happier than I've ever seen him! I'm so glad for you both, I'm sure you'll have a wonderful life together.'

Aida's teeth bit sharply into a trembling bottom lip as she fought against a misery of tears. She opened her clutch bag, took out the crumpled note she'd received before the ceremony and handed it to her friend. With that, finally, the battle she had been staunchly fighting all evening came to an end and she burst into tears.

'Oh, Aida, what is it? Don't cry.' Camelia placed an arm around her shoulders, looking curiously at the piece of paper. 'Whatever it is, it can't be that serious. Wait, let me read it.'

Having scrutinised the message, Camelia lifted her head and sighed. 'This has been written by a vicious, jealous woman, *habibti*. It doesn't surprise me, there have been so many women after Phares. You might not see him that way, but my brother is a good catch. Besides,' she smiled ruefully, 'the woman who marries my brother won't have a mother-in-law … always a plus in our society.' She nudged Aida and chuckled. 'Although Tante Halima is much worse than any mother-in-law.'

Aida dried her eyes and gave a shaky laugh. 'I know, I don't think she likes me much. She told me off at the reception because she thought I looked more like a mourner than a bride.'

'You did seem rather quiet. I thought you were just tired, but now that I've read this, I understand why.'

Aida looked her friend squarely in the eyes. 'Was Phares in Luxor last night?'

'No, he came home this morning on the first plane,' Camelia admitted. 'He was at the hospital … some patient on whom he'd performed a difficult operation a couple of weeks ago had an embolism. I think it was very serious, I mean deadly, and he spent the last two nights at the Anglo. He was catching up on his sleep right up until when he had to get ready for the wedding.'

Aida glanced away. 'I see.'

Camelia gripped her arm. 'Look here, Aida, you either trust Phares or you don't, and if you don't, I can't understand why you married him. Surely you wouldn't tie your life to someone in whom you don't have total confidence? I know you love him, you always have, even if your pride sometimes made you deny it. And Phares *adores* you. I wouldn't have let you marry him if I'd thought for a minute that he wasn't totally committed to you. Try and relax, and stop questioning everything all the time.'

But Aida was still tormented by doubt. 'He's so charming, so handsome, and he has a roving eye, you can't deny that.'

Camelia smiled and shook her head. 'That was before you came back. As long as you love him, and are not shy about showing it, he will be putty in your hands. All he wants is to make the people he loves happy.'

Aida let out a long sigh. 'I think the message was from Isis.'

'Maybe. I wouldn't put it past her,' Camelia said with a shrug. 'But that's not the point. From now on, you must ignore all rumours and nasty tittle-tattle that fills Luxor's drawing rooms because these women have nothing better to do. Don't let anybody come between the two of you. Mounir and I never let the sun go down on an argument, we always made peace before nightfall. That's a good way to keep your marriage happy, because when you're angry, hurtful thoughts continue to simmer until they reach boiling point. You know the saying, *dabbuur zann aala kharab essu*, through its buzzing, a wasp only ends up bringing about the destruction of its own nest. That's what you're in danger of doing, but if you stay true to your love and trust each other, there's no reason for Phares to stray.'

Camelia was right; she must lock all these dreadful suspicions in a drawer and throw away the key. Aida had no doubt that she loved Phares and that her life would be miserable without him. She had won the prize. She could see it in the eyes of the women who had been present at the reception – some of whom had been delighted to see Phares happily married, but others, like Isis, had looked at her with eyes full of envy as he proudly introduced Aida to his friends, his arm lovingly and protectively placed around her shoulders.

Tension ebbed away from her and Aida kissed her friend warmly on the cheek. 'Thank you, Camelia. You're such a wise and good friend. You're right, I must put aside my insecurities about Phares and have faith in our love for each other.'

Her friend grinned. 'Good. Now, let me help you get ready. Phares must be waiting for you *ala nar*, on fire. The car is at the front door, ready to take you to the Winter Palace. The suite he has reserved is out of this world, and tonight the stars have never been so bright … a real night for romance!'

Camelia took down a dress from the rail where it was hanging and took off its cover. 'This arrived yesterday morning, straight from Marcel Rochas in Paris.'

It was a magnificent silver lamé gown of pure, simple lines, with a plunging neckline at the front and back, and ruched shoulders.

Aida gasped. 'It's so elegant … Phares has already sent me so many presents!'

'It's his pleasure. He has chosen everything for you himself.'

'You didn't help him?'

'I showed him a few magazines and photographs, but he did it all himself, I swear. His taste is amazing. I never realised my brother was so knowledgeable about clothes.'

'Well, his last girlfriend *was* a model.'

Camelia looked at her friend reproachfully. 'Forget about Nairy. He never loved her, despite what people say.' She waved a hand dismissively. 'It makes a good drama and to her, Phares was just a meal ticket. She's renowned for being a social climber. The affair suited them both and now it's well in the past. I hear she's already replaced him with some Greek tycoon.'

Aida gave a wry smile as she began unfastening her tiara and veil. If that was so, what was the model doing coaxing a rendezvous out of Phares less than two weeks ago? But Camelia was right, she must forget Nairy, especially tonight. She flushed at the thought of what was to come. Phares and his kisses, his muscled arms pulling her against his hard body …

Aida slid out of her wedding attire and went to the bathroom to freshen up and retouch her make-up. She stared back at her reflection in the mirror. Her eyes, she thought, looked larger and bluer tonight, the excitement in them hard to disguise. Her hair, which *Dada* Amina had insisted she wash with chamomile to enhance its goldenness, was silky and glistening. She gave it fifty energetic brushstrokes and let it fall in soft curls over her shoulders.

She came back into the bedroom and put on the lamé gown. It fitted her to perfection. Slipping on the matching silk-and-silver-mesh peep-toe high-heeled shoes, she checked herself again in the mirror, hardly able to recognise herself.

'Beautiful!' Camelia exclaimed. 'Phares asked me to give you these, by the way.' She handed Aida a navy-blue velvet box. 'They belonged to my mother. It's the only thing he took of her jewellery, I have the rest.'

'But …'

'Mama said that he could choose one parure to give to his future wife and he chose this one.'

'Are you sure?'

'Of course I'm sure.'

'He's given me so much already.'

'That is Phares. He will shower you with love and presents, but he does also demand loyalty and total trust.'

Aida sat down at the dressing table and opened the large jewellery box. She sucked in her breath as she saw the spectacular double strand of pearls with three squares of diamond baguettes positioned midway on each side of the necklace. It lay on its velvet cushion alongside matching earrings, two bracelets and a ring. Tears welled up in her eyes. 'I don't deserve this.'

'Of course you do. Come on, there's no time to waste. Phares wants you to wear these with the dress. He's waiting downstairs to see them on you. Here, let me do up the necklace.'

Aida obeyed meekly, so moved by Phares's generosity that she was trembling, her heart pounding. Feeling guilty at how she had behaved today, she promised herself that she would make it up to him and be a truly loving wife.

'You look striking. Those pearls were made for you, I swear.'

Aida glanced at herself in the mirror. Suddenly she couldn't wait to be with Phares and to read the admiration and desire in his eyes. Grabbing the matching shawl and her mother's pearl clutch bag, she gave her friend one last hug.

'Let's go, Camelia. Thank you for everything.'

A few minutes later, a sea of smiling faces and a yell of welcome hailed Aida's appearance at the head of the staircase. Everyone had gathered in the big hall to see the couple off.

At the bottom of the stairs, Phares stood waiting for her. Dark and powerful, his eyes were afire, sweeping the full length of her hungrily. Aida felt herself blush at the smile of devilment she saw there as she arrived on the last step and he took her hand. Sliding his arm around her waist, he caged her with his hard, muscled body. Yells, whoops and cheers erupted the moment he took her lips with his, and Aida felt herself melt, her knees trembling, loins flooding with the familiar warmth only his proximity could provoke.

For a moment, pressed against him, she forgot the gathered guests, but Phares released her suddenly, leaving her covered in blushing confusion as he turned to them.

'Friends, colleagues, ladies and gentlemen, regretfully, it is time for us to leave you. This has been a wonderful day.' Then, with a twinkle in his eye, and wearing his most charming smile, he added, 'But we still have a long night in front of us.'

His unambiguous remark was greeted with laughter and whistles as he lifted Aida into his arms and made for the front door. With a final wave, he helped her into the waiting car as their guests threw rose petals, rice, sweet almonds and memento coins bearing Phares and Aida's names over the happy couple.

*       *       *

Luxor's Winter Palace occupied a wonderful position on the banks of the Nile, its elegant horseshoe terrace raised on colonnades with a sweeping double marble staircase leading down to the forecourt. The Victorian-style opulent hotel had become famous in the early 1920s with Howard Carter's discovery of the sealed tomb of Tutankhamun. The tremendous find had captured the imagination of a global audience, bringing hordes of foreigners knocking at its doors in those years between the wars.

The prestige suite that Phares had reserved for their wedding night was huge, its tall, elegant French windows leading on to a small terrace with a wonderful view of the Nile, and across it to the emerald-green fields and the old town of Thebes.

'You haven't eaten since lunchtime, *chérie*,' Phares noted, following Aida into the room. 'I saw you didn't touch any of the canapés that were going round at the reception. I'll call room service and have them bring up a bottle of champagne and a big bowl of caviar.'

She smiled at her husband. 'Thank you, though I'm really not very hungry, but go ahead and order it if you'd like something. You must be starving. I didn't see you eat much either.'

He grinned. 'Don't worry about me. I tasted every appetiser on offer, *chérie*. They were quite delicious.'

Aida's eyes fell on the huge bed, welcoming and inviting with its pure white silk sheets. On it, the beautiful nightdress that had been packed for her had been laid out. Phares followed her gaze and his full, sensual lips tilted at the corner in a wry smile of acknowledgement.

'How about we eat later? I'll leave you to undress,' he murmured, his voice thick. The expression in his eyes told her everything he had left unsaid, and a spark of awareness flared low in her belly, spreading quickly outwards.

Anticipation shivered through her as she ran herself a bath, into which she poured a few drops of the delicious bath oil the hotel had provided, called *Nuit de Noces*. It filled the bathroom with its heady fragrance of jasmine, rose, green oakmoss, fern, musk and *fougère accord*, impregnating her skin as she soaked in the hot water, leaving it soft and silky to the touch.

After towelling herself vigorously, Aida slipped into the delicate nightgown and stood in front of the mirror. The filmy chiffon and lace robe had a low, gathered neckline with romantic flowing sleeves and tight lace cuffs. It was so revealing, she went pink with a mixture of embarrassment and excitement, although she had to admit that she liked what she saw. Tying a robe around her, she walked barefoot on to the terrace and gazed at the beautiful scenery spread out in front of her.

Overhead, a huge silver moon hung like a great jewelled lamp suspended from a chain of brilliant stars. The whole world seemed a wonderful symphony of violet and silver, the shadows of rock and palm trees etched in deepest black upon a mauve canvas. Every small hillock on the opposite bank of the great dark expanse of the Nile stood out clearly, and the breeze blew deliciously over the sand and silver waters. Soft and balmy, it held the fragrance of a hundred southern gardens in its breath.

*     *     *

Phares let himself into the room quietly in case Aida was asleep. He would wake her, but he would do so tenderly, lovingly, preparing her slowly for the night he had in mind for them. He immediately saw that she wasn't in bed and moving to the open window, he saw that she had her back to him, her beautiful body silhouetted against the balustrade outside, every curve outlined through the flimsy material of her night clothes.

The night was so superb, the panorama of the great moon, silver behind the dark trees, so exquisite that he dared hardly breathe lest it all dissolved into mist, as so many of his dreams had done in the days gone by. Until the last minute he had been afraid that Aida would change her mind, and it wasn't until the priest had pronounced them man and wife that he could relax.

But now, her proximity and her sweetness went to his head like wine, with the knowledge that she was his, and that he had only to put out his hand to touch her arm, so soft and warm and smooth. The gentle sound of her breathing in the otherwise silent place filled him with an overwhelming desire to draw her close to him. Phares had always believed that even when a man loved, he should be proud – always the confident victor, though in reality a suppliant. But now he knew better. Pride had ruled him too much before. The fear he'd experienced at the idea of losing Aida had taught him that love meant a great humility, that a man who would demand of a woman the immense sacrifice of marriage, with all its attendant obligations, must make the demand diffidently, not arrogantly as he had done, realising that from its very nature the bond must press more heavily on her than it would ever do on him.

Slowly, he moved away from the window and went into the bathroom to prepare himself. Her sweet scent was everywhere. He found her towelling robe hanging up on the back of the bathroom door and couldn't resist burying his face in it, inhaling the smell of her mingling with the fragrances she was wearing. He closed his eyes. Something deep and powerful and primitive flooded every nerve in his body.

He washed, shaved and pulled on a robe. Already aroused, he was growing harder by the second, the throbbing of his loins almost painful, he wanted her so much. But he must be patient; he didn't want to hurt her – Aida must be given as much pleasure as he intended to take.

Padding lightly on to the terrace, he stood on the threshold. Aida shimmered like a pearl under the moonlight, and as she turned to look at him he read in her eyes the same desire that was torturing him. She tilted her head with a shy, flirtatious smile, and he saw her gaze travel slowly over his torso before it was drawn towards the bulge of his virility.

Phares watched the enticing sway of Aida's hips as she came slowly towards him, and caught a tantalising glimpse of her ripe, womanly cleavage as she let her robe slip open. It fell from her shoulders and she stood before him in just her transparent chiffon nightdress, revealing, like a mirage, the perfection of her naked frame, her taut nipples pushing against the thin silk.

He stared at her, dry-mouthed.

'Phares …'

Coming out of the silence, his name breathed by her voice, rough with passion, shivered along his senses like a caress.

His eyes flickered in the darkness. 'I want you naked,' he murmured hoarsely. 'I want to see all of you. Now. I want to feel you, taste you, love you, Aida.'

With a sensuous movement of her shoulder she pushed the nightgown down to her waist, baring her breasts to him, and then, as if she had always been an exotic dancer, he saw her let the flimsy cloth slip to the ground. Unbelievably beautiful in the moonlight, she stood there trembling, waiting ... yes, he could read it in her eyes ... for his touch.

Their eyes locked. She held him spellbound ... *the seduction of innocence*, he thought. There was such contradiction in her. Instinctively, she knew how to be sensuous ... yes, it was that combination of purity and wantonness that excited him, rousing his deep, genuine desire as no woman ever had. His blood buzzed, turning to molten lava as these thoughts rushed through his mind, but he didn't reach out for her.

'Anticipation is half the fun,' he murmured huskily and rid himself of his robe.

He was naked and Aida's gaze travelled over him, lingering on his manhood.

'You want me,' she whispered.

'I'm burning for you.'

'Then take me.'

'What are *you* feeling?'

'I want you to touch me, Phares. Touch me everywhere ...'

'Everywhere?

'Everywhere.' The word came out as no more than a whisper, but he heard her.

Fierce lust seared his veins and the throb in his groin was agonising. Ungovernable longing for her took hold of him, he needed some release. His legs threatened to buckle; pulling her against him, he fell to his knees and leaned his head against the small triangle of curls between her thighs. He longed to explore it, his fingers trembling with the need to feel her, to take what was his, and his alone. He heard her breath catch as her hands pressed him even closer, meeting him with her hips.

He ran the tip of his fingers along the inside of her thighs, up and down her silky skin, making her moan and shiver from top to toe as he trailed them over the dewy, delicate skin that no one but him had touched. His middle finger found her slick folds and thrust deep into her soft, moist core. She sucked in a breath and let it out on a whimpering sigh of pleasure. Her sensitive flesh enveloped his finger completely as he stroked her inside, feeling the heat and moisture of her. Then, putting his warm mouth to those same lips now swollen with her passion and need for him, he parted them, flicking his tongue between the hot, unfurled petals, passing it over the flooded glistening bud, making her shudder. She jerked. Her legs wobbled and she cried out his name.

'Phares, oh, Phares, don't stop!' Her passionate pleading resonated in the night as she reached out for something to hang on to, and he felt her nails digging into his shoulders to steady herself while he fondled her wetly with his lips and tongue, using his fingers to apply ruthless and almost painful pressure to intensify her pleasure. She was surrendering herself in her usual generous way, parting her legs so he could reach deeper into her, lustfully enjoying this rapturous torture. She tasted smooth and sweet and delicious. The scent of her, the warmth of her skin, her whimpering sounds of ecstasy all seemed designed to urge him on, and she rocked backwards and forwards in rhythm with his playful strokes. Cupping her bottom with both hands, he pulled her closer, holding her tightly against him ... he wanted to reach inside her with his tongue ... drink all of her ... devour her.

He could feel her climax was coming; her muscles contracting and relaxing faster. She was moving quicker, her moans becoming stronger. His lips now closed firmly around the throbbing bud of her desire as he sucked and delicately nibbled it gently between his teeth. Aida couldn't muffle her scream. She writhed and almost lost her balance, but Phares held her steady and continued to nip at the fiercely swollen bud until he thought every last burst of carnal pleasure had subsided. Only then did he let her fall to her knees in front of him, her arms clasped around his neck as her breaths came in heavy pants.

And then suddenly, he felt her hands leave his shoulders and move downwards tentatively over the dark hair sprinkled over his chest. Bending over a little, she trailed them sensuously lower, following the line of his hair to his navel, and below to the brazen statement of his arousal.

*Yes*, he thought, *touch me, Aida, release me, I'm burning for you!* And as she closed her fingers around his turgid sex he inhaled sharply, a hoarse groan escaping from deep in his throat. Her touch was firm, but tender, her palm warm and soft as she stroked him from base to tip, harder and faster in a steady rhythm, her other hand running over the curve of his buttock as she continued to torment him.

Before he had time to react, she'd pushed him against the bed and leaning down, had taken him in her mouth, licking and sucking, loving him with ferocious tenderness, using her hand, her tongue and lips, while the fingers of her other hand squeezed in turn each of his nipples.

'Oh, God, Aida, you're killing me,' he rasped.

She was moving him to the edge; any time now he would peak. His breathing deepened, his body quivered ... he could feel the rush coming.

Phares's groans clamped down into hard, primal grunts, which seemed to urge Aida on. Gradually she built up the speed of her fondling, the moisture from her mouth mingling with the heat of her palm. As she caressed the smooth head of his shaft, applying the right level of pressure to it, he could feel himself becoming even harder in her mouth, which she opened wider and wider at his frenzy for her to take him in; he felt himself thrusting, burying himself deeper in her throat, delirious with the pleasure it was giving him.

Aida's greedy insistence was driving him over the edge. He had not bargained for her voracious boldness. 'Aida, oh, God, *chérie*, I'm coming, please!' he panted, but she ignored him, pressing him against the bed to keep him from pulling away.

He closed his eyes in soul-deep obedience, surrendering wholly to her wild passion as she loved him with a ferocious tenderness with mouth and hands. Feverish, he spoke words he had never before dared to utter, taking what Aida was giving so generously, indulging wholly and selfishly in the rapture she was dealing him minute by minute.

Then, before he knew it, he exploded in her mouth, spasms of pleasure raking and heaving through him.

And now he sat back, his breathing ragged, his body heavy, languid, spent. He was a little ashamed that he hadn't withdrawn sooner. The deep hunger that had built so swiftly inside him had sapped his control, but that was no excuse.

He looked up at her sheepishly. 'I'm sorry,' he murmured.

Aida smiled at him tenderly. 'Oh, Phares, you shouldn't be … I'm so in love with you,' she whispered, still shaking and breathless with passion. 'You can't imagine the pleasure I took in loving you … You're so beautiful.'

He pressed a smiling kiss on the top of Aida's head, then tilted her chin upwards with his fingertips. Slowly brushing his lips to her forehead, eyelids and the tip of her nose, he pulled away and stood up, before sweeping her up in his powerful arms, nuzzling her as he carried her into the dimly lit bedroom and set her on the bed.

'I could never let another man have you, Aida,' he whispered, his dark eyes grave and passion-filled. 'That's the truth of it. I would kill anyone who tried to take you from me. And I will love you till the day I die.'

# CHAPTER 14

'So you're awake? That's a shame, I was looking forward to waking you up.'

Aida lifted half-sleepy eyes to see Phares standing over her. His smile had a naked openness – a mixture of love, tenderness and longing. He had just come out of the shower and had a small towel wrapped around his waist, his copper-bronze body glistening with health in the morning sunlight. They had made love all night, but Aida was still a virgin. He hadn't wanted to deflower her in one go, but had preferred to take it slowly, concerned to cause her as little pain as possible. She had almost cried tears of joy when he had told her that he loved her and now she felt as though she was truly living in a dream.

'Sorry to disappoint you, husband.' She smiled shyly, still unused to the sight of so much of his naked skin. 'You still haven't told me about our honeymoon trip. Where are we going?'

'Well, tonight we start with the opening of *Aida* at the Khedivial Opera House. We'll spend the night at Mena House and then tomorrow we'll begin our journey up the Nile on a *dahabeyeh*.'

Delighted surprise lit Aida's eyes. 'Oh, Phares!'

'I know how fond you are of opera, and you once told me, a long time ago, that the most romantic journey anyone could take was to travel up the Nile from Cairo to Aswan by boat.'

'You remember that?'

Phares looked at her with mock indignation. 'I remember all our conversations, *chérie*.'

She laughed. 'And we're using the Pharaony *dahabeyeh*?'

'Yes, of course.'

'But it hasn't been used for years.' She remembered the lovely teak flat-bottomed boat with its rust-coloured sails; it was so romantic.

'I've had it renovated. I intend for us to travel up the Nile as though we were the guests of Khedive Ismail himself.'

Now, as he looked down at her, Aida saw the fire of pride and love shining in his eyes and the joy inside her rose up like a warm wave.

She was the luckiest woman on earth!

Phares glanced at his watch: 'Ten o'clock! It's been a while since we ate, shall I call room service? We aren't meant to be at the airport until this afternoon. What does my beautiful bride feel like having this morning?'

Aida wasn't the least bit hungry. Only eight hours ago she had consumed almost a whole bottle of champagne and mounds of caviar. Now her gaze slid over her husband's lean torso. He really was a magnificent sight. His shoulders were broad, his chest covered in a light dusting of dark hair, and there wasn't an ounce of surplus flesh on him to blur the perfect muscle definition on display. He was so good to look at; so solid, so vividly alive that she couldn't resist lifting her hand to stroke the satin smoothness of his skin.

A ringlet of wet raven-black hair had slipped and curled on his forehead, his perfect lips were curved in that now-familiar enigmatic smile that told her exactly what sort of appetite he really felt like satisfying. The look of hunger in his gaze was unmistakable, and its power shook her to the core. Her face grew hot, and her eyes responded in kind.

Without a word, he slid down on to the bed beside her and pulled away the sheet covering her nakedness. The raw desire smouldering in his face only made the excitement pulsing inside her expand. She wanted to give herself to him more than she wanted to take her next breath. Instinctively, her arms went to wrap around his neck, but with a playful growl, he caught her wrists and held them firmly to her sides. His eyes glinted with lustful amusement.

'Let me look at you, Aida, my beautiful wife. Let me drink in the perfection of your body. Your delicate collarbones, the shape of your waist, the soft mounds of your luscious breasts … delicious, like sweet ripe apples.' She felt the twin peaks of her nipples harden in response to his voice which was thick with desire, and she arched her back, desperate for his touch. But he kept her arms clamped to her sides, his eyes saturated with the need for her. 'My words are exciting you, eh? You are longing for me to touch you, I know … but don't be ashamed of your desire, *chérie*. I can see those beautiful nipples are getting harder, calling for my attention.'

She felt a frisson ripple up her spine as his eyes held hers in an embrace as thrilling as the words he was murmuring.

'Phares …' she breathed.

'Shuush, *chérie*, let me continue my journey.' His warm, husky voice never rose higher than a whisper.

Desperately aroused, Aida moistened her lips.

'Your lips are dry? They're asking to be kissed but you'll have to wait. I haven't finished yet. I'm still on my journey. I can see that little vein in your throat beating, the pulse on your stomach is racing also.' His cheeks were flushed as his predatory gaze flicked down to the space between her legs, now wet with longing. 'And I don't need to tell you what's happening to that delicious rosebud my mouth feasted on yesterday.'

A moan escaped Aida's throat and she spread her legs, her eyes pleading.

'Yes, I know how hot and swollen and needy it's becoming. You want me down there, don't you? You want me to kiss you, lick you, taste you.' Phares's eyes darkened, his voice a low rasp. 'It felt good, eh?'

Again, Aida passed her tongue over her lips. She could see that the memory of some of the games they had played last night was exciting Phares and just the thought of it increased the painful ache between her thighs.

He lowered his head so that his voice was hoarse against her ear. 'I can still smell you. The taste of you is still in my mouth, sweet and womanly, but most of all wet … so hot and wet, chérie. My whole body is aching to be inside you, but you have to be patient. Think of me touching you, stroking, rubbing, faster and faster. You can feel that wave of ecstasy coming, can't you?'

Stabs of lustful heat slid through Aida, making her gasp, and the thought that he was soon going to touch her only added fuel to the blaze. He was right: she was close to climaxing. How was that possible? She was so close … She could hear herself moaning, her hips rising off the bed, urging him to touch her.

'Shuush, chérie! Just feel …' As he lifted his head, Phares's gaze held Aida's, his ardent black eyes burning into the deep blue ocean of hers; the firelight of passion flickered across her body in a golden caress of its own, and then, slowly, he released her wrists.

He touched her hair briefly, brushed his thumb over her lower lip. Bending his head, he lightly pressed his mouth to hers, then touched his moist lips to the pulsing vein on her throat, his thumbs stroking the sides of her neck and down to her shoulders. He was so close now that Aida could see the glitter in his eyes, feel his heat, smell his skin, hear his uneven breathing.

His strong hands slid to her trembling breasts. They closed over them, moulding them to his palms, his thumbs trailing circles around the pebbled nipples straining for his attention. Each teasing stroke drew a series of small, throaty gasps from Aida's parted lips as their demanding peaks stood higher.

Still watching her, now he let his fingers glide over her stomach in the lightest of caresses, getting closer to that part of her that ached for him so badly. There was something of the voyeur in him that drove her wild. The enjoyment she could read in his gaze at her exhibition of pleasure titillated her, intensifying the effect of every stroke, every caress. It was the most erotic image she had ever imagined, and she obliged, opening her legs, shamelessly displaying her craving for him and the pleasure he was giving her. She wanted him and she wanted him to know it.

His hands slipped down a little further and paused over the small triangle of her mound of Venus. On fire now, Aida arched her spine again, edging her legs even more wantonly apart, trying to push her swelling flesh into his palms, driven by the aching demands of her sensitised body.

'Please,' she moaned.

The back of his hand brushed between her legs, quickly, lightly – a frustrating, feather-like touch – and she gasped. He was deliberately not touching her where she wanted. By now he knew how that game drove her to peak. The ache was deliciously unbearable, but Aida trusted Phares's experience. Her climax each time it had come had been more ferocious for the waiting.

Now bending his head, he took her mouth, gently at first, his lips barely grazing against hers. He ran his tongue around her lips before allowing it to dart inside. And then he was on the bed, lying against the length of her, his kiss deepening as his hard torso pressed against her breast. A growl rumbled through his chest. He took her mouth savagely, as though branding her – letting her know that he would never allow another man touch her. His primitive way of showing her how he felt and who was master was so thrilling, Aida's instincts rose to meet his ravaging, insatiable demands. His towel had fallen away and she wanted to feel him inside her. Not his tongue this time, but that strong ridge of his manhood, which was straining against the side of her hip, hard, warm and velvety. With every breath the length of it twitched slightly as she felt it expand and harden, making her fully aware of the hot strength of his desire.

How much more torment was she supposed to take? Clutching his hand, she tried to pull it down to her widely spread legs, inviting him to touch her.

'See how wet I am,' she gasped, dragging her mouth from his.

Infuriatingly, his hand remained under hers, pressing his palm firmly down on her stomach, staying her.

'Please …' she begged again, as his mouth nuzzled her throat and carried on with its journey downwards until finally she felt his warm lips dance upon her nipples, his tongue swirling and licking them mercilessly as he suckled her. He groaned her name, and she clawed at his shoulders, writhing beneath his mouth. He moved on, breathing hot breaths over the silken flesh of her stomach. When she moaned and wriggled, the hand lying under hers finally made its way towards her quivering thighs.

'Yes,' she gasped, as his fingers found her and touched her at last.

'Yes,' Phares's throaty groan echoed as he slid down her body, his fingers and mouth no longer searching, but devouring Aida's essence. Slow kisses, languid licks and gentle nibbles became increasingly fevered as passion soared and took over from any other emotion between them.

Aida's moans were low, guttural, saturated with desire as Phares shifted, moving on top of her and pulling her hips against his. She felt the hard, thick length of his manhood, the hot, velvety tip brushing against her liquid folds. Little shockwaves rushed through her as muscles she didn't even know she had started to squeeze.

He moved his shaft up and down her saturated bud.

'Oh God, Phares,' she moaned, 'please do something, this is torture … I'm melting inside.'

'Hot cream, *chérie*,' he rasped, his voice deep and passion-rough. He moved up and down against her again. 'So smooth and soft and slick.' His sculpted features were taut, his eyes smouldering as he nudged her legs further apart, gently, sliding a little deeper into her yearning flesh, pressing the tip of his virility against the damp wall of her resistance.

He kissed her deeply. 'I don't want to hurt you,' he whispered against her mouth.

'Love me, Phares. I want to be yours … completely.'

His eyes burned hotter, but it was nothing like the tenderness she read in them.

'Take me,' she whispered against his mouth. 'I'm not afraid. I love you.'

For a moment Phares shifted to let his hand move down between her legs, drawing more wetness, continuing to stroke her as he penetrated her with one finger, testing her receptivity. He added a second, stretching her slightly, making sure she was ready.

'Take me,' Aida breathed again as she writhed against his hand. Everything in her was strung so tight she could hardly breathe, her body poised on the brink of cracking beneath the building of tormenting pleasure.

He kissed her again, as if gifting her his soul, and her body responded to his tenderness as instinctively as a flower opening to the sun. Inch by inch, he pressed forward until she felt him, full and hard, filling her, deeper and deeper still. Her breath caught at the slight burning, but at the same time it was wondrous, magical, sacred … and then she felt the hot fire start to give way to a different sensation, one of warmth and fullness, and heightened pleasure.

Phares groaned deeply. 'Wrap your legs around me.'

Aida complied and tilted her hips, giving him unlimited access to the very core of her. She felt him push into her with a smooth, sure thrust, causing her to cry out and then hold still. He was buried deep, so deep inside her, sweeping her with him into a whirlpool of raw passion, with a force that fused their souls.

Phares's pelvis rocked against hers and her hips lifted instinctively to meet his. Their bodies moved apart and came together in a dance of passion and love, the erotic heat spiralling up and up. The wave was gathering inside her and Aida met every stroke of him, each one pushing her further to the edge.

She heard him whisper her name, softly, reverently, and felt his engorged manhood pump mindlessly inside her. Then she was there, joining him in ecstasy, and she splintered into a thousand pieces as lightning streaked upwards through her flesh, magnifying downward to slam into her groin. She screamed his name, moulding herself to his loins as he pumped his love inside her, and her climax crashed over her in huge waves of pulsing intensity.

Rolling off her and collapsing by her side, Phares cradled Aida in his arms. 'You're mine,' he whispered against her hair. 'I'm finally home.'

Yes, his possession of her was complete, thought Aida as she nestled against him, blissfully replete. Every part of her exquisitely branded by Phares, she had never felt so much at peace.

\*     \*     \*

Cairo's Khedivial Royal Opera House had been built nearly a century before by Khedive Ismail for the inaugural celebrations of the opening of the Suez Canal. The wooden building had been designed by two Italian architects, Avoscani and Rossi, as a small-scale replica of Milan's La Scala. The blend of neo-classical columns and arches of its façade and the baroque and rococo interiors made it a beacon of Western aristocratic style.

The theatre was dear to Aida's heart for two reasons. First and foremost because she had cherished memories of accompanying her father each year, but also because of Verdi's opera *Aida*, after which she had been named. Commissioned especially by the Khedive himself, and its first performance in his new Opera

House, the story was set in Egypt during the period of the greatest power of the pharaohs. It had always appealed to Aida, and not just because she was named after the heroine. She found the hopeless love of the Ethiopian slave princess for the general of the Egyptian army that held her prisoner so tragic that she could never listen to the opera without crying.

As the curtain rose to reveal a stage-set of such breathtaking authenticity, Aida had to stifle a gasp. The temples depicted on the backdrop were not today's ruins, but had been restored to their initial glory. She had read in the theatre reviews how the set designers had made a careful study of the tombs and temples in Upper Egypt, wanting to reproduce them faithfully in every detail. Sitting comfortably in her box, her eyes roved over the sculptures and the paintings on the temple walls, the interiors rich with crimson hangings and golden brocade, and throughout the whole of the first two acts she found herself carried back four thousand years to the day when Isis and Osiris were the divinities of the land.

An hour later, as she stood in the foyer with Phares in the interval she felt particularly glamorous in her black silk jersey Balenciaga evening gown, tubular in style with a gathered sweetheart bodice and a wide green satin waistband. The embellished purple bolero she wore over it created a striking contrast, and she could sense heads turning as she and Phares sipped their champagne, the two of them standing out even among the select crowd of bejewelled and elegant leading figures of Cairo's international community.

She leaned towards Phares, who was engrossed in conversation with another surgeon, and whispered, 'I'm going to the cloakroom. If the bell rings, don't wait for me. I'll join you at the box.'

The cloakroom was full as Aida slipped inside, but her sharp eye didn't miss the tall, elegant redhead hurrying past her, wearing a fabulous, almost transparent, red-and-white chiffon gown. Aida recognised her immediately and froze: Nairy.

'Aida, it's you!' Suddenly she was jolted from her thoughts by the familiar voice of Shirley Saunders. 'I haven't seen you in ages, I'm so glad you've recovered from that nasty bug.' Aida forced a smile. 'Ah, Mrs Saunders! How nice to see you again.'

'Oh, I love your dress!' the other woman gushed. 'And do I understand congratulations are in order? You've just married that gorgeous young doctor, haven't you? What's his name? … Pharaony … Phares Pharaony.'

'Thank you.' Aida half breathed a sigh of relief that Shirley Saunders hadn't thought to say any more on the subject of their visit to Wahat El Nakheel. 'Yes, Phares and I were married yesterday in Luxor.'

'He is such a great surgeon. He saved so many lives during the war. Extremely compassionate, I'm told. Have you known him a long time?'

'Yes. In fact, Phares and I grew up together. Our properties are adjoining and his sister Camelia is my best friend.'

'Oh, I see … neighbouring properties. Yes, of course. That's how rich landowners make sure the money is kept among the few elite, isn't it?'

Aida didn't like the insinuation, but she knew everybody took Shirley Saunders's words with a pinch of salt. Anyhow, for the time being, she had other things on her mind.

'If you'll excuse me,' she said, noticing one of the cubicles had become free. 'The bell will be calling us soon.'

'Yes, yes, of course, go ahead … don't let me keep you,' the Englishwoman answered hurriedly, but Aida could tell she was disappointed not to have the opportunity to pry any further.

A few minutes later, Aida was making her way back to the foyer when she heard the end-of-interval bell. Hurrying back to her seat, she rounded a corner and stopped in her tracks. Phares was standing at the door of their box, leaning against the arched frame, in conversation with Nairy.

He was his same cool and collected self, and seemed to be listening quietly to Nairy's somewhat agitated monologue. Then he shook his head with an apologetic air while the model was insisting, gesticulating, obviously pleading with him.

Aida was deliberating whether or not to interrupt their tête-à-tête when she saw her husband take out a card from his inside pocket, scribble something on the back of it and hand it over to the young woman, who immediately smiled and threw her arms around him, kissing him hard on the lips.

Acid churned in Aida's stomach as she watched them together. Phares did not push Nairy away, but simply shook his head as the model disentangled herself from him with that half-amused, indulgent smile that raised one corner of his lips, a smile that had always made Aida feel weak at the knees.

Nairy walked away. Phares stood for a second looking after her, then went back into the box.

Aida could feel herself beginning to tremble. She remained frozen to the ground, while people pushed past her on the way to their boxes. Sick and angry at the same time, she felt foolishly close to tears.

*Would Nairy's shadow always be between her and Phares?*

The bell sounded for the third time, bringing Aida back down to earth. She took a deep breath and hurried back to her place just as the lights were dimming. Phares turned to her with the same loving expression that had lit up his face since she had become his wife.

'What kept you?' he whispered, concern warming his voice. 'I was worried. Are you all right?'

Aida nodded, grateful for the obscurity that cloaked them so he could not see her tears brimming. 'Nothing, nothing ... I'm fine, really.' She felt hot and cold at the same time, sick with an anger directed against herself for her foolish response to what she had just witnessed. Even now, the model was obviously running after her husband, and Phares, gentleman that he was, didn't want to hurt the young woman's feelings. He was probably hoping once she accepted he wasn't a free man, she would leave him alone. Aida wondered whether or not to calmly tell Phares of the day she had seen them at the hospital but she knew she wouldn't: pride forbade her to admit to him that she was capable of such a lowly feeling as jealousy.

During the entire final act of the opera, panic clawed at Aida's stomach. She sat on the edge of her seat, wondering what Phares had written on his card. Whatever it was, it seemed to have calmed the model down, and had been rewarded by a kiss of some exuberance.

'Aida, are you sure you're all right?'

She realised abruptly that the opera had come to an end. The lights had come on, and people were moving in their seats, the auditorium filling with the muted sound of their conversations. The grating noise of chairs, pushed back on the wooden floor in the neighbouring boxes, was painful to her ears. She felt suddenly as though her senses had been scraped raw, like a sore patch of tender skin.

'I'm fine,' she lied. 'Just a bit of a headache, that's all.'

She stood up shakily, outwardly composed, but inside seething with a multitude of confused emotions.

Phares looked down at her tenderly. 'We'll go straight to the hotel and you can go to bed. You've overdone it, *chérie*. You need a good night's sleep. I was selfish and greedy last night. You didn't get much rest, eh?' he said, placing an arm solicitously around her as they went down the few steps that led to the foyer. 'You'll feel better in the morning.'

They drove back to Mena House in silence. Though she was not looking at him, Aida felt Phares's gaze weighing heavily upon her. Once or twice he stretched out his hand to take hers, but she didn't move, her heart willing her body to become insensitive to his touch.

Once in their room, Phares took her in his arms. The way he was looking at her made her tremble. 'You're sure you're feeling all right?'

'Yes, yes, I'm feeling fine. It's as you said … I didn't get much sleep last night.' She was practically gabbling in her desperate need to escape his embrace without raising his suspicions.

His eyes scrutinised her. 'Why are you trembling so much, then?'

'I'm … I'm not,' she lied, protesting.

'I can feel it, Aida. Are you unwell? Is it a migraine?'

'Yes, yes, I can feel it coming on,' she answered quickly, relieved that he had given her a plausible excuse. 'I'll undress and take an aspirin.'

Gently, he pulled her closer as he murmured, 'I remember the migraines you used to get. You used to say that having your scalp massaged was always a far more effective cure than painkillers.'

Aida stared up at him. How did he remember? It was true that when she was younger she had always claimed massage worked better than painkillers for a headache, but it had only really been an excuse to have Phares touch her.

She wriggled in his arms. If he pressed her against him any more, she would be lost. 'No, no, it isn't the same thing,' she insisted, recognising the panic but also the longing in her voice and hoping he wouldn't notice it too. 'Honestly, I'll take an aspirin and get into bed,' she reiterated shakily.

His mouth twisted in a smile she found hard to understand. 'It's all right, Aida. I can take a hint.' He let his arms fall to his side. 'Go ahead and sleep. I'll be in the bar downstairs if you need anything. Just ring reception and they'll fetch me.'

Aida watched Phares close the door behind him and instantly felt bad. She had almost asked him to stay, but she needed to be alone; she needed time to think, needed to fight the tumult that had begun in her the moment she had seen Nairy coming out

of the cloakroom. She didn't want to doubt him. He had finally
declared his love for her, and surely he couldn't have made love
to her the way he had the night before if his feelings had not been
as deep as he claimed? Still, none of it added up; there was a part
of the puzzle that eluded her, and as long as the mystery went
unsolved, she couldn't relax.

\*       \*       \*

It was the low, insistent burr of the bedside telephone that
eventually woke Aida. The alarm clock showed one forty-five in
the morning. She was alone in bed. Groggily, she reached for
the receiver.

'Hello?'

'There is a phone call for Dr Phares Pharaony,' the hotel
receptionist's voice informed her.

'Umm … a phone call? But …'

'Shall I put the person through?'

'Yes, yes, of course. Dr Pharaony is at the bar downstairs, but
I'll take the call.'

*Who could it be at this hour? Camelia? Was she in trouble again?*

'Hello?' she said.

'Is Phares there?'

It was a woman, and although Aida had barely ever heard
Nairy's voice she knew immediately that it was the Armenian
model.

'No, who is this?'

'Where is Phares?'

'Who is this?'

'Then he must be on his way,' the woman murmured, and put
down the receiver.

For a few seconds Aida remained nonplussed, and paused
halfway out of bed, shivering a little. Then, without giving it

a second thought, she went to the wardrobe, pulled on some clothes and shoes, pulled a brush through her hair, and left the room.

She headed straight for the bar. Only a few English officers remained, who turned around as she entered. Ignoring the strange looks they gave her, she went up to the barman: 'Have you seen Dr Pharaony? I am his wife. I have an urgent telephone message to give him.'

The barman smiled obligingly. 'He received a phone call here just a moment ago, Mrs Pharaony. I saw him leave the hotel.'

Aida paled.

*So, he'd gone to her.*

They hadn't been married forty-eight hours and already he was cheating on her. How could he? He must be playing some kind of cruel game with her. Panic gripped her. This couldn't be happening. She must not let it happen. She would wait for him … face him … it was the only way. She needed to get to the bottom of this if she wanted to save her marriage.

\*       \*       \*

Dawn was pointing when Phares finally returned to the hotel. Despite Aida's agitation, exhaustion had got the better of her and she'd fallen asleep on the sofa. A hand touched her shoulder lightly, and she jerked awake.

'Aida, *chérie*, what are you doing, sleeping on the sofa like this?'

She opened her eyes and looked into her husband's face: he looked tired and drawn.

'Phares …? I was waiting up for you.'

'You shouldn't have.'

She sat up, trying to gather her wits. 'Where were you?'

'At the hospital, where else?'

She tried to speak composedly but her voice shook.

'Don't lie to me, Phares.'

He sank down into the chair opposite and looked her straight in the eye. 'I'm not lying to you,' he replied calmly.

'I'm asking you again. Where were you last night and this morning? I have a right to know.'

Phares went to the small minibar in the wall and took out a bottle of cognac. Pouring a large measure into a glass, he said, 'First, I was at the bar, as I told you I would be, and then I went to the hospital.' He took a gulp of brandy and studied her face, frowning. 'Although we have a life together, I also have a life that belongs to others, and you, my dear wife, will have to learn to accept it and trust me. You married a doctor, remember?'

The thought that he was reminding her of their marriage made her vision fill with a strange red haze. She laughed bitterly. 'Oh yes, the perfect alibi! Every time you need one, you can claim you were at the hospital. How convenient.'

Phares caught his breath, the knuckles of his right hand showing bone white against the crystal of the brandy glass in his hand. His brows lowered over dangerously glittering eyes. 'How dare you say such a thing to me!'

For an instant, Aida was afraid at the look on his face. His expression had never been so closed to her, as if all the muscles were iron, but she refused to cower away from him. His words were fuel upon the anger that she had left smouldering inside her for so long, showing its smoke now in her blazing blue irises.

'I will not have the wool pulled over my eyes. I was warned about you and about this affair of yours, but I *still* married you.'

'Stop this, Aida. You're overtired …' He reached out to touch her and in a flare of temper, she flung his hand away.

'Do *not* speak to me as if I'm a child! You and Nairy are lovers. You married me for my land, but *she's* the one you love. *She's* the one you can't live without. All you're thinking about is your Coptic pride, adding more riches to your family's wealth.'

Angry indignation flared fiercely in his eyes. 'By God, that isn't true!' He glowered down at her, barely in control of his emotions.

'Then give me an explanation, Phares. I saw you together at the hospital on the day you were supposed to meet me for lunch. I finished my errands early and went there to see you. As I got there, I saw you both … she was in your arms, and I heard you tell her you'd meet her that evening.' The words were tumbling out in a torrent of pain as she wiped the tears from her face angrily. 'Then on the way to the wedding, I received a note telling me not to marry you because your heart belonged to someone else … It said to ask you where you'd been for the two nights before the wedding. And then tonight, I saw you at the opera. You gave her a note … Was it possibly our room number, Phares?' Aida snapped back, her cheeks aflame with fury, all resolution to hold on to her dignity gone. 'She rang you in the middle of the night and I took the call, but when I went down to the bar you'd gone.' She put her head in her hands. 'We're supposed to be on our honeymoon,' she whispered. 'Then you come back to me at dawn. What am I supposed to think?'

Phares drained his glass in one go. Thrusting a hand through his black hair, he drew a deep, audible breath, like a man about to dive into the depths.

'Aida, I will give you the information you're after this time but make no mistake, I will not be put through an interrogation and asked to account for my whereabouts ever again. You have married a surgeon, but that is beside the point. Marriage in my opinion should be based on trust. If not, there is nothing there.' A strange look crossed his face and he hesitated before continuing. 'I could have put you through a thousand questions when you came back from Kasr El Nawafeer …'

Aida opened her mouth to say something, but Phares stopped her with a peremptory hand. 'Let me finish … But I trusted you, because I know you and I love you. If that wasn't the case,

I wouldn't have married you. I never hid from you that Nairy and I had an affair for a couple of years, but it ended over six months ago. Exactly what I told you before, and it hasn't changed. The day you saw me at the hospital, I was arranging to meet Nairy and her mother that evening to perform an emergency post-operative procedure on Mrs Paplosian, who'd had a serious embolism. I went there to make sure she was all right. She is *my* patient and whether you like it or not, she has priority over my personal life, especially if her life is in danger after an operation *I* have performed. Tonight, I went to the hospital because Nairy and her mother wanted to be reassured that she is out of danger. I would have passed by in the morning, but I preferred to finish with this tonight and be free for you today. I have never been away from the hospital for so long before, and it has unsettled a lot of the staff. It'll be almost impossible to get through to me on the *dahabeyeh*.'

Aida knew that she was hearing the truth.

'Y-you should have told me.'

He took another sip of cognac and shook his head. 'Maybe this time I was wrong in not telling you, but in all sincerity, you took so long in making up your mind to marry me, I didn't think you cared this deeply. You never told me you loved me before, I'm not a mind reader.' His expression softened. 'I only realised it fully when we made love yesterday. Aida, I love you, but I'm not one to answer questions about my whereabouts. You of all people should respect the principle of doctor-patient confidentiality so if I tell you I'm off on business, you must trust me. It's the foundation of all relationships, and especially of marriage.'

The look in Phares's eyes, his earnest words, wiped away any doubts in Aida's mind that she wasn't loved by her husband. Her heart swelled with emotion. This time the tears that ran down her face were ones of relief.

'Phares, I'm so sorry.'

Unable to stay away from him any longer, she went to him, sliding her arms around his waist and pressing her face against the buttoned fastening on his shirt. For a few moments they remained like that, Phares's body stiff and unyielding against hers. Then his control seemed to snap, and with a groan, he gathered her to him. One hard hand turned her face up to his, cupping the fragile hollows of her throat while his mouth played around the edge of hers, coaxing her lips apart before taking passionate possession of them, kissing her with a hungry need that bruised her lips. She kissed him back, wanting it never to stop, loving the feel of his body against hers, loving the smell and taste of him.

Finally, she drew away reluctantly.

'Phares, you look so tired. You need some sleep. Let's get into bed and we'll sleep for a few hours nestled against each other.'

'Yes, my wise little wife.' His eyes glinted mischievously. 'I think you're right. If we don't exercise some restraint, we won't be able to face the camel journey back to the *dahabeyeh* this afternoon.' He gave her a peck on the nose, lifted her into his arms and set her on the bed, before tearing off his clothes and sliding under the sheets next to her, naked.

\*     \*     \*

Moored at a tiny oasis on the banks of the Nile, *Matet*, the Pharaony *dahabeyeh*, was named after the sun boat of Ra, the sun god in Ancient Egyptian mythology. The sky was strewn with streamers of pale rose-coloured clouds, the afternoon light turning the calm river golden by the time Aida and Phares arrived. Leaving their camels with dragomen, they strolled down the hill, through palm groves, along the muddy footpath of the tiny oasis where lemon, guava and mango trees bloomed.

Several young *fellahas* passed them, bearing earthenware jars filled to the brim with river water. Straight-backed and barefooted, they were heading up the dune to the row of long, low mud-brick houses on the topmost ridge, with that easy carriage that comes from balancing heavy loads on one's head from childhood. A group of women seated on the bank of the Nile, not far from where the *dahabeyeh* was moored, were washing their clothes in the murky water. As Phares and Aida reached the bottom of the hill, they rose, coming forward in their long, black, full-sleeved garments, trains dragging over the sand behind them like court dresses. They smiled, flashing teeth in dark faces, and spoke between themselves in hushed, shy voices, curious big dark eyes surrounded by kohl staring almost reverently at the young couple.

Beyond them, the dark-green and gold Pharaony *dahabeyeh* floated on the water.

'It's an elegant yacht, yet a houseboat too,' breathed Aida in admiration as Phares took her on board for a tour.

'It's been converted from its original state. Once it would have needed to be towed by a steam launch if the winds were unfavourable, but now it has a steam engine of its own.' Phares grinned, clearly pleased with her response. He greeted the small crew, standing at the ready in their white *galaleeb*. 'They're part Nubian, part Arab. Fine sailors.'

The eight cabins were exceptionally spacious and opulent, fitted with everything luxurious modern civilisation required. The woodwork was white and the brass shone, the portholes placed so passengers could admire the passing landscape from their beds, which had brass bedsteads no different than some of the ones at home, Aida noticed with surprise. Each bed was spread with an eiderdown because although the days were hot, at night the temperature dropped drastically.

The main salon was on the upper deck, along with a dining room and smoking room. The decks were extremely spacious, spread with carpets and generously fitted with a few deckchairs and rattan chairs with comfy cushions, a table with a glass top and umbrella.

The magnificent houseboat's interior had murals illustrating Ra's sun boat at different stages of its daily journey to the sun, and the ceiling of the main sitting room featured the sacred ship cradled by the protective arms of the giant figure of Nut, goddess of protection. Ra was depicted at the prow, crowned by the sun disk, and in the company of the Ennead of Heliopolis, nine solar deities who featured in the creation myth.

Phares paused as Aida tilted her head back to gaze at the mural.

'It's wonderful, isn't it?'

'The whole of the myth is portrayed on these walls and ceilings.'

'The Boat of a Million Years,' she murmured. It was one of her favourite bedtime stories, which her father loved to tell. In it, Ra and his companion gods sailed through the sky, giving light and heat to the world, but the part of the story she liked most, which always gave her the shivers, was when they boarded another barge, *Sektet*, for the dangerous journey through the night, sailing to the terrifying realm of the Duat in the underworld. Here, they had to battle an evil serpent, Apep, and in defeating him, they kept the universe in order, with right triumphing over wrong.

'The Ancient Egyptians had a delightful and imaginative concept of the universe,' Phares told Aida later on as they sat watching the sunset, sipping champagne on deck in the pleasantly cool hours of the evening. 'They saw their world as confined in something resembling a large box, with a narrow, oblong floor with Egypt as its centre. The Nile, arising from the endless ocean in the south, flowed towards endless Mediterranean in the north. The sky seemed to them somewhat like an iron ceiling sprinkled with suspended stars. The people who lived within this protected, fertile area were *remej*, ordinary folk. All others were dune wanderers, people of the desert.'

To hear Phares explain the mythology of their land with such devotion brought back memories of learning those same stories and ancient beliefs at her father's lap. Aida felt moved, because all at once she felt as if she was home, with family she had known and loved all her life. Not for the first time did she recall how close he had been to Ayoub, how as a boy he had so enjoyed the company of her father. Now it was almost as if it was Ayoub's voice she was hearing, yet this was her husband, Phares; it felt so *right*, and her eyes misted over with grateful tears.

For the next few days, the river stretched endlessly away before them, smooth as glass. The sky was always cloudless, the days warm, the evenings exquisite. Every reach or bend of the river presented objects of delight and historical interest. Aida had started a diary and she spent much time observing and painting with words the vivid images she was seeing and the emotions they aroused in her.

Each morning, they sat on deck, Aida writing letters and her diary; Phares reading medical journals. Now and then, they raised their heads to watch the sunny riverside scenes sliding by at walking pace amid the palm groves, sandbanks, and patches of fuzzy-headed *doora*, maize, and cotton fields: a boy plodding along the bank between the papyrus and the stones, leading a camel laden with cotton; girls coming to the water's edge carrying great empty jars on their heads, waiting to fill them when the boat had gone by. Pigeon towers of mud villages peeped through clumps of *lebbek* trees; a solitary *fellah*, felt skullcap on his head and only a slip of scanty tunic fastened about his loins, working the long pole of a *shaduf*, stooping and rising again and again, with the regularity of a pendulum. This scene was no different to the paintings Aida had seen in the tombs of Thebes: the man so closely resembled an Ancient Egyptian that she found herself wondering fancifully how he had escaped being mummified four or five thousand years ago.

After lunch, replete with food and sunshine, Aida and Phares retired to their cabin for a siesta, where they alternated between lazily exploring each other's bodies and sleeping, reviving themselves for the evening hours. And the nights ... oh, such nights! The stars shone with a lustrous brilliancy that was so intense. Aida's senses were overwhelmed by the perfect little world that encompassed them ... the boat, with her broad sails and her long wake whitening in the moonlight, glided smoothly as her Arab crew, lying on deck, chanted their peculiar and plaintive songs. Sometimes the scream of a startled pelican or the gurgle of some huge fish as it wallowed in the water might disturb the silence for a moment, but it only made the calm that followed more profound.

Aida and Phares often sat up late into the night, quietly absorbing the sounds of the moonlit river before returning to the privacy of their cabin to explore further the delights of each other. Their hunger for one another was insatiable, and each tried to emulate the other in trying new ways and positions to maximise their mutual pleasure.

One night, Phares produced a book, the Kama Sutra. 'It's the bible of sex positions,' he told Aida, his intense dark irises dancing with wickedness. 'Inspiring, don't you think?' he added as he flipped the pages.

'Completely wanton,' she answered, though an illicit thrill chased a quivering path up her spine.

'Just like you, *chérie*,' he teased with a lazy amusement, pulling her against him and kissing the side of her neck. 'Were you a courtesan in another life?'

'That's not a very nice thing to say,' she dimpled.

He leaned back to look at her, trailing the backs of his fingers down her cheek. 'On the contrary ... You are never so beautiful as when you're enjoying giving yourself to me. The Kama Sutra is very wise when it comes to the power of a woman's sexual pleasure. Unlike men, those of your sex are mysterious, like a seashell, delicate and deep. When making love, they open up to show their beloved their core. Then they close their shell up again, away from other prying eyes. It makes the man feel special … proud and honoured.'

'Then why do so many men in our circle take mistresses after they are married? It seems to be the norm. Most women seem to accept it – in fact, some even welcome it.'

'That's because neither the man nor the woman in our stilted society understands the principle of lovemaking. When a wife becomes the mistress of her husband, and not a mere procreation machine, it is the most wonderful thing. Love is something you give, not take. So many Coptic couples tend to forget that. Our men are selfish, and our women have not been taught the art of seduction. The Coptic Church has much to answer for.' His fingers traced the outline of her jaw. 'I think nothing can be more beautiful than a wanton sharing of pleasure behind closed doors in the privacy of a husband and wife's bedroom.'

His touch on her skin was distracting her, making her pulse dance. 'Where on earth did you get all these ideas? I would have never thought you so broadminded.'

Phares gave a throaty laugh. 'This broadmindedness, as you call it, has strings attached.'

Aida's gaze was riveted to her husband.

His eyes raked over her as his fingers trailed down to the neckline of her cotton dress. 'I am a very possessive and jealous lover, *chérie*. If you ever gave me reason to doubt your faithfulness, I would never touch you again.'

Her breathing deepened. 'I will never give you cause to doubt my love or fidelity.'

Phares's hand went lower, his thumb lazily circling one nipple, which instantly hardened against the thin fabric of her dress. 'You are a very provocative woman, *chérie*. Men will pursue you,' he murmured huskily, staring down at her.

Aida gasped at his touch and countered breathily, 'What about you? You're not the celibate type. You have such a fierce sex drive.'

He laid a finger on her lips to keep her quiet, and bent over to whisper against her mouth, 'I love you. I want you. Now and always …' Then he silenced her in the most effective way possible by bringing his mouth down hard on hers.

Struggling to draw herself away a little, she gazed deep into his eyes. 'You won't tire of me?'

His hand slid down her body and slipped beneath her skirt, his dextrous fingers finding her feminine core, drawing a deep moan of need from his wife. 'Will you get tired of this, *chérie*?'

'No,' she breathed as waves of desire began to storm inside her.

His fingers worked backwards and forwards between her slick heat. 'Why would I ever feel the need to stray when I have you with me, feeling you throbbing and swelling under my touch, your warmth flooding my fingertips? As long as you lust for me, your cries of pleasure in my arms will come between me and any other woman.'

In an instant, he pulled his shirt over his head and intoxicated with excitement, Aida's eyes feasted on his naked torso, his muscles like bronzed marble. 'Take off your dress,' he growled. 'It's time you experienced just how inspiring the Kama Sutra can be.'

His hungry gaze travelled the length of Aida's body as her dress fell in a pool around her feet, and he quickly rid himself of the rest of his clothes.

Phares proceeded to sit on the bed with his legs crossed. Aida could see that he was totally aroused and that a muscle in his cheek was clenching and unclenching spasmodically. 'Come,' he said in a low, husky voice, leaning forwards as he extended his hand and pulled her towards him. 'Sit on my lap and wrap your legs around my waist.'

The aching emptiness low in her pelvis intensified as Aida stared at him, drinking in his magnificent arousal. 'You're beautiful,' she whispered.

She would gladly have taken a snapshot of him in this position; he was completely perfect: a classic pharaonic statue of flesh and blood.

'Take me inside you,' he ordered softly.

She gave a shocked gasp as she slid on to him. He felt so good, so hard, sinking into her with a depth that they hadn't experienced previously, and instinctively, she wrapped her legs even tighter around his waist, hugging him to her with her arms and her thighs.

'Yes,' he whispered, his hand at the small of her back, pushing into her further so he was buried to the hilt. They began to rock backwards and forward in unison.

'Yes, *chérie* ... wrap me up in your moist cocoon. You're so soft, so deliciously wet for me.' Phares thrust hard and deep inside her, and she was groaning, digging her nails into him, bucking convulsively as he took her to a level of pleasure so fierce it made their previous encounters seem almost tame. 'You want this, don't you? It feels good, eh?'

He lowered his head, and his mouth caught one taut pink peak and then the other. Aida's breathing came in rasps as she quivered, craving those magician's hands on her breasts. Attuned to her needs, Phares cupped them in his palms, hard and swollen, squeezing the aching flesh, and she jerked as his tongue swirled around each jutting crest in turn, gasping as he nibbled and sucked at them, sending lightning arcing through her all the way down to her womb.

And now he took her hand and placed it between their bodies, just at the point where he had entered her. 'Touch me here, and let me touch you,' he groaned as his fingers reached from underneath and started to tease her throbbing bud.

'Phares ... oh, Phares!' Words poured from her lips, words that in other conditions would have made her blush, they were so crude; all thought of preserving some propriety lost in the need for further erotic sensations. But she didn't care; she was shaking in every cell of her body, only aware of the amazing sensation of him filling her, of him stroking the crux of her need with measured, rhythmic strokes that made everything burn and tingle, tighten and clench inside her.

Phares placed his hot lips against her ear, nuzzled the side of her neck, drawing on her flesh, branding her with a small mark before nibbling at the lobe. 'You want more? I can feel it. You're getting hotter, and wetter ... I can feel you throbbing under my fingers, begging for release.'

'Yes, more ...' she groaned, rocking backwards and forwards, moving up and down frantically on top of him.

Phares responded intuitively, stroking her bottom, cupping the round, full cheeks, spreading them wider on top of him so his rigid shaft could delve deeper into her moist core, and she opened further in response to his caressing fingers.

'Yes, oh yes!' Aida panted as her hand joined the caressing. This spinning madness was just too much. She was dizzy, the tension in her body coiled like a spring; she was getting wetter and wetter. She passed her tongue over her lips, savouring the stimulating sensations mushrooming in her centre. Was she touching him or herself? She couldn't tell anymore. All she knew was they were one ... their bodies were one, their souls were one ... She didn't want this thrilling pleasure flooding her every nerve to stop.

And now he was taking her lips in his mouth in no gentle exploratory kiss, his agile tongue darting in and out, enacting what his hard manhood was doing within her while his fingers still fondled her moist, aching core. Aida burned from the inside out, certain she was about to ignite as he continued with his persistent rhythmic thrusts. It was as if her body was soaring high into space, waves of ecstasy washing over her, stronger and stronger. She was panting, desperate for completion.

'Please,' she sobbed.

'Soon, very soon, *chérie*,' he whispered in her ear as lifting himself up and holding her against him, he turned and laid her on the bed.

Phares's mouth returned to Aida's with a violence that made her gasp. Still, she gave herself up to his kiss with such ardour that a great shudder ran through him and he tightened his arms around her savagely, tipping her head back with the force of an overwhelming surge of passion that left them both helpless against its drive.

Aida was ready for his onslaught when, shoving her legs apart, he slammed inside her, pumping harder and faster, issuing the primitive male demand for her submission which she welcomed with every nerve, every sinew, every breath in her body. She pushed him as hard as he was pushing her. He was claiming her, possessing her, and that was what she wanted … what she craved.

Arching did not seem enough. Clinging was not enough either. Aida wanted to feel more of him inside her and parting her legs wider to give him further access, she lifted herself up on her elbows to meet his merciless thrusts.

Her body wept with pleasure, scalding tears of honey that made Phares groan. 'Yes, Aida … yes, *chérie*, open up for me … love me, Aida … never stop!' His thrusts were getting wilder as he pressed her down into the bed, setting a frantic rhythm of plunges, blotting out all thoughts except the pain and the ecstasy his body was administering.

And now Phares's body had become rigid. Aida knew that he was trying to control his climax. Hers was coming too, the waves growing stronger and stronger … she was almost there. Her internal muscles tightened like a fist around his flesh.

She heard him let out a fierce growl, then he erupted inside her with a groan that sounded like that of a wild animal, the hot liquid of his seed flooding her, and it was this last push that rushed Aida over the edge. She met him, exploding into tiny shards of fractured light, gasping and writhing on the bed in the throes of a climax that went on and on, softening finally into a series of delicious aftershocks as she floated down from the stars to which he had taken her.

They collapsed together and lay spent, panting, still trembling and moaning, replete with pleasure.

Aida purred as Phares's arm encircled her. The power of this magic between them was beyond measure.

'Still doubt the hold you have on me, *chérie*?'

'No,' she said, her voice shaky. She stroked his flushed face, feeling the heat in his skin, still excited by the evidence he had shown her of how he felt.

For a moment she lay there, her breathing calming gradually. 'Phares, when I think of how it nearly went wrong, how we might never have got together again …'

He laughed softly. 'Shuush, *chérie*. All that is in the past now. *Ehna welad el naharda*, we are today's children.'

\*     \*     \*

Aida and Phares spent the next few days visiting the monuments between Cairo and Assiut. First, they stopped at the Middle Kingdom necropolis of Beni Hassan, where a group of rock-cut tombs had been carved into the high limestone cliffs on the eastern banks of the river. Aida had been particularly delighted to find that it was on their itinerary because her father's next big excavation project would have taken them there. She couldn't help but feel a pang of sadness, though, as they walked through the subterranean burial chambers and gazed at the colourful

paintings of everyday life, hunting and warfare adorning the walls
of the tombs.

How she missed Ayoub!

Phares seemed to intuit her sorrow and encircled her shoulders
with his arm, drawing her closer to him. She looked up at him
with a grateful smile and vowed that, for his sake, she would try
not to dwell on what might have been – it was the here and now
that mattered.

The next day, they decided to press on to Denderah to visit
the Temple of Hathor, which her father had always praised for
the magnificence of its decoration. Given the Goddess Hathor
was the patron of the Pharaony home, it seemed only right that
she and Phares should visit. Both agreed that they couldn't pass
by without stopping, although it would take the whole day and
part of the night to get there. They didn't mind, though. They
loved every part of this leisurely cruise, discovering each other's
minds during the days and their bodies during the nights.

As if in some languid dream they passed the cool green reaches
of Manfalout on the west bank and its picturesque terraced
gardens by the waterside; they saw crested minarets and fretted
domes, and floated on to where the Arabian Desert again closed
in and precipitous mountain crags frowned over the river.

From time to time, a monotonous chant on three notes, which
must surely have been heard by the very first pharaohs themselves,
echoed at different places along the shore. Half-naked men on
the banks, with torsos of bronze and voices all alike, intoned it
in the morning when commencing their labours and continued
throughout the day, until the evening brought them repose. Aida
loved this song of the water drawers – the song of the *shaduf*,
accompanied by the slow cadences of creaking wet wood. She
found the movements of the men manoeuvring it to have
a singular beauty: one man would lower the wooden lever to
draw water from the river while the next would catch the filled

bucket in its ascent, emptying it into a basin made out of the mud of the riverbank.

With both sails set and flying before the wind, they saw the panorama unfold itself rapidly, mile after mile, hour after hour. Villages, palm groves, rock-cut sepulchres all flitted past and were left behind.

They arrived at Denderah in the early morning. In the pre-dawn, the Nile was the colour of ink, the current invisible on its glassy surface. Morning mists hung across the top of the water and the stillness was such that the silhouettes of the robed figures of the crew, huddled in blankets on the shore, seemed transfixed. A couple of feluccas had joined their *dahabeyeh* for the night and together, the boats moored at the side of the darkening river evoked the ancient and romantic scenes of a David Roberts painting.

Phares and Aida waited until the sun was up before starting their journey to the ruins, four kilometres away. A crowd of boys with their donkeys were waiting for any foreigners wanting to visit the temple, although today there were few people except some local guides sitting around smoking and *fellahin* in the neighbouring fields. The heat had dropped and there was a pleasant breeze, so unusual for a summer's day. Phares hired a couple of donkeys and, along with one of the boys, they made their way to the Temple of Hathor.

They came to a plain, green and level as a lake, widening out to the foot of the mountains – and the temple, islanded in that sea of rippling emerald, rose up before them upon its platform of stone and blackened mounds of earth. Although they were still far off, it looked enormous, a sharply defined mass of dead-white masonry. The walls sloped in slightly towards the top and the façade appeared to be supported on six massive columns, with the remnants of a large stone doorway still standing in the centre of the courtyard leading to the main temple building.

'It looks very naked and solemn,' Aida remarked. 'More like a tomb than a temple.'

'That's because we're too far away to distinguish any of the carvings or images of legends on the walls,' Phares answered, squinting into the distance. 'I've visited this temple before, and trust me, the paintings are remarkable and so well preserved.'

As they drew nearer and the ground rose, the details of the temple gradually became more distinct. It was surrounded by a hefty mud brick enclosure. Inside the boundary, rows of ruined walls showed the original position of the ancient streets and what was once their buildings.

And now they were close enough for Aida to see that the huge, round columns of the façade were topped with stone-headed Hathor capitals, the rays of the sun seeming to light a spark of life in their carved eyes and accentuate the melancholy smile that gives most Egyptian statues such a mysterious attraction. And the walls, instead of being smooth and tomb-like, were covered with a multitude of sculpted figures.

'It's one of the only temples with its roof intact,' Phares told her as they dismounted, leaving their donkeys with the boy. While he waved away a couple of men trying to sell them trinkets, Aida watched as the boy led the animals over to a man sitting by the ruins of the great doorway. Then she felt Phares take her hand, leading her quickly towards the pillared entrance of the imposing temple.

'Those zodiacs and murals on the ceilings are so detailed and vivid in colour, it's like they were painted only yesterday,' Aida murmured in awe as they entered the magnificent edifice. She felt dwarfed by the gargantuan columns rising up to the vaulted ceiling, each covered with elaborate carved reliefs set against exquisitely painted blue backgrounds.

Phares still held her hand. 'Come, let's climb up the staircase to the roof. You'll see how intricately the zodiac has been carved into the ceiling.'

The effect of the portico as Aida stood at the top of the staircase was one of overwhelming majesty. Hieroglyphs, emblems, strange forms of kings and gods covered every foot of wall space, frieze and pillar. Images of the sky goddess, Nut, swallowing Ra, the sun god, at dusk to birth him back to the world at dawn were spread out all along the walls.

Phares gestured towards one of the paintings, his mouth curving with amusement. 'I can tell you, the god Amon himself, the procreator, is often crudely drawn, but even he would seem chaste compared with the hosts of this temple.'

The beautiful goddess Hathor – her throat, her hips, her unveiled nakedness – was portrayed with a searching and lingering realism; her flesh seemed almost to quiver. She and her handsome spouse contemplated each other naked, their laughing eyes seemingly alive and intoxicated with love.

'Our ancestors, no doubt,' Aida added, raising her gaze to Phares with an intimate smile.

He slipped his hand around her waist and kissed her lightly on the lips before turning back to the depiction of Hathor and her husband Horus. 'Sex was an important part of life in Ancient Egypt, untainted by guilt. Both singles and married couples made love, and even the gods themselves were earthy enough to copulate. People think that the Kama Sutra was the first sex manual of its kind, but there is a famous Ancient Egyptian papyrus painting discovered at Deir el-Medina in the early nineteenth century, created during the Ramses period, that pre-dates it.' He grinned at her mischievously. 'It portrays in the most erotic way what went on between the bedsheets in Ancient Egypt.'

'Really? I've never heard of it.'

'It's in the Museo Egizio in Turin. I'm sure your father would have been familiar with it. The museum houses one of the largest collections of Egyptian antiquities, after Cairo, that is. I'd like to take you there one day.'

Aida glanced up at him with laughter in her eyes. 'I never knew that you were so knowledgeable about Ancient Egyptian erotica.'

Phares winked at her. 'There are many things you don't know about me, *chérie*.'

*I bet*, she thought, as they moved off to continue their walk through the temple. As each day passed, she was beginning to discover more and more about her new husband and she'd already realised that Phares had a deeper side to him that he didn't show off to the world, and she admired him for that. It made him seem mysterious, which only enhanced his appeal, but she wished that he would share more of himself with her. There were always things about him that felt out of reach.

It was as they were finally leaving the site that Aida noticed the Bedouin for the first time. She knew that he was a Bedouin, not only because he had a different build to the *fellahin* in the fields and the guides who hovered around the monuments, but also because of the way he dressed, his pure white *keffiyeh* shawl wrapped around his head and face, showing only his eyes. In his hand he held a string of blue beads and a knife was hung on a belt around his waist. He seemed to be following them and now that Aida thought about it, she realised he had been sitting by the entrance when they arrived, talking to the boy with the donkeys.

As they approached their young guide, Phares dropped back a little. When Aida looked back, she noticed that he was in deep conversation with the Bedouin, who appeared to be showing him something. Phares's tall frame was in the way and Aida couldn't make out what it was, but she noticed that the *keffiyeh* had now slipped from the man's face. His well-chiselled features, the thin, hooked nose and high cheekbones, were unmistakable – she had seen Bedouin tribesmen like this at the prince's oasis. A strange sense of foreboding crept over her, but she brushed it aside, putting it down to the memory of her unpleasant experience at Wahat El Nakheel, which was still vivid in her mind.

The two men did not speak for long, but then Aida saw Phares shove something in his pocket before making his way back to her.

'Who was that?'

He shrugged. 'Oh, one of those pedlars. They always hang around the sites, pestering people and trying to trick them into buying their stuff,' he told her lightly.

'He's a Bedouin.'

'Maybe … they're all Bedouins around here.'

She frowned. 'Did you buy anything from him?'

'No, why would I do that?'

Aida didn't insist, but she was sure that she had seen Phares put something in his pocket.

It had been a long and exhausting day. On the way back, the donkeys weren't particularly cooperative either. At one point, Aida's obstinate animal ran into a cornfield and refused to budge. She had to climb on to Phares's donkey for part of the way so it took them double the time to reach their *dahabeyeh*.

They had supper on deck as the twilight gloom lay warm upon the landscape and afterwards had an early night. For once, Phares seemed restless and not very talkative. Aida put it down to tiredness and she was so exhausted herself that she fell asleep as soon as her head hit the pillow.

It was three o'clock in the morning when she woke to find that Phares wasn't lying next to her. The *dahabeyeh* was at a standstill, and although it was dark outside, she could see through the porthole that they were at Luxor. Puzzled, she got up, slipped on her dressing gown and went up on deck.

Phares was nowhere to be seen, but she found Mahmoud, the head boatman, sitting on one of the steps to the boat, drinking a glass of ink-coloured tea and smoking.

'*Feen el Bey*? Where's the *Bey*?'

The Nubian shrugged. '*Maarafsh*, I don't know.'

'Has he been gone long? Has something happened?'

Before the man could answer, Aida saw Phares drive up in his Jeep. A moment later, he was hurrying up the steps to the boat.

'You're up, *chérie*,' he said, beaming.

'Yes, where have you been? I was rather worried when I woke up and didn't find you. And why are we in Luxor? Has anything happened? Aren't we going to Philae next?'

Phares placed an arm around her shoulders and smiled reassuringly. 'Slowly, slowly, so many questions ... I'll explain everything in good time, but for now, go and get dressed because we're going out.'

'*Out*?' Aida stared at him. 'Where?'

Taking her hand, he almost dragged her to the bedroom. 'Just throw anything on, we're not going far.'

His excitement was infectious. Aida found herself doing as he said and dressed quickly. While the mercurial side to her husband might have thrown other women, she found it fascinating as it suited her own taste for adventure.

She was ready in a few minutes and hand in hand, they almost ran to the Jeep, to the surprise of Mahmoud, who by now had risen and was standing at the bottom of the steps of the *dahabeyeh* with a bewildered expression on his face as they rushed past.

'Where are we going?' Aida asked again as Phares started up the Jeep.

But he wouldn't tell her, just threw her a smile and drove along the dark, quiet roads while she leant her head against the back of her seat and closed her eyes. She must have dozed a little as soon Aida heard Phares's voice again.

'Wake up, *chérie*, we're here!'

Quickly sitting up, Aida looked around her and saw that they were at the temple complex at Karnak. She gave Phares a puzzled look, but he was already coming around to the passenger side to help her out.

They walked up to the temple and a man appeared and opened a pair of tall, wrought-iron doors for them.

It was dark inside. Aida reached for Phares and his hand closed round hers – warm, reassuring.

'I don't understand,' she said in a whisper. 'Why have you brought me here now?'

'You'll see, *chérie*. Come on.'

Aida had visited the remains of the temple in daylight and knew that it was beautiful when the sun shone on it, bringing out the details of the hieroglyphics carved into the yellow sandstone. But, tonight, there was only a thin crescent of a moon and the ruins were engulfed in an eerie darkness. The guard had lit his lantern, and had given one to Phares, but their feeble glimmer only emphasised, rather than dissipated, the darkness in which they moved. In the dancing shadow of the moving lanterns the half-buried pylons, the solitary obelisk, the giant head of the pharaoh rising in ghastly resurrection before the entrance to the temple, floated before their eyes for a moment, then suddenly faded away and were reabsorbed by the darkness. A vague presence seemed to hover in the gloom, pursuing them along the avenue of sphinxes and from chamber to chamber. At any moment at the turn of a corridor, Aida half expected to meet the figure of a priest come back to his post after centuries of absence, or to hear the jingling of distant timbrels pierce the silence, announcing the coming of Tutankhamun.

By now, Phares had sent the guard away with a hefty *bakshish*, tip. But Phares seemed to know his way and led them unerringly along. Finally, he came to a stop and Aida was aware of the huge stone forest of papyrus-crowned columns all around her. They had entered the hypostyle hall of the Great Temple of Amun. Above them, stars glimmered in the night sky, visible through the roofing slabs lying across the mighty columns of this vast hall.

Phares gently pulled Aida against him. 'This is a special place, Aida. It can only be appreciated at this hour,' he murmured next to her ear. 'You need to imagine it as it used to be, feel the emotions it roused in the souls of the faithful. This is one of the most magical gifts I could think of giving you on our honeymoon.'

Suddenly, he let go of her and moved away. For a split second, Aida felt nervous, but her husband's warm voice came softly out of the darkness and began to tell her of the boy king Tutankhamun, who had come this way to his coronation, of the priests and court nobles who had led him in, a small child of nine, walking beneath these great columns. He told her of the musicians who had played for him, their music echoing among the stones as the great procession moved slowly on to the inner temple and into the presence of Amun, the god of gods.

'Close your eyes, Aida. Don't you hear the drums and the lutes and the reed pipes?'

Phares began to recite poetry to her, some in the original Ancient Egyptian, some that she could understand. His words danced in her head, telling of the young pharaoh, the living embodiment of a god, and the heroes and deities of these ancient lands.

There was silence as his voice died away, then he spoke again, 'Open your eyes, *chérie*. Look up.'

Aida did as he said and saw the first rays of dawn suddenly breaking through the sky, the rich golden light touching the carved heads of the columns, bringing to life the brilliant colours that still adorned them. She caught her breath as carved muscles seemed to flex, eyes to see, and mouths to smile, welcoming the new day.

The sun rose and the temple filled with glorious light, once again becoming the place of worship it was created to be, reaching out for the dawn's serenade, and as it had done for thousands of years, showing itself to be the greatest monument that man had ever made to their gods.

Aida stood and stared until the sun parted from the horizon, until the sky was completely blue, the glory of the dawn forever reaching out to another land. Her heart felt as if it would burst with the wonder of it and with love for her husband, who had come to stand next to her again. She turned to him, but was unable to speak. The love and tenderness Aida read in Phares's eyes surged through her every being. She felt it in the clamour of her heart, her yearning for the everlasting happiness that might be clutched at and coaxed into more than a fitful ray.

Placing an arm around her, Phares led her out into the wakening town and, without needing to speak a word, they drove back to the *dahabeyeh*.

*       *       *

The approach by water to the small island of Philae, the last stop of their honeymoon, was truly breathtaking. The river widened, flowing past gigantic black rocks of the most fantastic shape and form, and then suddenly, after a couple of sharp turns, Philae came suddenly into view, fringed by palms and crowned with a long line of temples and colonnades. Seen from the *dahabeyeh*, the island with its vegetation and its monuments seemed to rise out of the river like a chimera.

'It's incredible,' breathed Aida, standing on deck next to Phares while the boat glided nearer and the sculpted towers rose higher and higher against the sky. 'One can almost forget for a moment that the temple was built centuries ago. It all looks so solid, stately and perfect.'

Neither Phares nor Aida had visited the temple before and both stood in reverent awe.

'Right now, if we heard the sound of ancient chanting and a procession of white-robed priests was to appear now, I wouldn't think it so strange,' Phares observed. 'I can see now why Philae has been the subject of so many paintings. I've never seen anything so superb.'

The crew of the *dahabeyeh* scrambled off the boat to moor it in the shallows, allowing Aida and Phares down the steps.

'Do you know much about the island?' she asked, looking about her. Further up the shoreline, some fishing boats were moored and figures moved about slowly by the water's edge. 'The only thing I remember is that during pharaonic times it was known to be one of the burial places of Osiris, who became god of the afterlife.'

'Exactly. It was called the Holy Island and became known as the Pearl of Egypt. The ground was so sacred, only priests and temple attendants were allowed to live there, though it was still a pagan temple to the cult of Isis long after Christianity arrived here,' Phares told Aida as he helped her up the steep bank towards the monumental gateway of the great temple.

'The Ancient Egyptians thought that the Nile ended at Philae,' he went on. 'The Coptic-derived name was Pilak, meaning "the end" or "remote place", probably because it marked the boundary with Nubia. There are many legends connected to Philae, but the most famous one tells the story of how the almighty goddess Isis, wife of Osiris, found the heart of her husband here after he was murdered by his brother Seth. It was the last part of Osiris's body she'd gathered up, after they'd been strewn about the earth, and so, with her renowned magical powers, she was able to restore his body to life.'

'Perhaps that's why the island is called Philae, Greek for "beloved". Yes, I remember the story of Osiris's murder, but I didn't know there were others.'

'Are you familiar with the tale of the Angry Eye who abandoned Egypt?'

'No, whose eye was that?'

'It was a very popular myth during Greco-Roman times. After the god creator Atum had produced Shu and Tefnut, they became lost in the watery darkness of the *nun*, the waters of chaos. Atum sent his eye, the eye of Ra, to find them, thereby giving light to darkness. The eye returned with Shu and Tefnut, but went into a rage when she saw that Atum had grown a new solar eye. She ran away to a faraway land, thought to be Nubia. There, the eye took the form of a fiery lion that stalked the desert, killing and eating the flesh of her enemies. Recovered by the wise god Thoth, she was immersed in the Nile at Philae to cool her rage.'

Standing by the high stone gateway, entranced by the view, Aida's eyes were drawn to the still waters of the Nile, untroubled as they reflected the light blue of the sky. She didn't care to hear tales of jealousy and rage; she'd had her fill of those turbulent emotions for a lifetime. Her gaze slid to Phares, who had wandered on ahead, scrutinising the remnants of two granite lions guarding the entrance. Watching him run a hand through his hair distractedly, his handsome brow furrowed in thought, her heart gave a wrench as she realised that part of her still ached with uncertainty. *Surely I deserve a bit of happiness?* she thought to herself. *I only want Phares, nothing more.* But even now, when he was at last hers, Aida could not help but wonder if the fates would pluck him from her.

Later, after they had wandered around the island, Phares and Aida sat down to rest on a stone bench on a terrace overlooking the Nile. From there, they could see where the great river was divided into several channels by other rocky islands and beyond were the desert and the great granite hills of Assuan.

Phares drew her attention back to the ruins of Philae. 'These immense buildings have a certain solemn grandeur, don't they?'

Aida nodded pensively. 'When we walked through the Temple of Isis, I couldn't help but feel that tramping these sacred places is somehow profane,' she murmured. She glanced at the tall palms, their heavy branches seeming to bend over the ruins as though they were weeping, and gave a little shiver. 'Do you believe in the curse of the pharaohs? Do you think that in disturbing the tombs of the ancients, they signed their own death warrant, or that the strange number of deaths were caused by the release of bacterial spores, or whatever scientists now think?'

Phares shrugged. 'My father believes that Egyptian curses are a product of our superstitious culture and their psychological impact can be powerful. When you look at those curses, they were designed to strike terror into the hearts of tomb robbers. For example, there are some tombs where the pharaoh has inscribed a curse, like the one etched in the tomb of Khentika Ikhekhi, which reads something like: "*Who ever shall enter my tomb will be judged ... an end shall be made for him ... I shall seize his neck like a bird ... I shall cast the fear of myself into him.*" I can't remember the exact wording.' He turned to Aida and smiled, catching hold of her hand. 'Do you think we'll be cursed for coming here, is that it, *chérie*?'

She laughed and shook her head, thinking of the Victorians and their plundering of the sacred tombs and temples of the island. Her English forebears perhaps deserved a curse or two to fall on their heads, she thought wryly.

'The Temple of Philae was the last stronghold of the Ancient Egyptian priesthood, that's for sure,' continued Phares. 'It has a power that none can deny, but I don't think we'll be judged for coming here.' His gaze returned to the distant hills and Aida thought she caught a wistful undertone to his words.

It was as they were making their way down through the rocks at the foot of the temple complex to the *dahabeyeh*, which was moored further up the shoreline, that Aida noticed the Bedouin she had seen at Denderah. He sat smoking on one of the low boulders with a couple of fishermen, who were casting nets into the water. As they reached the river's edge, he did not move, but from the corner of her eye Aida saw him throwing away his cigarette. Moments later, she was aware that he was following them.

'There's that Bedouin again,' she told Phares.

His eyebrows drew together. 'What Bedouin?'

'You know, the man we saw at Denderah. The one who tried to sell you something.'

'How do you know he's the same man?'

'I recognised him.'

Phares kept walking. 'Don't take any notice.'

When they reached the boat, the Bedouin was still behind them, standing a few feet away, watching them intently.

'Wait here,' Phares told Aida.

He went over to the man. Although Aida could not hear what they were saying, she could see that they were having an obviously heated conversation. Finally, Phares came back, seemingly having sent the Bedouin away with a flea in his ear.

'What was all that about?'

Phares smiled, though there was something inscrutable in his eyes. 'You were right, it was the same seller offering the same stuff. They never give up. Anyhow, I doubt he'll bother us anymore. I told him if I saw him prowling around again, I would report him to the police.' Catching her around the waist, he gently kissed her forehead. 'There's nothing to worry about, *chérie*, I promise you.'

The honeymoon was almost over, and as they climbed to the *dahabeyeh*, Aida felt a strange sense of foreboding, quite different to the sadness that comes upon one at the end of an idyllic trip – an inexplicable apprehension of what was to come.

# Chapter 15

El Amal, Phares Pharaony's hospital on the edge of Luxor, stood in its own grounds overlooking the Nile. It was an attractive, new building with semicircular wings, watered lawns, and wide windows giving on to balconies where the patients could sit in the sun and enjoy its strengthening rays, especially during winter and springtime, or in summer sit in the bowers of shade provided by cascading purple bougainvillea. Zinnias and dahlias made vivid splashes of colour against the white-painted timber, and clumps of Egyptian papyrus grass raised their graceful heads in the afternoon sunlight, while drowsy butterflies flitted lazily among the flowers in the gardens and crickets chirruped incessantly on the slope to the river's edge.

This was Aida's third week at the hospital since their return from honeymoon. On their many nights aboard the *dahabeyeh*, talking about their experiences of the war and Aida's love of nursing, Phares had finally suggested that she come to work with him at El Amal. It was clear to him that Aida would never be happy simply running a household – she would need her own work and focus. He had no doubt at all that she would be a great asset to the hospital. After all, during her wartime training, she had been confronted with situations that went far beyond anything she might have learned in peacetime.

Aida had been thrilled by his suggestion, and settled into her new job immediately, observing the way things were done and learning the ropes easily. Each hospital she had been seconded to during the war had had its own idiosyncratic organisation and so, for her, learning to adapt quickly was familiar territory. She knew her work and loved it, and had such a way with patients and staff that she rapidly charmed everyone around her. Within a few days she began to feel as if she already belonged.

Still, it was early days and she hadn't yet started to work with Phares or any of the other surgeons. After her surgical nurse training in England, she knew that assisting in the operating theatre was where she really wanted to be, but she was in no hurry. Apart from anything, the theatre was a domain partially ruled over by Isis, and it hadn't taken Aida long to discover that the anaesthetist was universally disliked. Although first class at her job, Isis had no patience with the nurses, or compassion for the sick who needed reassurance. Of course, not one member of the staff had actually complained about Isis's behaviour – some of them even played up to her in a bid to gain her approval – but instinct told Aida that they were afraid of Isis and because they knew the anaesthetist was a personal friend of Phares's, they hadn't dared to be critical. Still, even if the nurses didn't dare grumble, the patients talked frankly enough.

Camelia, with her unerring perspicacity, had hit the nail on the head when she'd made the observation that Isis lacked any real love of humanity – 'I mean to say, how can someone be a healer without that? I think Phares has a blindness when it comes to that cold-hearted witch!'

It was clear to Aida from Isis's body language that her thwarted rival was simmering with fury; she was behaving like a sulky beauty queen who had failed to win the title. Scarcely addressing a word to Aida, unless it was to criticise her work, the tight-faced anaesthetist pored over patients' charts trying to find fault – some slip-up in the administering of medication or something that hadn't been filled in according to hospital procedure. Aida made a point of never answering back, instead gritting her teeth and going about her business quietly. Keeping her distance was the wisest course of action for now. The last thing she wanted was to create problems for Phares. Although she was his wife – and a good nurse into the bargain – she knew that Isis was far more indispensable to the hospital. If Aida couldn't make this work, then it was only right that she herself would have to go.

All the while Phares went about his business with a concentrated frown on his bronzed, handsome face, completely oblivious to Isis's sour face, or indeed that he had the nurses falling for him like ninepins. They giggled and simpered whenever he was in view, but he seemed oblivious to their flirtation. Aida wished – how she wished – that it wouldn't get to her, but occasionally she would sense a lump in her throat, her eyes misting. She couldn't help but recall a remark she had overheard one morning as she walked past the staffroom, where the nurses were gossiping over cups of tea. One of them had said laughingly, 'Dr Pharaony is one of those men who should be allowed a harem,' and Aida had felt startled for a moment, before dismissing the remark from her mind. She knew how popular Phares was with the nurses. With all women, in fact … but in this regard she was not one to share, and with that thought, her shoulders drooped dejectedly.

That morning, in the third week of her new job, Aida was at last given the chance she had been secretly longing for. She was in the corridor, about to enter a ward, when Phares stopped her.

'Nurse Pharaony, we have a crisis in the theatre. Nurse Younes has been taken ill and we have a young boy being brought in with an abdominal wound. It could be a case of peritonitis if we don't act fast. The ambulance will be arriving in twenty minutes. Are you able to assist?' He gave her a look that was both serious and encouraging.

'Of course, Doctor,' Aida replied without a moment's hesitation. She had assisted with similar operations before and the prospect of being Phares's third hand in the theatre didn't faze her.

His mouth curved into a satisfied smile. 'Can you please help get the theatre ready and check the equipment. The others will help you.'

She gave a decisive nod. 'I'll do it immediately.'

As she pulled a surgical gown over her uniform, Aida could hear Isis entering the adjacent theatre, her clipped voice issuing instructions to the orderlies and nursing staff. Even the thought of having to work with Isis couldn't stop the glow of happiness surging through her. Now, in a matter of moments, she would be in her rightful place: beside Phares at the operating table, organising, supplying, placing the instruments in his hand at exactly the right moment, following the split-second timing with a rhythm that was beautifully exact. Yes, she would be his third hand. She would prove to him how good she was at her job. This was her chance to show her worth, not only to Phares but to Isis too. If she came through with flying colours, maybe he would be prepared to move her to theatre duties permanently.

She had no doubt that Phares would save the young boy's life. Aida had come to appreciate his skill even more since working at El Amal, yet it was his humility that struck her most. He once told her when she praised him for the lives he had saved on the operating table, 'I can perform the surgery, *chérie*, but only God can perform the miracle of healing.'

*Well, she had better not let him – or God – down this morning.*

Through the glass, she could see Phares scrubbing up next door in his white gown, alongside his assistant surgeon, Dr Makloof. He was working fast, yet beneath his swift, sure movements, Aida knew he was cultivating that inner calm he found essential to his work and blocking everything out except the emergency case he was about to tackle.

The theatre was very quiet, the only sounds the whirr of fans doing their best to dispel some of the heat, the small clink of instruments, the bubbling of the autoclave steriliser and the tiny swish of starched gowns.

A nurse came in, wheeling a young boy on a trolley – he couldn't be more than six years old – and they lifted him on to the operating table.

In his cap and mask, Phares made a formidable figure, towering over the slight figure of the child. He extended his hands and thrust them into the rubber gloves held out for him by one of the assistant nurses.

'You know what to watch for,' Aida heard him murmur quietly to Isis, who gave a small nod. Then he raised his hand. Immediately Aida and the other white-gowned figures moved to their places, alert, silent. Someone exposed the small stomach, someone else swabbed quickly. Phares held out his hand without looking up and Aida firmly placed a scalpel in it. A thin red line appeared. The operation had begun and with it, the race to get the stomach cleaned out before the child's whole system became poisoned. Aida performed with robotic precision, never faltering for a second in supplying the outstretched hand with everything it required. Phares, in turn, was merely a pair of hands in thin rubber gloves – she was aware of nothing else as his deft fingers worked with a sureness and speed it was difficult to follow. They cut and probed, working against the clock, for the peritoneum hadn't ruptured quite yet, but it wasn't far off.

Clamps, retractors, swab, clamps … swab again. The scalpel bit deeply into the small cavity, through the skin, fat and peritoneum.

A nurse wiped Phares's forehead from behind, unobtrusively. His black eyes never left the cavity under his hands, and Isis's sharp gaze was similarly fixed on the boy's flushed face while her hand kept guard over the small, thread-like pulse.

There was a slight movement in the group around the table as the pus welled out, and though no one spoke it was like an exclamation of relief.

Swab, swab, drainage tubes inserted. Sutures passed through and drawn tight. Clamps and retractors released. Swab, suture.

The wide incision flushed, swabbed, and closed. Phares stood back, watchful, as Dr Makloof applied the dressing and taped it neatly. Then he glanced at Isis, who nodded.

'He's all right.'

The stomach was covered, the sheet drawn up over the small body. Around the table, the group became at once untidy, breaking up to perform their various tasks. Used instruments were taken away for cleaning; the soiled linen thrown into bins containing disinfectant; the rubbish burned. The little boy was wheeled swiftly to the recovery room, Isis and Dr Makloof accompanying him through the swing doors.

Phares joined Aida in the changing room. She untied the tapes of his mask and gown, then turned around so that he could do the same for her. She felt unusually hot and slightly lightheaded but put this down to her nerves. Above all else, Aida couldn't help but feel exhilarated.

'Sixteen minutes,' she said softly. 'Congratulations, Phares, I'm so proud of you.'

'I couldn't have done it in that time without you,' he replied soberly, and looked at her with a smile in his weary eyes. 'If he survives, half the credit is yours. We were partners in a different way today, *chérie*.'

Aida felt it too. To hear Phares's voice expressing the same thought filled her with pride. It seemed that today had brought them closer together.

\*    \*    \*

In his plain but spacious office on the ground floor of El Amal, Phares sighed quietly to himself as he sat across the desk from Isis, contemplating her thunderous expression. She had asked to see him first thing and he had obliged, sensing the storm was something to do with Aida and wanting to deal with it as quickly as possible. Following the surgery on the child a couple of days ago, when Aida had stepped in at the last minute to assist, he'd seen no reason not to promote her permanently to theatre nurse. Her calm professionalism was just what was needed in the operating theatre, and when he'd seen just how thrilled Aida had been by the experience, he acted immediately, without consulting Isis first. This, he realised, had brought things to a head.

Phares had experienced enough of Isis's tantrums in the past to know full well what he was up against. Looking at the stormy eyes glaring at him, he realised he would have to deal with her jealousy at some point, and better that it should be today – Aida was not at the hospital, having come down with the flu.

Phares smiled at Isis, resolutely ignoring the storm signals in her face. 'Shall I order some coffee?'

'I'm not here to have coffee, Phares. I'm here to have a serious conversation about your unreasonable decision to promote Aida to theatre. She is untried and untested. How could you promote her like this?'

'I experienced the way she handled that peritonitis operation.'

'Has she been properly trained for this sort of job?'

'Aida helped with much more traumatic situations in the hospitals in England during the war.'

'You only have her word as confirmation of that.'

His eyebrows shot up at this remark. 'Of course, and I trust Aida completely. It's quite clear from speaking to her, how deep her knowledge goes.'

Isis pinned him with a searing look. 'Look, Phares, we've worked together for years and you've always trusted my judgement. I think you're taking an unjustifiable risk. One false move and we could lose a life. This time was an emergency. We had no one else to replace Nurse Younes, so I can understand why you used Aida. And *hamdelellah*, thank God, the operation went without any hitch.'

Isis paused, and Phares took the opportunity to try and bring the discussion to a close. 'Yes, it did. Now please, don't worry, I know what I'm doing. And if you think I'm only promoting her because she's my wife, you'd be wrong.'

'I think you haven't overseen her work as I have,' Isis responded haughtily. 'I have seen her on the wards and she is not always punctilious. In fact, she can be quite slapdash. Once or twice I've noticed irregularities in her charts and Nurse Soraya has told me that Aida has made mistakes administering medication. As you know, we use different names here in Egypt for some of the medicines and I think she gets confused.'

Phares shook his head. 'I can't believe that. Aida is an intelligent woman and I'm sure she is well aware of all that.'

Isis lifted her chin angrily. 'She might be fit to work in hospitals in England, but she is quite lost here and certainly will not survive in theatre. The other day was nothing more than beginner's luck.'

Phares's eyes flashed. 'Well, as you know, I don't believe in luck. What I saw there was skill and experience and sound judgement. Look, Aida has told me about some of the cases she handled during the war and trust me, they were no small thing.'

Isis got up and walked impatiently about the room then turned to face Phares like a fighting bantam, her feathers ruffled.

'If you persist with this, then I will not attend any operations when she is on duty.'

Phares's mouth tightened to a thin line. 'Calm down, Isis. This helps no one. You know how much I count on your expertise … I trust you.'

Isis stood her ground, hands behind her back, her voice harsh. 'Yes, you trust me … you trust me … That's all well and good, but I don't feel secure entrusting a life to Aida when I know one small mistake could result in disaster. Not only would *I* feel responsible, but we would all be accountable if something untoward happened.'

There was silence in the office. It was a beautiful end-of-July morning, with blackbirds and thrushes singing their hearts out in the shrubs outside the open windows. It should have been peaceful, Phares thought with exasperation, but there was no peace under that belligerent stare; and he was perfectly aware of Isis's motives, she had been on Aida's case from day one. He gave an inward sigh, knowing this couldn't go on. Isis couldn't possibly continue to work under the same roof as him and Aida bearing this scale of resentment. Besides, much had reached him on the grapevine about the high-handedness with which she treated both the nurses and patients. The situation was unacceptable.

He flicked a Gitanes out of his cigarette pack and offered it to Isis, his face grave as he lit up for both of them. His best course of action was clear. 'Isis, you've been one of the pillars holding up this hospital. I couldn't have made it the success it is without you.'

She sniffed huffily, very much on her dignity, then treated him to a cautious smile.

'However ...' he went on '... I sense you're unhappy ...'

Isis opened her mouth to speak, but Phares held up a hand to stay her. 'As a friend and colleague, I think the best thing would be for you to try pastures new ... spread your wings, go for a promotion at another hospital, even travel a bit. Every hospital in the world needs a good anaesthetist.'

Isis's eyes widened in shock, then narrowed as she read the full implications of his words. 'Are you *firing* me? Has that wife of yours made you lose your mind?' she spat in disbelief.

At this, his mouth tightened. 'I think it best if we leave Aida out of this. She's said nothing to me, but this clearly isn't working, Isis.'

'So, you are asking me to leave. Go on, say it!'

'Very well, I am inviting you to tender your resignation. If you want to work out a notice period while you find another position, that's fine. We'll discuss the details. I will be sure to organise a generous settlement, that goes without saying.'

If Isis had broken down in tears Phares knew that it would have been a much tougher conversation for him, but she hadn't, and the look of pure malevolence she shot him only served to make him even more certain that he had done the right thing. He trusted Aida implicitly. How could he have Isis trying to undermine that trust at every opportunity? It was untenable ... not only bad for the hospital but ruinous to his marriage.

The relief Phares felt must have been reflected in his eyes because Isis met his gaze one final time, then stormed out of the office, slamming the door behind her.

*    *    *

It was on one of the days when Aida was off sick that the receptionist rang Phares to tell him there was a *fellaha* wanting to see him. Apparently, the woman had refused to see anybody but him.

Perplexed, he told the receptionist to send her in.

The woman was a *baladi* woman as opposed to a *fellaha* – most likely, she worked as a servant in a household rather than toiling in the fields. She was wearing the traditional *baladi* dress, a *melaya liff* – a cloth draped, sari-like, over her house dress, covering her hair and entire body, the ends of which were tucked under the arm. She immediately rushed over and bent forwards to kiss his hand, which he drew away quickly, not wishing to encourage the woman's excessive servility.

'May God protect you and protect your family and children, *ya Bey*,' she whined. 'May God give you everything your heart desires.'

'Enough ... enough. What can I do for you?'

'I want your indulgence.'

'Bottom line, please.'

'You saved my son Mohamed's life and I have come to thank you.'

Phares smiled, realising she meant the six-year-old child with peritonitis. 'You don't need to thank me. I am a doctor and it is a doctor's duty to save a life whenever God permits.'

'I am not worthy of you, or of *Sit* Aida.'

Phares frowned. 'What has my wife got to do with this?'

'I was told that she helped with the operation and then she looked after my boy.'

He nodded. 'That's correct. She's a very good nurse. Your son was in good hands.'

Curiously, the *baladi* woman still looked anguished, gabbling her next words so that he could hardly follow what she said.

'I was unable to come because I was at my mother's funeral in Aswan. As soon as I could, I hurried here to see you, to thank you ... and to tell you what must be said ...'

'That is very kind of you. What's your name?' Phares motioned for her to sit on the chair on the other side of his desk, but the woman merely stood, clasping her hands together at her chest.

'Your servant, Souma.'

*Souma* ... Phares stiffened. 'Your full name,' he demanded

'Souma Hassanein, *ya Bey*.' She began wringing her hands, her face a pitiful mask of anguish. 'I have come to make amends for a wrong I did your two families many years ago.'

Phares stared at her, for a moment nonplussed. This woman was the servant they had been looking for all this time, the one who, eight years before, had told Aida that it was *his* father who had brought the antique statue of Nefertari into Ayoub's house for him to authenticate, then disappeared before the trial and had never been found again.

'May God forgive me and bless you and your family with long life,' Souma whimpered. 'Ah, *ya Bey*, my conscience has been pricking me all this time. When I was told my son would have been taken from me if you hadn't saved his life, I knew it was a sign from God that I should come to speak to you.'

Phares fixed her with a stony look. 'I know who you are and what you did. It was you who planted that statue in Ayoub El Masri's house, was it not?'

'Yes, *ya Bey*, may *Allah* spare me,' the woman answered in a hoarse whisper, tears now gushing from her eyes.

'Why did you lie about my father?'

She shook her head miserably. '*El Shitan*, the Devil, *ya Bey*. Your father the *pasha* refused to give my brother Atef a job in his household …' Souma wiped her eyes with the edge of her head covering. 'I was angry, *ya Bey*, but God does not forget. He punished me for my sin, making my boy ill.'

'Someone must have paid you. Who was it?'

'They paid my brother Atef. These men … you have to do as they say, *ya Bey*. They threatened to kill me and my two daughters if I didn't do as I was told.'

'Who's the one in charge?'

'God only knows, *ya Bey*.'

Phares frowned. 'How do I know you're telling the truth? What do you want from me?'

Souma shook her head earnestly. 'No, no … I want only your indulgence. And to prove to you my goodwill. My brother Atef, he will take you to a place that will interest you.'

'What do you mean?'

Souma lowered her voice theatrically. 'My brother sometimes works for these smugglers of antiquities … We are poor and need the money.'

Phares gave nothing away in his expression. 'Are you saying there's some way he can undo some of the damage, prove that Ayoub El Masri was wrongly accused?' he asked, adding sharply, 'Though it's not as if he can bring him back, is it?'

'My brother can help you in other ways,' she answered, a sly look in her eyes. 'Atef, he knows that you and your English friends are interested in these smugglers, yes?'

He raised an eyebrow sceptically. 'May I remind you I'm a doctor, not a policeman.'

Souma flapped her hand, protesting she thought no such thing. 'And you're a very good doctor, *ya Bey* ... But I am telling you the truth. And there is nothing in it for us. This is out of the goodness of our hearts ... Atef can help you, *ya Bey*. And *in shah Allah*, God willing, you will let him.'

He considered her for a moment. 'If I were to take an interest in this, what would you propose I do?'

'My brother is prepared to take you to one of the hiding places of these people.'

'Why is he being so helpful suddenly?

'Because, he has the malignant illness, *beeid anack*, may you be preserved from it, *ya Bey*, and he wants to meet his maker with a clear conscience.'

He nodded. For these people, cancer, like the devil, was a fearful thing to call by its name.

'When?'

'Tonight, or tomorrow morning, if you want.'

'Tomorrow.'

'But you must promise not have a *kapsha*, a police raid, at the place while my brother is there, or for a few days after, because if these people realise he has betrayed them ...' Souma's eyes filled with genuine terror, '... *ma be yerhamoush*, they do not have any mercy. They will throw him to the wild dogs or they may burn him alive.'

Phares knew that she was telling the truth about these smugglers. There had been instances when mangled or charred corpses had been found in the desert. The top man, El Kébir, was ruthless and his guards known to be sadists.

'If I meet with your brother, be advised that there will be secret police watching me and if he tries any tricks, they will arrest him and you as well.'

'*Matkhafsh ya Bey*, don't be afraid, I swear as God is my witness that Atef will honour his side of it.'

'Where shall we meet? I don't want your brother to come to the hospital or my home.'

'He'll meet you at Karnak.'

'Fine. At what time?'

'After *Salat al-zuhr*, midday, after the sun passes its highest.'

'Very well. You can tell Atef that I'll be there but no stupid games, eh?'

'*Mafhoom, ya Bey*, understood, *ya Bey*. God bless you, *ya Bey*.'

After Souma left, Phares remained pensive. He debated whether or not to tell Aida about this strange visit, but decided that it was not the right time. First, he had to be sure this woman was telling the truth. Second, the authorities were very close to putting their hands on the head of the smuggling organisation and he was not yet at liberty to divulge to his new wife his role as secret agent. Tomorrow, he would go with Souma's brother Atef to this smugglers' den where they kept the loot and assess if what the woman had said was the truth, or whether she had an ulterior motive in telling her story.

*    *    *

At noon the next day, as Phares was getting out of his Jeep, he noticed a bus on which was written *Chiffons à la Mode* in large letters. There was obviously a fashion shoot at Karnak going on.

Clearly, British intelligence and senior police chiefs had managed to keep the prince's death a secret, even from his own company employees, or this event would have been pulled. They must have woven quite some cover story as to why Shams Sakr El Din was missing, Phares thought darkly.

Nairy Paplosian was almost certainly one of the girls posing for photographs. He muttered an oath. This was the last thing he needed and he hoped he could avoid bumping into her. After swiftly scanning the area around the Temple of Karnak, he was relieved to see that a man who had been leaning against the wall at the entrance was now coming towards him with a furtive smile of recognition.

Dressed in a faded *galabeya*, Souma's brother, Atef, was tall and wiry, with eyes that darted this way and that as he approached. Beneath his tan, his colour was sallow, probably due to his illness, Phares surmised, and his narrow face looked drawn, accentuated by a long, dishevelled beard.

He greeted Phares with the usual, s*alam aleykom*. 'My sister came to you, *ya Bey*.'

'Where can we talk safely? It is best if we talk first, and I don't want to be seen,' said Phares quickly.

'Come, there's a restaurant I know. We can sit at the back. No one will see us there, *ya Bey*.'

Atef led him to a traditional establishment, still quiet in these hours before lunch. Phares ordered coffee and forced himself to refrain from firing questions at his companion, whose eyes had lost none of their panicked expression. It was these nervous, darting glances above anything Souma had said that persuaded Phares that this was not a set-up – the man was too fearful. It seemed she and her brother were genuine in wanting to make amends for the damage they had done to the El Masri family.

'Tell me what you know,' Phares demanded, once two cups of Turkish coffee had been placed in front of them.

'We had no choice, *ya Bey*. Souma did what she must. They said they would kill our family. What else could we do? She didn't want to do it, to plant that *temthal*, statue.' He wiped his perspiring brow with the back of his sleeve. 'We had to do as they ordered,' he added hoarsely.

'I imagine money might have had something to do with it,' Phares responded coolly.

Atef glanced down at his hands. 'They would have killed us all,' he repeated, a plaintive whine creeping into his voice.

'So, you're still working with these smugglers ... What do you know? Who is El Kébir?'

Atef began to gabble, his words nervously tumbling over each other. '*Wallahi*, as God is my witness, I do not know. I have never seen him. No one sees him. I know nothing.'

Phares had thought as much – Atef was such small fry, he would never be given access to the ring's high command – but he'd wanted to check all the same. 'So, who is your link man in the operation? Where do you meet?'

'At Aysha the *ghazeya*'s coffee shop in Deir el-Medina, the workmen's village on the West Bank of the Nile. Word comes to me and that is where we always meet. A tall man – Egyptian, but dressed like an *effendi* ... suit ... a tie ... I don't know his name, *ya Bey. Wallahi, wallahi*!'

Again, Atef seemed to be telling the truth, as far as Phares could see. He drank the last of his coffee and slapped a few coins on the table, with a swift gesture to the proprietor who was making tea behind the counter to the jangling blare of a heavy wooden radio set.

Phares stood, pushing back his chair. 'Let's not waste time, Atef. You'd better take me to your contact. Remember, all you know is that I'm a buyer. I'll do the rest.' Phares hoped that Souma's brother would refrain from gabbling; he didn't want the man's nerves to give the game away.

Outside, once more, Atef gathered his shabby *galabeya* about him and led the way with his long, loping stride. They walked in silence to the town's edge and immediately plunged into a quarter riddled with narrow streets in which Phares felt lost in no time. *At least no one will recognise me here*, he thought grimly as they wound their way through garbage, stepped over goats and hens, threaded a route through a canyon of rundown houses, fought a plague of flies, and finally stopped before a shop where Oriental rugs were being woven.

'This place is safe,' said Atef. 'It is owned by my cousin, Ahmad. You will find what you are looking for here.'

Instinctively, Phares looked up. The crazy, white-painted Arab house with its projecting balconies, fretted windows and decorative excrescences appeared so top-heavy, it seemed as if it might to tumble into the street and engulf them at any moment.

They went through the shop and scrambled up a stone staircase as steep as a ladder, entering through a doorway at the top. Phares drew in his breath in amazement as they stepped into a fantastic shop of curiosities, a veritable treasure trove that held a mixture of old and new objects. There were nick-nacks as well as expensive items: semi-precious stone jewellery; old earthenware vases draped with gaudy silk fabrics; brass Aladdin lamps and a scattering of tourist trinkets – eye of Horus pendants and *hamsa* keyrings with their open hand symbol, both of which supposedly offered protection against the evil eye.

A small, thin man, whose skin was so yellow and shrivelled it looked as if he'd been unwrapped from the swathed bandages of an ancient mummy, blinked his way forward expectantly. A few murmured greetings and whispered words from Atef, then his cousin Ahmad led Phares through a beaded curtain to a room at the back.

His eyes widened to see the wealth of objects of archaeological importance that any European or American museum would give thousands to possess. Here, indeed, was history rifled from the tombs, and by the looks of it, a thriving family business.

Phares picked up a painted wooden head, badly chipped but which might originally have rivalled Nefertiti's bust, one of the beauties of the Berlin Museum. It lay among crude potsherds and a broken limestone carving. There were pieces of alabaster, scarabs, fragments of ivory and scraps of goldwork, all of which appeared genuine enough to Phares's untutored eye. Still, he didn't think this was the hiding place of the main cache.

*They'd have a strongroom elsewhere, much harder to access,* he thought.

'The tomb robbers have been busy,' Phares observed.

'One must live, even at the cost of the dead,' said the little man.

Phares was careful to disguise his distaste. 'Are there many of you engaged in this profession?'

A smile crossed Ahmad's wrinkled face. 'You cannot blame us if we try to hide a few treasures beneath our kaftans, *ya Bey.* How is it different to the men who work the diamond fields or goldmines? The diggers who try to extricate a few stones for themselves? We are poor and this is our land. Aren't we worthier of these small treasures than these *khawagat,* foreigners, who come to our country and gather our riches, just to take them back to their own?'

Phares thought it wise not to answer. He'd learned that the role of agent required a certain sangfroid to gain the trust of one's target. It had already entailed months of slow, careful steps. He couldn't blow it now if he was to have a hope of discovering the real hiding place for those larger, more important items, the likes of which he'd been used to handling since he had started work with the Embassy.

'Is this shop where you sell this stuff?'

'*Laa, laa.* No, no, *ya Bey.*' The man shook his head violently. 'The shop downstairs is purely for the sale of carpets. We don't bring buyers here, it would only draw attention to ourselves.'

'But then, how does this work? Surely, these nick-nacks, though of some value, are not the only things an expert like yourself would be selling?'

'You tell me what you are looking for and I will do my best to find it for you, *ya Bey*.'

'So, this is the way you always deal?'

'Yes. We must be careful. If a whisper reached the Department of Antiquities ...' The trader shook his head, his fingers wiping the sweat from his swarthy face. 'I only let you come here because of my cousin Atef. He tells me you are to be trusted, and now you have become known to the Bedouin dealers ...'

'Yes, indeed. You can rely on my discretion.'

'Sometimes a buyer is troublesome, he begins to ask questions, and when that happens, we take him to our shop of fakes in Qena. Excellent copies ...'

'Don't they recognise the good from the bad?'

The man grimaced. 'Usually the buyers are men of much wealth but no knowledge. Occasionally we are found out, but then we claim ignorance, as if we had also been deceived.' He shrugged and smiled. 'Better than getting caught, eh?'

Phares took a last glance at the room of deep shadows, where jumbled treasures of history were piled. He chose a gold rotatable seal ring with a lapis lazuli scarab, a symbol of the heart and the sun. The flat side was inscribed with the name of the owner, a man of an ancient race now consigned to the mists of time.

'I will buy this,' he told the man, turning the seal ring between his fingers. 'Once I've had it authenticated by my antique dealer in the Musky, if it's genuine as you claim, I will come back for a larger order.'

Having paid Ahmad the meagre sum of fifty Egyptian pounds for an item worth so much more, Phares took his leave of the two men and made his way down the stone staircase, through the carpet shop, and into the sunlight of Karnak. He had always known that tomb robbing in Luxor was a very profitable business but it never ceased to disturb him when he saw these undocumented riches for sale. Ahmad had hit the nail on the head when he compared this market with illicit diamond buying. Surely one couldn't always depend on the honesty of the guards left in charge of important finds while the archaeologists spent their time in hotel bars and nightclubs at the end of the excavation day? Knowing only too well the value of the objects they were supposed to protect, it would be such an overwhelming temptation to seize an item or two.

Phares suddenly felt bone-tired. It seemed suddenly as if this illegal trade was too big for anyone – certainly him – to thwart. Even if he were to find out the identity of El Kébir, there would only be another man, just as ruthless, ready to take his place. Like the Hydra's heads: if you cut them off, only more would grow back – in this case, stronger and cleverer than the ones before.

He drew a deep breath and thought of Aida. There was so much he was having to keep secret and it wore him down. How he longed to get back to her tender embrace. How happy she would be if only he could find out who it was that had framed her father. Sometimes, Phares wondered grimly if their marriage would stand or fall on his ability to do just that. He must keep going, he told himself, and continue this double life for a while longer, even if that meant he couldn't be wholly truthful to Aida.

*    *    *

That same afternoon, Aida sat in the drawing room of Hathor sorting through the post and suddenly paled. In her hand was a small yellow envelope similar to the one that had been handed to her on her wedding day. It was addressed to her in the same spidery scrawl as the first letter. With trembling hands, she opened it:

'*It only takes one person to make a marriage fail. Your nemesis is here, in Luxor. Remember the immortal words of Molière: "One is easily fooled by that which one loves."*'

Like the previous note, it was left unsigned.

Aida scrunched it into a ball, her mind racing. Previously, she had suspected Isis of writing the letters, but would the anaesthetist really dare to stoop so low? She had nothing to gain, except to drive a wedge between Aida and Phares by deliberately making mischief. There was no divorce in the Coptic Church, so even if their marriage broke up, Isis would never have a chance to marry him.

Aida reread the note. *Was Nairy actually in Luxor?* She remembered suddenly the posters she had noticed in town announcing that Chiffons à la Mode was coming to Luxor for a fashion shoot for the new season's catalogue at the Winter Palace.

She had been surprised, and relieved, that there was no word of Shams Sakr El Din. As far as Aida was aware, word hadn't got out of what truly happened that weekend at Wahat El Nakheel, but it could well be that the prince was keeping a low profile while any unpleasant rumours concerning his behaviour at the oasis palace died down. Aida had wondered about him, though she couldn't bring herself to mention his name to Phares. Since the wedding he had refused to talk any further about the prince, except to say that she herself had nothing to fear, and they had made no trips to Cairo where they might have seen him at the Gezireh Sporting Club.

Still, now in her mind the face of the model Nairy Paplosian swam painfully into focus. Her mouth went dry and it felt as though someone was crushing her chest, making it difficult to breathe.

She picked up the telephone and rang the hotel. Yes, the receptionist at the Winter Palace confirmed, ten models from

Chiffons à la Mode had arrived the day before for a fashion shoot at the Temple of Karnak and were staying at the hotel.

She had been feeling tired and nauseous all day and now a new sickening feeling rose up inside her, and with it, a dread of what she might discover in the days to come.

The queasiness and dizzy spells had started shortly after they had returned from their honeymoon. During that time, Aida had been able to hide her suspicions from Phares; she wanted to keep her pregnancy a surprise, giving him the good news only once she was sure. The day before, she'd had the confirmation she was waiting for and decided to stay at home because she had felt sick all night with a terrible migraine. Her father had told her that Eleanor had suffered migraines all through her pregnancy and the memory of their discussion was a bittersweet reminder that neither of her parents would be around to see their grandchild. With that thought, Aida felt suddenly alone.

She lay her head back on the cushion of the sofa and closed her eyes, trying to control the roller coaster of emotions rushing through her. Her mind returned to the poisonous letter. She trusted Phares, didn't she? She had to find it in herself to do so or their marriage would never stand a chance. Why should she believe a poison pen letter over the assurances of her husband whom she loved? It must be the pregnancy making her emotions so volatile, she told herself.

The wait for Phares seemed endless. On tenterhooks, Aida stood on the veranda, gazing down blindly at the river, feeling in turns hot and cold, unsure when and how she would tell him that he was about to be a father. Excitement and delight warred with a dark sense of dread, and conflicting thoughts assailed her … Perhaps tonight might not be the right time to broach such an important subject. She wished Camelia was here, but the whole family had left immediately after the wedding to spend the summer at the Pharaonys' house in Alexandria. Maybe her friend would have at least helped her put things in proportion.

Phares came in later than usual that evening. He looked tired and distracted, Aida thought.

'How was your day?'

He shrugged. 'Tiring.'

'Difficult operations?'

'Mmm …' He rubbed his hands over his eyes.

'Everybody's away. We don't need to have our dinner downstairs in the dining room. Shall we have it on the veranda up here? It's a beautiful night.'

He said nothing, staring over her shoulder into the distance.

'Phares …'

'Mmm …?'

'Didn't you hear me? Shall we have dinner on the veranda?'

'Whatever, *chérie*,' he answered, absentmindedly caressing her hair.

'Where have you been?'

'Where have I been?' he repeated, looking at Aida as if seeing her for the first time that evening.

In this pause, and what seemed to be an evasion of her question, Aida felt the sense of his betrayal rushing in on her, stifling her breath, making her dizzy with fear at what she might discover. She had to know if the warning in the letter had any foundation to it.

'Nairy's in town. Did you know?'

Phares turned away, frowning and walked over to the window. He lit a cigarette. 'So, what of it?' He wasn't looking at her – she couldn't see his eyes. Aida didn't like not being able to see his eyes. What was he hiding?

She swallowed. 'Did you know about it?'

Aida waited in silent agony, wondering why he wasn't answering her immediately. She felt adrift on a shoreless sea; it was impossible for her to discipline her thoughts. *Why was she still so haunted by uncertainty?* She had overestimated her resolution never to question him like a jealous wife and cursed her own weakness. If she didn't guard her emotions, she might find another kind of misery awaited her.

'I saw the buses parked at the Winter Palace as I was coming home,' he said eventually, still gazing out of the window. He offered nothing more but she felt the check behind his words and realised her questioning had brushed aside some of the usual enchantment they felt in each other's company. Now she wished she had never said anything.

'I'll pour you a whisky,' she said tentatively. 'And then I'll ask Gomaa to set the table on the veranda. It's a beautiful evening.'

'Yes, that'll be nice. Thank you.'

She poured him out two fingers of whisky. Phares seemed lost in thought and though she sensed he didn't want her to probe him, yet still she went on, trying to speak gently, but knowing she was driving him away.

'Don't quarrel with me tonight, Aida.'

'I'm not quarrelling with you, Phares. But I've never seen you so preoccupied. Has anything happened at the hospital? I'm worried about you.'

Phares sighed. 'Just trust me, *chérie.*'

He had smoked one Gitanes after another and hadn't touched the drink she'd poured him, she noticed. They sat together at dinner scarcely speaking, and when they did, it was to discuss matters at the hospital or to engage in small talk about the family. Any sense of happiness seemed to be slipping away with every minute of those silences between them. Once they had finished dinner, having scarcely touched the delicious food that had been brought to them, Phares got up – 'You'll probably want to stay up a little longer, so I'll see you in the morning. Goodnight, *chérie.*' And, with that, he yawned and headed upstairs.

A little later, as she undressed, angry with both Phares and herself, Aida repressed the hot tears that burned behind her eyes. In bed, she lay still, watching the figure of her husband lying with his perfectly muscled back to her in bed, apparently asleep.

Sleep eluded her. Her mind could not tear itself away from the note she had received, nor from Phares's closed expression all evening. She turned restlessly in bed and lay staring at the moonlight on the veranda. After plumping her pillows in an effort to get comfortable, she wondered why people wrote these cruel anonymous letters. What would they gain? She longed for the morning to come, hoping that the passing of the night would somehow drive away the turmoil in her mind.

Aida was just drifting off to sleep when the telephone on Phares's bedside table rang. He sat up and reached out for the receiver immediately, as if waiting for the call.

'Hello. Yes … yes … The cottage. Give me fifteen minutes and I'll be there,' Aida heard him whisper.

Phares slipped out of bed and went to the bathroom. A few minutes later, he emerged and hesitated before leaving the room. He came over to the bed and through the lashes of her half-closed eyes, Aida could tell he was looking down at her. Then he turned and padded quietly to the door, closing it carefully behind him.

She sat up, her heart racing. *So, he was going off to meet her … the beautiful Nairy.* Now it seemed whoever had written those poisonous letters had rendered her a service after all.

On impulse, Aida leapt out of bed and quickly threw on some clothes, wrapping a black shawl around her head. She stole down the big staircase like a thief, looking around her to make sure no one had heard herself or Phares moving around. The stairs were in darkness but a shaded lamp burned in the great hall below. There was no one about. She crept through the hall and into a small morning room from where she slipped out on to the terrace. Phares had said he would be at the cottage in fifteen minutes. The Jeep was still parked outside, which meant he had gone on foot and had probably taken the shortcut. They had spent a couple of afternoons picnicking at the cottage on his days off, so she knew the path well.

A seductive slip of a moon revealed her presence in the canopy of dark-blue velvet. Silent as a spirit, she ran across the grass and started down the narrow path leading to the cottage, overhung with sycamore trees whose leaves barely moved in the still air.

Aida walked quickly over the beaten ground, driven by an uneasiness she could not quell. It was as though someone were speaking in her ear, urging her to hasten if she really wanted to find out what Phares was up to. Her vivid imagination began to torture her with images of her husband with another woman behaving in some culpably indiscreet manner that would break her heart. Still, she needed to know ...

Now, as she reached the little house, the stars doming the night sky seemed to have increased in number, lighting up the silent spectral scene around her. The solitude was absolute. There were no lights filtering through the closed shutters of the cottage. *Maybe Phares hasn't arrived yet*, she thought. Was there another cottage perhaps ... another meeting place she didn't know about?

Then, just as she was thinking of leaving this peaceful place, there was a movement. A group of thick-leaved shadowy trees, the rustle of a silken garment, footfall on the beaten sand of the path, and then moments later, a shadow detached itself from the dense blackness.

Another second of suspense, and a silhouette appeared. As moonlight fell on the figure, Aida realised that it was not Nairy's shapely form, nor Phares's tall frame that crept out from the darkness. It was the shadow of a man, one she recognised immediately as the Bedouin who had been stalking them at Denderah and then again at Philae. He was stooping as if carrying something heavy.

The Bedouin approached the cottage and knocked three times on the door.

Through the trees, Aida saw a light turn on behind the shutters. Phares was in there … She stood very still, staring at the light so faint and yet so piercing in the heavy darkness. As she shivered in her thin dress, she pulled the shawl more tightly around her shoulders. *What was happening?*

The door opened and the man quickly entered the cottage. Aida's heart was racing at a rate of knots as she ran quietly across the lawn to the shuttered window. It was a warmer night than usual, Phares must have opened the window. As she came nearer, whispering voices could be heard on the quiet night air. She pricked up her ears.

'What brings you? I told you the other day not to get in touch with me unless I sent word to you …' Phares spoke in a low tone.

The voice of the Bedouin was harsh and raucous. 'I thought you might like to acquire something of value, something almost without price.'

'You're not trying to sell me some trash, like those scarabs you make by the thousand?'

'No, no! Believe me, I know you well enough now, master, not to sell such rubbish. I have the genuine objects. Funeral furniture, magnificently painted. Jewels of the dead … even a mummy, if you want it.'

Aida's heart sank.

'Have you been robbing a museum?'

Aida could not hear the Bedouin's answer. She was trembling from head to toe. Could it be possible? *Phares* was engaged in the trading of antiquities? No, it couldn't be! Not Phares. Yet here he was, meeting with a Bedouin in the dead of night, talking about buying stolen antiquities. The horror of such a thought overrode any other emotion she had been feeling. *What was her jealousy compared with what she was witnessing?*

'So, it's come to this,' Aida heard Phares murmur.

'By *Allah* ...' Again, she couldn't hear the remainder of the Bedouin's phrase.

'Show me what you have there.'

There was silence, then she heard Phares's voice again. 'Indeed, this is a beautiful piece you have here. What's it worth to you?'

'Let us say, master, it is worth the pleasure of dealing with you. I shall be honoured if you will accept it as a token of my loyalty to you.'

'*Min gheer laff wa dawaran*, without twists and turns, how much?' Phares rasped.

'For you, master, two hundred and fifty Egyptian pounds,' the Bedouin answered in the most dulcet of tones. 'Would you like me to bring you everything I have?'

'I would prefer you to take me to your shop, or rather, your main hiding place. I need to see *everything*. I have many European clients.'

The man laughed. '*Laa*, no, master. That would be very imprudent of me. Retribution would be swift. El Kébir would either throw me to the wolves in the *gebel*, desert mountains, or burn me alive, leaving my body in the desert for the vultures to pick at, so that none shall know to whom my dishonoured bones belong. As we say, *Ya nahla la tuqrusni wala ayiz minnik asal*, oh bee, don't sting me and I don't want your honey. Discretion is all.'

'So, you are part of El Kébir's men, are you?'

'We are all part of the *Kébir's* men. Who would dare go into competition with the emperor of antiquities?' The man laughed again, this time mockingly. 'Two water melons can't be carried in one hand. One mustn't attempt the impossible. Life is too precious, master.'

'I would like to meet the *Kébir*, do business on a bigger scale.'

The Bedouin gave a grunt. 'Many want to meet the *Kébir*, but to my knowledge, no one has been able to approach him

… Only a very small number know his identity. Trust me, master, that's a bad idea. We say *Ib'id'an ash-sharr wa ghanii lu*, keep away from trouble and sing to it. Why trouble trouble before it troubles you?'

'I see you are full of *hikam*, wise words, tonight.'

'He who has been scalded by soup, blows on yoghurt.'

Phares gave a rough laugh. 'All right, all right!' Then he added severely, 'Go now, don't get in touch with me unless I send for you.'

'*Mafhoom*, understood. *Salam, ya Bey*.'

The door opened and a shaft of light appeared on the threshold. Aida made herself as small as she could by crouching behind one of the shrubs that ran along the wall of the cottage as the Bedouin came out, disappearing stealthily into the darkness like a flitting ghost.

Silence lay over the garden. For a moment Aida stood frozen in the darkness. She would have given all she possessed for the power to blot from her mind – from her life – the conversation she had just heard. Then a big owl floated from one tamarisk tree to another and its hooting call woke her to the need to be gone before Phares should come out of the cottage. She had no time to lose if she was to get back to Hathor before him.

The blood coursed madly in her veins. As she ran, thoughts tumbled round her fevered head. She understood the significance of what she had witnessed tonight, and there was something so unexpected, so dreadful, about this revelation.

Time after time, everything she had thought to be true had been turned on its head. She was like a woman in a dream, the denizen of some strange unreal world where the light of the sun and the darkness of midnight were indistinguishable.

Her pride in her kind, wonderful husband, her reverential love for this man whom she admired so profoundly, her respect for the doctor who saved lives daily … all were swept away, proved a hollow sham. How could she have been so deceived? None of it made sense.

She smothered a sob. Now the agony of full realisation stabbed her very soul. *I shall die if I stay in this house any longer! I must get out – get away from all this treachery …* She had to leave … get far away from Phares and the tangled web of deception he had woven. Still, she must not be impulsive, she would bide her time and maybe ask for Alastair Carlisle's help.

She reached home as cautiously as she had left it barely an hour before, disrobing quickly and crawling into bed. Phares must not know what she had stumbled upon.

Suddenly she thought of the life growing inside her and with it came a tremendous sense of vulnerability. Phares's image came sharply into focus: haunting, taunting her with what they'd shared together. The excitement, the ecstasy … and her wantonness to experience it again, and again. She'd never experienced this depth of emotion before, nor felt so emotionally and mentally attuned to anyone. She wanted to rage against fate for being so unkind. And yet, even with everything she knew now, she still loved him.

She would not tell him about the pregnancy but would leave for England for good. He must never suspect her condition, never know her plans, for in Egypt the law precluded a woman from leaving the country without the consent of her father if she were unmarried, or her husband if she were married. Although she also had a British passport, Phares could stop her from leaving with the excuse that she was carrying his child.

As a single mother in England, what would be her fate? Divorce was frowned upon almost as much as in Egypt. She could always say she was a widow. Again, she thought of Alastair Carlisle – he would know what to do.

Phares came in just before dawn. Aida was awake when he slipped into bed beside her and took her in his arms. He would often reach for her in the middle of the night, just like this, and they would sleep cocooned together. Now her body reacted to the warmth of him, although his hands and feet were cold. But she didn't move as she usually did, pressing herself against him to feel more of him. She just lay there, eyes closed, agonising – her body and heart fighting with her mind.

Phares buried his face in her hair and neck. 'I love you,' he whispered. 'I love you … Never doubt it, *chérie*.'

Tears welled in Aida's closed eyes and as they ran down her cheeks, she was grateful for the darkness that shielded her misery.

*     *     *

A few days later, Aida sat in Alastair Carlisle's office waiting for him. She hadn't made an appointment, but when she had told his secretary who she was and that she wanted to see him on an urgent matter, the young assistant agreed to fit her into his schedule.

The day before, Phares had told Aida that he was leaving for Assiut and that he wouldn't be back for a week. After the night at the cottage, she had managed to hide her distress from him and when he had been surprised at her reluctance to make love, she had told him she had some sort of intestinal bug – not uncommon in Egypt, especially during the summer months. As soon as he'd left, she reserved a seat on the early plane to Cairo.

Alastair breezed into the room and on seeing her, a huge smile lit up his face.

'Aida, my dear, what a wonderful surprise!' he exclaimed as he put down his briefcase and greeted her with outstretched hands. 'I'm sorry I've kept you waiting, but something's come up and we've been at sixes and sevens since yesterday. Most of the staff are away during the summer months and everything is in chaos.' He stopped suddenly and glanced at her with a slight frown. 'You look a little peaky. All well with you? How is that charming husband of yours?'

Aida ignored the last question and sighed. 'Well, I really don't know where to begin. I need your help, Alastair.'

'Before we start, will you join me in a glass of lemonade? It's such a hot day, and Ismail whips up a jolly good one here at the Embassy.'

Aida smiled graciously. 'I'd love a glass, thank you.'

After a quick word with his secretary, Alastair took his seat behind the large mahogany desk. 'So, young lady, what can I do for you?'

'I want to leave for England.'

'I don't see any problem. There are planes to London every day, no restrictions on people travelling.'

Aida fidgeted uncomfortably in her chair. 'I want to leave in the next few days and I don't think Phares will give me permission. As you know, the laws in Egypt require a wife to have her husband's approval to leave the country.'

His fair eyebrows lowered over assessing eyes. 'I don't see why he wouldn't let you go. After all, you have family there.'

'It's complicated.'

'Look here, Aida, Phares is a good friend of mine. I don't understand what the problem is, but I can talk to him if you like.'

Suddenly panicked, Aida shook her head vigorously. 'No, no, please don't breathe a word of this.'

Ismail brought in the lemonades and left them on the table.

'*Shukran.*' When the man had left the room, Alastair leaned over his desk towards Aida, who had lowered her head, her throat burning, doing her best to control her emotions. 'There's something you're not telling me here. I don't wish to pry, but if you want me to help you, I also need to know what's going on.'

At that, she dissolved into tears.

He stood up and came around to her, perching on the edge of his desk. 'Come now, it can't be that bad.'

'It's terrible … terrible!' she sobbed.

'Will you tell me about it?'

Aida pulled a handkerchief from her pocket and dabbed at her eyes. 'I'm pregnant.'

'But that's a wonderful thing. Doesn't Phares want the child, or is it you who doesn't want it? Maybe a little early still to get bogged down with children?'

'No, no, I do want it … but … but … I haven't told Phares,' she hiccupped.

The consul looked at her kindly. 'I'm sure he'll be delighted.'

Aida shook her head again in desperation. *How could she explain the situation without landing Phares in it?* Suddenly, she remembered their conversation at Princess Nazek's charity ball. The consul had mentioned the trafficking of antiquities … and ironically, he was shadowing the wrong man, Aida thought bitterly. How could she tell him what she had witnessed without accusing her husband of being a thief and a smuggler?

Aida stood up. 'I'm sorry, Alastair. I shouldn't have come, I was wrong. Don't worry, I'll sort things out,' she said, wiping her tears and starting towards the door.

The consul laid a hand on her arm gently. 'Sit down, old girl, and let's talk about this calmly. You've worried me now and I can't let you go in this state. Phares would never forgive me.'

Aida hesitated before taking her seat again. 'He's gone off somewhere on business for a few days … who knows with whom,' she added, hoping that Alastair would think all this was about another woman.

*Better he thought that than the truth.*

'Is that what's upsetting you?'

'Yes.'

'I know Phares very well, my dear. I'll be honest now, as I can only guess what has made you upset. I'm quite certain he's not playing the field, if that's what's worrying you. He was like a madman when he thought you were in danger after your little jaunt into the desert.'

Her shoulders sagged. 'He disappears at night.'

Alastair looked thoughtful for a moment. 'He's a doctor, he's bound to be called out at all hours.'

Aida played restlessly with the handkerchief in her hands. There was nothing she could say without giving something away. She should have known this was futile. Alastair would never be able to help her – he and Phares were good friends. Of course he'd be loyal to him.

She stood up and gave a weak smile. 'You're right. Thank you … I'm just being foolish. I'm sorry I wasted your time.'

'Wait! You're not going anywhere.'

Alastair's countenance had sharpened, and Aida sensed he had come to a decision in that moment. She looked at him a little startled, for she had never seen anything other than a fraternal expression on the consul's face in all their previous dealings.

'I suspect I know what all this is about. Please, sit down, Aida.'

Wordlessly, she obeyed. Finding a cigarette from his pocket, Alastair seemed to deliberate as he lit it and moved away from his desk to stand by the window.

'I am sworn to secrecy, but in this case, I think I need to talk to you.' He turned and caught her eyes with a penetrating stare. 'In return, you *must* give me your solemn promise that you will not breathe a word of what I'm about to say. If you were to do so, you would put lives in danger. Especially your husband's.'

*Phares's life in danger?*

Horrified, Aida's heart twisted hard at these words. She sat bolt upright in her seat. 'I … I don't understand.'

'Do you give me your word of honour that you won't say anything, or act on any part of what I'm about to tell you?'

Aida smoothed a moist palm over the pleats of her skirt. With his question came the creeping realisation that her impulsive nature might have done her a disservice. Had she jumped to the wrong conclusions yet again? Doubted Phares before trusting her better instincts? *What on earth was going on here?*

'Yes, yes, of course, Alastair. You have my word of honour. Nothing you say will leave this room.'

The consul returned to his desk and ran a hand over his thinning blonde hair. 'We are talking here about trafficking. A ring of smugglers that extends from Greece, through Libya to Nubia. I seem to recall we touched on the subject a few months ago at Princess Nazek's ball?'

'Yes, I remember. I had the impression you suspected Prince Shams Sakr El Din was involved somehow.'

At the mention of the prince's name, Alastair shifted in his seat. 'Well, my dear, what I'm going to say next will come as a shock to you, I know. Your husband is playing a major part in catching these beggars. We recruited him a few months ago. He has enough knowledge of the desert and its tribesmen to be invaluable to us.'

'But Phares is a doctor, not a spy! Why would he do this?'

'Because he cares. He has a fervent belief that Egypt's antiquities must be protected for posterity and he doesn't want criminal organisations to run roughshod over the country he wants to protect.' He paused to smile at Aida. 'Young lady, I have grown to have a profound respect for that husband of yours.'

'Oh!' Wordless, she gave the tiniest gasp. Aida had come here suspecting treachery – base, criminal instincts in her husband, and now a hot rush of shame flooded her in the face of her own faithlessness.

Alastair's regard was full of gentle sympathy. He went on speaking, giving her time to recover herself. 'Phares has travelled all over the Western Desert and Upper Egypt, trying to gather intelligence. A man they call El Kébir. Phares was involved in a highly dangerous mission to apprehend one of the caravans transporting stolen antiquities, just before your honeymoon, in fact. We thought it might give us El Kébir.'

Aida's eyes widened, struggling with the meaning of his words. 'All that time before we got married … all that time he was away … He … he was a spy …?'

'Well, not officially, you understand. Though I must say, Phares being away on honeymoon was rather inconvenient for the agency.' The consul smiled at her as he stubbed out his cigarette. 'Still, it was clear he wouldn't have allowed anything to get in the way of being with you, Aida. So, I can assure you, his nightly escapades, poor man, have nothing to do with playing the field, but on the contrary, they are spent serving his country and the British government, risking his life to rid Egypt of this vermin.'

Aida remembered Phares's tired countenance, his distracted looks, and once again, she felt as small as a worm for ever having doubted him. 'So, you still don't know who El Kébir is?'

'We're getting closer. Phares is presently engaged on a vital part of what we hope will be the endgame. He has told you he is away travelling on business. In fact, he is posing as a dealer, working undercover on one of the most sensitive parts of this whole mission.'

She took a deep breath, too bemused to say anything for a few minutes, before sanity returned with a rush. 'Oh my God!' she exclaimed, burying her face in her hands. 'How utterly blind and foolish I've been.'

'Don't be too hard on yourself. It's tempting to jump to conclusions when you don't have all the facts.'

She swallowed. 'Where is he now?'

'I'm not at liberty to tell you that, but he is not alone and we are doing our best to protect him and the men with him.'

'How long will he be away?'

'That depends. But we are closer than we've ever been … so fingers crossed it shouldn't be long now.'

'Will you keep me posted?'

'That'll be a little difficult with you living in Luxor. We have reason to believe that some of the people involved in this racket are quite important. We can't talk on the telephone. One never knows who is listening at doors, so to speak.'

Aida's brow furrowed. She recalled again their conversation at the princess's ball. 'So, these "important" people you speak of …? Is one of them Prince Shams Sakr El Din? Is he involved?'

Alastair paused for a long moment, and she was about to apologise for having asked about what was surely classified information, but then he spoke: 'I have already given you sensitive details of our delicate operation so I suppose it won't hurt to give a few more … Yes, the prince was involved, and fought to avoid being apprehended. Fought your husband, in fact. In the skirmish, the prince was killed.'

'You mean *Phares* killed him?' Aida put a hand to her throat. 'B–but we never heard! Phares never said …'

'Even those close to the prince thought he had gone to Europe. We invented a cover story that was most effective in keeping tongues from wagging. It is imperative that El Kébir goes about his current mission feeling he is safe to do so. Otherwise, if he were to draw in his horns, we would never catch him. And this infernal tide of antiquities leaking out of the country through criminal hands will never be stopped.'

Aida felt faint. So many shocking things … she couldn't even start to process them in her mind.

Alastair rose from his seat and came over to her, laying a comforting hand on her shoulder: 'Now, go home, Aida. You have a good man for a husband, and a hero too. Be patient, and when Phares comes home, you will have a wonderful surprise to tell him.'

Her voice was quiet and a little shaky as she bade him goodbye. 'Thank you, Alastair. You've been a real friend. Don't tell him about this visit. I will in due course, when it's all behind us.'

'Of course, my dear. Mum's the word.'

*    *    *

That same afternoon, Aida took a flight back to Luxor and by late evening, she was back at Hathor. The house was quiet and suddenly she ached for Phares as never before. She felt empty, but not hungry, and asked only to have some soup taken up to her room.

As she sat on the veranda, her supper untouched, she watched the moonlight on the lawn casting shadows from the palms, making the garden seem like an enchanted fairyland. There was no stir of the trees, no sound; the motionless flowers in the beds lay open to the night. High up on a sycamore, a sleepy kite moved on his perch; a bat fluttered noiselessly across the starry sky. The peace of the night in the moonlight after the heat and the noise of the day should have stilled her troubled mind, but nothing could assuage the confusion and guilt that assailed her.

She took stock of the last few days. How utterly disloyal she must have seemed to Phares! She really didn't deserve him. Even confronted with what she had seen and heard at the cottage, she should have given him the benefit of the doubt. She couldn't blame the anonymous letter, which had sown the first seeds of distrust in her mind, because in her faithless heart, the truth of it was that she had been completely unjust towards her husband. That night when he seemed so aloof, she had been so preoccupied with her own jealousy and suspicions, she hadn't even tried to gently get to the bottom of what was making him so distracted. She had bombarded him with questions and had not listened when he had asked her to trust him.

She'd been cold, pushed him away whenever he'd wanted the comfort of her arms ... her warmth. Awake at night, she had heard him pace up and down the veranda, smoking one cigarette after the other – she found an ashtray full of the half-smoked butts the next morning. Now, it all made sense.

Aida looked into the night. Beyond the garden flowed the Nile, and behind that, the Western Mountains and the desert ... Phares's love. An entirely different world lying under the same moonlight: a vast expanse, stark as a moonscape under this peculiar luminosity.

*A dangerous place in which he was toiling right now for all she knew.*

Where was he now? Could he see the moon? Was he thinking of her? Did he feel the love she was sending to him across the night?

'Oh, Phares, I'm so very sorry,' she whispered as tears of regret and shame ran down her cheeks. 'God, please make him safe!'

*    *    *

The night was still, the full moon bringing its own unearthly pale glow to the quiet desert, outlining the eerie and lifeless scene of shadowy crevices, stark rocks and mountain ridges.

Phares felt the solid presence of Captain Charles Montgomery on horseback beside him, dressed similarly in Bedouin robes, and felt relieved that once again he had been teamed with this brave and experienced English officer. Montgomery had the requisite sharpness for the mission, paired with a genial humour that made him such a good companion. On first meeting it was perfectly possible to misjudge the man, with his loud laugh, bonhomie and cheery tone that seemed more suited to a British hunt breakfast than escapades into the desert of Upper Egypt. Still, Phares knew better. They'd had each other's back during their last escapade in the Western Desert – each saving the other's life in the face of enemy snipers – and he had no doubt, should things turn ugly tonight, they would protect each other again without hesitation.

Phares looked back along the line of eight camel-mounted Nubian guards and two more English officers. He felt confident that they would get the better of their elusive opponents this time, though the smugglers were as shifting and secretive as the desert sands in which they hid.

'We're not far now,' said Montgomery, his gaze roving ceaselessly from left to right, constantly on his guard. 'Lucky we got that tip-off … and all thanks to you, Pharaony.'

'Atef was a relatively lowly link in the chain, but proved useful,' Phares agreed. 'If he hadn't put me together with his cousin, we certainly wouldn't be here.'

Montgomery grinned. 'You're getting rather good at this. Are you sure you don't want to hang up your surgical gown and come and work for us permanently?' At Phares's amused, sceptical look, he laughed quietly. 'Well, your man came up trumps! We've never been able to trace dealers higher up the chain and have this kind of intelligence before. Let's hope it all comes good tonight.'

'I'm confident my informant knows his stuff and won't lead us on a wild goose chase. We know the size of the mission, the number of men involved, and the coordinates of their meeting place.'

'Not only that, this time we are assured that the King Rat himself will be here to officiate.'

*King Rat … That was a good name for El Kébir*, Phares mused. Clever, sinuous and devious, the boss of this criminal network was never to be found at any scene when the Egyptian police had made previous arrests.

'Let's hope so,' he agreed fervently. 'Because if we fail to run him to ground this time, there's little doubt El Kébir will go into hiding for good. He must have a sense that the net's closing in on him. I expect he's told himself this big operation will be his last for a while.'

Montgomery gave his usual easy grin, belying the astute sharpness behind his affable expression. 'Well, the man's greed will turn out to be his downfall, eh? Always a criminal's undoing … But let's not count our chickens yet – we've still got to apprehend the scoundrel.'

Phares and the three English officers rode for twenty minutes along the beaten desert track that led from Qena, confident their disguise and the group of Nubian guards would prevent any Bedouin agents of El Kébir noticing them. He'd learned from experience that, although true to its name the desert might look deserted, it could also be full of watchful eyes. Between still land and still sky, the only motion was a ballet of bats that glided in moonlight streams as if the sky was the most fabulous of fairground rides.

Like wildcats, the Nubians crouched on the high humps of their camels, carbines at the ready. From their shoulders floated the ends of their *keffiyehs*, which each wore wound about his head and neck. One of the men turned to confer with Montgomery, who raised his arm in a signal.

They had reached a plateau between a circle of flat-topped crags. Under the eerie light of the moon, everything appeared like a great white world of desolation. This was the place, they needed to get into position. According to their intelligence, the delivery – the biggest haul of priceless antiquities El Kébir had yet tried to shift – would be made here.

Seamlessly, the men divided into two detachments. They had prepared for this: one group with Phares and Montgomery would take one side, hidden among the shadowy outcrops of rock, while the other, led by the two English officers of Montgomery's close team, would take the other.

A whisper from one of the Nubian guards, and another arm signal from Montgomery, was met with a low whistle from the other detachment. Phares followed their line of sight, narrowing his eyes as he watched two pairs of advancing headlights approaching rapidly across the plateau.

Now the men were crouched, rifles in hand, behind the boulders at the base of the crag. Phares, craning his neck to see the ground above him, thought he had heard something – a rock fall – and it was then that he noticed the glint of a carbine shining in the moonlight. He signalled to Montgomery: men, hidden in the rocks above them. Both flattened down, assuming they had been lucky enough not to be spotted yet. Knowing the smugglers had their own snipers ready to pick them off once they had come into the open, the Nubian guards were in position further round the base of the circular crag with a good vantage point. Phares trusted the Nubians would be ready to cover them.

The two vehicles drew nearer and stopped about twenty yards away. Doors opened, and four Bedouins got out, two from each car. One of them was carrying a briefcase. They started towards a gaping hole in the nearby mountainside, which looked to be the mouth of a cave.

Like cockroaches from the cracks, two men in *galabeya* and *emma*, the national dress of the landowners of Upper Egypt, scurried out of the rocky grotto and all six men disappeared inside.

*A veritable Aladdin's cave*, thought Phares, wondering what treasures lay within.

In a trice, Phares and Montgomery broke cover, heading for a stack of boulders at the entrance to the cave. Immediately, shots cracked and bullets whistled overhead as the riflemen who had been hidden above them started to fire, and from the other side of the crag, the other two English officers and their men returned their volley without respite. As Phares crouched beside Montgomery behind the boulder, he turned to see a shadowy figure at the mouth of the cave lift his rifle in their direction, only to be felled instantly by a bullet from Montgomery.

Shots peppered the rocks around them and lit up the night sky, filling it with the pungent smell of gunpowder, but this time

Phares was convinced the team had their plan in place and were well organised. This was no more than they had expected and as his eyes followed the line of the track across the plateau, he gave a grim smile of relief.

A band of about fifty Nubian and Egyptian guards under the command of Egyptian officers was bringing up the rear. They swarmed in, the kind of amply sized reinforcement they had lacked last time but which now would help them defeat the criminal operation. Gunfire rang out as this great troop unleashed an unceasing volley of shots. From above, the enemy riflemen didn't have a hope of withstanding this level of firepower. The Nubian guards, which the English officers had left in the perfect strategic position, made sure that no one got away this time. Those who weren't wounded or killed staggered swiftly out of the rocks, hands in the air.

Inside the cave nothing stirred. No one else had attempted to flee. It was not until the gunfire had ceased and all that could be heard in the cool of the desert night were the cries of the wounded that there was any movement from within. Then a group of men – one behind the other – emerged, hands behind their heads in an indication of surrender. One of them, Phares saw, walked with a less submissive tread, and above the *keffiyeh* covering the lower part of his face burned a pair of furious eyes. This, he was sure, must be El Kébir.

A group of Egyptian officers who had entered the cave now returned to the open, bearing several large wooden packing crates. Phares let out a heavy breath and exchanged a smile with Montgomery. This had all gone to plan. There was a tension that remained in Phares, however, like a coiled wire in his gut. It would only be relieved once El Kébir, the man they had been hunting for so long, was unveiled.

He walked over to join the chief of police, one of whose officers was prodding the chest of this main suspect with his rifle ...

the leader of the whole criminal operation, one which led to a steady stream of contraband heading through Libya to Greece. The Bedouin lowered his scarf. There was nothing in his posture to denote shame or defeat, just a burning hatred emitted like a laser from a pair of hawkish light-brown eyes.

It took a moment for Phares to register the man without his usual round glasses.

Adly Geratly ... Isis's father ... a man he had known for the past twenty years. A neighbour, a guest of his father on many an occasion. A learned historian; after Aida's father, the most knowledgeable man Phares knew when it came to his country's wealth of antiquities ...

A wealth Geratly had been claiming for himself.

Phares's mind struggled to take in the enormity of it all. He approached with such a sickening dread, he couldn't find the words to express it. But it was Geratly who spoke first:

'You just couldn't stop yourself, could you? Always wanting to be the hero, eh, Pharaony? Surgeon ... spy ... scalpel ... gun ... You love it, don't you? And the ladies flocking around you ... I suppose you're proud of yourself.' Geratly's eyes were scorching, his voice a furious rasp.

Fury turned the moon-bleached desert around him red and Phares had to hold himself back from striking the man with his fist. Instead, he took a steadying breath. 'You disgust me,' he countered coldly. 'To think you caused the death of one of our noblest, finest intellects! Ayoub was a friend and mentor to me. I will never forgive what you did to that family. Nor will my wife, whom you've robbed of a father. Just tell me ... why?'

Geratly looked away from him. 'Ayoub had decided to talk to people he shouldn't have ... was getting too near the truth. I didn't know the man would have a heart attack. I thought framing him would put an end to his meddling.' He turned to stare at Phares with contempt. 'And to your betrothal to that half-breed, *khawagaya* El Masri girl.'

Understanding began to dawn in Phares's mind. 'I bet it was you who put the prince up to it. Drug Aida, put her in a harem … teach her a lesson – was that it? That *ibn kalb*, son of a bitch, was your partner in crime, after all. I wouldn't be surprised if you cooked the whole thing up together.' Phares, by now struggling to contain his savage fury, felt the full truth of it all wash over him. 'Hadn't you done enough to the El Masris? … I suppose you had me lined up to marry Isis? If Aida was no longer a suitable match, then your daughter would be next in line.'

Geratly's silence confirmed it all.

Phares was done. He gave his adversary one final glare of revulsion then turned on his heel, making a silent vow not to let this man's poison infect him a moment longer.

At last, here was an end to it. Months of watching, waiting, following, planning … Despite Geratly's taunting words, Phares did not relish playing the action hero – he was much more at home in an emergency room. A deep, honourable love for his country had led to his involvement in this whole business, and now he could retire from it all.

*More than anything, he just wanted to get back to Hathor, to the soft, sweet, safe harbour of Aida's arms.*

\*　　\*　　\*

Sunlight was streaming through Aida's bedroom window when she woke the next morning and for a split second, she wondered if yesterday had all been a dream. These days, her sense of reality seemed elusive as a desert mirage. For a moment she lay motionless, listening the chirping of birds in the trees. *I mustn't linger any longer*, she told herself. Jumping out of bed, she went to the bathroom to wash and dress. Even though she was not a surgeon or even a doctor, she made sure to be prompt, feeling she needed to be at El Amal in Phares's absence to represent him. Now that she was his wife, the hospital was her responsibility too.

The long white hospital building sat with its semicircular graceful wings, looking as though it were built of crystal in the clear morning sunlight. The two fountains in the garden were attracting sparrows, fighting noisily over the water, while the cooing of pacific doves from the tall eucalyptus trees added their own softer counterpoint.

Aida had done all her ward rounds for the morning and was just going back to the staffroom when she paused in the corridor. She had overheard something through the open door of Isis's office – part of a conversation which was obviously not intended for her ears.

'Here, Naima, take this,' the hard, abrupt voice of Isis Geratly said. 'Deliver it to the postbox outside the gates of Hathor, like you did the other day.'

Aida tiptoed closer to the door, praying the two women wouldn't realise she was there. Her heart was beating as though it might leap out of her throat any minute and she found herself holding her breath, wondering whether or not to go into the room.

'But …' Naima was protesting.

'No buts … Just do as you're told. I'll give you fifty piastres when you come back.'

'But Nurse Pharaony's here in the hospital, I can give it to her now. Why do I have to go all the way to Hathor? I have a lot of work today.'

'Don't argue with me, do as I say! Anyway, surely with your brother being sick, you could use the extra money?'

Spontaneously, Aida rapped on the half-open door to Isis's office and stepped inside without waiting for a response. Every bone in her body told her this had everything to do with those cruel anonymous notes. Tackling Isis face to face was the only way she had to confirm her suspicions and put a stop to the malicious hand that was writing them.

As she went in, Isis looked up and paled. Naima, the young nurse, was holding a small, familiar-looking yellow envelope. She was on the point of leaving the room, but Aida laid a hand on her arm: 'Just a second, Naima.'

Isis stood up, her perfect jaw clenched, her eyes shining with repressed anger. In fact, the anaesthetist looked so forbidding that Aida could almost imagine flames shooting from her mouth.

'I get the distinct impression you're not happy to see me, Isis.'

'I'm rather busy. Hasn't anyone ever told you to knock before entering?'

'The door was ajar. Anyhow, I won't take up much of your time.'

Isis addressed Naima sharply: 'You can go now.'

But Aida tightened her hold on the girl's arm. 'Stay here, please. If I'm not mistaken, this letter is addressed to me. No point in delivering it to Hathor. Since I'm here, I might as well spare you the journey.'

Naima nodded nervously and thrust the envelope into Aida's hand before scuttling quickly from the office.

Undaunted, Isis's dark eyes sparked with insolent disdain. 'How silly of me! I didn't know that you were going to be in this morning. That envelope is not from me, you know. Someone delivered it last night. I was just doing you a favour. I thought it might be important …'

Aida tried to keep her voice light. 'It's rather a coincidence, don't you think, that you should have a stack of similar yellow notepaper and envelopes on your desk? Also, it does appear that this is not the first time you've asked Naima to deliver a letter to Hathor.'

Like a cornered rat, Isis bared her teeth, her hands tightening into fists: 'How dare you doubt my words!'

'I not only doubt your words, Isis, but I'm accusing you of writing poisonous letters to me. I believe you have embarked on a campaign designed to destroy my marriage and you'd better tell me why.'

Isis shot her a cold stare. 'What are you talking about? Me wanting to destroy your marriage? Why on earth would I want to do that?'

'I can think of one obvious reason …'

'These accusations are total madness,' Isis sneered, stalking over to the doors that gave on to the raised terrace at the rear of the hospital. 'Please get out of my office.' She motioned brusquely for Aida to leave.

Although quivering inside with fury and apprehension, Aida maintained a deceptively calm veneer. She followed Isis, who had escaped the confines of her office to the terrace outside. Leaning against the balustrade, the anaesthetist glared out over the grounds below, arms folded across her chest, refusing to acknowledge Aida's presence.

'Before I leave, let's open this letter and read it together, shall we?' Aida said, tearing open the envelope.

The corner of Isis's mouth curled in a humourless smile. 'Why should I? It doesn't concern me.'

'*Having your heart broken is the easy part – knowing when to move on is the challenge. Go, before this man ruins your life.*' Aida read out. 'So … what do you make of that?'

Isis glanced back over her shoulder: 'That's not my writing.'

'Maybe not exactly. You're too intelligent for that.'

Aida stepped inside the office and picked up a notebook lying on the desk. She came back to stand next to Isis, who continued to stare woodenly ahead at the garden. Aida turned the first page and perused it closely.

'Look, that odd curly "C" in the letter. Doesn't it seem curiously similar to the ones in your notebook? Here, and here ...' Aida said with a deadly quietness, pointing to the page, then offering the open book for Isis to see.

'You bitch!'

Knocking the notebook from Aida's hand, Isis whirled round and seized Aida by the neck, pushing her backwards so that she was now the one leaning against the balustrade. 'It's you who stole Phares from *me*! We were planning to marry and then *you* came back. You don't belong here! Eight years ago, we thought we were rid of you ... All those years I've been waiting patiently for Phares to establish himself, get the hospital up and running, so he could ask me to marry him ... and then ... and then ...' Isis was shouting now, shaking Aida by the neck. 'We were happy... *everybody* was happy,' she snarled, '... but you had to come back and spoil it all!'

Taller, and with a much stronger build than Aida, Isis was bearing down on her, pushing her backwards over the balustrade. Aida struggled to prise away the anaesthetist's strong, gripping fingers, and at the same time was trying not to lose her balance. *It was a sheer drop to the gardens from the raised terrace: if she fell, she would surely break her neck.*

Aida faltered. Looking down, she was assailed by dizziness and a wave of terrible nausea but the other woman's grip was alarmingly strong. Blood pounded in her ears, her throat felt dry, her mouth so parched that she could barely get the words out.

'Let me go,' she rasped, almost inaudibly, as she felt her vocal cords being squeezed and crushed.

'You're afraid of me, aren't you?' Isis whispered the words close to her face, a strange, twisted smile hovering on her usually stunning features.

'Should I be scared of you?' Aida croaked, her need to breathe fighting with an impulse to retch.

'You should if you have any sense. If I push you over, people will think it's an accident.'

The picture in front of Aida blurred; she was vaguely conscious of Isis's face, its beauty marred by the two ugly patches of colour darkening her cheekbones. Her fingers started to tingle, she knew she was about to pass out.

She was dimly aware of voices behind her before blackness finally engulfed her.

# EPILOGUE

In the warm evening glow of the setting sun, Aida sat on the veranda, home again at Hathor. It was strange that she called the place 'home' in her thoughts; it showed how very different her frame of mind was now compared to the previous night. Two hours before, she had been discharged from hospital with little damage from Isis's assault other than a slight bruising around her neck. Nothing now – not even the shock of having been attacked – could still her singing heart. In front of her was a steak and a large salad and she found that she was properly hungry for the first time in a long while.

It had been a traumatic day, but at least the unpleasant episode with Isis had ended with the anaesthetist having gone for good. Dr Makloof, whom she was beginning to view as a firm friend, had told her that Isis had been fired with immediate effect from both Al Amal and the Anglo-American Hospital. Apparently, fearing legal retribution, she had caught a late-afternoon flight to Switzerland, doubtless planning to stay in Europe until the storm had died down.

*Well, she can hide her head under the covers there*, reflected Aida, determined not to let thoughts of the woman spoil the glow of wellbeing that spread through her body. Secure in Phares's love, she was almost disposed to feel generous to the anaesthetist who had been so warped by the bitterest jealousy.

She was excited in anticipation of Phares's return tomorrow. A little earlier, soon after Aida had arrived at Hathor, Alastair

Carlisle had called to tell her that the mission had been successful and her husband would be home soon. At the news, the last vestiges of fear and anxiety that had kept her muscles tense, her heart racing with disquiet, finally vanished. The consul, who of course knew of her pregnancy, told her to enjoy this special time.

'Nothing,' he insisted, 'will fill Phares with greater joy.'

Aida had heard that during the first weeks of pregnancy in many women the physical drive was sapped, but in her case, it was quite the reverse. Now, in this relaxed and expansive mood, bathed in the soft warmth of the evening, she found that she craved Phares more than ever; the mere thought of the way he sometimes looked at her had her melting with desire.

Fire burned in her blood … she felt completely alive.

Even the view spread before her eyes had taken a different aspect, as though in tune with her feelings. The west was aflame with reds and golds; against it, the ragged outline of the mountains glowed with a strange light of blended sapphire and opal. A blue mist gathered over the flat lands in the valley, out of which the palms lifted their bunched tops in silhouette against the sky. The drifting feluccas cast blurred reflections of their tall, graceful sails in the watery mirror of the Nile, which lay like a great sheet of iridescent glass. Along the riverbank, Aida could see field workers leading camels, donkeys, buffaloes and cattle – a dark, winding outline against the orange belt of the horizon. The colours of the picture were so vivid, something no painter could catch with his brush.

Aida rested her hand over her stomach where Phares's seed lay cocooned, the culmination of their love and desire. Her heart and mind were serene as never before. When the moon and stars came out, she went back inside, had a bath and then crawled into bed, too drowsy to stay awake. And as her eyes closed, she heaved a sigh of relief and smiled.

*Phares would be home soon.*

*     *     *

Phares let himself in to Hathor, adrenaline still coursing through his veins. After gulping down two large glasses of cold water in the kitchen, he made his way upstairs – he couldn't wait to take Aida into his arms.

He crept into the bedroom and tiptoed to the side of the bed. The night was warm and although the window and the shutters were open, Aida had thrown off the covers and was lying on her back, her beautiful honey-blonde hair spread out on the pillow, a few strands falling across one cheek. She was breathing softly. A moonbeam caressed her outstretched body, clad in a pale-blue clinging silk nightdress. He stood watching her sleeping form, his eyes drinking in her lovely feminine shape ... her breasts rising and falling with each soft breath, the outline of her stomach almost a mirage under the thin material; arms flung out to the sides, she looked as though she was offering herself to him, which brought Phares's senses into instant thrumming, blood rushing to his groin.

Sighing, he ran his fingers through his dark hair as he moved away from the bed. First, he needed a cold shower. Quietly shrugging out of his jacket, he tore off his tie, discarding his shirt and trousers before heading for the bathroom.

He stood under the spray of water a few long minutes; it ran down his burning, taut skin before he soaped himself. Slowly, his chaotic senses began to calm. He was still there, face lifted to the rivulets of water pouring down on him, when the shower curtain was pulled back and a naked Aida stepped in with him. When he felt her soft breasts against his back, he let out a husky groan.

'Ah, *chérie*,' he murmured as her arms slid round his waist, his inadequately subdued flesh already on the rise again at the brush of her hands.

'I've missed you,' Aida whispered against his back, pressing herself to him.

Twisting round, his manhood now aching with need, he bent his head and took one hard nipple in his mouth and then the other. He felt her shiver with pleasure.

'Oh, my love … I've been dreaming of you all night!'

Her voice, thick with desire, was almost too much for him, and cupping the soft round cheeks of her bottom, he lifted her against the wall.

Capturing her mouth with his, he kissed her long and hard, breaking off to murmur against her lips, 'You are my life, Aida. Nothing will ever harm you while you are with me.' Then, with the utmost care, he allowed her to slide down on to him.

She cried out as he entered her in one smooth, satisfying penetration, and he felt the convulsing shudder that immediately raced through her body, everything breaking within her, seconds before his own release, her flesh caught in wild spasms, her pleasure becoming instantly his pleasure. Together, they peaked in the most intense climax he'd ever had.

Panting, holding Aida in his embrace, her legs still straddling his waist, Phares walked back to the bedroom. After throwing a bath towel over the bedcover, he placed her gently down on the bed, then collapsed beside her, spent. He lay like that for several moments before levering himself up on one elbow to gaze down at her.

Aida's eyes opened on a low sigh. 'Oh, Phares, you're back, and safe … I've been so worried! I've been so blind … so unfair …'

'Shush, *chérie*! All is now well.'

Her gaze clung to his, her slow smile like the emergence of a beautiful desert sunrise. 'Alastair told me something of what you've been up to, my brave, wonderful husband. I know about the prince, I know about your work to catch the smugglers. I'm so proud of you … My father would have been so proud too.'

'Alastair already warned me that you'd been concerned by my absences. He did me a huge service in letting you into his confidence like that. I'd been sworn to secrecy ... Believe me, I wanted to tell you, but I couldn't.'

She placed a hand on his smooth chest, feeling his heart beating steadily. 'You're a good man, my love – and honourable. It was right that you didn't.'

'But there's more, and I will tell you, because it concerns you, *chérie*.'

Aida's eyes widened a little, unsure of what this might mean. He held a hand to her cheek. 'It's nothing bad, I promise you. It's everything you have been hoping for. Your father has been exonerated. Souma came to me, and through her and her brother Atef, we finally know the truth.' Aida took a breath to speak, but Phares put a finger to her lips to gently silence her. 'Listen, *chérie*, to what I have to say first ...'

He told her everything: how the smugglers had transported the stolen archaeological finds – many of them priceless museum-quality antiquities – to a disused tomb at the foot of a precipice, some distance from the Valley of Tombs. Aida's eyes sparkled as her husband told her a story worthy of the *Arabian Nights* tales.

'I wish you'd seen it,' he said, his eyes alight with the memory of discovery. 'The way into the tomb consisted of a shaft about forty feet deep, leading to a tunnel. At the end of this underground corridor, we found it – a burial chamber in the heart of the hillside.'

He went on to tell her how treasure upon treasure had been placed in this hidden tomb. The work was done at night and, furtively, the precious pieces of the tomb – the trinkets, the jewels and the funeral furniture – passed from one dealer to the next, transported by caravans across the desert and through the crooked streets of the Musky until they reached the admiring eyes of European collectors.

'A great price was paid for these objects, Aida,' he said, a shadow passing over his face as he thought of all that had already been lost to Egypt. His gaze refocused on her and she could see the fury spark in his eyes. 'And it was Adly Geratly who toasted each successful sale with champagne.'

At this, Aida's face became a mask of shock, her mind racing furiously to make sense of it all. When she heard how Geratly had been behind everything – including framing her poor father – her jaw tightened.

*So, he had masterminded the entire business. Isis's father …*

Now that Phares had come to the end of his account, it was Aida's turn to tell him what had happened while he had been away. She didn't choose to burden him with a description of her fevered jealousy, but when she came to Isis – her poisonous letters and the attack – it was his turn to feel shock and disgust.

And now it was Aida who placed a finger to his lips. 'Hush, I don't want to talk about it now! She has flown to Switzerland, and with luck, she won't return to Egypt for a good while. Let us not think of her again. Anyway, I have something that will take your mind off all these dark things … some news.' She lifted a hand to caress his face, the look in her eyes soft with tenderness and love.

'What news is that?' His taut face relaxed into a smile, but after one long look at her excited expression, the truth started to dawn on him.

*A question unvoiced … a wild hope …*

'It's true, Phares,' she murmured, smiling tremulously. 'We're going to have a child.'

For a long while, his eyes aglow, he couldn't speak, the strong emotions he felt choking his voice. He passed his hand lightly over her bare stomach in wonder. 'But this is incredible,' he breathed. 'What a gift you are giving me, *chérie!*'

Aida's eyes lit up. 'So, you're happy, Phares?'

'How can you ask?' Smiling, he bent his head and brushed Aida's lips with his. He then gathered her to him and drew the covers over them both. 'I'm the happiest man in the world, Aida.'

She beamed. 'I can't wait to tell Camelia …'

'And my father … He's been longing to be a grandfather, he'll be overjoyed.'

Aida lifted an arm over her eyes, flooded with guilt at the mention of Kamel Pharaony. 'Oh my God, Phares … when I think how unfair I've been! How I could ever have believed he'd owned that statue or had in any way been involved in framing his old friend? How am I ever going to be able to look your father in the eye? I'm so ashamed!'

Tenderly, he took her arm, drawing it away from her face.

'Don't be, *chérie*,' he insisted. 'All is well now and besides, making him a grandfather is the best present that you could have given this family. You and that little seed growing inside you will bring laughter back into our home and our hearts again.'

She turned to face him, a soft emotion filling her gaze.

'I love you, Phares.'

'And I you. More than you will ever know … Even though you agreed to be my wife, I knew that you were always wary of me. It hurt, I'll admit, but I also knew that one day, I would prove to you how much you mean to me.'

'I'm sorry if I hurt you. All that time, I was hurting myself even more. I guess this is the start of a whole new journey for us.'

Phares smiled enigmatically. 'A whole new honeymoon, *chérie*,' he whispered against her lips.

'Mmm …' she murmured sensually, moving to close the small gap between their bodies and stretching against him with a happy smile. Wriggling her hips against his, she instantly aroused him once more and he felt her tremble, her heart beating in a fast rhythm. 'I like the sound of that.'

Phares threw back his proud, dark head and laughed with rich appreciation. 'Whoever said that pregnancy dampened a woman's libido …' Then he brought his mouth down on hers and kissed her breathless.

As he lifted his head from her, a fleeting cloud passed over Aida's face. 'I love you, Phares. I know it now more than ever. I trust you utterly. I'll never doubt you again … Never, till the day I die.'

He smiled teasingly. 'No more doubts and jealous thoughts?'

'No. Those other thoughts, you know … I think they were only shadows, a kind of false dawn before the sun really rose.'

'Or mirages of your imagination,' he said gently. 'Sometimes just before the sun rises over the desert, a mirage hovers over the sand – a sort of forerunner to the genuine sunrise. The Bedouins call it the "Mirage of the Dawn" and say it foretells a cloudless day.'

'May it be the same with us,' Aida murmured, looking up at her husband fervently. 'Both of us have known the dawn mirage, now let's pass on to the perfect day.'

As she lifted her lips to receive Phares's kiss, the false dawn fled from the sky above, leaving them in the true and living sunshine of a mutual love.

# ABOUT THE AUTHOR

## Q AND A
## WITH HANNAH FIELDING

**What was it like for you, growing up in Egypt?**
My home town is the ancient and historic city of Alexandria, and although I left Egypt some time ago, the wonderful memories of it are still very vivid in my mind. Stretching some forty kilometres along the north coast of Egypt, it is known as the Bride of theMediterranean, and certainly in the 1950s and 1960s, the city was a beacon of Mediterranean culture.

The Alexandria of my childhood was so much more cosmopolitan than cities like Luxor, and even Cairo. Wherever you went, there was a wonderful mixture of Oriental and European dress and languages. Whether in the road, in restaurants or at the cinema, you would hear a medley of languages. There were Egyptians, French, Italians, Greeks, Armenians and English people, Christians, Muslims and Jews, all happily cohabitating under an azure sky, in beautiful old villas built in the Italian belle époque style, with lush gardens and fragrant orchards. For this community, and for most educated Egyptians, French was the lingua franca (at school, nuns drilled us in Arabic and French), while English was mostly used for business. So, my friends and I conversed in French – and those early childhood friends were mostly foreign, and every Friday afternoon, we would go to the cinema with my Greek, Armenian and Italian classmates.

Most shops and factories were family-owned by not only Egyptians but Greeks, Jews, Armenians, Syrians and Italians. Grand names come to mind, like Shamla and Cicurel, Gategno, Orosdi-Back, Benzion, Sidnawy and Hannaux department stores, where you could find all the latest fashions from Paris and the most beautiful silk fabrics; patisseries and tea shops such as Delices, Athineos, Pastroudis, Boudreaux and Fluckiger, which served the most mouth-watering cakes and ice creams; and Tomvaco, which sold delicious chocolates and candied fruits. (I especially remember its stuffed chocolate dates.)

Compared to the experience of the average child in Egypt in those days mine was in many senses a charmed childhood. We came from a well-connected family and lived in a sprawling house overlooking the shimmering Mediterranean, and my sister and I rode our bicycles around acres of lush grounds at my grandmother's house. We were also lucky enough to experience much of the culture that flourished in Alexandria at that time and my parents used to take us regularly to the theatre and to performances by world-class ballet companies like the Bolshoi and Leningrad, and La Comédie-Française. In many ways, I led a privileged and very cosmopolitan life but it was the quintessentially Egyptian flavour of life that was so dear to me, growing up in Egypt.

I loved the market in Alexandra too: an animated, good-humoured and crowded place, its veiled dim light filled with flickering shadows, the atmosphere redolent with exotic scents, the fragrance of oriental herbs and spices, orange blossom, musk and sandalwood; the guttural voice of stallholders and shouting hawkers calling out their produce. It was also a meeting place for all kinds of entertainment. There were the usual storytellers sitting cross-legged on the ground surrounded by children;

the fortune teller with her basket of shells accosting buyers and crying out *piééé-piaaa* (I still don't know what it means!); the seller of *baladi* bread riding his bicycle, zigzagging in and out of the crowd, balancing on his head a flat trellis with a heap of the delicious oatmeal loaves; or women carrying a goose, duck or chicken on their heads who, despite their burden, had the most magnificent carriage.

On the beaches, like San Stefano, Miami and Montazah (the fabulous grounds and beach of King Farouk's palace which, after the revolution in 1952, were opened to the public), and in the cafés and restaurants, the loudspeaker radio blasted out a medley of Italian, French, English and Greek songs to its international clientele. When I listen to songs from this era now, I am transported back in time, to a life that seemed light-hearted and full of mirth.

### The importance of family is a strong theme in *Song of the Nile* – is that true throughout Egyptian culture?

Yes, absolutely. Family is of the utmost importance in Egypt and family values are deeply engrained in the culture. Rich and poor alike will always put family first. Families are close-knit and supportive – and, typically, large. My grandparents on both sides had six children, and indeed, many of our relatives lived with us in the family house in individual apartments spread over the sprawling belle époque villa in Alexandria. In many families, marriages stay within the family circle; there is no ban on marrying cousins and it actually used to be encouraged. Newly married couples may well remain at home with the family rather than leave and start a new home. This way, several generations of a family live together, sharing the work of housekeeping and caring for each other, young and old.

For Christians, Christmas and Easter are events that bring families together. I lived in Alexandria, but most of my family

lived in Cairo, so every year we made the two-and-a-half-hour
drive through the desert to spend these feasts with the family in
Cairo. For Muslims, Eid is similar; it is an important time for
families to get together. By the time I was a teenager, many
members of my family had moved to Alexandria, and so every
year on Good Friday, after Mass, my father used to throw a big
family party at our home. I remember the adults around a very
long, grand table and we children around a smaller one; sometimes
there would be as many as eighty people.

*Sham El Nessim* is another time that families come together.
Dating from the time of the pharaohs, it is a festival to welcome
spring and it is celebrated by Muslims and Christians alike. On
that day you will see clusters of families picnicking in the parks,
by the Nile in Cairo, or on the beaches of Alexandria. How I loved
playing on the beach with all my cousins that day!

Determined to keep us close, my maternal grandparents
started a tradition: each Sunday, they hosted their children and
grandchildren for lunch. I remember those lunches so fondly:
the beautiful dining room, the delicious meals, the chatter,
the laughter. After my grandparents passed away, one of my aunts
continued the tradition, until we were all grown and some, like
me, had spread their wings. I hope that I will be able to
do something similar for my own children and grandchildren
someday, when we are all reunited in the same place.

**Why did you choose to set the book just after WWII?**
If Alexandria was a city with a European influence, one could
say that Cairo had the look of an Arabian city invaded by the West.
Here in the capital, the post-war era was a time of escapism and
making hay while the sun shone – of enjoying frivolity, glamour,
romance.

For the aristocracy, the British, and international officer class,
the Gezireh Club in Zamalek was a place for equestrian prowess,

for tennis tournaments, for polo and cricket. For the league of irregular troops of men and women for whom Cairo was a brief stopping-off place before a mission, the Shepheard's Hotel, the Mena House at Gizeh and the Villa Belle Epoque in Maadi were havens where legendary parties were held. There were shooting parties at the Oasis of Faiyum, extensive picnics at the Pyramids of Gizeh and Sakkara, and luxurious boat expeditions on the Nile in Luxor and Aswan, where the rich and famous congregated in their boating flannels or serge and linen skirts. The Palace and its various members held extravagant balls, where an elegant elite of Egyptian and foreign men and women in French designer outfits danced the night away. Bejewelled women, glittering in their long ballgowns, attended the very best ballet and opera performances at the Khedivial Opera House.

It was a time of beautiful, carefree people, a time of living for the moment, where past, present and future melded into one – a time when glittering Cairo was compared to Paris and when prosperity saw the Egyptian pound stronger than the Sterling pound. Indeed, I chose to set *Song of the Nile* in post-war Cairo for its bygone era of romanticism, when people lived oblivious of what was to come; a fairy-tale age of hedonism that would never return.

### What is it about Egyptian culture you love the most?

There is so much I love – that I miss – about Egypt. Dishes that are a staple in Egyptian culture, like *ful medames*, a hearty, creamy fava bean dish loaded with flavour from ground cumin, fresh herbs, tomatoes, a hard-boiled egg and zippy lemon juice; and *koshary*, a very popular street food made with rice, vermicelli, lentils, pasta, onions and tomato sauce. Wherever I have lived since leaving Egypt, I have looked for Egyptian ingredients in stores, but it is not always easy to find these.

I miss the warmth of the people – the man in the street who will rush to help you if you have a flat tyre or fetch you a glass of water, should you feel unwell; the *ghaffir*'s (porter's) wife in Upper Egypt, who will welcome you back home from your travels with her homemade *feteer meshaltet*, a pastry dish made with layer upon layer of pastry with ghee in between, or a plate of *basboussa*, a semolina cake sweetened with orange blossom water, rose water or syrup. The people are so kind, and curious too: Egyptians love to know what is going on, to be part of the community.

I miss the keen Egyptian sense of humour that is so revealing in proverbs like *'El erd fi ein omoh ghazal'* (The monkey is as beautiful as a gazelle in his mother's eyes), *'Ya wakhed el-erd ala maloh yeroh el-mal we yeod el-erd ala haloh'* (If you marry the monkey for his money, the money will go and you'll be left with the monkey) and *'En kan habibak asal matlhasoush kolo'* (If your sweetheart is made of honey, don't lap it all up; meaning don't take advantage of kindness).

I miss the Moorish architecture, with its elegant arches and domes, and its *mashrabiyas*, those lattice windows behind which one can imagine the beautiful women of the sultan's harem in *One Thousand and One Nights*. I miss the neoclassical buildings, the belle époque villas with their well-tended orchards and gardens, their magnificent gates edging palm-fringed avenues.

Last, but not least, I miss the landscape of Upper Egypt: the Nile, on which the feluccas (sailboats) glide serenely as they have since antiquity; the endless fields stretching afar, peppered with tiny villages with their mud walls and winding ways fringed with palms, where people still follow the traditions of their ancestors. Here is a place far removed from the trappings of everyday life; here is a place of deep-abiding peace.

**Why do you think people find Egypt so enduringly fascinating?**
To know from where we have come is a powerful driver for all

people, and so naturally Egypt, as one of the great ancient civilisations, is intriguing.

What makes Egypt special and its history and mythology and culture so enduring? I think it comes down to a single, very powerful feeling that Egypt inspires: wonder.

Of the Seven Wonders of the Ancient World, two were Egyptian: the Great Pyramid of Gizeh and the Lighthouse of Alexandria. Today, the Great Pyramid at Gizeh is the only one of these wonders to remain intact. This tomb, believed to have been built for the Pharaoh Khufu, dates back to *c.*2560 BC. To enter this structure today, thousands of years later, it is hard to put into words what an awe-inspiring experience it is.

To this day, Egyptologists are still uncovering treasures from the distant past, such as the well-preserved mummies in coffins recently discovered at the Saqqara necropolis in the desert outside Cairo. The ancient custom of burying the dead in beautifully decorated coffins and tombs (and, for the rich, with their treasure) means these relics from the past tell us colourful and compelling stories of the people who lived in this land long ago – romantic, dramatic stories of kings and queens, and of mighty gods and goddesses. By studying their hieroglyphics and artworks, we can know so much about these ancient people; we can work to unlock their secrets and mysteries.

It is this unearthing of the past, this thrill of discovery, that most draws us to Egypt, I think. For thousands of years, it was a glorious nation, at the heart of the Mediterranean world, but then Alexander III of Macedon built his great empire and Egypt's culture was eventually buried by Greek and Roman and Arabic influences. When we discover an artefact, then, we are unearthing a lost civilisation: a wonder indeed.

Beyond history, both ancient and more recent (the rebuilding of the Great Library of Alexandria has been particularly exciting), I think the allure of Egypt is the sense of timelessness here. Take a romantic felucca ride on the Nile with your loved one and you will see around you a landscape that seems so untouched, and people who have all the pride and values and warmth of their ancestors. Egypt is a place where past and present coexist; a magical place where it is easy to imagine that the blazing sun that watches over the land from above is the ancient king of gods, Ra, the giver of life.

**Find out more at www.hannahfielding.net**

# Egyptian food recipes

## Osta Ghaly's Basboussa

3 eggs
¾ cup granulated sugar (150g)
1 cup yoghurt or sour cream (245g)
½ cup butter, melted (113g)
1 tsp vanilla extract
1½ cups semolina (250g)
½ cup plain flour (65g)
1 cup shredded coconut (100g)
1 tsp baking soda
¼ tsp salt
Almonds to decorate

### For the syrup
1½ cups (250g) caster sugar
1½ cups (350ml) water
2 tbsp lemon juice
1 tsp rose water or orange blossom

1. Preheat the oven to 180°C/fan 160°C/gas mark 4.

2. Beat the eggs and sugar in a bowl with an electric mixer until light and pale. Mix in the yoghurt or sour cream and then

the melted butter, followed by the vanilla extract and beat on low speed. Finally, add the semolina, flour, shredded coconut, baking soda and salt. Mix gently until combined.

3. Transfer the mixture to a baking pan and spread evenly with a spatula. Score evenly into squares with a sharp knife. Place an almond in the middle of each square. Bake in the centre of the oven for 35–40 minutes or until golden.

4. While the cake is baking, make the syrup: add the sugar to the water in a saucepan and bring to a boil, stirring. Now stir in the lemon juice, then the rose water or orange blossom. Reduce the heat and simmer gently for 10 minutes. Cut the cake again and pour the syrup over the cake while still hot and leave to cool before serving.

## Koshari
One of Egypt's national dishes and a popular street food.

3 cups (700ml) of water for boiling the rice
Enough water for boiling the lentils and elbow macaroni separately
2 cups long-grain rice (400g)
2 cups black lentils (380g)
2 cups elbow macaroni (300g)
½ cup vermicelli pasta (75g)
3 tbsp vegetable oil
2 medium onions, peeled and diced (not too fine)
1 cup cooked chickpeas (170g)
Salt to taste

**For the sauce**
2 cups crushed tomatoes (450g)
1 cup (240ml) water
1 large diced tomato
1 tsp ground cumin
1 tsp ground coriander
1 tsp sugar
2 minced garlic cloves
Salt to taste

**For the dressing**
½ cup (120ml) white vinegar
1 cup (240ml) water
1 tsp ground cumin
1 tsp ground coriander
1 tsp paprika
½ tsp red pepper flakes
1 tbsp sugar
2 minced garlic cloves
Salt to taste

1. Boil the rice until almost done, and the lentils and pasta all separately until cooked, according to the packet instructions.

2. Heat the oil in a frying pan and fry the onions until transparent and lightly golden. Add the cooked pasta, fry until brown, then add the cooked rice. Add 3 cups (700ml) water. Cook for 3 minutes on high heat. Lower the heat and simmer until done, about 12 minutes in all. If needed, add extra water. Add salt to taste.

3. While the pasta mixture is cooking, make the sauce. Combine all the ingredients in a saucepan and cook over low heat, stirring.

If the sauce becomes too thick, add some water (the sauce for Koshari needs to be light). You can also make the dressing by combining all the ingredients in a separate bowl, then set aside.

4. Arrange the pasta mixture on a serving dish. Add the lentils, then the pasta/rice mixture and the chickpeas. Pour some of the sauce over the top, then the dressing. Alternatively, you can serve the sauce and the dressing separately.

# ALSO BY HANNAH FIELDING

# Burning Embers

### Hannah's mesmerizing debut novel

**Set in the heart of Africa, *Burning Embers* is a tale of unforgettable passion and fragile love tormented by secrets and betrayal.**

On the news of her estranged father's death, beautiful young photographer Coral Sinclair is forced to return to the family plantation in Kenya to claim her inheritance.

But the peace of her homecoming is disrupted when she encounters the mysterious yet fearsomely attractive Rafe de Montfort – owner of the neighbouring plantation and a reputed womanizer, who had an affair with her own stepmother. Despite this, a mystifying attraction ignites between them and shakes Coral to the core as circumstances conspire to bring them together.

It is when Coral delves into Rafe's past and discovers the truth about him that she questions his real motives. Does Rafe really care for her or is he hiding darker intentions? Should she listen to the warnings of those around her or should she trust her own instincts about this man with a secret past?

Paperback ISBN 978-0-9955667-9-8
Ebook ISBN 978-0-9929943-1-0

# The Echoes of Love

## Hannah's award-winning novel

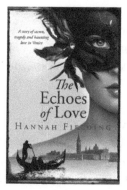

Set in the romantic and mysterious city of Venice and the beautiful landscape of Tuscany, *The Echoes of Love* is a poignant story of lost love and betrayal, unleashed passion and learning to love again, whatever the price.

Venetia Aston-Montague has escaped to Italy's most captivating city to work in her godmother's architecture firm, putting a lost love behind her.

Paolo Barone, a charismatic entrepreneur whose life has been turned upside down by a tragic past, is endeavouring to build a new one for himself.

Venice on a misty carnival night brings these two people together. Love blossoms in the beautiful hills of Tuscany and the wild Sardinian maquis; but before they can envisage a future together, they must not only confront their past but also dark forces in the shadows determined to come between them.

Will love triumph over their overwhelming demons? Or will Paolo's carefully guarded, devastating secret tear them apart forever?

Paperback ISBN 978-0-9926718-1-5
EBook ISBN 978-0-9926718-2-2

# Indiscretion

### The captivating first novel in the Andalucían Nights Trilogy

*Indiscretion* is a story of love and identity, and the clash of ideals in the pursuit of happiness. But can love survive in a world where scandal and danger are never far away?

Spring, 1950. Alexandra de Falla, a half-English, half-Spanish young writer, abandons her privileged but suffocating life in London and travels to Spain to be reunited with her long-estranged family. Instead of providing the sense of belonging she yearns for, the de Fallas are riven by seething emotions and in the grip of the wild customs and traditions of Andalucía, all of which are alien to Alexandra.

Among the strange characters and sultry heat of this country, she meets the man who awakens emotions she hardly knew existed. But their path is strewn with obstacles: dangerous rivals, unpredictable events and inevitable indiscretions.

What does Alexandra's destiny hold for her in this flamboyant land of drama and all-consuming passions, where blood is ritually poured on to the sands of sun-drenched bullfighting arenas, mysterious gypsies are embroiled in magic and revenge, and beautiful dark-eyed dancers hide their secrets behind elegant lacy fans?

Paperback ISBN 978-0-9926718-8-4
Ebook ISBN 978-0-9926718-9-1

# Masquerade

**The heartstopping second novel
in the Andalucían Nights Trilogy**

*Masquerade* **is a story of forbidden love,
truth and trust. Are appearances always
deceptive?**

Summer, 1976. Luz de Rueda returns
to her beloved Spain and takes a job as the
biographer of a famous artist. On her first day
back in Cádiz, she encounters a bewitching,
passionate young gypsy, Leandro, who
immediately captures her heart, even though
relationships with his kind are taboo.

Haunted by this forbidden love, she meets her new employer,
the sophisticated Andrés de Calderón. Reserved yet darkly
compelling, he is totally different to Leandro – but almost the
gypsy's double. Both men stir unfamiliar and exciting feelings
in Luz, although mystery and danger surround them in ways she
has still to discover.

Luz must decide what she truly desires as glistening Cádiz, with
its enigmatic moon and whispering turquoise shores, seeps back
into her blood. Why is she so drawn to the wild and magical sea
gypsies? What is behind the old fortune-teller's sinister warnings
about 'Gemini'? Through this maze of secrets and lies, will Luz
finally find her happiness … or her ruin?

Paperback ISBN 978-0-9929943-6-5
EBook ISBN 978-0-9929943-7-2

# Legacy

## The thrilling conclusion
## of the Andalucían Nights Trilogy

*Legacy* **is a story of truth, dreams and desire. But in a world of secrets, you need to be careful what you wish for.**

Spring, 2010. When Luna Ward, a science journalist from New York, travels halfway across the world to work undercover at an alternative health clinic in Cádiz, her ordered life is thrown into turmoil.

The doctor she is to investigate, the controversial Rodrigo Rueda de Calderón, is not what she expects. With his wild gypsy looks and devilish sense of humour, he is intent upon drawing her to him. But how can she surrender to a passion that threatens all reason – and how can he ever learn to trust her once he discovers her true identity? Then Luna finds that Ruy is carrying a corrosive secret of his own …

Luna's native Spanish blood begins to fire in this land of exotic legends, flamboyant gypsies and seductive flamenco guitars, as dazzling Cádiz weaves its own magic on her heart. Can Luna's and Ruy's love survive their families' legacy of feuding and tragedy, and rise like the phoenix from the ashes of the past?

Paperback ISBN 978-0-9932917-3-9
Ebook ISBN 978-0-9932917-6-0

# Aphrodite's Tears

**Hannah's powerful novel
of mystery and seduction**

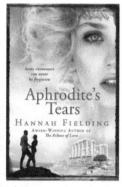

*Aphrodite's Tears* is a wildly romantic story of rediscovered love and unforgettable passion that will keep you turning the pages long into the night.

In ancient Greece, one of the twelve labours of Heracles was to bring back a golden apple from the Garden of Hesperides. To archaeologist Oriel Anderson, joining a team of Greek divers on the island of Helios seems like the golden apple of her dreams.

Yet the dream becomes a nightmare when she meets the devilish owner of the island, Damian Lekkas. In shocked recognition, she is flooded with the memory of a romantic night in a stranger's arms, six summers ago. A very different man stands before her now.

As they cross swords and passions mount, Oriel is aware that malevolent eyes watch her from the shadows. Dark rumours are whispered about the Lekkas family. What dangers lie in Helios, a bewitching land where ancient rituals are still enacted to appease the gods, young men risk their lives in the treacherous depths of the Ionian Sea, and the volatile earth can erupt at any moment?

Will Oriel find the hidden treasures she seeks? Or will Damian's tragic past catch up with them, threatening to engulf them both?

Paperback ISBN 978-0-9955667-6-7
Ebook ISBN 978-0-9955667-8-1

# Concerto

## Hannah's alluring novel of lost love and forgiveness

*Concerto* is a an unforgettable and moving love story – like an exquisitely haunting melody, it will stay with you forever.

When Catriona Drouot, a young music therapist, honours an opera diva's dying request to help her son, Umberto Monteverdi, recover his musical gift, she knows it will be a difficult assignment. Catriona had shared a night of passion with the once-celebrated composer ten years before, with unexpected consequences.

The extent of her challenge becomes apparent when she arrives at her client's estate on Lake Como. Robbed of his sight by a near fatal car accident, the man is arrogant, embittered and resistant to her every effort to help him. Still, Catriona sings a siren's call within him that cannot be ignored.

Caught up in the tempestuous intrigues at Umberto's Palladian mansion, Catriona discovers that her attraction to the blind musician is as powerful as ever. How can she share what she has hidden from him for the past decade?

Soon she realises that hers is not the only secret rippling uneasily below the surface. Dark forces haunt the sightless composer, threatening his life – for the second time.

Paperback ISBN 978-1-916489-51-6
Ebook ISBN 978-1-9164895-2-3